# Tunes and Grooves for Music Education

# Tunes and Grooves for Music Education

## Music for Classroom Use

Patricia Shehan Campbell
*University of Washington*

PEARSON

Prentice Hall

Upper Saddle River, New Jersey 07458

**Editor-in-Chief:** Sarah Touborg
**Executive Editor:** Richard Carlin
**Director of Marketing:** Brandy Dawson
**Marketing Assistant:** Irene Fraga
**Associate Marketing Manager:** Sasha Anderson Smith
**Senior Managing Editor:** Mary Rottino
**Production Liaison:** Jean Lapidus
**Text Permission Specialist:** Richard Kassel
**Composition/Full-Service Project Management:**
Preparé/Emilcomp
**Production Editor:** Francesca Monaco
**Senior Operations Supervisor:** Brian Mackey

**Art Director:** Jayne Conte
**Cover Design:** Bruce Kenselaar
**Cover Photo:** © Raeanne Rubenstein, 2007. Thank you to Principal Mary Lou Del Rio, and Music Teacher Barb Laifer, and all the teachers and students at the PARAGON MILLS ELEMENTARY SCHOOL in Nashville, TN, for their help and cooperation in the making of this photograph. Shown clockwise from left:  Zarius Phrance, Necoya Mathers, Anna Sharp, Mohamed Nur, Lila Rajasonbath, Kristi Trieu (center).
**Printer/Binder:** Bind-Rite Graphics
**Cover Printer:** Bind-Rite Graphics

Pearson Education LTD.
Pearson Education Singapore, Pte. Ltd.
Pearson Education Canada, Ltd.
Pearson Education—Japan

Pearson Education Australia, PTY, Limited
Pearson Education North Asia Ltd.
Pearson Educación De Mexico, S.A. De C.V.
Pearson Education Malaysia, Pte. Ltd.

10 9 8 7 6 5 4 3 2 1

ISBN-10 0-13-194146-1
ISBN-13 978-0-13-194146-5

To the music makers in my life

# Contents

# Acknowledgments

In the bigger scheme of things, book-writing—like music making—is rarely a solo venture. I have many to thank for their support and assistance with this project. There are the musicians whose songs, melodies, and rhythms are found within this collection, and whose recordings have inspired me. I am grateful to the work of the Lomaxes in their pioneering fieldwork in search of the American folk idiom, and am deeply obliged to the Seeger family for their efforts in preserving and transmitting this music through the generations. Their spirit of preservation and transmission is contagious, and I have been enticed into this compilation by their amazing contributions. The legacy of Ruth Crawford Seeger informed the project, too, as her landmark contributions to the dissemination of folk music, through sources like *American Folk Songs for Children*, are inspirational to all who value the music that real people make.

My gratitude extends to the music makers in my life, beginning at home. Mom and Dad were amazing singers and dancers, and it was all for the fun of it. They had no musical training (although they valued it in others), but their natural ability sent many a melody soaring after the beef stew was finished and we could turn from dialogue to song. My brother Jimmie and I chimed in as we could, and dancing lightened the clean-up time. There were also the aunts and uncles of the Sedar family who sang after every Sunday afternoon dinner at Grandma's house in East Cleveland, cousin Jerry and his accordion at the Kehoe communion parties, and all of the singing Kehoe uncles who could not help but render the same repertoire of Irish-American songs at every wake and funeral. Grandpa Kehoe was the leader of them all, with his Irish tenor sounding clearly through the groveling others. Their music is there for me even now, forever etched in memory, as is the music of summer camps, schooldays, and church functions.

The people outside the family with whom I have made merry with music over the years are too numerous to mention. There were the years of performance gigs as singer, guitarist, and keyboardist with "Lost St. John," "Corn Bred," and "The Fox River Trio." Janet Ban knows these years well, as do Denny Monroe, Dale Bendula, and Patrick "Deaver" Hoynes. The children at my teaching posts at St. Stanislaus School and Garfield Park School were amazing vessels of song, too, and with perked ears and exhuberant voices, we covered a good bit of musical ground. Members of choirs from St. John's Cathedral in Cleveland to St. John's College, Cambridge, were also my musical fellows and song bearers, and I am grateful to them for the music we made. I continue to trade songs with children in guest-teaching gigs at schools like Bryant in Seattle and Harrah on the Yakama Reservation. These and other musical exchanges are vital, rich, and varied.

I am grateful to Donald E. Peterson for the professorship he has afforded me to help in the development of this project. I am indebted to Robin McCabe, director of the University of Washington School of Music, for her support and encouragement of my efforts as a teacher and scholar. Sean Ichiro Manes was my research assistant for this project, and I am grateful to him for his library research, notations, and partial transcriptions. Chee-Hoo Lum provided much-needed assistance for further library research, and I thank him also for his organization of the glossary and indices. I sought and found support through conversations with my colleagues and friends, Carol Scott-Kassner, Rita Klinger, Patricia Costa Kim, and Barbara Lundquist.

On the home front, I am fortunate to know Charlie's steady presence as one who genuinely appreciates the music that I can muster "live" in our home, and son Andrew, whose own music making gives us tremendous hope that the music will live on into the foreseeable future.

# Introduction

Zoltán Kodály, Hungarian composer, folk song collector, educator, and advocate of "music for all," once predicted with confidence that the basic phenomena of music could be implanted in a child's soul through "fifty-four well-chosen songs." In the early twentieth century, various American educators praised the significance of a collection of fifty-five songs, and then *Twice 55*, for developing a community of enthusiastic singers. With these noble goals in mind for the cultivation of music in society, one still wonders: What could become of a slightly larger collection of melodies? Music that would be more diversified in origin, style, and language? Music of use to singers, and also to various other melodists, including those who play fiddle, flute, trumpet or tenor saxophone? What of the tremendous wealth of rhythmic ideas, too, for those who play percussion instruments of an array of timbral qualities? Could these be collected under one cover a grand variety of musical expressions that might set the music in motion for those who wish to make it? Could we know something more about the music, too, than what the noteheads deliver, all the way to understanding why a song *is*, and from whom it springs? And for the music that we know little of, could we listen in and get an earful of that which printed notation can only partially convey? With a broader brush on music in an era of globalization and multiculturalism, the wise and worthy recommendations of Kodály and the early American educators are launches to a more diversified musical palette that also offer answers to questions of cultural meaning.

## CULTURAL AND MUSICAL DIVERSITY

Even in a time of international border closings, there is increasing diversity within nations. In North America, both Canada and the United States know vast populations whose heritages can be traced to Africa, Asia, Europe, Latin America, and the Pacific. European countries have witnessed the growth of demographic diversity, with immigrants and asylum-seekers coming to them from other parts of Europe, Africa, and the Middle East. The populations of Australia and New Zealand are mixed, too, and include not only their indigenous peoples (the aboriginal Australians and the Maori) but also those from Europe, Asia, and other places in the Pacific. South Africa recognizes nine linguistic-cultural groups, and the political boundaries of many African nations have been redrawn to encompass multiple tribes, nations, and cultures. Shifting borders throughout the African continent, and the migrations of peoples into and out of China, Central Asia, and the Middle East add to the cross-fertilization of cultures. We live in a world of genuine diversity, a polyglot place of many-splendored expressions, both linguistic and artistic.

It is because there is such cultural diversity across the globe and within our very own local communities that there is musical diversity. Large American cities have long been ethnically and culturally diverse, where the music that emanates from neighborhoods includes Afro-pop, reggae-flavored music from the Caribbean, Indian film music, and hip-hop styles in Spanish, French, Khmer, and Korean. Increasingly, smaller cities and towns are diversifying, and the music of Serbs and Croats, Akan and Ewe, and Brazilians and Bolivians can be heard in homes, at weddings, and in restaurants in many locales far from the homelands of these cultures. Today, one can dial the radio, download a music sample, tune in an iPod, and watch videos of music from every land and nation. The world is multicultural, and it is accessible live or through various technological means.

Still, the music that is featured in university courses, school classes, and clinical settings is predominantly Eurocentric. Western art music of Europe and Euro-America is the mainstay of student orchestras and wind ensembles and of the choral music repertoire. While edging towards a wider world of possibilities, the music of school programs is yet anchored in styles that link to Western repertoire and performance techniques. Further, songs and instrumental selections from elsewhere in the world are often shared in a teaching–learning process that is not in keeping with the manner of its transmission within their cultures of origin. It is a time of enormous cultural change and musical variety within Western societies. But changes to the curricular content of music in schools, clinical settings, and higher education are yet in early stages of development, with many opportunities ahead to dig more deeply into musical styles and their avenues of transmission.

## TIME FOR THE WORLD MUSICS

Pioneering efforts in the United States to bring the music of the world's cultures into educational settings can be traced to the early part of the twentieth century, when the great European wave of immigration spurred a recognition of the many languages and cultures that were flowing into the American "melting pot." Folk songs and dances from across Europe joined European art music on school concert programs and in classroom lessons. The creation of the Pan-American Union in the 1930s brought Americans in touch with all of the Americas, and Spanish-language songs began to influence North American popular culture. Following World War II, the global aim of developing understanding across nations was reflected in schools, which began to explore musical expressions beyond Europe. The establishment of ethnomusicology as a field of study brought with it a growing awareness in universities of the rich variety of music that could be studied and performed. Fueled by the Civil Rights movement of the 1960s, the theme of cultural democracy began to be felt all the way to the content of school music textbooks that featured songs and listening selections from cultures in and beyond the United States. Classes in music for children added singing games of Ghana, Mexico, and Cambodia to the old standbys like "Bluebird" and "Looby Lou." By the 1980s, the full-fledged multicultural education movement had spurred those responsible for music in schools and communities to learn and share a broader selection of the world's music. In some schools and communities, the development of steel drum bands, West African drumming ensembles, Shona-style marimba groups, and gospel choirs were formed. Yet even now, the tunes and grooves of a wider variety of musical cultures are yet to be widely embraced as music that could be extensively and intensively studied and performed.

The time is past due for knowing music in its global and multicultural dimensions. Where music is experienced and learned, it must be with attention to how it is variously expressed. Musical cultures and styles must be studied for what they offer in the way of understanding music as a human phenomenon. In a democracy where every culture is meritorious and worthy of study, the presence of music in schools for its multiple sonic and cultural components is a natural outgrowth of such valuing. Music is to be experienced and understood as it is manifested within its culture, and for its comparative expression and use across cultures. The world's tunes and grooves belong in courses and classes at all levels, in clinical sessions, and in concerts whenever possible. It's no longer a question of "whether" music should be multiculturalized in learning experiences, but rather a matter of seeking responses to questions of "which music?" and how it might be brought into the lives of adults, adolescents, and children.

## CURRICULAR AND COMMUNITY USES OF THE WORLD'S MUSICS

For every musical expression, there are particular times and places in which it is made. Likewise, there are specific uses for the world's musical expressions in school and community settings. Genre by genre, every song and selection can make its way into lessons and sessions in music, and there is music that suits the interests of people of every age. For very young children, lullabies from the world's cultures can be experienced for their culture-specific and cross-cultural qualities. Children through elementary school age can enjoy the grand array of singing games and "story songs," or ballads. Songs of love, old-style courtship, and the contemporary negotiation of relationships run parallel to the everyday realities of adolescents. Dance music energizes the young and young at heart, motivating the rhythmic movement of arms, legs, and torso. There are songs of work and worship, war and peace, glad times and sad times that portray the human experience. Throughout the year, and in various classes and sessions, there are times and places for music of the world's cultures to be heard, learned, and performed.

In schools, an examination of music as a human phenomenon can proceed in a number of ways. A broad survey of music can be cross-cultural in nature, approaching a global reach that stretches far beyond the old-style survey of Western art music. Such a course can be colorful in its variety, relevant to courses in world history, geography, and language arts, and participatory enough to be enticing to children in the upper elementary and secondary school grades. In middle schools where exploratory "wheels" of curricular modules exist in music and the arts, a six-week or quarter-long course of intensive and focused musical experiences opens the doors to the musical cultures of Africa, Latin America, or Asia. Listening lessons give way to songs, percussive rhythms and instrumental pieces, dances, stories, and visits by community musicians. In secondary school ensembles, including choirs, bands, and orchestras, musical arrangements of the world's tunes and grooves can be prepared for programs. When conventional school ensembles are hard-pressed to perform standard repertoire that may not yet envelop some of the world's colorful musical expressions, there are still opportunities in class for experiences in the world's musics to be wedged in with the traditional musical fare, and made more central to learning. Guitar and keyboard classes can take on a multicultural flavor, too, with music from Columbia, Nigeria, Poland, and Thailand. Of course, there are also nonstandard secondary school music ensembles, too, that can be established, from mariachi bands to

Ghanian drumming ensembles, Polynesian choirs, and Brazilian samba groups. With so many options, the study of the world's music cultures in school is almost inevitable.

A word on authenticity: Music can (and does) change its sound as it shifts from one context to another. For example, the great tradition of samba music of Brazil may sound distinctively different in a middle school classroom than it does on the streets of Rio de Janeiro, just as an African American gospel song is rendered differently by a suburban high school choir than it is by the Kirk Franklin's professional gospel group, The Family, or by the Mississippi Mass Choir. So be it! So long as the ears are open to the sounds of musicians at the source of a tradition, and those who wish to learn the music and musical style are listening with frequency to recordings of the music, then a credible and musical performance can occur. To those who make the music, whoever they are and however removed they may be from the place where the music may have first originated, it is very real and thus as authentic as any music they have made and to which they have developed a connection. The time is past for withholding musical experiences from people for reasons of not having the proper instruments, or an inability over the short run of learning experiences to bring out the music-cultural nuances of a style. Thai music played on piano, Polish music on guitar, Filipino music for a string ensemble, a children's song turned into a rhythmic percussion piece, and Japanese music for school bands—why not? Music travels, and its timbres change in the hands of creative musicians everywhere. It is important to credit the traditional sound, and to listen with care (and even reverence) to the traditions, but the melodies and rhythms of great music can pass from adult choirs to children's choirs, from dueling banjos to concert band, and from a flute melody to one that is sung or played by a variety of musical instruments. Musical authenticity is music that is made with skill and personal or collective expression, such that the music is conveyed and received in meaningful—even powerful—ways, even as it may sound decidedly different from its origins.

The repertoire of music in use by community groups is also in a gradual process of change. Community choirs, whether for children, youth, adults, or intergenerational, resonate well with songs in new languages (and musical languages) from Eastern Europe, the Pacific, and southern Africa. The community bands and orchestras for youth, adults, and elders, including New Horizons bands for senior citizens, are grand opportunities for playing melodies from many cultures, whether in unison or in full harmonic arrangements. Community centers are hubs of activity for all ages, all day long and well into the evenings, and the short courses and workshops that pay tribute to the musical expressions of particular groups within the community are often broadly appealing (even as they also reach out to validate people who have been bypassed or underserved). It is not surprising that Brazilian samba music, played on percussion instruments, is a dynamic way of bringing people of an urban, suburban, or rural community together. Likewise, the old-time music of fiddle, guitars, and banjos is attractive to people who enjoy dancing and listening to standard melodies from the Appalachian and Ozark mountains. Drumming ensembles that feature West African rhythms, and marimba groups that perform melodies from Zimbabwe and Guatemala, are further examples of music that draws people together in communal ways.

Repertoire is important to music therapists who select music for its stimulative and sedative properties, its subject matter, and musical components that signal joy, sorrow, excitement, understanding, and peace. These emotional expressions are culture-specific, however, such that a client may derive meaning that is perceived differently from another client depending upon his or her cultural background. Knowing something of the client's musical experiences and interests can be useful in the determination by the therapist of which musical selections may be wisely applied to affect a change in behavior or mood. Given the increased extent of multicultural populations who require therapy in recent years, knowledge of a varied repertoire of songs and rhythms from Africa, Asia, the Caribbean and other parts of Latin America (for example) can be an important goal for therapists to realize. It may also be argued that music can transcend cultures, and that its musical potency to an individual may pertain to particular melodic and rhythmic dimensions regardless of whether this song is associated with his or her culture. This view offers good reason to develop a rich repertoire of songs, music for movement, and instrumental pieces that invite the participation of special populations. As in the case of music in schools and community settings, a more global expanse of repertoire in therapeutic sessions is certain to benefit those who listen and perform it.

## INSIDE THE BOOK

This book is intended as a compilation of some of the world's traditional songs, melodies, and rhythms for use by teachers, therapists, and leaders of various community organizations in their invitation of children, youth, and adults to music-making experiences. It is for those who will go professional—on various tracks—in their musical engagement, those who already are professional, and those who plainly want to make music alone and with others in whatever venues may open to them. While neither a "fake book" nor a "real book," it shares their function of providing musical notations to realize on various instruments. The contextualizations, the suggested experiences for self-instruction and group-learning, and the broad sampling of styles set it apart from these collections in use by popular and jazz musicians, and take it into the realm of classrooms, clinics, and community centers, and homes and hospitals, where music is taught, learned, and made.

As a text for undergraduate courses in music education methods, music therapy applications, and music/arts for classroom teachers, *Tunes and Grooves for Music Education* is appropriate for university students of music, education and therapy in need of a musical repertoire that they can personally use for shaping their music-making skills, and that they can then take on to lessons and sessions with children and adolescents in any number of contexts.

It is a resource of notated musical matter for stimulating music-making experiences from printed notation, from recorded excerpts, and from recommendations for further listening. In the recognition that melodies and rhythms are more than sonic properties but also have functions and meanings, the text serves to tell of the musicians and musical cultures from which the expressions have emerged. Importantly, the book serves as a collection of materials to be used by thoughtful musicians-in-the-making: music students who are honing their personal skills in singing and song leading, and learning to play piano, guitar, percussion instruments, and an assortment of band, orchestral, and folk instruments for now and in their future work.

Here are dozens of musical ideas, ready to be lifted from the page and fashioned into sonic form and personally meaningful expression. Heritage songs (that is, folk, traditional, orally transmitted "Tunes") from various musical cultures are featured within the compilation, including representative pieces from Africa, Asia, Europe, Latin America and the Caribbean, North America, and the southern Pacific, with texts in the original languages. The "Grooves" include a culturally diverse set of rhythmic segments from which percussion pieces are developed, from the interwoven dimensions of a fast mambo to the beat-keeping property of a hand-held gong. There is a heavy dose of Anglo-American folk songs and fiddle tunes and African-American spirituals and African-American folk songs, and a considerable number of Spanish-language songs and rhythms from popular dance forms of Latin America. To these selections are added Chinese percussion ensemble pieces, freedom songs from South Africa, traditional European rounds and canons, folk songs from the Pacific islands, and children's songs from many of the world's cultures. Covering an array of musical traditions, *Tunes and Grooves for Music Education* is an essential handbook of repertoire for music and education (and therapy) students, and community musicians, that should prove as useful in courses as in classrooms, clinical sessions, and community settings for inciting musical expression and skill-building from childhood onward.

The melodies and rhythms in the body of the text are transcriptions of music that are considered public domain and also from recordings where permission has been obtained from the artists, composers, arrangers, and publishers to portray the music in conventional staff notation. Transcriptions were also produced for music remembered by the author, including experiences long ago in her childhood (at school, on the playground, and at camp) and in her adult life (at community sings, during gatherings with friends and family, in workshops with musicians and teachers, and in fieldwork spent in the collection of songs). In most cases (although, not exclusively), more-intricate music was reduced to single melodic lines or foundational rhythms, while complex harmonic textures and rhythmic densities were somewhat minimized so that these could be read by all, including those with less-advanced musical training. In this way, music specialists as well as classroom teachers, community musicians, and therapists outside the realm of music would not feel blocked from the essence of the collection: to sing, chant, and play with immediacy—on sight—the songs, the melodies from larger works, and the rhythms.*

The text is organized alphabetically by title of the featured tunes and grooves. Many of the selections are intact songs, and their titles are known entities. A few of the melodies function as themes in larger works (such as the Copland's "Hoedown" theme, or Mozart's opening theme to his Symphony No. 40 in G Minor). Several of the rhythms for percussion ensemble are called by their genre name, for example, "Samba Groove." Each selection is described in ways that include the culture of origin, genre, composer, and/or performer(s) with whom the music is associated. Bulleted suggestions are offered for each notated song and musical excerpt for ways of motivating music making in song, instrumental play, eurhythmic movement, and creative improvisation. There are recommendations for further listening to fill out the experience, with the intention of leading users to further means of understanding the particular songs and musical cultures. Where some of the music will be familiar, or at least derived from cultures that have had considerable "play" in western contexts, the sound of the notation will already be in the ears of those who read it. Other music is further afield, or the notation provided for some could be helped immeasurably by the accessibility of its sound. Thus, the CDs store excerpts from about sixty selections that can be played and replayed, sung and played "to," in order to come to terms with the stylistic nuances of the music (and language). In some cases, 1 to 2 minute cuts are deemed entirely sufficient for "getting the groove" or the tune.

---

*The symbol (+) denotes the source recording on which the transcription was based.

The music is mostly of the genre that is referred to as "folk," or "traditional," or lately, "world" (although a few of the selections stem from composed or improvised art music, such as the "Minuet" from Haydn's Symphony No. 47 in G Major and the dutar-tabla duo from Afghanistan, or from the popular media, such as "La Bamba" and "John Wayne's Teeth" (from the film, *Smoke Signals*). In some sense, all of the music in the collection is popular, in that it is music people have liked for some time and are still making. It is music that is part of people's living and doing, whether they live on the high plains, in coastal towns, in mountain villages, in suburban split-levels, in ghettos and barrios, or on reservations. It is old-time music made fresh with every rendition, and newer music linked to history and heritage. There is rhythmic vitality in the music with (and without) melody, and there is a colorful palette of tones and timbres to sample in the rhythms (as well as in the melodies). When performed with feeling, this music holds the hearts and souls of people across time and culture.

Each song or melodic theme is approached through singing, even those that are primarily or purely instrumental. Neutral syllables, solfège syllables, and numbers are suggested. Moveable Do is the recommended solfège system, in which the tonic "home-tone" is always "do" or "1," regardless of the major key; for minor keys, the home tone is always "la" or "6." Only the seven syllables—do, re, mi, fa, sol, la, and ti—are used, and numbers 1 through 7; no "shadings" or alternate syllables are used for accidentals. (Of course, any system of sight-reading is applicable, including Fixed Do, Moveable Do with "fi"s (four: sharped) and "te"s (seven: flatted), numbers, and pitch letters—according to individual preference.) As vocalization is important in musical learning, even rhythms can be assigned a vocalized chant on syllables or words. The importance of internalizing the music cannot be overestimated, and is most readily accomplished through the intimate act of expressing it vocally.

A great majority of the songs and themes emanate from traditions that prize the use of harmonic accompaniment. Thus, piano and guitar accompaniments are suggested, including block chords, rolls, arpeggiations, and finger-picking possibilities. Dulcimer and autoharp are suitable for some of the selections, and for recorder and xylophone ensembles. Many of the melodies are well suited, albeit sometimes transposed, to orchestral and band instruments, including violin, flute, saxophone, trumpet, and trombone (among others). Percussion instruments, from finger cymbals and cowbells to congas and djembes, are appropriate for the performance of both "grooves" and selected melodies. New musical innovations lie in wait when instruments outside of a tradition are employed to sound the tune or groove. For example, the performance of a Vietnamese melody like "Qua Câu Gió Bay" on saxophone, the sound of the Brazilian "Cajueiro Pequenino" by a string ensemble (with percussion), and an arrangement of, Haere for a sixth grade band, are all enticing as cross-cultural encounters with musical cultures. These melodies may well be performed solo or in unison, or with harmonic progressions, clusters, or even in some sort of fugal fashion.

Many of the musical selections invite dancing or eurhythmic movement. Some of the songs are primarily associated with dancing, such as "Haliwa-Saponi Canoe Dance," "Hava Nagila," and "Allons Danser, Colinda." There are jigs and reels, waltzes, meringues and mambos, contra-dance tunes, and a rich variety of circle dances. Children's singing games require movement, too, of specific gestures that represent the song texts, and which are associated with jump-roping and hand-clapping activities. Various eurhythmic movements, including stepping, skipping, hopping, and jumping, are recommended as means of learning the music and feeling it to the fullest capacity. Movement with joy, with freedom and abandon, and within the strictures of cultural style are all potential experiences for knowing and expressing the essence of the music within the collection.

## *FOR GUITAR PLAYERS*

The melodies within the collection are playable by guitar, and of course where there are chords, there is always the potential for guitar chording. In a guitar class or private lessons, at any level, a rich variety of songs fit well within guitar-playing traditions. Melodies call out for chords, particularly those hailing from Anglo-American traditions such as "Old Joe Clark," "The Coo-Coo Bird," and "How Can I Keep from Singing?," African-American folk music ("Over My Head" and "The Buzzard Lope") and blues genres ("Walkin' Blues" and "Woke Up This Morning"), Mexican traditions ("A Mi Querido Austin," "La Bamba," and "Los Machetes") and other Latin American musical cultures ("Sambalele," "Tinga Layo" and "El Barreño"), as well as European traditions ("Dúlamán," "Kum Bachur Atzel," and "Ajde Jano"). Songs from the African continent ("Sansa Kroma," for example), and the Pacific Islands, such as "Tihore Mai," also fit well into the hands of guitarists who can play the requisite chords and/or melodies. Many of the selections require just three or four chords, and some even less than that, and then can be further colored by advanced players with sevenths, sixths, and suspensions. While most of the melodies sound well enough in standard tuning, D- and G-tunings, where the strings are adjusted to the relevant chord tones, may offer a pleasant sonic alternative. The selections can be played by an ensemble of guitarists, some on melody while others chord, or can be played and sung by the group just as so many of these songs would be performed within their traditions.

## FOR PIANO PLAYERS

When there are melodies and a piano nearby, there is the potential for music to be made. In piano classes, all melodies are possible, and many are potent for building skills and repertoire. The traditions of some of the melodies are more likely to inspire piano playing, such as the melodies from Western European classical music, (including themes from Mozart's first movement of Symphony No. 40 or Bach's "Little" Fugue in G Minor,) the songs of the African-American spiritual and gospel genres ("Go Down, Moses," "Joshua Fought the Battle of Jericho," "If You See My Savior," and "This Little Light of Mine"), and Anglo-American church and community songs ("Wondrous Love," "She's Like the Swallow," and "Salty Dog"). Latin American dance styles, particularly salsa music, naturally invite the use of piano, as in "Billie" and "Mi Bajo y Yo."

Musical genres that do not normally feature piano can nonetheless find themselves in the hands of pianists who can develop their musicianship and learn a broader array of musical expressions by playing (and singing) them. For a Cajun tune like "Bonjour, Mes Amis" to a Chinese melody like "Gong Xi Fa Cai," and from a Hungarian folk song like "Erdo, Erdo" to a Navajo melody like "I Walk in Beauty," the piano becomes a vehicle for conveying disparate melodic expressions in new sonic ways that are beyond the primary instruments of the folk culture. For students learning to play piano, or learning its function as a harmonic instrument, or with interests in expanding their repertoire beyond that of the conventional music of piano music collections, these collected tunes take them to new musical worlds.

## FOR PLAYERS OF PERCUSSION INSTRUMENTS

Percussion music, played by highly trained percussionists, falls into a variety of music categories—much of it within the realm of Western art music. Yet across the world, there is a vast array of styles and pitched and nonpitched percussion instruments by which to play them. The rhythmic grooves featured in this collection are derived largely from cultural groups in Africa and Latin America, with some examples from Asia, Europe, North America, and the Pacific. Many are meant to be played on non-pitched percussion instruments, such as drums, woodblocks, iron bells, and gongs, and some are fit for xylophones of wood or metal. They are playable by organized percussion ensembles or by students in university-level percussion methods classes, pick-up community percussion groups, or settings of young people in school classes or therapy sessions. Ideally, there are specific drums to offer the most culturally resonant sounds on these selections, and yet using what materials are available, merengue and samba grooves can be played on djembe drums, just as various African percussion pieces can be played on congas. A repertoire for a secondary school world percussion ensemble, or a community ensemble, could easily include "Wedding Dance Groove," "Caiqiu Wu," "Rumba Groove," "Reggae Groove," "Salsa Groove," and "Voice of Trong." Beginning players of conga drum in elementary school, or in a drumming circle on a Saturday morning, would do well with even one of these grooves, for example the rhythm for the salsa dance, learning it until it becomes second nature, and then playing it to accompany a variety of recorded selections by the likes of Tito Puente, Ruben Blades, Gloria Estefan, and Santana. In addition to full-out rhythm pieces, many of the selections in this collection can be dressed up with the addition of nonpitched instruments such as hand drum, shakers (such as maracas or shekere), woodblock, bell, or tambourine to spice up or clarify the rhythmic dimensions of the music. Thus, in performances by a group of singers, full mixed choir, band, orchestra, or a guitar or piano group, percussion instruments fill out and flavor the music.

## FOR SINGERS OF ALL SORTS

The songs beckon to singers, and beg for solo, small group, and full choral renditions. Many of them are intended as unison songs, with no need to harmonize them, and some by nature of their texts are meant as solos (for examples, "As I Roved Out," "Sometimes I Feel Like a Motherless Child," and "Poor Wayfaring Stranger"). The joy of a beautiful unison sound, when multiple singers move together across phonemes in precise rhythm, such that many voices sound as one, is something to behold in the group rendering of songs like "Johnny Has Gone for a Soldier," "Santa Clara," "Qiugaviit," "Jo'Ashila," and "Do Doc Do Ngang." There are rounds and canons fit for children who are gaining strength vocally and perceptually, such that they can hold their own part in a multi-layered song, starting as early as eight or nine (and sometimes as late as eleven or twelve) years. These songs include the likes of "Ah, Poor Bird," "Hotaru Koi," "Rise Up, O Flame," "Dowidzenia," and "Sumer Is Icumen In." Such canonic singing works well with groups of adolescent and adult singers, too, as warm-ups and "blending-songs" if not as actual performance pieces. Other more chorally oriented songs, sung from notated parts or created as singers become increasingly comfortable with the melodies and their harmonic potential, abound. There are the bona fide choral pieces such as "Northfield" and "Wai Bamba," and the imagined harmonies that can be realized in songs like "Kwaheri," "Keep Your Hand on that Plow," "Maramica Na Stazi," "'Ulili E," and "De Colores." Altogether, this collection is heavy on songs to be sung by singers alone and together, for the sheer joy and exhuberance of it, whether a cappella or with instrumental accompaniment.

## FOR ALL THE OTHER INSTRUMENTALISTS

Any tune that is sung can also be played—played on instruments alone, or played alongside the singing. A single flute (or recorder), or clarinet, trumpet, trombone, or violin, can offer expressive soloistic renderings of "Barb'ry Allen," "Cherokee Morning Song," "Khang Khaaw Kin Kluay," or "Le Jig Français," and while some timbres may seem to fit one melody or another more naturally (as in the case of a violin [fiddle] on "Soldier's Joy"), they may all be workable. It is entirely possible for a concert band, a brass quartet, a school orchestra or a makeshift ensemble of varied instruments to play melodies in unison, from "Turkey in the Straw" and "Sakura" to "Yo, Mamana, Yo" and "John Wayne's Teeth." Why? Because these selections help to diversify the music that players can share, because they are melodies that work as unison or harmonized pieces, and because they are relatively short musical pieces that work to tune players to one another in the course of playing them well.

There are wordless tunes in the collection meant principally for instrumental performance, including "Staliá, Staliá," Copland's "Hoedown," and "Tommy Peoples." Suggestions for instruments are offered, often with timbres in mind that might best fit the culture from which the tunes are derived. Yet any melody can be played by any instruments, in any number whatsoever. When the recordings can be paired with the live performances, wonderful things can happen, including that discriminating means of comparing "us" (the live players) with "them" (the recorded performers).

## MULTIMUSICAL SENSIBILITIES

The value of a book like *Tunes and Grooves for Music Education* is in how the music finds its way into the lives of those who wish to sing it, play it, and dance it. The plentiful expressions here have been meaningful to people over time and distance, and have the staying power that allows them to have been continued across the years even while they still sound fresh with each new rendition. They constitute a repertoire which is multicultural and global in perspective, whose purpose is to develop knowledge of music as culture, as well as a broader musicianship that leans towards multimusical sensibilities. That noble goal, cultivation of music in society, may well rest in the sorts of tunes and grooves gathered here with the potential to draw people of every age into the act of making music.

# Tunes and Grooves
# for Music Education

# A LA RUEDA DE SAN MIGUEL

Mexico

*To the wheel of San Miguel, Everyone brings a keg of honey.*
*So it will ripen, so it will ripen, and keep on turning Maria del burro.*

## The Tune

A well-known traditional children's song from Mexico, "A la Rueda de San Miguel" is sung and danced by young children—whether or not they have ever ridden a donkey or know precisely where San Miguel (St. Michael) is.

## The Music Culture

Mexico is a singing culture, where *cancion*es (songs characterized by romantic sentimentality and pathos) and a host of other vocal and instrumental forms are enjoyed by people of all ages—from mariachi to marimba ensembles, rock bands, and musica norteño groups comprised of guitars, accordion, and drums. Music is important to Mexicans, and children hear it on a daily basis and on special occasions such as baptism, quinceaños (a "coming-out" debutante party for fifteen-year-olds), weddings, birthdays, and even funerals. It is heard on national public holidays such as New Year's Day, Constitution Day (February 4), Independence Day (September 16), Día de los Muertos (Day of the Dead, November 1–2), and at Cinco de Mayo (May 5), a time for recognizing the Mexican national spirit and cultural identity. Of course, children will sing any time at all, and "A la Rueda de San Miguel" is as popular a singing game in Mexico as is "Ring Around the Rosy" in North America. Like its English-language counterpart, it is enjoyed for its associated game more than anything else. Interestingly, the song shares the same tune as another popular Spanish-language singing game, "A la Vibora de la Mar." Like many children's songs, this one makes only partial sense: San Miguel is a city in the province of Chiapas, Mexico (and there are ten other cities, towns, and villages in Mexico with this name, too).

### The Experiences

- Sing the melody on a neutral syllable such as "la," with solfège syllables (beginning on "sol") or scale numbers (beginning on "5").
- Sing the Spanish lyrics.

- Note the translation: "To the wheel of San Miguel, Everyone brings a keg of honey. So it will ripen, and the wheel will keep on turning Maria del burro." A keg of honey is a vast amount of that sweet substance to bring to a celebration; the honey ripens over time (even while) Maria continues to dance.
- Play the chords on the guitar, one chord per quarter-note beat, or in a down, down-up strum
- Play the guitar chords in an up-down fashion, to an eighth-note rhythm.
- Play the melody on violin, trumpet, flute, or recorder to the guitar chords.
- Play the game in a circle, facing in and holding hands. One player stands in center, while the others move right to the beat of the music. At the end of the song, the center player chooses someone to replace him/her in the center, and joins the circle, facing out. The game is repeated until all the players are moving with their backs to the circle.

## Recommended Listening
+*Children's Songs and Games from Ecuador, Mexico, and Puerto Rico*. Folkways FW 07854.
+*Disney Presenta Cantar y Jugar*. Disney ASIN: B0000894PR 20043.
*Al Lobo: Songs and Games of Latin America*. Rounder Kids CD 8078.

# A MI QUERIDO AUSTIN

Eva Ybarra

Quan - do voy pa - ra mi Aus - tin     me par - te mi co - ra - zon,

por - que to - dos me re - ci - ben     con ca - ri - no     y a - mor.

2. Mi capital del Estado
   Yo le doy mi inspiracion
   en este bonito Wapango
   tocando el Accordion.

1. *When I go to my Austin,*
   *My heart breaks just a bit,*
   *Because everyone welcomes me,*
   *With love and affection.*

2. *My capital of the state,*
   *I give my inspiration,*
   *In this beautiful Wapango,\**
   *Playing the accordion.*

\* Wapango (or Juapango) is the name for this genre of song.

Words and music by Eva Araiza Ybarra. Copyright 1995 Happy Valley Music. From Rounder CD 6062, *Romance Inolvidable* by Eva Ybarra y su Conjunto (1996). All rights reserved. Used with kind permission of Happy Valley Music.

# A MI QUERIDO AUSTIN

CD I, Track # 1

## The Tune

Eva Ybarra, *la reina de acordeón* (the queen of accordion), celebrates the capital city of Austin, Texas, with "A Mi Querido Austin" (To My Dear Austin). This is Tex-Mex music, also known as *Tejano conjunto*, that features accordion, *bajo sexto* (12-string bass guitar), bass guitar and drums.

## The Music Culture

*Tejano conjunto* is a popular genre of music developed in south and central Texas, which is now heard throughout Texas, in Mexican-American communities across the United States, and internationally. Conjunto music resulted from a general assimilation of European nineteenth-century dances, many of them brought to Texas by settlers from Germany and Czechoslovakia. The button accordion was used from the 1890s onward, first two-row buttons and then three-row buttons in the 1950s. The *bajo sexto*, electric guitar, and drums (or drum kit) became standard instrumentation by the 1960s. The *polca* (German and Czech polka) became a predominantly vocal genre in conjunto music, performed in a typically Hispanic style of two voices in parallel thirds and sixths. Conjunto is heard in clubs, dance halls, bars, and at a great variety of family gatherings, from Christmas and New Year's to weddings, birthdays, anniversaries, and reunions. "A Mi Querido Austin" pays tribute not only to the lively city known for its clubs and the highly regarded South-by-Southwest music (and film) festival, but also to the "wapango" (*juapango*) form—a term for peasant or rural music that is known for its plucked *rasgueado* technique on the instruments of the guitar family. Eva Ybarra is a San Antonio-based conjunto bandleader and accordionist who has been playing since she was six years old, and who enjoys integrating a little jazz and rock into her Tex-Mex tradition.

### The Experiences

- Listen to Track # 1, in order to hear Eva Ybarra and her conjunto group. Catch the pronunciation of the lyrics, the changing harmonies, the interplay of the instruments.
- Listen to the recording again, and hum the melody line while listening to the recording.
- Sing the song on solfège syllables, with scale numbers, and with Spanish text.
- Play the I–V chords on guitar or piano, exploring various left hand patterns in three:

- Add the bass line on string bass, electric bass, or piano.
- Listen again to get the feel of the music, and to pick up on the vocal harmonies and performance style.
- Using accordion or other available instruments (guitar, piano, bass), practice playing and singing the piece in a conjunto style.

### Recommended Listening

+*Romance Involvidable*, Eva Ybarra y su Conjunto. Rounder Select 6062.

*Los Dos Gilbertos, Roberto Pulido: Conjunto Classics*. Rounder Select.

# ABBOTS BROMLEY HORN DANCE
## (FIRST STRAIN)

England

CD I, Track # 2

## The Tune

Abbots Bromley is a town in Staffordshire, England, where a traditional dance of men holding antlers is performed. The melody, "Abbots Bromley Horn Dance" may be performed by an accordion or concertina, a pipe and tabor (drum), or a fiddle.

## The Music Culture

Local people maintain that the "Abbots Bromley Horn Dance" may have been performed around the time of winter solstice since the thirteenth century, possibly to mark the return of the sun. The festival at Abbots Bromley is now held in early September to coincide with the onset of the deer rutting season. The antlers used in the dance are usually reindeer horns that may weigh as much as twenty-five pounds and extend over three feet in width. They are mounted on wooden deer-heads, and poles are attached to the heads and horns to make them easier to carry. On the day of the festival, male dancers collect their horns at Abbots Bromley Church, where they have been stored. They receive an early morning blessing for the church vicar, and then they set off to perform the horn dance at twelve locations (including local houses and farms) across about ten miles in the vicinity of the village. The dancers each wear a cap, knee pants, knitted stockings, and a jersey. Their formation consists of two lines that face one another. They raise their antlers as if they are about to fight, then back away, advance, and lock horns. Along with the music and dancing, the festivities at Abbots Bromley include craft stalls, food stalls, and exhibitions.

### The Experiences

- While listening to Track # 2, sing the melody on "loo," noting its shorter and longer motifs and phrases.
- Listen again to the recording, and step the rhythm of the melody, feeling the rise and fall of the two-pitch motifs and the grace and glide of the longer phrase.
- Tap/pat the melodic rhythm while singing it.
- Play the melody on concertina, violin, flute, recorder, or other melody instrument.
- Create a verse to fit the melody and its rhythm. Sing it. Here is one example: "We dance the dance of deer who prance, to celebrate autumn and winter delight."

### Recommended Listening
+*John Langstaff: The Christmas Revels*. Revels Records 1078.
*English Customs and Traditions*. Saydisc 475.

# AEYAYA BALANO SAKKAD

India

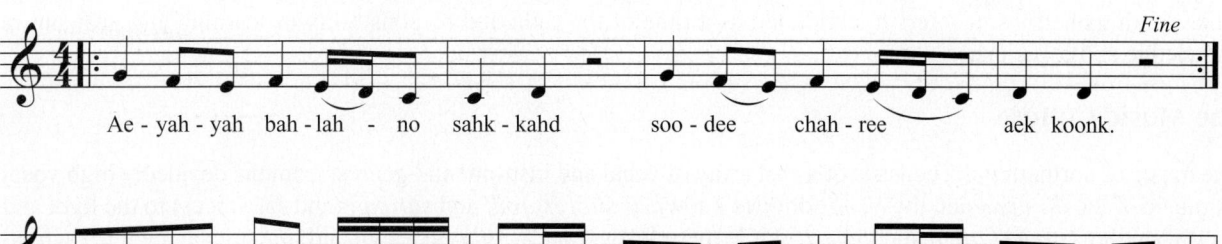

Ae - yah - yah bah - lah - no   sahk - kahd   soo - dee   chah - ree   aek  koonk.

Sahn - kah - tah  toom  kah   jee - vah   nah - nee - tee,  jee - vah - nah   nee - tee

Sahn - kah - tah  toom  kah   jee - vah - nah   nee - tee,  Sah - fahl   jah - vah   chahk

chohl  chee  ree  tee   Sah - fahl   jah - vah - chahk   chohl  chee  ree  tee.

*Come, children, gather near.*
*Come hear the secrets of life.*
*Childhood is a gift, it's passing by so fast,*
*We can never appreciate, something we really should celebrate.*
*This is the time when we have the power to learn and grow.*
*This is the time when we can build on the things we know.*

## AEYAYA BALANO SAKKAD (DRONE)

# AEYAYA BALANO SAKKAD

## The Tune

"Aeyaya Balano Sakkad" is a song for children and youth, intended to be sung by them at school, at festivals, or in other youth gatherings. It refers to childhood as a time of the right and responsibility of learning and growing in knowledge and experience.

## The Music Culture

The music of northern India consists of a vast array of vocal and instrumental genres, from the decidedly high vocal art music of the *dhrupad* and the *khyal* for lutes known as *sitar, sarod,* and *sarangi* (and for voices) to the light and playful rhythms of the *tarana* and *thumri*. While these forms vary greatly in design and function, and while each instrument and voice lends a distinctive performance quality to them, they all sound distinctively "Hindustani" by virtue of their underlying drone (played by *tambura* or *harmonium*), their percussive rhythms (played by drums such as *tabla*), and the tendency of their melodies to range from slightly decorated to highly melismatic. Yet these art music genres do not preclude the importance of folk and traditional music, including songs for entertainment, weddings, and for raising children who are morally bound to heed the lessons of their elders. "Aeyaya Balano Sakkad" is sung in Kankani, a language that is spoken in the western region, south of Bombay and along the coast of the Bay of Bengal. The song's melody is in the (Western) Mixolydian mode and its rhythm can be counted as an eight-beat rhythm cycle, or *tala*.

### The Experiences

- Sing the song on a neutral syllable such as "nah."
- Sing a Mixolydian scale, starting and ending on G. Think major scale, but with a lowered 7th degree: G A B C D E F G.
- Sing the song with the transliterated words, which sound close to the way they are spelled here.
- Consider the advice embedded in the song's lyrics: "Come children, gather near. Hear the secrets of life. Childhood is a gift, passing quickly by. We can never fully appreciate it, but we should celebrate it, knowing that this is the time when we have the power to learn and grow, and to build on the things we know."
- Play the drone throughout, on piano with sustain pedal, or by bowing D and G on a stringed instrument such as violin or cello.
- Play a drum pattern on conga drums that uses right (R), left (L), and both (B) hands. As some students play, others can "keep the tala" by clapping (C), tapping the fingers of the right hand one-by-one to the palm of the left hand (T), and waving (W) the right hand in the air for the *khali* (or empty) beat:

| Beat: | 1 | 2 | 3 | 4 | | 1 | 2 | 3 | 4 |
|---|---|---|---|---|---|---|---|---|---|
| Drum: | R | L | R L | B | | L R | L R | B | B |
| Clap: | C | T | T | T | | W | T | T | T |

- Combine drone and drum with sung melody.
- Intersperse the vocal line with solo or same instruments playing the melody; try violin, flute, saxophone, for example.

### Recommended Listening

*Folk Music of India.* Folkways FW 04409.

*World Library of Folk and Primitive Music, Volume 7: India* (compiled and edited by Alan Lomax). Rounder Select (Inventory ID: 8216117552).

*The Ravi Shankar Collection: India's Master Musician.* Angel 7243-5-67023-2-5.

# AFSHARI

Iran: Persian

## The Groove

In Persian classical music, "Afshari" is the name of a *dastgah,* or mode. It consists of these pitches: C D E♭ F G A♭ B♭ played by the *tar*, a lute with twenty-six moveable frets and six strings. A round single-headed frame drum known as *daff* performs the rhythm that is also derived from a mode but which finds its own interpretation in this piece by performer-composer Kamil Alipour of Tehran.

## The Music Culture

In Iran, classical Persian music is still widely performed in concert halls and in private chambers. Theoretical treatises on the music date back at least to the golden age of the Sassinad Dynasty of the third to the seventh centuries CE. Music has long been an intellectual as well as an expressive pursuit among the Persians. There are complex rules and techniques in learning to perform such instruments as the *tar* or the *setar* (a four-stringed lute), as well as the *daff*, particularly as it pertains to what is acceptable in the course of improvisation. The *daff* is integral to the music of many Muslim cultures, and is found in varying forms (*daf, def, duff*) across the Middle East, in northern Africa, central Asia and southeastern Europe. It has been connected with entertainment, celebration, religious festivities, battles, and poetry. Its membrane, often of goatskin, is glued to a wooden frame. The player holds the drum in one hand and beats with the fingers, thumb and palm of the other hand. While a goblet drum known as *tombak* almost replaced the *daff* in Persian classical music of the nineteenth century, the *daff* has been revived over the last twenty-five years.

### The Experiences

- Read the transcription. Play the rhythm on the *daff* or available hand drum, holding it in one hand while tapping with three fingers of the other hand. (Caution: there is much more to *daff*-playing than this single technique! Its performance practice requires training, to learn thumb, fingers, and palm techniques.)

### Recommended Listening

+*Music from Tea Lands*. Putamayo World Music PUT 180-2.
*Iran: Persian Classical Music*. Nonesuch 72060.
*Vision: Manoochehr Sadeghi*. Santur.com (Nakisa Records).
*Classical Music of Iran, Volumes I and II*. Smithsonian Folkways FW 08831, FW 08832.

# AH, POOR BIRD

England

From *Music in Childhood: From Preschool Through the Elementary Grade* with Audio CD 3rd edition by CAMPBELL/SCOTT-KASSNER, 2006. Reprinted with permission of Wadsworth, a Division of Thomson Learning: www. Thomsonrights.com. Fax 800-730-2215.

## The Tune

"Ah, Poor Bird" is a popular canon for choirs, school and community groups of singers. Thought to have originated in England, it is heard in many North American settings and is enjoyed in choirs of other English-speaking cultures.

## The Music Culture

As a canon, the performance of this melody provides a polyphonic texture of three voice parts, each one entering one measure after another, similar to the standard *round.* The canon is a fairly common song form in Western Europe, and was historically important in France, Italy, Germany, the Netherlands, and England. It dates to at least the thirteenth century, and at one point involved an inscribed formula or instruction, which the performer would implement in order to realize one or more parts from the given notation. The meaning of canon was relaxed later, and has come to refer to the process of imitation. *Chase* is a fourteenth-century term for canon, and for a small number of French-texted, three-voice canons that employed onomatopoeia and word-painting. *Catches* appeared in England from the late sixteenth century until 1800 as a type of common round for male voices, and catch clubs sprang up all over England by about 1750. The English folk music collector and editor, Cecil Sharp (1859–1924), included rounds, catches, chases, and canons in his collections of folk songs. He was instrumental in restoring this polyphonic form, as well as other song forms and dances, to the British people through their integration into schools.

### The Experiences

- Sing the song on a neutral syllable such as "bah", and on solfège syllables (beginning on "la") and scale numbers (beginning on "6").
- Sing the song with words, in unison, until it sounds fully in tune and solidly in ensemble.
- Break the group of singers into three groups, each one entering one measure after the previous group. Sing the song several times through, and then allow each part to finish in its time.
- Play a harmonic accompaniment on piano or guitar, choosing a light texture and dynamic level.

### Recommended Listening

+*The Rounds Galore and More Singers, Volumes I and II.* Astoria Productions. Available from <ukelady@prodigy.net>."
*Four-Voice Canons.* Cold Blue Label CB0011.

# AJDE JANO

Serbia

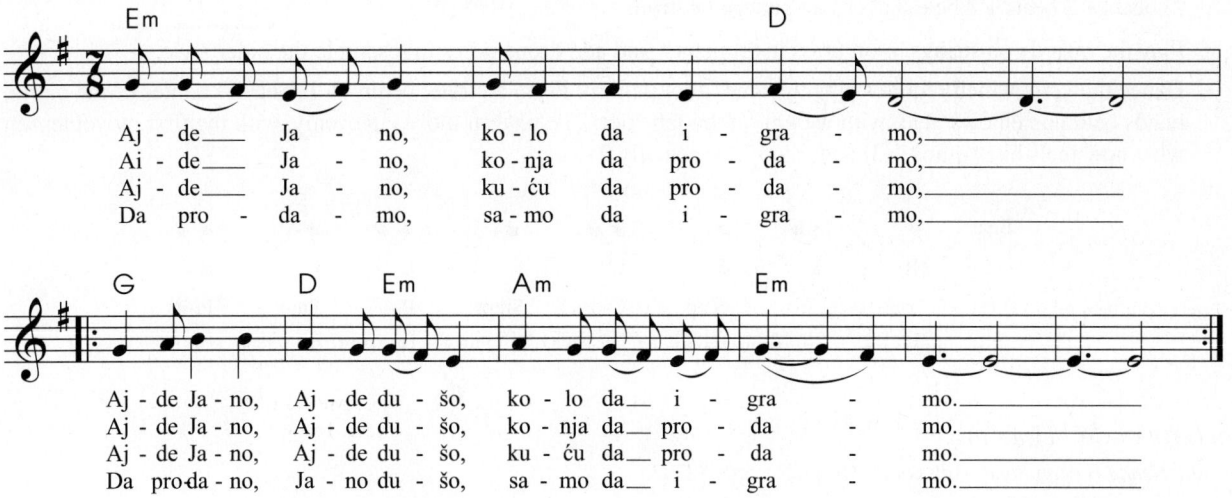

1. *Come on, Jana, dear one, let's dance the kolo.*
2. *Come on, Jana, dear one, let's sell the horse.*
3. *Come on, Jana, dear one, let's sell the house.*
4. *Let's sell them, Jana, dear one, just so we can dance.*

## The Tune

"Adje Jano" is a folk song from Serbia, whose very melody is an invitation to a traditional circle dance known as the *kolo*. As the lyrics reveal, this dance so enlivens its participants that they are willing to "sell the house" just so that they can give themselves entirely up to dancing.

## The Music Culture

Traditional songs of Serbia (and its neighboring countries of Croatia, Slovenia, Bosnia and Hercegovina, Montenegro, and Macedonia) are sung by girls and women without instrumental accompaniment, while the playing of musical instruments was (and in many cases still is) the work of men. Sometimes voices and instruments are combined, particularly in dance songs like "Adje Jano," in which case the powerful *gajde* (bagpipe) could sound a melody that would hold firmly in the outdoors. *Tamburas,* lutes with four strings, are popular at dances, too, to accompany singers or to play on their own, and brass bands are popular for local festivals and weddings. Traditional songs are dying out in Serbia due to the rapid modernization of even rural areas, and the "new" songs are breaking away from older drones and tight harmonies in seconds in order to allow for chordal harmonies. The use of asymmetric meter, for example 7/8 (in this case, in groups of 3+2+2 beats) may be a remainder of Turkish influence from the time of Serbia's status as part of the Ottoman Empire. As singer-dancers gather in a circle, they do not forget that their feet move in front and behind one another while keeping time to the subdivisions of the meter.

### The Experiences

- Sing the melody on a neutral syllables like "loo," and on solfège syllables (beginning on "do") or scale numbers (beginning on "3").

- Sing the song in Serbian, noting that the only unusual pronunciation for non-Serbians is "j" which is pronounced as "y." Thus "Ajde" is "Ay-deh" and "Jano" is "Ya-noh." Also, pronounce "dušo" as "doo-shoh," and kuću as "koo-choo." Following the chordal harmony, assign the drone to a small group of singers.

- Play through the chords of the song on piano or guitar. Punctuate the subdivisions, using a "slow-quick-quick" (3 beats + 2 beats + 2 beats) chording pattern or strum.

- Play the melody on strings or on brass instruments, and add drone notes to resemble the older style.

- Dance the *kolo*, which requires a "grapevine" foot pattern. Form a circle, begin by facing the center of the circle, hands held and elbows bent, with weight on the left foot. The pattern moves unevenly, with the first movement in what now feels like "quick" (3) and "slow" (4, actually 2+2).

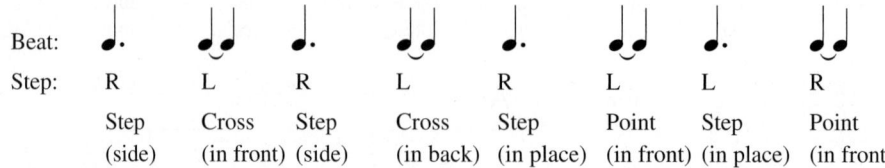

| Beat: | ♩. | ♩♩ | ♩. | ♩♩ | ♩. | ♩♩ | ♩. | ♩♩ |
|---|---|---|---|---|---|---|---|---|
| Step: | R | L | R | L | R | L | L | R |
| | Step | Cross | Step | Cross | Step | Point | Step | Point |
| | (side) | (in front) | (side) | (in back) | (in place) | (in front) | (in place) | (in front) |

## Recommended Listening

+*Vasilic Nenad Balkan Band, Folk Songs*. Origin Records 82392.

*Village Harmony: Traditional Songs of the Balkans*. Northern Harmony NHPC102-CD

*Folk Music of Yugoslavia*. Folkways FW 04434.

# ALA DE'LONA

Middle East: The Levant Region

A - la De'- lo - na, A - la De' - lo - na, Hi - war shi - ma -

li gha - yar ih - lo - na. Ma - ba - di i - mi ma - ba - di

ba - yi; Ba - di ha - bi - bi as - mar ih - lo - na.

*Fair De'lona with dark skin,*
*Chilled by the wind; I would*
*Leave my mother and father,*
*To visit my fair De'lona.*

## The Tune

One of the most well-known songs in the Arab Middle East, "Ala De'lona" is sung in Lebanon, Syria, Jordan, Egypt, Saudi Arabia, and neighboring countries. It is a love song originally sung by a young man smitten by the beauty of a girl named De'lona.

## The Music Culture

In the Levant region of the Middle East that includes Jordan, Lebanon, and Syria, songs are sung to express love, to voice social criticism, to lull a child to sleep, to mourn the deceased, to celebrate weddings. The traditional music of this region is essentially melodic in that it does not use the harmonic and contrapuntal devices of Western music. (However, popular music is likely to have accepted into its expressive palette the harmonic influences of the West.) Melodic, rhythmic, or timbral ornamentation is upheld in Middle Eastern music as a means of embellishing and supporting the melody. Short strophic forms are prevalent in the songs of the Levant, particularly four-line quatrains without refrains. The AABA rhyme scheme is less common than the AAAB form, but both of these forms stress the importance of sung poetry in Arab folk music where the text leads and helps shape the melody. Some songs are danced, and the 6-beat *dubka* rhythm spans the length of a line of verse (and a three-measure melodic unit).

### The Experiences

- Hum the melody of Ala De'lona, switching each time around to a different syllable ("lah," "mee," "doo") until the melody is familiar.
- Sing the melody on solfège syllables (beginning on "la") or scale numbers (beginning on "6").

- Play two chords per measure on guitar or piano, while singing.
- Using a hand drum or a goblet-shaped drum, play the rhythm ostinato. On "dumm," play a low-pitched sound, and on "takk," play a crispy, sharper, and higher sound.

dumm    takk    dumm    takk takk

## Recommended Listening

*Ali Jihad Racy: Mystical Legacies*. Lyrichord Discs, Inc. 7437.

*Arabic Songs of Lebanon and Egypt*. Folkways FW 06925.

# ALL AROUND THE KITCHEN

U. S.: Alabama

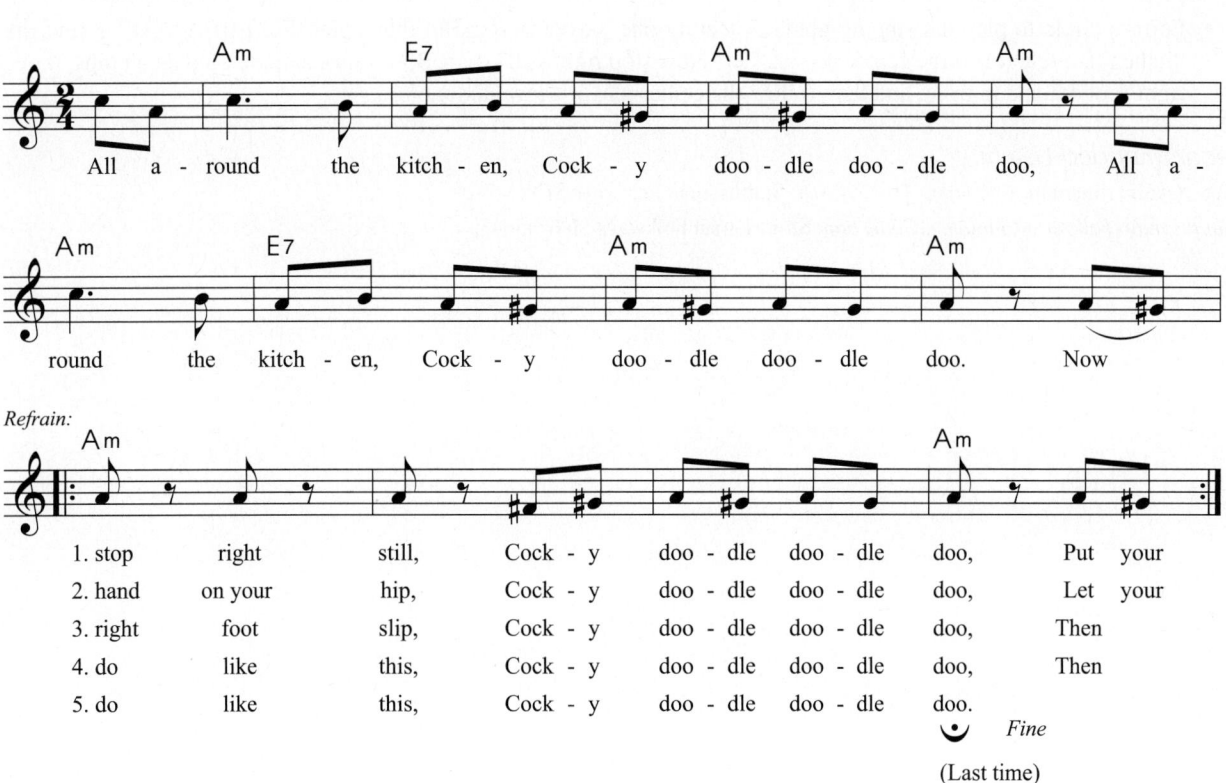

All a - round the kitch - en, Cock - y doo - dle doo - dle doo, All a -
round the kitch - en, Cock - y doo - dle doo - dle doo. Now

*Refrain:*

| 1. stop | right | still, | Cock - y | doo - dle doo - dle doo, | Put your |
| 2. hand | on your | hip, | Cock - y | doo - dle doo - dle doo, | Let your |
| 3. right | foot | slip, | Cock - y | doo - dle doo - dle doo, | Then |
| 4. do | like | this, | Cock - y | doo - dle doo - dle doo, | Then |
| 5. do | like | this, | Cock - y | doo - dle doo - dle doo. | |

*Fine*

(Last time)

## The Tune

This singing game was collected by the Lomaxes in Alabama, where children were seen imitating the movements of a leader in the center of the circle. Ruth Crawford Seeger included the song in her *American Folk Songs for Children* (1948), and Pete Seeger popularized the song through his singing of it with a lively banjo accompaniment.

## The Music Culture

Few names are better known in the collection and preservation of American folk songs—particularly Anglo-American and African-American songs—than the Lomaxes and the Seegers. Alan Lomax, son of John Lomax and brother of Bess Lomax Hawes, began collecting with his father for the Archive of American Folksong, Library of Congress, as early as 1937. He spent much of his time in the rural southern states, listening to and recording the blues, cowboy songs, children's songs, and songs heard on farms, in churches, prisons, and nightclubs. He invited Ruth Crawford Seeger, composer, educator, and wife of musicologist Charles Seeger, to transcribe the songs suitable for children. She set songs like "Oats Peas Beans," "I Got a Letter," "Hop Up My Ladies," and "Johnny Got a Haircut" as vocal lines with piano accompaniments. The Seeger children, Peggy and Mike (and Pete) performed them with banjos, 6- and 12-string guitars, and vocal harmonies. It is through the work of the Lomaxes and the Seegers that a rich repertoire of American folk songs—particular Anglo- and African-American songs—from the period of the Depression and World War II are known today.

## The Experiences

- Sing the song, noticing the small melodic range (g#–c′), that gives the song the character of speech—exaggerated.

- Play the chords on guitar, using a down-up movement of the left hand that provides four strums per measure.

- Form a circle to play the singing game, selecting one player to stand in the center. For part A ("All around the kitchen"), circle round the center person. On "Now stop right still" (part B, refrain), stop, put hands on hips, move right foot out and in front, and then follow the center player's invented motion.

## Recommended Listening

+*Pete Seeger: American Folk Songs for Children*. Smithsonian Folkways SFW 45020.

+*Smithsonian Folkways Children's Collection*. Smithsonian Folkways SFW 45043.

# ALL THE PRETTY LITTLE HORSES

United States

## The Tune

Lullabies like "All the Pretty Little Horses," a slumber song that is widespread in North America, continue to be alive and well as they are passed from parent to child.

## The Music Culture

Lulling a child to sleep by song is a universal phenomenon that knows no historical or cultural boundaries. The soothing sound of a lullaby emanates from those parents, grandparents, and others who are entrusted with the care of an infant, toddler, or small child. Melodies of lullabies are typically tonal, of a small range (an octave or less) and with fewer pitches overall than other song types, and undulating—rising and falling in a subtle rocking feeling. They tend to move quietly and gently in duple or triple meter, and their lyrics are about the familiar: mother and father, animals, the cradle, crib, or crèche. Well-known lullabies in North America include "Mockingbird" ("Hush little baby, don't say a word"), "Rock-a-bye Baby," Johannnes Brahms's song "Wiegenlied," and the French traditional berceuse. Lullabies are likely to be sung by women more than men (although this could be changing as men take on the challenges of child care), and are prized because of their potential to communicate to the wee ones in a direct, intimate, and intense manner. "All the Pretty Little Horses," long thought to be Anglo American in origin, is in fact rooted in an African-American lullaby that has been embraced by North Americans across the color divide.

### The Experiences

- Sing the song on a neutral syllable such as a soft "bah," and with solfège syllables (starting on "la") or scale numbers (starting on "6").
- Sing the song with the lyrics, articulating on the quick descending segments of each phrase.

- Play the chords on guitar, strumming up and down or plucking the strings in a steady eighth-note pattern (or six-teenth-note pattern, if a very slow singing tempo is selected) that continually begins with the root tone of the chord.

## Recommended Listening

+*Lullabies for Little People, Volume 1*. Columbia River Entertainment 191025.
*Lullabies of the World*. Folkways Records FW 04511.

# ALLONS DANSER, COLINDA

U. S.: Cajun

2. C'est pas tout le monde quit connait,
   Danser les danses du vieux temps.
   Allons, danser, Colinda
   Pour faire fâcher les vieilles femmes.

## The Tune

Within the repertoire of French-speaking Acadians, or "Cajuns" of Louisiana, "Allons Danser, Colinda" ranks as one of the the best known of all songs. Played on fiddle, accordion, and guitar, it invites dancing in restaurants, at festivals, and at "extended family" reunions.

## The Music Culture

From France to eastern Canada, the French carried their traditional customs, beliefs, oral lore, and tunes with them to the New World. Then from Nova Scotia to southwestern Louisiana (particularly in Lafayette and the bayou parishes west of New Orleans) and across the border into Beaumont, Texas, the French-speaking Cajuns migrated and took their music. French and French-Canadian music has, since the historic exodus of the Acadians from Canada to the bayou country, interacted with the music of the southern whites, Native Americans (particularly with their "terraced" singing style), and African Americans (adopting their syncopation, percussion idioms, improvisation, and blues style). Central to Cajun music is the fiddle, with its self-accompanying drone. Fiddlers like Dennis McGee, Dewey Balfa, and Rufus Thibodeaux helped shape the style in the middle of the twentieth century. Joseph Falcon and Ame'de' Ardoin popularized the accordion during the same period. Notable other musicians—fiddlers, and bands like Beausoleil, the Mamou Playboys and Ossun Express, reflect contemporary influences even as they replace their elders in the dance halls of southern Louisiana.

## The Experiences

- Sing the song on a neutral syllable such as "la," and on solfège syllables or scale numbers.
- Sing the song with words, noting that it is an exuberant invitation to "dance in the old-time style."
- Play the chords on guitar, strumming up and down in eighth notes so as to provide eight strums per measure.
- Play the Cajun-style "chinky-chink" rhythm on a triangle:
- Play the melody on fiddle. If an accordion is accessible, play the melody and chords on it, along with fiddle and guitar.
- If the music can be played live in a Cajun-style ensemble of fiddle, guitar, and accordian, try a couples dance called a "two-step" in a ballroom dance formation, with the couple circling round across the floor in a lightly bouncing "step-step-step-step"—four steps per measure.

## Recommended Listening

*+Roy Brule: Folk Music U.S.A., Volume 1*. Folkways FW 04530.

*+Joseph Falcon, Cajun Music Pioneer*. Arhoolie Records 459.

*15 Louisiana Cajun Classics*. American Masters Volume 3. Arhoolie 103.

## AMORES HALLARAS

Andean

## The Tune

"Amores Hallaras" ("You'll find another love") is a favorite tune of Andean musicians from Bolivia, Chile, Ecuador, and Peru. A Chilean ensemble called Inti-Illimani plays its rendition on *quena* (cane flute) and various stringed instruments, including the *charango*, a guitarlike instrument made from the hard-shelled body of an armadillo.

## The Music Culture

The Cordillera de los Andes are ragged mountains that stretch the entirety of the western length of South America. The high fertile valleys and plateaus there formed the region of the widespread and highly influential Incan empire.

The Incas were met, nearly obliterated, and dominated by the arrival of the Spanish conquistadores in the sixteenth century. The traditional customs of the indigenous Andean people up and down South America's mountainous west were altered by the presence of the Spanish, and over time their religious practices, economy, manner of dress, language, artistic expressions, and music blended with Spanish elements. The Andean pentatonic melodies were (and still are) performed on *quena* flute and *siku* panpipes, on guitars, violins, and other guitar-like instruments such as the *charango*.

## The Experiences

- Play the melody on flutes or recorders, or on violins, or on other melody instruments.

- Play guitar chords to accompany the melody, using a down, down-up strumming pattern.

- Stand with instruments in a circle facing center, as is traditionally done. While playing, shift the weight from one foot to the other, moving from side to side to the pulse.

## Recommended Listening

+*Music of the Andes*. Hemisphere 7243 828190 2 8.

*Latinoamerica Canta*. Yoyo Music 20016.

*The Best Instrumental Music from the Andes II*. San Antonio 018.

# ANDEAN PANPIPE MELODY

Andean

*Teaching Music Globally: Experiencing Music, Expressing Culture* by Campbell, P. S. (2004). By permission of Oxford University Press, Inc.

## The Tune

This Andean melody results from the *hocket* technique, the alternating back-and-forth sharing of the melodic pitches by two instruments (or groups of instruments). Two *siku* (panpipes, also known in Spanish as *zampoñas*) pair up to produce a dancing melody in Lydian mode.

## The Music Culture

Single-row and double-row panpipes are played in the region of the Andes mountains that stretches from Columbia and Venezuela, through Ecuador, Bolivia, Peru, and the northern parts of Argentina and Chile. The Aymara word *siku* is widely used to refer to panpipes, and panpipe players are known as *sikuris*. Most players are male. Women tend to dance to panpipe music rather than to play the instrument. Panpipes are linked to the agricultural cycle of the Andes, and various genres of panpipe music are also linked to the days of the saints. The high altitude of 4,000 or more meters explains the presence of the hocketing techniques; when sustained playing is not possible, two instruments are paired together to share the melody. The leading panpipe is the *ira,* and the follower is the *arca,* and one follows the other in piecing together a flowing pentatonic melody. Besides playing in alternating fashion, *siku* can be played in parallel octaves and sometimes in parallel fifths as well.

## The Experiences

- Sing the melody on a neutral syllable such as "loo," and on solfège syllables (beginning on "mi") or scale numbers (beginning on "3").

- Sing or play a Lydian mode on "F," with a raised fourth degree, playing "B" rather than "B♭"—just to solidify the scale on which the melody is based.

- Practice singing the melody in hocketed fashion, pairing up with another singer, or dividing a larger group into two parts. The *ira* (singer) sings the first pitch, the *arca* (singer) sings the second pitch, the *ira* the third pitch, and so on. Repeated pitches are sung by the same voice(s).

- Play the hocketed tune on flutes or recorders (if not panpipes), or on other available wind instruments.

- Try to play the melody while standing in a circle, and stepping from one foot to the other, in the traditional dance-and-play manner.

## Recommended Listening

*Mountain Music of Peru.* Smithsonian Folkways SFW 40020.

*Instruments and Music of Indians of Bolivia.* Folkways FW 04012.

*Music of the Andes.* Hemisphere 7243 8 28190 2 8.

# ARIRANG

Korea

> *Arirang, Arirang, Arariyo,*
> *Arirang, hills are calling to me.*
> *All my trials I know can be overcome.*
> *Daily I go to cross Arirang hills.*

## The Tune

In Korea and far beyond it, "Arirang" is the most widely identifiable of Korean folk songs. There are many versions of the song, which is known by its regional variations, and is performed in an array of arrangements by choirs, bands, orchestras, and nearly every kind of ensemble imaginable.

## The Music Culture

The original form of Arirang is "Jeongseon Arirang," a melody thought to have been sung in Jeongseon Country for over six centuries. The standard Arirang, or "Bonjo Arirang," is of relatively recent origin in Seoul. The text refers to the hills of Arirang, a Korean image similar to Shangri-la, Nirvana, and the Elysian Fields, a place to strive for where all troubles are left behind and all trials are overcome. Korean folk songs, called *minyo*, typically display a verse and refrain form (although Arirang does not), and include melodic improvisations or ornamentation of sustained pitches. The addition of various rhythms on *changgo* (an hourglass-shaped drum) offer a layer of musical complexity to otherwise smooth-flowing melodies in mostly triple meter.

## The Experiences

- Sing the melody on "noo" or other neutral syllable, and then in solfège or scale numbers, starting on "sol" or "5."

- Sing the melody with the Korean words. Note that it sounds much as it is written, with hard "g"s for "go" and "gae."

- Sing with words, or return to a neutral syllable, first in unison and then in four-part (or three-part, or two-part) canon, each part separated by just one measure.

- Play a drum part in keeping with the rhythm of the *changgo*, first chanting and then transferring the rhythmic chant to the drums. Use a double-headed drum, or place two tube-shaped single drums on the floor in front of the sitting player, with drum heads pointed out (to the left and to the right). Strike the drum heads with wooden mallets. The chant uses "Dong" (hitting both drum heads at once), "dak" (hitting the right head only, preferably with a thin, flat stick), "da" (a lighter version of "dak"), and "Kung" (hitting the left or right head—but not both heads—with a wooden mallet).

| Count: | 1 | 2 | 3 | 4 | 5 | 6 | 7 | 8 | 9 | 10 | 11 | 12 |
|---|---|---|---|---|---|---|---|---|---|---|---|---|
| Chant/Stroke: | Dong | | dak | Kung | da-da | dak | Kung | | dak | Kung | dak | |

## Recommended Listening

+*Arirang: Korean Song and Dance Ensemble*. MON00430.

*Korea: Folk Songs, Volumes 1 and 2*. Navarre Records.

# ARKANSAS TRAVELLER

U. S.: Appalachian and Ozark Mountains

Oh, once up-on a time in Ar-kan-saw, An old man sat in his lit-tle cab-in door, And he
fid-dled at a tune that he liked to hear, A jol-ly old tune that he played by ear. It was
rain-ing hard but the fid-dler did-n't care, He sawed a-way at the pop-u-lar air, Though his
roof-tree leaked like a wa-ter-fall, That did-n't seem to both-er the man at all.

2. A traveller was riding by that day,
   And stopped to hear him a-fiddling away;
   The cabin was afloat and his feet were wet,
   But still the old man didn't seem to fret.
   So the stranger said, "Now the way it seems to me,
   You'd better mend your roof," said he.
   But the old man said as he played away:
   "I couldn't mend it now, it's a rainy day."

3. The traveller replied, "That's all quite true,
   But this, I think is the thing for you to do;
   Get busy on a day that is fair and bright,
   Then patch the old roof till it's good and tight."
   But the old man kept on a-playing at his reel,
   And tapped the ground with his leathery heel.
   "Get along," said he, "for you give me a pain—
   My cabin never leaks when it doesn't rain!"

# ARKANSAS TRAVELLER

## The Tune

In the fiddle repertoire of the Appalachian and Ozark mountains, "Arkansas Traveller" ranks high among the tunes that fit well into the fiddler's hands. Whether the fiddler plays it alone, or with a blend of banjos and guitars, it moves quickly and with a definitive dance-like quality.

## The Music Culture

Music occupies a special place in the hearts of people living in the Appalachian and Ozark mountains of the eastern and south-central regions of the United States. There are traditional ballads and folk songs there, brought over by Anglo-Celtic immigrants, and *old-time music* that developed early in the twentieth century as a blend of the music of the immigrants with parlor and vaudeville music, African-American styles, and Minstrel Show tunes. Guitars, mandolins, banjos, hammered and plucked dulcimers, autoharps, fiddles, and other acoustic instruments join to create music today as it may have sounded in the hills and hollers for many generations. Electricity arrived later to the rural areas than to the cities, and thus it was not unusual for people in the mountain settlements to make their own entertainment. Their lives were wrapped up in farming, mining, and other manual labor, so that by the end of the day, a little music on back porches and in community dance halls gave balance to people's lives. Fiddlers learned from other fiddlers, picking up by ear a considerable repertoire of tunes that they could play alone or with others, and dance halls reverberated with the sounds of "Arkansas Traveller," "Cumberland Gap," "Turkey in the Straw," and other traditional tunes. The melodies were what set people to dancing, while the words to many of the fiddle tunes came later—almost as an afterthought. "Arkansas Traveler" was the state song of Arkansas from 1949 to 1963.

### The Experiences
- Sing the fast-moving melody on "dee" and "deedle-dee," the latter for sixteenth notes. Notice how the tune fits not only the harmonic language of a few chords but also the first-position pitches of the violin's A, D, and G strings.
- Play the chords on guitar or autoharp, maintaining a steady beat in a quarter- and eighth-note strumming pattern.
- Play the tune on violin—slowly, and gradually increase the speed.
- Alternate between playing and singing the melody, with harmonic accompaniment.

### Recommended Listening
+*Bluegrass All-Stars, Roger Sprung: Progressive Ragtime Bluegrass, Volume 1*. Folkways FW 02371.
+*Music of Roscoe Holcomb and Wade Ward*. Folkways FW 02371.
*A Treasury of Library of Congress Field Recordings*. Rounder CD 1500.1

## AS I ROVED OUT

Newfoundland

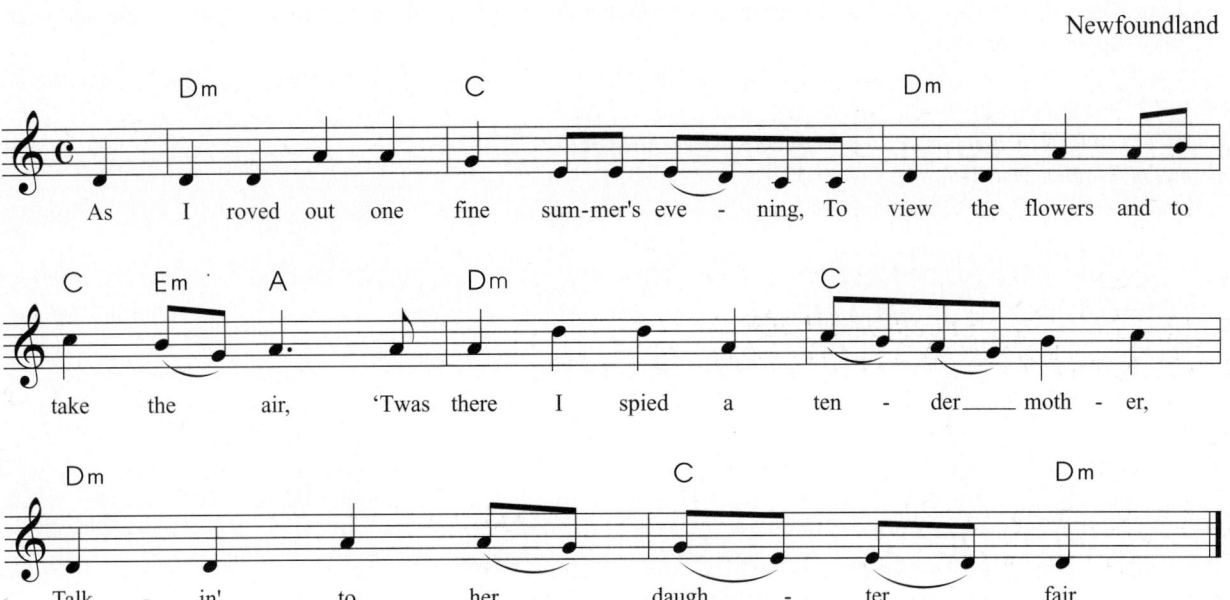

2. A sailor boy thinks for all to wander,

   And he will prove your overthrow.

   O daughter, you're better to wed with a farmer,

   For to sea he'll never go.

## The Tune

"As I Roved Out" is a sea shanty once sung by seafarers in Newfoundland who pulled together at oars or hauled on ropes. Their singing helped them to expel their breath and also distracted them from the strains of physical labor.

## The Music Culture

Located at the far eastern end of Canada, Newfoundland is a rugged land where people who settled there from Ireland, England, Scotland and Wales brought their traditional songs. Newfoundland and Nova Scotia are known for their sea shanties, songs of whaling, sealing and fishing, and ballads about shipwrecks and disasters at sea. Shanties were subordinate to the tasks they accompanied, and a command like "belay" or "avast heaving" instantly ended the singing and the work. Solo lines of shanties were often coarse, and sailors were known to disguise the words if they sang them in the presence of women. Shantymen improvised verses to set melodies, and were known to borrow from other sailors they met. Many of the texts spoke of "fair maidens," true love, infidelities, real and mythical heroes, and sailors' life onshore and afloat. The melodies of sea shanties often show modal influence, including Aeolian, Dorian, and Mixolydian modes.

### The Experiences

- Sing the song on a neutral syllable, on solfège syllables (beginning on "la" in a la-based minor) or on scale numbers (beginning on "6").
- Strum the chords on guitar, or play them on the piano, noticing the quick harmonic change at the end of the second phrase of text and melody. Experiment with a "down down-up" right-hand guitar strum, and try out the sound of open fifths rather than full chords in a left-hand piano accompaniment to the melody.

- Sing the song with accompaniment. Try other instruments as they are available, such as recorder (for melody), autoharp and concertina (for harmony), and plucked dulcimer (for melody and harmony).

- Improvise new verses, responding to questions of whether the daughter will or will not marry the sailor, and what may happen as a result.

## Recommended Listening

+*As I Roved Out: Field Trip Ireland.* (Sarah Makem) Folkways FW 08872.
*Folksongs of Newfoundland.* Folkways FW 06831.

# ATSIAGBEKO

Ghana

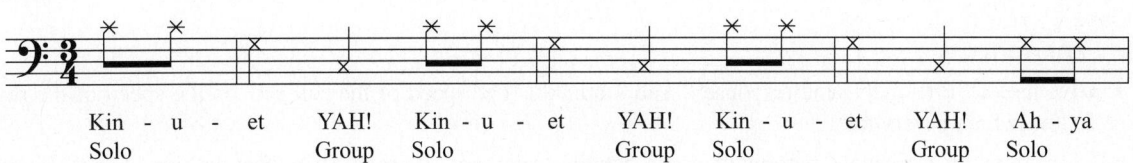

*Teaching Music Globally: Experiencing Music, Expressing Culture* by Campbell, P. S. (2004). By permission of Oxford University Press, Inc.

## The Groove

As the leader calls the group to attention, "Atsiagbeko" opens up to a full-fledged percussion piece featuring higher- and lower-pitched drums, *axatse* (a shaken gourd with external net of beads), and iron double bells called *agogo* bells.

## The Music Culture

The music of Ghana varies with the cultural and linguistic group. Yet be they the Akan, Asanti, Dagbani, Dagomba, Ewe, Fante, Franfra, Ga, Lobi, or Sisala, there is a tendency by people in the region to organize music in short repeated phrases on various instruments, each one layered in a complex web of multiple patterns that are played simultaneously. There is typically a bell pattern in the percussion that functions as a time line, or underlying meter, several drums of different pitch levels, and a rattle or shaker. Some rattles are made of gourd or wicker, with nets of beads, metals or coins strung across their surfaces; seed shell rattles and dried gourds with seeds inside are also used. Live music making is central to community activity in traditional societies within Ghana, and an identity marker in the lives of many throughout West Africa. Life cycle events such as birth, puberty initiation, and death are marked by musical performance, and music is likely to be a blended performance that includes dance, sung poetry, instrumental play, and the dramatic elements that are to be found in narratives, epics, and storytelling.

## The Experiences

- Give the call ("Kinuet") and response ("Yah") quickly. The speed of the call sets up the speed of the rhythms to follow, which is very fast.
- Learn the parts separately, patting, clapping, tapping, snapping, slapping (the chest with one hand). Begin slowly, internalizing the three-beat feeling. Think of words or syllables to vocalize while chanting, such as

    For the "agogo" bells: "Go-go bells, a-go-go! A-go-go bells, a-go-go-a!"

    For the "axatse" shaker: "Shake it. Stead-y." (2 times)

    For the tenor drums: "(Play) the high drum (whisper 'play' on rest; 4 times).

    For the bass drums: "The bass drum sounds like a thunder cloud when a storm is brewing."

- Play the time line on the "agogo" double (or single) bells, gradually layering in the axatse (shaker), tenor drum, and bass drum parts.
- Play continuously. As it is agreed to by the players, add and remove a part to change the texture, thus adding variety. The pattern of the bells should remain constant.

## Recommended Listening

*Master Drummer of Ghana* (Mustapha Tettey Addy). Lyrichord LLCT 7250.

*Africa, New York: Drum Masterpieces* (Ladji Camara). Lyrichord LYRCD 7345.

*Rhythms of Life, Songs of Wisdom: Akan Music from Ghana.* Smithsonian Folkways SFW 40463.

# BACH: BRANDENBURG CONCERTO NO. 2,
## IN F MAJOR, THIRD MOVEMENT
### (OPENING)

J. S. Bach

CD I, Track # 3

## The Tune

The third movement of J. S. Bach's "Brandenburg Concerto No. 2" is noted for its trumpet solo that rings out in a joyful fanfare. It is a decidedly difficult trumpet part, due to lack of valves on trumpets of the Baroque era. The movement is in fact a *fugue*, with the melody passed from trumpet to violin, flute, and oboe.

## The Music Culture

J. S. Bach dedicated the six Brandenburg Concertos to Margrave Christian Ludwig of Brandenburg, Germany, who was a friend and ally of Bach's employer, Leopold, Prince of Cöthen when he was *kappelmeister* (director of music). Bach wrote the pieces in 1718–1721, in the European historical period known as the Baroque. Unlike earlier concertos, the Brandenburg Concertos feature solo instruments extensively against a background of strings, harpsichord, and a few wind instruments such as flute and oboe. The concise head-motifs of the concertos are memorable, singable, and show the Italian melodic influence on Bach's style in their decorative and florid qualities. Throughout the six works, there is considerable ornamentation or embellishment of the melody, the presence of *polyphony*, and a continuous bass line and accompanying harmony, called *basso continuo*.

### The Experiences

- Listen to Track # 3 for the melody. Hum it or sing it on a neutral syllable like "doo" while tapping the melodic rhythm.
- Listen to the recording repeatedly, and sing the melody on "loo" until, with familiarity, it can be sung with solfège syllables or scale numbers.
- Play the melody on piano, with the fundamental chords sounding periodically to provide a harmonic framework.
- Play the melody on various instruments, including trumpet, violin, flute, and oboe (along with harmonic accompaniment).

### Recommended Listening

+*Bach: Brandenburg Concertos.* Benjamin Britten/English Chamber Orchestra. Decca 43847.

+*Stravinsky, Villa Lobos, and Bach.* New Orchestral Society-Boston. COOK01062.

## BACH: "LITTLE" FUGUE IN G MINOR
### (FIRST SUBJECT)

J. S. Bach

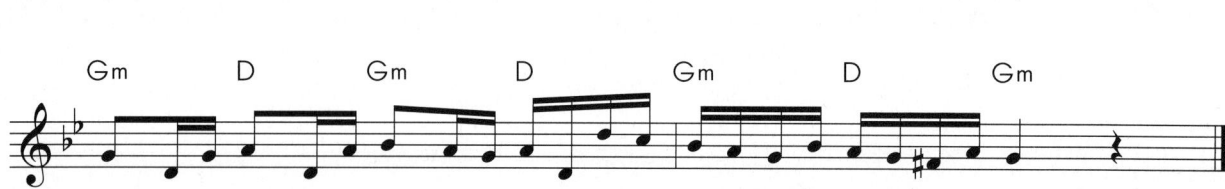

## The Tune

J. S. Bach was a master of the *fugue*, a compositional technique and form in which the melody of one voice or instrument is imitated by one or more others. His "'Little' Fugue in G Minor" is a prime example of how one voice chases another, as per the Latin word, "fugare": to chase.

## The Music Culture

In his long lifetime (1685–1750), J. S. Bach was known as a court musician, organist, composer, director of music (kappelmeister), choir director, and teacher (of singing and Latin). As a composer, he wrote Masses, large-scale choral works, chorales, organ works, chamber music, keyboard works, lute music, orchestral music, and canons. By all accounts, Bach was also known as master of the fugue, and could invent themes or subjects that he would then imitate through frequent uses of countersubjects and episodes, which could incorporate tonal harmony and modulation to related keys. Frederick the Great of Potsdam once played a theme for Bach, challenging him to improvise a fugue based on it. Not only did J. S. Bach improvise a three-part fugue on Frederick's pianoforte, but he later presented the king with *A Musical Offering* which consists of fugues, canons, and a trio based on the king's theme. Bach wrote *The Art of Fugue* just months before his death, a magnum opus of thematic transformation with eighteen complex fugues and canons based on a simple theme; it is believed to be the summation of polyphonic techniques of the European Baroque period. His "'Little' Fugue in G Minor" BWV 578, is so nicknamed not because it is short or of little importance but in order to distinguish it from his later "Great" G Minor Fantasia and Fugue, BWV 542.

### The Experiences

- Sing the theme of the fugue on a neutral syllable, "loo." Sing with solfège syllables (beginning on "la" in a la-based minor) or scale numbers (beginning on "6").
- "Dance" the theme by conducting it tapping the melodic rhythm, and even inventing four two-measure movements that can be performed alone, in pairs, or in a circle.
- Play the melody on piano, flute, violin, trumpet, or oboe, or other melody instrument.
- Add chords on piano, playing them in a rhythm that complements but does not overcome the melody.
- Perform the melody fugally. Start one voice or instrument, and bring in a second as the first part begins the third measure. Proceed with caution; there is a harmonic clash when the first part sounds the third beat of the fourth measure (B♭) and the second part sounds the third beat of second measure (F♯) yet the rest of it accomplishes resonant harmony.

### Recommended Listening

+*Bach: Organ Miniatures*. Hyperion CDA67211/2.
+*Bach: Orchestral Transcriptions Conducted by Stokowski*. EMI Classics 7243 5 57758 01.

# THE BALLAD OF CÉSAR CHÁVEZ

U. S.: Mexican American

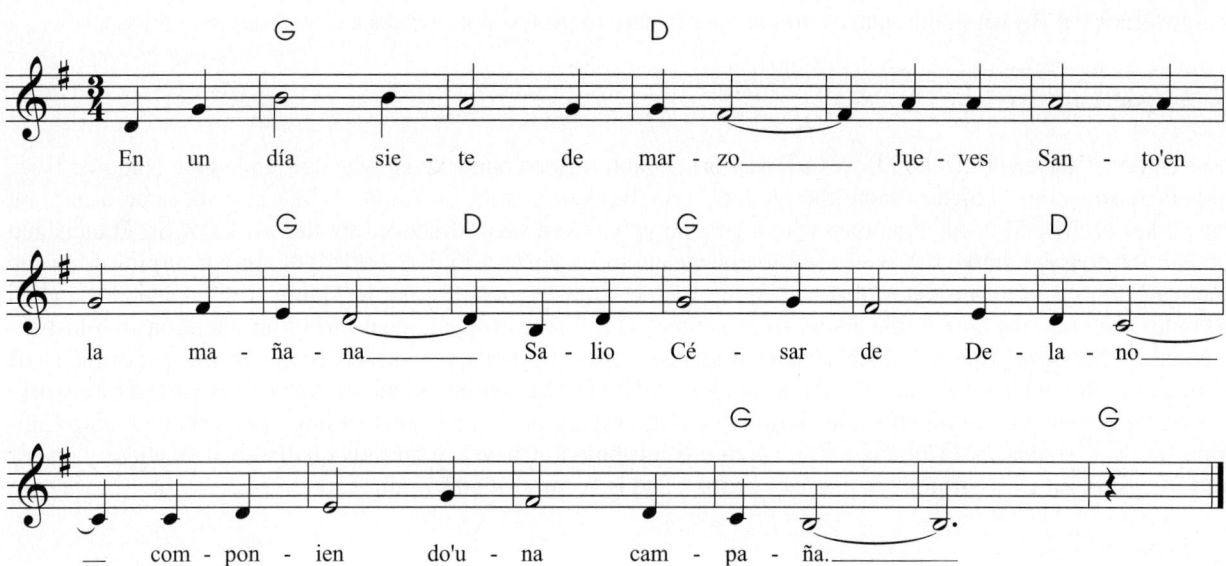

En un día sie - te de mar - zo_____ Jue - ves San - to'en
la ma - ña - na_____ Sa - lio Cé - sar de De - la - no_____
_ com - pon - ien do'u - na cam - pa - ña._____

2. Compañeros campesinos
este va a ser un ejemplo
esta marcha lallevamos
hasta mero Sacramento.

3. Cuando llegamos a Fresno
toda la gente gritaba
y que viva César Chávez
y las gente que llevaba

4. Nos despedismos de Fresno
nos despedismos con fe
para llegar muy contentos
hasta el pueblo de Merced.

5. Ya vamos llegando a Stockton
ya mero la luz se fue
pero mi gente gritaba
sigan con bastante fe.

6. Cuando llegamos Stockton
los mariachis no cantaban
que viva César Chávez
y la virgen que llevaba.

7. Ese Señor César Chávez
el es un hombre cabal
queria verse cara a cara
Con el gobernador Brown.

1. *On the seventh day of March*
*Good Thursday in the morning*
*César left Delano*
*organizing a campaign.*

2. *Companion farmers*
*this is going to be an example*
*this (protest) march we'll take*
*to Sacramento itself.*

3. *When we arrived in Fresno*
*all the people chanted*
*long live César Chávez*
*and the people that accompanied him.*

4. *We bid good-bye to Fresno*
*we bid good-bye with faith*
*so we would arrive safely*
*to the town of Merced.*

5. *We are almost in Stockton*
*sunlight is almost gone*
*but the people shouted*
*keep on with lots of faith.*

6. *When we arrived in Stockton*
*the mariachis were singing*
*long live César Chávez*
*and the Virgin of Guadalupe*

7. *That Mr. César Chávez*
*is a very strong man.*
*He wanted to speak face to face*
*with Governor Brown.*

*Teaching Music Globally: Experiencing Music, Expressing Culture* by Campbell, P. S. (2004). By permission of Oxford University Press, Inc.

## The Tune

This Mexican-American narrative ballad, or *corrido*, tells the story of farm laborers in California who sought fair treatment. Led by César Chávez, they left the orchards and groves of Fresno, Merced, and Stockton to meet with then-governor Pat Brown in the state capitol at Sacramento to protest poor wages and working conditions.

## The Music Culture

César Estrada Chávez (1927–1993) was a farmworker, labor leader, and activist who cofounded the National Farm Workers Association (which became the United Farm Workers). Born in Yuma, Arizona, he became a migrant farmworker at the end of his grammar-school education. Chávez was influenced by the works of St. Francis and Gandhi, and thus he worked through nonviolent means to organize a Latino civil rights group, urging Mexican Americans to give voice to issues of social equity by the votes they could cast. In March, 1969, Chávez marched 340 miles with seventy-five farmworkers from Delano, California, to Sacramento to bring attention to injustice-sendured by Mexican Americans. He organized grape-pickers' boycotts and strikes, protested the use of the short hoe that brought on back pain, and (later) pesticides, and he fasted to bring attention to the injustices of farmworkers. Chávez is honored on March 31, his birthday, by several states with a history of migrant work, including California, Texas, Arizona, and Colorado. The *corrido* is a tribute to Chávez, a narrative ballad that is sung by one or more voices (often with harmony in thirds or sixths), and is accompanied by guitar.

### The Experiences

- Sing the melody on "loo," and on solfège syllables or scale numbers.
- Sing the melody first with the Spanish verse. Note that "r"s are flipped (as in marzo), "z"s are pronounced as "ts," "e"s sound like long "a"s (as in sie-te), some syllables are elided (as in "tone" for "to-en", and "doh" for "do'u").
- Play the chordal accompaniment on guitar, giving emphasis to the first beat and lightening the touch on beats two and three.
- Play the melody and chords on piano, sounding at least one chord per measure. Explore the use of a bass tone on "one" and treble chords on beats two and three.
- Sing a harmony part, aiming to produce thirds or fourths that follow the chordal progression.

### Recommended Listening

+*Thinking Musically*. Bonnie C. Wade. Oxford University Press, 2004.

*Corrido de César Chávez*. Fonovisa Inc. ASIN: B00008F3KT.

*The Mexican Revolution*. Arhoolie Records 7041-44.

# BAMBODANSARNA

Olov Johansson

*Banbodansarna* is from *Världens Väsen* by Olov Johansson, 1997. Reprinted by permission of Olov Johansson.

CD I, Track # 4

## The Tune

A quartet of four Finnish musicians called Väsen create dance music with *nykelharpa* (keyed fiddle), viola, guitar, and percussion. Their tunes have the energy to set the body in motion, as in the case of a triple-metered *polska* called "Bambodansarna."

## The Music Culture

In contemporary Finland, instrumental folk-dance music enjoys much attention through festivals and competitions, and on recordings. Musical groups may be comprised of two fiddles, harmonium or accordion, and double bass, or just some (but not all) of these, in order to make room for Finnish traditional instruments such as the *kantele* (a plucked zither) and the *nykelharpa*, a fiddle whose melody and drone strings are played by pressing keys that then vibrate the strings to which they are attached. Such instruments are joined together in bands that perform polskas, mazurkas, waltzes, polkas, quadrilles, and other traditional circle and partner dances. The *polska* is the most widely known dance in Scandinavia, and dates from the Renaissance, with its roots in Polish dance forms and folk choruses. It spread to the North Sea region in the seventeenth and eighteenth centuries, when Sweden and Poland had close contact with one another. Today, the polska is considered one of the most characteristically national folk dances of Sweden. In Finland, polska refers more broadly to couple- and group-dances in triple meter.

### The Experiences

- Listen to Track # 4, and hum the drone pitch while catching the rise and fall of the melody.
- While listening, hum the melody in its four two-measure sections that form an "AABC" arrangement.
- Play the melody on violin, accordian, or other melody-producing instruments such as piano, viola, cello (and wind and brass instruments).
- Play the chords on guitar or piano, alongside the melody that may also be played (or sung). Accent the first beat of each measure, lightening up on the remaining beats by playing partial chords, or at least more softly.
- To the recording or live music, dance a three-step by making a full turn every three beats. Try this movement with a partner.

### Recommended Listening

+*Whirled: Väsen.* NorthSide NSD 6006.

*Tunes and Songs of Finland* (Adolf Stark). Folkways FW 06856.

# BARB'RY ALLEN

England

In Scar-let town, where I was born, There was a young maid dwell-in', Made

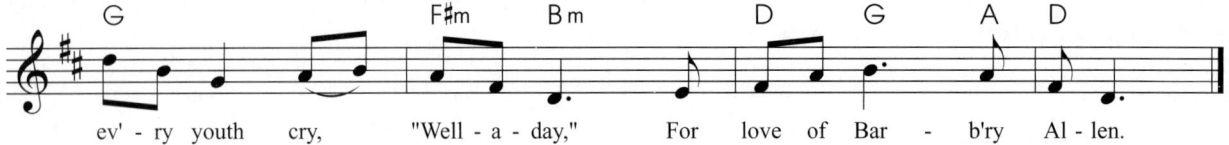

ev'-ry youth cry, "Well-a-day," For love of Bar - b'ry Al-len.

2. 'Twas in the merry month of May,
   When green buds they were swellin'
   Sweet William on his deathbed lay,
   For the love of Barb'ry Allen.

3. He sent his servant to the town,
   To the place where she was dwellin'
   Cried, "Master bids you come to him,
   If your name be Barb'ry Allen"

4. Then slowly, slowly she got up,
   And slowly went she nigh him,
   And when she pulled the curtains back,
   Said, "Young man, I think you're dyin'"

5. "Oh, yes, I'm sick, I'm very sick,
   And I'll never be better,
   Until I have the love of one,
   The love of Barb'ry Allen"

6. Then lighthy tipped she down the stairs,
   She trembled like an aspen.
   'Tis vain, 'tis vain, my dear young man.
   To wish for Barb'ry Allen.

7. She walked out in the green, green fields,
   She heard his death bells knellin'.
   And every stroke they seemed to say,
   "Hard-hearted Barb'ry Allen."

8. "Oh father, father, dig my grave,
   Go dig it deep and narrow.
   Sweet William died for me today;
   I'll die for him tomorrow."

9. They buried her in the old churchyard,
   Sweet William's grave was nigh her,
   And from his heart grew a red, red rose,
   And from her heart a brier.

10. They grew and grew o'er the old church wall,
    Till they could grow no higher,
    Until they tied a lover's knot,
    The red rose and the brier.

## The Tune

One of the most popular of the old British *ballads* is "Barb'ry Allen," which has been found in many variants across the United States. It tells of the romance between Barb'ry Allen and Sweet William, who died of a broken heart and was followed to his grave by the girl who loved him.

## The Music Culture

There are plenty of ballads from England, Scotland, and Wales, which have made their way across the waters to North America and are still known today. Among them are "The Two Sisters," "When Johnny Comes Marching Home," "The Derby Ram," "Lord Randall," "The Elfin Knight," and "Barb'ry Allen." They are known as Child ballads after Francis James Child, an American scholar who collected and devoted his life to the comparative study of British vernacular ballads. These ballads were widely varied by people who learned them orally—as neither their melodies nor their verses were in print for many centuries. Recordings and live renditions of "Barb'ry Allen" (Child Ballad No. 84) from Virginia to California, and Tennessee to Texas, and by Emma Rosten and Emmy Lou Harris, make it one of the best known of all the Child ballads. The song's popularity hails back to the time of General George Washington, who named it as one of his favorites. Even in the 1770s, "Barb'ry Allen" was already several hundred years old.

### The Experiences

- Sing the melody on a neutral syllable such as "bah," and on solfège syllables or scale numbers.
- Play the chords of the song on guitar, noting the fast harmonic changes in the last two measures. An autoharp is another suitable instrument for playing a chordal accompaniment, and a plucked dulcimer can play open fifths.
- Sing the melody unaccompanied, practicing the expressive manner of storytelling through song.
- Play a rendition of the melody as interlude every three or four verses, on fiddle or other melody instrument.

### Recommended Listening

+*British Traditional Ballads in the Southern Mountains, Volume 1* (Jean Ritchie). Folkways FW 02301.
+*Songcatcher*. Combustion 29586-2.
*Classic Ballads of Britain and Ireland, Volume 2*. Rounder Select ROUN 1776.
*Classic Scottish Ballads*. Tradition Records. ASIN: B0000058RE.

# BATMAN AND ROBIN

U. S.: Illinois

## The Tune

This patchwork song is the expression of playful children who create and re-create singing games on playgrounds, on the street, and in their backyards. "Batman and Robin" are comic book characters and movie heroes, as is Super-man, and the opening section of this singing games leads to other more familiar textual and melodic segments that are found in other children's songs.

## The Music Culture

Children are their own culture, separated from adulthood by age and experience, and quite content with the expressions, games, and lore that are their very own. Of their various diversions, the game of blindman's bluff, jacks, swings, and chase games date from at least 2,000 years ago. Some of the singing games, such as "Ring Around the Rosy," date back to medieval Europe. Children's music tends to involve their efforts at preserving some of the traditions passed to them while also creating new words, rhythms, and melodies. Thus, their repertoire of songs and singing games holds fast to traditions and changes, and a single song can thus mix the old (such as the melody to "I looked through the keyhole, what did I see. . . .") with the new (such as the Batman and Robin theme and the "oo-che-wa-che" motif). A generation or two onward, no doubt some components of this song will be somewhat different than they are now, even as other parts will remain the very same, for this is the way of children's culture that is always in transition and responsive to the popular media—and the language of "the street" (and playground).

### The Experiences

- Sing the song with the words, noting the following sections: (a) "Batman and Robin," mm. 1–5, (b) "Jump back Robin," mm. 6–9, (c) "I looked through the key hole," mm. 10–15, (d) "I got a pain," mm. 16–19, (e) "Row cherry," mm. 20–23, (f) "oo-che-wa-che," mm. 24–25.

- With the six sections in mind, designate one singer (or small group of singers) to each section, in performing the song. Mind the timing, so that each section proceeds smoothly from the preceding one.

- Apply a handclapping pattern while singing. Face a partner and clap: Beat 1: clap hands together; Beat 2: clap partner's right hand; Beat 3: clap hands together; Beat 4: clap partner's left hand together; Beat 5: clap hands together; Beat 6: clap partner's both hands.

- Play quarter-note chords on piano or guitar while singing. For the chanting parts, tap a quarter-note rhythm on the body of the piano or guitar, on desks, table tops, or the floor.

### Recommended Listening

*Skip Rope Games*. Folkways FW 07029.
*More Songs to Grow On*. Folkways FW 07676.

# BENJAMIN FRANKLIN

U. S.: Illinois

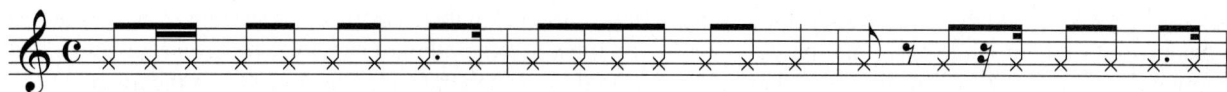

Ben - ja - min Frank - lin went to France, To teach the la - dies how to dance! Heel, toe, a - round you go! Sa -

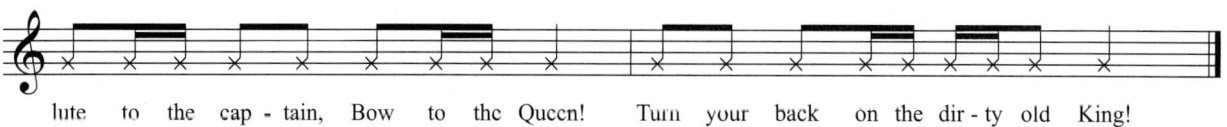

lute to the cap - tain, Bow to the Queen! Turn your back on the dir - ty old King!

CD I, Track # 5

## The Groove

For many generations, children have been singing and chanting as they jump (or skip) rope. "Benjamin Franklin Went to France" is a jump-rope verse chanted by schoolchildren in Edgewood, Illinois, as recorded by Pete Seeger in 1952.

## The Music Culture

The rope, ball, and stick are some of the oldest and most widespread of play implements known to children. Ropes have been used for skipping over and jumping with, for swinging, and for tug-of-war. They have been swung in circles, used in straight lines to connect folks up, and have been used for hopping, stamping, and balancing. When used alone, a child will hop over the rope on one foot or jump it on both feet jump. When one child jumps with two rope turners, hopping and jumping can happen alone, in pairs, in a succession of jumpers who move in and then out of the rope. "Double Dutch" requires two ropes turned alternately, one in each hand of the two turners, and "Egg Beater" utilizes four turners on two ropes that turn at right angles to each other. "Touching the ground" is a popular technique that requires the jumper to stoop down to the ground in between jumps, and "Peppers" is the call to jump rope at top speed. Through all the hopping and jumping, and in various formations, the chanted verses help to keep the jumpers rhythmically in the groove.

### The Experiences
- Listen to Track # 5 to the sounds of children in their jump-rope chant.
- Chant the jump-rope verse, clapping quarter-note beats throughout the verse.
- While chanting, switch from clapping quarter-note beats to clapping twice as fast, and then twice as slow.
- Chant while stepping, hopping, or jumping the quarter-note beat.
- Chant while jumping rope.
- Choose five percussion instruments, each with a distinctive timbre, for example, djembe or conga drum, claves, cowbell, shaker, finger cymbal (or triangle). Play the chant as a canon, with instruments coming in one measure at a time. Repeat the piece several times, both while chanting and without chanting.

### Recommended Listening
+*Skip Rope Games*. Folkways FW 07029.
*American Folksongs for Children*. Rounder Select CD ROUN 8001.

# BETTER DAYS

Sonny Terry and Brownie McGhee

2. Oh, look at your people
   I need a break
   Good things will come
   To those who wait.
   But that's all right, I don't worry,
   'Cause that'll be your better day.

3. When I had money,
   I had plenty friends
   No I don't have a dime
   Like a road without an end.
   But that's all right, I don't worry,
   'Cause that'll be your better day.

4. My burden's so heavy
   I don't hardly see
   Seems like everybody
   Down on me.
   But that's all right, I don't worry
   'Cause that'll be our better day.

# BETTER DAYS

CD I, Track # 6

## The Tune

*Blues* songs typically take the form of 12-bars, and sometimes 16-bars. But in "Better Day" as performed by Sonny Terry and Brownie McGhee, the blues are expressed in a statement-and-response form that relays a story of hard times that are expected to change course to a more positive period ahead.

## The Music Culture

Sometime in the late 1930s, Sanford "Sonny" Terry and Walter Brown "Brownie" McGhee became friends and struck a deal to make music together. Sonny had grown up on a farm listening to his father playing harmonica and his mother singing. Brownie had learned to play guitar from his father, who had made a career of playing at jukin' parties where blues and hollers brought on plenty of dancing. The two of them have done much to preserve and disseminate to a wide listening public the important African-American musical forms: gospel, spirituals, blues, and music that is part jazz, part rhythm and blues, and part rock-and-roll. Brownie's guitar style lays down strong rhythms with his chords, and walks and talks a boogie bass, while Sonny plays a personal style of blues guitar and harmonica. With backgrounds in singing spirituals and gospel (Sonny in Tennessee and Brownie in North Carolina), they both share in singing the songs of the genres they love.

### The Experiences

- Listen to Track # 6 for the interplay of the two voice parts and the chord changes that feature E major and E minor, and A major.
- Listen to the recording repeatedly, singing one of the two voice parts, and switching parts. The top voice is the "lead," and the second voice follows in imitation and harmony.
- Play the chords in quarter-note strums, and in a syncopated down-up left-hand strum that gives weight and greater length to the down strum.
- Sing the blues song melody while playing the guitar chords, and join with a partner to sing the two voice parts together.

### Recommended Listening

+*Sonny Terry & Brownie McGhee: Preachin' the Blues*. Folkways FW 31024.
+*Smithsonian Folkways American Roots Collection*. (Sonny Terry & Brownie McGhee) SFW 40062.
*Robert John: King of the Delta Blues Singers*. Columbia/Legacy CK 65746.

# BILLIE

Eddie Palmieri

CD I, Track # 7

## The Groove

Urban popular dance music was developing in New York City and in San Juan, Puerto Rico, during the 1960s and 70s. Based on both Cuban and Puerto Rican dance music, *salsa* was born and made manifest in high-energy music such as Eddie Palmieri's "Billie."

## The Music Culture

Salsa closely resembles its Cuban and Puerto Rican antecedents, and was shaped by Puerto Ricans living in New York City. West African rhythmic and textural traits were fused with Spanish melodic and harmonic structures to form salsa, even as many salsa compositions were also derived from the Cuban *son* and *guaracha* forms. In salsa, verses are sung by a lead vocalist, and a *montuno* section features call-and-response forms, driving rhythms, solo improvisation, and strong brass choruses that are called "mambos." Salsa bands include singers, percussion, piano, bass, trumpet, trombone, saxophone, guitar and *cuatro* (a small guitar). Important percussion instruments are the two-headed bongos, conga drums (known in Cuba as *tumbadoras*), timbales (a pair of toms that are mounted on a stand), claves, maracas, and güiro, a notched scraper that originated with the Arawak Indians who died away soon after the arrival of the Spanish to the Carribean. The interlocking rhythmic ostinati give salsa its unique feel. Innovators of salsa include Eddie Palmieri, Ray Barretto, Willie Colón, Johnny Pacheco, Celia Cruz, Tito Puente, and Mongo Santamaría.

### The Experiences

- Listen to Track # 7, and identify the instruments as they appear: singer, guitar, trumpet, trombone, cowbell, piano. Note the shift to the montuno midway, when strongly accented figures are played by the brass instruments, followed by a chorus that sings "mambo."

- Listen again to the recording, and tap, clap, or pat the accented figure played four times in succession by the brass instruments:

- Play the piano's montuno chord figure.

- Play the montuno along with basic rhythms of several key percussion instruments:

Claves:

Guiro:

(scrape the stick against the ridge in a down, down-up motion)

Cowbell:

open   close   open   close   open   close   open   close

- Dance the rhythm freestyle, feeling the groove.

## Recommended Listening

*Eddie Palmieri, Listen Here!* Concord Records (CCD-2276-2).

*Eddie Palmieri, Ritmo Caliente.* Concord Records (CCD-2180-2).

*Eddie Palmieri, La Perfecta.* Concord Picante CCD-2136-2.

# BILLY BOY

England

Where have ye been all the day?
Is she fit to be your wife? Bil - ly Boy, Bil - ly Boy? Where have
Can she cook an I - rish stew?

ye been all the day?
fit to be your wife me Bil - ly Boy? I've been
cook an I - rish stew? She's a

walk - in all the day with me char - min' Nan - cy Gray. She can
fit to be me wife as the fork is to___ the knife___ and me
cook an I - rish stew eye and sing in Hinnies toom

Nan - cy Kit - tle me - fan - cy. Oh, me char - min' Bil - ly Boy.___

## The Tune

"Billy Boy" moves rhythmically in compound meter, skipping along lightly. It utilizes the full diatonic scale—and more, as it sneaks in an F♯ and a stepwise excursion down to the fifth below the tonic "home tone."

## The Music Culture

England is a repository of ballads, folk songs and traditional dance tunes. The efforts of Cecil Sharp, an early collector, resulted in a collection of 3,000 tunes, including variants on the same song, between 1903 and 1924. "Billy Boy" is one of these songs, with its variants not only in England but also in other English-speaking parts of the world. There is the Appalachian-based folk song that is widely known, which begins with "Oh, where have you been Billy Boy, Billy Boy?" An English rendition shares the opening three pitches of the melody, the gist of the text about Billy and his wife, and the harmonic structure. Beyond that, the variants appear to be two distinctive songs, and not only the melody but also the lyrics are strikingly different. The earlier British folk song features "ye" for "you" and "me" for "my." Both renditions describe Billy Boy's wife as "fit" or "the darling of his life."

## The Experiences

- Sing the song on a neutral syllable like "doo," and with scale syllables (beginning on "mi") or scale numbers (beginning on "3"). Tap a "skip-ty" rhythm of quarter note/eighth note to accompany the melody.
- Sing the response or tag ending with its mix of syllables and words: "Nancy Kittle me fancy. Oh, me charmin' Billy Boy."
- Play the chords on guitar (or piano) while singing the melody, aiming for a light and bouncing quality.
- Play the melody on recorder while tapping a "skip-ty" rhythm on a hand drum, akin to the old English pipe-and-tabor (drum) sound.
- Sing other versions of the song, including the Appalachian variant.

## Recommended Listening

+*Andrew Rowan Summers: The Faulse Lady*. Folkways FW 02044.

+*Traditional Songs of Singing Culture: A World Sampler* (Campbell/Williamson/Perron). Warner Bros. Publications.

# BONJOUR, MES AMIS

U. S.: Cajun

2. Comment ça va, mes amis, comment ça va.
3. Ça va bien, mes amis, ça va bien.
4. Allons danser, mes amis, allons danser.
5. Allons chanter, mes amis, allons chanter.
6. Au revoir, mes amis, adieu.

1. *Good day, my friends, good day.*
2. *How are you, my friends, how are you?*
3. *I'm fine, my friends, I'm fine.*
4. *Let's dance, my friends, let's dance.*
5. *Let's sing, my friends, let's sing.*
6. *Goodbye, my friends, farewell.*

Traditional, Cajun, arranged by Bayou Seco. From Campbell, P. S., McCullough-Brabson, E., Tucker, J. C. (1994). *Roots & Branches: A Legacy of Multicultural Music for Children*. Danbury, CT: World Music Press. Courtesy World Music Press.

CD I, Track # 8

## The Tune

"Bonjour, Mes Amis" is a song of basic French phrases, all of which find their way into the language of the Cajun peoples of southwestern Louisiana. The vibrant and bouncy character of the music invites listeners to the dance floor to join in a Cajun two-step.

## The Music Culture

Cajun culture is a place of bayous and Cypress trees with hanging Spanish moss, a spread of spicy gumbo, couscous (a ricelike grain), and hot boudan sausage. The journey of the French-speaking peoples from Acadia (later called Nova Scotia) to Louisiana is the subject of Walt Whitman's famous poem, "Evangeline." The Acadians became the Cajuns, fashioning their culture near to the Gulf of Mexico in Louisiana (and the far southeastern coast of Texas), absorbing the cultural influences of immigrants from Europe and the Caribbean, as well as escaped slaves and free blacks, called Creoles. Like its food, Cajun music is a spicy blend. It features accordions, fiddles, and heavy iron triangles made of hay-rake tines—all meant to incite people's impulse to dance. Contemporary Cajun music is also performed on guitars, steel guitars, and drums. Groups like the late Balfa Brothers and Beausoleil have given people plenty of music to dance to in clubs and old-style dance halls, just as their elders had done when their fishing, trapping, hunting, and large-scale family cooking was completed.

## The Experiences

- Listen to Track # 8, humming along on the melody's tonic C-chord triad and the descending five-tone ending phrase.
- Sing the melody on a neutral syllable such as "bah," and on solfège syllables (beginning on "sol") or scale numbers (beginning on "5").
- Listen to the recording, and sing along with the French lyrics.
- Sing the melody while playing the chords on accordion, piano, guitar, or other harmony-producing instrument.
- Play a "chinky chink" ostinato on triangle:
- Dance the Cajun two-step. Link arms with a partner, and follow the pattern:

| 1 | 2 | 3 | 4 | 1 | 2 | 3 | 4 |
|------|------|------|-------|------|------|------|-------|
| step | step | step | pause | step | step | step | pause |
| L | R | L | pause | R | L | R | pause |

## Recommended Listening

+*Roots and Branches* (Campbell/McCullough-Brabson/Tucker). Danbury CT: World Music Press.

*Cajun Home Music*. Folkways FW02620.

*15 Louisiana Cajun Classics. American Masters Volume 3*. Arhoolie 103.

# THE BUZZARD LOPE

U. S.: Georgia Sea Islands

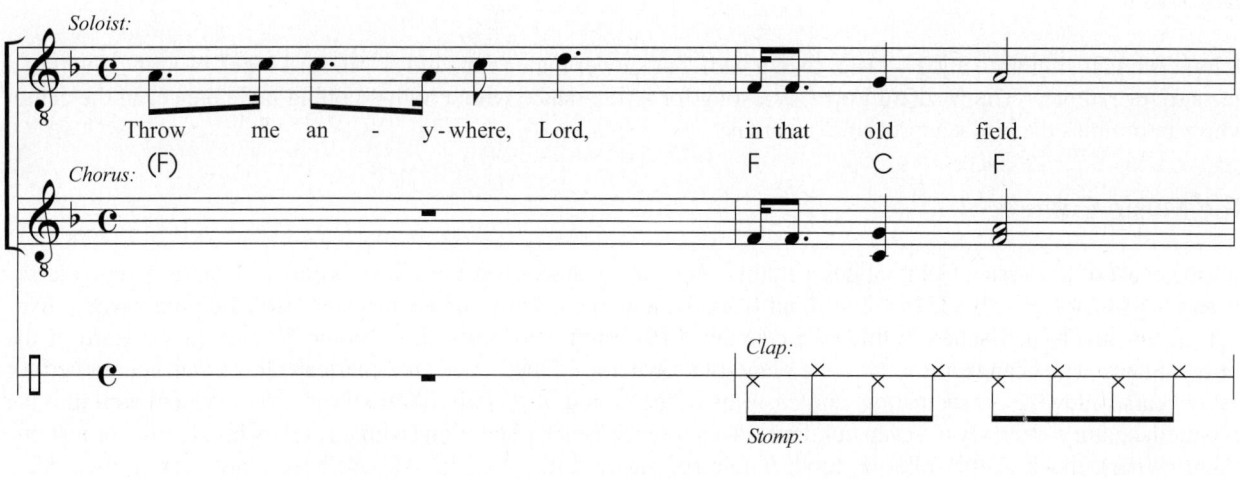

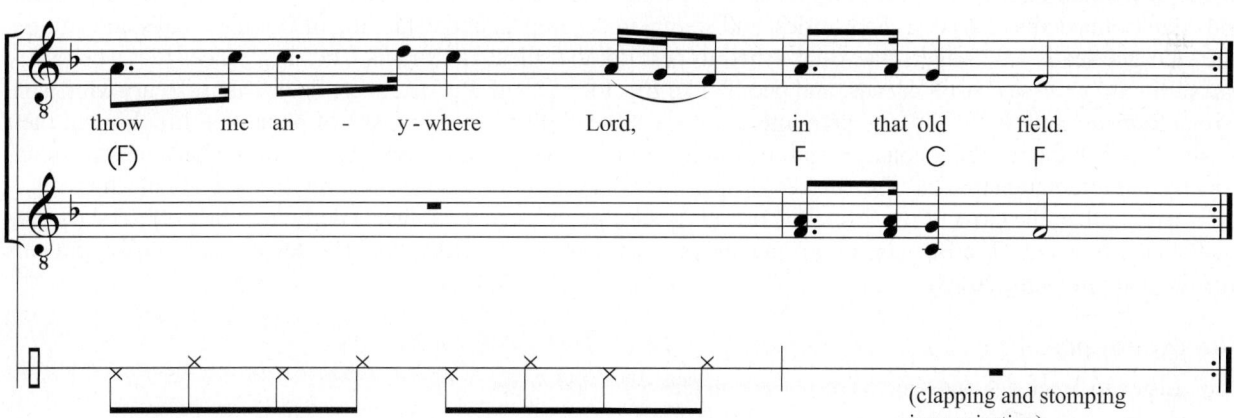

(clapping and stomping improvisation)

2. Don't care where you throw me,
   In that old field,
   Since my Jesus own me,
   In that old field.

3. You may beat an' bang me,
   In that old field,
   Since my Jesus save me,
   In that old field.

4. Don't care how you treat me
   In that old field,
   Since King Jesus meet me,
   In that old field.

5. Don't care how you do me,
   In that old field,
   Since King Jesus choose me,
   In that old field.

*(Repeat ad lib.)*

# THE BUZZARD LOPE

CD I, Track # 9

## The Tune

A lope is a gait similar to a jog—faster than a walk but slower than a run, and a "buzzard lope" is a movement of a buzzard, or vulture. "The Buzzard Lope" is a song for a ring dance with a high-stepping male dancer in the center who pantomimes the bird's approach to a carcass.

## The Music Culture

Off the coast of Savannah, Georgia, lies a chain of forested islands known as the Georgia Sea Islands, where marshes and bays historically made travel difficult from the mainland. Thus, the islands were isolated points where lives were lived largely untouched by life in Savannah, Charleston, and other cities along the eastern seaboard of the United States. The island culture of white plantation owners and their African-American slaves was maintained for many years following emancipation, and customs of the period of pre-Civil War slavery were evident well into the twentieth century. With six or seven hundred slaves living on each plantation (with a single white family, or just one white owner), much of the folklore, food, language, music, and art of the African homelands were preserved in work, play, and life at large. Lydia Parrish (wife of painter Maxfield Parrish), black folklorist Zora Neale Hurston, and Alan Lomax collected songs and stories, and sought to develop an understanding of Georgia Sea Island culture. The Georgia Sea Island Singers was established to perform the spirituals, shouts, and ring dances that were a key part of living on these coastal islands, and people like Big John David, Bessie Jones, Peter Davis, Henry Morrison, Emma Ramsay, and Mable Hillary were intent to "teach the chillun" the elements of plantation life through their music. Through the far-flung concerts and recordings of this group, Georgia Sea Island culture became known nationally and internationally. In "The Buzzard Lope," the dancing "bird" catches his prey (a slave), then whirls away a piece of cloth at the close of the dance to portray the casting off of a dead slave's body into the field. The point is made in the lyrics of "The Buzzard Lope" that despite whatever else may happen, the devout slave always puts his trust in God (and King Jesus).

### The Experiences

- Listen to Track # 9, and sing the response ("in that old field") to the calls.
- Listen to the recording, and add claps and stomps along with the sung response.
- Listening again to the recording, sing the call, separate from the sung response.
- Sing the song in its entirety, a cappella, with body percussion such as claps and stomps, or with piano accompaniment on the response.

### Recommended Listening

+*Georgia Sea Island Singers*. New World Records 80278.

*McIntosh County Shouters: Slave Shout Songs from the Coast of Georgia*. Folkways FW 04344.

# BY THE WATERS BABYLON

England and United States

## The Tune

In the sixth century BC, the Jews were exiled to Babylon, a city that figures prominently in some of the stories of the Old Testament. "By the Waters Babylon" is a tribute to the Jewish people, and to the steadfast manner in which they lived in memory of their homeland and with a yearning to return to it.

## The Music Culture

The song is a paraphrase of the opening lines of Psalm 137. It also recalls a prose poem published by Emma Lazarus in 1887 (who also wrote the poem on the Statue of Liberty). A sad, slow round, it has been recorded in various styles by Sweet Honey In The Rock and pop-folk singer Don McLean, among others. The text is directed to a historical time in the history of the world, and the melody is an old-English round.

After King Solomon's death in 930 BCE, his Jewish kingdom was divided into two pieces, Israel and Judah. These kingdoms lasted several centuries but were conquered by the Assyrian and Babylonian empires, and the Jewish people were carried off into exile and oblivion. This exile to Babylonia marked the beginning of the Jewish Diaspora. Babylon had been the holy city of Babylonia since 2300 BC In the region of Mesopotamia (now Iraq), and situated in equal parts along the left and right banks of the Euphrates River, Babylon was the hub of the kingdom of Nebuchadnezzar II (605 BCE–562 BCE). He directed the construction of the imperial grounds, including the spectacular Ishtar Gate—the most impressive of eight gates that ringed the perimeter of Babylon. The Hanging Gardens of Babylon were constructed during his reign for his wife, and were one of the seven wonders of the ancient world. Cyrus the Great, king of Persia, took Babylonia in 539 BCE without resistance, and it was he who permitted the exiled Jews to return to their own land. Yet during their captivity in Babylon, they wrote the substance of the holy scriptures known as the Torah. Judaism developed its framework there, and the Jewish people ensured their survival as a nation in exodus, as well as their spiritual identity, in their time together in Babylon.

### The Experiences

- Sing the song with solfège syllables (beginning on "la" in la-based minor) or scale numbers (beginning on "6").
- Sing the melody with its lyrics, noting the repetition of words and melodic motifs at different pitch levels.

- Play the chords while singing or playing the melody, one chord per quarter-note beat (or at least every two beats), on piano or guitar.
- Sing the song as an a cappella canon in three parts, with each part entering four measures after the one preceding it.

## Recommended Listening

+*By the Waters of Babylon*. Meridian Records 8447.

+*Paul Tate: Let All Creation Sing*! World Library Public Records 007470.

*Feel Something Drawing Me On* (Sweet Honey in the Rock). Flying Fish FF 70375.

# CAIQIU WU

China

Traditional, China, Arranged by Han Kuo Han.  From Han, K. H. & Campbell, P. S. (1992). *The Lion's Roar: Chinese Luogu Percussion Ensembles*. Danbury, CT: World Music Press. Courtesy World Music Press.

# CAIQIU WU
## (VERSION II)

China

# CAIQIU WU
## (VERSION III)

China

## The Tune

"Caiqiu Wu" translates as "flower-ball dance," a folk dance of China whose centerpiece is a handheld silk flower. The music for the dance is played by flute, woodblock, and a metallic instrument such as bell or triangle.

## The Music Culture

Music of the *luogu* percussion ensemble is widely performed in China and in Chinese communities around the world. Consisting of cymbals, drums, a variety of gongs, and various other percussion instruments, *luogu* is the music of parades, street festivals, and religious rituals. It may also be heard as the dramatic music of the theatre, as backstage accompaniment to the puppet theatre, at temples in Taoist, Buddhist, and (Taoist) Confucian rituals. Occasionally, a bamboo flute called *di* (or *di tze*) may be added for melodies, although a set of hanging gongs called *yunluo*, or cloud gongs, is used many of the melodic parts, too. "Luo" is the generic Chinese term for gongs made of copper, zinc, and tin, whose discs are typically "dished," appearing convex from the outside, so as to give a unique rising or falling tone when struck by a mallet. "Gu" refers to Chinese drums of all sizes, shapes, and functions, some of which are handheld, positioned on stands, or hung on the waists of dancers. *Luogu* is music of the people, less refined than the sound of "silk and bamboo" instruments such as fiddles, lutes, and zithers, and yet filled with spirit.

### The Experiences

- Sing the flute melody of the original version on a neutral syllable such as "loo," and on solfège syllables or scale numbers.
- Play the melody on flute, recorder, or other available melody instruments (including violin, saxophone, trumpet—any will do!). Play all three versions of the melody, noting the increasing density of ornamentation in the second and third versions.
- Chant and tap the rhythm of the woodblock, using the Chinese mnemonic syllables "da" or "go."
- Combine the percussion and melody instruments for all three versions.
- Make a flower-ball of large silk scarves. Tie them with their corners unfolding at the middle like flower petals. Move the silky flower-ball in curved lines to show the rise and fall of the melody.

### Recommended Listening

+*The Lion's Roar: Chinese Luogu Percussion Ensembles* (Han/Campbell). Danbury, CT: World Music Press.

*China's Instrumental Heritage.* Lyrichord LLST 7921.

*Drums—Chinese Percussion Music.* Hugo.

# CAJUEIRO PEQUENINO

Brazil

1. Ca - ju - ei - ro pe - que - ni - no ca - rre - ga - do de fu - lô. Eu tam -
bém sou pe - que - ni - no ca - rre - ga - do de a - mor.

2. Ai, meu ca - ju - ei - ro ven - to nor - te a - ba - lou, Que foi
is - to ca - ju - ei - ro se - ri - coi' a - nun - ci - ou.

1. *My little cashew tree,*
   *Filled with life,*
   *I am little, too,*
   *And filled with love.*

2. *Oh, my little cashew tree,*
   *That the north wind shook,*
   *Oh, what was that about?*
   *The story the bird told.*

*Cajueiro Pequenino* (As found in *Song of Latin America: from the Fields to the Classroom*) By PATRICIA CAMPBELL with ANA LUCIA FREGA. © 2001 WARNER BROS. PUBBLICATIONS. All Rights Reserved. Used by Permission of ALFRED PUBLISHING CO., INC.

## The Tune

The Brazilian children's song "Cajueiro Pequenino," tells of a little cashew tree that is filled with life as little children are filled with love. The singers are joined by the sounds of the guitar, accordion, *zabumba* (bass drum), *panderio* (small hand drums), bongos, and triangle.

## The Music Culture

Thoughts of Brazil conjure images of the beaches at Rio de Janeiro, lush rain forests of the Amazon region, soccer (or *futebol*), and street parades. Mention Brazilian music, and *samba, bossa nova*, and *choro* come to mind. So does the season of Carnaval, when the parade of *samba* schools fills the Sambadrome, the stadium constructed for samba performances. This is the time and place of costume dancers and musicians who perform on the towering floats to the music of samba bands. The polyphonic cross-rhythms of the *surdo* drums, friction drums (*cui'ca*), snare drums (*caixa*), and six-inch hand drums (*tamborim*) inspire all within earshot to celebrate. The brilliance of samba music is not the only sound of Brazil, however; the music of Milton Nascimento, Gilberto Gil, Clara Nunes, Martinho da Vila, Tom (Antonio Carlos) Jobim, and Joâo Gilberto represents many diverse musical voices and expressions—including *bossa nova*. The music of Brazilian children is straightforward and seemingly simple in its melody, rhythm, and harmonic progressions, yet the youngest children are exposed to the dynamic rhythms of the "adult music"—which seems to seep into their songs as underlying, pulsive patterns.

### The Experiences

- Sing the song on a neutral syllable like "nee," and then switch to solfège syllables or scale numbers.

- While singing the song on a neutral syllable, tap or clap an ostinato rhythm: ♪. ♪ ♩ or the more sophisticated samba sound of ♪. ♪ ♩

- Sing the song in Brazilian-style Portuguese, with special attention to pronunciation of "ju" (zhuh), "ei" (eh), "que" (kay), "eu" (uh), "meu" (muh), "foi" (fwah).

- Play the chords on guitar while singing or playing the melody. A steady rain of eighth notes is appropriate, accenting in this manner:

| Count: | 1 | + | 2 | + | 3 | + | 4 | + |
|--------|---|---|---|---|---|---|---|---|
| Accent: | > | | | > | > | | > | |

- Along with melody and chords, play an ostinato rhythm on conga or djembe drums: ♪. ♪ ♪ ♪

### Recommended Listening

+*Canciones de America Latina* (Campbell/Frega). Miami: Warner Bros.

*Songs and Dances of Brazil*. Folkways FW 06953.

*Putumayo Presents: Acoustic Brazil*. Putumayo World Music PUTU 234.

# CALYPSO FREEDOM

Sweet Honey in the Rock

*Teaching Music Globally: Experiencing Music, Expressing Culture* by Campbell, P. S. (2004). By permission of Oxford University Press, Inc.

# CALYPSO FREEDOM

## The Tune

Both *calypso* and *protest song*, "Calypso Freedom" is an expression with a Caribbean accent (in calypso style) of injustices done to people of color by society and the police forces that reinforce it.

## The Music Culture

Protest songs have sounded throughout American history: during the American Revolutionary War, the nineteenth-century abolitionist movement, the American Civil War, the union (labor) movement of the twentieth century, the Great Depression, the Civil Rights movement of the 1950s and 1960s, the Vietnam War, and in recent demonstrations against the Iraq War. Protest songs of the middle to late twentieth century include Woody Guthrie's "This Land is Your Land" (1940), Bob Dylan's "The Times They Are A-Changin'" (1964), Pete Seeger's "Waist Deep in the Big Muddy" (1967), and a host of songs by Joan Baez, Phil Ochs, Buffy Sainte-Marie, and Mimi and Richard Fariña. One of the best known and longest standing protest songs, "We Shall Overcome," has been a signature song for African Americans seeking full emancipation and fair treatment. The African-American female a cappella ensemble, Sweet Honey in the Rock, has done much to raise an awareness of social issues through song. Their signature sound is full choral harmony with a mixture of styles ranging from spirituals and gospel to blues and calypso. Of the last genre, a syncopated song of short verses with refrains, their "Calypso Freedom" functions as a protest song while offering a taste of the musical dynamism of the Caribbean islands.

### The Experiences

- Sing the "doo" section that functions as both harmonic accompaniment to the melody as well as chorus/response ("Freedom is coming and it won't be long") to the solo call.
- Sing the solo lines with the lyrics indicated.
- Sing the shared solo/chorus, "Freedom, freedom," in full harmony.
- Play the chorus part from start to finish on the piano.
- Add wood block and shakers.
- Create new verses on the topic of freedom. For example: "We're marching for our freedom and we won't take "no." We'll take it to the people, to the people we'll go."

### Recommended Listening

*Sweet Honey In The Rock: All for Freedom.* Music for Little People 42505D.

*Protest: Songs of Struggle and Resistance from Around the World.* Ellipsis Arts CD 1000.

*Calypso: Vintage Songs from the Caribbean.* Putumayo World Music.

# CHAANG

Thailand

*Elephant, elephant, elephant,*

*Have you, little (sister/brother), ever seen an elephant before?*

*Elephant is a big animal.*

*His nose is long, and is called nguang (trunk).*

*His teeth are underneath his trunk, and are called ngaa (teeth).*

*He has ears, eyes, and a long tail.*

Traditional, Thailand, arranged by Pornprapit Phoasavadi. From Phoasavadi, P. & Campbell, P. S. (2003). *From Bangkok and Beyond: Thai Children's Songs, Games and Customs.* Danbury, CT: World Music Press. Courtesy World Music Press.

## The Tune

Just as children in Thailand learn early on what an elephant is, they also learn how to sing the traditional action song, "Chaang."

## The Music Culture

In Thailand, elephants (*chaang*) are important historically, and they continue to be respected and cared for. They were the animals that Siamese and Burmese kings mounted for processionals in times of peace, and for surveying the land and calling the maneuvers during war. Elephants were once kept on the grounds of Thailand's royal palace, although now they are more likely to be found at zoos, at festivals, and at work in the logging industry. Thai children find elephants fascinating for their wide, flat, and flappy ears, their skinny tails, and their long and wrinkled trunks. "Chaang" is sung with delight by young Thai children who learn both vocabulary and coordination as they name the elephant's body parts whle tapping their own corresponding parts.

### The Experiences

- Sing the song on a neutral syllable such as "cha," and on solfège syllables (beginning on "solo") or scale numbers (beginning on "5").

- Chant the lyrics, with attention to all "aa"s sounding as "ah" and "i"s as "ee," and to the particular pronunciations of "nguang" (n[g]ooahng), "kheio" (kayo), and "taai" (tie).
- Sing the lyrics, noting that elisions must be heeded so that singers move quickly through several vowels on a single pitch.
- Add movements to depict the various parts of the elephant:

| | |
|---|---|
| Measure 1: "Chaang" | Take large side-to-side steps |
| Measure 2: "Koey hen" | Spread arms up, as if to ask a question |
| Measure 3: "Chaang man" | Extend arms, rounded, to show size |
| Measure 4: "Yaao riak waa nguang" | Place hands to nose, then extend arm from nose, to hand like a trunk |
| Measure 5: "Nguang riak waa ngaa" | Place hands at mouth, wiggle fingers, as if to show menacing teeth |
| Measure 6: "Taa haang yaao" | With hands, show big ears, eyes, and long tail, one after another |

- Although the song needs no accompaniment, and is not accompanied chordally in Thailand, play the chords on guitar, piano, or other harmony instrument.

### Recommended Listening

+*From Bangkok and Beyond* (Phoasavadi/Campbell). Danbury, CT: World Music Press.
*Land of 1000 Smiles: Classical Music of Thailand.* Sounds of the World 90172.
*Music of Thailand.* Folkways FW04463.

## CHAWE CHIDYO CHEM'CHERO

Zimbabwe

*It is the sound (of me) eating the food of the forest.*

Traditional, Zimbabwe, Arranged by Dumisani Maraire.  From Adzenya, A.K., Maraire, D., & Tucker, J. C. (1997). *Let Your Voice Be Heard: Songs from Ghana and Zimbabwe* (Rev. Ed.). Danbury, CT: World Music Press. Courtesy World Music Press.

## The Tune

As in many parts of sub-Saharan African, the Shona people of Zimbabwe blend songs and stories together. Dumisani Maraire, a master performer of *mbira* (thumb piano), was also a teller of tales who invited participation through singing by all.

## The Music Culture

In southeastern Africa lies the landlocked nation of Zimbabwe, formerly known as Rhodesia, whose majority people are the Shona. Zimbabwe means "houses of stone" in reference to the ruins of an ancient state in the southeastern part of the country which had been a major trading center from the ninth to the thirteenth century. Most Zimbabweans are farmers and miners, although a growing number work in industry. They continue to sing their songs and tell their tales, and play traditional instruments such as musical bows, flutes, and the *mbira*, even as the sounds of popular music from their African neighbors and the West play in the markets and at home. The well-known musician and educator Dumisani (Dumi) Maraire was raised in a musical family; all members from the eldest on down sang together and told stories at home in the evenings. Dumi learned "Chawe Chidyo Chem'chero," a story-song about the curly-horned *kudu* who sang for his supper, and countless other story-songs. Dumi performed on the *mbira*, a percussive instrument with flat, narrow iron keys that are attached to a hollowed-out gourd or a wooden box, playing the keys with his thumb and index finger. A consummate musician and teacher, Dumi played marimba and drums, too, and told his stories with an animation that captivated his listeners.

## The Experiences

- Sing the first, second, and third voice parts with solfège syllables or scale numbers, noting that G is the home tone ("do" or "1") and that the seventh scale degree is F rather than F♯.
- Sing each voice part with the words, noting the pronunciation as "chah-way" (chawe), "cheed-yo" (chidyo), "mwah-nah-wee-ay" (mwana i we).
- Layer in the three vocal parts to produce a chordal harmony.
- Tell the story, with pauses for the sung response "chawe chidyo chem'chero," which means "It is the sound (of me) eating the food of the forest."

## The Story:

Once there lived a family on a large farm on which they grew maize, wheat, yams, millet, and other crops. There was also a *kudu,* a wild antelope with curly horns and grey fur, who was lately coming upon the family's fields to eat the food they were cultivating. The family—father, mother, and little boy—puzzled about what to do with kudu to stop him from eating the food they grew to eat and to take to market in exchange for other goods. They agreed to send the boy deep into the field at the edge of the forest, to chase the kudu away. And so he went. He hid in the high grasses with an assemblage of metal pots and pans, waiting for the kudu. At sunset, who should slip out of the forest and into the family's field but a proud and hungry kudu. As the boy raised his pots and pans to frighten away the kudu, the clever kudu—who knew how much people enjoy music—began to sing. The boy was entranced, and stood frozen as he listened to the kudu's song: "Chawe chidyo chem'chero." [sing] The boy went home to his parents, happy to have heard the music, but with the news that he could not chase kudu away. At this point—[much more can be made of this in the telling of the story]—the mother went to the field with sticks to clack together. She hid, she heard the song [sing], she was entranced, and returned home. The father then went out to the field with his spear. He heard the song [sing], and then he, too, returned home.

The moral of the story is clear: The kudu sings for his supper, as he understands the power and magic of song, and the family learns to live alongside of—but not in command of or superior to—the kudu. In a performance of the story, "Chawe Chidyo Chem'chero" is sung three times in all, once at each musical "entrancement" by the kudu.

## Recommended Listening

+*Let Your Voice Be Heard: Songs from Ghana and Zimbabwe* (Adzenyah/Maraire/Tucker). Danbury, CT: World Music Press.

*Soul of Mbira: Traditions of the Shona People of Rhodesia.* Nonesuch H-72054.

# CHEROKEE MORNING SONG

U. S.: Cherokee

We de ya ho     wen de ya ho_____     wen de ya

wen de ya     ho ho ho ho     he ya ho, he ya ho     ya     ya     ya._____

CD I, Track # 10

## The Tune

Using text and vocables, "Cherokee Morning Song" offers a greeting to the morning in its gently rising and falling melodic phrases.

## The Music Culture

The Cherokee are estimated at 47,000 people. A core population still lives in North Carolina, but most live in Oklahoma as a result of their eviction and forced march in 1838–39 by the U.S. government in a mismanaged journey of 116 days known as the Trail of Tears. Early European encounters with the Cherokee in the mid-sixteenth century found them using stone implements, including knives, axes, and chisels. The Cherokee lived in bark-roofed log cabins, each with one door and a smoke hole in the roof. They cultivated maize, beans, and squash; hunted deer, bear, and elk for meat and clothing; made pottery; and wove baskets. Cherokee towns were comprised of 30–60 log cabins and a council house where meetings were held. After 1800, the Cherokee assimilated many aspects of their Anglo-American neighbors' culture, including methods of farming, weaving, and home building. The introduction of a Cherokee syllabary by Sequoyah in 1812 allowed them to develop a written constitution and a body of religious literature that included translations from the Christian scriptures. However, in spite of their efforts to assimilate, they were evicted from the Southeastern states under the Indian Removal Act of 1830 and resettled on reservations in the Oklahoma territory. Cherokee music, like the music of many of the Native American groups of the Eastern Woodlands, features brief, repetitive phrases and song texts that emphasize vocables.

### The Experiences

- Listen to Track # 10, tapping the pulse every beat, every other beat, or once every seven beats on the tambourine.
- Sing the song on solfège syllables (beginning on "mi") or scale numbers (beginning on "3").
- While listening to the recording, sing the Cherokee text and vocables.
- Add an F chord, or an F–C drone, once every two or four beats, depending upon how long the sound can be sustained.

- Play an ostinato rhythm of ♩ ♫ ♩ 𝅗𝅥 throughout on a hand drum. Add shakers and tambourines, as on the recording.
- Sing the song as a canon, with a new voice entering every two measures. Try the song as a canon with an entry at every measure.

## Recommended Listening

+*Tribal Dreams: Music from Native Americans*. EarthBeat R2 74269.

*Cry from the Earth: Music of the North American Indians* (Nancy & Mark Brown, Jamake Highwater). Folkways FW 37777.

*Creation's Journey: Native American Music*. Smithsonian Folkways SFW 40410.

# CIELITO LINDO

Mexico

*Verse:*

De la Sier - ra Mo - re - na, Cie - li - to lin - do, vie - nen ba - jan - do,

Un par de'o - ji - tos ne - gros, Cie - li - to lin - do, de con - tra - ban - do.

*Refrain:*

Ay, ay, ay, ay! Can - ta'y no llo - res. Por - que can -

ta - do se'a - le - gran, Cie - li - to lin do, los co - ra - zo - nes.

Ay, ay, ay, ay! Can - ta'y no llo - res. Por - que can -

tan - do se'a - le - gran, Cie - li - to lin - do, los co - ra - zo - nes.

1. *From the dark, distant mountain,*
   *Cielito lindo, I see descending,*
   *Your dark eyes flashing brightly,*
   *Cielito lindo, love's message sending.*

   *Refrain:*
   *Ay, sing with gladness*
   *For in those hearts that are singing,*
   *Cielito lindo, there is sadness.*

# CIELITO LINDO

## The Tune

For several generations, "Cielito Lindo" has been one of the best-known Mexican melodies, a love song that refers to the sweetheart as "Beautiful Heaven."

## The Music Culture

Evening serenades of a young man to a young lady were once customary courting practices in Spain and its former colonies, including Mexico. In the cool of the evening, a male singer with a guitar placed himself below the window of his prospective lover where he would perform verses of praise to her beauty and virtues. Quirino Mendoza y Cortez composed "Cielito Lindo" in the early twentieth century, receiving a copyright in 1929, yet there are indications that it is based on a traditional folk song from at least a century earlier. It quickly gained in popularity in Mexico and among Mexican Americans in the southwestern United States, and was soon a symbol of Mexican national identity around the world. Even while Mexican music has diversified and modernized, such that *discotecas* (record stores) abound in Mexican cities, with *música ranchera* (country music), *mariachi, salsa* (also called *música tropical*), and rock music sounding out into the streets, folk songs—simply sung to a guitar accompaniment—continue to be heard. As for "Cielito Lindo," it is still a song for serenading, and as it can be performed in various popular styles, as well.

### The Experiences
- Sing the song on a neutral syllable like "bah," noting the sustained rhythm that renders a syncopated feel in a triple meter. Sing it on solfège syllables or scale numbers.
- Sing the lyrics, with attention to these pronunciations: "e" (ay), "r" (flip), "j" (h), "ll" (y).
- Play the chords on guitar (or piano), accenting the first quarter-note beat in this strumming pattern:

### Recommended Listening
+*Canciones de Mi Padre* (Linda Ronstadt). Electra/Asylum Records 970765.
*Vamos a Cantar: A Collection of Children's Songs in Spanish.* Folkways FW 07747.

# ČIJA LI JE TARABA

Croatia

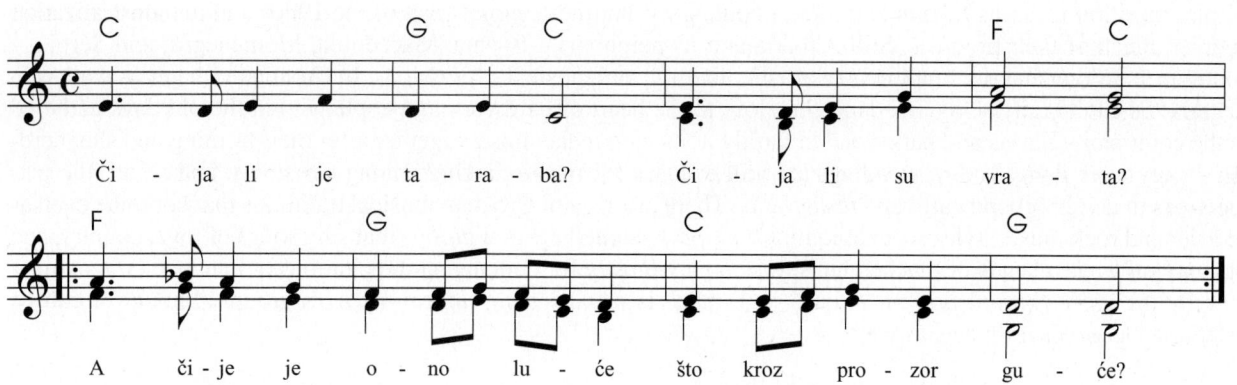

Či - ja li je ta - ra - ba? Či - ja li su vra - ta?

A či - je je o - no lu - će što kroz pro - zor gu - će?

| | |
|---|---|
| 1. Čija li je taraba? | 1. *Who is the fence?* |
| Čija li su vrata? | *Who is the door?* |
| A čije je ono luće | *And whose is that doll* |
| Što kroz prozor guće? | *Looking through the window?* |
| | |
| 2. Mamina je taraba | 2. *The fence is Mama's* |
| Tatina su vrata | *The door is Papa's* |
| A moje je ono luće | *The doll is mine* |
| Što kroz prozor guće. | *Looking through the window.* |
| | |
| 3. Srdiće se Mamica | 3. *Mama will get angry* |
| Sridiće se Tata | *So will Papa* |
| Ali neće ono luće | *But the doll looking out* |
| Što kroz prozor guće. | *The window won't.* |
| | |
| 4. Preskočiću tarabu, | 4. *I'll jump over the fence,* |
| Otvoriću vrata, | *Open the door,* |
| Polijubiću ono luće | *And kiss that doll* |
| Što kroz prozor guće | *Looking through the window.* |

Čija li je Taraba from *Village Harmony: Traditional Songs of the Balkans*, edited by Mary Cay Brass. Copyright 1995 Northern Harmony Publishing Company. Original transcription by Mary Cay Brass.

## The Tune

The text of this Croatian song, "Čija li je Taraba," opens with questions and resolves in a plan to "kiss the doll." What is uncertain is whether "the doll" is in fact a girl's toy or a girl of marriageable age.

## The Music Culture

In the countries of southeastern Europe that once comprised Yugoslavia, Croatia stands in the north and extends its Dalmatian coastline along the Adriatic Sea. Post-communist countries like Croatia moved quickly to make an economic transition that was favorable to their populations, but the regional wars of the 1990s and deindustralization derailed much of their progress. Still, Croatia and its neighbors—Bosnia, Macedonia, Montenegro, and Serbia—continue their long and rich traditions of artistic, literary, and musical expressions. In Croatian villages as well as in Zagreb, the capitol city, song and dance lie close to the heart of hardworking people who in the old days gathered in the community plazas and parks, and in family homes, to make music together after their farming and shepherding chores were done. Today, weddings are still excuses for music making among Croatians, and so are the get-togethers in neighborhood cafés and restaurants. There are several Croatian musical traditions that continue even as popular and rock music styles seem ubiquitous: *klapa*, a cappella choral groups that sing songs of love, country, and the sea; *tamburitza* bands of plucked lutes, which play mostly for dancing; and recitations of epic poetry accompanied by the *gusle* (bowed fiddle). "Cija li je Taraba" is usually sung informally by a group, although it can be performed as a concert piece, as well.

### The Experiences

- Sing the melody on a neutral syllable such as "see," and on solfège syllables or scale numbers. Follow the upper of the two pitches in the case of the harmonizing thirds.
- Sing the song's melody with Croat words, noting these pronunciations: "j"as "y" (as in chee-ya for "čija"), "c" as "s" (as in loo-chee for "luće"), "c" as "k" when followed by "u" (as in pres-ko-see-koo for "preskočiću," and similarly for "otvoriću" and "poljubiću").
- Sing the song's melody and harmony in thirds.
- Play the chords on accordion, piano, or guitar, while singing.
- Dance a simple *kolo* in a circle, using a "grapevine" foot pattern. Facing the center of the circle, hands held and elbows bent, place the weight on the left foot and move to the right.

| Beat: | 1 | 2 | 3 | 4 | 5 | 6 | 7 | 8 |
|---|---|---|---|---|---|---|---|---|
| Step: | R | L | R | L | R | L | L | R |
| | Step (side) | Cross (in front) | Step (side) | Cross (in back) | Step (in place) | Point (in front) | Step (in place) | Point (in front) |

### Recommended Listening

*Village Harmony: Traditional Songs of the Balkans.* Northern Harmony 4003BC.
*Folk Music of Yugoslavia.* Folkways FW 04434.

# CINDERELLA

United States

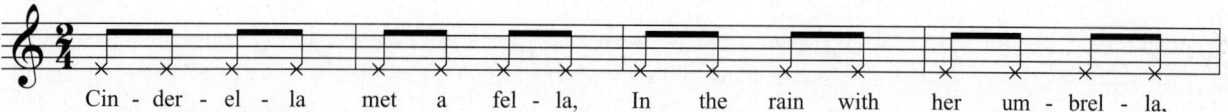

Cin - der - el - la  met  a  fel - la,  In  the  rain  with  her  um - brel - la,

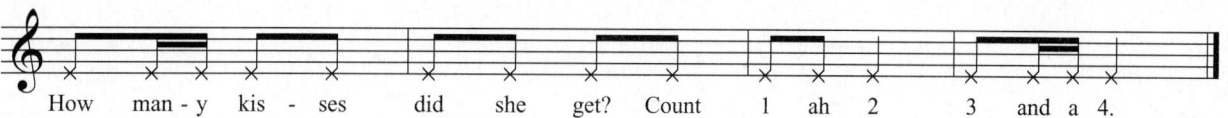

How  man - y  kis - ses  did  she  get?  Count  1  ah  2  3  and a  4.

## The Groove

Jump-rope chants like "Cinderella" offer children opportunities to vocalize in a rhythmic manner. They keep time with the beat of the rope as it repeatedly hits the pavement and invites them "in" to the rhythmic play of jumping rope.

## The Music Culture

Cinderella, the heroine of the fairy tale by the Brothers Grimm, has come a long way from her German-Romantic nineteenth-century origin to the contemporary appearances she has made in children's books, theatre productions, and films. She has been taken to the streets where children gather to jump rope, clap hands, and play various counting games. In the rope-jumping experience, children take turns hopping "inside" the center of a rope that is turned by a child at either end. This requires considerable coordination, as they must time themselves to hop just after the rope strikes the pavement (or gym floor). The sounds of the rope and of hopping feet form a steady rhythmic ostinato to accompany the chanted rhyme. Children can also enjoy "doing Cinderella" by facing a partner, clapping hands together in a recurring rhythm, and chanting the rhyme. The chant is easily adaptable to either activity.

### The Experience

- Tap a quarter-note pulse while vocalizing the "Cinderella" chant.
- Switch from the words of the chant to counting out the rhythm (1 + 2 +) or chanting with syllables systematically (ti-ti ti-ti).
- While chanting the words through several revolutions, clap hands with a partner:

| Say: | "lap" | "clap" | "partner" | "clap" |
|---|---|---|---|---|
| Do: | pat lap | clap own hands | clap partner's hands | clap own hands |
| Count: | 1 | + | 2 | + |

- Invent a new clapping pattern to accompany the chant, and consider adding stamping and snapping, too.
- Chant while jumping rope alone or with two rope-turners.

### Recommended Listening

+*Skip Rope Games*. Smithsonian Folkways SFW 07029.
*American Folk Songs for Children*. Smithsonian Folkways SFW 45020.

# CÔ HÀNG XÓM

Vietnam

*A green hedge separates our homes,*
*Neither of us has any attachments,*
*You and I long for each other,*
*If only there wasn't a hedge between us,*
*I'll have to come visit you.*

## The Tune

Popular music in Vietnam is just that: popular. "Cô Hàng Xóm" features the national instrument, *dan bao* (a monochord), with keyboards, drums, and a woodblock in a tribute to a neighborhood girl with whom a young man is enamored.

## The Music Culture

The music of Vietnam includes a wide array of traditional instrumental and vocal genres, Western art music, and popular music that has arisen from the merger of Vietnamese and Western idioms. Popular songs with romantic, folk, and historical themes are now widely known in Vietnam and in Vietnamese communities in the United States, France, Australia, and elsewhere in the world. Vietnamese popular music is readily available on commercial recordings, radio, television, and in live concerts. Often, this music sounds very Western, but the choice of traditional instruments, the use of Vietnamese lyrics, and a singing style that utilizes glottal techniques and a highly nasalized quality give Vietnamese music its own identity. While "Cô Hàng Xóm" is a long way from the traditional Vietnamese court music performed at Huê and the theater music (such as *hat cai luong*), it demonstrates how the essence of a traditional song's sound and subject matter can be carried forward in new forms.

## *The Experiences*

- Sing the melody.
- Play the chords on piano or guitar, exploring possibilities for playing them once, twice, or four times per measure, in block or arpeggiated form.
- Sing the melody while playing the harmony on piano or guitar. Add a soft beat on drum set or other available drums, and the woodblock ostinato.

## *Recommended Listening*

+*Cô Hàng Xóm*. (Tài Linh.) Mua Hong Production MHCD.

*The Music of Vietnam, Volume 1*. Celestial Harmonies 13082-2.

*From Rice Paddies and Temple Yards: Traditional Music of Vietnam* (Nguyen/Campbell). Danbury, CT: World Music Press.

# THE COO-COO BIRD

U. S.: Appalachian and Ozark Mountains

Gon - na build me log ca - bin On a moun - tain So

high So I can see Wil - lie as he goes on by.

Oh, the cuck - oo she's a pret - ty bird She wob - bles when she

flies. She ne - ver says coo - coo Till the fourth day Ju - ly.

2. I've played cards in England,
   I've played cards in Spain,
   I'll bet you ten dollars,
   I'll beat you the next game.

3. Jack-o'-Diamonds, Jack-o'-Diamonds,
   I knew you from old,
   You robbed my whole pocket,
   All my silver and my gold.

CD I, Track # 11

## The Tune

In the southern Appalachians and the Ozark mountains, banjo players call "The Coo-Coo Bird" one of their favorite pieces. The reference to "the fourth day of July" (Independence Day) suggests the freedom that is symbolized by a bird in flight.

## The Music Culture

The cuckoo tends to be a shy bird more often seen than heard, living in thick vegetation, especially in the temperate and tropical regions of Europe (including England). Cuckoos are known for laying single eggs in the nests of other birds to be incubated by the foster parents who rear the young cuckoo. They have been the subject of many musical expressions, including canons, strophic songs of multiple verses, and polyphonic and chordal arrangements. Some of these "cuckoo songs," found in England, Scotland, Wales, and in the mountains of the eastern United States, are sung a cappella. Others may be accompanied by guitar or banjo, or even played as instrumental solos on hammered dulcimer or fiddle—especially the American versions. This particular song is known for its haunting melody, anchored in the minor mode with a lowered seventh scale degree.

## The Experiences

- Listen to Track # 11, following the rise and fall of the undulating melody and the descending pattern of the accompanying banjo figure.

- Sing the song with the recording, noting the short phrases of only a few words to every breath.

- Experiment with possible G minor accompaniments on guitar, including strumming and finger-picking patterns. Choose one to play while singing the three verses of the melody. The chords can be played on other harmony instruments, too, including piano.

- As a transition between sung verses, play the melody on banjo, fiddle, or guitar.

## Recommended Listening

+*Doc Watson and Clarence Ashley: Smithsonian Folkways American Roots*. Collection SFW 40062.
+*Mike Seeger: True Vine*. Smithsonian Folkways SFW 40136.

## COPLAND: FANFARE FOR THE COMMON MAN

Aaron Copland

CD I, Track # 12

### The Tune

"Fanfare for the Common Man" was composed by Aaron Copland in 1942, with the intention of honoring less the heroes of war than those men and women who shared the labors and hopes of those who aimed for victory on the battlefield.

### The Music Culture

American composer Aaron Copland scored his famous fanfare for four French horns, four trumpets, three trombones, tuba, timpani, bass drum, and tam-tam. His sketches show that he had considered other titles as well for his composition: "Fanfare for a Solemn Ceremony, for the Day of Victory, for Our Heroes, for the Rebirth of Lidice, for the Spirit of Democracy, for the Paratroops, and for Four Freedoms." When the piece was premiered on March 12, 1943, the composer's sense of humor was evident in his comment: "I was all for honoring the common man at income tax time." Some have identified the character of American music with the "open" sound you hear in Copland's fanfare, the result of a scant use of thirds and a prevalence of fourths and fifths. The progression of the percussion's introductory call, followed by the wide open range of the trumpet's call, brings the listener to sharp attention and a realization that an important tribute is in progress.

#### The Experiences

- Listen to Track # 12, particularly for the ceremonial flair of the trumpets interspersed with and punctuated by the timpani.
- Play the fanfare melody on piano. Note the quick sixteenth-note motivic rise to sustained pitches.

- Experiment with sustained single notes played by the left hand (the first note of each motivic call) or open fifths as accompaniment. Note the effect of these sustained Cs, Gs, and Fs against the more active melody.
- Play the theme on various other melodic instruments, especially trumpet.

## Recommended Listening

+Copland: *Appalachian Spring Suite*, Fanfare for the Common Man. Bernstein/New York Philharmonic. Sony 37257.

# COPLAND: HOEDOWN

Aaron Copland

# COPLAND: HOEDOWN (CHORDS)

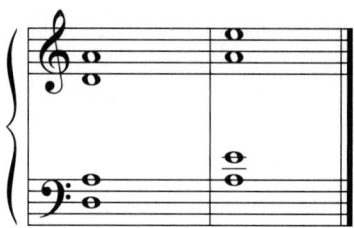

CD I, Track # 13

## The Tune

Composer Aaron Copland enjoyed writing for large public venues: the stage, screen, radio, TV, and the concert hall. Of his staged ballet music, he is noted for his ballets, and for components like "Hoedown" within the larger ballet works that have become standard fare in the orchestral repertoire.

## The Music Culture

As an American student and young professional in Paris, studying composition, conducting, and piano, Aaron Copland also attended many plays, concerts, and ballets. Even in his youth in New York, he regularly went to dance recitals, including performances by the legendary Isadora Duncan and the Ballets Russes. His first orchestral score was a ballet called *Grogh,* a macabre fantasy which he later refashioned into other works, including a second ballet, *Hear Ye! Hear Ye!* Three of Copland's best-known compositions were ballets: *Billy the Kid* (1938), *Rodeo* (1942), and *Appalachian Spring* (1943–44), which he wrote for dancer-choreographer Martha Graham. *Rodeo* is a poignant love story set against a frontier background, in which "Hoedown" appears as a fiddle tune for a country barn dance.

## The Experiences

- Listen to Track # 13 for the sounds of the bowing and plucking of violins, violas, cellos, and stringed basses.
- Play the theme on the piano, as they would be played quickly by a fiddle in a Saturday night barn dance.
- Experiment with playing chords, or just the open fifths of chords, as harmonic accompaniment for the melody.
- Play the theme on violin, with other violins playing open fifths (the D and A strings for the D chord, and the A and E strings for the A chord).
- Improvise upon the theme, embellishing the melody, or even sustaining selected pitches as a means of providing calming segments between fast-moving passages.

## Recommended Listening

+Copland: *Appalachian Spring Suite, Fanfare for the Common Man*. Bernstein/New York Philharmonic. Sony SMK 63082.

# CRIPPLE CREEK

U. S.: Appalachian and Ozark Mountains

*Verse:*

I got a gal and she loves me, She's as sweet as sweet can be.

She's got eyes of ba-by blue, Makes my gun shoot straight and true.

*Chorus:*

Goin' down Crip-ple Creek, Goin' in a run, Goin' down Crip-ple Creek to have some fun.

2. I got a beau and he loves me,

He's as sweet as sweet can be.

He's got eyes of darkest brown,

Makes my heart jump all around.

Chorus: Goin' down to Cripple Creek fast as I can go,

Goin' down to Cripple Creek, don't be slow.

Raise my britches above my knees,

Wade in Cripple Creek if I please.

## The Tune

In a list of fiddle tunes from the Appalachians and the Ozark mountains, "Cripple Creek" rises to the top of the list of favorites and is the most famous among them.

## The Music Culture

There are numerous Anglo- and Celtic-American tunes in the hands and fingers of American fiddlers, banjo players, and guitar pickers. Some of these derive directly from "the old countries" of England, Scotland, Ireland, and Wales; others are truly American, conceived and transmitted by the "mountain people" of the Appalachians and Ozarks. For fiddlers, the best tunes are often the ones that can be played with occasional double stops on the open D and A (or A and E, or even G and D) strings. "Cripple Creek" is a quintessential hoedown and a staple in the repertoire of Appalachian and Ozark mountain fiddlers and banjo players. For guitar players, it takes on a double persona as both a pickin' tune and a song to be sung and strummed. "Cripple Creek" has found its way into the repertoire of bluegrass and old-time bands, and is danced to by cloggers and square dancers alike.

## The Experiences

- Sing the melody on a neutral syllable like "dee" (for the eighth notes) and "deedle" (for the sixteenth notes).

- Play the melody on fiddle/violin (or banjo, guitar, or even piano), at a fast tempo.

- Harmonize the melody, articulating every quarter-note pulse. For violin players, use the open fifths of double-stops when possible.

- Sing the song with the lyrics, and play instrumental interludes between the verses.

## Recommended Listening

*American Banjo: Three-Finger and Scruggs Style* (Oren Jenkins). Smithsonian Folkways SFW 49937.

*Glen Neaves and the Virginia Mountain Boys: Country Bluegrass from Southwest Virginia*. Folkways FW 03830.

*Skillet Lickers: Old Time Fiddle Tunes and Songs from North Georgia*. County Records. CO-3509 CD.

# CUBAN RUMBA GROOVE

Cuba

## The Groove

The *rumba* (or rhumba), a popular dance of Afro-Cuban origin, can happen only when the right combination of percussion instruments are "in sync" in their interactions. A Cuban rumba percussion ensemble is key to the high energy of the rumba dance.

## The Music Culture

Rumba originated in the dances of the Kongo cult in Cuba. The *cumbia* and *guaguanco* were danced with extensive hip and shoulder movements, while the rumba was seen as an imitation of old people and housewives—yet still with expressive hip and torso movement. In Cuba, the rumba is defined by an accompaniment that includes conga, *tumbadora, quinto* or *salidor* drums, claves, and other stick-beaten resonant objects. The instruments perform complex duple-meter patterns that use extensive syncopation. The rumba became known in a modified form in the United States in 1914, but when it was toned down with less suggestive movements in the 1930s, it spread like wildfire across the country and in Europe. Characteristic movement of the rumba dance is a rocking of the hips to a quick-quick-slow rhythm. If there is a melody, it tends to be repetitive so that the principal musical character, the ostinato patterns on the percussion instruments, can be readily heard. The rumba is still popular as a ballroom dance.

## The Experiences

- Learn the distinctive rumba clave rhythm by stepping it (and clapping the complementary rhythms):

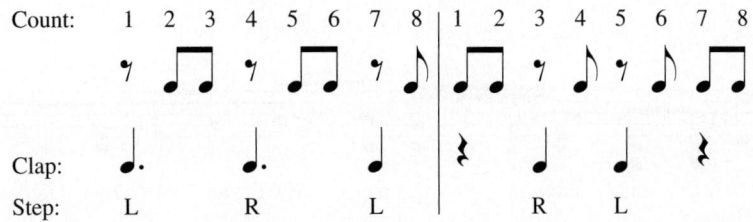

- Play the rhythms one by one, noting that all but the low drum are two-measure ostinati (the low drum's ostinato is just one measure in length).
- For the high and low drum, note that by playing with a cupped hand, the sound will be "muffled in center"; "open" means to play with a flat hand across the drum head.
- Play the parts together, repeatedly.
- Play to recordings of rumba music and musicans.

## Recommended Listening

*Afro-Cuban All Stars: A Toda Cuba Le Gusta*. Nonesuch 79476.
*Rhumbas & Mambos 1948–1951*. Tumbao Cuban Classix.
*Rhumba Favorites*. Eclipse Music Group 64440.

# CUMBERLAND GAP

U. S.: Tennessee and Kentucky

1. Lay down boys and take a lit-tle nap, We're all goin' down to Cum-ber-land Gap.

Cum-ber-land Gap, Cum-ber-land Gap, We're all go-in' down to Cum-ber-land Gap.

2. Me and my wife and my wife's pap,
   We all live down to Cumberland Gap.
   Cumberland Gap, Cumberland Gap,
   We all live down to Cumberland Gap.

3. I got a gal in Cumberland Gap,
   She's got a baby call me "pap"!
   Cumberland Gap, Cumberland Gap,
   We all live down to Cumberland Gap.

4. Cumberland Gap it ain't very fur,
   It's just three miles from Middlesboro.
   Cumberland Gap, Cumberland Gap.
   We're all goin' down to Cumberland Gap.

## The Tune

A well-known fiddle tune, "Cumberland Gap" makes reference to a natural pass cut through the Cumberland Plateau by stream activity near the point where the states of Kentucky, Virginia, and Tennessee meet.

## The Music Culture

The towns of Cumberland Gap, Tennessee and Middlesboro, Kentucky are as close as one gets to a remarkable 1,600-foot pass in a plateau at the edge of the Appalachian Mountains. The Cumberland Gap was discovered in the mid-eighteenth century, and Daniel Boone blazed the Wilderness Road through it. It opened up migration from the thirteen colonies to the Northwest Territory that stretched from Ohio all the way to the Mississippi River. The strategic gap was held by either the Confederate or Union troops at various times during the American Civil War. It was the inspiration for one of the best-known melodies from the Appalachian frontier, now a standard tune for fiddle players. Because the fiddle was a common instrument in England, it became an important instrument in the Anglo-American colonies and in the inland territories where pioneers sought new land on which to make their homes. They brought their pots and pans, food staples, hoes and shovels, a few field animals, and a stash of clothing—and fiddles. When time allowed, they used their fiddles for reflecting on the journeys behind and ahead of them.

## The Experiences

- Play the melody on piano or other melody instrument; note that the melody is always the top pitch.
- Play the melody and harmony as written on the piano.
- At the piano or on guitar, add chords to harmonize the melody with block chords or arpeggios at a steady pulse.
- Transfer the melody to violin, playing the chords on the guitar. Explore the possibilities of playing melody on other stringed instruments, as well as on wind and brass instruments.
- Sing the verses, providing instrumental interludes between them.

## Recommended Listening

+*Doc Boggs*, Volume 3. Folkways FW 03903.

+*Clawhammer Banjo* (David Johnson). Folkways FW 31094.

*Cathy Sisco: Rugged Road*. Voyager Recordings. CD 362.

# DE COLORES

Mexico

De___ co - lo - res,___ de co - lo - res se vis - ten los cam - pos en la pri - ma -

ve - ra.___ De___ co - lo - res,___ de co - lo - res son los pa - ja -

ri - tos que vie - nen de'a - fue - ra.___ De___ co - lo - res,___ de co -

lo - res es el ar - co i - ris que ve - mos lu - cir.___ Y por

e - so los gran - des a - mo - res de mu - chos co - lo - res me gus - tan a mì.

2. De colores,
   de colores es al arco iris que vemos lucir,
   Y por eso los grandes amores de muchos colores
   Me gustan a mì.

1. *The colors,*
   *The colors of countryside in the spring.*
   *The colors,*
   *The color appear as the sun shines through the rain clouds.*

2. *The colors,*
   *The colors of the rainbow that appears when a storm cloud is touched by the sun.*
   *And this great love of many colors*
   *Is pleasing to me.*

# DE COLORES

## The Tune

The splendors of springtime and the colors that come through the alternating rain and sunshine are the subject of this much-loved Mexican folk song, "De Colores."

## The Music Culture

The music of Mexico encompasses *mariachi, cumbia*, brass ensemble *banda* music, *norteña, ranchera*, and much more. There are three folk dances, too, that are widely popular in Mexico: the *huapango* from the Gulf coast province of Veracruz, which consists of singer, violin, small *jarana* guitar, and large *huapanguera* guitar; the *jarana* from the Yucatan peninsula, played by *jaranas,* drums, cornets, and *güiro;* and the *jarabe* of Jalisco state that has been popular with *charros* (Mexican cowboys) since the nineteenth century independence movement. Even as these ensembles and genres are associated with particular regions (for example, the *mariachi* of Guadalajara in the state of Jalisco), they are more widely known, too, through their spread by the media. Yet few pieces are better known throughout Mexico and Mexican-America than "De Colores." Like a chameleon, the song has taken on many renditions and styles, too, from a single singer's melody with guitar accompaniment to its performance by a full mariachi ensemble.

### The Experiences

- Sing the melody on a neutral syllable like "loo," and then with solfège syllables (beginning on "sol") or scale numbers (beginning on "5").
- Sing the song with words, remembering that in Spanish, "j" (in parajitos) sounds like "h."
- Add chordal accompaniment to the sung melody on guitar, providing one stronger and two lighter strums per measure.
- Continuing with the guitar's harmony, play the melody on violins and trumpets. If there are two or more of one or both instruments, experiment with harmonizing the melody in the characteristic thirds (usually a third lower than the melody).

### Recommended Listening

+*De Colores and Other Latin American Folk Songs* (Jose-Luis Orozco). Arco Iris.

+*Canciones de America Latina* (Campbell/Frega). Miami: Warner Bros.

*Mariachi Los Camperos de Nati Cano*. ¡Llegaron Los Camperos! Concert Favorites of Nati Cano's Mariachi Los Camperos. Smithsonian Folkways SFW 40517.

# DEIRDRE'S FANCY
## (SLIP JIG)

Ireland

## The Tune

In the Irish sessions of instrumentalists who gather together informally to play, "Deirdre's Fancy" is a slip jig, one of the tunes that comes around in the course of the evening to beckon fiddles, flutes, tin whistles, bagpipes, guitars, concertinas, and *bodhrans* to play.

## The Music Culture

Irish jig tunes have been a part of the instrumental traditions since the seventeenth century. They are defined by their compound meters in which each beat consists of a subgroup of three pulses. There are three types of jigs: single, double, and slip jigs. Single and double jigs sound in 6/8 time: the single jig uses a predominant ♩ ♪

pattern, while the double jig moves along in mostly two groups of three eighth notes ♪♪♪ ♪♪♪ per measure. The slip jig, or hop jig, is in 9/8, each measure consisting of at least one group (and often two groups) of triplets. While single and double jigs are traditionally danced solo or as couple dances, the slip jig is known today for its performance by female dancers who seem literally to fly across the floor in their soft shoes. In an Irish session of instrumentalists, several jigs may be played without a break, sometimes alongside reels or hornpipes.

### The Experiences
- Sing the melody on "dee" and "deedly-dee" (the latter for the three eighth-note figures), and also with solfège syllables (beginning on "la" in la-based minor) or scale numbers (beginning on "6").
- Play the melody on flute, recorder, tin whistle, violin, or other melody instruments.
- Add chordal accompaniment on concertina (accordion), harp, guitar or piano, playing three chords per measure.
- Play the two-measure ostinato rhythm on bodhran (or hand drum).

### Recommended Listening

*Irish Traditional Fiddle Music* (*Reels, Jigs, and Polkas*). Bescol 308.
*Willie and Michael Clancy: Irish Jigs, Reels, and Hornpipes.* Folkways FW 06819.
*Island Angel* (Altan). Green Linnnet Recordings GLCD 1137.

# DO DOC DO NGANG

Vietnam

1. Chorus: *(Sound of water whirling about the paddle.)*
   Girl: *I row the crossing boat.*
   Boy: *I row the current-flowing boat.*

2. *Tomorrow we will get together in the same stream.*
   *Why shouldn't our wish come true, to be married?*

Traditional, Vietnam, as sung and arranged by Phong Nguyen. From Nguyen, P. T. & Campbell, P. S. (1990). *From Rice Paddies and Temple Yards: Traditional Music of Vietnam.* Danbury, CT: World Music Press. Courtesy World Music Press.

CD I, Track # 14

## The Tune

The lyrical melodies of Vietnamese folk songs, like this one for "Do Doc Do Ngang," invite singers to find their parts as soloist or in the chorus. The text speaks to a need for people to look past differences to their confluences of ideals, attitudes, and dreams.

## The Music Culture

Vietnam is river country, particularly at the delta of the Mekong River in the southern region of the country. River fishing is common there, as is the cultivation of rice paddies in fields irrigated by rivers and canals. Rivers are the roadways of the Vietnamese people, and they use small boats called dò as their main means of transportation.

Songs are sung on boats, using traditional poems that contain riddles, analogies, and metaphors. As boatmen (and boatwomen) row along with or against the current of the river, they find songs useful in making their work more efficient. In fact, there are boats especially designed to flow with the current or to cross the river against the current. This particular song speaks to the two types of boats, each with its own flow and way of rowing, as a metaphor of a man and a woman coming from different backgrounds who might nonetheless find common ground and join together in marriage. A further metaphor can be imagined, given the time at which this song was popular, when the country was divided into North Vietnam and South Vietnam, such that reference to marriage was a gentle plea to look past political differences to the possibilities of unification.

## The Experiences

- Listen to Track # 14 for the glissandi of the *dan tranh* lute, followed by its plucked accompaniment to the vocal lines. Tap a steady pulse while listening also for melodic patterns.

- Sing the chorus sections, pronounced "kwan hoy ho-oh kwan;" note that there are four chorus sections, the first three of which are identical. This phrase is intended to sound like the water whirling as the boat is paddled.

- Sing the song's melody on a neutral syllable such as "lai," interspersing the vocables of the chorus section as it comes around.

- Play a "cluster-chord," using a combination of A–C–D–E–G, the pitches of the pentatonic scale, to accompany the song on piano, once every four beats and allowing the sounds to sustain and decay. Conclude the song with a final round of the chorus, measures 1–4.

- Create another harmonic accompaniment, using any number of pitches of the scale as drone or ostinato, on a selection of available instruments—from guitars to xylophones, flutes and clarinets, violins, and/or trombones and trumpets.

- Sing the lyrics, which begin with the soloist's verse, pronounced:

  Verse 1:    (Chorus) Aem lah-ee kawng daw ngahng,

  Ahn shhanhng kawng daw yaw-koo.

  Ahn lah-ee kawng daw yaw-koo,

  Aem trer kawng daw ngahng.

  Verse 2:    (Chorus) Mah-ee tah moh yawng (Chorus)

  Shah kohng dohng lawng mahng teeng hwaee trohng.

- Clarify the meaning of the song through its two verses. Further verses describe a marriage, when the couple is dressed in pink (the wedding color), and the husband and wife dream of a long life together with many children and grandchildren.

## Recommended Listening

+*From Rice Paddies and Temple Yards: Traditional Music of Vietnam* (Nguyen/Campbell). Danbury, CT: World Music Press.

*Eternal Voices: Traditional Vietnamese Voices in the United States.* New Alliance Records NAR CD 053.

*The Music of Vietnam, Volumes 1–3.* Celestial Harmonies 13083-13084.

## DOK DJAMPA

Laos

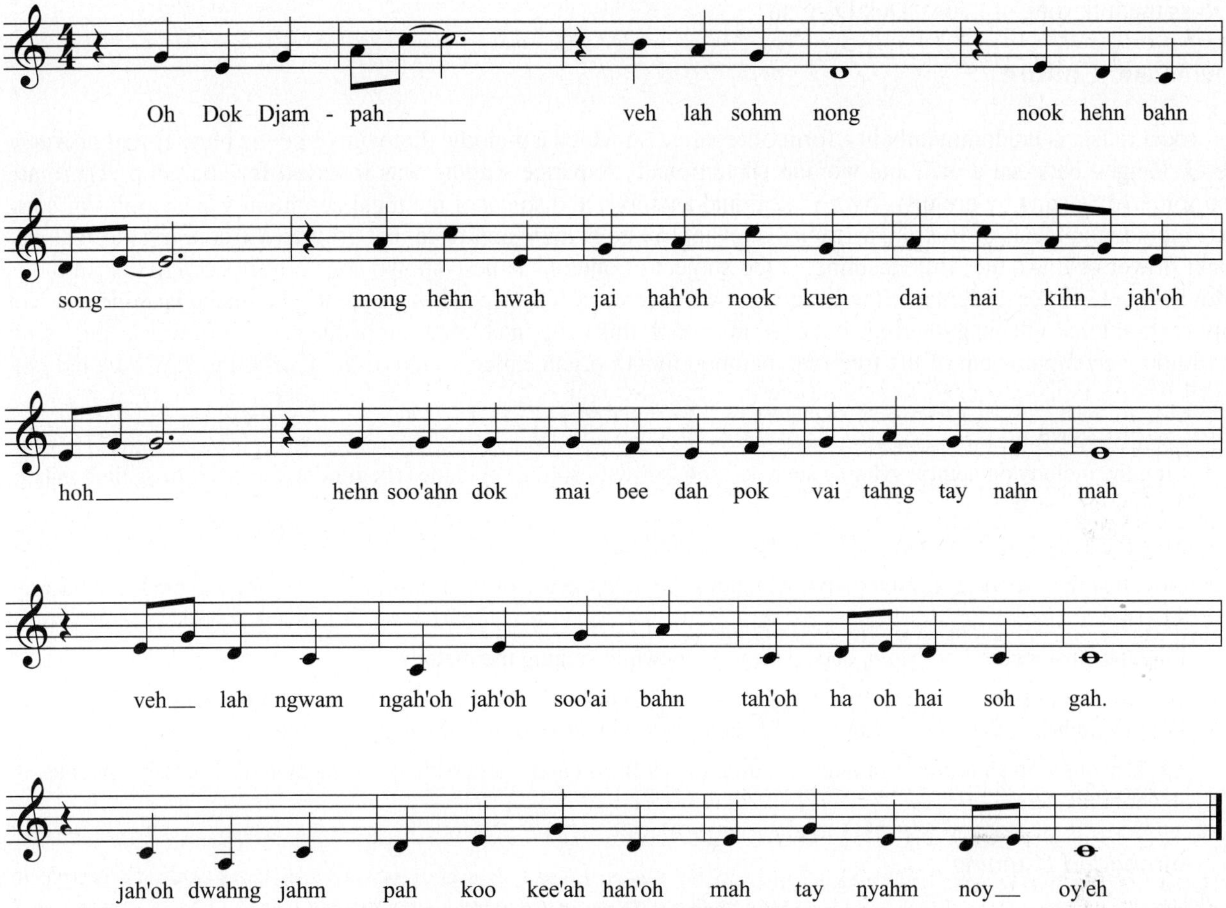

Oh  Dok  Djam - pah_____      veh  lah  sohm  nong          nook  hehn  bahn

song_____                    mong  hehn  hwah  jai  hah'oh  nook  kuen  dai  nai  kihn___  jah'oh

hoh_____              hehn  soo'ahn  dok  mai  bee  dah  pok  vai  tahng  tay  nahn  mah

veh___  lah  ngwam  ngah'oh  jah'oh  soo'ai  bahn  tah'oh  ha  oh  hai  soh  gah.

jah'oh  dwahng  jahm  pah  koo  kee'ah  hah'oh  mah  tay  nyahm  noy___  oy'eh

*Ah Dok Djampa, the Jasmine flower,*
*The sight of you brings throughts of home.*
*Your beauty and your sweet perfume*
*In father's garden we remember you so well.*
*In times of sadness you restore our hope and joy.*
*Ah, Dok Djampa, you'll always be with us each day.*

## DOK DJAMPA (DRONE)

# DOK DJAMPA

## The Tune

Jasmine is a fragrant, flowering, woody shrub that grows in many parts of Asia. It has inspired traditional music such as the folk song of Laos, "Dok Djampa."

## The Music Culture

Lao vocal music is predominantly in a form of repartee, in which a melodic dialogue of poetic phrases and proverbs are exchanged between a man and woman. Traditionally, repartee singing was reserved for courtship. There are also songs to be sung by groups—hymns, regional anthems, and songs of the local community. The topics of song texts include the ideals of Buddhism, topics relevant to Lao history, and flora that grow in the countryside. The national flower of Laos, the white jasmine, is the subject of one of the best-known songs of that country. Jasmine is cultivated in Laos for its delicate flower and its sweet scent, and its dried flowers are used to make jasmine tea. Not only at traditional village gatherings but even in school, this song in celebration of the revered flower is sung with or without accompaniment of the free-reed bamboo mouth organ called *khaen* or the four-stringed lute called *pin*.

### The Experiences

- Sing the melody on neutral syllable such as "noo," or with solfège syllables (beginning on "sol") or scale numbers (beginning on "5").
- Sing the song in its transliterated text (phonetic spelling).
- Note that the melody is mostly pentatonic, but shifts into the use of the fourth degree (F) for one phrase, measures 11–14.
- Play the cluster chord on piano, once per measure, while singing the melody.
- Improvise an ostinato (of one, two, or more measures) or progressive accompaniment for the sung melody, utilizing the pitches of the cluster chord. Add D and E occasionally, to fit the pentatonic melody.
- Experiment with an accompaniment on guitar, or violins in a melodic ostinato of separated, successive pitches, or in chord clusters.

### Recommended Listening

*Isan Slete: The Flower of Isan: Songs and Music from Northeast Thailand.* Global Style CDORBD051.
*Anthology of World Music: Music of Laos.* Rounder Select 5119.

# DOMINO

United States

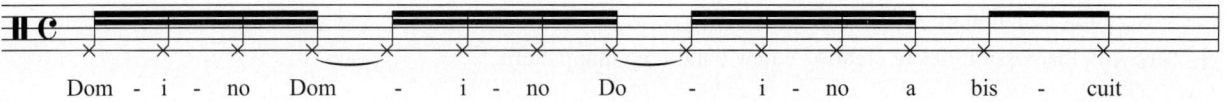

Dom - i - no   Dom - i - no   Do - i - no   a   bis - cuit

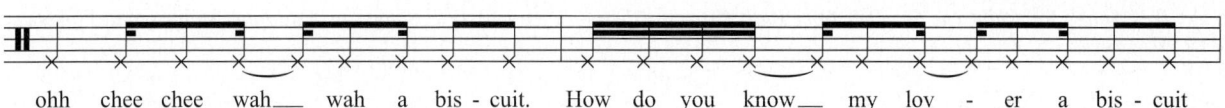

ohh   chee   chee   wah___ wah   a   bis - cuit.   How   do   you   know___ my   lov - er   a   bis - cuit

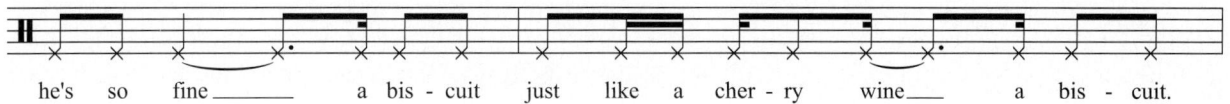

he's   so   fine_____   a   bis - cuit   just   like   a   cher - ry   wine___   a   bis - cuit.

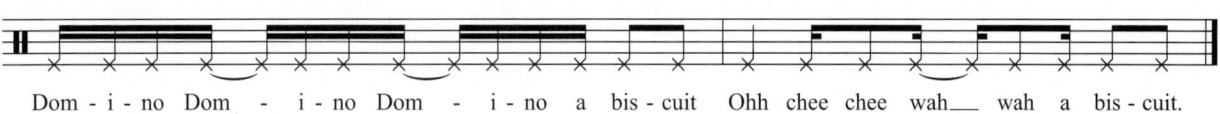

Dom - i - no   Dom - i - no   Dom - i - no   a   bis - cuit   Ohh   chee   chee   wah___ wah   a   bis - cuit.

## The Groove

"Domino" is a children's hand-clapping activity that utilizes words and syllables to create a rhythmic groove.

## The Music Culture

Syncopated and stretched-over-the-bar (and beat) rhythms are a good indicator of music with African-American origins. Dance and movement are intrinsic to African and African-derived musical expressions, too, and syncopation incites the sort of movement that is fluid, holistic, and far away from the more sedate nature of European dance styles with their straight and reserved posture (and more regular, straightforward rhythms). As African and African-American dances emphasize exaggerated shoulder and hip movements, so the musical play of African-American children is as much about the movement as it is about the song itself. Even a seemingly simple chant can feature percussive sounds in vocalizing some of the syllables ("chee," "bis-cuit," "just," "cherry"). This vocal percussion serves to accentuate the rhythm, and gives rise to the jump-roping and hand-clapping that requires precise movements in order to fit the groove.

### The Experiences

- Rhythmically chant the words, remembering to sustain the long rhythms and to clip the quick rhythms in a meticulous percussive style of enunciation.
- Pat, clap, or tap the rhythm of the chant, with and without the words.
- Add percussion accompaniment to the chant by playing select measures (for example, measure 1 and measure 2 as two distinctive ostinati that can be performed on drums, sticks, cowbells, and shakers).

- Perform a one-measure hand-clapping game with a partner, with one movement per eighth-note beat, in this sequence: a b c a b c d d

  (a) clap partner's hands, one hand up and the other down

  (b) clap partner's hands, reversing hands so that the up hand is now down and the down hand is now up

  (c) clap partner's two hands together

  (d) point both thumbs over the shoulder

- Play with the possibilities of creating a new hand-clapping pattern.

## Recommended Listening

*Skip Rope Games.* Smithsonian Folkways 07029.

*Animal Folk Songs for Children: Selected from Ruth Crawford Seeger's Animal Folk Songs for Children.* Smithsonian Folkways FW 07551.

# DORAJI

Korea

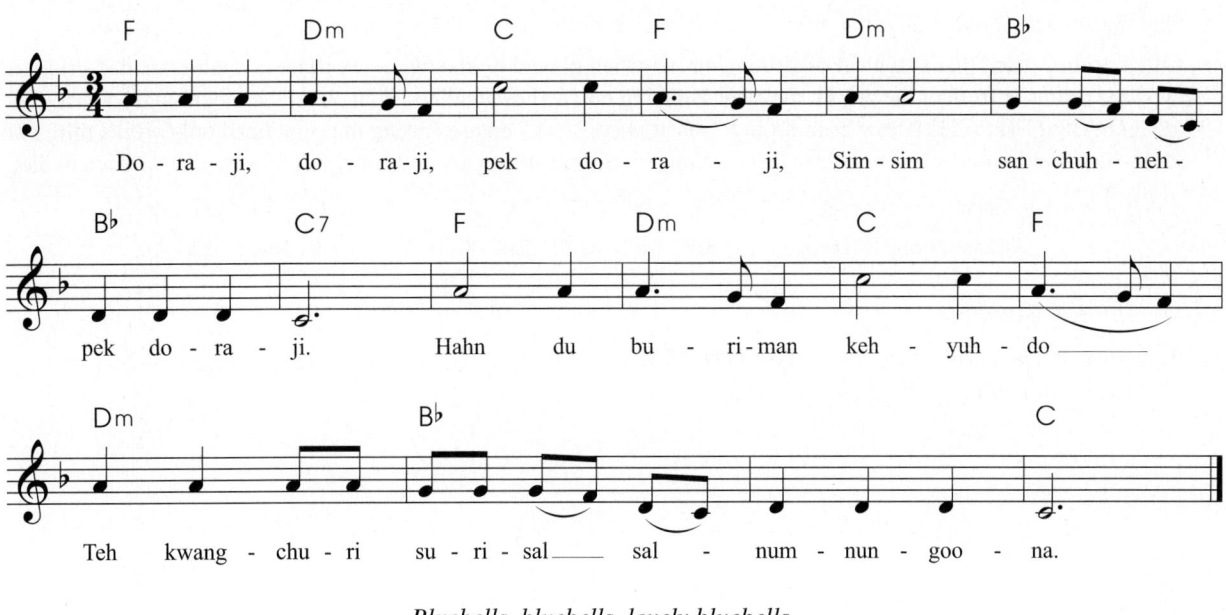

Do - ra - ji, do - ra - ji, pek do - ra - ji, Sim - sim san - chuh - neh -

pek do - ra - ji. Hahn du bu - ri - man keh - yuh - do

Teh kwang - chu - ri su - ri - sal____ sal - num - nun - goo - na.

*Bluebells, bluebells, lovely bluebells,*

*Deep in the mountains my bluebells grow.*

*Gathering bluebells in wide valleys,*

*Baskets of bluebells will overflow.*

From *Music in Childhood: From Preschool Through the Elementary Grade* with Audio CD 3rd edition by CAMPBELL/SCOTT-KASSNER, 2006. Reprinted with permission of Wadsworth, a Division of Thompson Learning: www. Thomsonrights.com. Fax: 800-730-2215

## The Tune

One folk song familiar to most Koreans is "Doraji," a song of springtime that celebrates the beautiful bluebells that fill the countryside and give good cheer to all who see them.

## The Music Culture

In Korea, both amateur and professional musicians perform folk songs, or *minyo*. These songs may be shaped in verse and refrain form, or as a single melody for one or more verses, or even as a solo improvisation of words for a verse in a group performance. Some folk songs are known only in a limited locality, while others such as "Doraji" are known throughout Korea and are part of Koreans' cultural identity. As opposed to traditional music of other parts of Asia, Korean songs are typically felt in triple (rather than in duple) meter. The highest artistry and training is required for *p'ansori*, a stylized dramatic narrative form for solo voice and drum, but *minyo* can be sung by all who wish to give voice and join in. While the currently popular music of Korea is Western in quality, and piano, violin, choral singing and orchestral music engage many young people in private lessons, school and community experiences, Koreans value *minyo* as part of their cultural heritage. These songs may be sung a cappella, or with accompaniment on piano or traditional instruments such as the *kayagum* (zither) and *changgo* (double-headed drum).

### The Experiences

- Sing the melody on a neutral syllable such as "doh," and on solfège syllables (beginning on "mi") or scale numbers (beginning on "3").

- While singing the melody on "loo," conduct the three-beat metric pattern. Try this sitting, and then while stepping to the quarter-note beat.
- Sing the song in Korean, following the transliterated text that sounds as written. Note that "ji" is "gee"—with a soft "g."
- Play the chords on piano or guitar, offering a soft and delicate quality through arpeggiation or broken chords.
- Add a drum pattern that is typical of Korean *minyo* when played by the *changgo*. Place a double-headed drum or two tube drums in front of the player, their heads facing out, and use mallets. First chant the mnemonic pattern, noting that "Dong" signifies hitting both drum heads at once, "Dak" entails hitting the right head only with a thin, flat stick, "Da" is a lighter version of "Dak," and "Kung" indicates hitting the left (or right) head with a wooden mallet.

| Count: | 1 | 2 | 3 | 4 | 5 | 6 | 7 | 8 | 9 | 10 | 11 | 12 |
|---|---|---|---|---|---|---|---|---|---|---|---|---|
| Chant/Stroke: | Dong | | dak | Kung | da-da | dak | Kung | | dak | Kung | dak | |

## Recommended Listening

*Korea: Folk Songs Volume 1.* Navarre Records ASIN: B000003MP8.

*Folk and Classical Music of Korea.* Folkways FW 04424.

# DOWIDZENIA

Poland

*Farewell, my friend, until we meet again.*

Words and Music by Andrea Schafer.  From Schafer, A. (1995). *My Harvest Home: A Celebration of Polish Songs, Dances, Games and Customs.* Danbury, CT: World Music Press. Courtesy World Music Press.

## The Tune

"Dowidzenia" is a traditional Polish song of farewell which can be sung as a round in four parts.

## The Music Culture

Poland was inhabited by various Slavic tribes long before the empire of Poland was established, which by the fifteenth century stretched across most of central Europe. By the eighteenth century, the powerful countries of Austria, Prussia, and Russia controlled and annexed parts of Poland, wiping the country (but not Polish culture) off the map. The Roman Catholic faith, language, and traditional arts were maintained by the Poles through the topsyturvy rise of Poland's sovereignty during World War I and loss of it again to the former Soviet Union in World War II. Through the solidarity of their free trade unions, the Polish people gained a freedom of expression and then worked to avert poor wages and poor working conditions so as to develop free enterprise. Through trying times and periods of greater ease, Polish folk music has been heard—vocally, and on accordions, violins, clarinets, and trumpets. Instrumental music for folk dances in both duple and triple meter abounds. While the *polka* is more Czech than it is Polish (although it has been adapted by Polish Americans), Polish *waltzes, trojaks* (dances for two girls and a boy), *mazurkas*, and *polonaises* are danced with great vigor. There are also many genres of Polish vocal music, among them the songs of greeting and farewell, seasonal carols, wedding songs, and lullabies. Some are sung in unison, while others are sung in full choral harmony, or as in the case of "Dowidzenia," in imitative style.

## The Experiences

- Sing the song on a neutral syllable, and solfège syllables (beginning on "la") or scale numbers (beginning on "6").

- Sing the song with the verse, which translates roughly as "Farewell, my friend, until we meet again." Note particular pronunciations: "wi" is "vee," "dze" is "jeh," and "cze" is "cheh."

- Play a harmony for the song, using D minor and C chords at the piano or on guitar, alternating between the root or bass note on the first beat and the upper voices of the chord on beats two and three.

- Sing the song as a four-part a cappella round, with each new part beginning four measures after the previous part.

### Recommended Listening

+*My Harvest Home* (Schafer). Danbury, CT: World Music Press.

*Polish Folk Songs and Dance*. Folkways FW 06848.

# DRUNKEN SAILOR

England

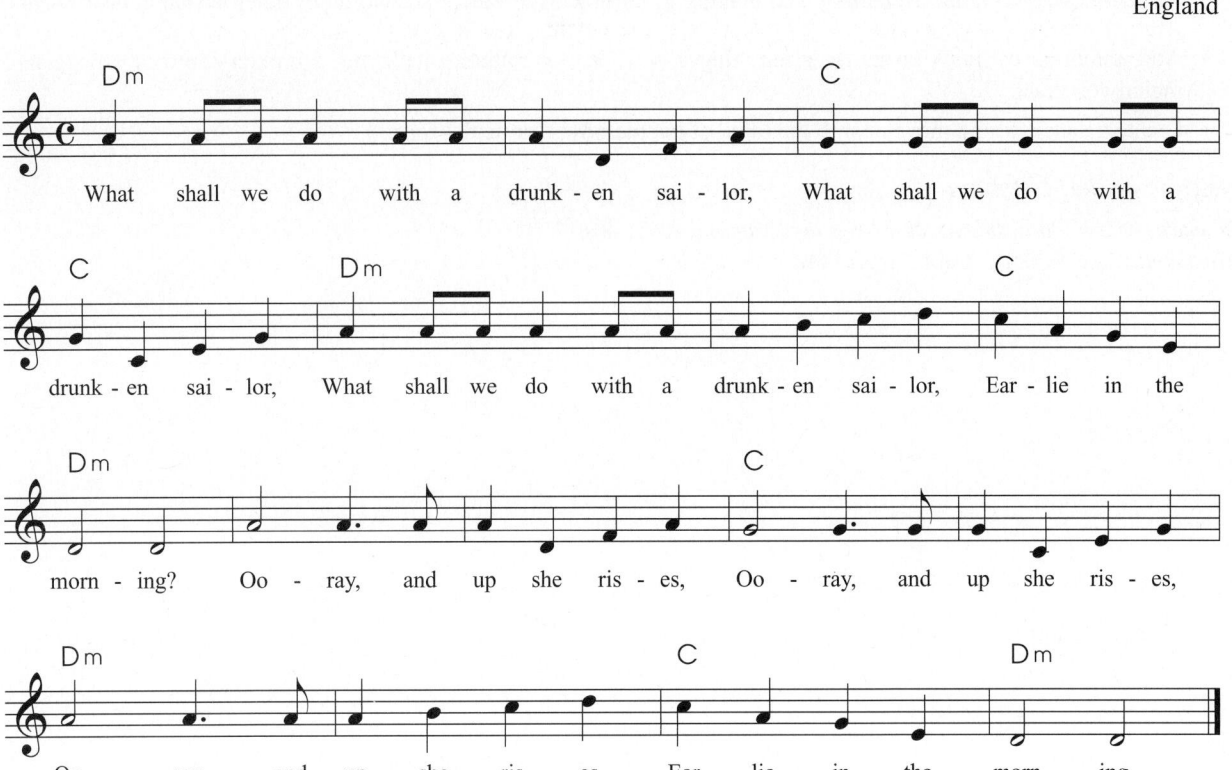

## The Tune

A well-known song to adults and children in England is "(What Shall We Do with a) Drunken Sailor?" the melody of which is the basis of a hornpipe dance.

## The Music Culture

Older layers of traditional music in England survive today in social dances, communal music making gatherings, and children's play. Such is the case of "What Shall We Do with a) Drunken Sailor?" which has known a history of treatment as a hornpipe (dance) melody in the early 1800s, a sea shanty by the mid-nineteenth century, and a singing game danced by children from Birmingham (England) to Glasgow (Scotland). It may have originated in Ireland, as it resembles the march tune "Oro Se do Bheatha 'Bhaile" ("Oro, you are welcome home"). In the children's game as in the hornpipe dance, singers join hands in a circle and "go 'round" (children may pantomime a drunkard's tipsy step). On "up she rises," various movements have been performed, from kicking one's legs in the air or bowing to one's partner, to hoisting an imaginary rope up into the air, as if it held the sail on an old-fashioned schooner. The repeating melody (in a symmetrical repeated ABAB:‖ of two measures per phrase) and text (three times on the title phrase, followed by a closing "Ear-lie in the morning") guarantee a built-in ease of learning this song. The tune has also made its way into the ears of British listeners through its use as a signaling "wake-up call" on BBC radio every morning.

### The Experiences

- As a warm-up exercise to the melody, sing triads on D minor and C major using solfège syllables (beginning on "mi" in la-based minor) or scale numbers (beginning on "3"), or on neutral syllables such as "dum" and "dee."
- Use the melody as a sight-reading exercise, noting the placement and extent of the triads in the melody.
- Sing the melody, being careful to sing "earl-lye" for "ear-lie."

- Sing additional verses such as "Take him and shake him and try to wake him" and "Give him a dose of salt and water." Create further verses.
- Switch between singing the melody and playing it on tin whistle, recorder, violin, or other available instruments.
- Add a chordal harmony on guitar, strumming a ♩ ♪♩ pattern, or playing a broken-chord or arpeggiated melody on piano.
- Create a dance, fitting movement to the logic of the melody's (or text's) form.

## Recommended Listening

+*Rogue's Gallery: Pirate Ballads, Sea Songs and Chanteys.* ANTI- 86817.
+*Cantus: Let Your Voice Be Heard.* Cantus 1201.

# DÚLAMÁN

Ireland

Du - la - man   na   Bin - ne bu - i,   Du - la - man____ Gae - lach,

Du - la - man   na   far - raige__   se - befehehearr   a   bhi   in   Ei - rinn.

*Seaweed from the yellow cliff, Irish seaweed,*
*Seaweed of the sea, the best in all of Ireland.*

CD I, Track # 15

## The Tune

In an island country like Ireland where there is plenty of rocky coastline, "Dulaman" is an apt song to sing about the seaweed that drapes the rocks, cliffs, and sandy beaches.

## The Music Culture

Now, as ever, the people of Ireland value music as a key component of their identity. A revival of traditional Irish music in the second half of the twentieth century has brought it to the ears of young people not only in Ireland but also in centers of Irish settlement abroad—chiefly in Britain, the United States, Canada, and Australia—as well as in continental Europe among people who are not necessarily of Irish descent. Traditional Irish music is largely Celtic (Gaelic or Irish) songs and instrumental airs and dance tunes. Now the music is primarily recreational, for listening and dancing, while in the past history of Ireland it also had mythic and seasonal ceremonial meaning. Irish music tends to be monophonic, with various instruments playing the same melody (or very close to it); the harmonic and percussive dimensions have developed in recent times. The Chieftains, a traditional Irish music band, have done well to preserve and popularize traditional music of Ireland, while groups like Altan have taken steps to re-create Irish music, taking traditional tunes and rearranging them for contemporary listeners and dancers.

### The Experiences
- Listen to Track # 15 for the sound of the *bodhran*, the stringed instruments, and the singers. Tap the *bodhran* rhythm, or at least keep a steady pulse.
- Sing the melody on solfège syllables (beginning on "la") or scale numbers (beginning on "6").
- Listen to the recording, and sing the melody with the Gaelic words.
- Play the melody on flute, violin, concertina, harp, or other melody instrument.
- Play the chords on guitar or piano, sounding them on beats one and four, while singing the melody. Explore the possibilities for an arpeggiated, broken-chord accompaniment.

- Listen to the recording again, and tap the underlying rhythm of the *bodhran* on a hand drum.
- Perform the song with melody, harmony, and percussion instruments, and sing the refrain multiple times. Allow the instruments to sound all together, and then to be featured in separate melodic solos.

## Recommended Listening

+*The Best of Altan*. Green Linnet Records 1177.
+*Island Angel* (Altan). Green Linnet Records GLCD 1137.
*Local Ground* (Altan). Narada 724387592728.

# DULCE, DULCE

Ella Jenkins

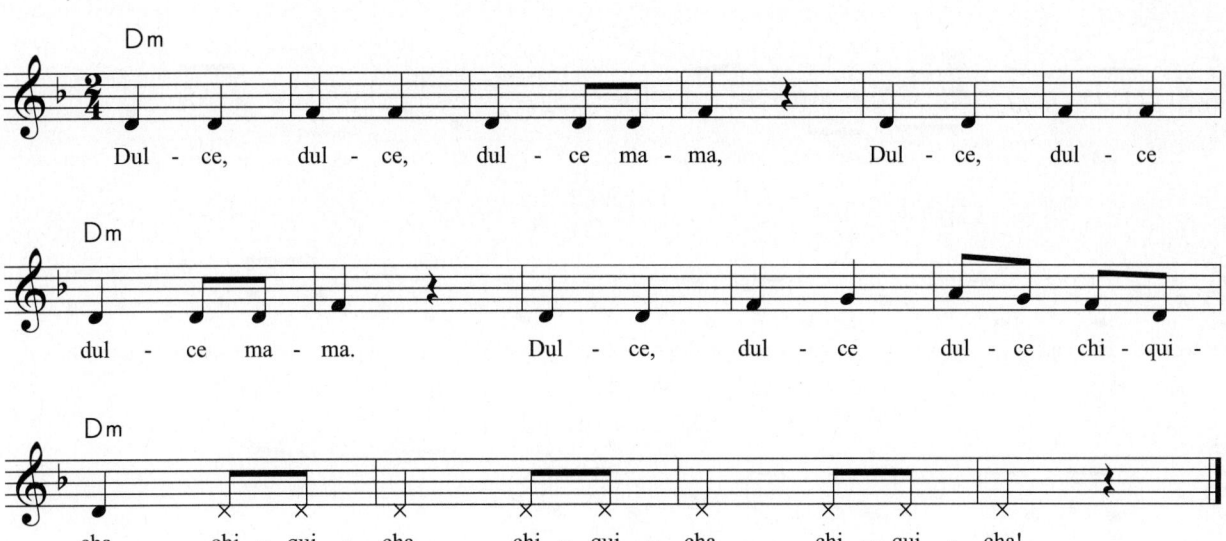

Words and music by Ella Jenkins. Copyright 1966 Ell-Bern Publishing Company (ASCAP). Used by kind permission of Ell-Bern Publishing Company.

## The Tune

This joyful children's song by singer and educator Ella Jenkins is about "sweets," or candies, which in Spanish are called "dulce."

## The Music Culture

In any Mexican village, town, or city, there are shops that feature large supplies of brightly colored sweets and candied cakes. There are outdoor tables of sweets on the plaza or in the streets as well, wedged between tables of handmade clothing, home-distilled *mescal*, straw hats, and small clay-colored figurines. The *mercados,* or merchants, sell *postres* (pastries, sweet breads, frosted buns, and powdered cookies), pecan clusters, dried mango, papaya cakes, sesame almond "bird nests," and fruit pickled in *mescal*. There is also homemade ice cream in flavors like coconut, lemon, strawberry, and mango. People enjoy sweets as desserts, after-school (and work) snacks, weekend treats, and on special occasions such as birthdays, holidays, and fiestas throughout the year.

### The Experiences

- Sing the song on solfège syllables (beginning on "la") or scale numbers (beginning on "6").
- Sing the song with the Spanish words, noting that "dulce" is pronounced "dool-say" and "chiquicha" is pronounced "chee-kee-chah."
- Pat the lap on the first beat and clap on the second beat of each measure.
- For "chiquicha," try a sequence of two quick claps and a pat.
- Play a basic harmonic accompaniment on guitar or piano, selecting a rhythmic pattern that works to support the melody. Explore possibilities for one chord per measure, a chord on "1" and a tap on "2," or an "oom-chink" pattern of bass note and chord for every measure.

### Recommended Listening

+Ella Jenkins: *You'll Sing a Song and I'll Sing a Song*. Smithsonian Folkways SFW 45010.

# EL BARREÑO

Guatemala

[Musical notation with chords C, G7, C, G7, C, F, G7, C, F, G7]

1. De los ca-ba-lli-tos que me tra-jo'us-ted, Nin-gu-no me gus-ta, So-lo'el que mon-

te. Ha-ga-se pa'a-ca, ha-ga-se pa'a-lla, Que mi ca-ba-lli-to lo'a-tro-pe-lla-
ma-ta Ay ba-rre-no si, Ay ba-rre-no no, Ay ba-rre-no due-no de mi co-ra-

ra. Ha-ga-se pa'a-ca, ha-ga-se pa'a-lla, Que mi ca-ba-lli-to lo'a-tro-pe-lla-ra.
zon. Ay ba-rre-no si, Ay ba-rre-no no, Ay ba-rre-no due-no de mi co-ra-zon.

2. Por a'hi vie-ne'un le-che-ri-to, con su can-ta-ro de pla-ta.

Y la ni-ña le res-pon-de: "E - sa le-che'a mí me."

1. *Of all the little horses you brought me,*
   *I don't like any other than the one that I can ride.*
   *Come over here, go over there,*
   *Watch out, for my little horse will trample you!*

2. *A little milkman arrives with his silver can of milk*
   *A small girl responds, "I love that milk!"*
   *Oh, the bowl, yes. Oh, the bowl, no.*
   *Oh, I adore my bowl.*

## The Tune

The title of this Guatemalan folk song, "El Barreño" refers to an earthen bowl that is treasured by a little girl, and the sweet, fresh milk that it contains. It is also about little horses that, while they may be beautiful to watch and to ride, must be carefully avoided, lest in their spirited cantering, they cannot stop themselves from running wild.

## The Music Culture

More than most countries in Central and South America, Guatemala has continued its traditional life of farming, and of small towns and rural villages. The Mayan Empire flourished for more than a thousand years in Guatemala, and almost half the people are descended from the Maya (while others are ladino or mestizo, mixed Spanish and indigenous). The country has not urbanized very quickly, and thus it is not unusual for whole families to be involved in working in the fields and taking time in the evening to have meals together, to talk, and to make music. The songs heard in the fields and in the homes are often the melodies of the notable *marimba* culture. Guatemalans play three types of marimbas, all of wood, and typically with the *charleo* or buzzing sound: the *marimba de tecomates* (marimba with gourds), the *marimba sencilla* (with 33 to 40 bars), and the *marimba doble* (the largest, with 68 bars, that is played by four musicians).

### The Experiences

- Sing the melody on a neutral syllable such as "noo," and on solfège syllables (beginning on "sol") or scale numbers (beginning on "5").
- Sing the song with the Spanish text, noting several pronunciations: "lli" in Guatemalan Spanish is "jee" (and "lla" is "ja"), and "pa'aca" is "pah-sah." Note also quickly moving elisions of syllables.
- Play the chords on guitar (or piano) in a triple meter pattern, while singing the melody.
- Using hard mallets on marimbas or wooden xylophones, improvise an arrangement that takes into account the melody and harmonic changes. While one or several instruments play the melody, divide the chord tones among other instruments. For a xylophone ensemble, the soprano, alto, and bass xylophones can be designated to play on the first, third, and fifth tones of the chords—all in a continuous eighth-note rhythm.

For example:

Soprano xylo
Alto xylo
Bass xylo

### Recommended Listening

+*Canciones de America Latina* (Campbell/Frega). Danbury, CT: World Music Press.
*Music of Guatemala, Volumes 1 and 2*. Folkways FW 04212 and 04213.

# EL JUEGO CHIRIMBOLO

Ecuador

> El jue - go chir - im - bo - lo, que bo - ni - to es, con un
> pie, o - tro pie, u - na ma - no, o - tra ma - no, un co - do, o - tro
> co - do. El co - do. El jue - go chir - im - bo - lo, que bo - ni - to es! Hey!

*The chirimbolo game, how beautiful it is!*
*With your right foot, your left foot,*
*Your right hand, your left hand,*
*Your right elbow, your left elbow.*

Traditional, Ecuador, as remembered and arranged by Elizabeth Villarreal Brennan. From Campbell, P. S., McCullough-Brabson, E., Tucker, J. C. (1994). *Roots & Branches: A Legacy of Multicultural Music for Children*. Danbury, CT: World Music Press. Courtesy World Music Press.

## The Tune

The title of the Ecuadorian children's singing game, "El Juego Chirimbolo," cannot be directly translated, except to say that it means "The Whatchamacallit Game." It is a favorite of children due to its social aspect as well as to the physical challenge of playing the game at ever-increasing speeds.

## The Music Culture

In the *altiplano* (high plains) region of Imbabura province, about two hours' drive north of the Ecuadorian capital city of Quito, indigenous Quichua-speaking people mix with the Spanish culture in the farming communities and market towns. Many Ecuadorians, along with other indigenous peoples throughout the Andean region, (which includes Peru and Bolivia), some who speak Quichua, Quechua, or Aymara, trace their history to the powerful Incan empire even as they live a bilingual and bicultural life. Even today, pre-Christian (pre-Spanish) customs and celebrations color the feasts of their Roman Catholic liturgical year, from Christmas (December) and New Year's Day (January) to Carnival (February), Lent (February–April), Easter (March–April), Corpus Cristi (June), and All Souls' Day (November). Popular instruments include the indigenous panpipes (*rondador*), flute (*quena*), small and large drums, as well as the European-styled violins, guitars, and *charango*s (small guitars with armadillo-shell bodies). Market villages and towns in the Imbabura province tend to specialize in one product or another, including woven cloth, straw hats, leather goods, and pottery, a likely influence of the Spanish who conquered the region and established these traditional crafts as commercial ventures to sustain village life and support its modernization. While the adult men and women of the Ecuadorian highlands farm, weave, or create various handicrafts, their children engage in play that includes singing games and chants like "El Juego Chirimbolo."

## The Experiences

- Sing the song on a neutral syllable such as "dah," and on solfège syllables (beginning on "mi") or scale numbers (beginning on "3").
- Sing the song in Spanish, remembering that "juego" is pronounced "hway-go," "que" is "kay," and "pie" is "pee-ay."
- Play the chordal accompaniment on guitar, with a basic down-up/down-up ♪♪ ♪♪ strum.
- Play the singing game, facing a partner and holding hands. The following movements coordinate with the phrases of music and text.

> "El juego chirimbolo, que bonito es": Holding hands with your partner, move four steps sideways, beginning with the left foot. Think (and practice by chanting aloud) "left-close, left-close, left-close, left-close."
>
> "Con un pie": Point right foot toward partner, tap the floor.
>
> "Otro pie": Point left foot toward partner, tap the floor.
>
> "Una mano, otro mano": Clap partners' right hand across, then left hand.
>
> "Un codo, otro codo": Tap partners' right elbow across, then left elbow.
>
> Repeat sequence. At the second ending, partners hold hands, raise them above their heads, and make one complete turn under the arms to the left. On "hey!" partners drop hands and jump up in the air.

- Sing and play the game three times, each time faster than the time before it.

## Recommended Listening

+*A Singing Wind* (Elizabeth Villareal Brennan). Danbury, CT: World Music Press.
*Bolivia Manta – Tinkuna*. A.S.P.I.C. X55511.
*The Best Instrumental Music from the Andes Two*. San Antonio Discos 018.
*Music of the Andes*. Hemisphere 7243-8-28190-2-8.

# EL RABEL

Chile

El ra - bel pa - ra ser fi - no'ha de ser de ver - de pi - no, la

vi - hue-la'd(e) du - ra he - bra y'el se - dal de mu - la ne - gra, la

vi - hue-la'd(e) du - ra he - bra y'el se - dal de mu - la ne - gra.

An - da mo - re - ni - ta re - co - je'e - se pa - ñue - lo.

Mi - ra que'es de se da'y lo'a - rras - tras por el sue - lo.

*For the violin to be the finest,*

*It must be made from the (wood of) the green pine tree.*

*The vihuela is made of hard wood,*

*With its strings made of hair of a black mule.*

*Come little girl (of tanned/brown skin),*

*Pick up the handkerchief.*

*You can see that it's made of silk as you drag it across the floor.*

## The Tune

Remnants of Spanish culture hold strong in Chile, particularly in the Zona de Chiloe in the southern part of the country, where traditional songs like "El Rabel" (The Violin) have been sung for many generations.

## The Music Culture

Like much of Latin America, the region that is now Chile was conquered by the Spanish in the sixteenth century (1536, precisely), and was ruled for almost three centuries, until the liberator José de San Martín helped Chileans win their independence in 1817. Spanish influences still remain, particularly in the official language, called "Castellano"; the predominance of the Catholic religion; the attitude towards the importance of the extended family; and the presence of the acoustic "Spanish" guitar in Chilean traditional music. Because the southernmost part of Chile, called Zona de Chiloe, was the last Hispanic bastion on the South American continent, Hispanic cultural and artistic traditions are particularly strong there. Popular Renaissance dances originating from central Spain persist there even today, a certain testimony and tribute to the old country. In the traditional Chilean song, "El Rabel," the Spanish influence is once again evident in the subject of the text, the violin and *vihuela*, all rooted in the Spanish culture and Chile's colonial heritage.

### The Experiences

- Sing the melody on a neutral syllable such as "la," and with solfège syllables (beginning on "sol") and scale numbers (beginning on "5").
- Sing the song with Spanish lyrics, noting the quick elisions of syllables ("no ha" as "noah," for example) and the pronunciation of "vihuela" as "vee-hway-lah," "pino" as "pee-noh," "hebra" as "hay-brah," "recoje'ese" as "ray-koh-hay-say."
- Play the chords on guitar in the fast down-down-up motion of a ♩ ♩ ♩ rhythm.
- Add an ostinato rhythm on hand drum: ♩. ♩ ♩
- Dance a circle dance. All dancers hold a small handerkerchief or scarf in their right hand (or tied to their right wrist). Count off "ones" and "twos" around the circle so that every other dancer moves in one of two sections at the end of the song. Begin facing inward to the circle, with arms down. As the song is sung, twirl scarves with the right hand above the head.

> Measures 1–4: All turn to the right, stepping eight times in that direction, arriving back in the original position on count 8.
>
> Measures 5–8: All turn to the left, stepping eight times in that directions, arriving back in the original position on count 8.
>
> Measures 9–12: Repeat movement of measures 1–4.
>
> Measures 13–16: All "ones" step eight steps forward into the center of the circle, and stay there.
>
> Measures 17–20: All "twos" step eight steps forward into the center of the circle, hold raised hands with the "ones" and bow.

### Recommended Listening

+*Canciones de America Latina* (Campbell/Frega). Miami, FL: Warner Brothers.

*Canta Para Una Semilla: Homages to Violeta Parra by Inti-Illimani*. Monitor MON 71821.

# EL SIQUISÍRI

Mexico

CD I, Track # 16

## The Tune

One of the great harp traditions of the world is found in Mexico, where folk songs like "El Siquisíri" are given a bright and lively "ring" by the harp.

## The Music Culture

There is a long tradition of stringed instruments in Mexico, including guitars and violins, *vihuelas,* and harps. They are played alone and together, in a variety of combinations, including the *mariachi* ensemble. In fact, the musical functions of melody, chordal accompaniment, and bass were completely fulfilled through the mariachi instrumentation in the years before 1940. Melodies were played by the violins and large harp, while rhythmic chordal accompaniment was provided by the curved-spined *vihuela.* The bass line was played on the low-pitched strings of the harp, or on the "big guitar" called the *guitarrón.* The guitar harmonically filled out the ensemble, doubling the *vihuela* as a harmony instrument. While modern *mariachi* ensembles have added trumpets, the stringed instruments (although not the harp anymore) are the core of the sound. Of course, other Mexican ensembles feature stringed instruments, too, including the trio of harp, *vihuela,* and guitar that play the bright and quick-tempoed *jarocho* style in "El Siquisíri."

### The Experiences

- Listen to Track # 16 for the sounds of string instruments: harp, two guitars (one playing the bass line and another a rapid strum), and *vihuela.* "Air-play" one of the instruments, imitating the performance of it in the air.
- Listening to the recording, hum the pitches of the bass line.
- Sing the bass line pitches on solfège syllables (beginning on "re") or scale numbers (beginning on "2").
- Play the two chords, G (dominant) and C (tonic) on guitar, *vihuela,* accordion, or other harmony-producing instrument.
- Play the bass line and chords on one or several guitars, or on piano. Find various ways to strum, pick, and play the two chords, to maintain musical interest (and avert monotony). Play without and then with the recording.

### Recommended Listening

*José Gutiérrez y Los Hermanos Ochoa: La Bamba: Sones Jarochos from Veracruz.* Smithsonian Folkways SFW 40505.
*Jarocho.* Para Musica 20013.

# EN CADA PRIMAVERA

Spain

En ca - da pri - ma - ve - ra el cu - cu can - ta - ra, y'a

su can - cion li - ge - ra mi voz se u - ni - ra.

Cu - cu, cu - cu, cu - cu.

*In each and every spring time,*
*The cuckoo it will sing.*
*To his light caroling I'm quite glad my voice to bring.*
*Cuckoo, cuckoo, cuckoo.*

## The Tune

"En Cada Primavera" is a seasonal canon in praise of the cuckoo, a song with a history that hails back to Renaissance Spain.

## The Music Culture

Major secular forms of music of the Spanish Renaissance were the *romance,* primarily a song that told a story (often legends of the border wars with the Moors), and the *villancico* (songs with repeated sections, which included almost all songs that were not romances). One of the most prolific composers of these songs was Juan del Encina, whose songs of a folklike character form the core of the secular Spanish repertory that survives from the reigns of Ferdinand and Isabella. Music for the *vihuela* was also prominent in Spain during the Renaissance, as a solo instrument, in company with the harp and keyboard, and as accompaniment to songs and dances. Of the sacred music of the period, the greatest Spanish Renaissance composers were Morales, Francisco Guerrero and Victoria, whose masses were of the polyphonic "Palestrina style" of the era that could be heard at the great cathedrals at Seville, Barcelona, and Madrid. Meanwhile, in an era when imitative techniques and the fugue were prominent, the canon emerged as a vocal form that was enjoyed by amateur groups of singers. "En Cada Primavera" is a song of spring's bird, the cuckoo. The cuckoo was widely known in Spain and throughout Europe for several millenia, and made its appearance in the Bible, in mythology, and in the classic works of Aristotle and Pliny. The bird's call of a descending minor third has found its way into the sound of the cuckoo clock, and into folk and composed music—including Beethoven's use of it in his Pastoral Symphony. It sounds again in this song of the Spanish Renaissance.

## The Experiences

- Sing the song on a neutral syllable such as "koo," and with solfège syllables (beginning on "sol") or scale numbers (beginning on "5").

- Sing the song with the Spanish-language lyrics, moving quickly through "cion" (of "cancion") by pronouncing it as "syon."

- While singing the melody, play the chords on piano, rolling and sustaining one chord per measure or arpeggiating the chords across the beats.

- Sing the song in a three-part canon several times through, with each voice part beginning four measures after the previous voice.

## Recommended Listening

*Chacona: Renaissance Spain in the Age of Empire*. Dorian Recordings ASIN: B00004TVAN.

*Children's Songs from Spain* (James/Alonso). Folkways FW 07746.

# ERDO, ERDO

Hungary

1. Er - do er - do de ma - gas a te - te - je.

Jaj, de re - gen le - hul - lot a le - ve - le.

Jaj, - de re - gen le - hu - lot - a le - ve - le.

Ar - va ma - dar par - jat ke re si ben - ne.

2. Buza koze szallt a dalos pacsirta,
   Mert odafenn a szemeit kisirta.
   Buzavirag, buzakalasz arnyaban
   Ragondolt a regi, els o parjara.

1. *In the silent forest sings the lonely bird,*
   *Cold winds blowing whisper secrets never heard,*
   *High above the moon reflects an icy light,*
   *Shadows fleeing swiftly through the autumn night.*

2. *Through the misty treetop flies the orphaned lark.*
   *Forest branches creaking stiffly, bare and stark.*
   *Sadly sounds the plaintive calling high above,*
   *Calling in the autumn shadow for his love.*

"Erdo, Erdo de magos," gr. 3, from MAKING MUSIC. Copyright © 2005 by Pearson Education, Inc. Reprinted by permission.

## The Tune

"Erdo, Erdo" is a Hungarian folk song with a poetic text that offers images of trees in late autumn, their leaves blown away, and the quiet and the loneliness that settles in as winter nears.

## The Music Culture

The Hungarian people have an impressive collection of folk music, recorded and documented in the early twentieth century by composers Béla Bartók and Zoltán Kodály. To them, Hungarian folk music was the unwritten music surviving among the peasants in the countryside. Much of their collected music is preserved in the national archives, and some of it became the basis of symphonic, choral, and chamber works they wrote—either by way of intact melodies and rhythms or compositional material such as small pitch intervals (for example, seconds) or rhythmic motifs. Because the Hungarians trace their history to the borders of Europe and Asia, and to close relationships with Turkic peoples (along with at least ten centuries of life in their central European homeland), their music is distinctive through these influences even as it is also varied. More than most people, the Hungarians have proudly maintained music as key to their identity, with an unusual extent of government-backed support for music education in the twentieth century.

## The Experiences

- Sing the melody on a neutral syllable such as "loo," and on solfège syllables (beginning with "F" as "do") and scale numbers (beginning with "F" as "1").
- Increase the tempo of the song while singing on "loo."
- Sing the Hungarian text, noting that "Jaj" is "yah," "szallt" approximates "jalt," and "g" is a hard "g."
- Play the chords on accordion, piano, guitar, or other harmony-producing instrument.
- Experiment with pedal points and drones, selecting one or several pitches from the song (for example, D, E, A) to play continuously on piano, xylophones, stringed, wind, or brass instruments, at a constant pulse to accompany the melody.
- Divide the melody into parts, singing in a two-measure canon, on "loo" or with the lyrics.
- Sing the song in a one-measure canon, so that each group enters one measure after the one before it.

## Recommended Listening

*The Rough Guide to Hungarian Music.* World Music Network RGNET1092 CD.

*Gyujtottam Gyertyat: Hungarian Folk Songs.* Hungariton 18054.

*Folk Music of Hungary.* Folkways FW 04000.

# FAST MAMBO GROOVE

Cuba

## The Groove

Like much of the dance music of Cuba and all the Caribbean, the polyrhythmic character of the *mambo* calls listeners to dance. A "Fast Mambo Groove" beckons listeners to respond via movement to multiple percussion instruments—each of which plays in its own dynamic pattern—that complement one another when joined together.

## The Music Culture

The mambo is derived from the Cuban *rumba*, which comes from a Spanish word for "party." The source of the rumba is the sound of Cubans of African descent, who have played percussion instruments alongside their singing and dancing since their arrival on the island. Conga drums, *cajones* (wooden boxes), and claves are common to the rumba, and the claves' fixed rhythm pattern, or time-line, is considered essential to the form so that solo improvisations can occur on the drums and vocally without chaos or confusion. In the 1940s, the mambo emerged in Cuban ballrooms as a blend of polyrhythmic percussion and swing music. By the mid-1950s, it had spread throughout North America and Europe. The dance uses forward and backward steps and a hip-rocking motion—a response to the polyrhythms of the maracas and claves.

## The Experiences

- In order to set the pulse (and tempo), tap, clap, or pat the rhythm of the maracas.

- Tap, clap, or pat the other rhythms one at a time: claves, cowbell 1, cowbell 2, conga drums, timbales. (For timbales, use two mallets. For cowbell, play open (O) at the end of the bell and closed (C) at the top of the bell that is muted by the hand that is holding it. For congas, "P" is pat with the palm of the hand, "S" is a sharp slap, and "F" is fingertips in the center of the drumhead.)

- Consider adding syllables and words to help internalize the rhythms:

| Maracas: | ch-ch-ch-ch | ch-ch-ch-ch | ch-ch-ch-ch | ch-ch-ch-ch |
|---|---|---|---|---|
| Claves: | mam- | bo | fast | mam-bo |
| Cowbell 1: | dance | rhy-thm | dance | rhy-thm |
| Cowbell 2: | play the | rhy-thm and | dance the | mam-bo |
| Conga: | low high | low con-ga | low high | low con-ga |
| Timbales: | play both | hands tim-ba-les play | both hands | tim-ba-les |

- Once the rhythm is learned and can be played in a coordinated fashion, add an improvised melodic groove on various instruments—trumpet, saxophone, trombone, and other available melodic instruments. This groove may be a four- or eight-beat phrase of just three pitches, repeating, and breaking for any instrument which would like to "go solo" in its own improvisation.

## Recommended Listening

*Bomba: Monitor Presents Music of the Caribbean.* Monitor MON51355.

*¡Mambo Mania! The Kings and Queens of Mambo.* Rhino/Wea 71881.

*¡Cubanismo! Reencarnación.* Hannibal HNCD 1429.

# FENG YANG

China

*Verse:*

Zuo - sho__ luo    you - sho - gu    shou na - luo - gu

lai - chang - ge    Bie de__ ge er - wo ye bu hui chang

Zhi hui - chang - ge    Feng - yang - ge    Feng feng - yang - ge -

yi - yo - ya.    *Refrain:* Drr ling dang piao e piao    drr ling dang piao e piao

Drr piao    Drr piao    Drr piao drr piao piao you drr ling dang piao e piao.

*Left hand gong, right and drum,*

*with drum and gong in hand, I come to sing;*

*Other tunes I don not know,*

*But Feng Yang song . . .*

## The Tune

From the Feng Yang farming region of China comes "Feng Yang," a folk song about street vendors who sell their wares and make their music.

## The Music Culture

In the vast country that is China, there are many musical expressions. Inside concert halls and theatres, the music tends toward symphonic and chamber ensembles of stringed instruments. Out in the streets, and particularly in the markets, the music is rhythmic, percussive, and loud. The latest popular music sails through speakers into the market, and drums and gongs are played by *luogu* ensembles. Occasionally, a one-man band may make his way through the market, calling out, singing, and playing music to draw attention to the toys and trinkets he sells. Vendors' songs may be traced to the time of the Ming dynasty (1368–1644), when famine struck the Feng Yang area in

Anhui province and farmers began to wander the countryside, begging and singing their songs to attract attention. Some of their songs are thought to have been adopted by vendors even then, and were passed down through the generations.

*The Experiences*

- Sing the melody on "zuo" (zoh) or "shou" (show), and on solfège syllables (beginning on "sol") or scale numbers (beginning on "5").
- Sing the words and "sounds" of the refrain, while continuing to sing the verse on a neutral syllable. Note that "drr" is essentially a rolled "r," and "piao" is pronounced as "pee-ow." Note that the refrain is largely the onomatapoeic sounds of the various instruments played by the vendor.
- Sing the verse in Chinese, with this pronunciation:

    Zoh shoh low, yoh shoh guh. Show nah low guh lah-ee chahng geh.

    Bee-eh di geh ehr woh yeh buh hoo-ee chahng. Zhe hoo-ee chahng, geh Feng Yang geh.

    Feng feng yang geh ye yo yah.

- Play the chords on piano or other harmony instrument while singing the melody.
- As a variation, play the melody of the verse on flute, violin, or high-pitched xylophone (glockenspiel), thus approximating some Chinese instruments with light and bright tone qualities.

*Recommended Listening*

*Chinese Instrumental Heritage.* Lyrichord LLST 7921.
*Flower Drum and Other Chinese Folk Songs.* Monitor MON 71420.

# FISH AND CHIPS

United States

## The Tune

In the spirit of songs sung around the campfire, "Fish and Chips" is a playful three-part song that includes sections on "one bottle of pop" and "backyard junk."

## The Music Culture

Songfests once happened regularly in North American families, in churches, and at schools, but technology has allowed for music to be made by others such that people no longer need to perform "live" to entertain themselves. Still, at summer camps, where children spend a week or more in rustic, forested surroundings, there are times and occasions for singing together. They swim, boat, make crafts, play at archery, and sometimes ride horses. They take meals together, often in an old farmhouse or under a covered pavilion. In the evenings, after the sun sets, it is not unusual for campers and counselors to build a bonfire to gather around, keep the mosquitos away, toast marshmallows, tell stories, play guitars, and sing songs. More than popular songs and songs from musical theater, it is the traditional songs like "Kumbaya," "The Crawdad Song," "Down by the Riverside," "New River Train," "Swing Low, Sweet Chariot," and "Fish and Chips" that people of several generations will find themselves singing in the great outdoors, releasing their last bit of energy before retiring to their cabins and tents.

## The Experiences

- Sing the melody on a neutral syllable like "tee," or with solfège syllables or scale numbers.
- Sing the melody with the lyrics. Notice how the syllables easily fit the rhythms of the melodies, especially "bottle of pop."
- Play one melody on piano while singing another. Also, sing one melody while playing the other two.
- Sing the songs as one long melody in canon, with the second group coming in eight beats after the first (as the first group begins to sing the "bottle of pop" melody), and so on.
- Accompany the song with chords on guitar or on piano, emphasizing the triple meter by accenting the first of every three pulses, or playing octaves or a bass tone on beat one.

## Recommended Listening

*Skip Rope Games*. Smithsonian Folkways SFW 45015.
*Growing Up with Ella Jenkins*. Smithsonian Folkways SFW 45032.

# FOLLOW THE DRINKIN' GOURD

U. S.: African American

2. Now the river bank'll make a mighty good road,

   The dead trees will show you the way.

   And the left foot, pegfoot traveling on,

   Just you follow the Drinkin' Gourd.

   (Refrain)

3. Now the river ends between two hills.

   Follow the Drinkin' Gourd.

   And there's another river on the other side,

   Just you follow the Drinkin' Gourd.

   (Refrain)

## The Tune

One of the most poignant of African-American historical songs, "Follow the Drinking Gourd" is a reminder of the attempts by slaves to escape the southern United States for freedom in the North.

## The Music Culture

In the years preceding the Civil War, a system called the Underground Railroad existed by which African-American slaves from the southern United States were secretly helped to freedom by sympathetic Northerners. In defiance of the Fugitive Slaves Acts, the slaves went by night or in disguise. There was no actual railway, nor was it underground, but there were back roads and pathways with stopping places called "stations." The Northern abolitionists who sought to banish slavery were called "conductors," and they aided travelers (called "packages") along the way. The destination of the travelers was the fourteen northern states and beyond into Canada, which was known as "the promised land" because it was beyond the reach of fugitive-slave hunters. Many tales were told of the brave men and women who reached their freedom, and as a consequence, Northern sympathy for emancipation of slavery grew stronger until freedom was declared by President Abraham Lincoln in his Emancipation Proclamation of 1863.

## The Experiences

- Sing the melody on a neutral syllable like "noo," and with solfège syllables (beginning on "la") or scale numbers (beginning on "6").
- Check the precision of the syncopated rhythm while singing, and keep time by tapping a steady quarter-note pulse.
- Read the lyrics for the historical content, with references to time of escape ("when the sun comes back"), the Northern abolitionists ("Old Man"), and of course the advisory to "follow the drinkin' gourd" (the constellation of stars in the sky that could show travelers the way north).
- Play the harmony in whole-note or quarter-note chords on piano or guitar while singing the melody.
- Play a collective harmonic accompaniment on strings, winds, or brass instruments, with each player selecting a chord tone to sustain or play in quarter notes, for each chord as indicated.

## Recommended Listening

+*Steal Away: Music of the Underground Railway* (Kim and Reggie Harris). Appleseed Records 1022.
+*Fifty Sail on Newburgh Bay* (Pete Seeger, Ed Renehan). Folkways FW 07557.

# FORTY-NINER

Haliwa-Saponi

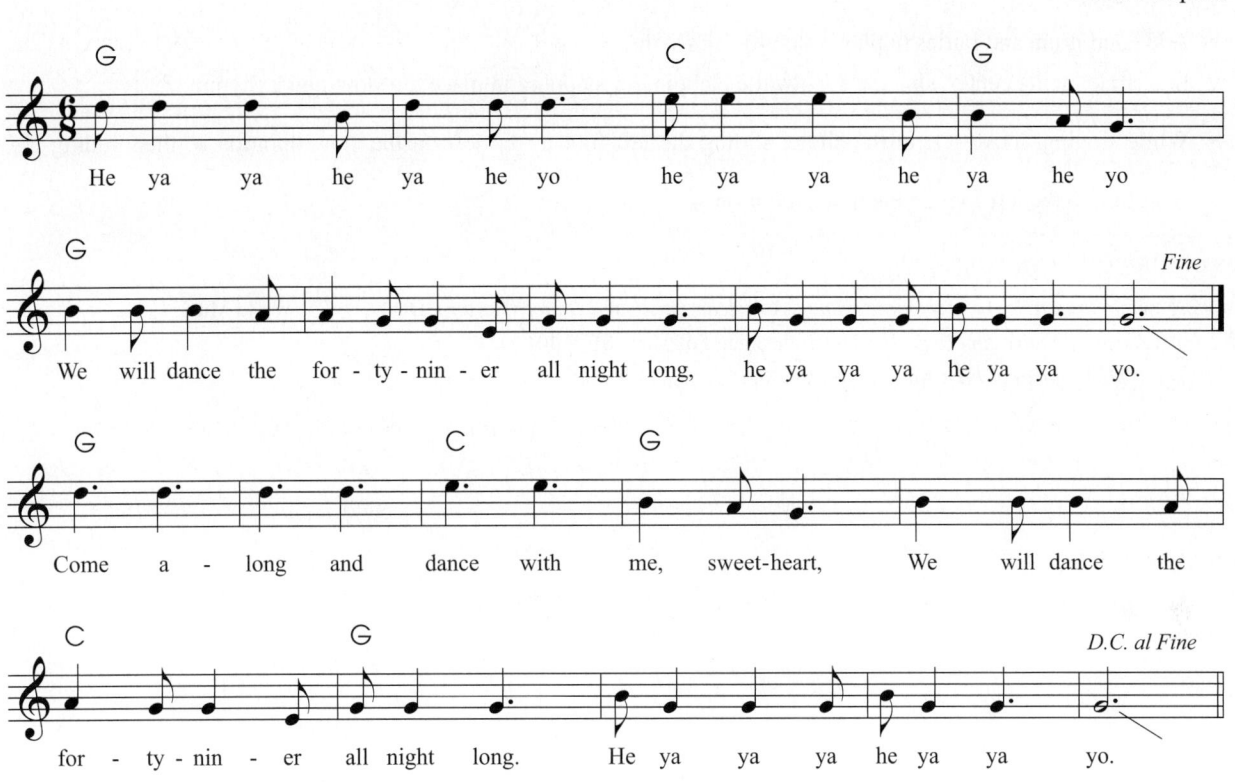

He ya   ya   he ya   he yo   he ya   ya   he ya   he yo

We will dance the for - ty - nin - er all night long, he ya ya ya he ya ya yo.

Come a - long and dance with me, sweet-heart, We will dance the

for - ty - nin - er all night long. He ya ya ya he ya ya yo.

Traditional, "Pan Indian," as sung to Bryan Burton by the Hailwa-Saponi Dancers. From Burton, B. (1998). *Voices of the Wind: Native American Flute Songs for Recorder*. Danbury, CT: World Music Press. Courtesy World Music Press.

## The Tune

"Forty-Niner" is a social dance song of the Haliwa-Saponi people, a Native American group in the mid-Atlantic region of the Eastern Woodlands.

## The Music Culture

Forty-Niner dances are popular among Native Americans, especially among the younger people. Not only are they social dances that entail choosing a partner, but the words to the songs are typically humorous or at least lighthearted in character. The lyrics of Forty-Niner songs usually combine English, vocables, and sometimes Native language, and refer to courtship or events in daily life. The Haliwa-Saponi people, with bands living in North Carolina, Pennsylvania, and New York state, sing and dance this particular "Forty-Niner." They maintain a tribal office in North Carolina, and take "Haliwa" from the first syllables of Halifax and Warren counties, in which many of the group reside.

### The Experiences

- While tapping, clapping, or patting a ♩. pulse, sing the melody on a neutral  syllable like "doo," and on solfège syllables (beginning on "sol") or scale numbers (beginning on "5").
- If the changing rhythms become confusing, slow the tempo down and tap every eighth-note pulse.
- Step the rhythm of the song while singing the melody on a neutral syllable.

- Sing the song with text, pronouncing "he" as "hay," "ya" as "yah," and "yo" as "yoh."
- Play the chordal accompaniment on guitar or other harmony instrument, remembering that contemporary Native American music is often harmonized and played in styles ranging from country to rock.
- Add hand drum and rattles to play a slow-quick rhythm ♩ ♪
- In a circle facing center, sing the song while clapping or stepping in place the slow-quick rhythm.
- While singing, move left in the circle, sliding the left foot to the left on the slow duration ♩, then sliding the right foot to the left foot on the quick duration ♪

## Recommended Listening

+*Moving Within the Circle: Contemporary Native American Music and Dance* (Burton). Danbury, CT: World Music Press.
*Creation's Journey: Native American Music*. Smithsonian Folkways SFW 40410.
*Heartbeat 2: More Voices of First Nations Women*. Smithsonian Folkwasy SFW 40455.

# FREIGHT TRAIN

Elizabeth Cotten

1. Freight train, freight train, run so fast, Freight train, freight train, run so fast,

Please don't tell what train I'm on, They won't know what route I've gone.

2. When I'm dead and in my grave,
   No more good times here I crave,
   Place the stones at my head and feet,
   Tell them that I've gone to sleep.

3. When I die, Lord, bury me deep,
   Way down on old Chestnut Street,
   Then I can hear old Number Eight
   As she come rolling by.

CD I, Track # 17

## The Tune

Elizabeth Cotten (1895–1987) wrote "Freight Train" when she was just twelve years old, and sang it throughout her life—even while numerous other singers and bands copied her.

## The Music Culture

Train songs were once as popular as trains themselves, particularly in the late 1800s to the mid-twentieth century, when they were the main mode of transport from one small town to the next. Some songwriters were inspired by the sounds of train whistles, their steam engines, and their rolling wheels on tracks, while others found themselves entranced by the literal and figurative function of "going places," escaping troubles, seeking love and adventure, and taking the journey of a lifetime. "Freight Train" is one of Elizabeth Cotten's songs, first recorded in 1958. She had been playing banjo and guitar when she was quite young, and lived near enough to the railroad in Chapel Hill, North Carolina, that it would wake her up at night—thus came the song. Later, when working at a department store, she found and returned little Peggy Seeger who had become separated from her mother, composer Ruth Crawford Seeger. The Seegers hired Elizabeth to work for them soon after, and she rediscovered how to play guitar. By the 1960s, she was playing "Freight Train" and various other songs and instrumentals at folk festivals across the country, first with Mike Seeger (son of Ruth and Charles Seeger) and later on her own. She continued to perform and record into her early nineties, and was honored with numerous awards.

## The Experiences

- Listen to Track # 17, with attention to her guitar-picking style, for which Elizabeth Cotten was known to use primarily her thumb (on melody) and first finger (on the three lowest strings).
- Sing the melody on a neutral syllable like "bah," and with solfège syllables (starting on "sol") or scale numbers (starting on "5").
- Sing the lyrics of the three verses, adding vocal harmony on the chord tones.
- Play the chords on guitar, autoharp, banjo, or other harmony instrument.
- Listen to the recording for ideas on how to shift from strumming to finger-picking the chords, and experiment with possibilities.

## Recommended Listening

+*Elizabeth Cotten: Freight Train and Other North Carolina Folk Songs and Tunes*. Smithsonian Folkways SFW 40009.

*Shake Sugaree: Elizabeth Cotten*. Smithsonian Folkways SFW 40147.

## FROGGIE WENT A-COURTIN'

England

1. Frog-gie went a-court-in' and he did ride, Mm-hmm, Mm-hmm, Frog-gie went a-court-in' and he did ride, Mm-hmm, Mm-hmm, Frog-gie went a-court-in' and he did ride, A sword and pis-tol by his side, Mm-hmm, Mm-hmm.

2. He said, "Miss Mousie, are you within?" Mm-hmm.
   (continue throughout verses)

   "Oh yes, sir, here I sit and spin." Mm-hmm. (continue throughout verses)

3. He took Miss Mousie upon his knee.
   And he said, "Miss Mousie, will you marry me?"

4. "You'll have to ask my Uncle Rat,
   And see what he will say to that."

5. Uncle Rat gave his consent,
   And the moles inscribed the document.

6. "Oh, where will the wedding supper be?"
   "Away down yonder in a hollow tree."

7. "What will the wedding supper be?"
   "Two green beans and a black-eyed pea."

8. The first came in was a little white moth.
   He spread out the tablecloth.

9. The next came in was a bumblebee.
   With a fiddle on his knee.

10. The next came in was a little flea.
    To take a jig with the bumblebee.

11. The next came in was a pesky old fly.
    He ate up the wedding pie.

12. The next came in was an old tomcat.
    He took up after Uncle Rat.

13. He ate up all the wedding cake.
    And chased the party into the lake.

14. Then Frog and Mousie left for France.
    And that is the end of this romance.

## The Tune

One of the best known of English-language *ballads,* "Froggie Went A-Courtin'" tells the story of the courtship and wedding of Froggie and Miss Mousie.

## The Music Culture

The oldest group of English-language songs in the oral tradition are ballads. Many of them classified by Francis James Child in *The English and Scottish Popular Ballads* predate 1750, and tell the stories of true love, and false love, and the lives, loves, and tragic losses of hunters, sailors, carpenters, parsons, and merchants, as well as numerous "fair maidens." Ballads function to tell stories of single events such as shipwrecks, battles, weddings, and funerals, as opposed to the multiple events that are told in sung *narratives.* Many of the British (English, Scottish, and Welsh) and Irish ballads found their way into the southern Appalachian Mountains, and were preserved there in isolated hills and "hollers," sung even after they had disappeared in Europe. "Froggie Went A-Courtin'" has been sung in many variants for at least four hundred years, first in England and then in the Appalachians. An interpretation of one variant of the song holds that Miss Mousie represented Queen Elizabeth I (1533–1603) of England and that Frog was "Monsieur Frog," a French ambassador to the English court; this particular variant was a social protest against that marriage. Many of the song versions end "happily ever after," although some end tragically when a cat swallows both frog and mouse.

## The Experiences

- Sing the melody on a neutral syllable such as "mah," and on solfège syllables or scale tones.
- Sing the multiple verses of the ballad, dividing them between solo singers who tell the story and respondents who join together to sing the "mm-hmm" response that encourages the spinning-out of the tale.
- Play the chords on guitar, strumming up-and-down strokes twice per measure ♩ ♩ ♩ ♩ or double time ♫♫ ♫♫. Or play a bass line and chord pattern:

Chord:

Bass:

## Recommended Listening

+*John Jacob Niles Sings Folksongs.* Folkways FW 02373.
+*Alan Mills, More Animals, Volume 2.* Folkways FW 07642.
+*Bruce Springsteen: We Shall Overcome: The Seeger Sessions.* Columbia 82876-82867-2.

# GALBI

Ofra Haza

*What is the cause of this pain?*

*Who is the one who does not know that I exist?*

"Galbi." Words by Aharon Amram and Gogly Music Publ. Acum, Ltd.

CD I, Track # 18

## The Tune

Tradition is combined with state-of-the-art recording techniques in the music of Ofra Haza, a Yemenite Jewish singer, who shaped "Galbi" into a style that has been played in dance clubs around the world.

## The Music Culture

In the southwestern part of the Arabian peninsula, Yemen lies at the junction of the Arabian and Red seas. One of the oldest Jewish communities in the world, the Yemenite Jews, lived there as minorities in a Muslim culture for at least a millennium. Jews from Yemen began to move north into the area of Palestine at the end of the nineteenth century, and almost the entire Yemenite Jewish population—some 50,000—were airlifted to Israel after the founding of that nation in 1948. They brought with them their poetry, their songs, their liturgical practices, and their mixed languages of Hebrew, Aramaic, and Arabic. Born in 1957, Ofra Haza immigrated on foot with her family from Yemen to Israel. She sang songs of everyday life, and became interested in enhancing them with dynamic percussive rhythms and technology that would give them a contemporary sound and feel. An immensely popular singer, she received the Israeli equivalent of the Grammy three times for best female singer. As a song of unrequited love, "Galbi" is a sonic envelope of tremendous energy and passion.

## *The Experiences*

- Listen to Track # 18, humming along to the Phrygian melody.
- Listen again to the recording, tracking and tapping the rhythm of a selected percussion instrument. Some of the percussion timbres and techniques emanate from the use of oil cans and household trays that were once played by Jews in Yemen to circumvent the ban on musical instruments imposed by orthodox Muslims.
- Sing the notation on a neutral syllable such as "lah," while patting a steady beat.
- Play the two-chord harmonic accompaniment on piano, guitar, or other harmony instrument.
- Listen to the recording, and use hand drums or tambourines to play a fast ostinato pattern of

## *Recommended Listening*

+*Ofra Haza: Fifth Gates of Wisdom*. Shanachie Records SH 64002.
*Ofra Haza: Shaday*. Warner 25816.

# GIMPEL THE FOOL

U. S.: Yiddish

CD I, Track # 19

## The Tune

A short story published in Yiddish by Isaac Bashevis Singer in 1945 inspired the title of this *klezmer*-styled music: "Gimpel the Fool."

## The Music Culture

The Yiddish term klezmer (from *klezmorim*, the Hebrew word for musical instruments) originated in the older Ashkenazi centers of cities in central and eastern Europe. Early instruments included lead violin, contra-violin, *cimbalom* (a hammered dulcimer), bass or cello, and sometimes a flute. The clarinet was added in the early nineteenth century, and brass instruments appeared later in the century. Landowners in Poland, Lithuania, the Ukraine, Romania, Hungary, and old Czechoslovakia encouraged the development of klezmorim as a Jewish guild. In North America, a revival of klezmer music (along with Yiddish theater) began in 1970 in New York, Philadelphia, Boston, and Toronto. Rock-style klezmer took its influential shape with Frank London and Alicia Svigals and the Klezmatics, and clarinetist David Krakauer developed a sophisticated style of klezmer jazz. Commonly klezmer tunes are created in either a minor scale or a scale employing an augmented second degree. Harmonization and syncopation are typically a part of klezmer music, too. The klezmer piece "Gimple the Fool" refers to the short story about Gimpel, a gullible man who responded to a lifetime of deception and betrayal with childlike acceptance and a steadfast belief in human goodness.

### The Experiences

- Listen to Track # 19, and hum the melody that is played first by the trumpet and later is joined in harmony by the clarinet.
- Sing the melody on a neutral syllable such as "lah," and on solfège syllables (beginning on "mi" and utilizing sol-mi syllables without alteration) or scale numbers (beginning on "3").
- Practice singing the augmented second by repeating measures 1 and 2.
- Follow the "oompah" of the low brass instruments on beats one and three, and the flamlike drum roll on beats two and four. Pat on beats one and three, and clap on beats two and four.

| Beat: | 1 | 2 | 3 | 4 |
|-------|------|------|------|------|
| Move: | step | bend | step | bend |

- Step in place or across the floor, on beats one and three, bending the knees on beats two and four.
- Play the melody on trumpet or clarinet, or on violin, cello, or flute, or other melody-producing instrument.
- Play the chords on piano, playing the root or bass tone of the chord on beats one and three and the chord on beats two and four.

| Beat: | 1 | 2 | 3 | 4 |
|---|---|---|---|---|
| Piano: | root/bass | chord | root/bass | chord |

## Recommended Listening

+*Dancing in the Aisles* (Klezmer Conservatory Band). Rounder 3155.

*The Klezmorim: First Recordings.* Arhoolie CD 309.

# GO DOWN, MOSES

U. S.: African American

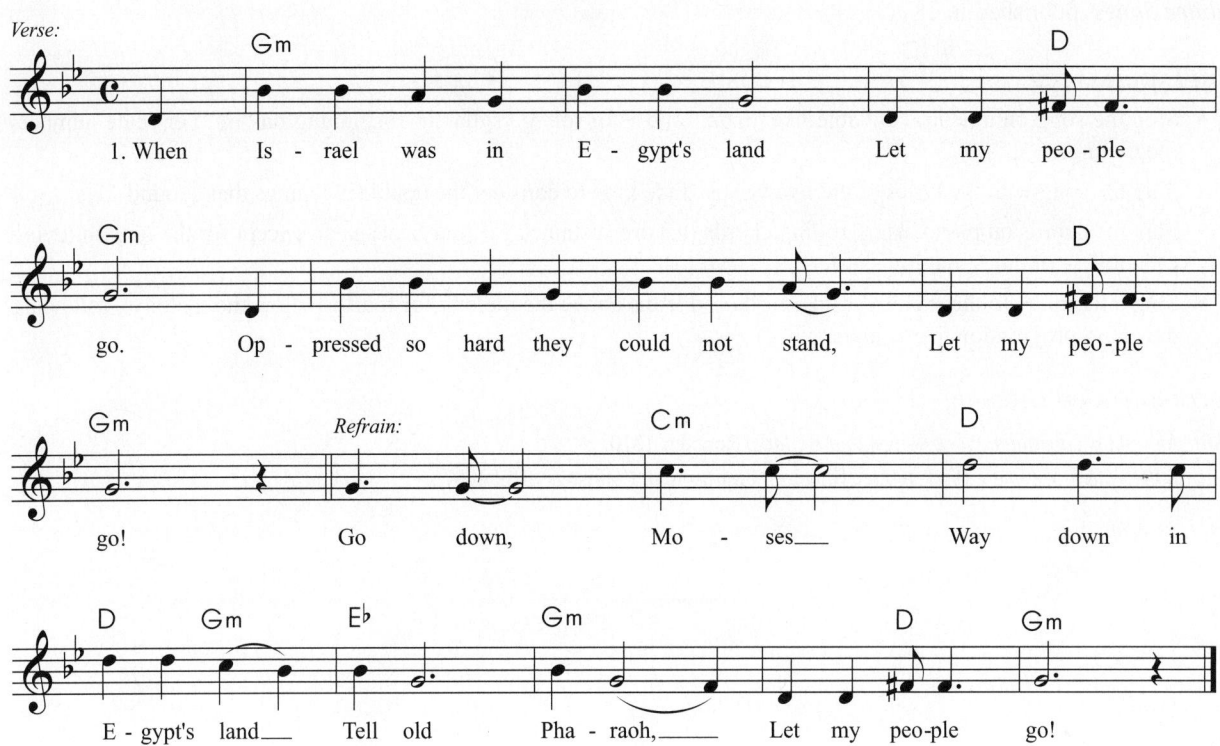

2. Thus saith the Lord, bold Moses said,
   Let my people go;
   If not, I'll smite your first-born dead,
   Let may people go.
   (Refrain)

3. No more shall they in bondage toil,
   Let my people go;
   Let them come out with Egypt's spoil,
   Let my people go.
   (Refrain)

4. The Lord told Moses what to do,
   Let my people go;
   To lead the chilrdren of Israel thro,
   Let my people go.
   (Refrain)

5. When they had reached the other shore,
   Let my people go;
   They sang a song of triumph o'er
   Let my people go.
   (Refrain)

## The Tune

The spiritual, "Go Down, Moses," was created by African Americans to compare their enslavement with the captivity of the Hebrews by Pharoah in Egypt.

## The Music Culture

"Go Down, Moses" is the first well-known African-American spiritual to have appeared in print. In 1861, the Reverend Lockwood, a chaplain at Fortress Monroe in Virginia, was credited with having offered the words and music from a melody he had heard sung by African-American slaves. As in so many spirituals, the lyrics have both a Biblical reference and a relevance to slavery and the freedom the slaves so dearly desired. In "Go Down, Moses," the prophet was seen as the great emancipator, leading his people out of Egypt and from the bonds of slavery to their freedom across the Red Sea (or the Sea of Reeds, as biblical scholars have called it). The Jubilee Singers of Fisk University, in Nashville, Tenessee, sang their own version of the song, which is found in their collection of *Jubilee Songs*, published in 1872.

## The Experiences

- Sing the song on a neutral syllable like "mah," and with solfège syllables (beginning on "mi") or scale numbers (beginning on "3").
- Sing the song with the lyrics of the five verses. Take time to consider the double meanings that abound.
- Play the chords on piano, using rolling chords that are sustained for four beats each (except for the quick-moving cadential harmonies that run shorter).
- Sing a harmony to the melody, using thirds and fifths above the melody (or fourths below the melody), following the chord progression that is marked.

## Recommended Listening

+*Afro-American Spirituals, Work Songs, and Ballads*. Rounder 1510.

*Wade in the Water, Volume 1* (Fisk Jubilee Singers). Smithsonian Folkways SFW 40072.

# GONG XI FA CAI

China

Mei - tiao da jie shi - ao shiang,    Mei ge ren de tsu - i li.

Jian mian di - i chu - u hua    Jui shi gong xi gong xi.

Gong xi gong xi gong xi ni ya!    Gong xi gong xi gong xi ni!

*In the time of New Year's joy,*
*In the streets you'll hear the cry:*
*(Festive words for family,*
*Friends and neighbors, too, oh!)*
*"Happy New Year time is here, oh,*
*Happy New Year time is here."*

## The Tune

Embedded within this song is the Chinese greeting for a happy new year, "Gong Xi Fa Cai," for that celebration time in late January or early February.

## The Music Culture

The Lunar New Year is the most important event in the Chinese calendar of festivals. Once known as Chun Jie (Spring Festival), it was a farmer's time to celebrate the coming of a renewed fertility of the earth, the period of the land's reawakening to the new life of all that grows from the soil. The pursuit of happiness through prosperity is especially important to the Chinese. Accordingly, gifts are given, and people flock to the shops to purchase lanterns, porcelain, clay, "china" plates, clothing, books, games, and cards. No New Year's celebration is complete without the traditional gift of money wrapped up in a red packet called *hong bao*. Parents give this packet to their children in denominations of two monetary units, or larger amounts divisible by two. The common greeting of the Chinese New Year is "Gong xi fa cai," which means "Congratulations! May your wealth and prosperity increase!" The Chinese prefer wishes to resolutions, for if wishes do not come true, the gods are to blame.

### The Experiences

- Sing the melody on neutral syllable such as "nah," and with solfège syllables (beginning on "la") or scale numbers (beginning on "6").

- Sing the Chinese lyrics with these pronunciations in mind:

    May tee-ow dah jee shee-ow shee-ahng, May guh run duh tsoo-ee lee.

    Tchin meen dee-ee jay-oo hwah Jwee shih gung shee gung shee.

    Gung shee gung shee gung shee nee yah!

    Gung shee gung shee gung shee nee!

- Play the chords to harmonize the melody, on piano or guitar. Determine a preferred style: chords at the indicated chord changes (only), chords every pulse, or arpeggiated or broken chords.
- Add percussion instruments in one-measure ostinati:

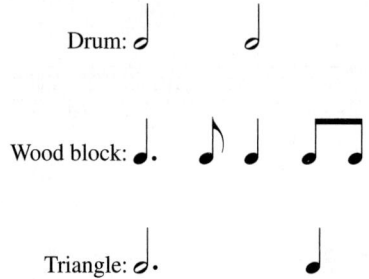

## Recommended Listening

*An Anthology of Chinese Folk Songs* (Ellie Mao). Folkways FW 088077.
*Chinese Folk Songs.* Lyrichord LLCT 7152.

# GUAJIRA GUANTANAMERA

Cuba

*Refrain:* Guantanamera, guajira Guantanamera
Guantanamera, guajira Guantanamera.

1. Yo soy un hombre sincero
   de donde crece la palma.
   Y antes de morirme quiero
   Cantar los versos del alma.

2. Cultivo una rosa blanca
   en junio como en enero.
   Para el amigo sincero
   que me da su mano franca.

3. Mi verso es de un verde claro
   Y de un carmin encendido.
   Mi verso es un siervo herido
   que busca del monte amparo.

*Guantanamera, rustic guantanamera*
*Guantanamera, rustic guantanamera*

1. *I am a sincere man*
   *From the land of the palm trees*
   *And before I die I want*
   *To sing these verses of the soul.*

2. *I grew a white rose*
   *In June as in January*
   *For a genuine friend*
   *Who gives me his hand freely.*

3. *My verse is a clear green*
   *And bright red carmine*
   *My verse is a wounded servant*
   *Who looks for the protection of the mountain.*

# GUAJIRA GUANTANAMERA

CD I, Track # 20

## The Tune

One of the best known Cuban songs is "Guantanamera," with lyrics based upon the poem by the revered Cuban poet, José Martí. Its performance suggests a communal sensibility that was much in keeping with the spirit of independence in which Martí so thoroughly believed.

## The Music Culture

The story behind the song "Guantanamera" features contributions by several poets, singers, and players. While the lyrics are based on the first poem in a collection called *Simple Verses* by nationalist poet José Martí, the poem was adapted by Julián Orbón. The tune was composed by Joseíto Fernández, and was sung in 1962 by Hector Angulo, a young Cuban music student at Camp Woodland in the Catskills of New York state. Folksinger Pete Seeger heard the young Hector sing, and was so enamoured of it that he added the song to his repertoire, which he then took on his international concert tours. The song was a hit for the Sandpipers in 1967, and has been performed by Joan Baez, Tito Puente, the Paul Winter Consort, José Feliciano, Los Lobos, Nana Mouskouri, and rap musician Wyclef Jean (among others).

### The Experiences

- Listen to Track # 20, humming the sung melody and following the use of guitar and bongos, in this live performance recorded in Washington D.C. by the Cuarteto Patria with singer Compay Segundo.
- Sing the melody on neutral syllable such as "lee," and on solfège syllables (beginning on "la") or scale numbers (beginning on "6").
- Sing the melody with the Spanish-language words, noting that "gu" is "gw," "hombre" is "ohm-bray," and "crece" is "cray-say."
- Listen again to the recording, tapping the bongo rhythm:
- Play the chords on guitar, strumming a leisurely down down-up pattern of
- Add the bongos (or congas) for the rhythm, as they are played on the recording.
- Improvise rhythmic patterns on Cuban percussion instruments such as claves, güiro, and cowbell.

### Recommended Listening

+*Smithsonian Folkways World Music Collection*. Smithsonian Folkways SF 40471.
+*Guantanamera! Latin American Hits*. Monitor MO 61490.
+*Le World Cuba: Havana Noches*. Suave 6942085.

# HAERE, HAERE

New Zealand: Maori

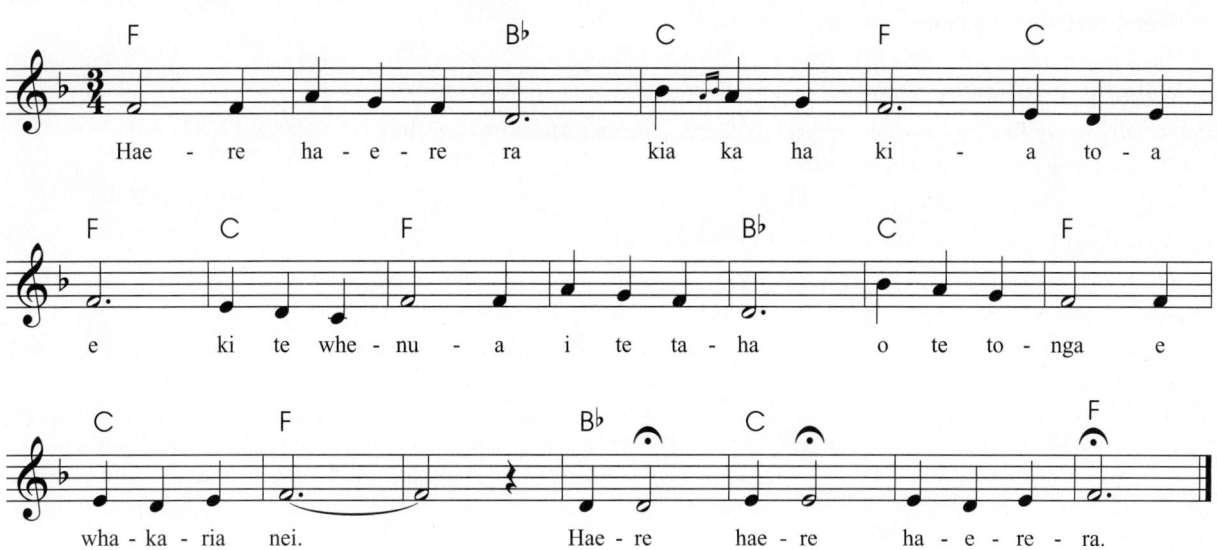

Hae - re   ha - e - re   ra   kia   ka   ha   ki - a   to - a

e   ki   te   whe - nu - a   i   te   ta - ha   o   te   to - nga   e

wha - ka - ria   nei.   Hae - re   hae - re   ha - e - re - ra.

*Farewell, go with strength and courage*

*To that chosen direction (south)*

*Illuminated for you.*

## The Tune

The Maori of the islands of Aotearoa, also known as New Zealand, hold fast to their language, traditional culture, and artistic expressions. For them, music is linked to many of their social occasions, including welcome songs and farewell songs like "Haere, Haere."

## The Music Culture

Long before Captain James Cook surveyed the coastline of New Zealand and claimed the land for England in the late eighteenth century, the islands were settled by Polynesians who became the Maori people. The Treaty of Waitangi was signed between the British Crown and the Maori tribes to recognize what rightfully belonged to the indigenous people, but it was not until recent decades that the New Zealand government established New Zealand/Aortorea as a bicultural (and even a multicultural) nation. There are two forms of Maori music, the "action song" (*waiata-a-ringa* or *waiata kori*) that blends European melodies with Maori words and actions, and the in- digenous Maori chant that remains uninfluenced by European music. Non-Maori are struck by the colorful style of the shouted *haka* posture dances, with their foot stamping, out-thrust tongue, and distorted eyes. Still, it is the *waiata*, including welcome songs, laments, blessings, and farewell songs, as well as the *poi* dances with sung accompaniment and the slapping rhythm of tethered *poi* balls, that are most commonly performed by the Maori. Even as the *pakeha*, or white Europeans, have developed their institutions throughout the country, the Maori are prominent among the indigenous peoples of the world for persevering in efforts to keep their traditions alive and very well—all the way to the music they make.

### The Experiences

- Sing the melody on neutral syllable such as "ha," and on solfège syllables or scale numbers.
- Sing the Maori words to the song, noting these pronunciations: "haere" is "hah-eh-ray" (quickly), "kia," is "kya," "wh" is "f" (as in "fenooah"—whenua, and "fakarya"—whakaria).

- Play the chords on the guitar as is typical of Maori-style performance, accenting the first pulse of each measure in ♩ ♫ ♫ pattern.
- Gather in several lines of singers, with guitars in the back, standing shoulder to shoulder. Transfer the weight of the feet from left to right once per every three beats.

## Recommended Listening

+*Traditional Songs of Singing Cultures* (Campbell/Williamson/Perron). Miami: Warner Bros.

*Maori Songs of New Zealand*. Mastersong 500132.

# HAI WEDI

Algeria

## The Groove

Combine the music of traditional Algerian song with the use of synthesizers, guitars, and electronic rhythms, and the sound that emerges is *pop-rai*. Cheb Hamid's "Hai Wedi" is a sorrowful song about the loss of one's girlfriend to another man.

## The Music Culture

In Algeria, *pop-rai* (or just *rai*) is a revolution in music that has blended local traditions with the influences of rock, soul, funk, and reggae. A number of complex traditional rhythms are retained within the style, while the use of drum machines and a layering of various other audio technology techniques gives the music a decidedly contemporary sound. The songs are sung in the Arabic language, and may be comprised of a small range of pitches. Rachid Bab Ahmed is one of the preeminent *rai* producers, who raised Cheb Khaled, or just Khaled (also known as the "King of Rai") and Cheb Hamid to international fame in the *pop-rai* he recorded. In Algeria, France and throughout North Africa and the Middle East, *pop-rai* is top-ranked dance-club music.

### The Experiences

- In a fast four-count, follow the rhythm that emphasizes the fourth count: 𝄽 𝄽 𝄽 ♩
- Play the bass ostinato on stringed bass, tuba, baritone, bassoon, bass trombone, or the low octave on the piano.
- Hum the melody, noticing its tight range of a third.

- Consider how the music expresses deep sadness. In translation:

    My eyes are crying, you've gone with my rival.

    I have eaten the whole fish including the bones.

    You taught me to love you and now you're gone.

    The pigeon flying around will find his mate.

- Create a dance movement that reflects the groove, keeping hand-clapping or foot-stepping (stamp or shuffle) movements in mind. Two possibilities follow, each one of which can be performed throughout, or performed alternately.

| Count: | 1 | 2 | 3 | 4 |
|---|---|---|---|---|
| Movement 1: | R step | L step | R step | jump (both feet) |
| Movement 2: | R sway | L sway | R sway | clap-clap |

## Recommended Listening

+*Pop-Rai and Rachid Style*. Virgin Records 2-91407.

*Hada Raykoum* (Cheb Khaled). Triple Earth Terra 102.

*Absolute Rai*. EMI International 8508622.

# HAIDA

Jewish

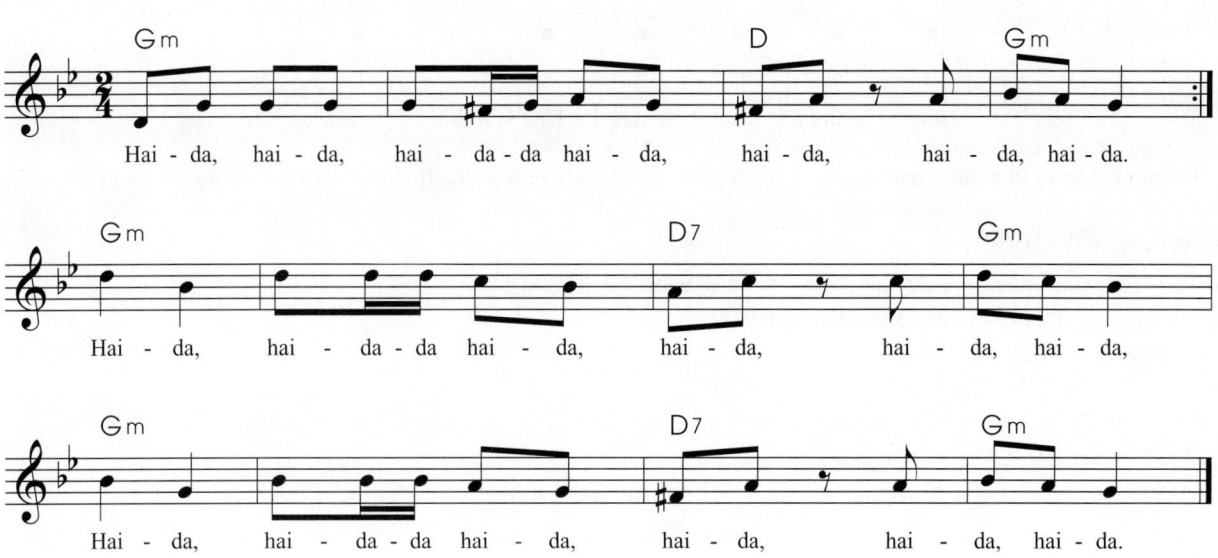

## The Tune

Among the Eastern European Hasidic Jews, a *nigun* such as "Haida" is a melody of syllables that is accompanied by dancing.

## The Music Culture

Numerous minor-key melodies exist among the Ashkenazi Jews of Eastern Europe. These *nigunim* (the plural of *nigun*) are typically modal, either Dorian or Aeolian, and may be sung to prose texts or to syllables that are not translatable. Often they are simple combinations of melodic formulae, and their lyrics or syllables may be the last section of a prayer. Some *nigunim* are thought to have been in existence since the sixteenth century, but because the music of Ashkenazi communities was not notated until the nineteenth century, their history is in fact uncertain. A few of the *nigunim* shift out of the realm of liturgical chant and prayer and into the secular folkways of people who enjoy singing them solo and in groups.

### The Experiences

- Sing the melody on solfège syllables (beginning on "mi") or scale numbers (beginning on "3").
- Sing the *nigun* syllables, noting that "hai" is pronounced "hi."
- Clap after the fifth beat of each phrase, at the rest, just before brief phrase ending.
- Play the chords on piano or guitar in a "boom-chick" pattern that features the root or bass note on the beat and the chord on the offbeat.

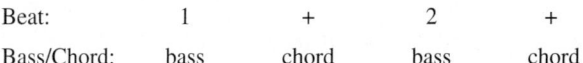

| Beat: | 1 | + | 2 | + |
|---|---|---|---|---|
| Bass/Chord: | bass | chord | bass | chord |

- Reinforce this rhythm by playing eighth notes on drum set or tambourine.
- Dance a simple grapevine step while singing the song. In a circle, with hands held, arms up, and weight on the left foot, move to the right:

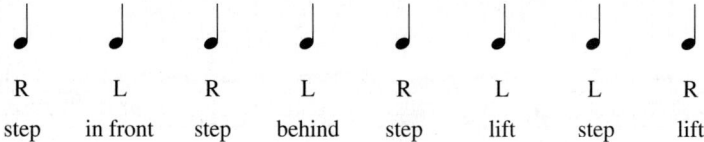

| R | L | R | L | R | L | L | R |
|---|---|---|---|---|---|---|---|
| step | in front | step | behind | step | lift | step | lift |

- Sing the song in a three-part canon. The second voice part begins as the first part moves into the second phrase.

## Recommended Listening

*New York City: Global Beat of the Boroughs.* Smithsonian Folkways SFW 40493.

*Nigun Anthology.* Transcontinental Music Publications 950114.

*Alter Rebbe's Nigun.* Tzadik 7131.

# HALIWA-SAPONI CANOE DANCE

Haliwa-Saponi

Traditional, as sung to Bryan Burton by the Hailwa-Saponi Dancers.  From Burton, B. (1993) *Moving Within the Circle: Contemporary Native American Music and Dance*. Danbury, CT: World Music Press. Courtesy World Music Press.

## The Tune

Native American groups like the Haliwa-Saponi Singers of Pennsylvania have long used songs to teach hunting, fishing, and household skills. Such may have been the origin of the "Haliwa-Saponi Canoe Dance" song for its functional purpose of reliving and relating the group's once-considerable time spent at work and in sport on the rivers.

## The Music Culture

The Haliwa-Saponi are a Native American tribe living in the Piedmont region of North Carolina and in Pennsylvania and New York. Originally called Saponi, "Haliwa" was added to refer to the counties of Halifax ("Hali") and Warren ("wa") in North Carolina, where many of the group reside. While they are all singers and dancers for communal events and seasonal celebrations, the Haliwa-Saponi also designate those among them who will continue with skill and knowledge in the performance of traditional songs and dances reminiscent of the time in their history when the days were filled with hunting, fishing, and the preparation of food for their family meals. The canoe was once their main mode of transportation along the rivers of the eastern woodlands. The dance that accompanies this song is performed in a column of dancers who line up one behind the other as paddlers in a canoe.

### The Experiences

- Sing the melody on a neutral syllable such as "ya," and on solfège syllables (beginning on "la") or scale numbers (beginning on "6").
- Sing the song with the vocables, or sung (and nontranslatable) syllables, noting that "we" is pronounced "way."
- Play the chords, or the open fifths, of designed chords, on piano, guitar, violin, cello, or other harmony- (and fifth-) producing instrument.

- Play steady pulses on a large hand drum held centrally by several people, each one with a mallet.
- Form single-file lines of three or more dancers, with a lead dancer in front. Dancers place their hands on the upper arms of the dancer in front of them, and appear as paddlers in a canoe. Side-step to the left for eight beats (across two measures), then to the right, and so on. The stepping movement follows.

| L | R | L | R | L | R | L | R |
|---|---|---|---|---|---|---|---|
| 1 | 2 | 3 | 4 | 5 | 6 | 7 | 8 |
| R | L | R | L | R | L | R | L |
| 1 | 2 | 3 | 4 | 5 | 6 | 7 | 8 |

## Recommended Listening

+*Moving within the Circle: Contemporary Native American Music and Dance* (Burton). Danbury, CT: World Music Press.

*Heartbeat: Voices of First Nations Women.* Smithsonian Folkways SFW 40415.

# HANDEL: MINUET NO. 2

G.F. Handel

## The Tune

The Baroque composer George Frideric Handel composed this "Minuet No. 2." The minuet was a popular social dance in seventeenth-century England.

## The Music Culture

George Frideric Handel (1685–1759) was a leading composer of concerti grossi, operas and oratorios. Born in Germany, he lived most of his life in England. He was famous for writing the *Messiah* oratorio, as well as *Water Music* and *Music for the Royal Fireworks*. He grew up in a time when dances like the bourrée, gavotte, sarabande, and minuet were commonly performed at social events. The triple-metered minuet was an aristocratic social dance that was dignified yet graceful and relaxed. The musical form was incorporated into keyboard and ensemble suites by Handel and J. S. Bach and their contemporaries, and in the Classical period, it became a standard form for the third movement of symphonies and sonatas.

### The Experiences

- Sing the melody on a neutral syllable such as "loo," and on solfège syllables or scale numbers.
- Play the melody on piano or other melody instrument such as violin, flute, trumpet, or clarinet.
- Harmonize the melody with the chords indicated, on piano or guitar.
- Arrange the melody and harmony for available instruments, dispersing the pitches of the chords. For example, in a band, dole the melody out to trumpets, the chord roots to flutes, clarinets, and oboes, thirds to French horns and saxophones, and fifths to trombones, bassoons, baritones, and tubas. Switch parts, allowing various instruments to take turns playing the melody.

### Recommended Listening

+*Age of Elegance* (Philadelphia Orchestra). Sony 1 MLK 62369.
+*Handel: Greatest Hits*. Sony MLK 64066.

# THE HANDS

Gina Valdez

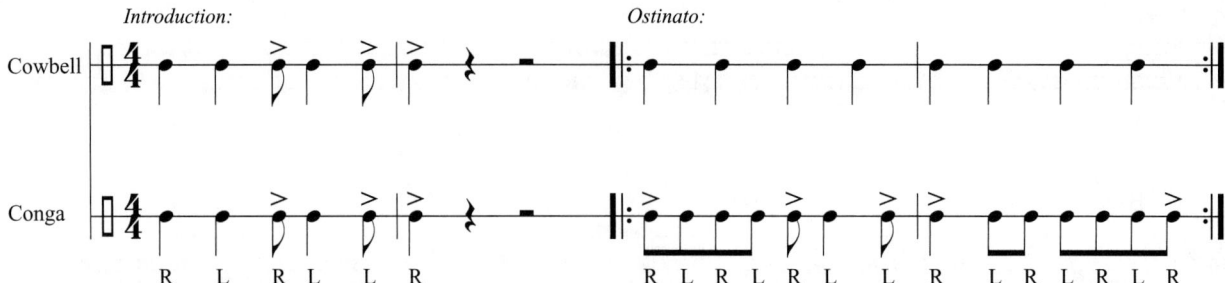

Depending on the light of the hairy sun or the moon,
Or the shade of the tamarinded noon or the chapel at dusk,
The hands, these hands, my hands, your hands,
Will appear cream or cinnamon, pink, red, black, or yellow.
Our heritage.

These are hands of congas, of requintos, guiros, claves, bongos and timbales.
Of maracas, charangos, guitarrones, and marimbas, castanets, tambourines, and cymbals.
Tin-tin-timbalao, tingo.
These hands sing, dance, clap to the beat of corn
On its way to becoming a tortilla.

These hands around *albondingas* and dreams
Circle waists, sides, and hips,
Peel bananas, masks, and mangos,
Add, subtract, multiply on blackboards, beds and griddles.

These hands speak fluent Spanish.
They warm. They reduce fevers.
Sometimes they write poetry.
Sometimes they recite it.
These hands could take away all pain.

These hands tied by centuries of rope to ovens, tables, and to diapers,
To brooms, mops, trays, and dusters,
To saw and hammers, to picks, hoes, and shovels.
They scrub floors, plates, and lies,
Pick strawberries, grapes, insults, and onions.
Plant corn, mint, hope, and cilantro.
Piece by piece, they honor us with our history.

These hands, so large, so small.
Two hummingbirds, quiet, still, joined, pierced by a nail of U.S. steel.
Unbind, shout, close into a fist of sorrow, of anger, or impatience.
These raised hands open, demand the same as they produce, as they are giving.
These hands smile in triumph.

Music, Steve Loza Sextet, from *Red Car Blues*, Merrimack 10102, 2000; copyright 2000 Steve Loza: Poem, "The Hands" (Los Manos), by Gina Valdés, from *Comiendo Lumbre = Eating Fire*. Colorado Springs, CO: Maize Press, 1986 (now at Bilingual Press). Copyright 1986 by Gina Valdés. All rights reserved. English translation by Gina Valdés.

# THE HANDS

CD II, Track # 1

## The Groove

Gina Valdez, an important Chicana poet, wrote "The Hands" to express the soul of Chicanos and Latinos living in the United States.

## The Music Culture

Gina Valdez is a Mexican-American poet whose images of Latin Americans are vivid depictions of their lives and values. In her *Comiendo Lumbre: Eating Fire*, "The Hands" is one of a collection of poems that offer diverse images of Latin Americans, their folkways, philosophies, and styles. She gets to the heart of Latino identity with visual and aural images in lines that speak to the activity of the hands as they "sing, dance, clap to the beat of corn on its way to becoming a tortilla," "peel bananas, masks, and mangos," "speak fluent Spanish," and "scub floors, plates, and lies." When Steven Loza, an ethnomusicologist and jazz musician, read the poem (and met the poet), he was impressed with the spirit and energy of Gina Valdez, and was inspired to set the poem to music: a rhythmic reading with cowbell and conga.

### The Experiences

- Listen to Track # 1, paying attention to the images of Latin American peoples, while tapping, clapping, or patting the steady beat of the cowbell.
- Listen to the recording again, and read the verse aloud.
- Play the introduction on cowbells and conga, as notated.
- Play the basic structure of the conga accompaniment as notated, or by finding a higher and lower pitched sound to play a steady rain of eighth notes.

- Practice reading the poem alone or with others in a "choral recitation." Divide the poem into verses for multiple readers to share, while others play the percussive accompaniment.

### Recommended Listening

+*Red Car Blues* (Steve Loza Sextet). Merrimack Records MR 10102.
*Rough Guide to Salsa de Puerto Rico.* World Music Network RGNET 1130 CD.
*La Salsa de Cuba.* Milan Records 35871.

# HASHEWIE

Eritrea

Traditional, Eritrea, new words and arrangement by Hidaat Ephrem. From Campbell, P. S., McCullough-Brabson, E., Tucker, J. C. (1994). *Roots & Branches: A Legacy of Multicultural Music for Children*. Danbury, CT: World Music Press. Courtesy World Music Press.

## The Tune

The songs of a community are often shared in full circle, as in the case of "Hashewie," an Eritrean song in celebration of membership in a group of friends and family members.

## The Music Culture

In the Cape Horn region of eastern Africa lies Eritrea, a small nation bordering the Red Sea that lies south of Egypt, east of Ethiopia, and north of Sudan. Eritrea was for many years an Italian colony (1889–1945), followed by forced occupation by Ethiopia in 1951, and then a war for independence from Ethiopia that resulted in its nationhood in

1993. Eritreans are Christian (predominantly Greek Orthodox) or Islam, and are comprised of nine language groups that include Tigrinya, Tigre, and Arabic.  While in the process of modernization, Eritrean homes are often two-room structures of stone with tin roofs, an outside kitchen, and a yard where children play. Eritrean children understand their world, and learn important cultural values, through songs, chants, and stories.  They need little encouragement to sing and to spontaneously create new songs, as music is integrated within their families and neighborhoods. Singing voices and clapping hands are the most popular instruments, while a five-string guitar called *kirar* and a two-headed drum called the *keboro* are played at weddings and other festive occasions at which everyone dances, from the youngest children to the elders. "Hashewie" is the song of Hidaat Ephrem, an Eritrean poet now living in Seattle, who remembers holding hands with her friends in the yard of her family home, circling and singing.

## The Experiences

- Sing the words of the solo and response parts in antiphonal fashion, back and forth between singers, while clapping.
- Follow this pronunciation: Hah-show-ee-ay  (Show-ee-ay)

   Bih-hah-deh-hah-beer-nah

   Hah-show-ee-ay-nah-behl-nah

   Ah-lem kit-fel-toe

   Koo-loo-meh-nin-et-nah

   Hah-show-ee-ay nih-bel

   Neh-fa-lit-ah-dih-nah

   Bih-hah-deh-hah-beer-nah

- Note the translation: "Going round, all together (round), Saying round (round), So the world will know (round), Who we are (round), Let's say (round), All together (round)."
- Sing the response in a triadic or "cluster" harmony.
- Play the chordal harmony on guitar or keyboard, with a bass note on "one" and the chord on "two."
- Standing in a circle, step the pulse in place while singing; then, use a traveling step while singing, moving to the right.

## Recommended Listening

+*Roots and Branches*.  Campbell/McCullough-Brabson/Tucker. Danbury, CT: World Music Press, 1994.

*Éthiopiques, Vol. 5: Tigrigna Music*. Buda Musique.

*Semai* (Abraham Afewerki).  Negarit 5421.

# HAVA NAGILA

Israel

*Let's be happy. Let's sing and be happy.*
*Rise up, brothers and sisters, with happy hearts.*

## The Tune

"Hava Nagila" is a popular song of celebration among Jewish people. It is performed at weddings, folk dance, and other festive gatherings.

## The Music Culture

The Hebrew words to "Hava Nagila" are a straightforward declaration of happiness, of rejoicing in song, and awakening in the joy of being alive. It is the best known of Jewish folk songs by those who are not Jewish, and is heard at various occasions in Jewish communities across the world. It is particularly known as dance music, and is played by various combinations of instruments that include violin, clarinet, accordion, keyboards, brass, electric guitars, synthesizers, and drum set. The Israeli *hora*, a circle dance imported from the Balkans, is an expression of happiness that is performed with grapevine steps.

## The Experiences

- Sing the song on a neutral syllable such as "lai," paying attention to accurate singing of intervals such as the augmented second (between $E^\flat$ and $F\sharp$).
- Sing the song with lyrics, noting these pronunciations: "gi" is "gee" (with a hard "g"), and "chim" is "khim" (with a somewhat guttural quality).
- Play the chords on piano or guitar with a two-beat , root-and-chord pattern (or a four-beat, root-chord-chord-chord) pattern. The faster the tempo, the more fitting is the two-beat pattern.
- Dance the *hora* in a circle, holding hands that are lifted up, with arms bent at the elbow. Use the signature grapevine steps and a lifting of each foot, as follows.

| Count: | 1 | 2 | 3 | 4 | 5 | 6 | 7 | 8 |
|---|---|---|---|---|---|---|---|---|
| Foot: | R | L | R | L | R | L | L | R |
| Movement: | step | in front | step | behind | step | lift | step | lift |

## Recommended Listening

+*Songs of Israel*. Monitor MON71364.

*Klezmer: Early Yiddish Instrumental Music 1908–1927*. Arhoolie Records 7034.

# HAVA NASHIRA

Israel

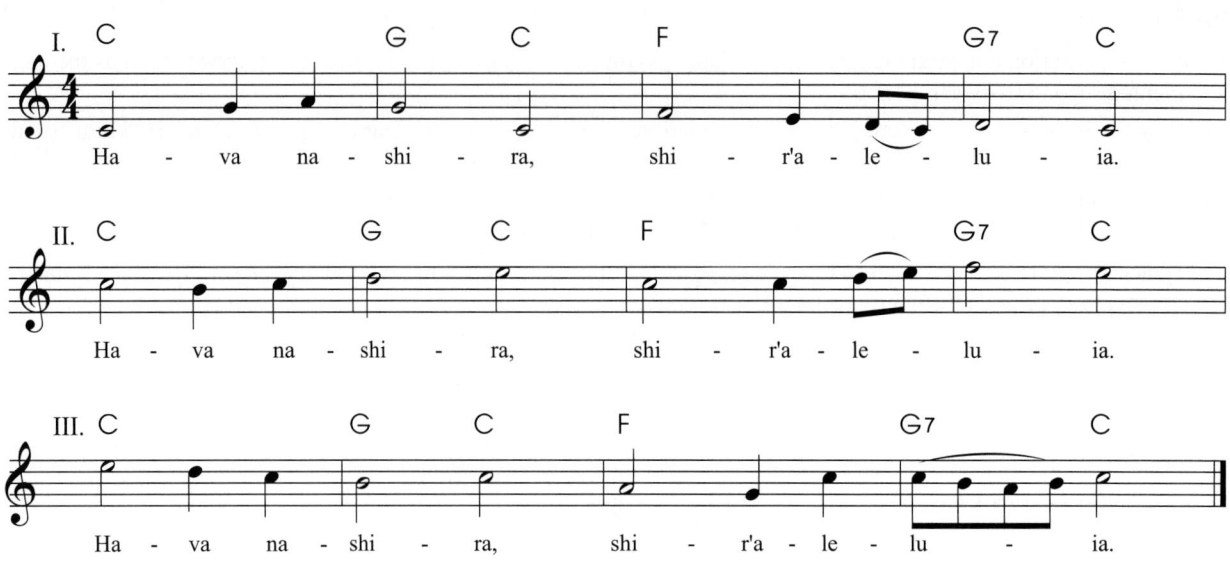

*Come, let us sing, Alleluia.*

## The Tune

A well-known song of Jewish communal celebration, "Hava Nashira" is sung in canon and is danced as well.

## The Music Culture

With the founding of the nation of Israel at the eastern end of the Mediterranean, many Jews from Europe, Russia, North Africa, and the Arabian Peninsula migrated to the area. They sought freedom from centuries of prejudice and harsh treatment, and saw the journey to Israel as a means of moving past the madness of the holocaust during World War II. They shaped a movement of national liberation known as Zionism that supported the establishment of a homeland for the Jewish people in the land of Israel, where the Jewish nation had originated over 3,200 years earlier. Along with focused attention to developing a governing body, commerce and industry, jobs, and education, they made time to celebrate their cultural identity and the communities they were developing through music and dance. Families, friends, and neighbors in cities and on *kibbutzim*, enclosed communities that lived and worked together, joined together regularly to sing folk songs and dance joyfully. "Hava Nashira" celebrates life and the community of people who make it meaningful.

## *The Experiences*

- Sing the melody on a neutral syllable such as "loo," and on solfège syllables or scale numbers.
- Sing the song with the lyrics, pronouncing "shi" as "she."
- Play the chords on guitar, strumming four beats per measure or using a down, down-up pattern
- Sing the song as a three-part canon, such that the second voice part begins as the first part is starting the second phrase, and so on.
- In a circle, hold hands and step a steady (quarter note) beat to the right, swinging the arms in and out on alternating beats. Drop hands between two people, such that one becomes the leader and the other the last member of a long line that spirals and "snakes" wherever the lead dancer will go. In the best of timing, the line can spiral inward, forming a tight coil as the song comes to closure, and as hands go up in a final triumphant "hurrah!"

## *Recommended Listening*

+*We've Got Some Singing To Do*. Folkways FW 02407.
*Songs of Israel*. Monitor MON71364.

## HAYDN: SYMPHONY NO. 47 IN G MAJOR, MINUET AND TRIO

Franz Josef Haydn

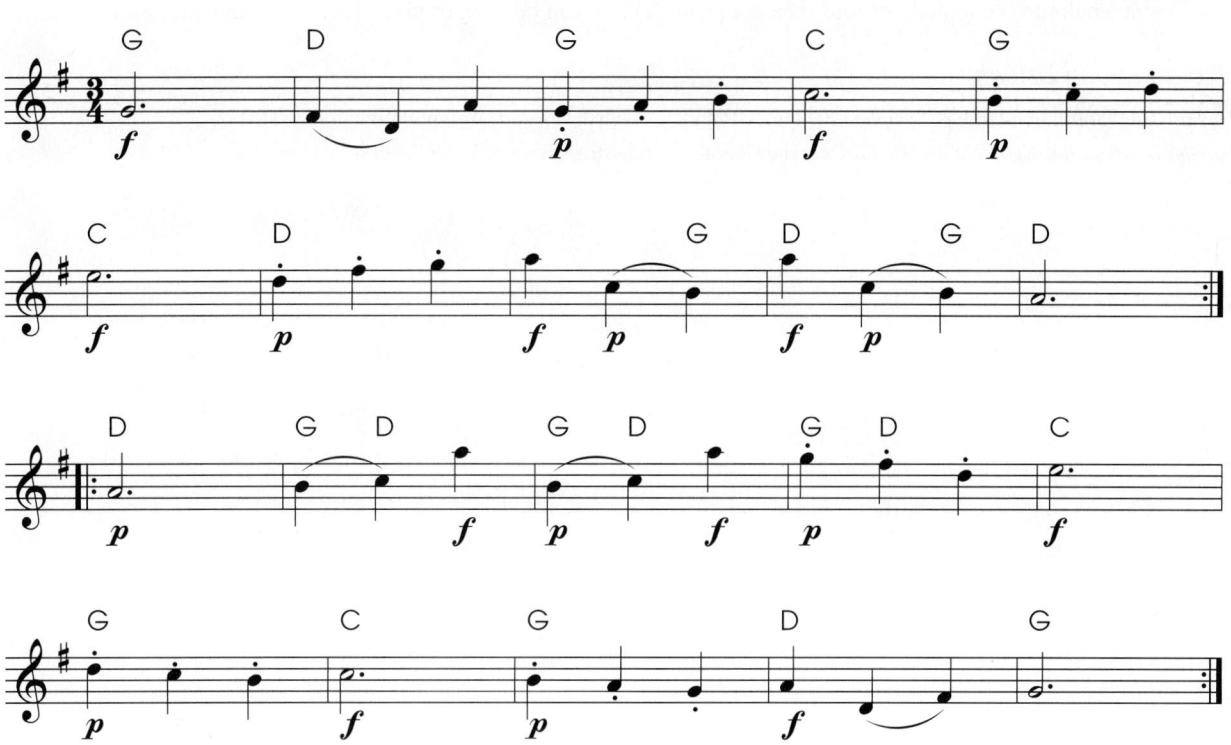

CD II, Track # 2

## The Tune

The Austrian composer Franz Josef Haydn playfully wrote this symphonic movement as a palindromic "al roverso," such that the second melody is an exact reverse of the first melody.

## The Music Culture

Franz Josef Haydn is often described as the "father" of the Classical symphony and string quartet. His music is characterized by short musical motifs that develop into full-fledged structures. He invented the string quartet, and his symphonies are the earliest written that still remain in the standard repertoire. He codified the formal organization of first-movement sonata form, and expanded the length and complexity of this form over the course of his lifetime. His compositional practice influenced both Mozart and Beethoven. He is known for his musical jokes, including the sudden loud *forte* chord in his "Surprise" symphony, No. 94, and the fake endings in his quartets (Op. 33, No. 2 and Op. 50, No. 3). In this Minuet and Trio, he creates a palindrome. The players read their music twice for ten bars, and then they read it twice backwards, arriving at the beginning. The placement of dynamic markings help one to recognize the music when it is played in reverse.

### The Experiences
- Listen to Track # 2, humming the melody's rise and fall, and following its dynamics and articulation and its reversal.
- Sing the melody on a neutral syllable such as "mah," and on solfège syllables or scale numbers. Perform with dynamics and articulation details.

- Play the melody on violin, flute, saxophone, trumpet, xylophone, and other melody instruments, carefully ensuring that the sudden dynamic changes and proper articulation are sounded.

- Play the chords on piano, once per measure or in an arpeggiated manner.

- Invent a palindrome melody of four measures (in 4/4) that can be sung or played forwards and backwards.

## Recommended Listening

+*Haydn: The "Sturm und Drang" Symphonies*. Trevor Pinnock, English Consort. Archiv Production 463731-2.

+*Haydn: Symphonies, Numbers 43, 46, 47*. Cologne Chamber Orchestra. Naxos 8.554767.

## HERE COMES SALLY

U. S.: African American

## The Tune

This children's song is a combination of two well-known melodies, "Here Comes Sally" and "Shortnin' Bread."

## The Music Culture

Like many of the songs that children sing, the two that intermingle here have a built-in redundancy in their lyrics, a relatively small melodic range, and a select set of pitches that are repeatedly used. The melody for "Here Comes Sally," with its even rhythm and pentatonic pitch set, is decidedly "straight" compared to that of "Shortnin' Bread." This second melody is rooted in African-American culture, with its bouncing and syncopated rhythms, the flat third degree of the scale, and the chromatic slide up from G through G♯ to A. (In fact, there are variants to these songs, too, such that the first melody has been heard with the flatted third degree and a fairly syncopated rhythm. ) "Shortnin' Bread" was an African-American plantation song that enjoyed a revival in the early days of radio. The phrase refers to the preparation of many southern quick breads, from banana to pumpkin, with butter, lard, and solid shortening.

## The Experiences

- Sing the melody on a neutral syllable such as "doo," and with solfège syllables or scale numbers.

- Sing the song with the lyrics, ensuring a spirited bounce on the dotted rhythms of the second melody.

- While singing, snap fingers on beats 1 and 3 and clap hands on beats 2 and 4. Variations on this include patting or stepping (stamping) on beats 1 and 3, while continuing the clapping on beats 2 and 4. Still another variation is a stamp-clap-snap-clap pattern:

| Beat: | 1 | 2 | 3 | 4 |
|---|---|---|---|---|
| Var. 1: | snap | clap | snap | clap |
| Var. 2: | stamp (or pat) | clap | stamp (or pat) | clap |
| Var. 3: | stamp | clap | snap | clap |

- Harmonize the melody on piano, using the designated chords, playing whole (or partial) chords on every beat.

- Form two lines, partners facing one another. In a simple contradance formation, the head couple moves together up and down the line in freestyle fashion, making their way to the bottom of the line in 12 measures. On "Mama's little baby," all partners step in and improvise a hand-clapping pattern. A new head couple moves down the line the second time around, and so on.

## Recommended Listening

*Smithsonian Folkways Children's Collection*. Smithsonian Folkways SFW 45043.

*Lady Bug, Lady Bug and More Children's Songs*. Folkways Records FW 0754.

# HINDEWHU

Congo: Mbuti

CD II, Track # 3

## The Tune

Some of the most striking music in sub-Saharan Africa results from the characteristic Mbuti technique of alternating a sung voice with the sound of a bamboo flute, as is heard in "Hindewhu."

## The Music Culture

The Mbuti are a group of indigenous hunter-gatherers living in the forested Congo region in the heart of Africa. Once called "Pygmies," this group prefers to be called Mbuti, which means "forest people" or "children of the forest." They live in small bands of fifteen to sixty people, in small, circular, temporary huts that each house a family unit. As the dry season arrives, they move out into the tropical rain forest to forage the foods it yields: crabs, shellfish, snails, fruits, roots, cola nuts, bananas, yams, and peanuts. They hunt animals for meat using bows and arrows, or large nets and traps. The music of the Mbuti is often wordless yodelling that results in disjunct melodies. Their communal singing is densely textured, with pentatonic melodies and harmonies in fourths, fifths, and occasional seconds. The music is primarily vocal, although there are solo instruments that are played at quiet times, including a three-stringed harp, a musical bow, and a three-hole bamboo flute that can be played in alternation with singing.

### The Experiences

- Listen to Track # 3, and follow the sound of the flute by tapping each time that it is played.
- Listen again to the recording, and follow the voice by tapping as it sings in between the sound of the flute.
- See the notation of the general layout of flute and vocal pitches, which is less an accurate rhythmic representation than a guide to pitches. Note that after an introductory phase, the flute settles into a periodic rhythm even as the voice continues to fluctuate rhythmically, depending upon the breath that is taken.
- Sing the four pitches of the sung melody: E ("i"), F♯ ("fu"), A (also "fu"), and one high E ("ya").
- Sing the melody on the syllables (noting that "i" is pronounced as "ee"), and tap every time the flute sounds.
- Experiment with the technique of singing and playing (only the high "D") on a flute, recorder, or other wind instrument.
- Create a musical piece that utilizes just three pitches, three syllables, and a recurring pitch (a high "D") on a wind instrument.

### Recommended Listening

+*Anthology of World Music: Africa, Ba-Benzele*. Rounder Select 5107.

*Mbuti Pygmies of the Ituri Rainforest*. Smithsonian Folkways SFW 40401.

## HOTARU KOI

Japan

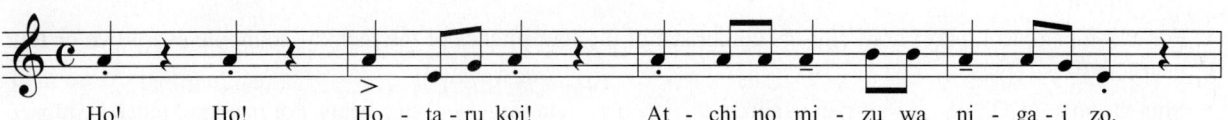

Ho!    Ho!    Ho - ta - ru koi!    At - chi no mi - zu wa ni - ga - i zo,

Kot - chi no mi - zu wa a - ma - i zo.    Ho!    Ho!    Ho - ta - ru koi!

*Come, firefly, come!*
*The water over there is bitter,*
*The water over here is sweet,*
*Come, firefly, come!*

## HOTARU KOI (DRONE)

## The Tune

The Japanese folk song "Hotaru Koi" pays tribute to the luminous firefly (or lightning bug) that lights up the summer nights.

## The Music Culture

Nearly 2,000 species of fireflies are known in the world, with about thirty species in Japan alone. They are small flying insects that light up and then go dark again, blinking away through the night. The Japanese have associated *hotaru* with the Chinese legend of a poor scholar who studied by the glow of fireflies, since he could not afford an oil lamp. As early as the eighth century, the *hotaru* became a poetic metaphor for passionate love. A Japanese folk belief is that the spirit of a living person or the ghost of the dead assumes the shape of a *hotaru*. During the Edo period (1603–1868), firefly-viewing was a popular summer pastime. "Hotaru Koi" has long been enjoyed as a canon by Japanese singers.

## The Experiences

- Sing the melody on a neutral syllable such as "ho" or "ha," and on solfège syllables (beginning on "la") or scale numbers (beginning on "6").

- Sing the melody with the lyrics, noting that the Japanese transliteration is straightforward, with "i" sounding as "ee" and "a" as "ah."

- For accompaniment, play chord clusters comprised of the four pitches of the melody, sounding every two or four beats.

- Sing the song in a three- or four-part canon, with new parts entering every two beats. For maximal musical impact, sing the song as a canon with a new voice (or group of voices) entering every beat.

## Recommended Listening

+*Mizuyo Koyima: Lullaby* [Japanese Children's Songs]. Pacific Moon PMR-0015.

*Traditional Folk Songs of Japan*. Folkways FW 03434.

# HOW CAN I KEEP FROM SINGING?

United States

*Verse:*

1. My life flows on in end-less song,___ A-bove earth's lam-en-ta-tion._____ I
2. Through all the tu-mult and the strife,___ I hear that mu-sic ring-ing._____ It

hear the real though far-off hymn___ That hails a new cre-a-tion.___
sounds and ech-oes in my soul,___ How can I keep from sing-ing?___

*Refrain:*

No storm can shake my in-most calm,___ While to that rock I'm cling-ing_____ Since

Love is Lord of__ heav-en and earth, How can I keep from sing-ing?_____

## The Tune

The sentiments of singing for the joy of it, and in celebration of life itself, are expressed in this traditional Anglo-American hymn, "How Can I Keep from Singing?"

## The Music Culture

In the Protestant churches of eighteenth-century America, the hymn emerged as a means of arousing the emotions of a religiously awakened congregation by words and by tune. (This period followed the singing of metrical psalms and the florid "fuguing tunes.") The invigorating hymns of the Methodists, the Baptists, and other Christian denominations were intended to bring people to their feet and to sing with all their hearts. By the nineteenth century, composed and traditional hymns were making their way into hymnbooks, so long as they were suitable theologically, aesthetically, and practically. Choir singing continued in some denominations, and for some services, but the benefits of having full congregational participation in singing outweighed the losses. Singing with gusto (if not entirely accurately and always in tune) was prized. Some of the hymns came from the folkways of the people at the pulpit—the ministers—or others active in the liturgical ritual, while other hymns initially intended for church alone went home with people and were sung in the fields, in nurseries, on porches and in parlors. "How Can I Keep from Singing?" is a folk hymn proudly "owned" and kept alive by the people—even though it was written by Robert Wadsworth Lowry in 1860.

### The Experiences

- Sing the melody on a neutral syllable such as "lee," and on solfège syllables (beginning on "sol") or scale numbers (beginning on "5").
- Sing two verses of the song's lyrics, heeding the syncopations and sustained pitches.

- Play the chordal accompaniment on piano, using an arpeggiated or broken-chord pattern. On guitar, strum in a down, down-up fashion, or fingerpick eighth notes for a fluid accompaniment.
- Explore the possibilities for vocal harmony, singing thirds and fifths of the designated chords.

## Recommended Listening

+*How Can I Keep from Singing?* (Olympia's Daughters). (Available from olympiasd@juno.com.)

+*Abide with Me* (David Phillips). Gentle Spirit Music. (Available from FAX 541-344-7508.)

## I WALK IN BEAUTY

Navajo

Words & music: Arlene Nofchissey Williams. From Burton, B. (1993). *Moving Within the Circle: Contemporary Native American Music and Dance*. Danbury, CT: World Music Press. Courtesy World Music Press.

## The Tune

The message of the Navajo song "I Walk in Beauty" is that a person is beautiful when he or she has peace within. This song is frequently heard at *powwows* that draw Native Americans from many different tribes and nations.

## The Music Culture

The songs of the Navajo are sung in an open and relaxed style that emphasizes the lower end of a vocal range. They are often pentatonic melodies, although 6- and 7-tone scales are also evident, with melodies typically proceeding stepwise. Vocables are mixed with Navajo or English-language lyrics, which often mention spirits, the land, and living in harmony with family and friends. The traditional composition method of the Navajo involves the creation of a song by an individual, a process of collective revision when the song is revealed to the group, and further adaption of the song to fit particular performance settings. Arlene Nofchissey Williams, a Navajo woman, is credited with having composed this song, which was first recorded at Brigham Young University in Utah, where many Native American students are enrolled for study.

### The Experiences

- Sing the melody of the song (the top pitch of the thirds) on a neutral syllable such as "nay," and on solfège syllables (starting on "sol") or scale numbers (starting on "5").

- Sing the song with the vocables and English-language text.
- Add the vocal harmony, one third lower than the pitches of the melody. Measure 7–15, are sung solo or in unison.
- Play the chords on piano or guitar, with full or partial chords sounding every beat.
- Add a rhythm ostinato on hand drum
- Add a rhythm ostinato on rattles:
- Play the melody on recorder or flute (especially a wooden flute).

## Recommended Listening

+*Stars in the Desert*. Soar Records 152.

*Navajo Songs*. Smithsonian Folkways SFW40403.

# I WENT TO CALIFORNIA

United States

I went to Cal - i - for - nia    far, far a - way;    I met a sen - or - i - ta    with

flow - ers in her hair, Oh! shake it, shake it, shake it,    shake it if you can,    and

if you can not shake it,    you do the best you can, Oh!    shake it to the bot - tom

shake it to the top    and turn a - round and turn a - round,    till you make a stop.

## The Tune

This familiar melody has been linked to the children's song, "I Went to California" and its many variants such as "I Went to Mississippi" and "Shake It, Baby, Shake It."

## The Music Culture

Hand-clapping songs hold a special appeal for children, especially for girls between the ages of six and nine years. The clapping, slapping, finger-snapping, and stamping that they do, facing one another, singing to each other, smiling and laughing, are a means of social interaction. For North American children, the songs typically fall with in a small pitch range, are felt with a duple (rather than triple) meter, and fluctuate harmonically between tonic and dominant. They are learned by children who watch and listen to other children, and then imitate what they have observed. There is a built-in evaluation system, too, such that the children who "mess up" the movements, the words, or the melody, may sometimes face severe criticism by the "experts" among them. Hand-clapping patterns range from a simple two-gesture movement of clapping one's own hands and then the hands of the partner to intricate patterns that include not only clapping up and down an imaginary column between the partners but also hand-shaking, finger-snapping, and brushing the backs of each other's hands. Some hand-clapping songs stay in the repertoire for generations, even while new songs are generated by children as a result of their live and mediated experiences.

### *The Experiences*

- Sing the melody on a neutral syllable such as "bah," and on solfège syllables (starting on "sol") or scale numbers (starting on "5").
- Sing the lyrics of the song, with careful attention to the ♩. ♪ rhythm.

- Play the chords on piano or guitar, one chord to a beat (even though it is common knowledge that such accompaniment is not necessary for children's singing games).
- Sing and perform the associated hand-clapping movement:

| Beat: | 1 | 2 | 3 | 4 | 5 | 6 | 7 | 8 |
|---|---|---|---|---|---|---|---|---|
| | Pat hands in lap | Clap own hands | Clap partner's right hand | Clap own hands | Clap partner's left hand | Clap own hands | Clap both of partner's hands | Clap own hands |

- Invent a more complex hand-clapping pattern that features hand-shaking, finger-snapping, and brushing the backs of the hands.

## Recommended Listening

*Skip Rope Games*. Smithsonian Folkways SFW07029.
*Children's Singing Games*. Saydisc CD-SDL338.

# IF ALL THE WORLD WERE PAPER

England

## The Tune

Even as some traditional songs express a sentiment or tell a story, others may pose riddles, as in the case of the English traditional song "If All the World Were Paper."

## The Music Culture

Traditional songs of England are performed today, thanks to those who have collected and disseminated them to children and adults alike, in schools, churches, and at seasonal gatherings and community events. Through efforts such as the collection of ballads by Francis James Child; the classification of folk songs by Cecil Sharp; and the public dissemination of traditional songs and pipe, flute, and fiddle tunes by John Langstaff in theatrical productions, songbooks, and recordings, the repertoire of the English people is preserved and transmitted. Langstaff himself (1920–2005) was the founder of the Christmas Revels, a project intended to develop an appreciation of English medieval (and more recent) traditional music and dance in theatrical pageantry. Morris dancing, mummers, bagpipers, guitar and dulcimer players, and large choruses of men, women, and children called "revelers" still perform English music during the Christmas season for audiences from Boston and New York to Tacoma—with lots of audience participation. So popular were the Christmas Revels that other seasonal and not-so-seasonal Revels productions were also created. Through live performances as well as through published collections of English (and Anglo-American) music such as *Sally Go Round the Moon*, folk songs like "If All the World Were Paper" can be brought out of the archives and to the attention of enthusiastic young singers.

### The Experiences

- Sing the melody of the song on a neutral syllable such as "pa," and on solfège syllables (beginning on "sol") or scale numbers (beginning on "5").
- Sing the song with the English-language text; at the end of the second time around, shout the answer to the riddle.
- Play the chords for the song on piano, guitar, autoharp, or dulcimer, sounding them twice per measure (or once every ♩. pulse). Play a chord cluster loudly at the end to give emphasis to the riddle's answer.
- Recall familiar riddles, or invent them, and creatively set them to verse and melody that can be sung and played. In the style of this "riddle song," keep the 6/8 meter and the C major diatonic scale.

## Recommended Listening

+*Old English Nursery Rhymes*. Saydisc CD-SDL 419.

*The Jackfish and More Songs for Singing Children* (John Langstaff). Revels Records CD 2201.

*The Wild Mountain Thyme* (John Langstaff). Revels Records CD 1094.

## IF YOU SEE MY SAVIOR

Thomas A. Dorsey

3. Oh, you'll have to make this journey on without me.

   Pay back the debt sooner or later, must be paid.

   You may see some old friends who may ask about me.

   Whoa, tell them I'll be coming home someday.

4. If you see the Savior, tell him that you saw me,

   When you saw me, I was on my way.

   You, when you reach that golden city, think about me.

   Don't forget to tell the Savior what I said.

CD II, Track # 4

## The Tune

Gospel composer Thomas A. Dorsey wrote "If You See My Savior" as a tribute to a friend he met in the hospital. Dorsey came out of the hospital and resumed his work, but his friend passed away.

## The Music Culture

Thomas A. Dorsey (1899–1993) is known as the "Father of Gospel Music," having cracked the combination of hymns of Christian praise with the style and rhythms of jazz and the blues. Some of his best known compositions are "Take My Hand, Precious Lord," as performed by Mahalia Jackson, and "There'll be Peace in the Valley," as performed by the Carter Family and, later, Johnny Cash. Dorsey published "If You See My Savior" in 1929, and it brought the house down at the National Baptist Convention in 1930. With this song and his establishment of the first gospel choir at the Ebenezer Baptist Church in Chicago, gospel music was on its way. Sweet Honey in the Rock was founded by Bernice Johnson Reagon in 1973 as an all-woman a cappella ensemble focused on singing the long-standing music of African Americans: spirituals, hymns, children's songs, freedom and justice songs, and gospel (as in this rendition of "If You See My Savior," retitled "I was Standing by the Bedside," with guitar by Toshi Reagon).

## The Experiences

- Listen to Track # 4 to the lead singer and the rhythmic harmony of the backup voices, and to the single guitar that reinforces the harmony. Tap, clap, or pat the steady rhythm of voices or guitar.

- Sing the melody on a neutral syllable such as "doo," and the solfège syllables (starting on "mi") or scale numbers (starting on "3").

- Sing the song with the lyrics, noting the many references to salvation.

- Play the chords on guitar in steady down strokes, or in a down, down-up motion in a ♩ ♫ rhythm.

- Listen to the recording, and attempt to sing the chordal changes of the backup voices in a "doo-doo wop" in a ♫ ♩ rhythm.

## Recommended Listening

+*Wade in the Water, Volume 3: Sweet Honey in the Rock*. Smithsonian Folkways SFW40074.
+*Precious Lord: The Great Gospel Songs of Thomas A. Dorsey*. Legacy 057164.
*Gospel Music*. Folkways Records FW 32426.
*Essential Mahalia Jackson*. Legacy 89067.

# IKOKOU

Gabon

CD II, Track # 5

## The Groove

A clapped rhythm, a soloist's calls, and a repeated choral response comprise this song of the Pounou people of southern Gabon.

## The Music Culture

On the West coast of the African continent lies Gabon, a nation-state whose people are of many linguistic and cultural groups. Despite their distinctions, the various cultural groups share a high regard for the place of music in their lives. The people of Gabon, like the people of other West African nations—Ghana, the Gambia, the Ivory Coast (Côte d'Ivoire), Liberia, and Benin—are drawn to expressing themselves musically as they pray and perform rituals, as they work and study, as they prepare for the hunt or for the meal they will share. Because Gabon is to Africa what Tibet is to Asia—the spiritual center of religious initiations—the sacred music of the Bwiti (whether attributed to the Mitsogo or the Fang peoples) is highly regarded and continues to attract much attention. There are drums, iron bells, shakers, and xylophones in Gabon, but sometimes voices and some body percussion are all that is necessary for making music. The Gabonese city of Libreville arose in the 1980s as a center for recording African popular music (at Studio Mademba), where it rivaled Johannesburg and Abidjan in the production of pan-African hits. "Ikokou" involves a continuous clapped rhythm and the sung phrase "Ngang Madouar Malumba." The song is sung by the Pounou while dancers are preparing for a performance in their community, donning their masks and applying their makeup.

### The Experiences

- Listen to Track # 5, and follow the clapped rhythm that continues even as the soloist's voice is heard quickly singing over it.
- With the recording, tap, clap, or pat the ostinato rhythm.
- With the recording, sing the response with this pronunciation: "Nahng ma-dwar ma-lum-bah."

### Recommended Listening

+*Lambarena: Bach to Africa.* Sony 64542.

*Music from an Equatorial Microcosm: Fang Bwiti Music from Gabon Republic, Africa.* Folkways FW 04214.

# IN THE PINES

U. S.: Appalachian Mountains

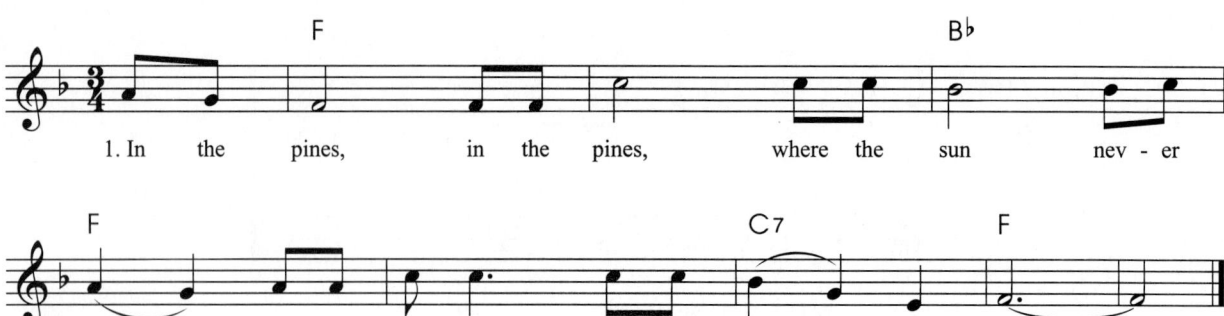

2. Oh, if I'd minded what grandma said,
   Oh, where would I been tonight?

3. I'd a been in the pines, where the sun never shine,
   And shivered when the cold wind blow.

4. The longest train I ever saw
   Went down the Georgia line.

5. The engine it stopped at a six-mile post,
   The cabin never left the town.

6. Now darling, now darling, don't tell me no lie,
   Where did you stay last night?

7. I stayed in the pines, where the sun never shine,
   And I shivered when the cold wind blow.

8. The prettiest little girl that I ever saw
   Went walking down the line.

9. Her hair it was of a curly type,
   Her cheeks was rosy red.

10. Now darling, now darling, don't tell no lie,
    Where did you stay last night?

11. The train run back one mile from town,
    And killed my girl, you know.

12. Her head was caught in the driver wheel,
    Her body I never could find.

13. Oh darling, oh darling, don't tell no lie,
    Where did you stay last night?

14. I stayed in the pines, where the sun never shine,
    And I shivered when the cold wind blow.

15. The best of friends is to part sometimes,
    And why not you and I?

16. Now darling, oh darling, don't tell no lie,
    Where did you stay last night?

17. I stayed in the pines, where the sun never shine,
    And I shivered when the cold wind blow.

18. Oh, transportation has brought me here,
    Take a money for to carry me away.

19. Oh darling, now darling, don't tell no lie,
    Where did you stay last night?

20. I stayed in the pines, where the sun never shine,
    And I shivered when the cold wind blow.

## The Tune

Variants occur in the melody, lyrics, and performance style of many folk songs. This version of "In the Pines" was popularized by *bluegrass* legend Bill Monroe.

## The Music Culture

Hundreds of variants of "In the Pines" have been found by folklorists and folk song collectors. They form a lyric folk song cluster, related by subject (the context of the lyrics), general melodic contour, and particular melodic or rhythmic patterns. They vary, too, sometimes even by name, as is the case with "In the Pines," which goes also by the names "The Longest Train" and "Black Girl." Bill Monroe and his Blue Grass Boys recorded "In the Pines" first in 1941 for RCA Victor, and later in 1952 for Decca. Sounding on mandolin, guitar, fiddle, stringed bass, and with a whining vocal line of hollowed-out harmonies of fourths and fifths, his version of "In the Pines" stands firm even today. Monroe's leading role in the evolution of bluegrass as a musical genre is further reason that his version is seen as a standard one.

## The Experiences

- Sing the melody on a neutral syllable such as "lah," and with solfège syllables (beginning on "mi") or scale numbers (beginning on "3").

- Sing the song with the lyrics, with attention to the slurs and the single dotted rhythm.

- Add a bluegrass harmony to the melody, aiming for the use of fourths and fiths on the sustained notes (on words like "pines," "sun," "shivered," "blow").

- Play the chords on guitar, autoharp, or dulcimer.

- Add a stringed bass for "bottom" and violin, banjo, or mandolin as harmony or during the interludes to give the song a bluegrass flair.

## Recommended Listening

+*Bill Monroe: Anthology*. MCA Nashville Album 4/22/2003.

*Hand-picked: 25 Years of Bluegrass on Rounder Records*. Rounder CD AN 22/23.

# JO'ASHILA

Navajo

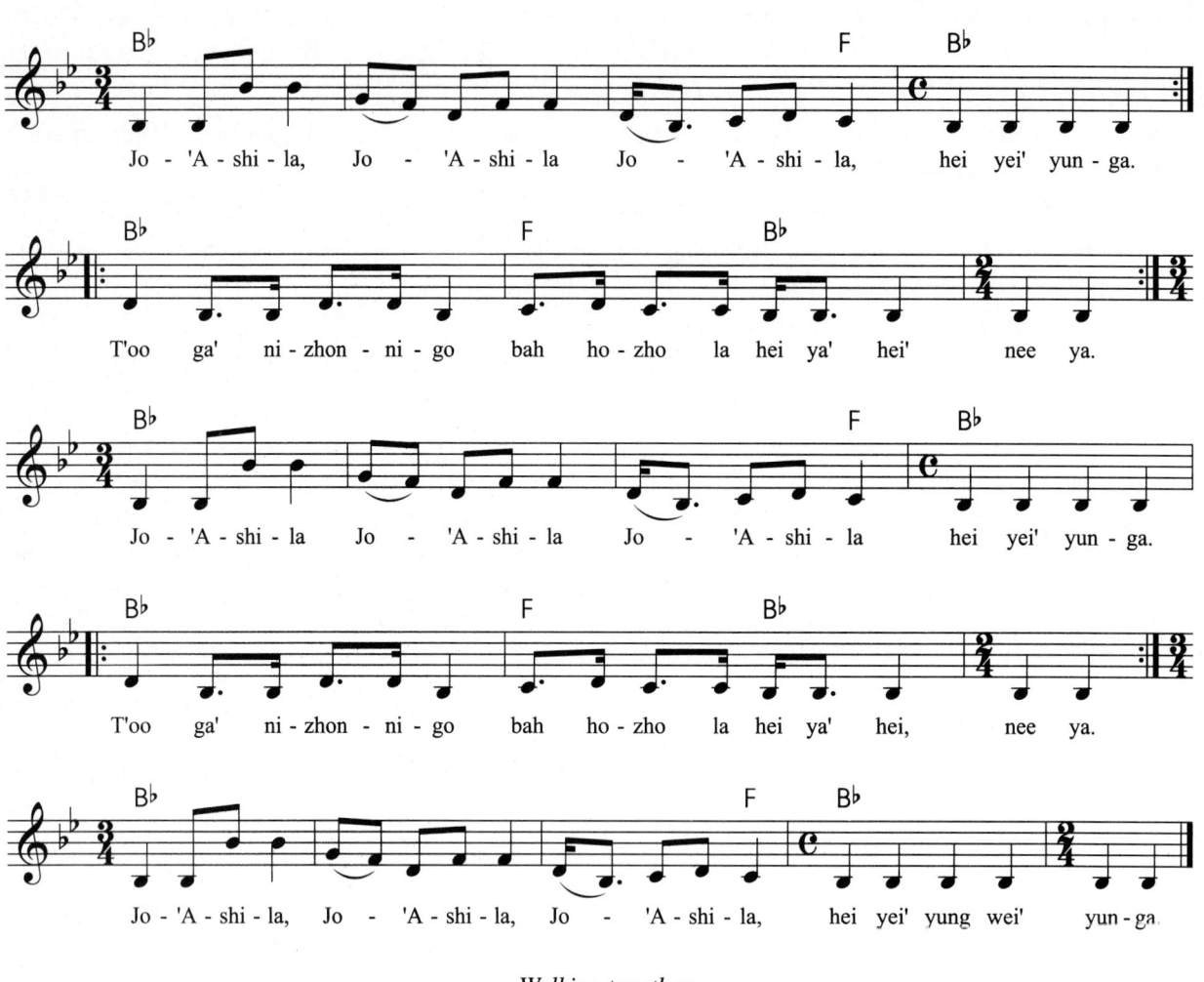

Jo - 'A - shi - la, Jo - 'A - shi - la Jo - 'A - shi - la, hei yei' yun - ga.

T'oo ga' ni - zhon - ni - go bah ho - zho la hei ya' hei' nee ya.

Jo - 'A - shi - la Jo - 'A - shi - la Jo - 'A - shi - la hei yei' yun - ga.

T'oo ga' ni - zhon - ni - go bah ho - zho la hei ya' hei, nee ya.

Jo - 'A - shi - la, Jo - 'A - shi - la, Jo - 'A - shi - la, hei yei' yung wei' yun - ga.

*Walking together,*
*Happy about beauty.*

Traditional, Navajo, as sung and arranged by Marilyn Hood. From Campbell, P. S., McCullough-Brabson, E., Tucker, J. C. (1994). *Roots & Branches: A Legacy of Multicultural Music for Children*. Danbury, CT: World Music Press. Courtesy World Music Press.

CD II, Track # 7

## The Tune

Expressed within the text of Jo'Ashila are the traditional Navajo values of support to family and community and a balanced and healthy life as something of beauty to experience and behold.

## The Music Culture

The Dinéh, or "the People," is how the Navajo refer to themselves. Theirs is the largest population of Native Americans within bounds of the United States, with a reservation that extends from northeastern Arizona to northwestern New Mexico and southwestern Utah. Some Navajo continue their traditional economy of farming, raising livestock (especially sheep), and the extraction of minerals, coal, gas, and sand, while others work in business and industry, and as teachers and artists. The traditions continue, including the society's matrilineal leaning, with the grandmother at the center of each clan and the mother as owner of livestock and crops. Ceremonies continue the essence of Navajo life, including those that feature chanting by shamans or medical practitioners—often with the sounds of rattles and a water drum—to restore health to the community or to individuals, to bless and pay tribute to individuals, and to honor life passages (such as the coming-of-age for young people and the passing of the elders). Traditional social songs like "Jo'Ashila" are sung to the accompaniment of a hand drum (played with a padded drumstick), and are danced in a two-step arrangement of couples who bounce lightly in a clockwise formation.

## The Experiences

- Listen to Track # 7, tapping the beat and following the melody's octave jump.
- Listen to the recording, humming along and singing only on the "Jo'Ashila" phrases.
- The Navajo lyrics are pronounced as follows:

  Jo-ah-shee-la (3x), hay yay yoon gah.

  Toh-oh gah nee-zhon-nee-goh

  Bah ho-zho lah hay yah hay nee yah.

- Dance these movements in a circle, with the women choosing their partners, forming a circle of couples facing clockwise (left) with the woman on the circle's inside. Men hold their right arms at chest level, and the women place their arms on top. The movement to the pulse shows a slight rhythmic bounce.
- Play the melody on flute, and add chordal accompaniment (block chords or broken chords) on keyboard or guitar.

## Recommended Listening

+*Roots and Branches*. Campbell, P. S.; McCullough-Brabson, E.; Tucker, J. C. Danbury, CT: World Music Press, 1994.

+*We'll Be in Your Mountains, We'll Be in Your Songs: A Navajo Woman Sings*. Marilyn Help and Ellen McCullough-Brabson. Albequerque: University of New Mexico Press.

# JOHN WAYNE'S TEETH

Sherman Alexie and Vaughn Eaglebear

John Wayne's tee - th, John Wayne's tee - th, are they plas - tic or are____ they steel?

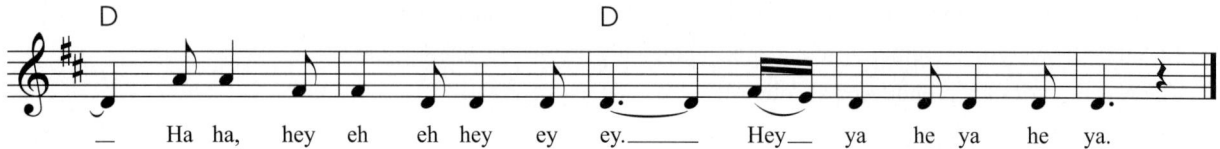

____ Ha ha, hey eh eh hey ey ey.____ Hey__ ya he ya he ya.

## The Tune

The combination of vocables and English-language lyrics is a fairly common characteristic of contemporary Native American music, and "John Wayne's Teeth" provides just that balance with a touch of humor as well.

## The Music Culture

Award-winning poet and novelist Sherman Alexie worked with the Eaglebear Singers to produce "John Wayne's Teeth" for the movie *Smoke Signals*. Alexie, who is part Spokane and part Coeur d'Alene Indian, grew up on the Spokane Indian Reservation in Washington, and later became the best-selling author of numerous books, including *Reservation Blues* and *Indian Killer*. He wrote the screenplay for *Smoke Signals*, coproduced the movie, and collaborated with a songwriter on four of the songs on the soundtrack. True to an important function of Native American music, the songs are an organic part of the film rather than an afterthought; they are a way of telling a story. Alexie's childhood and youth on the reservation, in the region of the Spokane and Columbia rivers, are the source for this film, and the books, short stories, and poetry he writes today.

### The Experiences

- Tap the beat and following the contour of the melody with its vocables and English lyrics.
- Hum the melody while noticing the prominence of the tonic triad.
- Sing the melody on a neutral syllable such as "hey," and on solfège syllables (beginning on "sol") or scale numbers (beginning on "5").
- Play a steady pulse on a hand drum while singing the song with vocables and lyrics.
- Play a guitar accompaniment to the melody. Although the recording of this song does not feature guitar, the instrument has become fairly standard in contemporary Native American songs (as evidenced by other songs on the film's soundtrack).

### Recommended Listening

+*Smoke Signals*. Miramax TVT (USA) 8260.
*A Native American Odyssey*. Putumayo PUTU 144-2.

# JOHNNY HAS GONE FOR A SOLDIER

United States

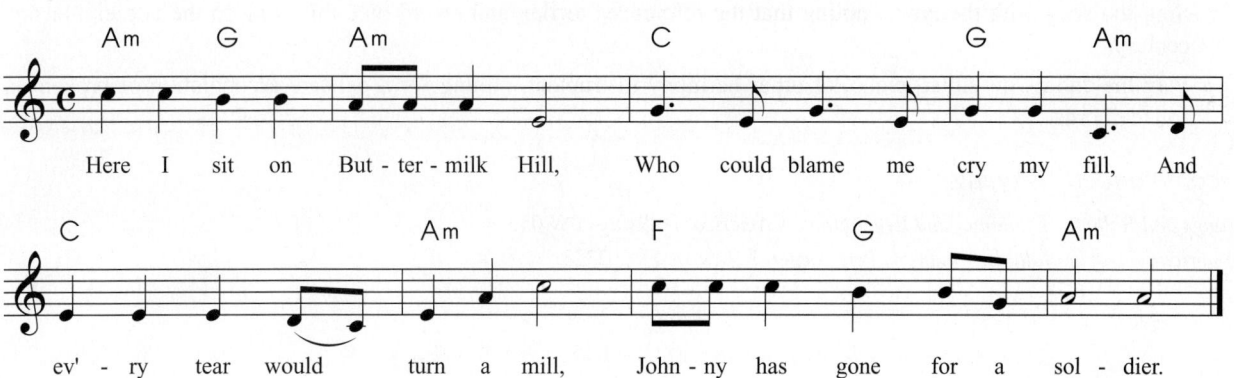

Here I sit on But - ter - milk Hill, Who could blame me cry my fill, And ev' - ry tear would turn a mill, John - ny has gone for a sol - dier.

2. Me, oh my, I loved him so,
   Broke my heart to see him go
   And only time will heal my woe,
   Johnny has gone for a solider.

3. I'll sell my flax, I'll sell my wheel,
   To my love a sword of steel,
   So it in battle he may wield,
   Johnny has gone for a soldier.

4. Here I sit on Buttermilk Hill,
   Who could blame me cry my fill,
   And ev'ry tear would turn a mill,
   Johnny has gone for a solider.
   (reprise of verse 1)

## The Tune

One of lyrical songs of the American Revolution, "Johnny Has Gone for a Soldier" tells of the sorrows of helplessly watching a loved one go to war.

## The Music Culture

Songs of war are plentiful, and they not just the stuff of battle cries and military might. There is the tender side of war that has inspired romantic songs that tell of the departure of a friend or lover, songs of yearning, and songs of sacrifice. "Johnny Has Gone for a Soldier" and "The Cruel War" are exemplars of romantic songs, both a far stretch from spirited war songs like "When Johnny Comes Marching Home" and "Battle Hymn of the Republic." Based on an old Irish tune entitled "Shule Aroon" and sometimes referred to as "Buttermilk Hill," "Johnny Has Gone for a Soldier" paints the picture of a girl during the period of the American Revolution who waits longingly at home for her lover who is off to war. The song is hauntingly beautiful, an expression of the grief that is felt by people in every war when friends, families, and lovers are split apart.

## The Experiences

- Sing the song on a neutral syllable such as "lah," and on solfège syllables (beginning on "do") or scale numbers (beginning on "3").

- Sing the song with the lyrics, noting that the references to flax and sword date this song to the late eighteenth century.

- Play the chords on guitar, piano, or other harmony instrument, aiming for a delicate arpeggiation of broken or rolled chords.

## Recommended Listening

+*Songs and Ballads of Colonial and Revolutionary America*. Folkways FW 05274.

+*American Favorite Ballads, Volume 4: Pete Seeger*. Folkways FW 02323.

# JOSHUA FOUGHT THE BATTLE OF JERICHO

U. S.: African American

## The Tune

African-American spirituals often reference events and figures in the Bible. "Joshua Fought the Battle of Jericho" tells the story of the leader of the Israelite tribes whose campaigns helped to move them across the Jordan River so that their mobile community might finally settle down.

## The Music Culture

The Bible is the source and inspiration of many African-American spirituals. "Joshua Fought [or Fit] the Battle of Jericho" is just one of the Biblical spirituals, alongside "Didn't My Lord Deliver Daniel?," "Blow your Trumpet, Gabriel," "Swing Low, Sweet Chariot," and "Roll Jordan Roll." In historical accounts, Joshua succeeded Moses in leading the Jews into the land of Canaan and distributing its territories to the twelve tribes of Israel. In what was a gradual process of infiltration and acculturation, Joshua moved the Israelites ever westward into Canaan, and they increasingly became a force to be reckoned with, within the spaces between the walled cities of that region. Jericho was one of these walled cities of the Canaanites which, rather than by a single calculated plan of conquest in which "the walls came tumbling down," was more gradually negotiated and eventually opened to the Israelites. While there are also white spirituals that feature stories from the Bible, the music of black spirituals is defined by syncopation, microtonally flatted notes, counter-rhythms marked by hand clapping, and cries of "Glory," "Hallelujah," and other words of affirmation.

## The Experiences

- Sing the melody on a neutral syllable such as "tah," and with solfège syllables or scale numbers.
- Draw attention to the syncopation by tapping the melodic rhythm with one hand while tapping the steady beat with the other.
- Sing the song with the lyrics, with keen attention to the syncopation of the dotted eighth and sixteenth note figures.
- Play the chords on piano, guitar, or other harmony instrument, sounding the full chord or parts of it every beat (for example, alternating the root tone with the third and fifth tones).

## Recommended Listening

+*I Sing Because I'm Happy: Mahalia Jackson.* Smithsonian Folkways SFW 90002.

+*Wade in the Water, Volume 1: African-American Spirituals: The Concert Tradition* (Fisk Jubilee Singers). Smithsonian Folkways SFW 40072.

# JUANATIA

Ecuador

Jua - na - ti - a - ta ta - push - pa,   ah,  Tu - tay   pun - ya - mi  pu - ri -

ni,   ah,   Jua - na - ti - a - ta  ta - push - pa,   ah, - Tu - tay   pun - ya - mi  pu - ri -

ni.   Can - baj   tu - nu - ta  ya - rish - pa   ah,   Tu - cuy   pun - ya - mi  lla - qui -

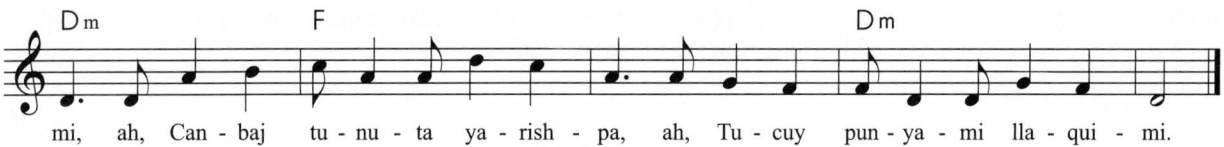

mi,  ah,  Can - baj   tu - nu - ta  ya - rish - pa,   ah,  Tu - cuy   pun - ya - mi  lla - qui - mi.

*"Looking for Miss Juana,*
*I'm walking night and day,*
*Remembering your sweet singing,*
*I weep night and day,*
*Night and day I remember.*
*But when Mr. Mariano arrived,*
*He told me all about it:*
*That woman with her six children was abandoned.*
*That's why I'm crying,*
*That's why I remember."*

## The Tune

In the high Andes mountains of Ecuador, "Juanatia" is performed by singers alongside wooden-flute players, guitarists, violinists, and bomba drummers.

## The Music Culture

The indigenous population of Andean Indians spills across the national boundaries of Ecuador, Peru, Bolivia, Argentina, and Chile, with some living in the high elevations of Columbia and Venezuela as well. Their ancestors hail from the Incan Empire, which the Spanish encountered on their arrival to the west coast of South America in the early sixteenth century. Andean Indians up and down the west coast constitute a somewhat united musical culture, but with regional variations. The languages spoken are Aymara, Quechua, and Quichua (in Ecuador), and the instruments include panpipes (sicu or zampoña), end-blown notched flutes (quena), lutes made of armadillo shells (charango), drums (bomba), guitars, and violins. The musicians play for dancing (and dance as they play) and for the pleasure of their listeners on plazas, in restaurants, and at festivals. "Juanatia" is a favorite of musicians in Ecuador, and nearly every band in the high market town of Otavalo (about two hours north of the Quito) includes it in their repertoire. The song tells of a woman with six children who was sadly left to raise them alone.

## The Experiences

- Sing the melody on a neutral syllable such as "lah," and on solfège syllables (beginning on "la" in la-based minor) or scale numbers (beginning on "6").
- Tap, clap, or pat the rhythm of the melody while singing, and then only the pattern: ♪ ♩ ♪
- Sing the melody with words:

  > Wahn-nah-tee-ah-tah  tah-poosh-pah
  > Too-tay poon-yah-mee poo-ree-nee (repeat lines 1 and 2)
  > Cahn bye too-noo-tah yah-rish-pah
  > Too-coo-ee poon-yah-mee yah-kee-mee (repeat lines 3 and 4)

- Play the melody on flute or violin, or other melody instruments.
- Accompany the singing and playing with chords on guitar, using a pattern of down and down-up strokes in this rhythm: ♩ ♫
- Gather singers and players in a circle, and step to the pulse in place, randomly turning one way and then the other. A small shuffling step to the left is also a typical movement for the music.

## Recommended Listening

*+Bolivia Manta—Tinkuna*. A.S.P.I.C. X 55511.

*Music of the Andes*. Hemisphere 7243 8 28190 2 8.

# JUBILEE

U. S.: Anglo-American

Verse:

All out on the old rail - road, All out on the sea;

All out on the old rail - road, Far as eye can see.

Refrain:

Swing an' turn, Ju - bi - lee! Live an' learn, Ju - bi - lee!

2. Hardest work I've ever done.
   Workin' on the farm.
   Easiest work I've ever done.
   Swinging my true love's arm!
   (Refrain)

3. If I had a needle and thread,
   Fine as I could sew,
   Sew my true love to my side,
   And down this creek I'd go!
   (Refrain)

4. If I had no horse to ride,
   I'd be found a-crawlin'
   Up and down this rocky road,
   Lookin' for my darlin'.
   (Refrain)

5. All out on the old railroad,
   All out on the sea;
   All out on the old railroad,
   Far as eye can see.
   (Refrain)

# JUBILEE

## The Tune

A *jubilee* is both a gathering for purposes of celebration, and an energetic song that celebrates life, love, peace, and all good works, as in the case of this "Jubilee" of considerable exuberance.

## The Music Culture

As a genre of song, the jubilee is a spiritual that was once monophonic and a cappella, and an antecedent of the blues; it was a term used by African Americans to refer to spirituals, even as whites often called them *slave songs*. Mention "jubilee" in a conversation on music, and thoughts turn towards the African-American choral group, the Fisk Jubilee Singers, who organized in 1872 at Fisk University in Nashville, Tennessee, to sing mostly four-part arrangements of spirituals. They were former slaves singing the songs they had first learned in enslavement, establishing the black spiritual in the history of American music through the many concert tours they made to Europe and across the United States. Jubilee quartets were also developed in the first half of the twentieth century at Fisk University and other historically black schools—Hampton Institute, Tuskegee Institute, Wilberforce University—and then in black churches, too, to further spread the Negro spirituals and later, gospel standards. Still, the jubilee has crossed racial boundaries, such that white Southerners took it upon themselves to sing and play spirited spiritual melodies in church and outside of it, on guitars, banjos, and fiddles in an "old-time" barn-dance way. The "Jubilee" featured here appears to be Anglo American in style, based upon the major-key melody, the straight-ahead duple meter, and the language ("my true love," "darlin'").

### The Experiences

- Sing the melody on a neutral syllable such as "see," and on solfège syllables (beginning on "mi") or scale numbers (beginning on "3").
- Sing the melody with lyrics, noting the nineteenth-century rural images of the railroad, sewing with needle and thread, "no horse to ride," and traveling down the "creek."
- Play the chords on guitar, autoharp, or dulcimer, strumming once, twice, or even four times per beat; the faster the strum, the more the impression of motion as called for by the phrase, "swinging my true love's arm."
- For the more rural Anglo-American sound, add string bass, violin, and banjo.
- In a contradance formation of one line facing the other, with partners standing directly opposite one another, move to these basic dance steps:

> Measures 1–2: Step four counts inward, towards partner.
>
> Measures 3–4: Step four counts out, away from partner.
>
> Measures 5–8: Repeat.
>
> Measures 9–10: Link elbow to partner's elbow and swing four counts to the right.
>
> Measures 11–12: Swing four counts to the left.
>
> Repeat measures 9–12.

### Recommended Listening

+*This Little Light of Mine*. Folkways FW 03552.

*Afro-American Spirituals, Work Songs & Ballads*. Rounder Select 1510.

# JUMP IN THE FIRE

U. S.: African American

He's a li - ar jump in the fi - re. Fi - re so hot, he jump in the pot, he

jump in the pot. The pot so cold, he jump in the hole. The hole so nar - row, he

jump in the bar - rel. The bar - rel so high, he jump in the sky. The sky so blue, he start like new.

## The Groove

The lyrics to children's chants are made of images both real and imagined, as in the case of "Jump in the Fire."

## The Music Culture

Children's chants are frequently voiced with remarkably sophisticated rhythm that include a steady pulse, a constant meter, and syncopation. Their spoken words are elongated or squashed into durations that precisely fit the meter. Their voices can hold a constant monotone as they motor through the verse like automatons, or can show fluctuations of pitch that denote passion when they are excited. The oral lore of children as expressed in their chants and songs are seldom without movement, and "Jump in the Fire" is no exception. It is intended by African-American children to be clapped by partners who face one another, find their rhythms, chant together, and clap hands with the precision of moving together like cogs in a wheel. The lyrics tell the story of an unnamed but confused character in rhyming words like "fire" and "liar," and "high" and "sky."

### The Experiences

- Tap, clap, or pat the rhythms of the chant.
- Rhythmically chant the words while tapping, clapping, or patting.
- Play the rhythms on sticks or other percussion instruments, chanting the words and then silencing them.
- Accompany the chant with a hand-clapping pattern with a partner.

| Beat: | 1 | 2 | 3 | 4 |
|---|---|---|---|---|
| Move: | Pat hands on lap | Clap own hands | Clap partner's hands | Clap own hands |

• In a more sophisticated hand-clapping pattern, add to the first four gestures these next gestures, for an eight-beat pattern altogether.

| Beat: | 5 | 6 | 7 | 8 |
|---|---|---|---|---|
| | Brush hands together (in prayer form) to partner's left side | Brush hands together (in prayer form) to partner's right side | With right hand, shake partner's right hand | With left hand, snap fingers in the air |

## Recommended Listening

*Skip Rope Games.* Smithsonian Folkways SFW 07029.

*Children's Singing Games.* Saydisc CD-SDL 338.

# KALINKA

Russia

*Under the pine tree, under the green tree,*

*Lay me down to sleep. Ailiuli, liuli . . .*

*Kalinka, Kalinka, Kalinka of mine,*

*In the garden grows a raspberry tree.*

Traditional, Russia, as sung and arranged by Beth Cohen. From Campbell, P. S., McCullough-Brabson, E., Tucker, J. C. (1994). *Roots & Branches: A Legacy of Multicultural Music for Children*. Danbury, CT: World Music Press. Courtesy World Music Press.

# KALINKA

## The Tune

In Russia, "Kalinka" is a green bush with puffy white "snowball" flowers and bitter berries; it is also a girl's name.

## The Music Culture

Russian folk music is as diverse as the people with whom Russia has had long historical ties. There are many dialects and various kinds of folklore coming from the surrounding peoples, many who also live within Russia's boundaries, including the Slavonic, Finno-Urgric, and Turkish peoples. Thus, regional musical traditions continue instrumentally and in the use of various languages and dialects, even as national characteristics of Russian folk song are also notable: songs in minor key, rhythmic patterns linked to the verse, and polychoral textures that may include a static, dronelike part. The traditional performance style features strong voices that project well, which may arise from the rustic practice Slavic farmworkers share of singing outdoors in the fields. There is a Russian folk repertoire of songs for work, the seasons and the holidays (winter, New Year, Shrovetide, St. George's Day, summer solstice), weddings, lullabies, and laments. Russia's unique folk instrument is the *balalaika*, a triangular three-stringed instrument, played alone to accompany singing or in instrumental groups to reflect the collective and communal nature of music that is close to the Russian heart. "Kalinka" is known by Russians at home and now living abroad, and is more likely to be performed on guitar and piano than on *balalaika*, although the melody and language remain intact.

### The Experiences

- Sing the song on a neutral syllable such as "loo," and on solfège syllables (beginning on "mi") or scale numbers (beginning on "3").
- Sing the song with Russian lyrics, noting the following pronunciations: *iu* is "yu," *zhi* is "zhee," *vy* is "vee," *ai* is "ay," *ia* is "ya,", and *ty* is "tee."
- Play the chords on guitar or piano, elongating the strum or rolling an arpeggiation of the chords for the verse section. At the chorus section, begin slowly in an "oom-chink" bass-and-chord pattern that gradually increases in speed.
- Add tambourine at the chorus, playing a "tap-shake" pattern throughout.

### Recommended Listening

+*Roots and Branches.* (Campbell, P. S.; McCullough-Brabson, E.; Tucker, J. C.). Danbury, CT: World Music Press.
+*Kalinka: Balalaika Ensemble "Wolga."* Arc Music EUCD 1499.

# KARAW
## (OSTINATO)

Ali Farka Touré

## The Groove

The "Bluesman of Africa," Mali's Ali Farka Touré, plays a guitar style in works like "Karaw" that not only reflects his attraction to the American blues tradition but also has done much to set a generation of Malian musicians on course to continuing the exchange of ideas between Mali and the West.

## The Music Culture

The largest contingent of contemporary African musicians signed to record labels in the United States are from Mali. A vast, dry, landlocked nation in the interior of West Africa, Mali is a crossroads of traditional and modern music. One reason may be that some of the American music listened to today, including folk, blues, jazz, and rock styles, have roots in Mali going back to the time of the slave trade. Thus Malians like Ali Farka Touré, Toumani Diabate, Oumou Sangare, and the Super Rail Band sound both "African" and vaguely Western. Malian musicians today blur the distinction between traditional and modern, and their experimentation with guitar is uniquely oriented towards blues (even as blues may have evolved from Malian traditional music). Mali is also still the land of the *griot*—singer, instrumentalist, and storyteller all wrapped into one—and a place of remarkable melodic music on the 21-stringed *kora* harp and the wooden *balafon* (xylophone). In brilliant fashion, Ali Farka Touré and others perform Malian musical themes and instrumental techniques on the electric guitar to create a hypnotic and dynamic music that stands between (and extends across) the cultures.

### The Experiences

- Tap the ♩♩♩ triplet rhythm of the sticks, accenting the first of every three sounds.
- Hum the principal ostinato figure.
- Play the ostinato figure on a guitar, xylophone, piano, or other melody instrument.
- Improvise on another melody instrument while continuing the ostinato figure.

### Recommended Listening

+*Ali Farka Touré: The Source*. Hannibal #1375.
*Ali Farka Touré*. Mango Records 9826.
*Mali Lolo! Stars of Mali*. Smithsonian Folkways SFW 40508.

# KEEP YOUR HAND ON THAT PLOW

U. S.: African American

2. Ain't but one chain a man can stand,
   That's the chain of a hand in hand.
   Hold on . . .

3. Freedom's name is mighty sweet,
   Black and white are gonna meet.
   Hold on . . .

4. Ain't but one thing we did wrong,
   Was staying in the wilderness too long. . . .
   Hold on . . .

5. Only one thing that we did right
   Was to organize and fight. . . .
   Hold on . . .

## The Tune

"Keep Your Hand on That Plow" is a classic African-American spiritual. With very few modifications to the original text, the song is now loaded with meaning for people of all ages and walks of life.

## The Music Culture

A popular rendition of an older spiritual arose from one whose original text was in keeping with the times of its first appearance in the nineteenth century: "Got my hand on the gospel plow, Wouldn't take nothin' for my journey now, Keep your hand on the plow, hold on." Alice Wine of South Carolina is credited with adding a new power-packed line in 1965, "Keep your eyes on the prize." The context of a rural farm was immediately shed for an image that would evoke a message that could work for anyone, in any setting. For adults working with youths in African-American communities, the line became a slogan to challenge and also encourage them to believe that no sights could be set too high, and no accomplishment was beyond the reach of those who gave focus to "the prize": education, a good job, and strong, positive contributions to society.

### The Experiences

- Sing the song on a neutral syllable such as "mah," and on solfège syllables (beginning on "la") or scale numbers (beginning on "6").
- Sing the song with lyrics, noting references to Biblical figures, oppression, and the call for freedom through organization and struggle. Heed the long durations of some of the notes (and words).
- Play the chords on piano or guitar, giving accent to beats two and four.
- Sing the melody of the first two lines in unison, and offer a vocal harmony to the last two lines (beginning with "hold on"), selecting the chord tones for the sustained notes.
- While singing, move from side to side, shifting the weight from one foot to the other, and clapping on beats two and four.

| Count: | 1 | 2 | 3 | 4 |
|---|---|---|---|---|
| Chords: | bass (or rest) | chord | bass (or rest) | chord |

### Recommended Listening

+*Sing for Freedom* (Cordell Reagon, Charles Jones). Smithsonian Folkways SFW 40032.

+*Freedom Voices: WNEW's Story of Selma* (Pete Seeger). Folkways FW 05595.

+*Bruce Springsteen: We Shall Overcome. The Seeger Sessions*. Columbia 82876.

# KHAANG KHAAW KIN KLUAY

Thailand

Traditional, Thailand, arranged by Pornprapit Phoasavadi.  From Phoasavadi, P. & Campbell, P. S. (2003). *From Bangkok and Beyond: Thai Children's Songs, Games and Customs*. Danbury, CT: World Music Press.  Courtesy World Music Press.

CD II, Track # 8

## The Tune

The crocodile zither, called *ca-khee*, is a revered instrument of the Thai people, capable of virtuosic performances of pieces such as "Khaang Khaaw Kin Kluay" (Bats Eating Bananas).

## The Music Culture

Thai music is "group music" that features ensembles of xylophones, gongs, zithers, fiddles, flutes, and oboes in various combinations. Yet a number of instruments have also risen to solo status, including the *ca-khee*, a three stringed zither with eleven high frets. The strings are played with a two-inch ivory plectrum that is tied to the right index finger with a silk cord. The *ca-khee* is shaped like a crocodile, and variations of this crocodile zither are found in Burma (*mi gyaung*) and the Phillipines (*krajappi*). The performance technique requires that the right hand strums with the plectrum while the left hand stops the strings on the frets. The *ca-khee* is prominent in the performance of Thai court music in *mahoorii* and *khrüng saai* ensembles, but it is also a soloistic instrument. The popular piece "Khaang Khaaw Kin Kluay" is the final and fast section of a longer composition that functions as an exercise to build up the performer's muscle strength and memory. It is played not only on *ca-khee* (with the hand cymbals called *ching*) but also on various jazz, popular, and rock instruments by Thai musicians.

### The Experiences

- Listen to Track # 8, and follow the steady pulse of the bell-like ching by tapping along. Clap on the bright sound ("ching") and pat the back of one hand into the palm of the other on the more muted sound ("chop").
- Sing the melody on a neutral syllable such as "nee," and on solfège syllables (beginning on "la") or scale numbers (beginning on "6").
- Listen to the recording, and follow the rise and fall of the melody by singing along.
- Play the melody on guitar, xylophone, violin—all instruments whose timbres are familiar to Thai people.
- Add the ching part by tapping a bell in alternating ringing and dampened timbres, saying "ching" (bright) and "chop" (dampened) while playing. Compare with the recording.

### Recommended Listening

+*From Bangkok and Beyond* (Phaosavadi, P. and Campbell, P. S.). Danbury, CT: World Music Press.
*Music of Thailand*. Folkways FW 04463.

# KHMER CHANGKEH REAV

Cambodia

Traditional, Cambodia, Arranged by Sam-Ang Sam. From Sam, S. A. & Campbell, P. S. (1991). *Silent Temples, Songful Hearts: Traditional Music of Cambodia*. Danbury, CT: World Music Press. Courtesy World Music Press.

# KHMER CHANGKEH REAV

CD II, Track # 9

## The Tune

For centuries, the *mohori* ensemble of Cambodia was the court ensemble that played for the entertainment of the king and queen and their guests. "Khmer Changkeh Reav" (Slim-Waisted Khmer) features the wooden xylophone and circular bronze gongs.

## The Music Culture

In Cambodia, the *roneat* (a wooden xylophone of 16 or 21 keys) historically played lead melody in the court music ensembles at Phnomm Penh. The *korng tauch* and *korng thomm* are high- and low-pitched embossed gongs, each of the 16 or 21 gongs resting horizontally in a circular wood frame. They play simultaneous variations of the *roneat* melody in the ensembles of the court in what is linearly organized music that allows embellishment according to the idiosyncratic makeup of each instrument. All three pitched percussion instruments use padded mallets wrapped in cloth or yarn to soften the sound on the wood keys and bronze gongs. Along with flute, several stringed instruments and a battery of percussion instruments (including the bell-like bronze hand cymbals called *chhing*) comprise the *mohori* ensemble that is played for the court dance, shadow-puppet plays, and masked dramas that were always so highly valued by the Khmer of Cambodia.

### The Experiences

- Listen to Track # 9, and follow the steady pulse of the bell-like *chhing* by tapping along. Clap on the bright sound ("ching") while patting the back of the hand into the palm of the other on the more muted sound ("chop").

- Listen to the recording, and hum the principal pitches of the basic melody on beats 1 and 3 of the *roneat* xylophone (top) part; note that the pitches of the gongs coincide on these beats, too.

- Sing the principal pitches of the basic melody on a neutral syllable such as "bah," and on solfège syllables (beginning on "la") or scale numbers (beginning on "6").

- Play the principal pitches of the basic melody for two beats each on xylophone, or other melody instrument. A possible stopping point is the first note of measure 9, or proceed to the end.

- When the principal pitches are learned, experiment with the possibility of improvising between them. The musical "rules" of classical Khmer music of Cambodia are (a) to maintain the pentatonic melody, and (b) to play the principal pitches of beats 1 and 3.

- Add the *chhing* part on beats 1 and 3.

### Recommended Listening

+*Silent Temples, Songful Hearts: Traditional Music of Cambodia* (Sam, S. A. and Campbell, P. S.). Danbury, CT: World Music Press.
*Mohori: Khmer Music from Cambodia* (Sam-Ang Sam Ensemble). Latitudes LAT 50609.

# KNEEBONE

Bessie Jones and the Georgia Sea Island Singers

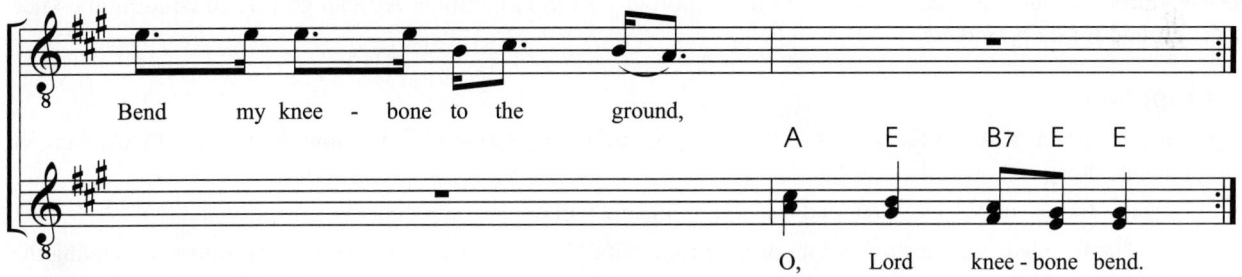

2. Kneebone didn't I tell you,
   Ah, kneebone,
   Kneebone didn't I tell you,
   O Lord, kneebone bend.

3. Kneebone, didn't I call you,
   Ah, kneebone,
   Kneebone didn't I call you,
   O Lord, kneebone bend.

4. I call you in the mornin',
   Ah, kneebone,
   Call you in the evenin',
   O Lord, kneebone bend.

5. Bend my kneebone to the ground,
   Ah, kneebone,
   Bend my kneebone to the ground,
   O Lord, kneebone bend.

6. Kneebone, Zachariah,
   Oh, kneebone,
   Kneebone, Zachariah,
   O Lord, kneebone bend.

7. Kneebone, didn't I call you,
   Oh, kneebone,
   Kneebone didn't I call you,
   O Lord, kneebone bend.

# KNEEBONE

CD II, Track # 10

## The Tune

Bessie Jones and the Georgia Sea Island Singers made it their mission to preserve "Kneebone" and countless other folk songs and spirituals of the Gullah people.

## The Music Culture

The Gullah culture is preserved on plantations and in the towns of the Georgia Sea Islands off the coast of Georgia, South Carolina, and Florida. The residents are African Americans directly descended from slaves who were brought in the 1700s from the "Rice Coast" region of West Africa at the border of Liberia and Sierra Leone. During the American Civil War, when the Union navy occupied the islands, the white southerners fled to the mainland, leaving the blacks there to run their own lives, freed from the bondage of their masters. Isolated from the mainland, the Gullah have preserved African influences in their language, religion, storytelling, cuisine, and music. Alan Lomax met Gullah singers as early as the 1930s, and returned in the 1960s to record them. Among others of the Georgia Sea Island Singers he recorded, Bessie Jones emerged as a leader with a passion to "teach the chillun" their heritage through song. "Kneebone" refers to the importance of the traditional African gesture of bending the knee to the ground for daily prayers.

### The Experiences

*   Listen to Track # 10 for the sounds of the solo call and group response, and follow the ostinato by clapping or tapping along.
*   Sing the chorus in two- and three-part harmony, with and without the recording.
*   Sing the melody of the solo voice solo or in unison, with lyrics that pertain to the prayer position of bending the kneebone to the ground.
*   Play chords on piano or guitar for the chorus part, interspersing this response with the a cappella solo.
*   Listen to the recording, and clap one of several clapping ostinati. Then, add the singing atop the clapping.
*   Sing the solo and response, adding harmony instrument and clapping.

### Recommended Listening

+*Bessie Jones et al.: Georgia Sea Island Songs*. New World Records 80278.
+*Slave Shout Songs from the Coast of Georgia* (McIntosh County Shouters). Folkways FW 04344.

# KOMMT EIN VOGEL

Austria

Kommt ein Vo - gel ge - flo - gen, setzt sich nie - der auf mein

Fuss, hat's ein Brif - chen im Schna - bel, von der Mut - ter ei - nen

Gruss. Lie - ber Vo - gel, fling wei - ter, bring ein Gruss mit ei - nen

Kuss, denn ich kann dich nicht be - glei - ten, weil ich hier blei - den muss.

*A bird flies to me and lights on my foot.*
*He has a letter in his beak, and greetings from my mother.*
*Dear little bird, fly and take a greeting and a kiss.*
*I cannot go with you now, for I must stay here.*

## The Tune

This Austrian song about a gentle bird who visits as a messenger is a reminder of the "close to home" content of the first songs in the lives of young children, where animals, family, and playthings are principal topics of interest to them.

## The Music Culture

Austrians who live in Vienna, Innsbruck, Salzburg, and numerous alpine and lowland towns and villages continue to perform "their music." Be it Mozart's music (not only in his hometown of Salzburg but throughout the country), *The Sound of Music* (the true story in the form of musical theater of a musical family in Salzburg), or folk traditions like the *jodler* (yodel) and the *landler* (a dance in triple time), the experiences begin early and live long as the Austrians perform and participate in music making, and patronize others who do so as well. Austrian folk music is frequently set in triple meter, and features triadic and stepwise melodies in major keys. The rich mountainous region of the Tyrol is a repository even today of *jodlers*, and *landlers* that are played on fiddles, button-box accordions, stringed bass, and the increasingly rare wooden-keyed xylophones. Folk song singing continues in the homes, in schools, and in the restaurants and beer gardens.

## The Experiences

- Sing the melody on a neutral syllable such as "lee," and on solfège syllables (beginning on "mi") or scale numbers (beginning on "3").

- Sing the song with German lyrics, with attention to this pronunciation:

  Kohmt ine foh-gle geh-floh-gehn,

  Zetst zik nee-der auf mine foos,

  Hahts ine brif-ken im shnah-ble,

  Fohn der moo-ter ine-nen groos.

  Lee-ber foh-gle fling vi-ter,

  Brink ine groos mit ine-nen koos,

  Den ik kahn dik nisht beh-gli-ten,

  Vile ik heer bli-ben moos.

- Play the chords on guitar, autoharp, accordion, piano, or xylophones, giving accent and/or playing the chord root on the first beat and the higher chord notes as lighter sound on beats two and three.

| Count: | 1 | 2 | 3 |
|---|---|---|---|
| Chords: | root (or bass) | chord | chord |

- Add a "pat-clap-click" body percussion rhythm to accompany the singing.

## Recommended Listening

+*Traditional Songs of Singing Cultures* (Campbell, P. S.; Williamson S.; Perron P.). Miami: Warner Bros.

+*Children's Folk Songs of Germany*. Folkways FW 07742.

# KUM BACHUR ATZEL

Israel

*Get up, lazy boy, and get to work.*

*Kukuriku kukuriku, the rooster is calling.*

"Kum Bachur Atzel" gr. 3 from MAKING MUSIC. Copyright © 2005 by Pearson Education, Inc. Reprinted by permission.

## The Tune

The Hebrew lyrics for the Israeli song "Kum Bachur Atzel" are literally a rooster's wake-up call ("kukuriku") to rise and commence work.

## The Music Culture

Jewish folk songs from Israel are sung in Hebrew, the country's national language and one of the oldest in the world. They were once sung unaccompanied, or with a tambourine or hand drum for rhythmic interest. In the Zionist movement of the late 1940s and 50s, guitars were played to add harmonic support to folk melodies. Today, anything goes, such that violins, brass, winds, and fully electric instruments of rock and popular genres may also come into play in creating new renditions of old music. The klezmer traditions of Eastern Europe have become widespread in Jewish communities throughout Europe and in North America, and have made their way to Israel, too. Beyond the repertoire specific to weddings and certain Holy Days, klezmer style has been applied to much of the older folk song repertoire. Where a song about a rooster has never been a part of the klezmer tradition, Jewish folk songs appear in a range of styles that defy a single characterization or a single acceptable sound ideal.

### *The Experiences*

- Sing the melody on a neutral syllable such as "da," and on solfège syllables or scale numbers.
- Sing the lyrics for the song, which are pronounced as follows:

  Koom ba-kur at-zel, vuh-tzay la-a-vo-da.

  Koo-koo-ree-koo, koo-koo-ree-koo, tar in-gol ka-ra.

- Play the chords on guitar, piano, or other harmony instrument.
- Add a stringed bass for an oom-pah bass line.
- Experiment with the use of clarinet, violin, trumpet, and trombone to play the melody (or the third above or below it) in klezmer style.

### *Recommended Listening*

+*Shiron L'gan*. Transcontinental 950013.

*You Should Be So Lucky* (Maxwell Street Klezmer Band). Shenachie 67006.

*The Klezmorim: First Recordings 1976–78*. Arhoolie CD 309.

# KWAHERI

Kenya

Kwa - he - ri, kwa - he - ri, m-pen-zi kwa - he - ri, kwa - he - ri

tu - ta-o-na-na te - na tu - ki - ja - ri - wa.

*Goodbye, dear friend.*
*We will meet again if God wille.*

From *Fire Within*, Libana, 1990. Arrangement by Susan Robbins and Libana. www.libana.com.

## The Tune

Music making is an integral part of life for the people of Kenya. The farewell song, "Kwaheri," is often sung spontaneously at the end of a party.

## The Music Culture

Situated in East Africa, Kenya was one of a number of countries on the continent that was formed by the British into a single colony with numerous territories of people and cultures. In addition to many groups of indigenous people, there are also descendents of Arab, Indian, and European settlers living there today. Music and music making in Kenya reflect this diversity, with many instruments and styles heard in the neighborhoods of Nairobi and across the nation's towns and villages. As Western instruments such as trumpets, flutes, guitars, accordions, and saxophones were introduced to Kenya during European colonization, local instruments ranging from rattles and drums to lyres, flutes, and horns were the target of nationally sponsored preservation programs. Yet as some of the local and international styles vie for the attention of Kenyans today, vocal music in multipart forms continues on. Singing—whether in the widely recognized Swahili national language or in a more local dialect—is seen as something every every citizen can do—and does do, with considerable frequency.

### The Experiences

- Sing the melody on a neutral syllable such as "too," and with solfège syllables or scale numbers.
- Sing the lyrics, noting this pronunciation:

  Kwah-heh-ree, kwah-heh-ree, im-pen-zee kwah-heh-ree.

  Too-ta-oh-na-na tay-nah too-kee-jah-reewah.

- Play the chords on piano or guitar, following the rhythm of the melody.
- Experiment with singing multipart harmony above and below the melody, using the designated chords as guide to harmony parts.
- Step and clap a basic rhythm:

| left | right | clap |
|------|-------|------|
| foot | foot | (hold) |
| step | step | (hold) |

## Recommended Listening

*Luo Roots: Musical Currents from Western Kenya*. GlobeStyle CDORBD 061.
*Missa Luba: An African Mass: Kenyan Folk Melodies*. Phillips 426 836-2.
*Rough Guide to the Music of Kenya*. World Music Network RGNET 1137 CD.
*Music from the Nonesuch Explorer Series: Africa*. Nonesuch 79793-2.

# KWA-NU-TE

Mic Mac

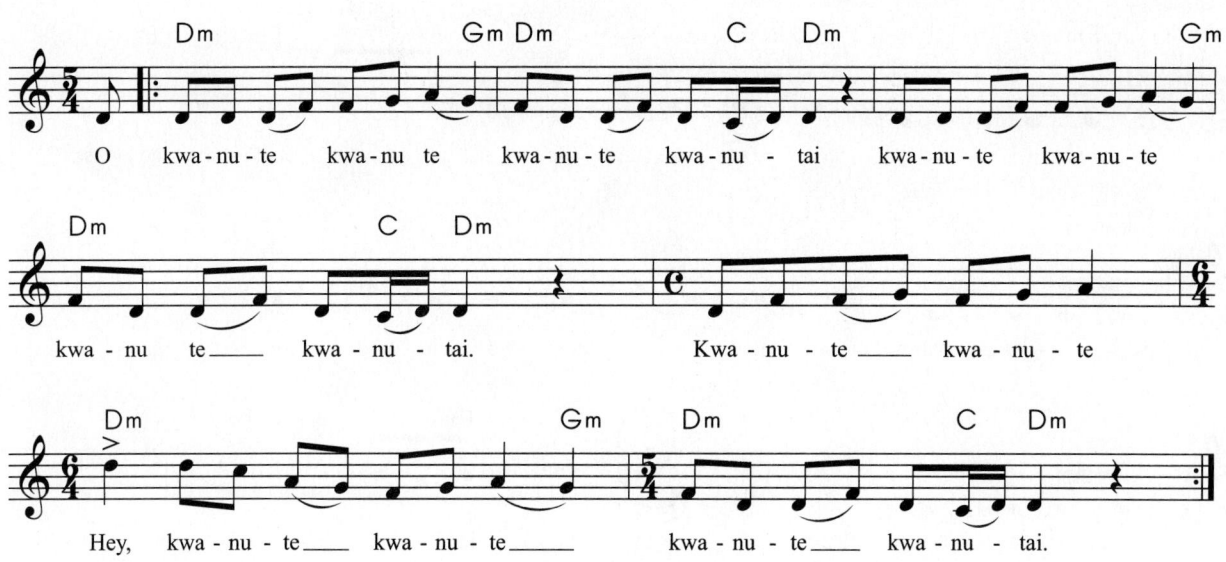

Traditional, Mic Mac, as sung to Bryan Burton. From Burton, B. (1998). *Voices of the Wind: Native American Flute Songs for Recorder.* Danbury, CT: World Music Press. Courtesy World Music Press.

## The Tune

A gathering song of the Mic Mac Indians of Nova Scotia, "Kwa-Nu-Te" calls people together for prayer, community announcements, presentations, and speeches.

## The Music Culture

The Mic Mac (also known as M'ikmaq) are a First Nations people living in bands in Maine, the Gaspé Peninsula of Quebec, and Canada's Maritime Provinces of New Brunswick, Nova Scotia, and Prince Edward Island. There about 40,000 Mic Mac in all, about a third of whom still speak the Algonquin Micmaq language, and use its system of hieroglyphic writing. Many more speak English or French. They embrace Christianity while holding to some of the traditional rituals, ceremonies, and music and dance that define them as a people. The word "wigwam" comes from the Micmaq to refer to a dwelling of five spruce poles, a hoop of moosewood to brace the poles, and birchbark sheets laid over the poles like shingles. In their river country, on lakes, and even far out to sea, the Mic Mac traveled in wide-bottomed canoes, and fashioned sleds for land travel in the winter. They still entertain each other with storytelling, and often integrate the stories with songs and dances. "Kwa-Nu-Te" is a Mic Mac gathering song, or a song used as grand entrance music to initiate a communal event.

### The Experiences

- Sing the song on "noo," and on solfège syllables (beginning on "la") or scale numbers (beginning on "6").
- Sing the lyrics, with attention to the pronunciation of "te" as "tay" and "tai" as "tie."
- Play the chords on guitar or piano, sounding one chord to a beat.
- Add a drum to play even eighth notes across the length of the song.
- Holding hands in a circle formation and facing into the circle, perform a simple shuffle step at quarter-note speed that proceeds left while stepping low to the ground in a left-right rhythm.

### Recommended Listening

+*Voices of the Wind* (B. Burton). Danbury, CT: World Music Press.

*Creation's Journey: Native American Music.* Smithsonian Folkways SFW 40410.

# K'WEJINA CH'ING CH'ING

Korea

*(Musical notation: Fm — "K'we-ji-na ch'ing ch'ing na-ne, — no-se no-se chol-mo no-se")*

*(Musical notation: Fm ... Eb — "K'we-ji-na ch'ing ch'ing na-ne, — nulg-o chi-myon mot-no-na-ni")*

*(Musical notation: Fm ... Eb Fm Eb — "K'we-ji-na ch'ing ch'ing na-ne, — u-ju-ui sam-na-man sang,")*

*(Musical notation: Fm ... Eb Fm — "K'we-ji-na ch'ing ch'ing na-ne, — hyong-hyong sek sek")*

*(Musical notation: Fm Eb Fm — "gak gak-i-yo, K'we-ji-na ch'ing ch'ing na-ne.—")*

*Hear the sound of the gong ringing.*
*Play while we are still young and healthy.*
*Hear the sound of the gong ringing.*
*As we grow up, time is precious.*
*Hear the sound of the gong ringing.*
*All living things on the earth,*
*Hear the sound of the gong ringing.*
*Each one different, special too.*
*Hear the sound of the gong ringing.*

## The Tune

One of the characteristic instruments in East Asian ensembles is a flat gong. "K'wejina Ch'ing Ch'ing" is a Korean harvest song that celebrates the sound of the gong whether it is played alone, in a percussion ensemble, or in a full-sized orchestra of strings, winds, and percussion.

## The Music Culture

In Korean *nong-ak*, or farmer's music, a small ensemble of eight musicians play various types of drums, gongs, woodblocks, and bells. To these outdoor instruments is sometimes added a conical oboe. Meanwhile, the ensemble also includes eight dancers performing on hand-held drums and eight actors who play the parts of various characters in Korean folklore. At the celebrated Korean holiday of *Ch'usok*, known as Mid-Autumn or Thanksgiving Festival, traditional work songs are performed by the *nong-ak* ensemble to commemorate the harvest workers who prepare for the festival as well as for the cold weather of the winter ahead. A transformation of *nong-ak* came with the development of high-energy music known as *samulnori*, from the Korean words *sa* and *mul* (meaning four objects or instruments) and *nori* (meaning play). Even in this contemporary ensemble, the flat gong rings out loudly and clearly at *Ch'usok*, for other festivals, in parades, and on concert stages throughout the world that have been venues for helping to popularize this Korean music.

### The Experiences

- Sing the melody on a neutral syllable such as "jee," and on solfège syllables (beginning on "la") or scale numbers (beginning on "6").
- Sing the constant response, "K'wejina ch'ing chi'ing nane" (pronounced "kewh-jee-na ching ching nah-nay") while singing the remainder of the melody on a neutral syllable.
- Sing the lines of verse between the response phrase, remembering that *e* sounds as "ay," *i* sounds as "ee," and *u* sounds as "oo."
- While harmony is not present in traditional Korean music, contemporary renditions of folk songs do utilize guitars and keyboards. With this in mind, play the chords on piano or guitar, twice per measure.
- While singing, pat and clap ♩., one pat and one clap per measure.
- Play a two-measure rhythmic ostinato on percussion instruments.

### Recommended Listening

*Arirang: Korean Song and Dance Ensemble*. Monitor MON00430.
*Korea: Vocal and Instrumental Music*. Folkways FW 04325.

## KYE KYE KULE

Ghana

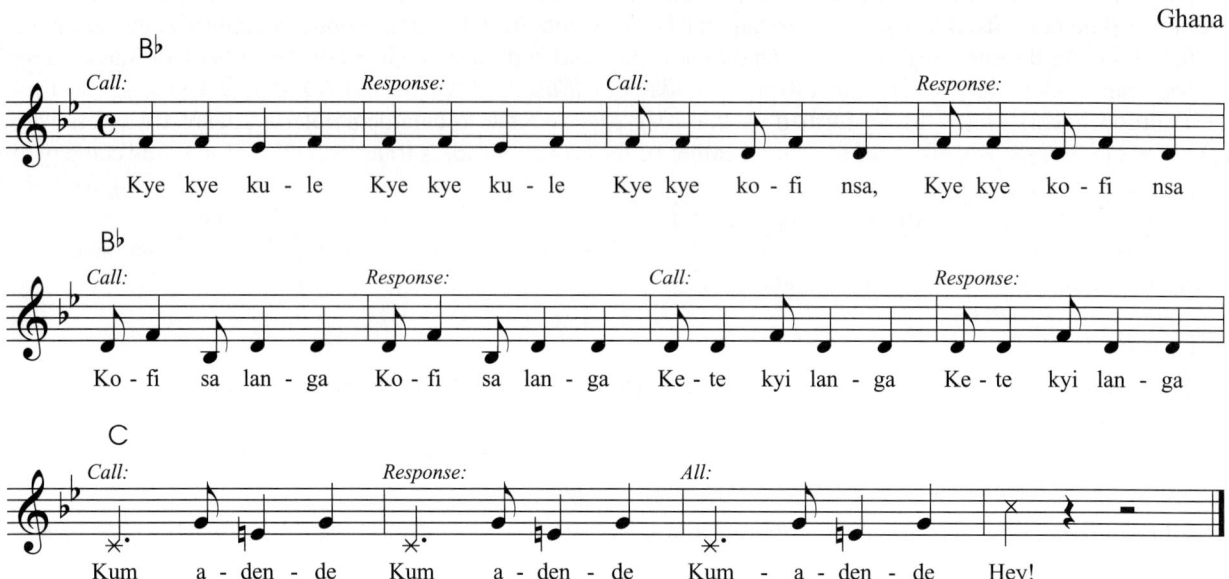

Traditional, Ghana, as sung by Abraham Zobena Adenyah. From Adzenya, A. K., Maraire, D., & Tucker, J. C. (1997). *Let Your Voice Be Heard: Songs from Ghana and Zimbabwe* (Rev. Ed.). Danbury, CT: World Music Press. Courtesy World Music Press.

### The Tune

Although the "words" of this children's singing game are not translatable, the song remains popular among Akan and other children in Ghana.

### The Music Culture

Singing games are standard fare for children everywhere in the world. Be they of specific types such as counting, jump-roping, hand-clapping, or ball-bouncing, they engage children to not only sing or chant but also to "do." The songs may feature ostinati rhythms that accompany the song or chant, or cross-rhythms in which what is clapped or jumped is not the same but complements what is sung. In some of these playful children's songs, an acceleration of the pulse challenges children to sing ever faster as the song progresses or is repeated. In Ghana and throughout sub-Saharan Africa, children's singing games often utilize call-and-response singing in two parts. In "Kye Kye Kule," there is a built-in follow-the-leader function of the call-and-response technique.

### *The Experiences*

- Sing the melody on neutral syllable such as "chay," and on solfège syllables (starting on "sol") or scale numbers (starting on "5").
- Sing the lyrics, noting these pronunciations:

  Chay chay koo-lay

  Chay chay ko-fee sah

  Ko-fee sah lan-gah

  Kay-tay kee lan-gah

  Koom ah-den-day (Hey!)

- While singing a cappella is typical for all children's songs, their melodies and harmonies can also be played as "a different rendition" on piano, guitar, or other harmony instrument. Arrange this song for any instrument of choice.
- Play the singing game: (1) tap the head four times, (2) tap the shoulders four times (while twisting the torso one way and then the other), (3) tap hands on the waist four times (while twisting the torso one way and then the other), (4) pat the knees four times, and (5) tap the toes on the floor four times, (6) jump up and throw arms up in the air like a cheer.

## Recommended Listening

+*Children's Songs for Games from Africa* (Kojo Fosu/Edwina Hunter). Folkways FW 77855.
*African Songs and Rhythms for Children*. W. K. Amoaku. Smithsonian Folkways SFW 45011.

# LA BAMBA

Ritchie Valens

*Let's dance with the music!*
*To dance the bamba,*
*One must have a bit of grace,*
*A little grace for me and you,*
*Higher and higher,*
*You and I shall be.*
*I'm not a sailor, but a captain.*

# LA BAMBA

CD II, Track # 11 and # 12

## The Tune

A well-known Mexican folk song, "La Bamba," became widely known when Ritchie Valens popularized it with his rock band in the late 1950s.

## The Music Culture

Richard Valenzuela grew up in Los Angeles hearing the traditional music of Mexico even as a new style of music called rock and roll was emerging. He was playing in a band and making recordings while he was still in high school. In 1958, he turned a traditional Mexican song, "La Bamba," into a rock-and-roll hit, becoming the first star to come out of California's Mexican-American community. (He also became known by his anglicized stage name, Ritchie Valens.) The song is one of the most performed Spanish-language songs, by singer-guitarists and rock bands as well as by traditional *jarocha* musicians on *arpa* (harp), guitar, and two smaller guitars known as *requinto* (a four-stringed guitar), and *jarana* (an eight-stringed guitar). Of the traditional *son jarocho* style of which "La Bamba" is an example, it can be said the strophic form of the song, with multiple verses, invites improvisation of the singers and instrumentalists over the underlying rhythmic and harmonic framework. While the more traditional form of "La Bamba" hails from the state of Veracruz in the eastern part of Mexico, it is Ritchie Valens's version that is best known.

## *The Experiences*

- Listen to Track # 11 and Track # 12 to the two renditions. Identify the instrumentation of the former (harp, four-stringed bass, *jarana*, and *requinto*), and the latter (guitars, bass guitar, drum set, woodblock).
- Listen to Track # 12, and tap, clap, or pat the rhythmic ostinato on woodblock: ♩ ♩ ♫ ♩
- Sing the melody on a neutral syllable such as "bah," and on solfège syllables (beginning on "fa") or scale numbers (beginning on "4").
- Sing the lyrics, following Track # 12 as the rendition closest to the notation, and for help on pronunciation. Remember to flip the *r*s (or double *rr*s, as in "arriba").
- Play the chords on guitar, using Track # 12 as a guide.
- Add a bass line, and a percussion accompaniment (preferably on drum set).
- Compare the rock-and-roll version (Track # 12 to the traditional *jarocho* version (Track # 12). Note changes in melody and lyrics by way of the improvisational quality, and the different feel of movement that the two versions engender.
- Move in a style that the musical quality inspires. Create a basic dance for the two versions that a group of dancers can perform.

## *Recommended Listening*

+*La Bamba: Sones Jarochos from Veracruz*. Smithsonian Folkways SFW 40505.
+*Ritchie Valens: La Bamba and Other Hits*. Rhino Flashback 78172.

# LA MACCHINA DEL CAPO

Italy

La mac - chi - na del ca - po, ha un bu - co nel - la gom - ma, La

mac - chi - na del ca - po ha un bu - co nel - la gom - ma. La

mac - chi - na del ca - po ha un bu - co nel - la gom - ma Ri - pa -

ria - mo ri - pa - ria - mo - la col chew - ing gum!

*The boss's car has a hole in its tire,*
*Let's all fix it, let's all fix it with chewing gum!*

Traditional, Italy, as sung by Rosella Diliberto. From Diliberto, R & Burton, B. (1999). *Welcome to Mussomeli: Children's Songs from an Italian Country Town*, Danbury, CT: World Music Press. Courtesy World Music Press.

## The Tune

In Italy, children sing "La Macchina del Capo" (The Boss's Car) with high energy and good humor, since it tells of repairing a flat tire with chewing gum.

## The Music Culture

Italy became a unified nation in the latter nineteenth century, until which time the region consisted of principalities, duchies, and papal states. Even as a politically united nation today, however, there are northern and southern cultural distinctions. From a musical perspective, the north sounds more "Central European," with Alpine influences, while the south takes its musical influences from the Mediterranean, North Africa, and the Middle East. As choral singing and harmony are predominant in northern Italian music, melismatic solo singing is characteristic of southern Italian music. Children's music in Italy is less differentiated by regions than is adult music, however, and the important matter to them is whether or not the songs can also be played or danced. In the case of "La Macchina del Capo," the humor and the game itself compels Italian children to choose it as one of their favorite songs.

## The Experiences

- Sing the melody on a neutral syllable such as "ma," and on solfège syllables (beginning on "sol") or scale numbers (beginning on "6").

- Sing the song with lyrics, noting that *ch* is pronounced as "k" (as in ma-kee-no) and that elisions are performed quickly (as in "ha-un").

- Play the chords on guitar or piano. The guitar can be strummed in a down, down-up ♩ ♫ rhythm. One fitting pattern at the piano is a root/bass and chord on alternating beats.

- Play the singing game that requires the progressive elimination of words and phrases each time it is sung, in this order: (1) sing all the words, (2) omit "macchina" but sing all other words, (3) omit "macchina" and "capo," (4) omit "buco," (5) omit "gomma," (6) eliminate all words.

- With each word that is eliminated, silently pantomime a gesture:

| | | |
|---|---|---|
| "macchina" | (car) | steer the car with a driving wheel |
| "capo" | (boss) | salute the "boss" with the right hand to the head |
| "buco" | (hole) | poke a hole with the index finger through a "tire" |
| "gomma" | (tire) | use two hands to make a circle |
| "chewing gum" | | use one hand to pull a long string of gum from the mouth |

## Recommended Listening

+*Welcome to Mussomeli: Children's Songs from an Italian Country Town* (Diliberto, R. and Burton, B.). Danbury, CT: World Music Press.

*Festa Italiana: Songs and Dances*. Monitor MON71345.

# LAK GEI MOLI

Taiwan

Lak gei— mo li jin jian shui. Long gun— si(n) zui—

jin— go zhui. Ho hui lan———— die———— xien— xiang—

dui Xin bin(n)— mou——— gun—— xiung———— ka———— kui.

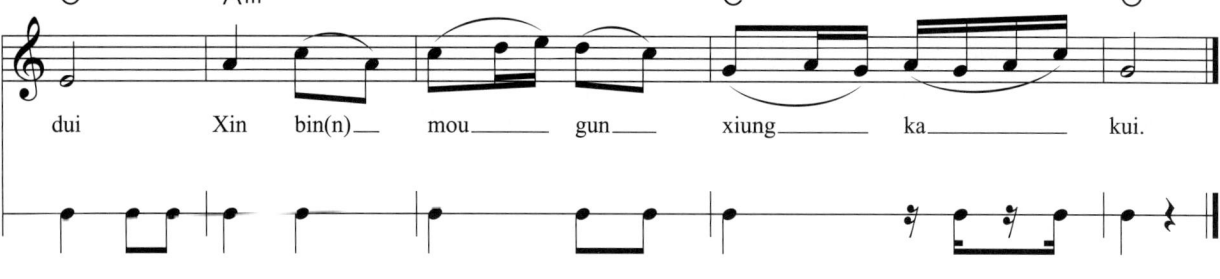

*White jasmine flowers of the Sixth Moon are fair,*
*And there's a young lad who's noble and fine.*
*Lovely flowers rarely ever grow all alone,*
*Fair and lonely lass can be sad, so sad.*

Traditional, China, Arranged by Han Kuo Han. From Han, K. H. & Campbell, P. S. (1992). *The Lion's Roar: Chinese Luogu Percussion Ensembles*. Danbury, CT: World Music Press. Courtesy World Music Press.

CD II, Track # 13

## The Tune

One of the best-known traditional songs in Taiwan is "Lak Gei Moli" (Jasmine Flowers of the Sixth Moon), sung a cappella or punctuated with woodblock and bell.

## The Music Culture

Chinese music is heard not only in the People's Republic of China (China) but also in the Republic of China (Taiwan) as well as in Chinese communities elsewhere in the world. Traditional songs of southern China and Taiwan tend to be lyrical, gently flowing, with an emphasis on melodic intervals of a third and fourth. They typically move in duple meter, and either the melody or its accompanying percussive patterns will contain syncopated rhythms. The *di* or *di-tze* (flute) may double a sung melody, or play alternating verses, and instruments like *xing* (bell), *bangzi* (woodblock), or various drums and gongs may accompany the song. "Lak Gei Moli" is a song of springtime (as the sixth moon appears in June) when "lovely flowers rarely grow all alone," a phrase that implies that young men and women should be together.

### The Experiences

- Listen to Track # 13 to the delicate and graceful melody and the contrasting sound of the syncopated percussion rhythm.
- Sing the melody on a neutral syllable such as "lee," and on solfège syllables (beginning on "sol") or scale numbers (beginning on "5").
- Sing the lyrics, using this pronunciation:

  Lak gay mo lee jeen jan shwee.

  Long goon seen zwee jeen go zhu-wee.

  Ho hoo-ee lan dee shen shahng dwee

  Seen been moo goon shung ka kwee.

- Play the chords on piano or guitar, with full knowledge of the fact that contemporary Chinese music utilizes harmony but traditional music does not.
- Chant and tap out the rhythm of the woodblock.
- While singing the melody, add a bell on the first of every two beats throughout the song, and the woodblock rhythm.
- Sing the verse, then play it on flute, recorder, glockenspiel, violin, or on instruments further afield, including saxophone and trumpet.

### Recommended Listening

+*The Lion's Roar: Chinese Luogu Percussion Ensembles* (Han, K. H. and Campbell, P. S.). Danbury, CT: World Music Press.

*An Anthology of Chinese Folk Songs* (Ellie Mao). Folkways FW 08877.

## LAS MAÑANITAS

Mexico

Es - tas son las ma - ña - ni - tas que can - ta - ba'el rey Da -
vid; las mu - cha - chas tan bo - ni - tas tam - bien las can - tan a
sí; Des - pier - ta, mi bien des - pier - ta! Mi - ra que ya a - ma -
ne - cio! Ya los pa - ja - ri - tos can - tan la lu - na ya se tio.

*There are songs sung at daybreak that King David used to sing.*

*The girls who are so pretty also sing them this way:*

*"Wake up, my dear, wake up!*

*Look, it has dawned already!*

*The little birds are now singing,*

*The moon has already disappeared."*

*Teaching Music Globally: Experiencing Music, Expressing Culture* by Campbell, P. S. (2004). By permission of Oxford University Press, Inc.

## The Tune

Known as "the birthday song," "Las Mañanitas" has been sung (and clapped) in Mexican and Mexican-American families for generations.

## The Music Culture

There is an abundance of music in Mexico, and for those Mexican Americans who continue to live out their familial traditions in the United States and elsewhere. City life in Mexico is replete with music in concert halls, at dances, at political rallies, in the music of itinerant musicians on sidewalks and on buses, and on television programming. Where 90 percent of 100 million citizens of Mexico are Catholic, there is also choir music and mariachi music to heighten their worship at Catholic masses. No family gathering is complete without music, either, as it accompanies baptisms, celebrations of *quince años* (for fifteen-year-old debutantes), weddings, birthdays, funerals, and festivals. Whether supplied by a *mariachi* band, a *jarocha* ensemble of harps and guitars, a salsa or rock band, or simply by family members who enjoy singing together, the music is there in the everyday life and special events of Mexican families. To celebrate birthdays, Mexican families sing a traditional birthday song, "Las Mañanitas."

## The Experiences

- Sing the song on a neutral syllable such as "mah," and on solfège syllables (beginning on "sol") or scale numbers (beginning on "5").

- Sing the lyrics, noting the pronunciations of the following: "que" is "kay," "David" is "dah-veed," and "pajaritos" is "pa-ha-ree-tos."

- Play the chords on guitar, strumming in a rhythm that allows the root note or bass strings to sound on "1" and the chords on the upper strings on the second and third beats:

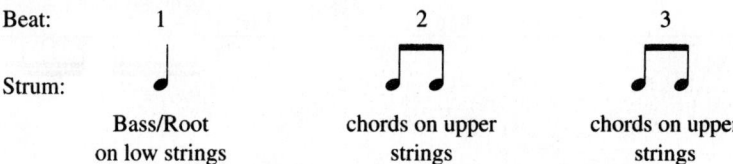

| Beat: | 1 | 2 | 3 |
|---|---|---|---|
| Strum: | Bass/Root on low strings | chords on upper strings | chords on upper strings |

- In a *mariachi* style, play the melody and harmony (which is mostly a third higher than the melody) on trumpets and violins.

## Recommended Listening

*Mariachi Vargas de Tecalitlán. 100 Años de Música.* BMG 7-4321902742-9.

*Mariachi Vargas de Tecalitlán. La Fiesta del Mariachi.* PolyGram Discos 7-31452-69462-1.

*Mariachi Los Camperos de Nati Cano. ¡Llegaron Los Camperos! Concert Favorites of Nati Cano's Mariachi Los Camperos.* Smithsonian Folkways SFW 40517.

# LE JIG FRANÇAIS

U. S.: Cajun

CD II, Track # 14

## The Tune

Cajun music continues the traditions of the French and French Canadian dance genres, notably the reels, hornpipes, and jigs such as "Le Jig Français."

## The Music Culture

Descendents of the eighteenth century Acadian exiles from Nova Scotia fashioned a unique culture called "Cajun" in New Orleans and in the parishes of southwestern Louisiana. They spilled over into the east Texas cities of Beaumont and Port Arthur, especially with the discovery of oil there in the 1920s and 30s, when they moved their language, cuisine, music, and dance with them. Cajun culture has preserved and continued the expressions of their forebears, all the way back to French Canada and France itself. Fiddles and accordions are used to play folk tunes and dance melodies, especially of the quadrilles of old France. Because music travels, and the Acadians of Canada heard plenty of British music (as did the French in their historical exchanges across the British channel), reels, hornipes, and jigs also slipped into the Cajun repertoire. When the first commercial recordings of Cajun music appeared in the 1920s, tunes were standardized. Contemporary groups like Beausoleil, the Mamou Playboys and Ossun Express continue to perform traditional tunes like "Le Jig Français" even as they invent contemporary expressions all their own.

### The Experiences

- Listen to Track # 14, and follow the arpeggiated broken chords of the fiddle while also tapping the sound of the triangle.
- Tap out a steady quarter-note pulse, while humming just the first pitch of every beat.
- Play the melody on violin, mandolin, flute, piano, or other available melody instrument.
- To the melody, add a bass line (on piano, stringed bass, bass guitar), playing the pitches "on" the beat as quarter-notes.
- Play the triangle in a continuous ♪♪♪♪ pattern.
- Experiment with a shuffle step in a heel-to-toe dance, in place, in response to the recorded or live music; this step

  sounds a ♩ ♪ rhythm. In a circle formation, holding hands and facing center, move in four-measure phrases:

    Measures 1–4    Circle right
    Measures 5–8    Step to center
    Measures 9–12   Step back from center
    Measures 13–16  Circle right
    Measures 17–20  Find a partner and swing
    Measures 21–24  Move back to original space
    Repeat sequence

- Another dance involves an inside and an outside circle, and what becomes inside-outside partners connected by a "skater's hold," facing right.
    Measures 1–4    Shuffle right (forward)
    Measures 5–8    Swing partners
                    Inside-circle person moves immediately "up" and to the right, to a new outside-circle partner
    Repeat sequence

### Recommended Listening

+*Louisiana Cajun Classics: America's Masters, Volume 3*. Arhoolie 103.
*Bayou Deluxe* (Michael Doucet and Beausoleil). Rhino/WEA 71169.

# LET'S GET THE RHYTHM OF THE BAND

United States

Let's get the rhy-thm of the band, oh yeah, We got the rhy-thm of the band.____

Let's get the rhy-thm of the hand, clap your hands now, We got the rhy-thm of the hand.____

Let's get the rhy-thm of the feet, stomp it out with me, we got the rhy-thym of the feet,____

Let's get the rhy-thm of the band. Let's get the rhy-thm of the band.

## The Tune

Rhythm is primal in music, and especially so for children who enjoy its pulse and energy. They encourage each other's movement in "Let's Get the Rhythm of the Band."

## The Music Culture

Children's musical lore is comprised of their own invented songs and chants and those that they make their own through modifications of what they have experienced. They take from the songs they have heard sung to them, and from the media that offer daily exposure to rhythms and melodies. They may incorporate something as unexpected as cheerleaders' cheers into their own repertoire. A long-time crowd-pleaser at high school football and basketball games is a cheer that invites fans to clap, stamp, and snap their fingers in support of their team. This cheer is chanted without pitch, with time allowed for enthusiastic body percussion, or in a style that is sung in a blues-y manner. In the case of "Let's Get the Rhythm of the Band," it is likely that children heard the chant at games, and fashioned it into a "cheering-song" that fits well within the repertoire of their singing games.

### The Experiences
- Sing the melody of the song on a neutral syllable, and on solfège syllables (beginning on "la") or scale numbers (beginning on "6").
- Sing the lyrics to the song, noting that at the end of every phrase, there is "space" for improvising a clapped, stamped, or finger-snapped rhythm.

- Play the harmony on piano or guitar, just to hear how the chords fall—even though children's songs are not in need of harmonization.

- Create new verses for the melody—whether about a band, a team, a friend, a favorite food. Leave time for an improvised rhythm at every phrase ending.

## Recommended Listening

*Shake It To the One That You Love the Best: Play Songs and Lullabies from Black Musical Traditions*. Cheryl Warren Maddox. El Sobrante, CA: Warren-Mattox Productions. ISBN: 0962338109.

*Children's Singing Games*. Multicultural Media SDL-338.

## LIAN XI QU
### (PART I)

China

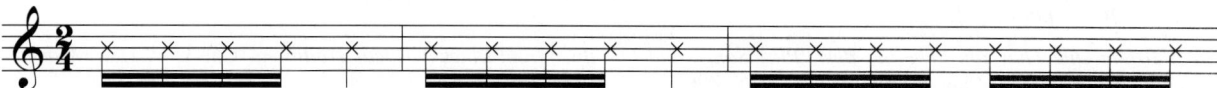

Dong, dong, dong, dong, chahng,   Dong, dong, dong, dong, chahng,   dong, dong, dong, dong, dong, dong, dong, dong,

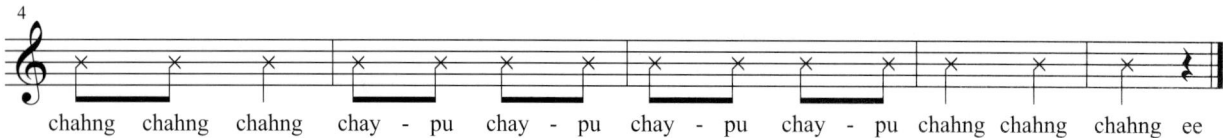

chahng   chahng   chahng   chay - pu   chay - pu   chay - pu   chay - pu   chahng  chahng  chahng  ee

## LIAN XI QU
### (PART II)

China

Chay   tay   ee   chay   chahng   ee   Dong   dong dong tay   tay   chahng   ee

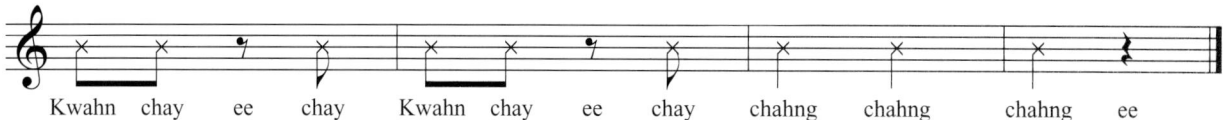

Kwahn   chay   ee   chay   Kwahn   chay   ee   chay   chahng   chahng   chahng   ee

Traditional, China, Arranged by Han Kuo Han. From Han, K. H. & Campbell, P. S. (1992). *The Lion's Roar: Chinese Luogu Percussion Ensembles*. Danbury, CT: World Music Press. Courtesy World Music Press.

CD II, Track # 15

## The Tune

A popular *luogu* (percussion ensemble) festival piece from south-central China is "Lian Xi Qu," a two-part étude.

## The Music Culture

Among the finds of archeological digs in China instruments dating from the Shang dynasty (16th–11th centuries BCE), are stone chimes and bronze bells—testimony to the importance of percussion instruments for many millennia. During the Six Dynasties (220–581 CE), gongs and cymbals were introduced from Central Asia. By the Tang Dynasty (618–907 CE), there were seven drums in the court orchestra, as well as bells and wooden clappers. Of the eight categories of Chinese musical instruments within the Ba Yin system, four are percussion instruments (metal, stone, wood, and skin). Percussion instruments make up the *luogu* ensembles that are heard in Chinese street parades, at the lion and dragon dances, for music of the theater (and puppet theater), and in religious ceremonies. Two festival pieces of the *luogu*, popular in the lower Yangzi River area of China, are combined in "Lian Xi Qu."

## The Experiences

- Listen to Track # 15 for the varied drum and gong sounds, and tap the pulse—be it ♩, ♫ ♩ or ♬
- Slowly chant the mnemonic vocables of the two parts, with an understanding that each syllable represents a particular instrument, its timbre, and how it is performed.
- Note that these rhythms are notated with letters that stand for mnemonic sounds.

> Part I:  2/4  D D D D K | D D D D K | D D D D D D D D | K K K | C P C P | C P C P | K K | K O
>
> Part II: 2/4  C T O C | K O | D DD T T | K O | Q C O C | Q C O C | K K | K O

> Key:  D = dong (drum)
>
> K = chang (all percussion instruments)
>
> C = chay (cymbals, open)
>
> P = pu (cymbals, muted)
>
> T = tay (small gong)
>
> Q = kwang (large gong)
>
> O = ee (silence, rest)

- Chant the syllables slowly at first, gradually increasing the tempo of the chanted syllables per each run-through.
- Play the chant on instruments, differentiating between drum, cymbals, and gongs, while continuing to chant the mnemonic vocables.
- Play the piece in ABA form.

## Recommended Listening

+*The Lion's Roar: Chinese Luogu Percussion Ensembles.* (Han, K. H. and Campbell, P. S.). Danbury, CT: World Music Press.

*Chinese Percussion Music.* Marco Polo 8-223652.

# LO YISA GOY

Israel

*Nation will not lift up sword against nation,*
*Nor will they learn war anymore.*

From *Fire Within*, Libana, 1990. Arrangement by Susan Robbins and Libana. www.libana.com

## The Tune

The text of this traditional Jewish song is from the Old Testament. "Lo Yisa Goy" is a plea for peace.

## The Music Culture

Because of their migrations to Europe and across North Africa, the Jewish people transported their musical traditions to places far from their homeland on the eastern edge of the Mediterranean Sea: to Russia, Germany, France, Lithuania, and Morocco, among other places. They were also influenced by the music they heard over the centuries in their communities in these far-flung places. Yet despite their integration into the surrounding culture, the Jews also continued their customary practices. The music of Moroccan Jews and Russian Jews alike is evidence of their widely spread penchant for minor and modal melodies, their use of florid recitatives in their worship ceremonies, and their attunement to the verses of the Old Testament. Their advocacy of peace has come in various musical forms, emanating from grave historical circumstances of the holocaust and the Russian pograms. This setting of Isaiah 2:4, from the Old Testament, has taken hold as a song shared by many who advocate peace across the world.

### The Experiences

- Sing the song on a neutral syllable such as "lo," and on solfège syllables (beginning on "la") or on scale numbers (beginning on "6")
- Sing the lyrics, with attention to these pronunciations: "yisa" is "yee-sah," "cherev" is "kay-ref," "yil'm" is "yeel-im," and "michama" is "mil-kah-mah."
- Sing as a round, or in three parts; start a new part every four beats.

- Play the chords on guitar, piano, or other harmony instrument, sounding once every two beats.
- Add tambourine and hand drum accompaniment:

- Move in a circle, holding hands, to this simple set of dance steps—one movement to every eight-beat, two-measure phrase:

  1. 8 steps to the right
  2. 8 steps to turn in an individual circle (drop hands)
  3. 8 steps to the middle of the circle
  4. 8 steps back out of the circle

## Recommended Listening

+*Our Rock and Our Redeemer*. Monitor MON00720.
*Songs of Israel*. Folkways FW 06847.

## LOOP DE LOO

U. S.: Alabama

Here____ we go loop de loo. _____ Here____ we go loop de loo. _____ Here

__ we go loop de loo all on a Sat - ur - day night. I put my *right hand in, I

put my right hand out, I give my right hand a shake shake shake and turn my bo - dy a - bout.

*1. right hand
2. left hand
3. right leg
4. left leg
5. big head
6. whole self

## The Tune

Children enjoy action songs that require their interactive rhythmic movement, as in the case of this traditional African-American tune, "Loop de Loo."

## The Music Culture

Across the world, children have a way of taking from their surroundings the music that pleases them, and of tinkering with that music to make it all their own. They borrow from adults and from children, from the music that filters live into their homes and from the mediated music of TV, DVD and videos, CDs, and the Internet. "Looby Loo" can be traced to eighteenth-century England, when children would circle while they sang, holding hands and swinging arms back and forth as high as they could go. "Hokey Pokey" is a singing game embraced by children and teachers alike, played as often in school as on the playground outside; it is embraced by preschool and kindergarten teachers who have goals of teaching right and left (hands and legs). In a pastiche of the two songs together, African-American children created "Loop de Loo" for playground performances from Birmingham, Alabama to St. Louis, Missouri, and in Chicago and Los Angeles as well. They preserved parts of the text and most of the second song's melody ("Hokey Pokey"), while dressing up the first song ("Looby Loo") with a syncopated rhythm and a la-based melody. The song's movement combines the swinging arms and the shaking of arms and legs, the head, and the whole self, as mentioned by the singers.

## The Experiences

- Recall versions of "Looby Loo" and "Hokey Pokey," and sing them.

- While tapping subdivisions of the pulse (eighth notes), chant the song text in rhythm.

- Separate into pulse-tappers and rhythm-clappers who clap the melodic rhythm, then perform the two parts simultaneously.  Switch parts and experiment with other body percussion sounds and with percussion instruments.

- Sing a la-do-mi triad repeatedly, and also a major triad in first inversion (sol-do-mi), in preparation for singing the melodies of the two songs.

- Sing the song on a neutral syllable such as "loo," and with solfège syllables beginning on "la" or scale numbers beginning on "6."

- While singing the song, gather to swing arms while walking in a circle (measures 1–4) and stand at attention to play the "Hokey Pokey" (measures 5–8).  Note that there is a sequence of shaking movements: right hand, left hand, right leg, left leg, big head, whole self.

## Recommended Listening

+*A Tisket, A Tasket*. Kimbo recordings, 1563461269 9781563461262.

+*Hokey Pokey Rock*. Collector Records 4715904.

*Children's Singing Games*. Saydisc CD-SDL 338.

# LOS MACHETES

Mexico

CD II, Track # 16

## The Tune

With guitars, trumpets, and violins, "Los Machetes" is considered by many Mexicans and Mexican Americans to be one of the finest *mariachi* dance tunes.

## The Music Culture

When the music of Mexico comes to mind, it is often mariachi music that heads the list. Despite the regional varieties of instruments and genres of music in Mexico, mariachi is widespread—particularly as it has found its way into the world at large. Once a local and isolated tradition of the people of the Jalisco province, headquartered at Guadalajara, mariachi became a commercial commodity by the 1940s when it was broadast over radio and tracked into films that received national and international attention. The modern mariachi instrumentation consists of two trumpets, three to six violins, guitar, *vihuela* (a five-stringed guitar), and *guitarrón* (bass guitar). The ensemble plays a range of pieces, one of the most common being the *canción ranchera*, a song in either triple waltz meter or in slow and fast tempo versions of duple meter. There is also the slow, romantic music of the *bolero,* and the *son,* a wildly popular song with a simple, repeated vocal melody that is applied to multiple verses.

### The Experiences
- Listen to Track # 16, humming the melodies played by the trumpet and violins and tapping the beat (or off-beat).
- Play the melody and harmony of a third below, on trumpets and violins.

- Listen to the recording, and note this organization of instruments:

    A: (trumpets)

    A: repeated (violins)

    B: (measure 1 on trumpets, measure 2 on violins, measure 3 on trumpets, measure 4 on violins)

    B: repeated.

- Play the piece in the order of the recording's arrangement, switching between instrument groups.

- Play the chords on guitar, giving a fast off-beat strum four times per measure, in this manner:

## Recommended Listening

+*Mariachi Nuevo Tecalitan: Mexico Y Sus Valses*. Delta DTA0044110.

*Mariachi Los Camperos de Nati Cano. ¡Llegaron Los Camperos! Concert Favorites of Nati Cano's Mariachi Los Camperos.* Smithsonian Folkways SFW 40517.

*Mariachi Vargas de Tecalitlán. 100 Años de Música.* BMG 7-4321902742-9.

# LOY KRATHONG

Thailand

*In the twelfth month when the full moon shines,*

*Water overflows the canal.*

*All of us, men and women*

*Have lots of fun on Loy Krathong Day!*

*Let's celebrate Loy and float the dainty Thai creations.*

*We ask the girls to dance ramwong.\**

*Let's dance on Loy Krathong Day!*

*Good deeds will bring us happiness.*

\*Ramwong is a popular social dance performed
by partners gathered in a large circle.

Traditional, Thailand, arranged by Pornprapit Phoasavadi. From Phoasavadi, P. & Campbell, P. S. (2003). *From Bangkok and Beyond: Thai Children's Songs, Games and Customs.* Danbury, CT: World Music Press. Courtesy World Music Press

# LOY KRATHONG

## The Tune

Thailand's November festival of lights is called "Loy Krathong," when this song of the same name is played by traditional and Western instruments and is sung live by children and adults alike, and is broadcast over TV and radio, too.

## The Music Culture

People celebrate Loy Krathong in November, when the full moon of the twelfth month shines over Thailand. The monsoon season comes to closure then, and people take the time to give thanks to the spirit of water for her abundant supply (as well as to apologize for pollution of the rivers and canals). Thai people carry small lotus-shaped banana-leaf (or foam) vessels to the rivers and lakes, and set them to sail in the water with their candles, incense sticks, coins, and flowers. People dance the *ramwong*, a popular partner dance that moves around a large circle with a shuffling step and graceful upturned hands and fingers. Sometimes the music will sound from traditional instruments such as *ranaat* (xylophone), *khluoy* (fipple flute), *khoong wong* (circle of gongs), and *ching* (thick brass cymbals), and sometimes from high-decibel rock bands.

### The Experiences

- Sing the melody on neutral syllable such as "loy," and on solfège syllables and scale numbers.
- While singing the melody, alternately clap and clasp the hands so as to make a sharper sound on beats 1 and 3 and a more muffled sound on beats 2 and 4.
- Use cymbals to produce the ching's sharper ringing tone ("ching") by touching the edges of the two cymbals together, and the muffled tone ("chop") by striking one cymbal to the other and holding it tightly.
- Chant the lyrics, with attention to the following pronunciations: *c* is "ch" as in "cing" and "ca," and the final two phrases sound as "boon cha sohng hee row suk cha-ee."
- Sing the lyrics, noting the occasional two-pitch phrases to a single syllable.
- Play the melody on wooden xylophones, or recorder or flute, Western instruments with timbral qualities that approximate those of *ranaat* and *khluoy*.
- While Thai music is not harmonic except in some contemporary forms, explore the sounds of chords on piano or guitar with the traditional melody and sound of the *ching*.

### Recommended Listening

+*From Bangkok and Beyond* (Phoasavadi, P. and Campbell, P. S.). Danbury, CT: World Music Press.
*Sleeping Angel: Thai Classical Music*. Nimbus NI5319.
*The Rough Guide to the Music of Thailand*. World Music Network RGNET 1095 CD.

# LUA AFE

Tuvalu, Polynesia

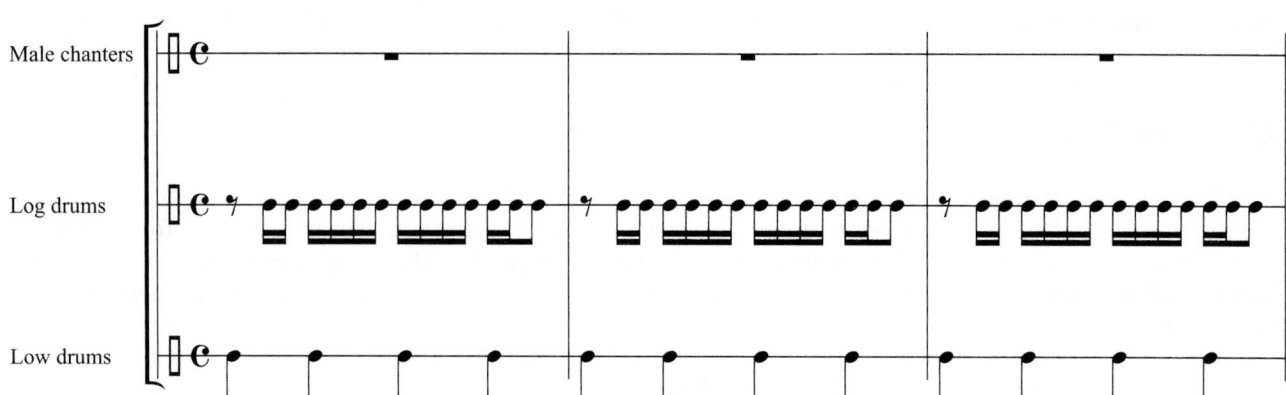

"Lua Afe" by Opetaia Foai from the album *Te Vaka, Ki mua* WMCD1002 by Te Vaka. Copyright 1999 by Spirit of Play Productions Ltd. www.tevaka.com

## The Groove

On the islands and atolls of the southern Pacific Ocean, log drums and rhythmic chants are important musical expressions. From the people of Tuvalu comes "Lua Afe," a celebration of the wish that people of all colors and creeds may come together without prejudice.

## The Music Culture

Located midway between Hawaii and Australia is the Polynesian island nation of Tuvalu, with its ten square miles of land comprised of four reef islands and five atolls. It is a beautiful yet tenuous place, given that the low elevation of the land poses a threat to the people there; a rise in the sea level through global warming could necessitate evacuation to neighboring Fiji, Samoa, or New Zealand. Governed by Britain from 1892 to 1978, Tuvalu is a constitutional monarchy within the Commonweath of England. There are 12,000 Tuvaluans who live in a traditional community system in which each family has its own task to perform for others, be it fishing, house building, or defense. Skills are passed from father to son. The traditional music of Tuvalu, as is also the case of other Polynesian island communities, is largely comprised of vocal chants and the sounds of log drums. Te Vaka of New Zealand, led by Tuvaluan Opetaia Foa'I, values the traditional sounds and stories of their elders, and the group has been inspired to forge a contemporary expression complete with drum set, and guitars.

## The Experiences

- Using hard mallets or wood dowels on the floor or metal surface (rungs of a metal chair, edge of a metal desk), play the log drum parts.
- Add the steady beat of a drum.

## Recommended Listening

+*Te Vaka: Ki Mua*. Creative New Zealand. WMCD1002.

*Tuvalu: A Polynesian Atoll Society*. Pan Records 2055.

# MAITREEM

India

*Let us conquer the world through friendship and love.*

*Let us think of others in the same way we think of ourselves.*

*Let us banish wars.*

*Let us eschew envious rivalry.*

*Let God almighty show mercy and save this mother earth from lust and grief.*

*Give and receive kindness from all people.*

*Let all the people of the world be blessed with happiness and fulfillment.*

# MAITREEM

CD II, Track # 17

## The Tune

A song advocating world peace, "Maitreem" is oriented toward a fusion of the sounds and sensibilities of both Carnatic South India and the Islamic Middle East.

## The Music Culture

Musical cultures collide when musicians perform for and listen to one another. They bring their own styles, listen to the music of others, and see what emerges when they play together—or experiment with music that is new to their ears. Musical influences have always traveled from one culture to the next, resulting in fusion. Salsa is a blend of Afro-Cuban, Puerto Rican, and European components; jazz mixes African-based rhythms with European-based harmonies; Andulusian music of medieval Spain was a fusion of the musical expressions of Muslim, Jews, and Christians. "Maitreem" arose from the crossroads of South Indian and Islamic elements, when the ensemble Al-Andalus sought a musical merger that would convey the Sanskrit prayer as a cross-cultural, even universal, message. It is a traditional South Indian melody within a tuning called "Subalakshmi."

### The Experiences

- Listen to Track # 17, following the *oud*, *darabuka*, and cymbals, along with the singer's melody. Tap out the pulse or a selected rhythm.
- Listen to the recording, and hum along with the vocal melody.
- Sing the lyrics, noting that all *as* sound as "ah."
- Play the chords on guitar, using a down-down-up strum:
- Add a percussion ostinato as accompaniment:

Drum 1:

Drum 2:

Wdbl:

Cymbal:

### Recommended Listening

+*Al-Andalus: Illumination.* Al-Andalus (FAX: 503-234-1341).

*Ramnad Krishnan, Vidwan: Music of South India (Songs of the Carnatic Tradition).* Nonesuch Explorer Recordings.

*Music from South India, Tavil Nadaswaram Group.* Moers Music 01090.

# MAJKA RADA

Bulgaria

Maj - ka Ra - da sit - no ple - te sit - no ple - te — lju - to kul - ne

Maj - ka Ra - da sit - no ple - te sit - no ple - te — lju - to kul - ne

Šter - ko Ra - do bja - la Ra - do Tvoj - ta Ra - do — ru - sa ko - sa

Šter - ko Ra - do bja - la Ra - do Tvoj - ta Ra - do ru - sa ko - sa.

2. Tvojta Rado rusa kosa, koj šte I e purvo libe
   Dali ergen ili vdovets, ili turchin drugoverets.

3. Rada mama, tikhom duma, mamo, mamo, milna mamo
   Ne e ergen, nito vdovets, nito turchin drugoverets.

4. Naj šte mi e naj junache, naj junatsi bajraktarče (repeat).


1. *Rada's mother complains while she knits:*
   *Rada, my beautiful daughter, your fair hair, who will be its first admirer?*
2. *Will he be a bachelor, a widower, or a Turkish infidel?*
3. *Rada answers her mother softly:*
   *Sweet mother, he will be neither a bachelor, a widower, nor a Turkish infidel.*
4. *He will be no less than the bravest of the brave (repeat).*

# MAJKA RADA

## The Tune

"Majka Rada" is typical of the songs sung by Bulgarian women who once, in the preindustrial Balkan region, sang dreamily of brave and handsome suitors as they gathered together to sew, knit, and spin.

## The Music Culture

In the Balkan villages of Bulgaria, old Yugoslavia, Romania, and Greece, until World War II, singing and dancing was not "performance" but rather an integral aspect of everyone's daily experience. Music was part of the social life. Women sang while they worked in the fields, sewed and knitted together at home, or shucked corn. Men made music on pipes and flutes while they tended sheep and cattle, and visited with one another at the local café. Music was also intertwined with courtship and flirtation between men and women, and was integrated within celebrations of calendrical and life-cycle events. Songs were often linked to romantic subjects, particularly those sung by women for women, often about suitable and not-so-suitable suitors—including "Turkish infidels." It was not unusual for song lyrics to refer to the Turks in a derogatory manner, particularly in that the Ottoman (or Turkish) Empire ruled the Balkans, sometimes harshly, for more than seven centuries.

### The Experiences

* Sing the melody on a neutral syllable such as "mah," and on solfège syllables or scale numbers.
* Sing the lyrics of the song, giving attention to the pronuncation of *j* as "y" (as in "my-kah" for Majka, "lyu-toh" for ljuto, "byah-lah" for bjala, "shterko" for "šterko," and "tvoy-ta" for Tvojta).
* Add the vocal harmony as notated in the third phrase.
* Play chords on a harmony instrument such as accordion, guitar, or piano.
* Perform the dance in a circle, holding hands up with arms bent, moving to the right on these steps. Begin with the weight on the left foot, facing center and slightly to the right.

| Beat: | 1 | 2 | 3 | 4 | 5 | 6 | 7 | 8 |
|---|---|---|---|---|---|---|---|---|
| Step: | R | L | L | R | R | L | R | L |
| | step | slide | step | slide | step | step in front | step | step behind |

| Beat: | 9 | 10 | 11 | 12 | 13 | 14 | 15 | 16 |
|---|---|---|---|---|---|---|---|---|
| Step: | R | L | R | L | R | L | L | R |
| | step | step in front | step | step | step behind | slide | step | slide |

### Recommended Listening

*Village Harmony: Traditional Songs of the Balkans.* Northern Harmony NHPC102-CD.

*Village and Folk Music of Bulgaria.* Nonesuch 79195.

*Le Mystère des Voix Bulgares.* Nonesuch 79165.

## MAMA LAMA

United States

Ma-ma la-ma cu-ma la-ma ma-ma la-ma piz-za  Ma-ma la-ma cu-ma la-ma ma-ma la-ma piz-za.

Oh,  no,  no,  no,  no,  la  piz - za.  Oh,  no,  no,  no,  no,  la  piz - za.

Ee - nie mee - nie - dix - a pee - nie Ooh va da ohh ba ne ne  A ba katch - ee a ba watch - ee  X - Y - Z.

## The Tune

Children's musical lore is a living poetry in motion, as they orally transmit their songs and chants such as "Mama Lama," improvise upon them, and re-create them to suit their needs.

## The Music Culture

Where children gather, they often share a repertoire of songs and chants that is known by other children far and beyond them. English-speaking children from the United Kingdom to North America, and from Australia and New Zealand to South Africa, share some of the same repertoire. In nations and cultures where a dialect of English, a *patois,* is present (as in Caribbean countries such as Trinidad, Barbados, Jamaica, and the Bahamas), still a repertoire of children's lore comes through that is known on playgrounds as far away as London and Los Angeles. Words and syllables may shift slightly, small variances may occur in rhythms and melodies, and sometimes movements and games are shaped to local preferences, yet still the piece is recognizable, re-created in the living tradition of poetry, music, and movement. "Mama Lama," not in any way translatable, is nonetheless alive and well in children's culture.

### The Experiences

- Sing the melody on the two syllable "lama," and on solfège syllables or scale numbers.
- Clap, tap, or pat the quarter-note or eighth-note pulse while singing.
- Sing the lyrics of the song, articulating the fast-moving syllables.
- Add chords on guitar, piano, or other harmony instrument, with an understanding that such chords are not really necessary for children's engagement in the singing game.
- While singing, play a hand-clapping game with a partner, one gesture to each beat.

| Beat: | 1 | 2 | 3 | 4 |
|---|---|---|---|---|
| | slap right hip | clap right hand to own left (in front, near belt line) | hands together, slap back of left hand to back of partner's left hand ("prayer-hands") | clap right hand to own left hand |

| Beat: | 5 | 6 | 7 | 8 |
|---|---|---|---|---|
| | (repeat #1) | (repeat #2) | hands together, move them up (above belt line) and slap back of left hand to back of partner's left hand; see #3) ("prayer-hands") | hands together, move them down (below belt line) and slap back of right hand to back of partner's right hand; see #3) |

## Recommended Listening

*Skip Rope Games*. Smithsonian Folkways SFW 45015.
*Children's Sing Games*. Multicultural Media. SDL-338.
*cELLAbration*. Smithsonian Folkways SFW 45059.

# MARAMICA NA STAZI

Croatia

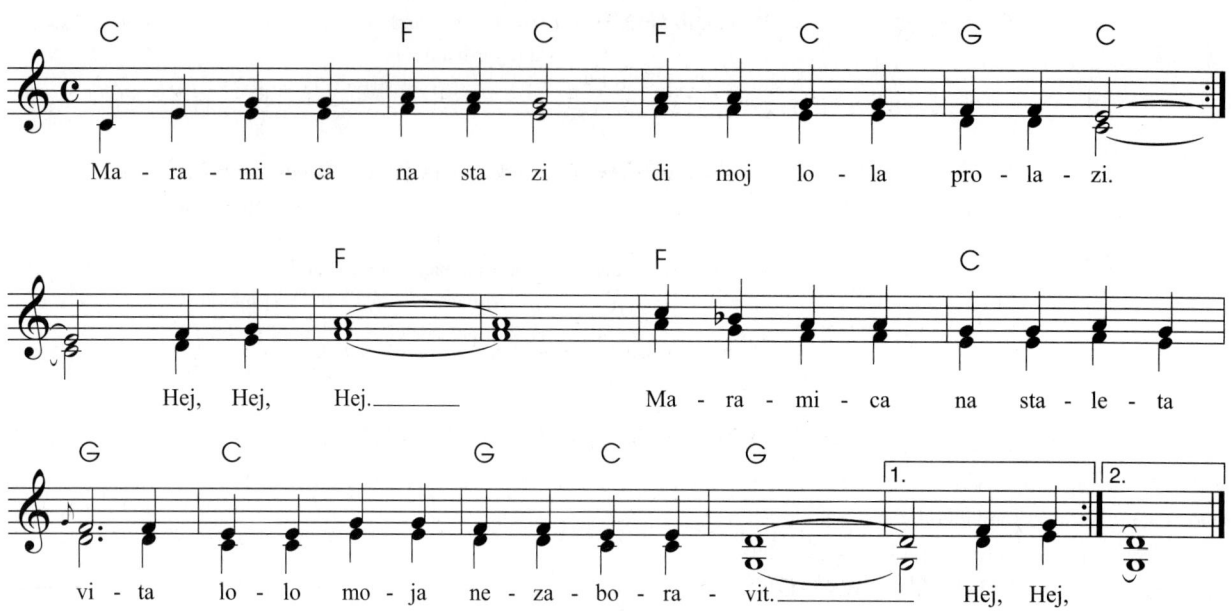

2. Moj se lola šalio, nova kola pravio
   Hej . . . i uprego šalaj dva čiljaša
   Dva čiljaša nema koǎjaš.

3. Lolo moja, di si ti, želna sam te viditi.
   Hej . . . lol moja, što mi se ne javis
   Da te pitam kako žvotariš?

1. *There's a handkerchief on the road where my dear one passes.*
2. *He made a new cart with two horses and no driver.*
3. *Oh, sweetheart, why don't you call me so I can ask you how life is?*

"Maramica Na Stazi". From *Village Harmony: Traditional Songs of the Balkans*, edited by Mary Cay Brass, copyright 1995 Northern Harmony Publishing Company. Original transcription by Mary Cay Brass.

CD II, Track # 18

## The Tune

Like many traditional songs of Croatian village women, "Maramica Na Stazi" is in a style that allowed them express their thoughts of love and romance while spinning, knitting, and sewing together.

## The Music Culture

In the pre-socialist agrarian musical cultures of the Balkan countries of southeastern Europe—Bulgaria, Greece, Romania, and old Yugoslavia—song formed the basis of village musical culture. Croatian men played instruments such as *gusle* (bowed lute) and *tamburitza* (plucked lute), while women—whose hands were constantly occupied—sang. Because women worked in the fields to plant and harvest vegetables, and in their homes they prepared the food and produced textiles, their hands were never free to play instruments. Young Croatian girls grew up in the fields and in the kitchen, listening to their mothers, grandmothers, aunts, and older siblings and cousins, and learned the lyrics and melodies so as to perform them. While men sang, too, it was the women's role to be the primary bearers of the singing tradition, passing on songs of their sweethearts, their lives in the village, and their work in the countryside.

## The Experiences

- Listen to Track # 18 for the gentle undulation of thirds as played by the accordion and then sung by the mixed choir.
- Sing the melody (the upper pitch of the thirds) on a neutral syllable such as "zee," and on solfège syllables or scale numbers.
- Sing the lyrics, pronouncing *j* as "y" in "moj," "moja" and *š* as "sh."
- Sing the vocal harmony, the lower pitch of the thirds.
- As an interlude, play the melody and harmony on accordion, clarinets, violins, or trumpets—standard instruments in Croatian village bands.
- Add a bass line on trombone or tuba, following the movement of the chords.

## Recommended Listening

+*Village Harmony: Traditional Songs of the Balkans*. Northern Harmony HNPC102-CD.

*Songs and Dances from Croatia*. Arc Music 1550.

*Folk Music from Croatia*. Arc Music 1078.

# MÁRU-BIHÁG
## (RAGA)

India

## MÁRU-BIHÁG (DRONE)

CD II, Track # 19

## The Tune

Hindustani music of North India is notable for its improvisatory use of intricate melodic material based upon *ragas* like "Máru-Bihág."

- A simple May Day celebration dance can be danced in concentric circles, the inside circle group members facing a partner in the outside circle group. Partners place their right hands together, shoulder high with palms flat, with left hands behind their backs.

| Beat: | 1 | 2 | 3 | 4 | 5 | 6 | 7 | 8 |
|---|---|---|---|---|---|---|---|---|
| Move: | Step forward | Close | Step back | Close | Step forward | Close | Step back | Close |

| Beat: | 9 | 10 | 11 | 12 | 13 | 14 | 15 | 16 |
|---|---|---|---|---|---|---|---|---|
| Move: | Right palms still touching, walk with partner in a clockwise circle | | | | | | | |

| Beat: | 17 | 18 | 19 | 20 | 21 | 22 | 23 | 24 |
|---|---|---|---|---|---|---|---|---|
| Move: | Bow to old partner | | | | Step to the right and face new partner | | | |

## Recommended Listening

*The Wild Mountain Thyme* (John Langstaff). Revels Records CD 1094.
*Song Links, Volume 2: A Celebration of English Songs*. Fellside FECD 190D.

# MBUBE

South Africa

From *Music in Childhood: From Preschool Through the Elementary Grade* with Audio CD 3rd edition by CAMPBELL/SCOTT-KASSNER, 2006. Reprinted with permission of Wadsworth, a Division of Thompson Learning: www. Thomsonrights.com. Fax 800-730-2215.

## The Tune

One of the most widely known of the world's songs, "Mbube" is a South African song from the Zulu heartland of South Africa. It has come to be known as "The Lion Sleeps Tonight."

## The Music Culture

Solomon Linda first recorded "Mbube" in 1939 as a melody with three chords, few words, and baritones chanting in four parts in the background. Linda was a Zulu, born and raised in South Africa, and as a child he worked as a herder protecting cattle from lions in the untamed wilderness. This may have been what inspired his song, although it originally included only two Zulu words, "mbube" (lion) and "zimba" (stop). His 78 rpm recording of "Mbube" was the first record on the African continent to sell 100,000 copies, and the harmonies and chant came to define a style of Zulu a cappella singing known as *mbube*. Folksinger Pete Singer heard the song, and in his effort to develop an international movement of peace and unity, he recorded the song in 1952 with the Weavers, adding to Solomon Linda's tenor descant and bringing more words into what became a folk song staple. A reworking of the song by George Weiss in the 1960s further transformed the song, who turned the twenty improvised seconds of Linda's performance into a melody and added "in the jungle, the mighty jungle." Some 150 artists have recorded the song in languages from Dutch to Japanese, and groups like The Kingston Trio, the Tokens, and the Nylons have popularized it further. It stands as a song of the lion as a brave and proud animal, but also one who needs to be contained and controlled so as not to cause harm.

## The Experiences

- Sing the chords for "mbube" by listening and then picking out the parts that are notated.
- Play the chords for "mbube," providing support to the singing.
- Sing a wordless melismatic melody on "ee," over the chords that are sounded by the three lower voice parts.
- Play the chords on piano or guitar, or divided among stringed instruments, alone and along with singing.
- Arrange to perform the song with singers, chording instruments, strings (or other melody instruments) on the wordless melody, and singing again for the melody with words.
- Add drums on an ostinato rhythm of steady eight notes: ♩ ♩ ♫ ♩ ♫ ♩ ♫
- Repeat sections, as desired.
- Invent new words to the melody, about lions, bravery, pride, and the balance of control and freedom.

## Recommended Listening

+*Soweto String Quartet: Renaissance.* BMG BSP7009.

+*The Best of Ladysmith Black Mambazo, Volume 2.* Shanachie 66012

# MEDA WAWA ASE

Ghana

*I am lying under the wawa tree.*
*A young man/woman such as I,*
*I am lying under the wawa tree.*

Traditional, Ghana, arranged by Abraham Zobena Adzenyah.  From Adzenya, A. K., Maraire, D., & Tucker, J. C. (1997). *Let Your Voice Be Heard: Songs from Ghana and Zimbabwe* (Rev. Ed.). Danbury, CT: World Music Press. Courtesy World Music Press.

# MEDA WAWA ASE

## The Tune

The Akan of Ghana sing this "Meda Wawa Ase" as a warning to take time to reflect on one's life, and to consider how one's actions will affect other people—and oneself as well.

## The Music Culture

Many of the teachings of traditional societies such as the Akan in Ghana are embedded in songs, parables, and proverbs. Young people learn their moral values and social roles within the community through the sung and story-told lessons that come to them on a daily basis. School is but one context of learning; elders, including parents, grandparents, older siblings, and various members of their villages, towns, and urban communities also hold themselves responsible for setting children and youth on the right course. One traditional Akan song, "Meda Wawa Ase," is sung as a single melody, or in two (or more) parts, delivering the message to think about living in harmony with the values of the community. As the words suggest, the boy or girl is "lying under the wawa tree, reflecting." One version continues, "I am in the hands of my enemies, what should I do?" This suggests that he or she must live responsibly, and that inappropriate behavior will bring just punishments by those who are offended. The song expresses the need to think before acting, and to strive to do good works.

### The Experiences
- Sing the melody of the song on a neutral syllable such as "wah," and on solfège syllables or scale numbers.
- Sing the vocal harmony on a neutral syllable, and on solfège syllables (beginning on "la") or scale numbers (beginning on "6").
- Sing the lyrics, with attention to words like "tse-ba'a" (pronounced "say-bah"), "otse" (pronounced "oats"), and "nye'i" (pronounced "nyay").
- Sing the two vocal lines together, and note that the lower voice breaks into two parts for a few measures.
- Play the chords on piano or guitar, even though neither is typical in an Akan rendition of this song.
- Following the chords, explore the possibility of singing the song in three-part harmony.

### Recommended Listening

*Children's Songs for Games from Africa* (Kojo Fosu/Edwina Hunter). Folkways FW 77855.
*The Rough Guide to the Music of Nigeria and Ghana*. World Music Network RGNET 1075CD.

## MERENGUE GROOVE

Dominican Republic

Notes:
Guiro:                        Conga:
D = down stroke        O = strike open head—let ring
U = up stroke            S = slap (L.H. remains on head)

## The Tune

A popular dance form of Venezuela, Haiti, and the Dominican Republic, the *merengue* originated with the poor Dominican peasants.

## The Music Culture

The Carribean island-nations have inspired much of the Latin dance craze that has taken the clubs of Latin America, North America, and Europe by storm. In fact, Carribean rhythms of *salsa, merengue, guanguanco,* and *cumbia* are heard across the world. *Merengue* dance music combines rural, folk and urban popular traditions. Rising out of the politically and economically marginalized populations of the Dominican Republic, the music grew to become the symbol of national identity for the Dominican people. *Merengue* is played on accordion, sometimes the marimba, and in the old days on stringed instruments. Yet it is the variety of percussion instruments that gives the dance ever more "punch" today, including *claves, bongo* and *conga* drums, cowbell, *guiro*, and *timbales*. A call-and-response vocal structure is typical of the song and dance form, and the European-style couple dance takes on an African influence through the use of the hip and pelvis movements. *Merengue* is "hot" rhythms, unmistakable on the dance floor or in the hands of the players.

## The Experiences

- Tap, clap, or pat out the rhythms of the *merengue* instruments, one after another.
- Chant the parts rhythmically:

- Play the rhythms on instruments, chanting and then gradually fading out the chant.
- Gradually layer in the rhythms, beginning with claves and adding in the others.
- Substitute pitched instruments for the rhythms, each one playing one designated rhythm on one designated pitch, or a mixture of pitches from a designated chord.

## Recommended Listening

*Merengue Super Hits*. Disco Fuentes 10024.

*Merengue Fiesta*. Sony International 12417.

*The Rough Guide to Merengue*. World Muisc Network RGNET 1171 CD.

# MI BAJO Y YO

Oscar D'Leon

*Teaching Music Globally: Experiencing Music, Expressing Culture* by Campbell, P. S. (2004). By permission of Oxford University Press, Inc.

## The Tune

Among the sounds to emerge from Venezuela's dance halls of the 1960s and '70s was Oscar D'Leon, whose *salsa* style set people to moving to tunes like "Mi Bajo y Yo."

## The Music Culture

The identity and beauty of salsa is its rhythmic vitality. *Ritmo* (rhythms) is a concept of polyrhythmic organization that refers to the timing, volume, and timbre of the instruments that play it. The interlocking patterns of claves, guiro, and conga drums around the sounds of piano and bass are what compel listeners to want to dance. Salsa and other Caribbean dance forms are grouped around the constant claves rhythm, much as West African rhythms revolve around the unchanging rhythm pattern of a bell. Oscar D'Leon, bassist, bandleader, composer, and arranger, is credited with some of the most rhythmically driven salsa sound of all time. He performed as a founding member of Venezuela's top salsa band, Dimensión Latina, and with Salsa Mayor and much-recorded salsa artists like Beny Moré. "Mi Bajo y Yo" was a salsa hit when recorded by Oscar D'Leon in the late 1970s.

## The Experiences

- Tap, clap, or pat the rhythms of clave, guiro, and conga drums.
- Vocally chant the rhythms for each instrument:

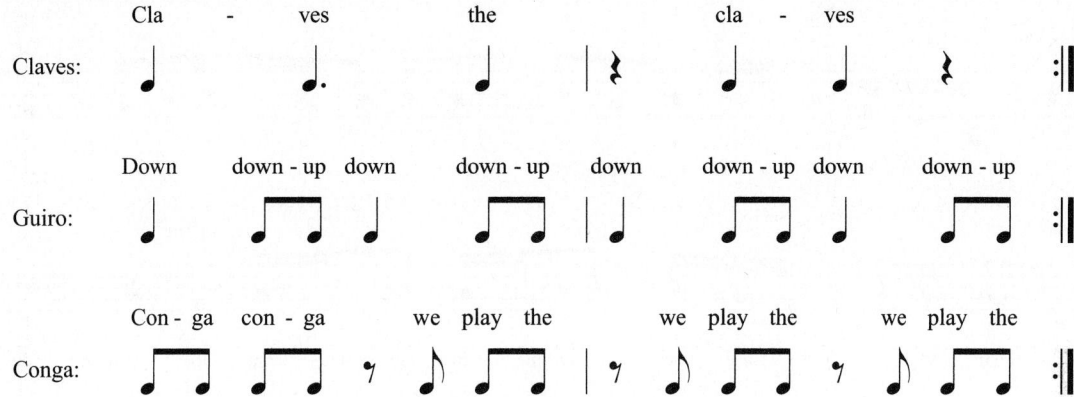

- Chant and play the percussion instruments, slowly fading out the chant.
- Play the piano part and bass line for the salsa piece.
- Add percussion instruments to the piano and bass lines.
- Dance the salsa, using this simple step while moving the hips.

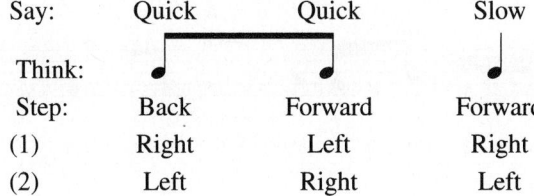

| Say: | Quick | Quick | Slow |
|------|-------|-------|------|
| Think: | | | |
| Step: | Back | Forward | Forward |
| (1) | Right | Left | Right |
| (2) | Left | Right | Left |

## Recommended Listening

+*Oscar d'Leon: Verdadero Leon*. T. H. Balboa 2102.
*The Best: Oscar d'Leon*. RMM 440017757.

# MI TIERRA

Fabio Alonso Salgado

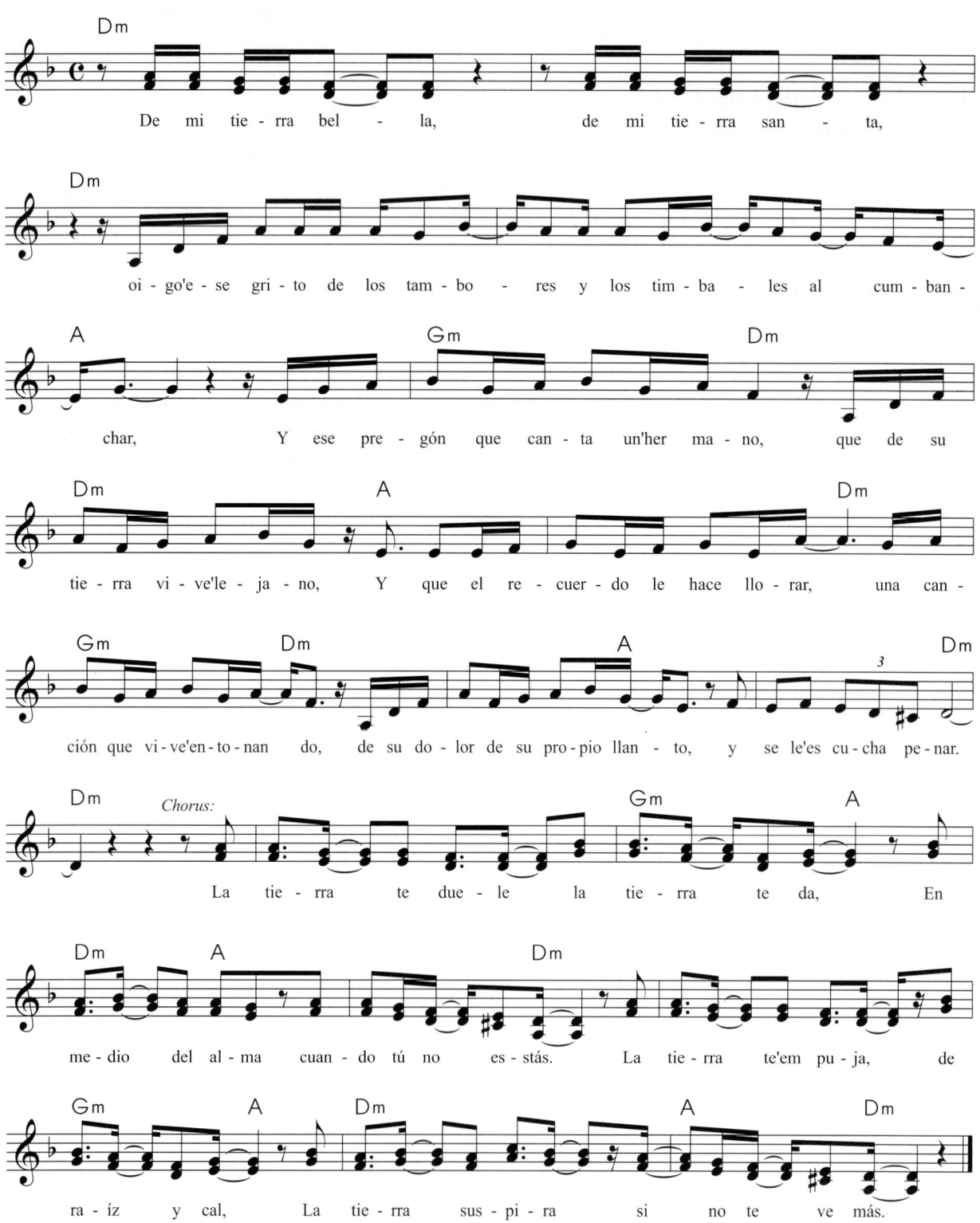

De mi tie-rra bel - la, de mi tie-rra san - ta,

oi-go'e-se gri-to de los tam-bo - res y los tim-ba - les al cum-ban-

char, Y ese pre-gón que can-ta un'her ma-no, que de su

tie-rra vi-ve'le-ja-no, Y que el re-cuer-do le hace llo-rar, una can-

ción que vi-ve'en-to-nan do, de su do-lor de su pro-pio llan-to, y se le'es cu-cha pe-nar.

*Chorus:*

La tie-rra te due-le la tie-rra te da, En

me-dio del al-ma cuan-do tú no es-stás. La tie-rra te'em pu-ja, de

ra-íz y cal, La tie-rra sus-pi-ra si no te ve más.

# MI TIERRA

CD II, Track # 20

## The Tune

Gloria Estefan sang "Mi Tierra" as a poignant tribute to the beauty of her homeland, Cuba. While it swings in Cuban salsa style, it is a universal statement of the deep connection that people make with the land of their birth—regardless of where they may be.

## The Music Culture

Cuba is the source of the *rumba*, the *mambo*, the *cha-cha-chá*, the *danson*, and the *habanera*. While Spanish colonization in Cuba began in 1511 (which essentially devastated the Indian culture through diseases brought by the Spaniards), the influx of slaves from Nigeria, Cameroon, Benin, and the Congo in the mid-eighteenth and nineteenth centuries brought the merging of European and African sensibilities into Cuban cultural expressions. Musically speaking, complex African rhythms were interlocked with the harmonies of Spain, forming what became the heartbeat of Cuban music. The island's dance music became world-renowned, and big bands, jazz combos, and pop/rock groups kept a close watch on the spirited music that arose from Havana. Following the revolution of 1959, musical artists went into self-imposed exile in Miami and New York, along with hundreds of thousands of others who sought refugee status in the United States. From the Cuban-American communities came musical talent of the status of Gloria Estefan known as the "Queen of Latin Pop." Gloria Estefan is a Havana-born singer-songwriter who began with the Spanish-language band Miami Sound Machine in the 1970s and crossed over to English-speaking audiences in the 1980s. Estefan's "Mi Tierra" is salsa-styled music that was wildly successful when it was recorded in 1993.

### The Experiences

- Listen to Track # 20 for the sounds of the cowbell, conga, sticks, the entrance of the guitar, and singer. Tap the beat and hum the melody.
- Listen to the recording again, and tap, clap, or pat the rhythm of the cowbell and sticks:

- Add a steady rhythm on the congas, finding places on the drum to play higher and lower pitch qualities.

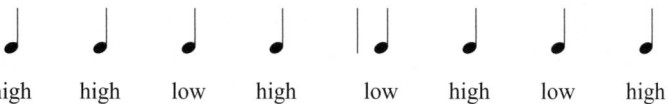

  high    high    low    high    low    high    low    high

- Perform together the cowbell, sticks, and drum parts.
- Sing with the recording to learn the lyrics, noting the pronunciation of elisions: "go-e" (gway), "un her" (oon-er), "ve-le" (blay), "ve-en" (bayn), and "le-es" (lays).
- Add the vocal harmony atop the melody.
- Play the chords on guitar in a down, down-up rhythm of ♩ ♩♪

### Recommended Listening

+*Gloria Estefan*: Mi Tierra. Sony 53807.

*The Rough Guide to Salsa Dance* (Second Edition). World Music Network. RGNET 1156 CD.

# MORE SOKOL PIE

Macedonia

*Verse:*

Mo - re    so - kol    pi - e ____

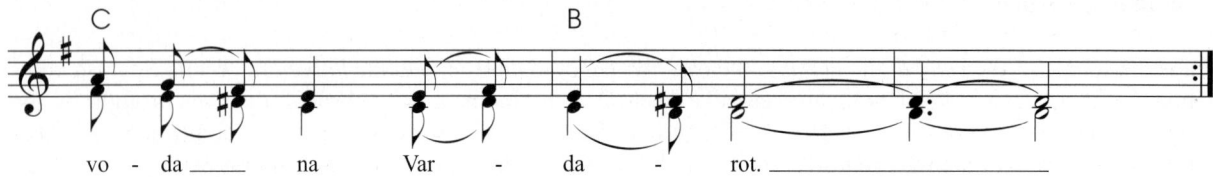

vo - da ____ na    Var - da - rot. ____

*Refrain:*

Ja - ne, ____    Ja - ne le be - lo ____ gr - lo.

*Instrumental Interlude:*

1. More sokol pie voda na Vardarot.
   Refrain: Jane, Jane le belo grlo.

2. More oj sokole, ti junacko pile,
   (Refrain)

3. More ne vide li junak da premine?
   (Refrain)

4. Junak da premine s devet ljuti rani,
   (Refrain)

5. S devet ljuti rani, site kuršumlii,
   (Refrain)

6. A deseta rana s nož e probodena.
   (Refrain)

1. A falcon drinks from the Vardar river.
   *Ref: Jana, Jana, fair throat.*

2. *Falcon, you heroic bird.*

3. *Have you seen a hero pass by?*

4. *With nine deep wounds,*

5. *All of them bullet wounds,*

6. *And the tenth, a fatal knife wound.*

# MORE SOKOL PIE

CD II, Track # 21

## The Tune

Songs in Macedonia cover love, harvest, seasonal ceremonies, and poignant memories of brave warriors, as in the case of "More Sokol Pie."

## The Music Culture

The crooked Vardar River flows northeast from Greece to Macedonia, and then south again at Skopje, the capital city of Macedonia, back into Greece. The river and its mountainous surroundings have been venues for historical encounters of both love and war. The geography and lore of the region have inspired Macedonians to sing of brave heroes, fair maidens, and fierce battles with the Turks during the five centuries of their ruling of the Macedonians during the Ottoman Empire. Macedonian women's songs evolved separately from men's songs, and given the context of women's work together in the field or in the home, they are often associated with birth, courtship, marriage, and death. They tend to be strophic, with one melody continuing for multiple verses, and parallel movement of seconds and thirds comprise the vocal lines. In "More Sokol Pie," the falcon, the fastest bird on earth (and also among the most intelligent) passes information as to the fate of the mortally wounded Macedonian hero.

### The Experiences

- Listen to Track # 21 for the prominent sound of the augmented second between the sixth and seventh scale degrees, as played by the accordion and sung by the choir.
- Tap, clap, or pat the 7/8 pattern, separating into subgroups of 3 + 2 + 2, as in 1–2–3, 1–2, 1–2.
- Sing the melody on a neutral syllable such as "moh," and on solfège syllables (starting on "re") or scale numbers (starting on "2").
- Add the vocal harmony on the neutral syllable, which tends to run a third below the melody. When there is no harmony, two voice parts sing in unison.
- Sing the lyrics of the song, noting that "pie" is pronounced "pee-ay," "š" is "sh," "ž" is "zh," "grlo" is "gril-loh," and "j"s are pronounced as "y"s (as in "Jane," or "yah-nay").
- Add chords on accordion, piano, or guitar, one to a beat (with accents on 1, 4, and 6).
- Add an ostinato rhythm on drums:

| Beat: | 1 | 2 | 3 | 4 | 5 | 6 | 7 |
|---|---|---|---|---|---|---|---|
| Pitch: | Low | high | high | Low | high | Low | high |
|  | > |  |  | > |  | > |  |

- Dance a simple movement of grapevine steps, holding hands in a line that can weave at the discretion of the leader and eventually turn into a tight coil of dancers. Start with hands held, facing front, and with weight on the left foot. (The movement runs its course across four measures, and repeats.)

| Beat: | 1–2–3 | 4–5–6–7 | 1–2–3 | 4–5–6–7 | 1–2–3 | 4–5–6–7 | 1–2–3 | 1–2–3–4 |
|---|---|---|---|---|---|---|---|---|
| Move: | R | L | R | L | R | L | L | R |
|  | step | step in front | step | step behind | step | lift | step | lift |

### Recommended Listening

+*Balkan Mixed Salad.* (Slavonia Traveling Band). Orchard 3039.
+*Pirin Folk Songs.* Gega 1727.
*Balkan Journeys Close to Home.* Golden Horn GHP004-2.

# MOZART: EINE KLEINE NACHTMUSIK
## (THEME, FIRST MOVEMENT)

W. A. Mozart

CD II, Track # 22

## The Tune

One of the most popular compositions by Wolfgang Amadeus Mozart is the chamber work "Eine Kleine Nacht-musik." The theme of the first movement is widely recognized.

## The Music Culture

One of the most enduringly popular composers of European art music, Wolfgang Amadeus Mozart, produced an enormous set of piano, symphonic, operatic, chamber, and choral music during the high Classical period of the late eighteenth century. The serenade "Eine Kleine Nachtmusik" was composed for violins, viola, and cello, with optional bass. It is widely recognized for its melodic beauty across the five movements. The theme of the first movement is sometimes referred to as a "rocket theme" due to its aggressive ascending direction. It has been used in television advertisements, movies, and video games.

### The Experiences

- Listen to Track # 22 for the signal sound of the rocket theme as played by the violins.
- Sing the melody on a neutral syllable such as "loo," and with scale syllables or scale numbers. Due to its range, drop the first ten measures an octave lower.

- Play the melody on instruments such as violins, violas, and cellos, or on flutes, clarinets, trumpets, or even piano.
- Add a harmonic accompaniment, using the chord symbols as a guide.

## Recommended Listening

+*Mozart: Eine Kleine Nacthmusik.* (Herbert von Karajan/Berlin Philharmonic) Deutsche Grammophon 29805.

+*Mozart: Eine Kleine Nachtmusik.* (Bruno Walter/Columbia Symphony Orchestra) Sony 37774.

# MOZART: THE MARRIAGE OF FIGARO
## (OVERTURE)

W. A. Mozart

## The Tune

Of the many operas that Mozart wrote, "The Marriage of Figaro" is among the most successful. Its "Overture" has become a standard concert piece for orchestras.

## The Music Culture

"Le Nozze di Figaro" (The Marriage of Figaro), an *opera buffa* (or comic opera), was composed by Wolfgang Amadeus Mozart and premiered in Vienna in 1786. The story recounts a single day in the palace, where the Count is seeking the favors of Susanna who is to be wed to Figaro, the Count's valet. Meanwhile, Cherubino, the young court page, is interested in the Countess, and the Count attempts to remove him by commissioning him into his regiment. Meanwhile, Figaro is surprised to find that he is the son of Bartolo and Marcellina, even as Figaro, Susanna, and the Countess threaten to embarrass the Count in his infidelity. A series of mistaken identities results in the Count's humiliation and then forgiveness by the Countess. The overture to the opera is unique, in that it does not use any music from the opera itself, but stands on its own themes as a favorite concert piece in the orchestral repertoire.

### The Experiences

- Sing the melody on a neutral syllable such as "lah," and with scale syllables (beginning on "mi") or scale numbers (beginning on "3").
- Play the melody on instruments such as violins, violas, and cellos, or on flutes, clarinets, trumpets, or even on piano.
- Add a harmonic accompaniment on piano, following the chord indications.

### Recommended Listening

+*Mozart: Eine Kleine Nacthmusik and Overture to The Marriage of Figaro.* (Bruno Walter/Columbia Symphony Orchestra) Sony 37774.

+*Mozart: Symphonies No. 38 and No. 41 and Overture to The Marriage of Figaro.* (Leonard Bernstein/New York Philharmonic) Sony 60973.

# MOZART: SYMPHONY NO. 40 IN G MINOR
## (FIRST MOVEMENT)

W. A. Mozart

CD III, Track # 1

## The Tune

Among the most singable orchestral themes of all time is the melody from the first movement of Mozart's "Symphony No. 40."

## The Music Culture

Born in Salzburg, Austria, in 1756, Wolfgang Amadeus Mozart was a musical prodigy, a boy wonder who was performing and composing regularly under the direction of his father, Leopold, all through his childhood. His compositions show the central traits of the Classical style: clarity, balance, and a decidedly delicate and transparent quality. He had a rare gift for imitating the music he heard, and through his European travels as a boy, he shaped a compositional language that showed Austrian-German, Italian, French, and British sensibilities. His symphonies, including No. 40, remain in the standard repertoire for orchestras everywhere in the world, due to their melodic and harmonic integrity. Mozart composed No. 40 in 1788 in just a few weeks, during which time he also completed symphonies No. 39 and No. 41. Symphony No. 40 is sometimes referred to as the "Great" G minor symphony to distinguish it from the "Little" G minor symphony, No. 25.

## The Experiences

- Listen to Track # 1 for the rhythmic motif of the theme, ♩ ♩ ♩, and tap, clap, or pat it each time it recurs.
- Sing the melody on a neutral syllable such as "noo," and on solfège syllables (beginning on "la") or scale numbers (beginning on "6").
- Play the melody on various instruments, including violin, flute, trumpet, trombone, saxophone, and piano.
- Add a harmonic accompaniment, using the chord symbols as a guide.

## Recommended Listening

*Mozart: Symphony No. 40 (Beethoven Symphony No. 5).* (New Orchestral Society of Boston) COOK 01657.
*Mozart: Symphonies No. 35–41.* (Herbert von Karajan). Deutsche Grammophone 453046.

# MUTUBARUKE EMIHANDA

Uganda

*When we heard that you wanted to visit,*

*We were extremely happy,*

*In a way we cannot say in words.*

## The Tune

In Uganda, the Bakiga people sing "Mutubaruke Emihanda" as a means of welcoming visitors to their home.

## The Music Culture

Uganda is a landlocked country in the equatorial region of East Africa, and home to many ethnic peoples, including the Bakiga, the Nyoro, the Baganda, and the Nubian. Even as the official spoken language of Uganda is English, the songs of the various people are sung in family tongues as well as in Swahili and Luganda (the language of "Mutubaruke Emihanda.") Many of the traditional songs of Uganda bear societal wisdom, as do the proverbs and stories, with messages of respect and tolerance, giving to others, welcoming the weary into their homes and lives, and sending them onward in peace. Songs of of the Bakiga people are frequently hand-clapped and danced, and may be performed on drums, beaded gourds, animal horns, and small bows and fiddles.

### The Experiences

- Sing the melody on a neutral syllable such as "ta," or on solfège syllables (beginning on "sol") or scale numbers (beginning on "5").

- Sing the lyrics to the melody, with attention to the pronuciation of *j* as "j," "rii" as "ree," "ngu" as "ngoo" (swallowing the "ng" into a sound not unlike the closed second half of the sound of "ring").

- Tap or pat and then play *djembe* or conga drums, and rattle, using these hand strokes as rhythm ostinati:

Drum 1:

Drum 2:

Rattle:

- Add the ostinato rhythms of the percussion instruments to the sung melody.

- Play the chords on piano or keyboard, even though the Bakiga need no harmonic accompaniment to perform this song.

## Recommended Listening

+Traditional Songs of Singing Cultures (Campbell, P. S.; Williamson, S.; Perron, P.). Miami: Warner Brothers.

*Music from Uganda, Volume 2: Modern Traditional.* Caprice 21553.

*Ouganda: Aux Sources du Nil.* Ocora C560032.

*Ngoma: Music from Uganda.* Music of the World CDT-142.

# MY MOTHER, YOUR MOTHER

United States

## The Tune

Children tease and taunt, and trade ideas in rhyme and in vocalized chants such as "My Mother, Your Mother" that they share and "play" in their jump-rope routines.

## The Music Culture

The ropes of backyard clotheslines were invitation enough to American children in the nineteenth and early twentieth centuries to "do something" with them. Particularly when the clothes were already dried and picked from the lines, the ropes then became objects of play for swirling, lassoing, and jumping over, under, and around. An everyday object soon became the basis of an important sporting activity: jump-rope (or "skip-rope"). With a child twirling at each end of a rope, other children would jump into the rope, jumping with it, or twice as fast, and in straightforward or "fancy" ways that include turning, touching the ground, and offering body percussion such as clapping in addition to the stamped-out sound of their feet. Children still do "jump-rope" for fun and for competition across playgrounds, schools, and even cities, at times jumping with two ropes in a "double-dutch" arrangement of two layers of motion rather than one. All they while, they chant rhymes and verses that are the oral lore of the "sport" of jump-rope.

## The Experiences

- Tap, clap, or pat the rhythm of the chant.
- Chant the lyrics while tapping, clapping, or patting the rhythm.
- On verbal cue from a leader, chant aloud ("chant") OR tap/clap/pat ("tap") the rhythm of the chant. Do one or the other, but not both, and without missing a beat.
- Play the rhythm of the chant on percussion instruments.
- Step a steady beat while chanting the rhythm. Then, jump the steady beat to match the timing of the rope.

## Recommended Listening

*Skip Rope Games*. Smithsonian Folkways SFW 07029.

*Children's Singing Games*. Multicultural Media SDL-338.

# NINE HUNDRED MILES

United States

I'm a - rid - ing on this train, I've got tears in my eyes, Tryin' to read a
let - ter from my home. _____ If this train run me right, I'll be home Sat - ur - day
night, 'Cause I'm nine hun - dred miles from my home. And I hate to hear that
lone - some whis - tle blow. It's that long lone - some train a - whis - tl - in' down.

2. Well, this train that I ride on is a hundred coaches long,
   You can hear the whistle blow a hundred miles.
   And the lonesome whistle call is the mournfulest of all,
   'Cause it's nine hundred miles from my home.
   (Chorus)

3. Well, I'll pawn you my watch, and I'll pawn you my chain,
   Pawn you my gold diamond ring.
   'Cause if this train runs me right, I'll be home Saturday night,
   'Cause I'm nine hundred miles from my home.
   (Chorus)

4. If my woman says so, I'll railroad no more,
   I'll side-tracker this wheeler and go home.
   If this train runs me right, I'll be home Saturday night,
   'Cause I'm nine hundred miles from my home.
   (Chorus)

# NINE HUNDRED MILES

## The Tune

The romance and mystery of a train ride often provoked songs like "Nine Hundred Miles," played on guitar, and sometimes with the harmonica on cue to deliver the sound of a train's distant, lonely sounding whistle.

## The Music Culture

In the years when trains were a main means of transportation from one North American hometown to the next, or to the big city depot, songs of the railroad were commonly sung, played, and heard. Railroads spread rapidly across the United States from the early 1800s, and by 1869, the east and west coasts were connected by the first transcontinental route. From 1870 to 1916, total track miles grew exponentially from 53,000 to 245,000 miles. But then as the automobile developed and paved roads expanded between the two world wars, railroad travel was reduced. Still, nostalgia for train transportation grew in those years and in the decades to follow, and music was one way to express the romance of rail travel. Songs were sung, played on guitar, and the cluster chords of a harmonica were added to standards like "Take the 'A' Train" and "Chattanooga Choo Choo" for full-sized jazz bands. "Nine Hundred Miles" harkens to a time when young men ventured far from home during the Great Depression of the 1930s, hopping trains and working the jobs they could find in the fields and factories to help them make a living to send home to their families—their parents and younger siblings, or their young wives and children. The minor key, the do-la relationship of a minor third, and the expression of destitution (so as to offer for sale the watch and ring) suggests that the song may have been of African-American origin.

### The Experiences

- Sing the song on a neutral syllable such as "nah," and on solfège syllables (beginning on "la") or scale numbers (beginning on "6").
- Sing the song with lyrics, noticing the match of the lonesome lyrics with the minor melody.
- Play the chords on guitar, giving emphasis to the bass/root pitch in the sustained verse section of thirteen measures

  with this plucked string and strumming pattern:

  Bass chord strums    -    -
  note

### Recommended Listening

+*Asch Recordings, 1939–1945, Volume 2*. (Woody Guthrie/Cisco Houston). Folkways FW 00AA4.
+*Billy Edd: USA* (Billy Edd Wheeler, Joan Summer). Monitor MON 00354.
*Hills of Home: 25 Years of Folk Music on Rounder Records*. Rounder CD AN 16/17.

# THE NOBLE DUKE OF YORK

England

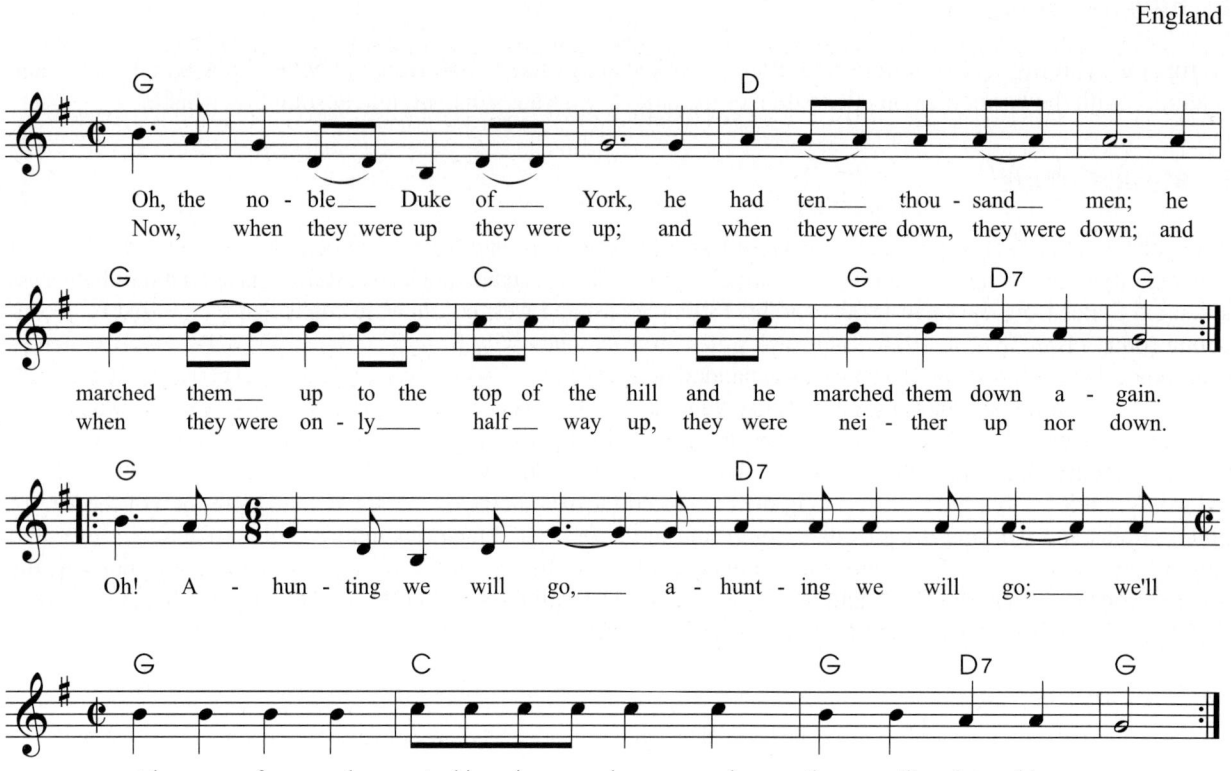

Oh, the no - ble___ Duke of___ York, he had ten___ thou - sand___ men; he
Now, when they were up they were up; and when they were down, they were down; and

marched them___ up to the top of the hill and he marched them down a - gain.
when they were on - ly___ half___ way up, they were nei - ther up nor down.

Oh! A - hun - ting we will go,___ a - hunt - ing we will go;___ we'll

catch a fox and put him in a box, and then we'll let him go.

## The Tune

A children's singing game, "The Noble Duke of York," can be traced to its British roots in the northern city of York, England.

## The Music Culture

In the United Kingdom, the inherited office of a duke offers dignities and privileges, but never independent rule. Dukes were once military commanders, often responsible for the defense of a region. As the central town of one region, York, England, is located at the confluence of the Ouse and Foss rivers. It functions as the traditional center of Yorkshire, an area of marshes and floodmeadows. There are currently twenty-four dukes in Great Britain, and while they are no longer military commanders, they continue to enjoy the privileges of nobility at the highest grade of British peerage. The duke referred to in the singing game may well be Frederick Duke of York, who was commander in chief of the British Army during most of the conflict with revolutionary France during the period 1793–1815. For those who perform the singing game, some of the fun and challenge is in changing meters from simple to compound, jigging to the phrase, "Oh, A hunting we will go."

## The Experiences

- Sing the melody of the song on a neutral syllable such as "dah," and on solfège syllalbles (beginning on "mi") or scale numbers (beginning on "3").

- Sing the lyrics of the song, tapping a steady pulse that does not change as the melody moves from a simple to a compound duple feeling.

- Play the chords on guitar or piano, with strums or arpeggiated chords making the metric shift in this manner:

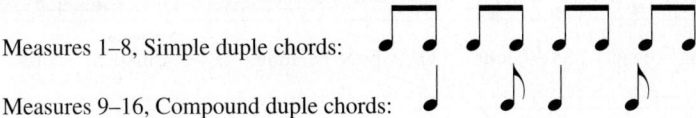

Measures 1–8, Simple duple chords:

Measures 9–16, Compound duple chords:

- In contra-dance order of two lines of partners facing one another, perform the dance inside and around these lines. The top couple takes hands and marches (or gallops) down between the lines, turning on the word "men" and returning to the original place. They then skip around the outside, down to the bottom place, and form an arch. All other couples join hands and skip to the bottom, proceed under the arch, and move back into place. The game is repeated with a new head couple; the old head couple stays at the bottom of the lines.

## Recommended Listening

+*More Music Time and Stories*. Folkways FW 07528.
+*You Can Sing It Yourself, Volume 2*. Folkways FW 07625.
*The Wild Mountain Thyme* (John Langstaff). Revels Records CD 1094.

# NORTHFIELD

United States
Lyrics: Isaac Watts, 1701
Music: Jeremiah Ingalls, 1804

# NORTHFIELD

CD III, Track # 2

## The Tune

The shape-note system of notation made its way into hymnbooks of the American heartland in the nineteenth century. "Northfield," with lyrics by Isaac Watts and melody by Jeremiah Ingalls, and other shape-note tunes survive in the small churches of the rural south and in shape-note singing circles.

## The Music Culture

William Little and William Smith published *The Easy Instructor* in 1801, based upon four-syllable solmization, and it made its way with a migration of settlers into the American South and Midwest. Four shapes—triangles (for the first and fourth scale degrees), circles (for the second and fifth degrees), squares (for the third and sixth degrees), and a diamond (for the leading, seventh, tone)—comprised the four-syllable system. Known also as "fasola" with reference to the three syllables used twice over within the octave, the diatonic scale of pitches was thus sung as "fa sol la fa sol la mi fa." By the 1820s, shape-note publications appeared in three areas: from the Shenandoah Valley through Cincinnati to St. Louis, at the center of German-language hymnody, particularly in the Philadelphia area, and the southern states, particularly in South Carolina and Georgia. Regular sessions were designed to learn to read the hymns through the designated shape notes, so that Sunday morning worship services of various Protestant denominations could be a fully participatory session of all people in the congregation. Many of the hymns were from the folk tradition of modal melodies, and when shape-note reading began to fade, the melodies were nonetheless established in the oral tradition of many church congregations. Some hymns were composed, as is the case of "Northfield," but in the style of modal folk tunes prevalent in the early nineteenth century. *The Missouri Harmony*, *Kentucky Harmony*, and *The Southern Harmony and Musical Companion* are historic collections of shape-note tunes still in use in some singing circles.

### The Experiences

- Listen to Track # 2, following the fasola syllables that are sung by the four vocal groups.
- Sing the main melody in the tenor line, using the seven-syllable solfège system or scale numbers. For the challenge of knowing the historic system, sing the melody with fasola syllables.
- Sing the harmony parts in soprano, alto, and bass lines, with solfège syllables or scale numbers, or with fasola syllables.
- Reduce the four parts to piano, playing them with two hands.

### Recommended Listening

+*Old Harp Singing*. Folkways FW 07528.

+*Nineteenth Century American Sacred Music* (Isaiah Thomas Singers). Folkways FW 32381.

+*The New England Harmony: A Collection of Early American Choral Music* (Old Sturbridge Singers). Folkways FW 32377.

# OATS, PEAS, BEANS (AND BARLEY GROW)

England

## The Tune

One long-standing singing game of children in England (and New England) is "Oats, Peas, Beans (and Barley grow)." Performed in the round, the players take their clues from the text as to what will comprise their pantomime.

## The Music Culture

Hailing back to at least the 1870s, "Oats, Peas, Beans (and Barley Grows)" is notable for its quaint references to the work of farmers in their sowing and tending of crops through the growing season, and making merry in the social dances that occurred as communities of farmers, wives, and children gathered together. The song was sung by adults at harvest suppers in nineteenth-century Sussex, England, and then (as is the tendency of many adult songs) was usurped by children and fashioned into a singing game. Variants of the song are known in England, the United States, Canada (including French Canada), France, Belgium, Sweden, Denmark, and Italy.

## The Experiences

- Sing the melody on a neutral syllable such as "bah," and on solfège syllables (beginning on "sol") or scale numbers (beginning on "5").
- Sing the lyrics to the melody. Note that there are three verses and an interlude section at "waiting for a partner" with a different melody.
- Play the chords on guitar, piano, or other harmony instrument, playing on the ♩. pulse or arpeggiating the chord tones in a ♩ ♩ ♩ rhythm.
- Select a one-measure rhythm to tap, clap, pat, and play as an ostinato on percussion instruments. Examples are (1) ♩ ♪ ♩ ♪ (2) ♩ ♪ ♩. (3) ♫♫ ♩. (4) ♩ ♪ ♫♩
- Play the singing game in a circle formation, all players facing center. A "farmer" is designated, who takes a center spot to act out the images of sowing seed, folding arms at ease, stamping and clapping on the beat, and turning around with one hand above his eyes in a "search" gesture. People then join hands in verse three ("waiting for a partner), swinging their arms back and forth, and on the fourth verse, they skip clockwise while the farmer and his "wife" (whom he has just selected) swing in the center.

## Recommended Listening

+*Old English Nursery Rhymes*. Saydisc CD-SDL419.

*The Jackfish and More Songs for Singing Children* (John Langstaff). Revels Records CD-2201.

# OH, FREEDOM

U. S.: African American

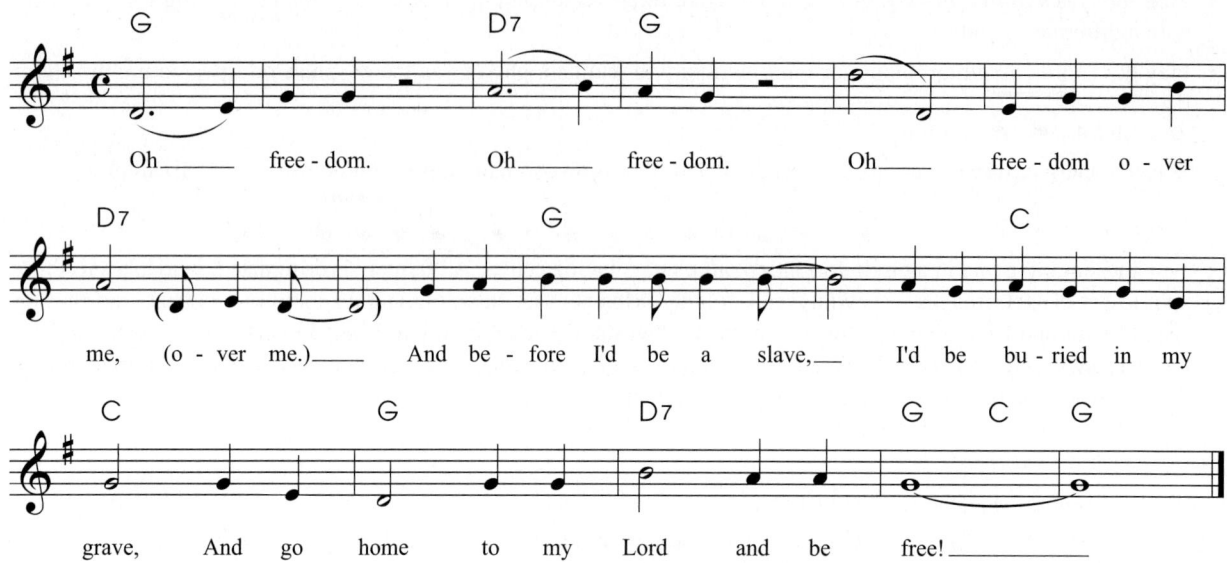

2. No more moanin', No more moanin',
   No more moanin' over me (over me).
   And before I'd be a slave,
   I'd be buried in my grave,
   And go home to my Lord and be free.

3. No more slavery, No more slavery,
   No more slavery over me (over me).
   And before I'd be a slave,
   I'd be buried in my grave,
   And go home to my Lord and be free.

4. There'll be singing. There'll be singing.
   There'll be singing over me (over me).
   And before I'd be a slave,
   I'd be buried in my grave,
   And go home to my Lord and be free.

## The Tune

Freedom songs have been vital to oppressed people, and African Americans led the way through the communal singing of songs like "Oh Freedom" through their struggle for freedom in the nineteenth century.

## The Music Culture

Freedom is a precious state of mind, a way of being. It is taken for granted by those who have it, and is much sought after by those who do not know it. The capture, transport, and selling of Africans in the trade markets of American cities and towns in the eighteenth and nineteenth centuries reinforced the perspective of people as property whom "buyers" could assign to various tasks to aid their work on farms and plantations. The enslavement of

African people as the property of their white landowners and bosses ensured their loss of freedom, such that they were at the mercy of a schedule and set of tasks that were not their own to choose. In these challenging times, music was a means of making free, at least in the mind, and African Americans took to singing as they worked in the fields and in the home, in the evenings, and at worship. They sang their songs of freedom without instruments, but sometimes with hand-hewn guitars, banjos, and fiddles, and often with the accompaniment of their own clapping and stamping.

## The Experiences

- Sing the song on a neutral syllable such as "lah," and on solfège syllables (beginning on "sol") or scale numbers (beginning on "5").
- Sing the lyrics of the melody, with a deep breath for the octave descent at "Oh" (measure 4). Note also the imitation of "over me"; a second vocal part can sing this as the lead voices sustain the pitch for "me."
- Play the chords on piano, guitar, or banjo, keeping a solid quarter-note pulse.
- Explore possibilities for vocal harmony, striving to sing the thirds and fifths of the chords indicated.
- Possibilities abound for percussion accompaniment, especially with tambourine (on beats 2 and 4) and a drum in a supportive ostinato rhythm such as ♩ ♩ ♪ ♩ ♪

## Recommended Listening

+*Call for Freedom*. Folkways FW 07566.

+*Wade in the Water, Volume 1*. Smithsonian Folkways SFW40072.

# OLD JOE CLARK

U. S.: Appalachian and Ozark Mountains

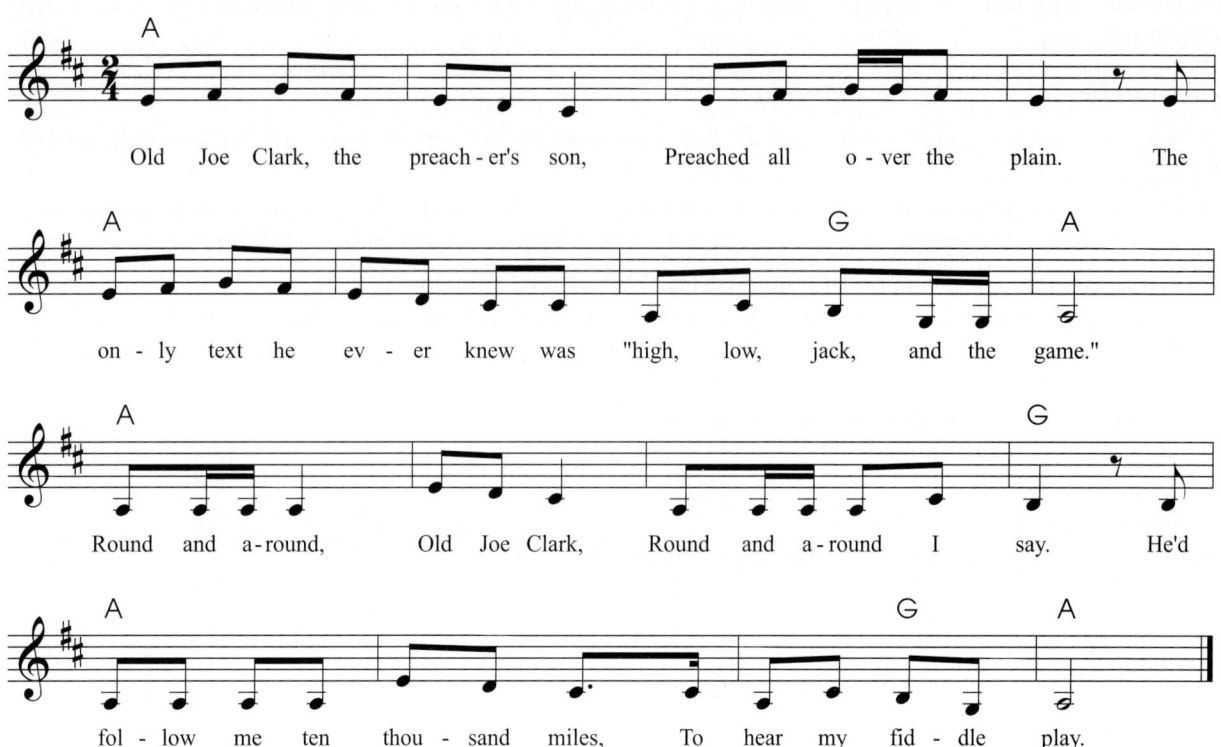

Old Joe Clark, the preach-er's son, Preached all o-ver the plain. The

on-ly text he ev-er knew was "high, low, jack, and the game."

Round and a-round, Old Joe Clark, Round and a-round I say. He'd

fol-low me ten thou-sand miles, To hear my fid-dle play.

2. Old Joe Clark he had a mule,
   His name was Morgan Brown,
   And every tooth in that mule's head
   Was sixteen inches round.

3. Old Joe Clark had a yellow cat,
   She would neither sing nor pray.
   She stuck her head in a buttermilk jar
   And washed her sins away.

4. Old Joe Clark he had a house,
   fifteen stories high.
   And every story in that house
   Was filled with chicken pie.

5. Sixteen horses in my team,
   The leaders, they are blind,
   And every time the sun goes down,
   There's a pretty girl on my mind.

CD III, Track # 3

## The Tune

The popular fiddle tune "Old Joe Clark" was "mountain music" to American people in the southern Appalachians, the Alleghenies, the Smokies, the Ozarks, and the Piedmont region of the Carolinas. It traveled to other instruments, too, finding its way into the hands of mandolin, banjo, and guitar players.

## The Music Culture

Some refer to "Old Joe Clark" as a square dance, while others call it a fiddle tune. In fact, many fiddle tunes—from "Cripple Creek" to "Soldier's Joy"—made their way into the dance repertoire of reels, waltzes, square and contra-dances of rural America. This tune seems to have been popular in Tennessee, and Alan Lomax found that it had been recorded solely by Nashville-area musicians from 1927 to 1942. The harmonic language of the verse's melody is standard in the Southern musical repertory: a six-tone (hexatonic) Mixolydian mode on A (A–B–C–D–E–F–G). The two sections, comprised of verse and refrain, invite dancers to emit an energetic bounce. The words (which typically are added later to a fiddle tune) are not without humor, telling of Joe Clark as the preacher's gambling son, his mule's large teeth, his cat's penchant for buttermilk, and his house full of chicken pie.

### The Experiences

- Listen to Track # 3, hum the Mixolydian mode, whose pitches resemble a major scale except for the lowered seventh degree.
- Sing the song on a neutral syllable such as "dah," and on solfège syllables (beginning the verse on "sol") or scale numbers (beginning the verse on "5").
- Sing the lyrics slowly at first, and then gradually increasing to the quick tempo of a fiddle tune.
- Play the chords on guitar, piano, mandolin, dulcimer, or other harmony instrument. Use a lively ♪ ♪ rhythm that gives rise to a dancing feeling.
- Play the melody on violin while continuing the chording, as introduction and interludes between the sung verses.

### Recommended Listening

+*Bluegrass from the Blue Ridge: A Half-Century of Change: Country Band Music of Virginia* (Bluegrass Buddies). Folkways FW 03832.

+*Clark Kessinger Live at Union Grove* (Clark Kessinger, Gene Meade, Gene Parker). Folkways FW 02337.

*Appalachian Stomp: Bluegrass Classics.* Rhino R2-71870.

# OLD ROGER

England

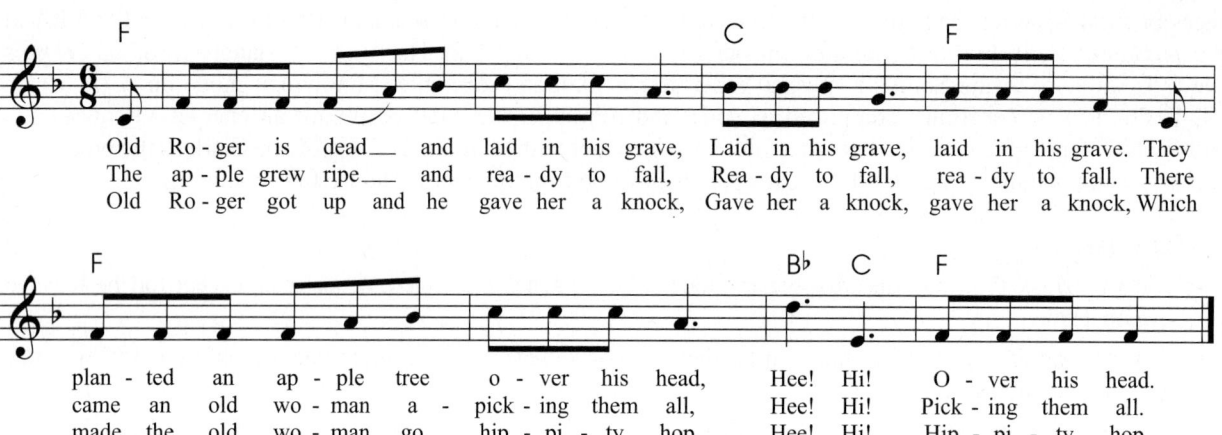

```
Old   Ro - ger   is    dead__   and   laid   in   his   grave,   Laid   in   his   grave,   laid   in   his   grave. They
The   ap - ple   grew   ripe__   and   rea - dy    to   fall,    Rea - dy    to   fall,    rea - dy    to   fall. There
Old   Ro - ger   got    up    and   he    gave  her   a    knock,  Gave  her    a   knock,  gave  her    a   knock, Which
```

```
plan - ted    an    ap - ple   tree    o - ver   his   head,   Hee!  Hi!   O - ver   his   head.
came   an     old   wo - man   a -  pick - ing  them   all,   Hee!  Hi!   Pick - ing  them   all.
made   the    old   wo - man   go   hip - pi - ty   hop,    Hee!  Hi!   Hip - pi - ty   hop.
```

## The Tune

"Old Roger" is a playful song sung by children in England, Ireland, Canada, and the United States. It may once have been a means for restoring a lightness of being to a community following a mourning period for someone in their midst who had passed on.

## The Music Culture

Like ballads, carols, and narrative songs of old England, children's songs and singing games also have histories that precede record keeping and whose origins can only be surmised. In the case of "Old Roger," folklorists have deduced its age (at least 400 years, possibly dating to the late 1500s) by nature of its antiquated language, in particular the phrase "dead and laid in his grave." The song is often acted out rather than danced, with many reported instances of Old Roger lying flat on his back in the middle of a circle. A second child stands in the circle, representing an apple tree, and another child pretends to be the old woman picking apples. There is a chase, and Old Roger taps (knocks) the old woman; the old woman becomes Old Roger in the next performance. There are numerous variants of the song, with added verses, changes of name (including "Poor Johnnie," "Old Cromley," and "Old Grumbler"), and various exclamations ("Heigh-ho" and "Hee-haw"). Further, there is an association of "Old Roger" by way of intent and text to the well-known folk song, "Cock Robin." Such is the nature of the oral tradition in which songs are passed from one singer to another, their essence preserved through many renditions.

### The Experiences

- Sing the song on a neutral syllable such as "tee," and on solfège syllables (beginning on "sol") or scale numbers (beginning on "5").
- Take special note of the descending leap of the seventh in the penultimate measure, "la" to "ti," and practice singing it accurately.
- Tap out an ostinato rhythm while singing the verses:

- Play the chords on concertina, guitar, or piano, two chords per measure or an arpeggiated pattern of fast but steady pulses.
- As described previously, the song can be enacted dramatically.

## Recommended Listening

+*Wild Mountain Thyme*. Revels CA 1094.
+*Folk Songs with the Seegers*. Prestige PR 7375.

# ONE AUGUST MORN

Jamaica

## The Tune

Children in Jamaica sing the pentachordal "One August Morn," and when together in a group they offer their spontaneous imitations of the lead singer's part.

## The Music Culture

Jamaica, a Caribbean island nation, is located south of Cuba and west of Haiti and the Dominican Republic. The third most populous English-speaking country in the Americas, after the United States and Canada, it sits out in a sea where other islanders speak Spanish, French, Dutch, or even Hindi. Jamaica's language, like those of other Caribbean islands, is a remnant of the colonization efforts of the region by Europeans. The British period of rule of a massive population of Africans imported into slave labor brought Jamaica its reputation in the nineteenth century as the world's largest sugar-exporting nation. A series of revolts by the disproportionately large black population (the black to white ratio was 20:1) for over a century led finally to full independence of the Jamaicans. Today there remains a severe economic inequality in Jamaica, and a cycle of violence, drugs, and poverty that has not yet been overcome. The music of Jamaica is inspired by its history and present conditions, such that British elements are found in some of the folk songs while African-inspired music (in Jamaican *reggae*, for example) is prominent in social, work, ritual, and recreational/dance forms. Much of the music is participatory, improvisation is welcome, and many songs are linked to games and dances.

## The Experiences

- Sing the melody on a neutral syllable such as "mah," and on solfège syllables (beginning on "sol") or scale numbers (beginning on "5").
- Sing the melody of just five pitches (a pentachord of "sol" to "re," or 5 to 2) with lyrics.
- Add the imitative phrases at the close of each melodic line. For harmony, sustain the last pitch of each lead-line phrase while the imitative phrase is sung.
- Play the chords on guitar or piano, utilizing a pattern of bass and chord, and accenting beats 2 and 4.

| Beat: | 1 | 2 | 3 | 4 |
|---|---|---|---|---|
| Play: | bass tone | chord | bass tone | chord |

- Explore other imitative phrases, ones that imitate the words but that utilize different pitch material. For example, instead of singing only Gs on "One August Morn," sing an exact pitch replication of the lead voice.

## Recommended Listening

*Children's Jamaican Songs and Games*. Folkways FW 07250.

*Folk Music of Jamaica*. Folkways FW 04453.

*Jamaican Folk Songs*. Folkways FW 06846.

# ONE COLD AND FROSTY MORNING

U. S.: South

One cold and fros - ty morn - ing, just as the sun did rise, The

poss - um roared, the rac - coon howled, 'Cause he be - gan to freeze, He

drew him - self up in a knot, with his knees up to his chin, and

ev' - ry thing had to clear the track when he stretched out a - gain. Old

Jes - sie was a gen - tle - man a - mong the old - en times.

## The Tune

A full diatonic scale is embedded within the melody of this morning wake-up song from the American south, "One Cold and Frosty Morning."

## The Music Culture

The work of folklorists in the 1930s and 40s brought about a stream of songs from rural areas and small towns of America. The Lomax family—father John and son Alan (and daughter Bess Lomax Hawes)—were important in building the Archive of American Folk Song at the Library of Congress. They traveled the southern United States in the 1930s and 1940s with primitive recording equipment (including a 300-pound recorder) to farms, churches, cafés and bars, and documented folk song and instrumental music, blues, and cowboy lore. Several generations of the Seeger family were instrumental in preserving and disseminating American folk music. Charles Seeger was appointed to the music division of the Resettlement Agency, a federal New Deal organization. His wife, Ruth Crawford Seeger, shifted from composing in the 1930s to working closely with the Lomaxes in transcribing and then writing the classic *American Folksongs for Children* in 1948. Her stepson, Pete Seeger, led a revival in folk music performance in the 1940s and 1950s, and her children Mike Seeger and Peggy Seeger became professional musicians who joined in the course of disseminating folk music through performance for many decades forward. Songs like "One Cold and Frosty Morning" can be traced to the folklore, transcriptions, and dissemination efforts of the Lomaxes and Seegers.

## The Experiences

- Sing the melody on neutral syllable such as "dee," and on solfège syllables or scale numbers.

- Sing the lyrics, giving energy to this bouncy tune with clear and articulate pronunciation.

- Play chords on guitar, autoharp, dulcimer, piano, or other harmonic instrument. For the stringed folk instruments, steady eighth-note strums are functional and fitting, while the piano can play a "boom-chink" figure of a bass note on beat 1 and a chord on beat 2.

- Add a two-measure percussion ostinato accompaniment of available instruments such as drum, sticks, and metal objects (cowbell, pots and pans):

## Recommended Listening

+*American Folk Songs for Children* (Peggy and Mike Seeger). Rounder Select 11543.

*The Jackfish and More Songs for Singing Children* (John Langstaff). Revels Records CD-2201.

# OVER MY HEAD

U. S.: African American

2. Over my head, there is dancing in the street.
   There must be joy somewhere.

3. Over my head, there's a play about to start,
   There must be joy somewhere.

4. Over my head, there's a rainbow of surprise,
   There must be joy somewhere.

## The Tune

The traditional songs of African Americans are frequently sacred in tone, or at least suggestive of a "higher power," as in the case in "Over My Head" where music, dance, a play, and a rainbow are believed to be unfolding in the heavens above.

## The Music Culture

Religion and churches have been central to the lives of African Americans, and their many religious, social, and cultural functions continue to this day. Through the sacred songs they sang at church and in their lives beyond it, they found refuge for unrestricted cultural and personal expression. Secular and sacred worlds became intertwined, too, so that thoughts of salvation and the heavens, as well as Biblical stories of the oppressed Hebrew people and the cruel Egyptians, permeated their folk spirituals and songs. The promise of a better life was a regular theme in their pre-emancipation songs (many of which continue in the repertoire even now), and these songs were vital in providing a forum for social commentary and criticism. Hope resonated through the songs, with words to the effect that there was joy to be had beyond troubles of their daily experience.

## The Experiences

- Sing the melody on a neutral syllable such as "mah," and on solfège syllables or scale numbers.

- Sing the lyrics, with attention to the sustained as well as short and syncopated rhythms.

- For a more relaxed swing, treat the notation as a jazz piece, translating the ♩. ♪ to a ♩ ♪ feeling of a triplet swing. Convert the 4/4 to 12/8, allowing the triplet feeling to permeate throughout.

- Sing a vocal harmony, finding chord tones to "dress up" the melody.

- While singing, clap on the off-beats 2 and 4, and step side-to-side in a step-close movement that shifts the weight from right to left sides.

- Play the chords on piano and guitar, exploring the potential for full chords and broken chords played steadily on the beat. Note that there are several quick harmonic shift at the cadences.

## Recommended Listening

+*Praise the Lord: Gospel Music in Washington D.C.* Smithsonian Folkways SFW 40113.

+*Spirituals in Concert* (Kathleen Battle/Jessye Norman). Deutsche Grammophon 429 790-2.

*When Gospel Was Gospel*. Shanachie SHA-CD-6064.

# PADDY WORKS ON THE RAILWAY

United States

Eight-een hun-dred and for-ty-one, That's the year my trou-bles be-gun, That's the year my

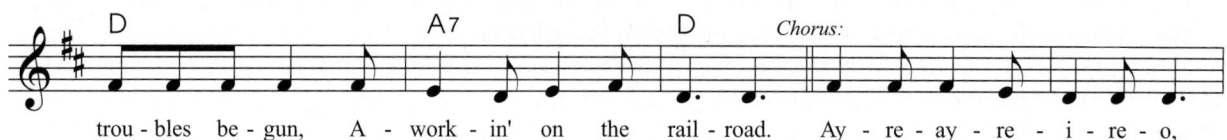

trou-bles be-gun, A - work-in' on the rail-road. Ay - re - ay - re - i - re - o,

Ay - re - ay - re - i - re - o, Ay - re - ay - re - i - re - o, A - work-in' on the rail-road.

2. Eighteen hundred and forty-two,
   That's the year I lost my shoe,
   That's the year I lost my shoe,
   A-workin' on the railroad.

3. Eighteen hundred and forty-three,
   That's the year I crossed the sea,
   That's the year I crossed the sea,
   A-workin' on the railroad.

4. Eighteen hundred and forty-four
   That's the year I reached the shore,
   That's the year I reached the shore,
   A-workin' on the railroad.

5. Eighteen hundred and forty-five,
   I'd rather be dead than be alive,
   I'd rather be dead than be alive,
   A-workin' on the railroad.

6. Eighteen hundred and forty-six,
   Picked up my shovel and picked up my picks.
   Picked up my shovel and picked up my picks,
   A-workin' on the railroad.

7. Eighteen hundred and forty-seven,
   That's the year I went to heaven,
   That's the year I went to heaven,
   A-workin' on the railroad.

8. Eighteen hundred and forty-eight,
   Saint Peter said I was too late,
   Saint Peter said I was too late,
   A-workin' on the railroad.

9. Eighteen hundred and forty-nine,
   The devil said that I was just in time,
   The devil said that I was just in time,
   A-workin' on the railroad.

# PADDY WORKS ON THE RAILWAY

## The Tune

Irish immigrants arriving to America in the nineteenth century took the jobs that they could get, including hard labor in the construction of the American railroad. "Paddy Works on the Railway" gives an account of one Irish worker's time in the railroad enterprise.

## The Music Culture

Some of the industrial underpinnings of America were built through the work of immigrant Irish tarriers, shanty-men, and jerries. The waves of Irish immigration began during the Irish potato famine (1845–1849) and continued through the nineteenth and into the twentieth century. These immigrants desired to escape not only famine and poverty but also British oppression. "Paddy Works on the Railway" is likely to have taken a route similar to other Irish traditional songs, beginning on land in the "ould sod" and later shanghaied into service at sea (and collected by some as a *sea shantey*) before arriving again on land in the New World. While the text states 1841 as the year of Paddy's emigration (with several versions citing 1861), folklorists place the song as first popular in the 1850s. There are two principal tunes for the shantey, with this older one sung in a major mode while a more popular one published by the Lomaxes in *American Ballads and Folk Songs* traces the minor-key melody of "When Johnny Comes Marching Home." The sung has been much recorded, by the Clancy Brothers, Ewan MacColl, Pete Seeger, Tom Glazer, the Dubliners, and the Weavers.

### The Experiences

- Sing the melody on a natural syllable such as "pah," and on solfège syllables (beginning on "mi") or scale numbers (beginning on "3").
- Sing the lyrics, with recognition that it is the combination of the clearly enunciated words with the melody, rather than the melody alone, that gives interest to the song, and that the chorus is like a light *vocalise*, or vocal exercise, that should just bounce along.
- Play chords on guitar, piano or other harmony instrument to accompany the song, sounding (at least) two chords per measure on the ♩· of the compound meter.
- Tap, clap, or pat a steady ♩· with the left hand, and with the right hand, a bouncing rhythmic ostinato of ♩ ♪ ♫♫
- Transfer the body percussion to playing the two rhythms on hand drums.
- Trade the verses, parceling them out among solo singers, and bringing the full chorus in on "Ay-re-ay-re-i-re-o."
- Invent new verses to describe Paddy's work, or create a new set of lyrics on the same melody to describe a different line of work.
- Experiment with singing the text to the other "Paddy" melody, "When Johnny Comes Marching Home."

### Recommended Listening

+*Sea Chanties and Forecastle Songs at Mystic Seaport* (Stuart M. Franck). Folkways FW 37300.

+*Cisco Houston Sings American Folksongs*. Folkways FW 02919.

*Far from the Shamrock Shore: Mick Maloney*. NY: Crown Publishers 2002. (Book with CD).

# PIKI MAI

Maori

CD III, Track # 4

## The Tune

For the Maori, the offical greeting is a vital component for starting a meeting of friends and visitors to their homes and *marai* (community center). "Piki Mai" is an up-tempo Maori song of welcome.

## The Music Culture

As one version of oral history tells it, the Maori people arrived from eastern Polynesia about 1,000 years ago in seven great canoes to "the land of the long white cloud" which they named Aotearoa. That name has been returned to designations of the country, sitting side-by-side with New Zealand in honor of the bicultural history that is both Maori and British. The Maori have retained their language, their folkways, and much of their music and dance as emblematic of their identity as the first people of the island nation. Their traditional music consists of action songs of European melodies with Maori words and actions, called *waita-a-ringa* or *waiata kori*, that date to the beginning of the twentieth century, and the wholly indigenous Maori chant. *Waita* is in fact a term loosely used to refer to all sung styles, although they are categorized according to functions that include laments for the dead, love songs, aids to speech making, and songs of welcome and farewell. Movement and dance are integral to Maori song, and the *poi* style of dance with sung accompaniment features fast-tempo melodies within a small range, to which *poi* balls (puffy white balls on strings) are swung rhythmically by dancers against their bodies. The Maori dancers wear skirts, called *piu piu*, that are traditionally made from long fibrous leaves that are scraped, buried in a muddy marsh so as to dye them dark brown, and then washed and curled into slender tubes. The image of singing dancers who stamp their feet, clap their hands, slap their *poi* balls, and swing the tubes of the *piu piu* are fitting to the "Piki Mai" greeting song.

## The Experiences

- Listen to Track # 4 for the percussive rhythms and the choral sound of the men's and women's voices, while tapping a steady pulse.
- Sing the melody of the first (notated) section on a neutral syllable such as "loo," and on solfège syllables (beginning on "mi") or scale numbers (beginning on "3").
- Listen to the recording while singing the lyrics to the first notated section; note that the phrase "piki nuku" in measures 12–13 is chanted rather than sung.
- Play the chords on guitar or ukelele in a fast rhythm of quarter notes.
- Add vocal harmony to coincide with the chords that accompany the melody.
- Dance a basic movement, gradually layering in these movements:

|  |  |
|---|---|
| Beat 1: | stamp |
| Beat 2: | clap |
| Beat 3: | shake hands front right |
| Beat 4: | shake hands front left |

For every first beat, shift the weight of the feet from left to right. Note that "shake hands front" requires arms to extend across the body and parallel to one another, first to the right and then to the left.

- With handmade *poi* balls of tissue and string, practice small circular and figure-eight movements that extend across two or four beats.

## Recommended Listening

*Kahurangi: Music of the New Zealand Maori*. Monitor MON 71827.
*Maori Songs of New Zealand*. Folkways FW 04433.

# POOR WAYFARING STRANGER

John Jacob Niles

2. I know dark clouds will gather 'round me,

    I know my way is steep and rough,

    But beauteous fields lie just beyond me,

    Where souls redeemed their vigil keep;

    I'm goin' there to meet my mother,

    She said she'd meet me when I come.

    I'm only goin' over Jordan,

    I'm only goin' over home.

3. I want to wear a crown of glory,

    When I get home to that bright land,

    I want to shout Salvation's story,

    In concert with that bloodwashed band;

    I'm goin' there to  meet my Saviour,

    To sing his praise forever more,

    Im only goin' over Jordan

    I'm only goin' over home.

# POOR WAYFARING STRANGER

## The Tune

Not all traditional songs are of unknown origin and untraceable to a composer, preserver, or transmitter. "Poor Wayfaring Stranger" is a folk spiritual attributed to John Jacob Niles that reflects the music that surrounded him in his youth.

## The Music Culture

Ballads and folk songs need balladeers and folksingers to preserve and transmit them, and to create and shape them as well. John Jacob Niles (1892–1980) made his contribution as composer, collector, and balladeer. Growing up in rural Kentucky, he heard the songs of the farmworkers his father employed, and was influenced by these songs. He published a number of influential folk song collections, including *Songs My Mother Never Taught Me* (1929) (collected from soldiers he had met while in the service) and *The Ballad Book* (1961). Following conservatory studies in vocal performance, Niles sang with the Lyric Opera of Chicago, but returned to the mountains of North Carolina (and later back to rural Kentucky) to write songs that grew from music that surrounded him. He made his own lutes and Appalachian dulcimers, recorded for RCA Victor, and toured widely from the 1930s onward. His musical sensibilities retained a folk song style in his songs, including minor and modal melodies in "Black is the Color of My True Love's Hair," "Go Way from My Window," "I Wonder as I Wander," and "Poor Wayfaring Stranger." His songs have become prominent in the repertoire of the American folk song tradition.

### The Experiences

- Sing the melody on a neutral syllable such as "lah," and on solfège syllables (beginning on "la") or scale numbers (beginning on "6").
- Sing the lyrics of the song, noting its syllabic character (one pitch per syllable) and the references to spiritual salvation.
- Play the chords on guitar, autoharp, dulcimer, or piano. Use an arpeggiated or plucking accompaniment in ♩ or ♪ ♩ pulses.
- Explore possibilities for vocal harmony, sounding open fifths (or fourths) on "ah" at the beginning of each measure.

### Recommended Listening

*My Precarious Life in the Public Domain* (John Jacob Niles). Revola CRREVI38.

*I Wonder as I Wander* (John Jacob Niles). Empire 7005063.

# PULLIN' A SKIFF

U. S.: Ora Dell Graham

I went down - town, to get my grip. I come back home, just a -

pull - in' a skiff, just a - pull in' a skiff. I went up - stairs, to

make my bed. I made a mis - take and I bumped my head, just a -

pul - in' a skiff, just a - pull - in' a skiff. I went down - stairs to

meet my cow. I made a mis - take and I miss'd that stile, just a -

pull - in' a skiff, just a - pull - in' a skiff. To - mor - row, to - mor - row, to -

mor - row ne - ver come. To - mor - row, to - mor - row, to - mor - row and a

bone. And a hm mm, and a hm mm, and a hm mm hm mm hm mm!

# PULLIN' A SKIFF

CD III, Track # 5

## The Groove

Children were engaged in rhythmic speech long before the hip-hop culture had established itself. An example of their rhythmically driven play is the jump-rope chant of Ora Dell Graham, "Pullin' the Skiff."

## The Music Culture

The establishment of a national folk music archive was a long time in the making, beginning in 1928 with the advocacy of Carl Engle, chief of the Library of Congress Music Division. Engle was followed by folklorist Robert Winslow Gordon, who made 1,000 field recordings all the way from North Carolina's mountain banjoists to San Francisco's waterfront windjammers. John A. Lomax replaced Gordon in 1933, and with his then eighteen-year-old son, Alan, he began a series of journeys down America's backroads to record over 3,200 discs and 75 cylinders of songs, instrumental music, folktales, sermons, and prayers. The Lomaxes recorded performances on a 315-pound machine that they carried in the rear of their Ford sedan. There are eighty-six recordings in a series they called "Folk Music in the United States," which includes the music of fiddlers, Sacred Harp singers, players of banjo, harmonica, and blues guitar, and children. One excursion to the Drew Colored High School in Drew, Mississippi, in 1940, brought them to a group of black school children, including Ora Dell Graham, a little girl who offered her jump-rope chant, "Pullin' the Skiff," to be recorded. In conversation on the original recording with John Lomax, she responds to his question as to the source of her knowledge of the chant: "I just learned it by—just by go on singin' it."

### The Experiences

- Listen to Track # 5 and follow the child's verse and the steady pulse of the rope as it strikes the pavement.
- Chant the words rhythmically, noting the extent of syncopation and the mention of everyday items and events. A "skiff" is a wheeled or wheelless platform for transporting heavy loads.
- Listen to the recording, and chant along with attention to the rhythmic nuances.
- Chant the speech rhythm with soloists on "the verse lines" and group response on the "chorus" section, "just a-pullin' a skiff, just a-pullin' a skiff."
- Improvise a percussion track of body percussion or drums, rattles, and bells, to accompany the chant.

### Recommended Listening

+*A Treasury of Library of Congress Field Recordings* (Alan Lomax). Rounder Records ROUN 1500.
*Deep River of Song: Alabama.* Rounder Select 1829.

# QIUGAVIIT

Inuit: John Park Wheeler

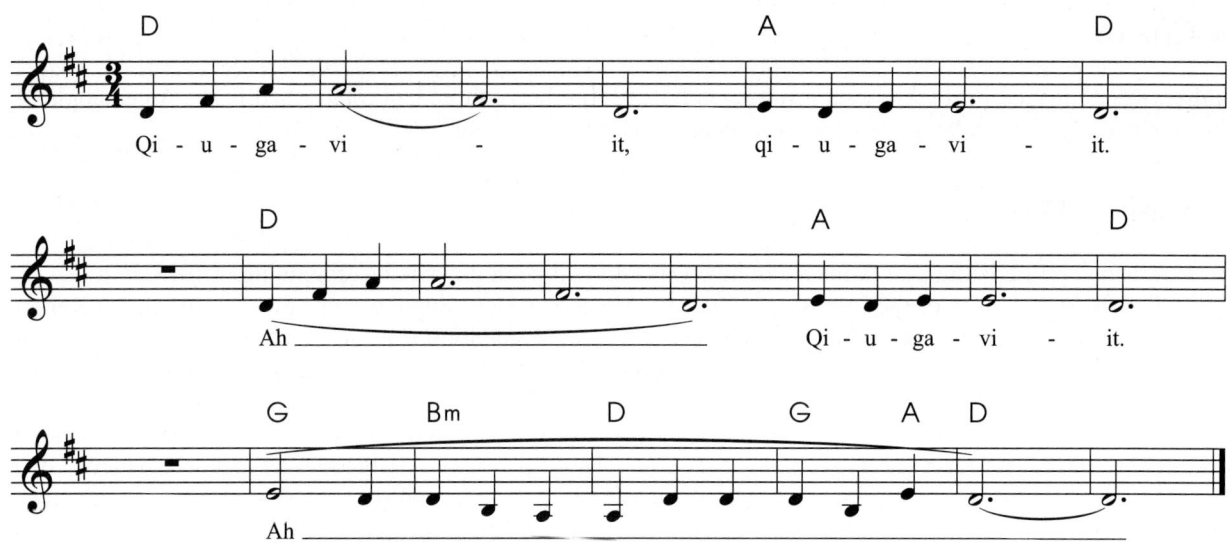

*Do you know now?*

CD III, Track # 6

## The Tune

The Inuit people of the Arctic region of Canada and Alaska embrace both traditional and contemporary sounds in their music. "Qiugaviit," (called "Quijujavit" by composer Jon Park Wheeler), combines Inuit language and melody with contemporary instrumentation and technology in a song that scolds a hunter for not dressing warmly for the weather.

## The Music Culture

There are a number of Inuit cultures spread across Arctic Canada and Alaska. They adapted to the harsh climate by developing hunting and fishing skills, including whaling technology, and building ice houses, called igloos, and sea canoes. Once called Eskimos, the Inuit trace their history in the region to about 2000 BCE. While most Inuit nowadays are connected to the wider world cable TV and the Internet, they connect with their past by singing songs to the accompaniment of a large drum of caribou skin that is played with a bone/antler or wooden beater. Their vocal music ranges from a soft and breathy quality to a guttural throat-singing technique, learned from the elders and practiced on the dark winter days when there is plenty of time for indoor practice. They sing a traditional song form called *pisik*, fitting their words precisely with the drumbeat, and sometimes dancing or swaying as they sing. A singing duo, Tudjaat, adapted an old *pisik* to their performance "Qiugaviit." The Inuit word translates as "Do you know now?"—the question raised by the Inuit elder to a man who went hunting without dressing for the cold, and nearly froze to death. The song is intended to underscore the importance of thoughtful action, of rising above ignorance, of listening to the elders and to the forces of nature.

## The Experiences

- Listen to Track # 6 to hear the sounds of the arctic wind, the caribou drum, the singers, the accordion, and the electric guitar. Follow the pulse of the drum by tapping along.
- Sing the melody on a neutral syllable such as "vah," and on solfège syllables or scale numbers.
- Listen to the recording, and sing only the repeated "qiugaviit" ("Do you know now?") when it occurs, pronouncing it as "quay-yoo-yah-vay." The rest of the melody may be sung on a neutral syllable such as "ah."
- Play the ongoing pulse on hand drum.
- Add chords on guitar, accordion, or piano, strummed or rolled once per measure or as the chords change.

## Recommended Listening

+*A Native American Odyssey*. Putumayo PUTU 144-2.

+*Tudjaat*. Rescue Records 80226.

*Eskimos of Hudson Bay and Alaska*. Folkways FW 04444.

# QUA CẦU GIÓ BAY

Vietnam

Yêu  nhau  còi___  áo  ý  a  cho  nhau  Về  nhà  dối  rằng  cha  dối

me  a  ý  a  Rằng  a  ý  a  qua  cầu  Rằng  a  ý  a  qua

cầu.  Tình  tình  tình  gió_____  bay  Tình  tình  tình  gió_____  bay.

2. Yêu nhau còi nón ý a cho nhau.
   Về nhà dôi rằng cha dối me a ý a.
   Rằng a ý a qua câu. Rằng ý a qua cầu.

3. Yêu nhau còi nhẫn ý a cho nhau.
   Về nhà dôi rang cha dối me a ý a.
   Rằng a ý a qua câu. Rằng ý a qua cầu.

Final chorus:
Tình, tình, tình, gió bay.
Tình, tình, tình, dánh roi.

1. *Loving you, I give my coat,*
   *Coming back home, I lie to father and mother,*
   *"On the bridge, the wind has taken it away."*

2. *Loving you, I give you my hat,*
   *Coming back home, I lie to father and mother,*
   *"On the bridge, the wind has taken it away."*

3. *Loving you, I give you my ring,*
   *Coming back home, I lie to father and mother,*
   *"On the bridge, because of the wind.*
   *it has dropped into the river."*

Traditional, Vietnam, as sung by Phong Nguyen.  From Nguyen, P. T. & Campbell, P. S. (1990). *From Rice Paddies and Temple Yards: Traditional Music of Vietnam.* Danbury, CT: World Music Press. Courtesy World Music Press.

CD III, Track # 7

## The Tune

Even in cultures where marriages are traditionally arranged by parents, it is not unusual to have other friendships before the time of marriage itself. The Vietnamese song, "Qua Cầu Gió Bay," tells of discreet gift-giving between a young boy and girl—and the stories they make up to keep the friendship to themselves.

## The Music Culture

The music of the Vietnamese is rich with highly melodic vocal forms, including lullabies, children's songs, and the songs of peasant-workers in the rice paddies. There are antiphonal songs sung by boys and girls, and *quan ho*, a competition song that is particular to the northern province of Ha Bac near Hanoi. During the spring and autumn festivals, groups of young people gather by a lake or river, or in a temple yard, to sing songs that are partly improvised. They practice their verses in advance, but also strive to keep a spontaneity about the singing. Girls may sing songs that are then personally interpreted and improvised upon by boys; hence, the antiphony. At the actual *quan ho* competition, participants don traditional dress to represent their homes and villages, and sing within the strictures of the song form and yet improvise with an originality that brands the songs as their own. "Qua Cầu Gió Bay" is one of the best known of the old *quan ho* competition songs, complete with a call-and-response style. Its message communicates youthful defiance of traditional customs, even when, in the end, parent-arranged marriages continue to hold sway past the friendship-making period of adolescence. Sung unaccompanied or with the support of a *dan tranh* (zither), the song offers a contagious, lyrical melody.

## The Experiences

- Listen to Track # 7 for the sound of the *dan tranh* and the singers, and hum the melody of the chorus.
- Sing the melody on neutral syllable such as "nah," and on solfège syllables (beginning on "la") or scale numbers (beginning on "6").
- Listen to the recording and follow this pronunciation to guide singing of the lyrics.

    Yoo nyah-oo ker-ree aw ee ah tsaw nyah-oo vay nyah.

    Zoh-ee zahng tsah zoh-ee may ah ee ah.

    Zahng ah ee ah kwa kah-oo.

    Zahng ah ee ah kwa kah-oo.

    Ting ting ting zaw bay-ee.

    Ting ting ting zaw bay-ee.

    (For verse 2, substitute "non" (hat) for "ao" (coat), and for verse 3, substitute "nhan" (ring).)

- Sing the verses solo, with choral response on the "tinh tinh" sound of the wind.
- Play chords on piano or guitar, providing arpeggiation. In the case of the guitar, fingerpicking can provide a fitting accompaniment.
- Explore possibilities for melodic improvisation, particularly on the sustained tones, to include vocal trills or the use of upper and lower neighboring tones.
- With the melody as foundation, create new verses in English, of kind gestures to loved ones.

## Recommended Listening

+*From Rice Paddies and Temple Yards: Traditional Music of Vietnam* (Nguyen/Campbell). Danbury, CT: World Music Press.

*Eternal Voices: Traditional Vietnamese Music in the United States.* New Alliance Records NAR CD 053.

*Songs and Dances of Vietnam.* Monitor MON 00731.

# QUIEN ES ESE PAJARITO?

Argentina

1. *Who is that little bird,*
   *That sings over the lemon tree?*
   *Go and tell him to stop singing,*
   *Because he is stealing my heart.*

2. *If you want to know me better,*
   *Come along my garden.*
   *There is my name written*
   *On the jasmine leaf.*

## The Tune

"Quien es ese Pajarito?" is a *chaya*, an Argentinian traditional dance song about a little bird. The performance of this song can include movements of the dancer's own creation, without a designated or predetermined form.

## The Music Culture

In the decidedly large and diverse country of Argentina, various musical forms vie for the attention of listeners young and old, urban and rural. The population embraces various cultures that include *mestizos* (Spanish and indigenous mix), Italians, Germans, Japanese, Jews, French, and Russians. There is the music of the national dance form, the tango (which arose in the port areas of Buenos Aires where descendants of Europeans, Africans, and native South Americans mixed culturally), in addition to popular dance music such as the *cuarteto* (similar to the *merengue*), and the adopted Columbian *cumbia*. The folk music of Argentina takes on many instrumental flavors including the Andean sounds of *charango*, *zampoñas* (panpipes), and flute in the north of the country near the borders with Bolivia and Chile. The *chaya* is a folk song meant to be danced, but freely and according to the whims of the singer, and is accompanied by *charango* or guitar and *bomba* drum.

## The Experiences

- Sing the song on neutral syllable such as "es," and on solfège syllables (beginning on "la") or scale numbers (beginning on "6").
- Sing the lyrics of the song, remembering to pronounce *j* as "h" and "qui" as "k."
- Play chords on guitar with a ♩ ♫ ♩ ♫ rhythmic strum.
- While singing the song, tap, clap, or pat the first pulse of every measure, swaying left or right every three beats. As an extension, pat on beat 1 and clap on beats 2 and 3.
- Play an ostinato rhythm on drum and maracas:

| Beat: | 1 | 2 | 3 |
|---|---|---|---|
| | drum | maracas | maracas |

- Play the melody on flute or recorder, with guitar accompaniment.

## Recommended Listening

+*Canciones de America Latina* (Campbell, P. S.; Frega, A. L.). Miami: Warner Bros. Publications.
*Argentine Folk Songs*. Smithsonian Folkways FW 06810.

# RABBIT DANCE: "UNCLE SAM"

Iroquois

Traditional, Seneca, as sung to Bryan Burton. From Burton, B. (1993). *Moving Within the Circle: Contemporary Native American Music and Dance.* Danbury, CT: World Music Press. Courtesy World Music Press.

## The Tune

An Iroquois Rabbit Dance called "Uncle Sam" expresses the views of young Native Americans who were called off to the armed service in World Wars I and II.

## The Music Culture

The Seneca Nation of Native Americans is part of the Iroquois Confederacy that lives on reservations in the states of New York and Pennsylvania, and in Canada. They once warred with the Oneida, Onondaga, Cayuga, and Mohawk tribes, but have been united for centuries (along with the Tuscarora) under an agreement known as the Great Law of Peace. With their dual roles as citizens of their first nation and of the United States, the Seneca (and the Iroquois at large) speak English as well as their mother-tongue language, adhere to the values of their tribal and national cultures, and follow traditions that are both Seneca and American in nature. They uphold two histories, abide by two constitutions, pay respect to two flags, and defend and protect two nations. The lyrics to the "Uncle Sam" Rabbit Dance are indicative of the draft or volunteer efforts of Seneca solders to join with other Americans in the armed forces during the two world wars (I and II) to defend American interests. In general, Rabbit Dances are popular social dances among the Iroquois, and among other groups as far as the Plains and in the Southwest. They are ladies' choice dances, where the woman selects her dance partner, and their songs combine vocables with humorous commentary on courtship. Couples link arms and dance a two-step in a large circle.

## The Experiences

- Sing the melody on a neutral syllable such as "hey," and on solfège syllables (beginning on "la" in la-based minor) or scale numbers (beginning on "6").
- Tap, clap, or pat the rhythm of the melody, noting the frequent use of the ♩ ♪ and its reversal, the ♪ ♩ patterns.
- Sing the lyrics of the melody's vocables and English-language text.
- Sing the melody while stepping the melodic rhythm, in place.
- Add a drum to play the slow ♩. pulse while singing.
- Play the melody on flute, and explore the effect of the sound on clarinet, trombone, cello, and saxophone (among other instruments).
- Play an accompaniment on piano, guitar, or other harmony instrument, denoting the six quick pulses per measure through intact or broken chords.
- Dance the two-step with partners facing right in a large circle, holding inside hands. Move to the right, swinging arms easily forward and back, stepping two steps forward, one step back, and one in place:

| Beat: | 1 | 2 | 1 | 2 |
|-------|---|---|---|---|
| Step: | forward | forward | back | touch in place |

## Recommended Listening

+*Moving Within the Circle* (Burton, B.). Danbury, CT: World Music Press.

*Seneca Social Dance Music*. Smithsonian Folkways FW 04072.

# REGGAE GROOVE

Jamaica

## The Groove

Jamaica has been the home of "Reggae Groove" for four decades, and has fixed its place solidly within the realm of the world's popular music.

## The Music Culture

As an island nation in the Caribbean Sea, Jamaica has long been known for its mixed African-British traditions of language, culture, and music. When R&B came to the island, it was transformed into genres like *ska* (with its accents on the off-beats in jazzy horn lines), *rock steady* (with its off-beats accentuated by bass and rhythm guitar), and *reggae*. By the late 1960s, reggae had established itself as a slowed-down and laid-back style of club music, stylized by its emphasis on the off-beat as a regular pattern of accentuation. Of the various *reggae* groups that established the style, The Wailers (Bob Marley, Peter Tosh, and Bunney Wailer) are credited with leading the wave of popular interest in the style, with Bob Marley continuing to foster a solo career until his death due to cancer in 1981. *Reggae*'s appeal, in the hands of Marley and other artists, was not only its groove but also its function of spreading the message of political rebellion, peace, and brotherhood. *Reggae*, and the legacy of Bob Marley, is revered then and even now in and beyond Jamaica to Jamaican communities in London and New York, and in African countries such as Nigeria, Ghana, Zimbabwe, and South Africa, where it has influenced popular music.

## The Experiences

- Chant the single lines of rhythm on a neutral syllable such as "bah" or "tah."
- Chant the parts using short phrases, which correspond to the notated rhythms.

- In playing the cowbell part, "X" indicates playing at the closed end of the bell and "O" indicates playing at the open end of the bell.
- In playing the conga drum, note that "P" (beat one) indicates a press stroke, "S" (beat two) is a slap with the right hand on the drum head (while holding the left hand on the head), and "O" is a strike of the open drum head so that it rings.
- Gradually layer in the percussion parts, chanting aloud and fading the chants to silence.
- Explore the possibility of playing the *reggae* percussion parts with a *reggae* recording.
- When the rhythm can be performed in a tight ensemble, invite trumpet, saxophone, flute, piano, and various other instruments to improvise a melody, short "riff," or groove above it.

## Recommended Listening

*Bob Marley: Reggae Fever*. Madacy Records 5434.

*Reggae Gold 2005*. VP/Universal 1729.

*The Fabulous Wailers*. Norton 901.

*20th Century Masters: The Millenium Collection: The Best of Peter Tosh*. Hip-O Records 000241102.

# RUMBA GROOVE

Cuba

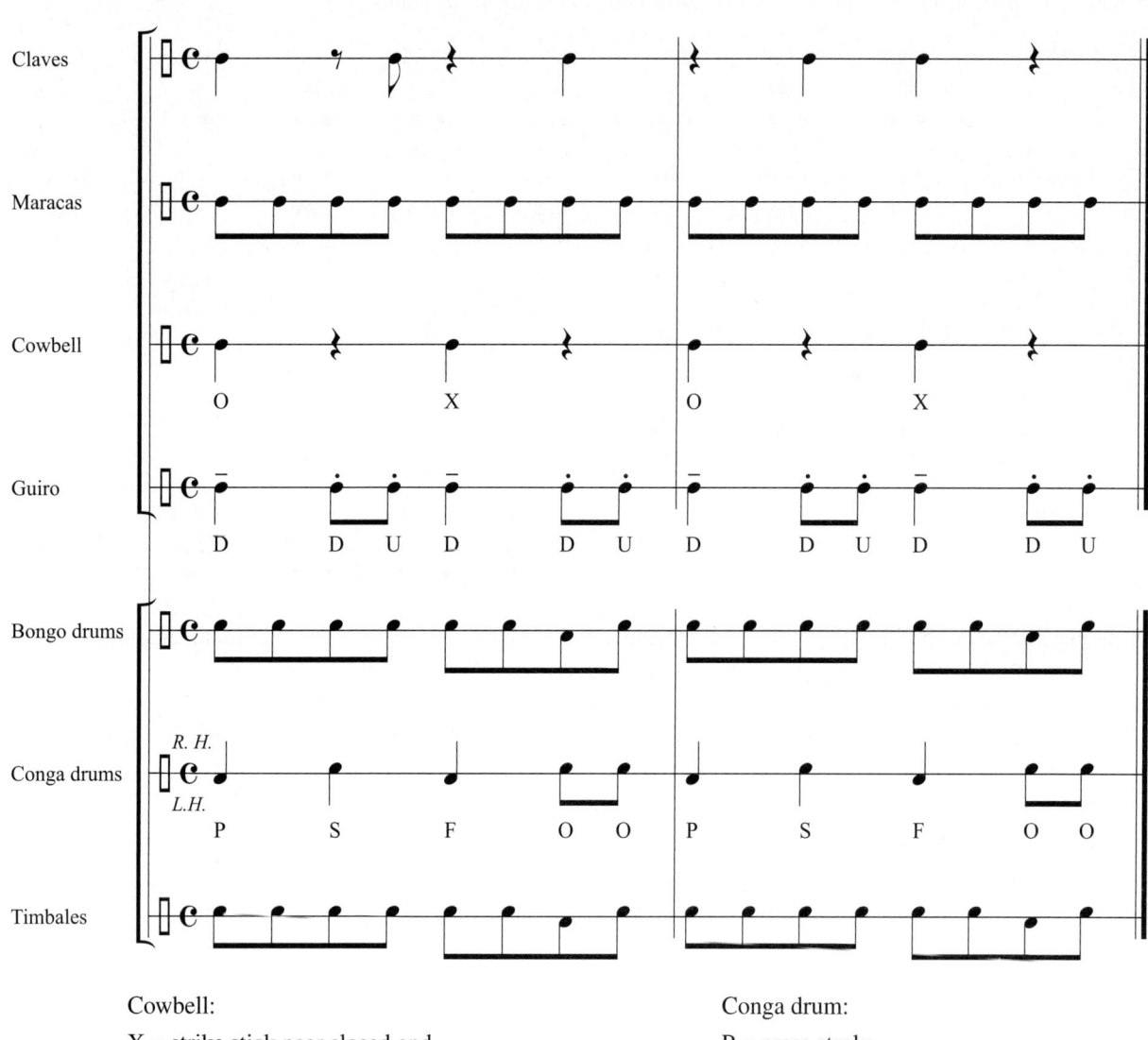

Cowbell:

X = strike stick near closed end

O = strike stick near open end

Guiro:

D = down stroke

U = up stroke

Conga drum:

P = press stroke

S = slap (L.H. remain on head)

F = finger tips

O = strike open head and let ring

## The Groove

The dance music known as "Rumba Groove" is found at its purest on Cuba's north coast, where the descendants of former slaves from West Africa (expecially the Yoruba) were brought to work in the sugar cane fields, still dance, drum, and sing the lively form.

# The Music Culture

*Rumba* is the Spanish word for party, and to hear an Afro-Cuban rumba band's percussion and voices is to get a real sense of celebration in music. Long before there was the ballroom dance style, there was the *rumba* (or rhumba) of informal parties on Cuban's north coast, where people gathered to play percussion instruments, to sing, and to dance. The interlocking rhythms of *rumba* are played by *claves* (a pair of sticks that always start the rumba by playing the "clave" pattern), cowbell, *maracas, guiro, conga* drums and various other drums such as *bongos, timbales,* and (for religious occasions) the *batà* drums. There are three types of traditional *rumba* that are distinguished by tempo, rhythmic density, and who may dance it. A variety of themes are explored by the *rumba* song, too: love and desire, friendship, unrequited or rejected love, local pride, surival in the face of adversity, and the actuality of *rumba* music and dance. The shape of *rumba* is commonly a long lyrical vocal melody that is sung by a soloist or duet of voices over the murmuring of percussion instruments which, on cue from the band leader, tightens up, is joined by a chorus of singers, a call-and-response section, and the unfolding of improvisational singing. The dance style of the *rumba* features a rocking of the hips in a quick-quick-slow rhythm that is at cross-rhythms with the accompaniment. *Rumba* is contagious music and highly participatory.

## The Experiences

- Chant the single lines of rhythm on a neutral syllable such as "dah" or "pah."
- Chant the short rhythmic phrases of the percussion instruments, which correspond to the notated rhythms.

- In playing the conga, note that "P" means to press into the drumhead, "S" is to slap the drumhead with right hand while holding the left hand on the head. "O" is to strike the drumhead so that it rings, and "F" is a stroke that requires the sharp precision of the finger tips in striking the drumhead.
- The cowbell is alternately played at the open end (O) and the closed end (X).
- Gradually layer in the percussion parts, chanting aloud and then fading the chant as the rhythm is internalized.
- Play the rumba rhythmic complex without and later with a recording.

## Recommended Listening

*Rumba Favorites*. Eclipse Music Group 64440.

*Buena Vista Social Club*. World Circuit/Nonesuch 79478-2.

# A RICH IRISH LADY

Canada, United States

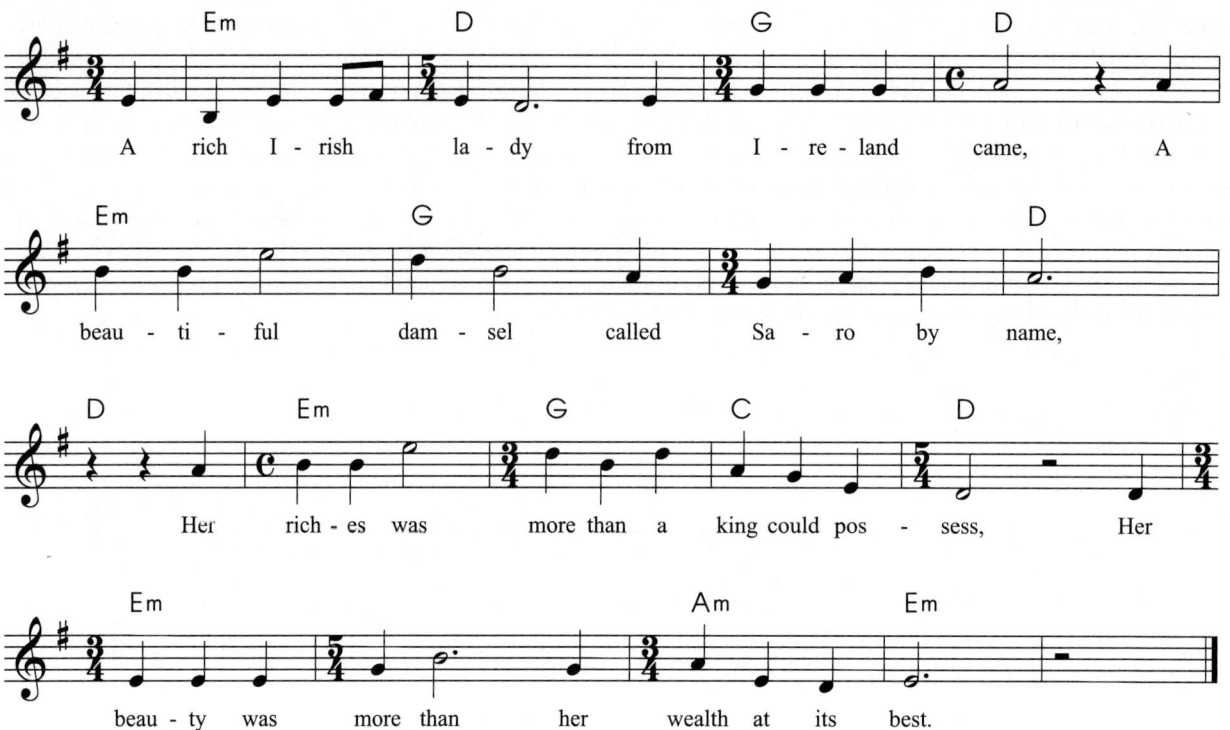

2. A lofty young gentleman courtin' her came,
   Courtin' this lady called Saro by name.
   "Oh, Saro! Oh, Saro! Oh, Saro!" said he,
   "I'm afraid that my ruin forever you'll be."

3. "I'm afraid that my ruin forever you'll prove,
   Unless you turn all your hatred to love."
   "No hatred to you nor to no other man,
   But this, for to love you, is more than I can."

3. So end all your sorrows, and drop your discourse,
   I never shall have you unless I am forced."
   Six months appeared and five years had passed,
   When I heard of this lady's misfortune at last.

4. She lay wounded by love, and she knew not for why.
   She sent for this young man whom she had denied.
   And by her bedside these words they were said,
   "There's a pain in your side, love,
   There's a pain in your head."

5. "Oh no, kind sir, the right you've not guessed,
   The pain that you speak of lies here in my breast"
   "For I know how foolish a young maid can be,
   I knew not the way to give love, lovingly."

6. "You are my doctor, and you are my cure,
   Without your protection I'll die I am sure."
   "Oh, Saro! Oh, Saro! Oh, Saro!" said he,
   "Don't you remember when I first courted thee?"

7. "I asked you in kindness, you answered in scorn,
   I'll never forgive you for times past and gone."
   "Times past and gone I hope you'll forgive,
   And grant me some longer comfort to live."

8. "I'll never forgive you as long as I live,
   I'll dance on your grave, love, when you're laid in
      ground."
   Then off of her fingers bold rings she pulled three,
   Saying, "Take them and wear them,
   When your're dancing on me."

9. "Adieu, kind friends, adieu all around,
   Adieu my true love. God make him a crown.
   I freely forgive him, although he won't me,
   My follies ten thousand times over I see."

# A RICH IRISH LADY

## The Tune

"A Rich Irish Lady" tells the story of a woman's denial of love, and the heartache it brings her years later when, too late, she appeals to the same suitor in an attempt to rekindle his interests in her.

## The Music Culture

The *ballad* began to appear in the Middle Ages, and flourished as a narrative genre in England, Scotland, Ireland, Wales, France, and the Low Countries (Netherlands, Belgium) in the sixteenth and seventeenth centuries. Ballads traveled with people in their transatlantic crossings, and many were maintained as traditional entertainment pieces in the English, Irish, Scottish, and French communities of Canada and the United States. Love, unrequited love, elopement, bride-stealing, adultery, and death appear as themes in ballad stories. The loyalty to a partner until and beyond death, including the reuniting of lovers in their grave, is another prominent ballad theme. The musical content of ballads varies, embracing major (Ionian) and minor (Aeolian) modes, as well as a fair share of Dorian and Mixolydian melodies. Ballads are usually sung solo, although various instruments such as guitar, banjo, dulcimer, fiddle, and harp are sometimes used to accompany singers. The melody and verse shape one another, such that rhythm, pitch content and singing style are dependent upon the text, just as the ballad tune helps to shape every word of the verse. "A Rich Irish Lady" is unusual for its mixture of 3/4, 4/4, and 5/4 meters, and yet it reflects the singing style that comes from the flexibility of a storytelling style that ebbs and flows with the singer's breath.

### The Experiences

- Sing the melody on netural syllable such as "ree," and on solfège syllables (beginning on "la") or scale numbers (beginning on "6").
- Hum the melody while keeping time through the various meter changes. For each meter, pat the first beat, and clap or tap the remaining beats, in every measure.
- Sing the lyrics of the song, fitting the syllables into the melody.
- Play chords on guitar, autoharp, dulcimer, or piano, strumming or rolling chords on the beat (with emphasis on the first beat of each measure). Explore the sound of open fifths to convey the text's conveyance of emptiness.
- Play the melody on flute or violin, as interludes between the verses.

### Recommended Listening

+*American Folk Songs Sung by the Seegers* (Peggy Seeger). Smithsonian Folkways FW 04432.
*Classic Scots Ballads: Ewan MacColl.* Visionary 450764.
*Ballads from Her Appalachian Family Tradition: Jean Ritchie.* Smithsonian Folkways SFW 40145.

# THE RIDDLE SONG

U. S.: Appalachian Mountains

I gave my love a cher - ry that has no stone, I

gave my love a chick - en that has no bone, I gave my love a ring that

has no end, I gave my love a ba - by that's not cry - ing.

2. How can there be a cherry that has no stone?

   How can there be a chicken that has no bone?

   How can there be a ring that has no end?

   How can there be a baby that's not crying?

3. A cherry when it's blooming, it has no stone,

   A chicken when it's pipping, it has no bone,

   A ring when it's rolling, it has no end,

   A baby when it's sleeping, there's no crying.

## The Tune

A well-known tune from the Appalachian Mountains, "The Riddle Song" is traceable to at least the seventeenth century, when it was sung as entertainment at the courts during the British Renaissance.

## The Music Culture

The mountain range known as the Appalachians encompasses eighteen American states from Maine to Georgia, and embrace as well the mountains known as the Berkshires (Connecticut), the Green Mountains (New Hampshire), the Catskills (New York), the Blue Ridge (Virginia), and the Great Smoky Mountains (Tennessee). While widely spread, there are cultural identities that connect people across this area, including speech, dialect, supersititions, crafts, and music. Poor people from England, Scotland, Ireland, and Wales, looking for cheap (or free) land, found it on the steep ridges of agriculturally useless land. They brought their Anglo-Celtic folk songs and ballads and instrumental dance tunes, and the vocal music within the realm of women to keep, often unaccompanied and during their work at home and in the fields, as bearers of their families' cultural heritage. Up until the 1920s, before the the advent of recorded sound and radio, the musical repertoire of the Appalachians continued in the oral lore of people who sang for work, worship, and also for group enjoyment. "The Riddle Song" was one such piece of musical life of people living in the Appalachians, with evidence of it all across the 1,500 miles of that region.

## The Experiences

- Sing the melody on a neutral syllable such as "loo," and on solfège syllables (beginning on "sol") or scale numbers (beginning on "5").
- Sing the lyrics, with attention to the three verses that comprise the riddle's contextual statement, question, and answer.
- Play the chords on guitar, autoharp, dulcimer, or piano, one to a beat.
- Add musical interludes by way of playing the melody on violin, or picking it out on the guitar, dulcimer, or banjo.

## Recommended Listening

+*American Favorite Ballads, Volume 2* (Pete Seeger). Smithsonian Folkways FW 02005.

+*Josh White: Remaining Title, 1941–1947*. Document 1013.

*Very Early Joan* (Joan Brez). Vanguard VCD 79446/7.

# RIO GRANDE

United States

Were you ev - er in Ri - o Grande?    Ri - o, 'way Ri - o.    Oh
Where the Port - u - gee girls can be found,    And

were ____ you ev - er on ____ that strand?    We're bound for the Ri - o
they are the girls to waltz ____ a - round,

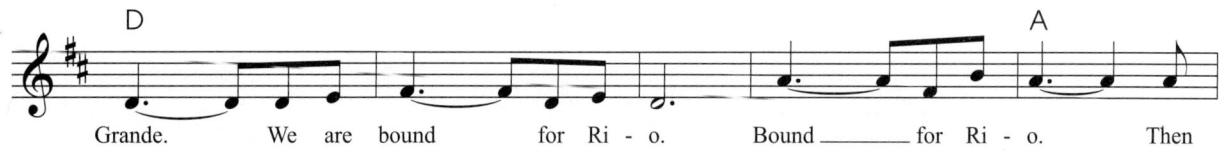

Grande.    We are bound for Ri - o.    Bound ____ for Ri - o.    Then

fare ____ you well, my pret - ty young girl,    We are bound for the Ri - o Grande.

## The Tune

Not only sea songs but also river songs qualify as shanties. "Rio Grande" functioned for sailors as a kind of work song on the water to help sailors alleviate the monotony and lift the air of fatigue that would settle around the hoisting of sails, the swabbing of decks, and the stoking of the steam engine.

## The Music Culture

Sailors worked hard to coordinate their effort and lighten their labor while working aboard ships powered through the mid-nineteenth century by human muscles and the natural elements of the wind and sea. The sea shanty was characteristic of sailors' work, and they would sing with unusual volume and energy into the wind, themselves in solo leads to which roaring choruses responded from the sails, across the decks, and from down under in the engine room. The colorful (and sometimes obscene) verses about their lives afloat on the high seas and down the great rivers were captured in tunes like "Blow the Man Down," "Storm Along," "The Ship Neptune," "Drunken Sailor," and "Shenandoah." When steam power ended the need for extensive manual labor, sea shanties made their way into an onshore revival as early as 1900 in concert halls and schools. A second revival of sea shanties, starting in the 1950s, brought back the crusty sound of real sailors in high spirit and rugged tone.

## The Experiences

- Sing the melody on a neutral syllable such as "ree," and on solfège syllables (beginning on "mi") or scale numbers (beginning on "3").

- Sing the lyrics, dividing between solo phrases and group response (on "Rio, 'way Rio") and through the chorus that begins "We're bound for Rio."

- Play chords on guitar, concertina, or piano, following a 6/8 pattern:

Beat:   1  2  3    4  5  6

Chord:

- Sway to each side on the ♩. pulse, while singing.

## Recommended Listening

*Conjunto! Texas-Mexican Border Music, Volume 1*. Rounder 116160232.

*Border Bash: Tex-Mex Dance Music, Volume 2*. Folkways FW 0652B.

# RISE UP, O FLAME

United States

Rise up, O flame, _____ by __ thy __ light glow - ing.

Bring to us beau - - ty, ___ vi - sion, __ and joy.

From *Fire Within*, Libana, 1990. Arrangement by Susan Robbins and Libana. www.libana.com.

## The Tune

Whether sung in unison or in canon, "Rise Up, O Flame" is a much-loved song that brings a sense of unity and comaraderie in the singing of it.

## The Music Culture

Singing has a way of bonding people together. Singing around a campfire is a kind of double bonding, as the combination of resonant voices raised in song and a fire's flickering flame are as mesmerizing as they are socially satisfying. For children and adults alike, memories of summer camps are more than hot dogs and beans, arts and crafts, hiking and horseback riding; they are also about the songs sung every night around the campfire. Songs (or parodies of songs) like "B-I-N-G-O," "Sloop John B.," "Dem Bones," "This Land Is Your Land," "She'll be Coming Around the Mountain," "Good Night, Irene," "Jet Plane," and "Kumbaya" keep campfire sessions humming, with singers swaying to the songs' rhythms, their arms around each other, staring into the flames of the fire. Sometimes camp songs have a spiritual or mysterious side to them, too, such as "Amazing Grace," "Down by the Riverside," or a song attributed to the seventeenth century composer Christoph Praetorius, "Rise Up, O Flame." With all of these songs, there is the strumming and picking of guitars to keep the singers on key and in time.

### The Experiences

- Sing the melody of the song on a neutral syllable such as "bah," and on solfège syllables (beginning on "la") or scale numbers (beginning on "6").
- Sing the lyrics of the song, with attention to the melismatic way of several pitches sounding for a single syllable.
- Sing the song in canon. Begin with two parts, the second group entering two measures after the first group. Then, sing the song in a four-part canon, with each group entering one measure after the one before it.
- Play just the Dm chord (or just the tonic and fifth tones) once every three beats as a kind of drone accompaniment, on guitar, dulcimer, authoharp, or piano.
- Explore possibilities for accompaniment on violins and cellos, or wind instruments, or xylophones, with each player determining which pitch of the Dm triad he or she will play, and for how long.

### Recommended Listening

+*Libana: Fire Within*. Ladyslipper 108.

*Camp Songs: The Song Swappers*. Folkways FW 07628.

# SAKURA

Japan

## The Tune

The Japanese name for ornamental cherry trees is "Sakura," and the song is a tribute to the soft pink blossoms that fill the parks and gardens of Japan every spring.

## The Music Culture

As a symbol of Japan, the blossoms of the cherry trees known as *sakura* are depicted on kimonos, dishware, and stationery. The most commonly found blossoms are nearly white but tinged with the palest pink, and while they only bloom for about a week, they are a lasting symbol of the ephemeral nature of life that is considered brief but beautiful. Given the long south-to-north span of Japan's islands, the festivals of the cherry blossoms begin in Okinawa in February, reach Kyoto and Tokyo at the end of March, and arrive in Hokkaido in mid-April. People go to parks, shrines, and temples with family and friends, holding flower-viewing parties known as *hanami*. In 1912, Japan gave 3,000 *sakura* as a gift to the United States, and renewed the gift with another 3,800 trees in 1956; they line the shore of the Tidal Basin in Washington D.C., and are the focal point of an annual Cherry Blossom Festival. *Sakura* are depicted in art and song, and the well-known song, "Sakura," is performed vocally and on traditional Japanese instruments (such as *koto, shakuhachi*, and *shamisen*), as well as on Western instruments.

### The Experiences

- Sing the melody on neutral syllable such as "ya," and on solfège syllables (beginning on "la") or scale numbers (beginning on "6").
- Sing the lyrics, noting that *i* sounds as "ee" and *u* sounds as "oo."

- Play the chords on guitar or piano, rolling them at the rate of once or twice per measure. For a more transparent sound, play just the first and fifth note of the chord.
- Play the melody on flute or recorder as interludes between the sung verse.
- Add a two-measure percussion ostinato:

## Recommended Listening

+*Sakura: A Musical Celebration of the Cherry Blossoms.* Smithsonian Folkways SFW 40509.
+*Traditional Folk Songs of Japan.* Smithsonian Folkways FW 04534.

## SALSA GROOVE

Puerto Rico

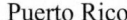

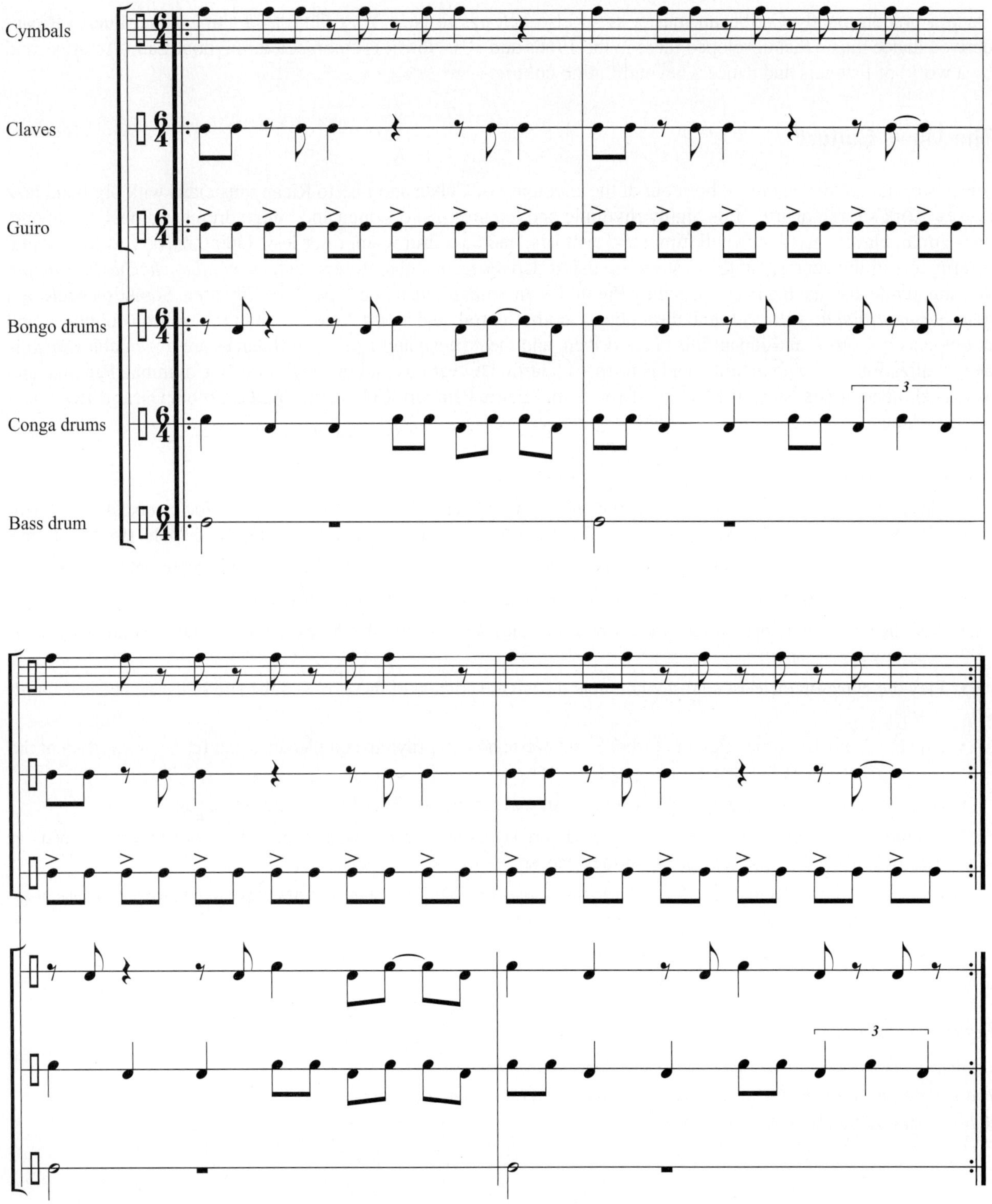


*Teaching Music Globally: Experiencing Music, Expressing Culture* by Campbell, P. S. (2004). By permission of Oxford University Press, Inc.

# SALSA GROOVE

## The Groove

Once a predominantly Caribbean music, *salsa* also belongs to New York City, as a Cuban- and Puerto Rican-derived dance music that developed there in the 1960s and 70s. Now it is embraced throughout Latin America, and by a world of listeners and dancers beyond Latino culture.

## The Music Culture

*Salsa* is up-tempo dance music, born out of the encounter of Cuban and Puerto Rican musicians with big-band jazz in New York's Latin quarter. It is highly rhythmic and features piano, conga and bongo drums, trumpet, trombone, bass guitar, claves, guiro, cowbell, timbales, cymbals, and bass drum—more or less. Opinions vary as to absolute forerunners of the genres, but there is a sense that it derives from Cuban forms such as *mambo, chachachá, rumba,* and *son*, while also having been shaped by Puerto Rican immigrants in the New York City area. Sometimes referred to as *música tropical, salsa* is found throughout South, Central, and North America, in the Caribbean countries, and in outposts in Europe and Japan. It is *clave*-driven, and the African and Spanish influences are undeniable. *Salsa* is a crystallization of Latino identity, and is further identified by various national styles (as in Columbia, Panama, and Venezuela) and artists (such as Machito, Tito Puente, Eddie Palmieri, Celiz Cruz, Willie Colon, Oscar d'Leon, and Ruben Blades).

### The Experiences
- Chant the rhythms of the various instruments, using selected vocables such as "tee" (for cymbals), "vay" (for *claves*), "gwee-do" (for *guiro*), "goh" for (for *bongo* drums), "kah" (for *conga* drums), and "boh" (for low drum).
- Play the *conga* part; note the higher and lower notes and find places on the drum that will represent them well.
- Layer the *bongos* in over the *conga*, again finding higher- and lower-pitched timbres to play.
- Add the low drum (a bass drum, or a low *conga* sound), and rehearse the three drum parts until they are in tight ensemble with one another.
- Play the *claves* in their ostinato rhythm; note the slight variation of the ♪♩ at the end of the second and fourth measures.
- Add the cymbals (or triangles, or cowbell), and notice how this rhythm complements and fits between much of the *claves*' rhythm.
- Add the *guiro* part playing up and down the ridges, accenting the first of each eighth-note pair.
- Explore a performance arrangement that gradually layers in instruments, and that allows instruments to "rest" at their own discretion, coming back in as they choose.
- Use the rhythm as a foundation for melodic improvisation, inviting a pianist, brass players, guitarists and bass players to join in, creating a groove on a progression such as:

| Measure: | 1 | 2 | 3 | 4 |
|---|---|---|---|---|
| Chord: | Am | G | F | E |

### Recommended Listening
*Tito Puente: Oye Como Va: The Dance Collection.* Concord Records 4780.
*The Sun of Latin Music: Eddie Palmieri and Lalo Rodiguez.* Musical Productions 56253.
*Ruben Blades: El Que La Hace La Paga.* Fania JM 624.

# SALTY DOG

United States

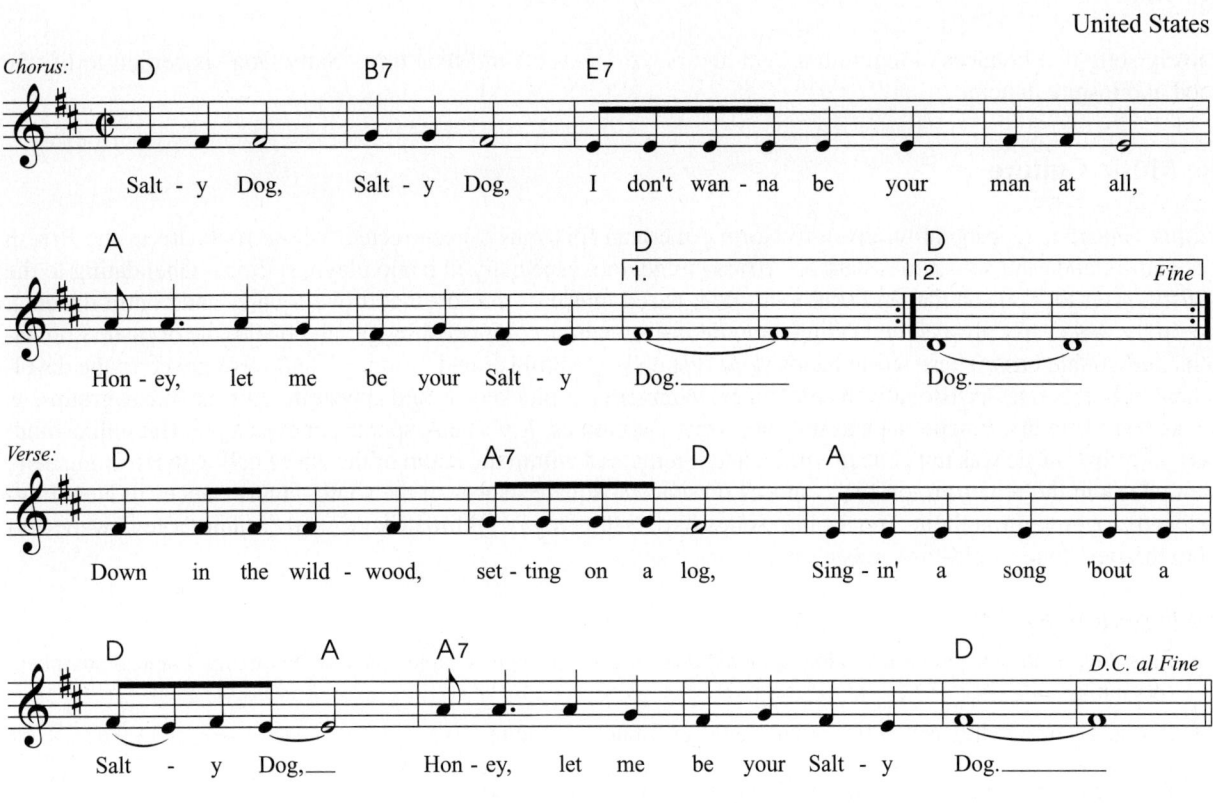

*Chorus:*

Salt - y Dog,   Salt - y Dog,   I don't wan - na be   your   man at all,

Hon - ey,   let   me   be your Salt - y   Dog._____   Dog._____

*Verse:*

Down   in the wild - wood,   set - ting on a log,   Sing - in' a   song   'bout a

Salt - y Dog,___   Hon - ey,   let   me   be your Salt - y   Dog._____

(Chorus)

2. Two old maids a-sitting in the sand,
   Each one wishing that the other was a man.
   Honey, let me be your Salty Dog.

   (Chorus)

3. Worst day I ever had in my life,
   When my best friend caught me kissing his wife.
   Honey, let me be your Salty Dog.

   (Chorus)

4. God made a woman and He made her mighty funny,
   When you kiss her round the mouth, just as sweet as any honey.
   Honey, let me be your Salty Dog.

   (Chorus)

# SALTY DOG

## The Tune

A lively song that bounces along with a light and playful text, the *old-time* tune "Salty Dog" is certain to lift the mood and inspire dancing.

## The Music Culture

*Old-time music* is a designation given to North American folk music, resurrected, whose roots are in the British Isles and Ireland (and sometimes with an African tinge, too, especially in banjo playing). It is a label dating to the 1920s to refer to Appalachian and southern fiddle-based music of the sort that drove square- and contra-dancing. The fiddle was nearly always the leading melodic instrument, accompanied by guitars, banjo, the occasional mandolin, and double bass. These string bands were first called "hillbilly" and "country," and were linked to the development of bluegrass. Occasionally, the dulcimer (hammered or plucked) would appear in old-time music groups, as well as non string instruments such as the concertina, harmonica, jew's harp, spoons, or even a jug. But unlike bluegrass, old-time music was not concert music; and it remained within the realm of the dance hall with its strong beat, its emphasis in the repertoire on reels, and its presence at square dances in the south, contra dances in New England, and clogging throughout Appalachia. Songs like "Salty Dog," "Old Joe Clark," and "Soldier's Joy" were central to the repertoire of old-time music groups.

### The Experiences

- Sing the melody on a neutral syllable such as "dah," and on solfège syllables (beginning on "mi") or scale numbers (beginning on "3").
- Sing the lyrics, lightly and with a bounce, at a moderately fast tempo.
- Play the chords on guitar, strumming on the off-beats:
- Play the melody on fiddle, mandolin, banjo, or guitar, as interludes between the sung verses.
- Play a bass that plucks out the changes of the chords.
- For flavor, put the backs of two metal or wooden spoons together, hold with the knuckle of the index finger in between them, and play a rhythmic ostinato on spoons:

### Recommended Listening

*This Little Light of Mine* (Guy Carawan). Smithsonian Folkways FW 03552.
*I Bid You Goodnight*. Arhoolie Records 433.

## SAMBA GROOVE

Brazil

## The Groove

*Samba* is the national music and dance of Brazil, a style that attracts participants not only during the pre-Lenten period of Carnaval but all through the year.

## The Music Culture

Brazilian music is played across the world, and its *samba* and *bossa nova* styles stand on their own as well as in influencing American and European jazz expressions. In the grand old city of Rio de Janeiro, and in the northeastern cities of Salvador de Bahia and Recife, the music of *samba* is a way of life. Neighborhoods, called *blocos*, support the participation of young and old in *samba* schools, where people who want to play a percussion instrument, choreograph a routine, or write a song can learn to do so. While these *samba* schools target the Carnaval celebration of (typically) February as their coming-out time for five days of elaborate parades and competitions, *samba* music is played all year round. The music of *samba* is loud, even boisterous, with call-and-response techniques operating between the various drums, rattles, and bells. It is outdoor music, and compelling enough to get everyone within earshot to move to its groove. For jazz musicians working in the 1950s, such as Charlie Parker, Stan Kenton, Oscar Peterson, and Horace Silver, *samba* was irresistible, and along with the more sedate *bossa nova*, it continued to be embraced through the 1960s by the likes of Stan Getz, Charlie Byrd, and Cannonball Adderly.

## The Experiences

- Chant the individual lines of the percussion instruments, each one on a vocable: "cah" for *cabasa* (a shaken gourd with an external net of beads), "bah" for *agogo bells* (a double iron bell), "wee" for *guiro* (a notched gourd or wood block that is often shaped like a fish), "wah" for *conga* drum 1, "tah" for *conga* drum 2, "dah" for *conga* drum 3, and "lee" for *timbales*.

- Gradually layer in the instruments, continuing to chant and then fading it out when the rhythmic pattern is completely internalized.

- For the *agogo* bells, find the higher- and lower-sounding bells to correspond with the indications in the pattern.

- For the *conga* drums, which can be played with alternating right and left hands, using palms and fingertips, there are also more sophisticated techniques to utilize: "S" is a slap of the hand while holding the other hand on the drum head; "O" is striking the open head and letting it ring; "H" is striking with the heel of the palm; "F" is striking with the fingertips; and "P" is pressing into the drum.

- Note that various instruments—including *maracas*, cowbell, and snare drum—can be substituted for the *timbales*.

- Explore the possibilities of creating a repeated four-bar melody, or a short, repeated melodic motif to meld with the *samba* rhythm, along with a harmonic progression such as

| Measure: | 1 | 2 | 3 | 4 |
|---|---|---|---|---|
| Chord: | D | Em | A7 | D |

## Recommended Listening

*This is Samba! Volume 1*. Rounder CD 5091.

*Samba Brasil*. Polygram Records 15761.

*The Rough Guide to Samba*. World Music Network RGNET 1058 CD.

# SAMBALELE

Brazil

Sam - ba - le - le ta do - en - te, tac - oa - ca - be - ca que bra - da

Sam - ba - le - le pre - ci - sa - va de'u - mas de zoi - to lam - ba - das, Sam -

ba - le - le ta do - en - te, tac - oa ca - be - ca, que bra - da

Sam - ba - le - le pre - ci - sa - va de'u - mas de zoi - to lam - ba - das, Sam -

ba sam - ba sam - ba - le - le, Pi - sa - na ba - ra da sa - ia le - le!

Sam - ba sam - ba - sam - ba - le - le! Pi - sa - na bar - ra da sa - ia.

*Sambalele is a fellow, who rarely gets to his pillow,*

*He spends his time loudly playing, no one can tell where he's staying.*

*Sambalele went out dancing, with his new cart he went prancing,*

*Then he arrived at the market, but he forgot how to park it.*

*Sambalele, sambalele, we wish your neighbors could tell where you stay.*

*Sambalele, sambalele, often we just cannot find you.*

# SAMBALELE

## The Tune

A continuous syncopated rhythm is what characterizes "Sambalele," a Brazilian folk song about a man who plays and dances the samba.

## The Music Culture

Brazilian music is wrapped into *samba* culture, including the percussive rhythms of the *samba* drums (and the *samba* schools that train them); the formal parades at the time of Carnaval; and the hundreds of thousands of participants (*not* spectators) who dance in the streets to the sounds of the passing *samba* schools. The pre-Lenten Carnaval season is a national period of celebration, and offices and schools shut down so that Brazilians can focus on celebrating—singing, dancing, and playing. The radio and TV pick up and disperse new Carnaval hit songs, giving national exposure to songs that were created by individuals within their local *samba* schools. Folk songs like "Sambalele" are revived, too, and given attention at this peak time of music making, so that the older-layer traditional songs can hold their place alongside the late-breaking new songs. In this way, there is music for every generation, because the old songs are not retired, but resurrected.

### The Experiences

- Tap, clap, or pat the syncopated pattern:
- Sing the melody on a neutral syllable such as "lay," and on solfège syllables or scale numbers.
- Sing the lyrics, recognizing that Portuguese-Brazilian language has distinctive sounds in *oa* ("wah"), *oi* ("awng"), *ia* ("yah"), and *ça* ("s").
- Play chords on guitar or piano in a ♩ ♩♩ pattern of complete or partial chords.
- Play the syncopated pattern on drum, shakers, and wood block.
- Perform a basic dance movement, the right hand out with the elbow bent at a right angle and the left hand over the stomach, with a two-measure stepping pattern.

| Beat: | 1 | 2 | 1 | 3 |
|-------|---|---|---|---|
| Move: | L step | touch right toe | R step | touch left toe |

### Recommended Listening

*Samba Bossa Nova*. Putumayo World Music PUTU 195-2.
*Afro Brasil*. Verve 845 326 2.

# SAN SERENÍ

Spain

*San Sereni of the good, good life.*
*The shoemakers do like this.*
*I like it this way!*

## The Tune

Widely known in Spain and other Spanish-speaking parts of the world, "San Sereni" tells of some of the traditional occupations of people in neighborhoods and villages.

## The Music Culture

Old Spain continues its long and proud history, even as a cultural evolution of many centuries has brought a mixed population of European and North African peoples to the country. This mix is responsible for many musical genres, including that soulful musical style known as *flamenco*. Highly emotive singing at the edge of pain, Spanish flamenco singing interacts with guitars, hand-claps, and shouts. Yet there is much more to Spanish music, including the folk songs of the people that are preserved by parents and grandparents singing within the vicinity of their children's hearing. There are guitar-accompanied song forms such as the *romance, décima,* and *canción*, and there are the songs of children and for children by adults. "San Sereni" has made its way through the centuries and across many countries from Chile to Venezuela as "the shoemaker song," and it invariably brings with it opportunities for children to imitate the actions of what it is that people do all day.

### The Experiences

- Sing the song on a neutral syllable such as "zah," and on solfège syllables (beginning on "sol") or scale numbers (beginning on "5").
- Sing the lyrics, noting these pronunciation points: "buena" is pronounced "bway-nah," "hacen" is "ah-sen," "me" is "may," "campañeros" is "cahm-pahn-yay-ros."
- Play the chord on piano or guitar, using a down, down-up strum for guitar:

- Following the first verse, all other verses remain the same except for the substitution of words for "los zapateros:"

    Verse  2: las bailadoras (the folk dancers)

    3: los carpinteros (the carpenters)

    4: las pianistas (the pianists)

    5: los campañeros (the bell-ringers)

    6: las costureras (the seamstresses)

- As pantomime is part of the performance of this song, act out each occupation as it is sung.

## Recommended Listening

+*Latin American Children's Game Songs*. Folkways FW 07851.

+*Roots and Branches* (Campbell, P. S.; McCullough-Brabson, E.; Tucker, J. C.). Danbury, CT: World Music Press.

# SANSA KROMA

Ghana

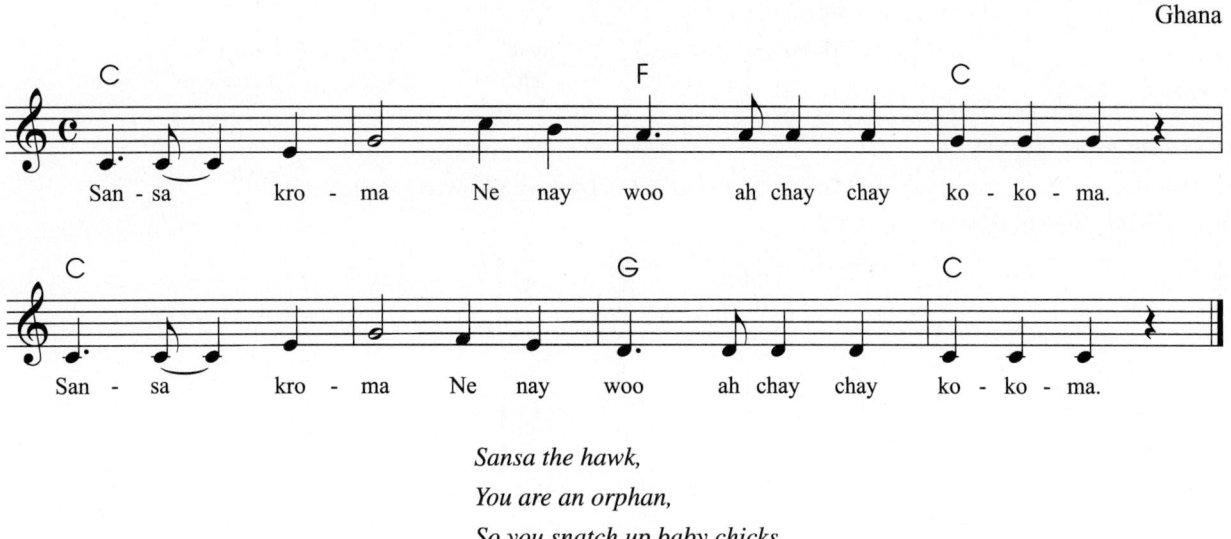

*Sansa the hawk,*

*You are an orphan,*

*So you snatch up baby chicks.*

## The Tune

Akan children of Ghana enjoy "Sansa Kroma" as a song and a game that involves them in passing rocks around a circle, always rhythmically and hooked to the beat.

## The Music Culture

In the West African nation of Ghana, the Akan, Asanti, Ewe, Ga, and various other cultural groups find uses for music throughout the day and across the calendar. Children are no exception, as they, too, sing songs of many functions that include play, work, learning (such as counting, or body parts, or colors, or appropriate moral behavior), and initiation into adult society. They have a repertoire of playful singing games that require hand-clapping, stepping, stomping, and finger-snapping. Some games have them passing an object (a rock, block, pebble, seed, or ball) to one another around a circle. "Sansa Kroma" is such a rock-passing game. Its Akan-language lyrics speak of a hawk who, orphaned at birth, roams around in search of baby chicks to kill and eat, since no one else can provide for him. It is a warning to the young to stay close to home, for fear of predators.

### The Experiences

- Sing the melody on a neutral syllable such as "mah," and on solfège syllables or scale numbers.
- Move to the rhythm pattern while singing:

  step  step  clap

  R     L

- Sing the lyrics of the song, which have been transliterated from the spoken Akan language.
- Play the chords on guitar or piano, intact or arpeggiated—even though such chords are not necessary for songs of Ghana, or children's songs.

• Play the rock-passing game in a sitting circle, each player with a rock (or pebble, ball, or block) in front of him/her self (or placed slightly to the left). After chanting "take-right-left-pass," slowly practice a four-beat motion:

| Beat: | 1 | 2 | 3 | 4 |
|---|---|---|---|---|
| Move: | pick up<br>(from left) | tap to<br>right | tap to<br>left | pass on<br>to the right |

## Recommended Listening

+*Let Your Voice Be Heard* (Adzenyah, A.; Maraire, D.; Tucker, J. C.). Danbury, CT: World Music Press.

*Ghana: Children at Play*. Folkways FW 07853.

# SANTA LUCIA

Italy

Sul ma - re luc - ci - ca L'a - stro d'ar - gen - to, Pla - ci - da è l'on - da, Pro - spe - ro è il ven - to, Ve - ni - te al - l'a - gi le, Bar - chet - ta mi - a! San - ta - Lu - ci - a! San - ta Lu - ci - a! San - ta Lu - ci - a!

*On the sea shines,*
*The star of silver*
*Placid is the wave*
*The wind prospers,*
*Come to the agile*
*Little boat of mine!*
*Santa Lucia,*
*Santa Lucia!*

## The Tune

One of the most famous folk songs of Italy, "Santa Lucia" is an ode to the city of Naples, and to the Santa Lucia area, which faces the Gulf of Naples. The song was embraced by the Scandinavians who celebrate St. Lucy (Lucia) Day on December 13.

## The Music Culture

In Sweden, Denmark, Norway and Finland, St. Lucy (called Sankta Lucia in Swedish) is venerated in a ceremony where girls dressed in white robes carry candles, led by one girl who poses as the saint with a crown of candles on her head. Sankta Lucia is the festival of lights fit for a winter's night which, before the reform of the Gregorian calendar in the sixteenth century, fell on the winter solstice—the longest and darkest night of the year. The candles symbolize the fire that refused to take the life of St. Lucy, while they are also interpreted as the light which overcomes the darkness. On December 13, the Swedish tradition is that girls (and now boys, too, known as "star boys") go from house to house carrying baked goods to every door. Within Swedish families, daughters go to each room to wake their sleeping family with saffron buns and coffee. (There are variants of this practice in other Scandinavian countries.) Along with other seasonal carols of the coming Christmas, "Santa Lucia" is sung and played in homes, churches, on the streets, and in the shops. The song's original lyrics describe the beautiful view of the Naples harbor area, but they have been changed in Sweden and elsewhere in Scandinavia to express St. Lucy's ability to overcome the fire and to convey the belief that by doing good works one can rise out of darkness and despair.

## The Experiences

- Sing the melody on a neutral syllable such as "loo," and on solfège syllables (beginning on "sol") and numbers (beginning on "5").
- Sing the lyrics, noting these pronunciations: *a* ("ah"), *e* ("ay"), *i* ("ee"), *u* ("oo"), "luccica" ("loo-chee-kah"), "Lucia"("loo-chee-ah"). The *g* is soft.
- Play the chords on guitar or piano, intact on every beat or in arpeggiated fashion in eighth notes throughout.
- Play the melody as an interlude on violins, cellos, or other melody instruments.
- In a circle or freely, move to a basic dance step:

| Beat: | 1 | 2 | 3 |
|---|---|---|---|
| Step: | R | L | - |
| | step | close | bounce both knees |

## Recommended Listening

+*Neapolitan Songs*. Smithsonian Folkways FW 08770

*Christmas in Sweden* (Jules Stjarna). Naxos 8-557790.

## SANTO DE OTAVALO

Ecuador

San - to San Jua - ni - to, San - to de O - ta - va - lo,

Ma - na ku - yak Pi - ca, Da - le con el pa - lo

Traditional, Ecuador, Arranged by Elizabeth Villarreal Brennan. From Brennan, E. V. (1988). *A Singing Wind: songs and Melodies from Ecuador*. Danbury, CT: World Music Press. Courtesy World Music Press.

## The Tune

St. John is the "Santo de Otavalo," the patron saint of Otavalo, a market town high in the Andean mountains of Ecuador, where young girls sing this song of potential suitors.

## The Music Culture

*Los Indígenas* is the preferred name of the Quichua-speaking people of Ecuador, whether they are fully Indian or *mestizos* (of mixed indigenous and Spanish ancestry). Before the arrival of the Spanish, Ecuador had been absorbed into the pan-Andean empire of the Incas. When they were colonized, they were converted to Catholicism and also assembled into communities with specific economic emphases. People in some villages were taught weaving skills, while in other villages they learned how to craft leather goods, or earthen pottery, or to carve wooden statues and furniture. On farms, they grew corn, peppers, and plantains, and raised sheep and cows. The people of Otavalo carried on their weaving of textiles, which had begun at least 1,500 years before the Spanish conquered the region. The town, located in a valley surrounded by the Andean peaks of Imbabura, Cotacachi, and Mojanda volcanoes, grew into a Saturday market where people from the surrounding communities would come to trade their goods. Now the largest daily market in South America, Otavalo is also known for its Andean traditional music and musicians. One of the traditional songs is "Santo de Otavalo," which is sung as a prayer to San Juanito (St. John), particularly during his feast-day celebration in September, when young girls light candles, dance on the plaza, and express their hope of finding someone to love them. The words are in Spanish and Quechua. The song's melody finds its way as well into the instrumental music played by panpipes known as *zampoñas, quena* flutes, guitars, violins, and the *bomba* drum.

### The Experiences

- Sing the song on a neutral syllable such as "nee," and on solfège syllables (beginning on "la") or scale numbers (beginning on "6").
- Sing the lyrics, noticing the need for elision of two syllables, "de" and "O," in the third measure.
- Play the chords on guitar, piano, or other harmony instrument. For guitar, play one of several strums:

 or

- Play a basic one-measure drum pattern:
- Play the melody on flutes or recorder, with guitar accompaniment.
- Add a harmony (vocally or on flutes/recorders), one that follows the melody at an interval of a third (or occasionally a fourth) lower.
- Perform a traditional circle dance, facing center, holding hands, and following these steps across the four melodic phrases:

    Phrase 1: Step four steps into the center of the circle

    Phrase 2: Step four steps out of the center of the circle

    Phrase 3: Step four steps to the right

    Phrase 4: Drop hands, and step four steps around in a personal circle, landing face-forward on the fourth step

## Recommended Listening

+*A Singing Wind: Five Melodies from Ecuador* (Brennan, E.). Danbury, CT: World Music Press.

*Music of the Andes*. Hemisphere 7243 8 28190 2 8.

# SARIKA KEO

Cambodia

Oh, Sarika keo,

What are you eating?

You are eating cactus fruits,

You are playfully nipping at each other.

Traditional, Cambodia, Arranged by Sam-Ang Sam. From Sam, S. A. & Campbell, P. S. (1991). *Silent Temples, Songful Hearts: Traditional Music of Cambodia*. Danbury, CT: World Music Press. Courtesy World Music Press.

## The Tune

There is a talking bird in Cambodia known as *sarika keo*, and children enjoy singing a song about this bird of many colors.

## The Music Culture

The *sarika keo* is a small black bird with white and yellow markings on the side of its head. Its home is in Cambodia, where it resides in the wooded areas and tall grasses of the Mekong River Delta. Sometimes, the Khmer people keep the bird as a pet, and train it to speak phrases such as "Teou na?" (Where are you going?) and "Arkun" (Thank you). The song is sung by children in Cambodian and Cambodian-American communities, as they learn about what the bird eats and how it plays. The song is typically sung in two parts, with girls (or boys) singing the the verse and the remaining group singing the untranslatable phrases, "ey sariyaing" and "euy keo keo euy." While Khmer folk songs are performed without instrumental accompaniment, it is also conceivable to play their melodies on two- and three-stringed fiddles, wooden xylophones called *roneat*, and end-blown flutes called *khloy*, and to hear also the sound of the *chhing* (bronze cymbals) and various sizes and shapes of drums.

338 Tunes and Grooves for Music Education

## The Experiences

- Sing the melody on a neutral syllable such as "lah," and solfège syllables (beginning on "mi") or scale numbers (beginning on "3").

- Sing the lyrics, noting these pronunciations: "keo" ("koy"), "euy" ("oy"), "yaing" ("yahng"), "choeuk" ("chook"), and "knea" ("k'nay").

- Sing the song in two groups, dividing into verse and response parts.

- Play the chords on piano or guitar, even though harmony is not typically heard in the traditional music of Cambodia.

- Play the melody on recorder or flute, "or on" violin, "or on" wooden xylophones, as a doubling of singing voices, and as introduction, interlude, and closing.

- Add the *chhing* (cymbals), playing on beats 1 and 3, alternating between the muffled (+) and ringing (o) sounds.

## Recommended Listening

+*Silent Temples, Songful Hearts: Traditional Music of Cambodia* (Sam, S. A. and Campbell, P. S.). Danbury, CT: World Music Press.

*Cambodia. Musical Atlas.* EMI C-064-17841.

*Royal Music of Cambodia.* Philips 6586 002.

# SAVALIVALAH

Samoa

# SAVALIVALAH

## The Tune

One avenue to learning a language is by singing it, and "Savalivalah" mixes into its lyrics Samoan phrases with their English translations. Samoan music is primarily vocal, and its uses are both public and private.

## The Music Culture

The Samoan Islands is a nation of nine inhabited Polynesian islands that includes the four islands of the independent state of Samoa and the five islands that comprise the territory of American Samoa. Samoans live a communal life with little privacy, choosing instead to work, eat, study, and pray together, and the absence of walls in their traditional homes support these practices. Musically, the Samoas have been described as cousins to the Maoris of New Zealand, the Cook Islanders, and the Tahitians. They sing in harmony of the everyday, the ocean, fishing, canoes, and of praise to a Christian God. Much Samoan history and culture are communicated through songs and dances like the *siva* and *sasa*. Instruments are minimalized in Samoan music, but movement is an important component to singing together in groups. Before the arrival of Europeans, they played hollowed-out logs to accompany songs, adding guitar and ukulele as they were brought to the islands by missionaries and travelers. Those instruments are now being replaced by the electronic keyboard. Yet the choral sound of multiple voices in harmony is maintained as central to Samoan musical identity.

### The Experiences

- Sing the melody on a neutral syllable such as "fai," and on solfège syllables or scale numbers.
- Sing the melody with lyrics, noting that *a*s are pronounced as "ah," *i* as "ee," "ia" as "yah," "te" as "tay," "oe" as "oy," and "fai" as "fah-ee."
- Sing the song in three-part harmony, as notated.
- Standing in lines or a circle, move to the beat in a step-close movement from right to left, thinking, chanting, and doing "step-close" twice per measure in each direction.

| Beat: | 1 | 2 | 3 | 4 | 1 | 2 | 3 | 4 |
|-------|---|------|---|-------|---|------|---|-------|
| Move: | R | step | R | close | L | step | L | close |

- Play the chords on guitar, piano, or other harmony instrument.
- Using a pair of sticks, tap them on the floor and click them together in an ostinato rhythmic movement. Choose from these pattern possibilities.

| Beat: | | 1 | 2 | 3 | 4 |
|-------|------|----------------------------------|----------------------------------|----------------------------------|----------------------------------|
| Sticks: | (a) | tap floor | tap floor | click together | tap floor or |
| Sticks: | (b) | click together | click together | tap floor | click together or |
| Sticks: | (c) | tap floor at hand-end of stick | tap floor at far-end of stick | tap floor at far-end of stick | tap floor at hand-end of stick |

### Recommended Listening

*Music of Oceania: Samoan Songs*. Musicaphon 52705.
*Music from Western Samoa: From Conch Shell to Disco*. Folkways FW 04270.

# SEA LION WOMAN

U. S.: Christine and Katherine Schipp

Sea lion wo-man (sea lion), She drank cof-fee (sea lion), She drank tea (sea lion)

And the gam-bler lie (sea lion). Way down yon-der (sea lion), 'Hind the wall (sea lion),

And the roos-ter crow (sea lion), and the gam-bler lie (sea lion). Sea lion wo-man (sea lion),

She drank cof-fee (sea lion), She drank tea (sea lion), and the gam-bler lie (sea lion).

Sea lion wo-man (sea lion), She drank cof-fee (sea lion),

She drank tea (sea lion) And the gam-bler lie (sea lion).

CD III, Track # 8

## The Tune

Recorded in Mississippi in 1939, "Sea Lion Woman" was the song of two sisters who described it as a part of their repertoire of play.

## The Music Culture

Christine and Katherine Shipp were the two daughters of a family of fourteen children when Alan Lomax met them in his folk song research of the 1940s. Their father was a sharecropping minister, and their mother was a choir director. They sang at their father's church as members of not only his family but also of their mother's family-made choir. They also learned the playground songs of their friends, adding to their home, family and church repertoire. Such is the way of children's culture, to acquire songs early in their childhood and in a variety of contexts. Because it is a part of the oral lore, it may never be known whether the song is "Sea Lion Woman," "C-line Woman," or "See Lyin' Woman." The African-Americanisms stand out in the dialect, the call-and-response format, and the repeated use of the minor third between the "do" and "la" pitches. As the girls explained it, there is no particular game, actions, or movement involved, as they simply sang to "have something to be saying" as they played and jumped about.

### The Experiences

- Listen to Track # 8, and sing the "sea lion" response to the sung various phrases.
- Sing the melody on a neutral syllable such as "see," and on solfège syllables (beginning on "mi") or scale numbers (beginning on "3").
- Sing the lyrics of the song without the "sea lion" response.
- Share the singing of the song, dividing among two or more singers the phrases of changing text with the "sea lion" response.
- Play the single Dm chord on guitar, piano, or other harmony instrument. Explore rhythms that can set the song into an attractive groove.
- Explore possibilities for playing a percussive track to accompany the song, as well as a bass line. Body percussion, or percussion instruments, may be effective.
- Create new text phrases for the melody, using subjects as far afield as the marine animal (sea lion) to "lies and truths"(See lyin') to travel on a bus line (C-line).

### Recommended Listening

+*A Treasury of Library of Congress Field Recordings* (Alan Lomax). Rounder ROUN 1500.

*Bessie Jones: Put Your Hand on Your Hip and Let Your Backbone Slip: Songs and Games from the Georgia Sea Islands*. Rounder 11587.

*Folk Visions and Voices: Traditional Music and Song in Northern Georgia, Volumes 1–2*. Folkways FW 34161, 34162.

# SEPARALA TAMBIEN

Jose Ramon Sanchez and Tito Puente

CD III, Track # 9

## The Groove

The music of Tito Puente is music-with-a-groove, driving rhythms that invariably beckon people to the floor as participants rather than as passive listeners. "Separala Tambien" is more than a suggestion: it is a flat-out invitation to dance.

## The Music Culture

New York City has long been a center for musical innovations, and it is home to the birth and development of a whole culture of Latin American music. The contributions of Cubans and Puerto Ricans to the evolution of Latin dance music and Latin jazz there are undeniable, and among the giants who shaped the sound was Tito Puente (1923–2000). Known as "El Rey" (the king), Puente was a *timbales* player and band leader. He grew up in Spanish Harlem, studied piano as a child, and then drum set and *timbales*. He played in various bands, including Machito's Afro-Cubans in 1941. He studied composition and orchestration at the Julliard School, and formed his own group, the Picadilly Boys, that played through the 1950s and 60s with a heavy brass sound and energetic Afro-Cuban percussive rhythms. Puente was a leading figure in the *salsa* movement of the 1970s, as well as an influence in the Latino rock sound of Carlos Santana. He formed the Latin Percussion Jazz Ensemble (later called the Latin Jazz Ensemble) that toured internationally and spread *salsa* near and far, from Monterey, California to Montreux, Switzerland—and to Japan as well. To many who play, dance, and listen to Latin dance, jazz, and *salsa* music, Tito Puente's sound is classic and seminal.

### The Experiences

- Listen to Track # 9, tapping a steady pulse while following the entrance and activity of the saxophones, trumpets and trombones, and the vocal line.
- While listening to the recording, alternate between tapping the cowbell (with its steady quarter notes) and the *guiro* (with its quarter and eighth-note pattern) parts.

- Play the eighth-note pattern of the *conga* drum, finding a higher-pitched "ringing" sound for the last two eighths of each measure.
- For a more authentic conga drum sound, chant and then play this pattern of eighth notes:

| Beat: | 1 | 2 | 3 | 4 | 5 | 6 | 7 | 8 |
|-------|------|-----|-----|-----|------|-----|------|------|
| Chant: | heel | tip | cup | tip | heel | tip | flat | flat |
| Hand: | L | L | R | L | L | L | R | R |

"heel"—heel of the palm of the left hand

"tip"—finger tips of the left hand

"cup"—cupped palm of the right hand

"flat"—flattened-out palm of the right hand

- Play the *conga* drum with the cowbell and *guiro*, until it is locked in and tight.
- While listening to the recording, play the percussion parts.

### Recommended Listening

*Tito Puente: Oye Como Va: The Dance Collection*. Concord Records 4780.
*King of Kings: The Very Best of Tito Puente*. BMG Heritage 99001.

# SHALOM CHAVERIM

Israel

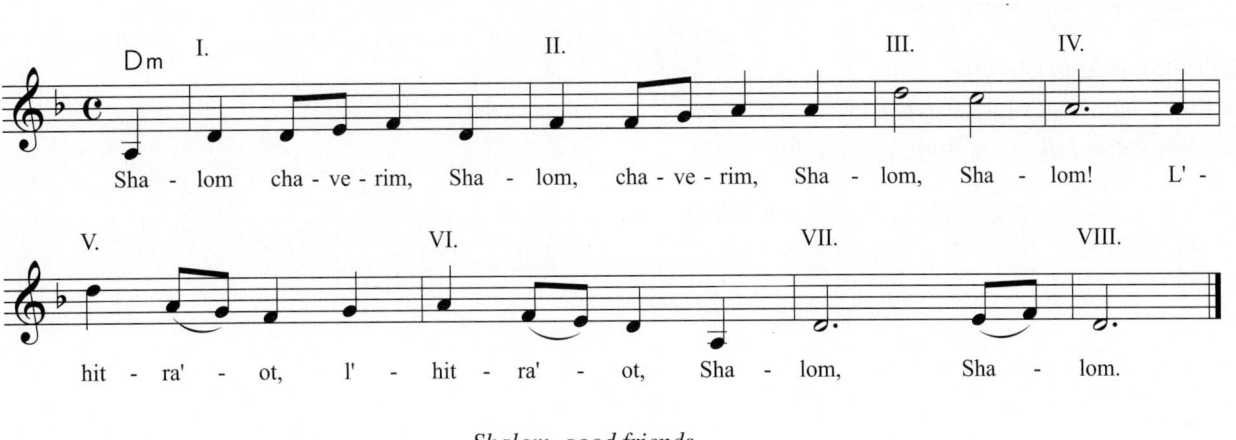

Shalom chaverim, Shalom, chaverim, Shalom, Shalom! L'-
hit - ra' - ot, l' - hit - ra' - ot, Shalom, Shalom.

*Shalom, good friends,*
*Shalom, good friends,*
*Shalom, Shalom,*
*Until we meet again, Shalom.*

## The Tune

The meanings of the Hebrew word "shalom" are multiple, including "hello," "goodbye," and "peace."

## The Music Culture

Israel is situated at the eastern edge of the Mediterranean Sea, a modern nation that is distinguished from others in the region by language, religion, and culture. Hebrew is spoken in Israel (and in Jewish communities around the world); it is a Semitic language of the Afro-Asiatic language family whose classical dialect was used in writing the Tanakh (the Hebrew Bible). The Neo-Babylonian Empire destroyed Jerusalem and exiled its population to Babylon, and the Persian Empire later allowed them to return to their region, at which point newer Hebrew dialects replaced the older Biblical Hebrew. When the Roman Empire exiled the Jewish population of Jerusalem, even these spoken Hebrew dialects faded and were used only for legal documents, science, medicine, poetry, and liturgical prayer. It was not until the advent of Zionism at the end of the nineteenth century, when Jews sought to establish a homeland in Israel, that Hebrew was restored as a spoken language to replace Yiddish, Russian, Ladino, and other languages of the Jewish diaspora. Now the language, religion, and culture of the Jews are revived in Israel, after so many years following the scattering of the people from their historical origin.

### The Experiences

- Sing the song on a netural syllable such as "lah," and on solfège syllables (beginning on "mi") or scale numbers (beginning on "3").
- Sing the lyrics, noting that there is a long "o" in "shalom" and that "chaverim" is pronounced "kah-veh-reem."
- Sing the song in canon, beginning with a two-part canon and extending to eight parts that can be layered in, measure by measure.

- Play the Dm chord on guitar, piano, or other harmony instrument, rolling it slowly once every four beats.
- Explore a variety of accompaniment possibilities, including various rhythmic patterns for chording and the ostinati that can be drawn from single measures of the melody and played on flutes and recorders, xylophones, and string, wind, and brass instruments.

## Recommended Listening

*Jewish Folksongs*. Folkways FW 08740.

*Mountain So Far: Folkways of Israel*. Folkways FW 31305.

# SHEHUO GUDIEN

China

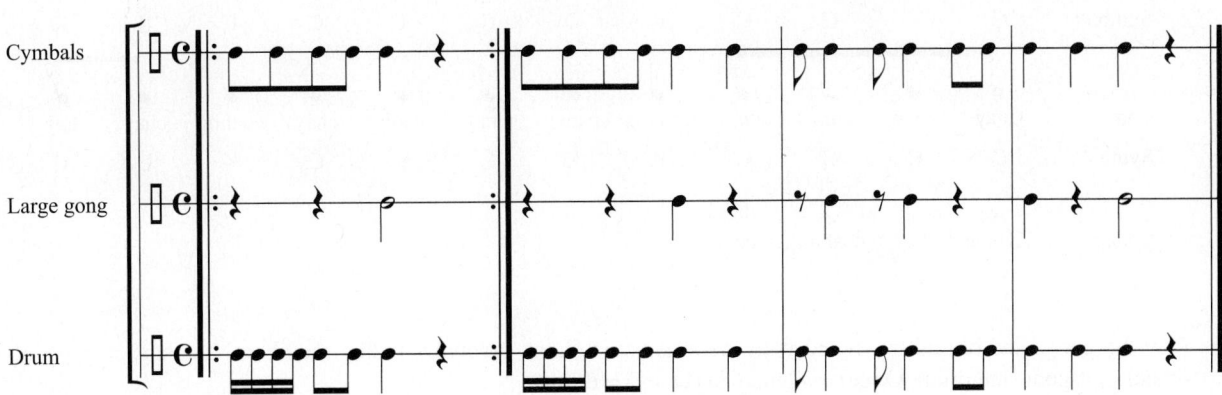

Traditional, China, Arranged by Han Kuo Han. From Han, K. H. & Campbell, P. S. (1992). *The Lion's Roar: Chinese Luogu Percussion Ensembles*. Danbury, CT: World Music Press. Courtesy World Music Press.

CD III, Track # 11

## The Groove

In northwestern China, a piece of parade music known as "Shehuo Gudien" is performed for festivals at the New Year, and in spring planting and autumn harvest seasons.

## The Music Culture

Chinese festivals can be found all through the year, from New Year's Day in late January to mid-February to the Buddhist *La Ba* Festival in late December. Between these holidays are the celebrations of the Spring Festival, the Lantern Festival, the Clear and Bright Festival of the planting season, summertime's Dragon Boat Festival and Double Seventh Festival, the Mid-Autumn Festival of the bright harvest moon, and the Double Ninth Festival of chrysanthemums for avoiding disaster. For all of these festivals, families set time aside to decorate their homes, eat specially prepared foods, sing songs, participate in or watch parades of dancing lions and dragons, and listen for the music of the *luogu* ensemble. Players of gongs and drums dress in elaborate costumes, landing in the village square, park, or city center. The music of "Shehuo Gudien" is but one example of *luogu* processional music, a piece from Gansu Provence in northwestern China that is associated with songs and dances of planting or transplanting.

### The Experiences
- Listen to Track # 11, tapping the pulse while focusing on the intermingling of gongs and drums.
- While listening to the recording, follow the mnemonics that are typically chanted by those who are learning the piece.

- Chant the mnemonics without the recording, gradually increasing the speed. The top line of notation is the one to which the following chant refers.

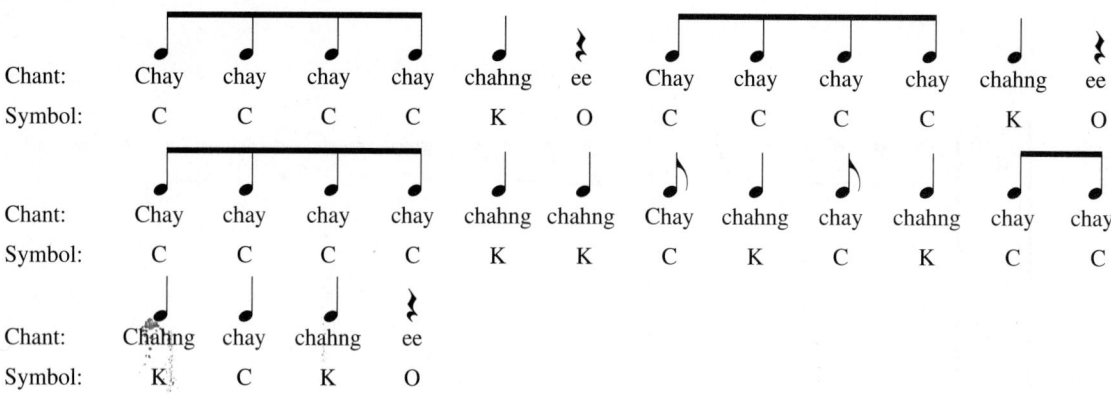

| Chant: | Chay | chay | chay | chay | chahng | ee | Chay | chay | chay | chay | chahng | ee |
|---|---|---|---|---|---|---|---|---|---|---|---|---|
| Symbol: | C | C | C | C | K | O | C | C | C | C | K | O |

| Chant: | Chay | chay | chay | chay | chahng | chahng | Chay | chahng | chay | chahng | chay | chay |
|---|---|---|---|---|---|---|---|---|---|---|---|---|
| Symbol: | C | C | C | C | K | K | C | K | C | K | C | C |

| Chant: | Chahng | chay | chahng | ee |
|---|---|---|---|---|
| Symbol: | K | C | K | O |

- Play the gongs and drums associated with the mnemonic chant, gradually fading the chant. C (chay) = gong, K (chahng) = gong and drum, O (ee) = silence, D (Dong) = drum
- Play another large gong for the music of the second line of notation.
- After numerous repetitions, when the top-line pattern is learned, a separate drum can be designated to play the third line of notation.
- The three lines of rhythm are played repeatedly, until the drum cues what will be the end by playing this pattern in the final measure:

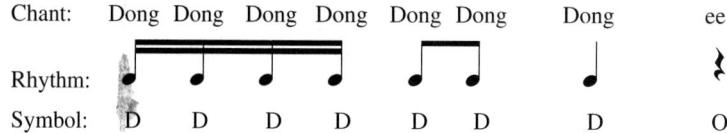

| Chant: | Dong | Dong | Dong | Dong | Dong | Dong | Dong | ee |
|---|---|---|---|---|---|---|---|---|
| Rhythm: | | | | | | | | |
| Symbol: | D | D | D | D | D | D | D | O |

## Recommended Listening

+*The Lion's Roar: Chinese Luogu Percussion Ensembles* (Han, K. H. and Campbell, P. S.). Danbury, CT: World Music Press. *Chinese Percussion Music*. Marco Polo 8-223652.

# SHENANDOAH

United States

O Shen - an - doah,____ I love your daugh - ter A - way,____ you roll - ing

ri - ver For her I've crossed the roll - ing wa - ter, A -

way,____ we're bound a - way,____ A - cross the wide____ Mis - sou - ri.____

2. The trader loved this Indian maiden.
   Away, you rolling river.
   With presents his canoe was laden.
      (Refrain)

3. O Shenandoah, I'm bound to leave you.
   Away, you rolling river.
   O Shenandoah, I'll not deceive you.
   (Refrain)

4. O Shenandoah, I long to hear you.
   Away, you rolling river.
   O Shenandoah, I long to hear you.
   (Refrain)

## The Tune

Slow in tempo and of the character of an expressive love song, "Shenandoah" is a shanty once sung by boatmen who worked on the Shenandoah River on its course through Virginia and West Virginia.

## The Music Culture

The Shenandoah River is the principal tributary of the Potomac River, running approximately 150 miles through several eastern U.S. states. It drains some of the valleys in the Appalachians on the west side of Virginia's Blue Ridge Mountains. The fertile soil that lie just beyond its banks made it a compelling place for early settlements, and even now it is a prime agricultural area. When boats were a major means of transport, those who worked them, hauling sails and heaving cargo, sang to pass time and alleviate the fatigue of their manual labor. The verse-refrain form of "Shenandoah" allowed for a lead singer to present new ideas (the trader's love for an Indian maiden, the sailor's promise not to deceive, his longing to hear the river) for the group to contemplate as they sang the refrain.

## The Experiences

- Sing the melody on a neutral syllable such as "doh," and on solfège syllables (beginning with "sol") or scale numbers (beginning with "5").
- Sing the lyrics of the song, adhering to the syncopations and the longer, sustained notes.
- Play the chords on guitar, bango, or piano, picking out individual notes in an eighth-note arpeggiation.
- Sing the song as it was originally intended, for solo verse and group refrain.

## Recommended Listening

+*Pete Seeger: American Favorite Ballads, Volume 1*. Smithsonian Folkways SFW 40150.

+*Sea Chanties and Forecastle Songs at Mystic Seaport*. Folkways FW 37300.

+*Bruce Springsteen: We Shall Overcome. The Seeger Sessions*. Columbia 82876.

# SHE'S LIKE THE SWALLOW

England

2. Maiden into her garden did go

   For to  pluck her some wild primrose

   The more she plucked, the more she did pull

   Until this maiden's apron was full.

3. Then out of these roses she made a bed

   A scarlet pillow for her head

   She laid her down, no word she did spake

   Until then this maiden's heart, it did break.

CD III, Track # 10

## The Tune

Traditional songs and ballads of England frequently tell of the unrequited love of young men and maidens. In "She's Like the Swallow," the depth of the beautiful maiden's sorrow is poetically described.

## The Music Culture

The oldest songs in England's oral tradition are the ballads, many of which predate 1750 and were collected and classified by Francis James Child. Hence the designation "Child ballads" for the classic songs of his collection, including the well-known stories of "The Elfin Knight" (Child 4), "The Twa Sisters" (Child 10), and "Edward" (Child 13). Cecil Sharp collected folk songs that entered the English oral tradition in the late eighteenth and nineteenth centuries, the largest group comprising narrative songs with tragic, historic, or comic themes based on a single encounter, such as "The Death of Bill Brown," "The Dark-Eyed Sailor," and "The Bold Grenadier." Others of these folk songs were nonnarrative and lyrical in character (for example, "I Wish, I Wish"), associated with drinking (for example, "The Barley Mow"), related to a specific occupations (for example, "The Old Weaver's Lament") or the sport of hunting (for example, "The Horn of the Hunter"), or were shanties sung on sailing ships (for example, "Sally Brown"). While the verses to "She's Like a Swallow" only hint of a story, the portrayal of the young maiden and her broken heart recalls the intent and function of ballads and more than a few folk songs of old England.

## The Experiences

- Listen to Track # 10, noting the infrequent sounding of a synthesized chordal accompaniment.
- Sing the melody on a neutral syllable such as "low," and on solfège syllables (beginning on "mi") or scale numbers (beginning on "3").
- Listen to the recording, and follow the lyrics and notation to detect the extent to which the singer improvises a melismatic passage more decorative than what is written.
- Sing the lyrics according to the notation, and then in an ornamented fashion as on the recording.
- Play the chords on piano, guitar, or dulcimer, rolling or strumming them every two beats so as allow the voice to be the prominent sound between the chords.

## Recommended Listening

+*Alan Mills and Jean Carignan: Songs, Fiddle Tunes, and a Folk-Tale from Canada*. Smithsonian Folkways FW 03532.
+*The Jupiter Book of Ballads* (Isla Cameron, Jill Balcon, Pauline Letts, John Laurie). Smithsonian Folkways FW 09890.
*The Best of British Folk*. Castle Communications CCSCD222.

# SHI NAASHA

Navajo

*I am going.*

*Beauty is all around me. I am going in freedom.*

From Anderson, W. M. & Campbell, P. S. (Eds.). Multicultural Perspectives in Music Education. Reston, VA: MENC, 1989.  Used by permission.

## The Tune

The "Long Walk Home" of the Navajo people inspired "Shi Naasha," so that despite their attempted removal from their native lands by the United States government, the Navajo saw beauty as they courageously walked back from their period of exile to their homeland.

## The Music Culture

In 1863 and 1864, the United States government attempted to remove the Navajo from Dinatah, their traditional territory in northeastern Arizona, western New Mexico, and southern Utah and Colorado. Early relations between Anglo-American settlers in New Mexico and the Navajo were peaceful enough, but peace disintegrated to raids and counterraids following the killing of Navajo leader, Narbona, in 1849. A destructive cycle of battles was followed by short-lived treaties, until a plan was hatched by the U.S. military leaders to pacify the Navajo by relocating them from their homeland (thought to be rich in gold and other minerals) to a place in the Pecos River Valley (which had insufficient water and minimal firewood). At least 200 died along the 300-mile march, and the reservation of forty square miles was little more than a prison camp. In 1868, following crop infestation and disease, the experiment was declared a disaster and the Navajo were granted 3.5 million acres in their previous homeland. Their return journey, the "Long Walk Home," brought the separate bands of Navajo together into a united Diné, or "The People." The text of "Shi Naasha" translates is a celebration of beauty and freedom.

### The Experiences

- Sing the melody on a neutral syllable such as "nah," and on solfège syllables or scale numbers.
- Sing the lyrics, following this pronunciation guide: "shi naasha" ("shee nah-shah"), "eiya" ("ay-yah"), "hei" ("hay").

- Play the quarter-note beat on a hand drum, or arrange a bass drum in a position with the head of the drum facing upwards so that multiple drummers can beat their mallets.
- Dance in circle formation, moving to the beat clockwise, stepping long (the left foot stepping and holding on beats one and two), then short (the right stepping up to the left foot on beat three).

## Recommended Listening

+*Navajo Songs from Canyon De Chelly*. New World Records 80406.

*Navajo Songs*. Smithsonian Folkways SFW 40403.

*Tribal Dreams: Music from Native Americans*. EarthBeat! R2 74269.

## THE SHIP'S CARPENTEER

England

'Twas in Lis-burgh of late a — fair dam-sel did dwell; Her wit and her

beau-ty — no one could e'er tell. She — was loved by a fair one — who

called her his dear And he by his trade was — a ship's car-pen-teer.

2. Early one morning before it was day,
   He went to his Polly, these words he did say:
   "O Polly, O Polly, you must go with me,
   Before we are married my friends for to see."

3. He led her through woods and through valleys so deep,
   Which caused this poor maiden to sigh and to weep:
   "O Billy, O Billy, you have led me astray
   On purpose my innocent life to betray."

4. "O Billy, O Billy, O pardon my life,
   I never will covet for to be your wife;
   I'll travel the whole world to set myself free,
   If you will pardon my baby and me."

5. "There's no time for pardon, there's no time to save,
   For all the night long I've been digging your grave.
   Your grave is now open and the spade is standing by";
   Which caused this young damsel to weep and to cry.

6. He covered her up so safe and secure,
   Thinking no one could find her, he was sure.
   Then he went on board to sail the world round,
   Before the murder could ever be found.

7. Early one morning before it was day,
   The captain he came up and these words did say:
   "There's a murderer on board and he must be known.
   Our ship is in mourning, we cannot sail on."

8. Then up steps the first man, "I'm sure it's not me."
   Then up steps the second, "I'm sure it's not me."
   Then up steps bold William to stamp and to swear:
   "I'm sure it's not me, sir. I vow and declare."

9. Now as he was turning from captain with speed,
   He met with his Polly, which made his heart bleed.
   She ripped him and tore him, she tore him in three,
   Because that he murdered her baby and she.

From *Music in Childhood: From Preschool Through the Elementary Grade* with Audio CD 3rd edition by CAMPBELL/SCOTT-KASSNER, 2006. Reprinted with permission of Wadsworth, a Division of Thompson Learning: www. Thomsonrights.com. Fax 800-730-2215.

## The Tune

A tragic story in song, "The Ship's Carpenteer" is an English broadside ballad with numerous variants depending upon who, where, and when it was sung.

## The Music Culture

Songs that tell a story have been widespread in England and elsewhere in Europe since at least the Middle Ages. Some of the early ballads tell of Tristram and Iseult, the hero Roland, and Olufa, daughter of the French King Pipin, and Sigurd and Brynhild. Their stories may extend thirty sung verses, and some as many as a hundred verses, with many repetitions and long drawn-out descriptions. Yet many ballads tell of unnamed (or only first-named) maidens and men of various occupations. "The Ship's Carpenteer" is known by many titles, including "The Gosport Tragedy," "The Cruel Ship Carpenter," "The Fog-bound Vessel," "Pretty Polly," and "Molly Girl," and has been documented by folk song collectors from Staffordshire, England, to Fayetteville, Arkansas. It relates the tale of a carpenter who seduces a woman, promising marriage, but she becomes pregnant, he murders her and joins the navy as a ship's carpenter. The crew sees the ghosts of the woman and her baby, and after vehement denials, the carpenter sinks into madness and despair, and dies. Cecil Sharp, the British collector of folk songs and ballads, claimed that this was one of the few "supernatural folk-ballads" that was still popular with country singers well into twentieth-century England.

### The Experiences

- Sing the melody on a neutral syllable such as "tee," and on solfège syllables (beginning on "mi") or scale numbers (beginning on "3").
- To internalize the 5/8 feeling, hum the melody while patting the lap (or on a tabletop or other surface) and clapping the subdivision of 2 beats and 3 beats:

| Beat: | 1 | 2 | 3 | 4 | 5 |
|---|---|---|---|---|---|
| Movement: | pat | snap | snap | pat | snap |

- Sing the lyrics of the song, noting that outside of the occasional sixteenth-note ornament, the song is typically syllabic.
- Play the chords on guitar, piano, or other harmony instrument. Follow the same 3-beat and 2-beat subdivision, chording at beats 1 and 4, or accenting those beats while giving a lighter sound with arpeggiation or broken chords to the remaining beats.

### Recommended Listening

+*George Dunn: Chainmaker*. Musical Traditions Records MTCD317-8.

*Sea Chanties and Forecastle Songs at Mystic Seaport*. Folkways FW 37300.

*The Best of British Folk*. Castle Communications CCSCD222.

# SHORTNIN' BREAD

U. S.: African American

## The Tune

The call-and-response form of "Shortnin' Bread," as well as the subject of this particular food, is a certain sign of its African-American origin.

## The Music Culture

For African Americans living in the rural south up through the mid-twentieth century, shortening bread was a dietary staple. Shortening is lard, the coagulated oils gathered from frying or cooking pork, chicken, or beef. It was spread like butter on bread, and eaten for breakfast (or any other time of day, including as snacks). Shortening bread was a favorite treat for children coming home from school, or in from their play. The song "Shortnin' Bread" was a Negro plantation song that was later revived on radio. In 1937, it was featured in the movie "Maytime" as "Mammy's L'il Baby Loves Shortnin' Bread," and was associated with Nelson Eddy. Its African-Americanisms include the call-and-response form of solo and group singers, the "do"–"la" pitch relationship, and the syncopated rhythms.

## The Experiences

- Sing the melody on a neutral syllable such as "doo," and on solfège syllables (beginning on "la") or scale numbers (beginning on "6").
- Sing the lyrics, with attention to the syncopated and quick sixteenth-note rhythms.
- Divide the singing of the song between a soloist and group.
- Add guitar to play rhythmically punctuated chords.
- For every measure in the refrain, snap on the first beat, clap on the second beat, and shift the weight of the feet from one side to the other on every beat.

| Step: | 1 | 2 |
|---|---|---|
|  | L | R |
| Snap: | 1 | - |
| Clap: | - | 2 |

- On the verses, turn to the right for four beats (steps) and then back again to the original position over four more beats (steps). Hang the arms down, drop the hands from the wrists, and shake them.
- Create a hand-clapping movement that extends two, four, or eight beats in a repeating ostinato movement; feature the clapping of partner's hands and own hands, single right and/or left hands, finger-snapping, and vertical columns of hand-clapping and hand-shaking at face, chest, and belt-line levels.

## Recommended Listening

+*Sonny Terry's New Sound: Jawharp in Blues and Folk Music* (Sonny Terry, Brownie McGhee). Folkways FW 03821.

+*Black Banjo Songsters of North Carolina and Virginia*. Smithsonian Folkways SFW 40079.

*Bessie Jones: Put Your Hand on Your Hip and Let Your Backbone Slip; Songs and Games from the Georgia Sea Islands*. Rounder 11587.

# SINGABAHAMBAYO

South Africa

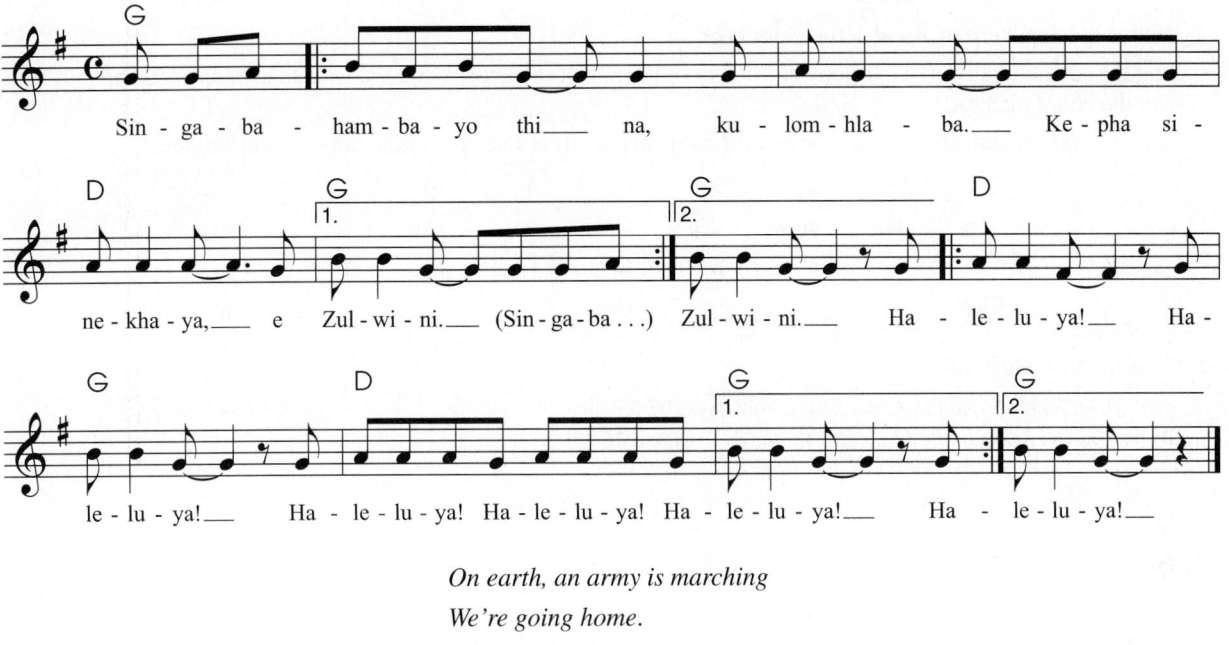

Sin - ga - ba - ham - ba - yo thi___ na, ku - lom - hla - ba.___ Ke - pha si -

ne - kha - ya,___ e Zul - wi - ni.___ (Sin - ga - ba . . .) Zul - wi - ni.___ Ha - le - lu - ya!___ Ha -

le - lu - ya!___ Ha - le - lu - ya! Ha - le - lu - ya! Ha - le - lu - ya!___ Ha - le - lu - ya!___

*On earth, an army is marching*

*We're going home.*

*Our longing bears a song.*

*So sing unto the Lord! Halleluya!*

From *Music in Childhood: From Preschool Through the Elementary Grade* with Audio CD 3rd edition by CAMPBELL/SCOTT-KASSNER, 2006. Reprinted with permission of Wadsworth, a Division of Thompson Learning: www. Thomsonrights.com. Fax 800-730-2215.

## The Tune

During the period of the anti-apartheid movement in South Africa, protest and freedom songs such as "Singaba-hambayo" were sung as a symbol of unity and passionate commitment to the cause of establishing a fully representative democracy inclusive of people of color.

## The Music Culture

The musical glory of South Africa is its vocal tradition, with songs communally sung in full harmony to accompany rituals and rites of passage from birth to death. Bantu-speaking peoples, including the Sotho, Xhosa, and Zulu, utilized call-and-response forms in their music prior to the advent of European travelers, and made prominent use of two or more linked melodic phrases that they could sing (or play) repeatedly, with high rhythmic energy. Christian missionaries who arrived to "convert the heathens" introduced choral hymns to South Africa, and visits by African-American jubilee singers such as the Fisk University and Orpheus McAddoo groups brought models of the choral harmonies that could be sung by South African groups. These musical components were consolidated in the freedom songs that black South Africans sang in their struggle against apartheid, and were heard not only in churches but also in the spirited protest marches and public rallies, particularly in the 1970s, 80s, and 90s. These freedom songs were prominent through the course of Nelson Mandela's lifetime struggle, in a nonviolent activism, for the equal opportunities and fair treatment of all South Africans of every color.

## *The Experiences*

- Sing the melody on a neutral syllable such as "ha," and on solfège syllables and scale numbers.
- Sing the lyrics, with attention to these pronunciations: "thi" ("tee"), "hla" ("lah"), all "*e*"s ("ay").
- Play the chords on piano, guitar, or other harmony instrument. For piano, play one chord per beat, and for guitar, strum a quick pattern of ♪ ♪♪ for every beat.
- Sing the song chorally, in a harmony consisting of pitches of the chords. Sing slowly so as to hear the melody's fit over the chord pitches.
- In a basic movement, step in place or in a forward shuffle, from one side to the other, while singing.

| Beat: | 1 | 2 | 3 | 4 | 5 | 6 | 7 | 8 |
|-------|------|-------|------|-------|------|-------|------|-------|
| Step: | step | close | step | touch | step | close | step | touch |
|       | R | L | R | L | L | R | L | R |
| Clap: | - | - | - | clap | - | - | - | clap |

## *Recommended Listening*

*This Land is Mine: South African Freedom Songs.* Folkways FW 05588.
*South African Choral: Songs of the Alexandra Youth Choir.* Naxos 76025-2.

# SOLDIER, SOLDIER, WILL YOU MARRY ME?

United States

*2. hat

*3. gloves

*4. boots

## The Tune

A song of the ill-clad soldier, "Soldier, Soldier, Will You Marry Me?" was sung at the time of the American Revolution and the Civil War.

## The Music Culture

During the period of the American Revolution, 1775–83, but also as late as 1861–65, the American Civil War, there was plenty of music to be made. Music was used to rally troops, as recreation, and to march by. Songs of love and war, and of heroes and humorous tales, comprised the repertoire of soldiers and those they left behind. They were sung without accompaniment, or doubled on fife, or played on instruments like guitars, banjos, and fiddles when these were available. At the edge of the battlefield, soldiers would hear and even borrow the tunes or lyrics of the other side's songs. They were known to serenade the other side, or to stop a battle to stage an impromptu concert.

Some songs became emblematic of a particular war, such as Julia Ward Howe's "The Battle Hymn of the Republic" (based upon the tune of the abolitionist song "John Brown's Body"), while some songs held universal themes that were fitting for any war, at any age. "Soldier, Soldier, Will You Marry Me?" is one of those songs that was fervently sung in the eighteenth-century Revolutionary War and was then rejuvenated during the Civil War.

## The Experiences

- Sing the song on a neutral syllable such as "me," and on solfège syllables (beginning on "sol") or scale numbers (beginning on "5").
- Sing the song with lyrics, noting that it is sung four times with only a substitution of the name of a garment (measure 7). Note the "zinger" of a response by the soldier in the final two measures.
- Play the chords on guitar or piano. On guitar, a down, down-up strumming pattern of ♩  ♫ is fitting; on piano, try rolling chords played every two beats.
- Play the melody on violin or flute, with guitar (and banjo) accompaniment.

## Recommended Listening

+*Folk Songs of the Catskills* (Barbara Moncure). Folkways FW 05311.

+*Old Timey Songs for Children* (New Lost City Ramblers). Folkways FW 07064.

## SOLDIER'S JOY

United States

Well, you chase___ the___ Rab - bit, and you chase the squir - rel,

Chase - that___ pret - ty girl a - round the world. Then you load___ your___ gun___ and you

aim it right, Let's___ hur - ry up___ boys,___ don't you take all night. Now you

chase that pos - sum and you chase that coon,___ and you chase that great___ big___

old___ ba - boon. Coup - le up,___ two,___ then you buck - le up___ four___ and___

cir - cle to your left,___ in the mid - dle of the floor. Now you mid - dle of the floor.

CD III, Track # 12

## The Tune

The American dance tune "Soldier's Joy" is heard at square dances and contra dances on fiddle as well as on mandolin, guitar, and banjo. Lyrics were added later to the tune, so that singers could also join in on the melody making.

## The Music Culture

The early history of instrumental music in the United States is quite naturally based upon the instruments and forms that were brought from Europe to the colonies and the newly formed American nation. Settlers from England, Ireland, and Germany were among the first Americans, and they brought to the New World the portable instruments they could pack or carry on their backs, such as the violin, flute, concertina and accordion, and various small percussion instruments such as the *tabor* or hand drum. The enslaved Africans fashioned the banjo in memory of the *halaam* they left behind, a percussively plucked lute of three strings with a skin-covered body. The music of early Americans was often dance music (including reels, jigs, hornpipes, polkas, and waltzes), which was played in barns, community centers, church "fellowship halls," and out on in the town square on summer nights. Fiddle tunes were created that, while they fit perfectly in the fingers and bowing patterns of the player, were also traded from one instrument to the other. "Soldier's Joy" is one such fiddle tune to which words were added so that even a singer could participate in the sharing of the melody for the dance. Fiddler Mark O'Connor's renditions of this and other early American dance tunes capture the character and style of colonial America.

## The Experiences

- Listen to Track # 12, and follow the melody as it is played successively by the fiddle, guitar, and banjo.
- Listen to the recording, and with alternate hands on a flat surface, tap the eighth-note pulse, switching to twice as fast (sixteenth notes) and twice as slow (quarter notes).
- Sing the melody slowly on a neutral syllable such as "loo," and on solfège syllables (beginning on "mi") or scale numbers (beginning on "3").
- If it feels high, try singing all but the first two lines (measures 1–5) an octave lower.
- Play the melody on violin, guitar, piano, banjo, flute, or other melody instrument; or in an ensemble of multiple instruments.
- Play intact or broken chords in eighth notes on guitar or piano.
- Explore various square- and contra-dance movements, each extending 4 (or 8) beats. For example, in squares of eight persons in four couples, try the following sequence of movements.

| | |
|---|---|
| Phrase 1 (4 beats/2 measures): | Couples 1 and 3 move to center in four steps |
| Phrase 2: | Couples 1 and 3 move back to place in four steps |
| Phrase 3: | Couples 2 and 4 move to center in four steps |
| Phrase 4: | Couples 2 and 4 move back to place in four steps |
| Phrases 5–6: | Right partner of couples 1–4 steps into center, extends left arm to center/places hands on top of other hands for a "western star," steps right for 8 beats/4 measures |
| Phrases 7–8: | Left partner of couples 1–4 moves in same fashion as noted above (Phrases 5–6) |
| Phrases 9–10: | Couples face right, hold hands in a crossed-arm skater's fashion, move eight steps |
| Phrases 11–12: | Couples turn left, move eight steps as noted above (Phrases 9–10) |

## Recommended Listening

+*Legends of the Fiddle: 20 Bluegrass Classics*. King 318.

+*Appalachian Journey* (Mark O'Connor). Sony Classical 66782.

*Heartland: An Appalachian Anthology*. Sony Classical 89683.

# SOMEBODY'S KNOCKING

U. S.: African American

## The Tune

In the *spiritual* "Somebody's Knocking," the message is that there are constant reminders of ethical ways to think and act. The internalized conscience is there to advise and direct the individual to the right path.

## The Music Culture

A century before Thomas A. Dorsey was writing "gospel songs" in Chicago, African slaves in the southern United States were listening to white Protestant hymns of the open-air camp meetings during America's religious revival, the "Great Awakening." They applied their syncopated rhythms and vocal slides, and thus produced the new sound of the spiritual. There were the more complicated spirituals like "Steal Away" and "He Never Said a Mumblin' Word" that were sung by studied choristers, as well as songs that even children could tune to and sing, like "Get on Board, Chillun" and "Somebody's Knockin' at Your Door." The spiritual matured, and came into the voices of The Fisk (University) Jubilee Singers in the latter part of the nineteenth century, who performed with the finesse of a professional choir, traveled the world, and spread the form and its style far and wide. Once validated by European royalty, spirituals became favorite pieces in all-white American choirs. Even as gospel music grew to a multi-million-dollar industry, the spiritual continued to develop as an art music for church and concert hall performances well into the twentieth century. From the highly complex to the straightforward, as in "Somebody's Knocking," spirituals have staying power.

### The Experiences

- Sing the melody on a neutral syllable such as "doo," and on solfège syllables or scale numbers.
- Sing the lyrics, sustaining the pitch on "door" for its full rhythmic value.
- Play the chords on piano, featuring a left-hand bass line comprised of chord roots that moves in quarter-note pulses, while playing chords in the right hand on the off-beat:

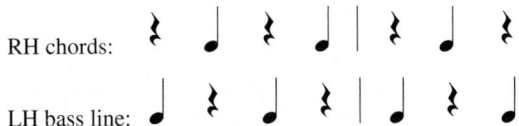

- While singing, clap and pat (on a flat surface, or lap) an ostinato rhythm:

## Recommended Listening

+*Celebration: It Is Well*. Intersound Records 5304

*Wade in the Water, Volume 1: African American Spirituals: The Concert Tradition*. Smithsonian Folkways SFW 40072.

# SOMETIMES I FEEL LIKE A MOTHERLESS CHILD

U. S.: African American

Some - times I feel like a mo - ther - less child,___ Some - times I feel like a

mo - ther - less child.___ Some - times I feel like a mo - ther - less child,___ a

long way___ from home,_____ a long way___ from home.

2. Sometimes I feel like I'm almost gone,

Sometimes I feel like I'm almost gone,

Sometimes I feel like I'm almost gone,

A long way from home, a long way from home.

CD III, Track # 13

## The Tune

African-American *spirituals* are further classified as *sorrow songs* when their texts are suffused with melancholy and the tempo of their performance is particularly slow. Few spirituals meet these criteria better than "Sometimes I Feel Like a Motherless Child."

## The Music Culture

Themes of loneliness, loss, and even death run through many African-American spirituals, and the intensely slow moving sorrow songs like "Were You There?" and "Sometimes I Feel Like a Motherless Child" are examples of this type of spiritual. They contrast with *jubilees,* spirituals that are quick in tempo, highly rhythmic, syncopated, and performed as *call-and-response* forms, such as "Didn't My Lord Deliver Daniel" and "Down by the Riverside." Gospel singer Mahalia Jackson (1911–1972), is associated with riveting performances of "Sometimes I Feel Like a Motherless Child." Although she was dubbed the "Gospel Queen," her rich contralto voice could shape spirituals in her own uniquely expressive style. She was associated with the gospel composer Thomas A. Dorsey for fourteen years, touring with him to promote his songs (including the gospel hit "Move on Up a Little Higher" that was recorded in 1947). She recorded in 1958 with Duke Ellington and his orchestra in "Black, Brown, and Beige," and in 1961, she sang at John F. Kennedy's presidential inauguration. It was the bending of the notes, the ornamentation of the pitches, and the deep vocal timbre (as revealed in this very spiritual) that earned Mahalia Jackson her place as a pioneer interpreter of African-American vocal music.

## The Experiences

- Listen to Track # 13, following the vocal slides that ornament the melody.
- Sing the melody on a netural syllable such as "ma," and on solfège syllables (beginning on "do") or scale numbers (beginning on "1").
- Sing the lyrics, attending to producing a sustained sound on "child," "long," and "home." Add a second verse, "Sometimes I feel like I'm almost gone," sung three times followed by the last four measures as in the first verse.
- Play the chords on piano, one chord per quarter-note beat.
- Using the chord indications as guide, add a choral harmony on "ooh" or "ah" as support to the melody.

## Recommended Listening

+*The Best of Mahalia Jackson*. Legacy Recordings 074646691120.

+*Wade in the Water: African American Sacred Music Traditions, Volumes I–IV*. Smithsonian Folkways SFW 40076.

+*John's Island, South Carolina: Its People and Songs*. Folkways FW 03840.

# SORAN BUSHI

Japan

2. Yahren, soran, soran, soran, soran. Hai! Hai!
   Okino kamome no nakukoe kikeba,
   Funanori kagyo wa yamerarenu,
   Yasa en ya-an sah no dokkoisho.
   Ah, dokkoisho, dokkoisho!

1. *Will we be able to catch herrings,*
   *If you were to ask a fox,*
   *Each and every fox will cry,*
   *"Kon," "won't come!"*

2. *Hear the songs of seagulls*
   *Out over the ocean waves*
   *And you can't give up being a boatman,*
   *The life on the sea.*

## The Tune

A traditional song (with dance) from the north of Japan, "Soran Bushi" recalls a life of working on the sea: herrings, seagulls, and ocean waves.

## The Music Culture

Japan was once a nation of farmers and fisherman, and each community knew its own local celebrations of nature and of prayers for good harvest and fishing seasons. Japanese festivals, called *matsuri*, reflect the ancient religious beliefs of the people, while also providing occasions for people to show and celebrate their traditional customs, which include food, dress, ritual, music, drama, and dance. There are festivals for: winter snow sculptures (in Hokkaido), spring and the blossoming of the cherry trees, rice planting time in May and June, summer (including boat racing festivals), and the autumn harvest. Shogatsu (December 31 and January 1) is the important festival to welcome the new year, and the Bon-Odori festival in August takes people back to their hometowns and families to honor their ancestors and to participate in folk dancing. Traditional instruments that appear at festivals include the various drums and gongs of the *matsuri bayashi* (festival music ensembles), a three-stringed plucked lute (*shamisen*), a plucked zither (*koto*), and a thick wooden flute (*shakuhachi*). Dances feature the actions of farmers and fisherman, and the two-person Lion Dance. "Soran Bushi" has been traced to a seacoast town, Otaru, northeast of Sapporo, on the northern island of Hokkaido. It originated as a work song of the herring fishermen to relieve their solitude, and gradually made its way into the repertoire of songs and dances performed at festivals.

## The Experiences

- Sing the melody on a neutral syllable such as "doe" or "soe," and on solfège syllables (beginning on "sol") or scale numbers (beginning on "5").
- Notice that the song appears in several parts: measures 1–6 open with a syncopated rhythmic pattern within a six-note range; measures 8–11, following the "hai! hai!" shout comprise a somewhat static phrase centered on "re" and "mi" (A and B); measures 12–21 sound as the longest melodic phrase that extends an octave and moves smoothly through an emphasis on "sol," "la," "do," and "re" (D, E, G and A); the final two measures are the punctuated ending.
- Sing the song with this guide in mind: "a" sounds as "ah," "i" sounds as "ee," "u" sounds as "oo," "koi" is "koy," "hai" is "high," and the "nn"s are intended as a close-mouthed hum.
- Play a chordal accompaniment, or just the open fifths of the indicated chords, on piano or guitar, pulsing once per beat.
- Perform these modified movements of the traditional dance.

| | |
|---|---|
| Measures 1–6: | Row the boat in slow motion, with arms out for two beats and arms in for two beats; repeat three times |
| Measure 7: | Clap twice for "hai! hai!" |
| Measures 8–11: | Throw the net out over the head with the right hand while stepping right and then left on alternate beats; repeat two times |
| Measures 12–16: | Tie the rope with hands in front, first with the right hand over and then with the left hand over while stepping right and left on alternate beats; repeat four times |
| Measures 17–21: | Bend over in place to pick up net and haul in over the shoulder in slow motion (two beats to bend and two beats to haul); repeat two times |
| Measure 22–23: | Wipe sweat from brow on "Ah, dok-koi-sho," clap rhythm for second "dok-koi-sho." |

## Recommended Listening

+*Minyo: Folk Songs from Japan*. Nimbus NI 5618.

*Matsuri*. Celestial Harmonies 13081.

# STALIÁ, STALIÁ

Greece

## The Tune

The film *My Big Fat Greek Wedding* did much to raise an awareness of Greek culture, customs, and music. "Staliá" is a dance piece that continues the tradition of minor-keyed and modal melodies as performed by the Greek lute known as *bouzoúki.*

## The Music Culture

The music of Greece combines Eastern and Western instruments and influences. From the West come the clarinet, guitar, violin, and drum set, while neighboring Turkey, the eastern Mediterranean, and North Africa are sources of the *kaval* (flute), *defí* (tambourine), *zoúrna* (double-reed*), daoúli* (deep-toned drum), *laoúto* and *bouzoúki* (plucked lutes). There is a Western-styled harmony in some Greek music, but also a tendency toward highly ornamented melodies with little or no harmony whatsoever. As for content of Greek melody, the *makámia* (modes) are prominent, particularly the harmonic minor of the Aeolian mode and the augmented second interval between the second and third degrees of the scale. Rhythms vary, from the duple meter of Western Europe to the 7/8 of the *kalamatianós* dance, a meter that is fairly common in Middle Eastern music. While there are regional styles within Greece, the music of the 2002 romantic comedy film *My Big Fat Greek Wedding* is of a pan-Greek style that is the result of media influence and the Americanization of the Greek immigrant community. Still, there is no denying the sound of the *bouzoúki* nor the modal minor quality of the melody.

### The Experiences

- Hum the melody while keeping time.
- While still humming, play the melody on guitar, piano, clarinet, violin, or other melody instrument.
- Play the chords on guitar, piano, or other harmony instrument, using the root of the chord on beats 1 and 3 and the third and fifth on beats 2 and 4.
- Combine the melody and harmony instruments and parts.

- While holding hands in a circle, perform a basic Greek "grapevine" dance step; start with the weight on the left foot and move to the right.

| Beat: | 1 | 2 | 3 | 4 | 5 | 6 | 7 | 8 |
|---|---|---|---|---|---|---|---|---|
| Step: | R | L | R | L | L | R | L | R |
| | step | close | step | touch | step | close | step | touch |

## Recommended Listening

+*My Big Fat Greek Wedding.* Sony 86823.

*Zorba's Dance: Memories of Greece.* Laserlight (USA) 15180.

# STREETS OF LAREDO

U. S.: Texas

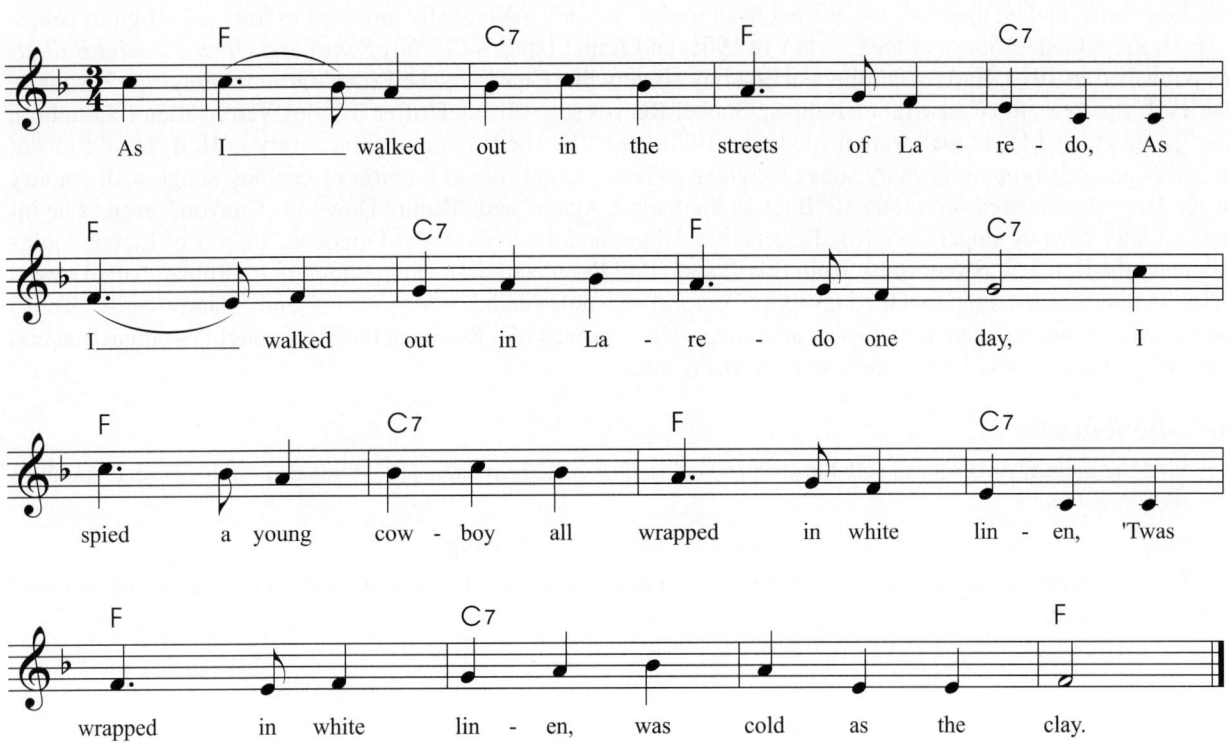

2. "I see by your outfit that you are a cowboy,"
   These words he did say as I boldly walked by;
   "Come set down beside me and hear my sad story,
   I'm shot in the breast and I know I must die."

3. "Twas once in the saddle I used to go ridin'
   Once in the saddle I used to go gay;
   First lead to drinkin', and then to card-playin',
   I'm shot in the breast and I'm dying today.

4. "Let six jolly cowboys come carry my coffin,
   Let six pretty gals come to carry my pall,
   Throw branches of roses all over my coffin,
   Throw roses to deaden the clods as they fall.

5. "Oh, beat the drum slowly, and play the fife lowly,
   And play the dead march as you carry me along.
   Take me to the green valley and lay the earth o'er me"
   For I'm a poor cowboy and I know I've done wrong.

6. We beat the drum slowly and played the fife lowly
   And bitterly wept as we carried him along.
   For we all loved our comrade, so brave, young and handsome,
   We all loved our comrade although he done wrong.

## The Tune

*Cowboy songs* relate the life of men's work on the open range and at the far frontiers of Texas and the western United States, particularly in the early to middle twentieth century. "Streets of Laredo" tells the story of a dying cowboy in Laredo, Texas, on the banks of the Rio Grande.

## The Music Culture

Cowboy songs began to appear as broadsides, in newspapers, and in songbooks in the late nineteenth century. They are related to the old English, Scottish, and Irish ballads in that they tell stories of men at work on their horses and with their cattle, and on their various diversions in town. They are melodically indebted to folk and religious songs. N. H. Thorp published *Songs of the Cowboy* in 1908, and John Lomax's *Cowboy Songs and Other Frontier Ballads* was published in 1910. Early recordings of cowboy singers like Charles Nabell (the "Original Singing Cowboy"), Charles T. Sprague, the Cartwright Brothers, Goebel Reeves (the "Texas Drifter"), Jules Verne Allen ("Longhorn Luke"), and Harry McClintock were made in the 1920s and 30s. The singing of Gene Autry in Hollywood films of the 1930s and 40s brought cowboy songs to wider audiences, and forged a union of cowboy songs with country music. Autry popularized such song as "Back in the Saddle Again" and "Riding Down the Canyon," even as he influenced later cowboy singers like Roy Rogers, Tex Ritter, and the Sons of the Pioneers. "Streets of Laredo" joins "Home on the Range," "Sweet Betsy from Pike," and "Red River Valley" as long-standing traditional ballads, even as Hollywood beamed out popular songs like "Tumbling Tumbleweeds," "Cool Water," and "Happy Trails." Traditional cowboy songs needed only a voice and guitar, while groups like Riders in the Sky brought in percussion and a full array of guitars and bass in their *western swing* style.

### The Experiences

- Sing the melody on a neutral syllable such as "la," and on solfège syllables (beginning on "sol") or scale numbers (beginning on "5").
- Sing the lyrics, giving accent to the first of three beats in the triple meter melody.
- Play the chords on guitar, accenting the first of three beats by either a strong strum or plucking the bass of the chord in this manner:

| Beat: | 1 | 2 | 3 |
|---|---|---|---|
| | > | | |
| Bass/strum: | bass | strum | strum |

- Add a triangle (the cowboy's dinner bell) to accent the first beat.

### Recommended Listening

+*John Lomax: Songs of Texas*. Folkways FW 05328.

+*The Cowboy: His Songs, Ballads and Brag Talk*. Folkways FW 05723.

*The Sons of the Pioneers Essential Collection*. Varese Saraband 066439.

*A Great Big Western Howdy from Riders in the Sky*. Rounder Records 610430.

# SUMER IS ICUMEN IN

England

## The Tune

One of the most celebrated medieval compositions of all time is "Sumer Is Icumen In," popular in its time and a notable song still in use today.

## The Music Culture

*Rota is* the term used in thirteenth-century England for a round or canon, a form in which voices enter successively with the same melody. This summer canon was composed around 1250 in the southern England town of Reading, just east of London. Part of the melody resembles a Gregorian *cantus firmus* or principal melody, and it is possible that the piece was conceived as a motet. The proper mode of performance is explained in the source as "a round sung by four fellows, but must not be performed by fewer than three." There is no specified ending for the piece, although a convenient conclusion is when the leading voice has sung the song twice. Typical of thirteenth-century polyphonic song, "Sumer is Icumen In" utilizes the major mode, frequent triads, emphasis on tonic, and dancelike rhythms that bounce and swing in a 6/8 metric feeling. The text is in Middle English, which was spoken as the true vernacular language of the majority between the Norman invasion in 1066 and the fifteenth century. Middle English is best known today as presented by Geoffrey Chaucer in his *Canterbury Tales*. The lyrics, roughly translated, celebrate the coming of summer and the loud and clear song of the cuckoo, a time when seeds are planted and grown and when lambs and calves are weaned.

## The Experiences

- Sing the melody on a neutral syllable such as "ihn," and on solfège syllables or scale numbers.
- Sing the lyrics, following this pronunciation guide:

  Su-merh is Ih-cuh-mehn ihn

  luh-deh sing koo-koo.

  Grow-eth sehd and blow-eth mehd

  and springth the wuh-deh noo.

  Sing koo-koo.

  Ah-way bleh-teth af-ter lomb,

  lout after cal-vay koo.

  Boo-lok stert-eth

  boo-key vert-eth

  moo-ree sing koo-koo.

  Koo-koo koo-koo,

  Wehl sing-es too coo-koo

  neh swik tho na-ver noo.

- Sing the song in a four-part round, with voice parts entering every two measures; sing twice through, ending when the first voice completes its second time through.
- Sing the song in a round with eight parts, with voice parts entering every two measures.
- Alternate between the C and Dm chords on piano or guitar.
- Explore the effect of voices entering every measure (rather than two measures).
- Play chords on piano or guitar, using a ♩. rhythm.

## Recommended Listening

+*Reading Abbey: Music of the Age of Chivalry*. Sound Alive Music 101.

+*Between March and April: Music of Medieval England*. Winged Horse Music 510.

# SWING LOW, SWEET CHARIOT

U. S.: African American

Swing low, sweet cha - ri - ot,___ co - min' for to car - ry me home.

Swing___ low, sweet cha - ri - ot,___ co - min' for to car - ry me home.

2. I looked over Jordan

And what did I see,

Comin' for to carry me home?

A band of angels

Comin' after me,

Comin' for to carry me home.

3. If you get there

Before I do,

(Comin' for to carry me home)

Tell all my friends

I'm comin' too,

(Comin' for to carry me home)

4. Sometimes I'm up

And sometimes I'm down.

(Comin' for to carry me home)

But still my soul

Feels heavenly bound.

(Comin' for to carry me home)

CD III, Track # 14

## The Tune

One of most famous of African-American *spirituals* is "Swing Low, Sweet Chariot," complete with a lively syncopated rhythm, Biblical references, and the good hope of salvation in the afterlife.

## The Music Culture

African Americans who journeyed from slavery into freedom wove their experiences into their music, particularly in secular expressions known as the *blues* and prayerful religious expressions known as *spirituals*. The designation "spiritual" came about because these songs were linked to stories, scenes, and characters from the Bible. Spirituals began in the cries, shouts, and hallelujahs of people striving to be free of their shackles. They were sung in plantation fields and houses as well as in churches, from the late eighteenth century onward. Even with the advent of gospel song, they are still sung today in churches and on the concert stage, particularly in the sensitive arrangements prepared for choral groups by knowledgeable composers such as William Dawson, founder of the Tuskeegee Institute's 100-voice choir in Alabama. "Swing Low, Sweet Chariot" first appeared in print in *Jubilee Songs* in 1872 as sung by the Jubilee Singers of Fisk University in Nashville, Tennessee. It is a widely known spiritual with numerous arrangements, and one with its own musical essence even when sung solo or in unison.

## The Experiences

- Listen to Track # 14, Sing the melody on a neutral syllable such as "low," and with solfège syllables (beginning on "mi") and scale numbers (beginning on "3").
- Sing the lyrics, swinging the rhythm while keeping the syncopated rhythms crisp and precise.
- Clap on the backbeat, or off-beat, while singing.
- Play the chords on piano, using four intact or partial chords per measure.
- Explore the full extent of vocal harmony, singing various pitches as denoted by the chord designations.

## Recommended Listening

+*The Collector's Paul Robeson*. Monitor MON 61580.
+*Lead Belly Sings for Children*. Smithsonian Folkways SFW 45047.
+*Spirituals in Concert* (Kathleen Battle, Jessye Norman). Deutsche Grammophon 429 790-2.

## TABLA SOLO IN JHAPTAL

Afghanistan

Tala count:   1          2          /  1          2          3          /  1          2          3          4          5

CD III, Track # 15

## The Tune

The traditional music of Afghanistan features several plucked lutes, including the *dutar* and *rabab*, and a pair of drums called *tabla*. While it is typical for the melodic instrument to seem to lead the music, sometimes the *dutar* (or *raba*) will play a basic melody to mark the rhythmic cycle (*tala*) of a *tabla* solo, as is the case here in the sound of the 10-beat *tala*.

## The Music Culture

Situated between Iran and Pakistan, with "the stans" nations (Turkmenistan, Uzbekistan, and Tajikistan) to the north, Afghanistan today is the product of its own tribal groups—Pastun, Tajik, Hazara, and Uzbek—and the influences of many centuries of Persian rule and proximity to India. In the nineteenth and twentieth centuries, Indian classical musicians were invited to become court musicians in Kabul, and their music and musical instruments were established as the elite art tradition of Afghanistan. A government radio station was important in shaping the music that most Afghans today identify as their own, including the Indian-sounding art music, the Soviet-inspired orchestral ensembles of regional folk instruments brought together to perform regional and newly composed songs, and a jazz orchestra based upon the principles of Western harmony. Ustad Mohammad Omar (d. 1980) is to most Afghans the embodiment of Afghan art music. He is known for his virtuosic performance on *rabab*, a plucked lute with a deep, waisted body carved out of mulberry wood. The instrument has three main playing strings that are plucked with a wooden plectrum, and from twelve to fifteen sympathetic vibrating strings. In 1974, Zakir Hussain, a world-renown *tabla* player (originally from India), joined Ustad Mohammad Omar for a public concert in Seattle, which resulted in a remarkable and rare recording of the two masters.

### The Experiences

- Listen to Track # 15 for the sound of the *rabab* and *tabla*, and tap the pulse as the *tala* is counted out.
- Sing on "loo" the "dutar melody" that is actually played on *rabab*; note that there appear to be an upper tetrachord (A–B–C–D) and a lower tetrachord (E–F–G#–A), with the A as the connector pitch.
- Listen to the recording, and try to keep the 10-beat *tala* in mind by counting and clapping "1" and ticking off the remaining counts on the fingers. "Ticking" is touching the thumb to the designated finger, in order to keep the pulse.

|  | 1 | 2 | 1 | 2 | 3 | 1 | 2 | 3 | 4 | 5 |
|---|---|---|---|---|---|---|---|---|---|---|
|  | Clap | tick | Clap | tick | tick | Clap | tick | tick | tick | tick |
| Finger: |  | little |  | little | middle |  | little | middle | ring | index |

- Take turns singing or playing the "dutar melody" and keeping the tala.

- On a drum, play subdivisions of the pulse ♩ ♩ while someone keeps the *tala*, and then four times as fast ♪♪♪♪.

- While someone keeps the *tala*, improvise rhythms on the drum, mixing ♩, ♩ ♩, and ♪♪♪♪.

- Layer in the *tala*-keeping, melody-playing (or singing), and rhythmic improvisation.

## Recommended Listening

+*Ustad Mohammad Omar.* Smithsonian Folkways SFW 40439.

*Music of Afghanistan.* Folkways 04561.

*Anthology of World Music: Afghanistan.* Rounder Select 5121.

*Heart to Heart: Afghan Songs of Love and Marriage.* Bolbol CD 02.

# TAFTA HINDI

The Levant: Jordan, Lebanon, and Syria

*"Tafta Hindi, Tafta Hindi."*
*Who will buy my clothes to wear?*
*Silks and satins, lovely laces,*
*Gold and silver for your hair.*

## The Tune

"Tafta Hindi" is an Arabic-language song of traders with goods from as far as India and China that they bring to villages along their caravan route in the Middle East.

## The Music Culture

Caravans are a mode of trade in the Middle East that stretches back to ancient civilizations. Such goods as spices, jewels, metals, ivory, oils, rare woods, and silk are associated with caravan trade on the Silk Road that linked China, Japan, and Korea with inner Asia, the Middle East, and eastern Africa. Groups of merchants organized themselves for mutual assistance and protection from hostile peoples as they traveled great distances of desert trail where defense could not be guaranteed by local governments against tribes who might pillage and loot their stocks. Camels, horses, and donkeys were the main carriers, and empires provided for the establishment of inns to accommodate travelers along the way. In the Middle East, these goods made their way to bazaars—markets consisting of a street lined with shops and stalls. In Arabic-speaking countries such as Lebanon, Jordan, and Syria, "Tafta Hindi" is still sung today as a popular folk song that recalls the caravan traders as a noteworthy historic event that brought the exchange not only of goods but also of expressive culture.

## The Experiences

- Sing the melody on a neutral syllable such as "dee," and on solfège syllables (beginning on "la") and scale numbers (beginning on "6").

- Sing the lyrics, noting that *a* is pronounced as "ah" and *i* sounds closer to "e."

- Play the chords on guitar, plucking the root or bass tone and strumming the chord:

| Beat: | 1 | + | 2 | + |
|---|---|---|---|---|
| Chord: | bass tone | chord strum | bass tone | chord strum |

- Play a two-measure rhythmic ostinato on drum (hand drum or goblet drum), tambourine, and finger cymbals.

## Recommended Listening

*Arabic Songs of Lebanon and Egypt* (George Sawa Trio). Folkways FW 06925.

*Anthology of World Music: Lebanon.* Rounder Select 5148.

*The Silk Road: A Musical Caravan.* Smithsonian Folkways SFW 40438.

## TAMBORCITA

Guatemala

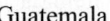

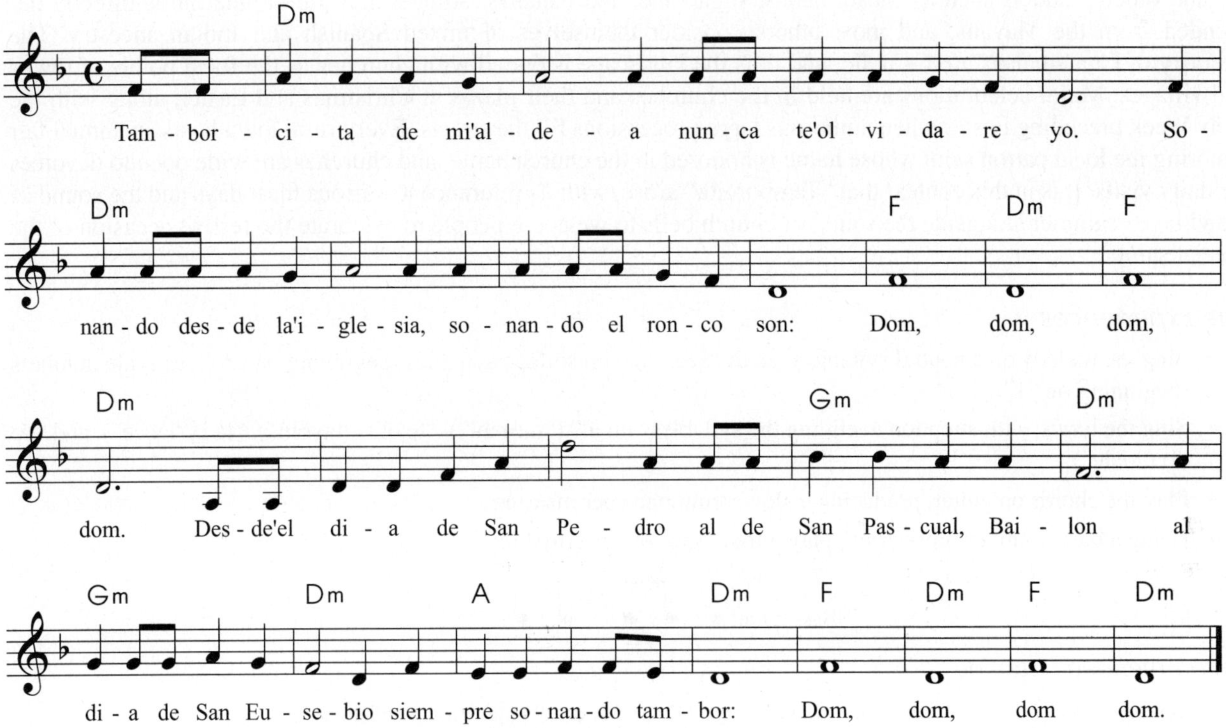
Dm
Tam - bor - ci - ta de mi'al - de - a nun - ca te'ol - vi - da - re - yo. So -
Dm F Dm F
nan - do des - de la'i - gle - sia, so - nan - do el ron - co son: Dom, dom, dom,
Dm Gm Dm
dom. Des - de'el di - a de San Pe - dro al de San Pas - cual, Bai - lon al
Gm Dm A Dm F Dm F Dm
di - a de San Eu - se - bio siem - pre so - nan - do tam - bor: Dom, dom, dom dom.

*Little Drummer from my village,*
*I shall never forget,*
*Sounding from the church,*
*Sounding the heavy beat,*
*Dom, dom, dom, dom.*

*From the feast day of San Pedro**
*To the feast day of San Pasqual***
*To the feast day of San Eusebio,****
*Always sounding the drum,*
*Dom, dom, dom, dom.*

** St. Peter*
*** St. Pascal Bailon, patron of cooks*
**** St. Eusebius*



## The Tune

The provocative aural image of church bells resounding in a Guatemalan village, and of a little drummer beating away on his bass drum, is brought into focus in the traditional song, "Tamborcita."

## The Music Culture

Guatemala is a Central American nation known for its mountainous volcanoes, its long and colorful period of Mayan rule, and its hard working population of farmers who contribute to the country's export earnings from coffee and other products such as cacao, beans, sugarcane, and bananas. Almost half the population is directly descended from the Mayans, and most others consider themselves of mixed Spanish and Indian ancestry. The majority of Guatemalans are Catholic, and thus the landscape is dotted with churches as the focal points of towns and villages. Major celebrations are held in the churches and their plazas at Christmas and Easter, along with the Holy Week preceding Easter when numerous large processions fill the streets. Every rural town hosts an annual fair honoring the local patron saint whose name is honored in the church name, and churches are wide open to devotees for daily visits. It is in this context that "Tamborcita" arose, with its reference to various feast days and the sound of the village drummer alongside the sound of church bells to welcome people to celebrate the festive occasion of the special saint.

### The Experiences

- Sing the melody on a neutral syllable such as "see," and on solfège syllables (beginning on "do") or scale numbers (beginning on "1").
- Sing the lyrics, with attention to eliding the syllables "mi al" ("meeahl"), "te ol" ("tayohl"), "la i ("lahee"), and "de el) ("dale").
- Play the chords on guitar, producing a slow strum once per measure.
- Using a bass drum, or other drum, play a four-beat ostinato rhythm:

Bass drum:

### Recommended Listening

+*Canciones de America Latina* (Campbell, P. S. with Frega, A. L.). Miami: Warner Bros. Publishers.
*Music of Guatemala, Volumes 1 and 2.* Folkways FW 04212, FW 04213.

# THIS LITTLE LIGHT OF MINE

U. S.: African American

## The Tune

During the American Civil Rights movement, "This Little Light of Mine" became one of the banner songs sung at protest marches and gatherings across the south, in the northern industrial cities, and all the way to Washington D.C.

## The Music Culture

From 1954 to 1968, a series of events and reform movements in the United States were aimed at abolishing racial discrimination against African Americans. Collectively known as the American Civil Rights Movement, it began with the case of *Brown v. Board of Education* in Topeka, Kansas, when the education of black children in separate public schools from their white counterparts was declared unconstitutional. The arrest of Rosa Parks in Montgomery, Alabama, for her refusal to give up her bus seat to white passengers fueled the fire, and led to an era of boycotts, sit-ins, and other means of protest across the Deep South. The campaign to desegregate schools, buses, restaurants, and various other public places was on, as was the drive by the early 1960s to register African Americans to vote. By the time of the March on Washington for Jobs and Freedom, in 1963, a collaborative of major civil rights organizations and the progressive wing of the labor movement raised their voices on the passage and enforcement of civil rights laws. More than 200,000 demonstrators gathered in front of the Lincoln Memorial, where Martin Luther King Jr. delivered his famous "I Have a Dream" speech. There was music, principally protest songs, at this and various other demonstrations, among them "We Shall Overcome," "Oh Freedom," "I Shall Not Be Moved," and "This Little Light of Mine." This last is an old spiritual tune that brings attention to the importance of unity, of standing up alone or together with strength in the knowledge that striving for justice and freedom is always "the right thing to do."

## The Experiences

- Sing the song on a neutral syllable such as "mah," and on solfège syllables (beginning on "sol") or scale numbers (beginning on "5").

- Sing the lyrics, watching for syncopations and sustained words and syllables.

- Clap on the off-beats while singing.

- Play the chords on piano or guitar. Use a pattern that accents beats 2 and 4: ♪♪ ♩ ♪♪ ♩

- Sing while walking, stepping, marching in freestyle fashion, in lines, or in a circle.

- Following the chordal progression, create vocal harmony.

## Recommended Listening

+*This Little Light of Mine* (Guy Carawan). Folkways FW 03552.

+*Sing for Freedom: The Story of the Civil Rights Movement through Its Songs*. Smithsonian Folkways 40032.

+*Voices of the Civil Rights Movement: Black American Freedom Songs, 1960–1966*. Smithsonian Folkways SFW 40084.

# THREE SISTERS

England

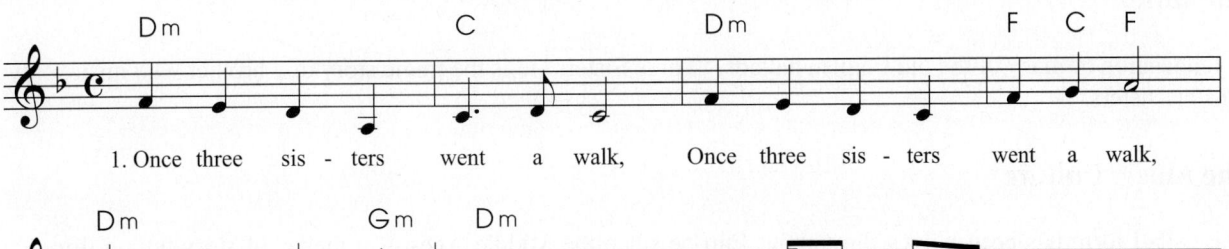

1. Once three sis - ters went a walk, Once three sis - ters went a walk,

Once three sis - ters went a walk, Down by the bon - nie banks of Air - drie, O.

2. They met a robber on the way,
   They met a robber on the way,
   They met a robber on the way,
   Down by the bonnie banks of Airdrie, O.

3. He took the first one by the hand,
   He birled her round till she could not stand,
   He birled her round till she could not stand,
   Down by the bonnie banks of Airdrie, O.

4. Will you be a robber's wife,
   Or will you die by my penknife?
   Will you be a robber's wife?
   Down by the bonnie banks of Airdrie, O.

5. I'll not be a robber's wife,
   I'd rather die by your penknife,
   I'll not be a robber's wife,
   Down by the bonnie banks of Airdrie, O.

6. Then he took out his penknife,
   Then he ended her sweet life,
   Then he ended her sweet life,
   Down by the bonnie banks of Airdrie, O.

7. He took the second one by the hand,
   He birled her round till she could not stand,
   He birled her round till she could not stand,
   Down by the bonnie banks of Airdrie, O.

8. He took the third one by the hand,
   He birled her till she could not stand,
   He birled her till she could not stand,
   Down by the bonnie banks of Airdrie, O.

9. I wish that my two brothers were here,
   I wish that my two brothers were here,
   I wish that my two brothers were here,
   Down by the bonnie banks of Airdrie, O.

10. What are your two brothers like?
    What are your two brothers like?
    What are your two brothers like?
    Down by the bonnie banks of Airdrie, O.

11. One's a minister, and the other's like you,
    One's a minister, and the other's like you,
    One's a minister, and the other's like you,
    Down by the bonnie banks of Airdrie, O.

12. God, O God, what have I done!
    Killed my sisters all but one,
    Killed my sisters all but one,
    Down by the bonnie banks of Airdrie, O.

13. Then he took out his penknife,
    Then he ended his sweet life,
    Then he ended his sweet life,
    Down by the bonnie banks of Airdrie, O.

# THREE SISTERS

## The Tune

In the fashion of many of the old English ballads, "Three Sisters" tells the tragic story of a brother who mistakenly kills his sisters.

## The Music Culture

The ballad form has been known throughout Europe since the Middle Ages as a means of story telling through song. The British have enjoyed a rich treasury of ballads, many of which have survived to the present day—in Britain as well as in other English-speaking countries where the British traveled to, settled in, and "set up house." Francis Child, the well-known ballad historian who collected and categorized English ballads, found some ballads to be familiar to people far beyond England itself. "Three Sisters" is one of them, also called "The Bonnie Banks o' Fordie" and "Twa Sisters" (and Child Ballad #10), which is known in Scotland and Wales, Scandinavia (in the local languages), and Appalachian America. The song was turned into a game version by children sometime in the early twentieth century, in which children played the parts of the robber-brother and each of the three sisters. Each sister was "birled" or spun around by the brother, and then would fall to the ground. The dramatization occurred as a small chorus of children would sing and sometimes clap a rhythm to the recurrent refrain.

### The Experiences

- Sing the song on a neutral syllable such as "loo," and with scale syllables (beginning on "do" in la-based minor) or scale numbers (beginning on "1")
- Sing the text of the thirteen verses of the ballad; pronounce the name of the river, the Airdrie as "air-dree."
- Take turns singing the verses solo or in small groups, but always joined en force by the full chorus on the refrain.
- Play the chords on guitar or keyboard to accompany the melody, choosing a roll or slow-strum just once per measure, or an arpeggiated "rain" of eighth notes that feature the chord tones in a regular pattern.
- Play the full melody as occasional interludes between the verses, on flute, violin, or other melody instrument.
- Add a percussion pattern on hand-drum:
- Dramatize the ballad, as British children might do.

### Recommended Listening

+*Three Sisters* (Peggy Seeger). Prestige International 13029.
+*Scottish Ballads and Folk Songs* (Jeannie Robertson). Prestige International 13006.

# TIHORE MAI

Maori

*Clear the sky.*
*Clear away.*
*Let the rain stop*
*And the sun shine.*

*Fly kingfisher on to a bush.*
*Ruffle the rain drops from your wings*
*Lest you catch a chill.*

*Clear the sky.*
*Clear away.*
*Let the rain stop*
*And the sun shine.*

*Flee worm from your burrow.*
*It might fill with water and you will drown.*

*Clear the sky.*
*Clear away.*
*Let the rain stop*
*And the sun shine.*
*e . . . i . . . e*
*Let the sun shine.*

# TIHORE MAI

## The Tune

"Tihore Mai" is Maori for an appeal to "clear the sky" of rain and allow the sun to come out, a song made popular by Moana and the Moahunters of New Zealand.

## The Music Culture

The Maori of New Zealand have long been a singing culture. Their repertoire can be variously classified and subclassified according to function, poetic text, who performs it, and whether it is integrated with dance—and much of it is. The two forms of indigenous Maori music, action song (called *waiata*) and chant, are continued today, even as more contemporary forms (from blues and rock to country) are performed intact or in fusion with traditional practices. The full choral sound is widespread at Maori gatherings in church, on the *marae*, or community center, and in schools, and their body movements and hand trembling, called *wiri*, are consistent in their performances. Contemporary groups like Moana and the Moahunters, a trio of young women vocalists who are backed by a male trio on guitar, bass, and drums, are keen to claim a Maori cultural identity that is deeply rooted in melodic chant and traditional polyphonic song while also drawing on popular and rock music styles.

### The Experiences

- Tap, clap, or pat the pulse.
- Sing the lyrics of the melody line, pronouncing the following vowels, consonants, and syllables in this way: *a* ("ah"), *e* ("ay"), *i* ("ee"), *o* ("oh"), "wh" ("f", as in "fa" for "wha" and "fee" for "whi"), "mai" ("my"), *g* (semi-hard "gh").
- Keep the loose translation in mind: "1, 2, 3, 4: Clear up, sky. Stop, rain. Come out, sun."
- Add the vocal harmony to the melody, with its fluctuation between C major and D minor.
- While singing in a circle, with arms at side, shake the hands in place from the wrist to the fingertips; this is *wiri*, which is believed to generate and communicate the spirit that protects and inspires.
- Note that the words for the first verse were taken from a traditional chant, while the reminder of the lyrics and the melody were added by the composer.

### Recommended Listening

*+Tahi: Moana and the Moahunters*. Southside Records D30787.
*Kahurangi: Music of the New Zealand Maori*. Monitor MON 71827.
*Maori Songs of New Zealand*. Folkways FW 04433.

# TINGA LAYO

Dominican Republic

Tin - ga Lay - o! Ven, mi bur - ri - to, ven! Tin - ga Lay - o! Ven, mi bur - ri - to,

ven! Bur - ri - to sí, bur - ri - to no. Bur - ri - to co - me con - te - ne - dor!

*Run, little donkey.*
*How contented you are.*

## The Tune

A reflection of rural life in the Dominican Republic, "Tinga Layo" has been enjoyed by children there as "the song about the donkey" for many generations.

## The Music Culture

Located next to Haiti on the Caribbean island of Hispaniola, the Dominican Republic is a Spanish-speaking country of approximately nine million people, the vast majority of whom are of mixed European and African ancestry. The Spanish heritage is evident in the predominant religion, Catholicism, as well as in the language, while African cultural elements are prominent in the musical expressions. The Dominican music of *merengue,* a mass-mediated dance style utilizing Latin percussion, brass instruments, bass and electric guitars, has been popular since the middle of the twentieth century, while the Dominican *bachata* is a form of slow and romantic folk music whose prominent sound is the Spanish-style guitar. Young people enjoy *reggaeton* and Dominican rock, and still younger people—children—enjoy the songs (like "Tinga Layo") that they can sing with their games and dances.

*The Experiences*

- Sing the melody on a neutral syllable such as "lay," and on solfège syllables (beginning on "mi") or scale numbers (beginning on "3").
- Sing the lyrics, pronouncing "ven" as "bayn."
- Tap, clap, and pat the rhythm for "ven, mi burrito" (and "come contenedor"), and play it on claves and sticks:
- Play the chords on guitar or piano, using eighth-note strums (a down-up stroke on the guitar) or broken chords (playing the root on the pulse and the third and fifth of the chord on the off-beat).

- Add a one-measure percussion accompaniment:

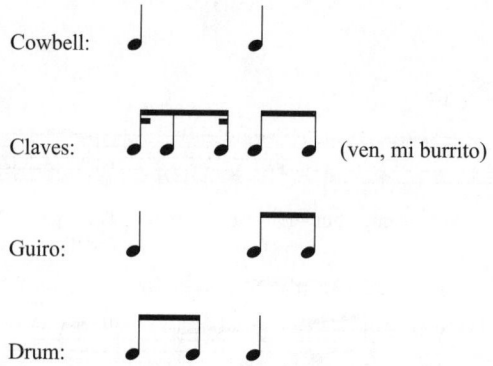

Cowbell:

Claves:                (ven, mi burrito)

Guiro:

Drum:

## Recommended Listening

*Music from the Dominican Republic*, *Volumes 1–4*. Folkways FW 04281-04284.

*Dominican Republic: La Hora Esta Llegando!* Expresion Joven CD. P-1025 (world music store.com)

# TITO TIMBERO

Tito Puente

CD III, Track # 16

## The Groove

Like so much of the music of the great Latin band leader, Tito Puente, "Tito Timbero" is a display of a percussionist's virtuosity atop a basic groove pattern.

## The Music Culture

In the New York City of the 1940s and 50s, big band music was taking on a Latin tinge, much to the credit of Machito, José Curbelo, and two Titos: Tito Rodriguez and Tito Puente. As a *timbalero* (*timbale* player), Tito Puente was much attuned to the big band music of the 1930s, and by 1950 he was a recognized composer and arranger with his band, the Picadilly Boys. More than just a backseat drummer as in the older-style bands, Puente got rid of the drum set and moved the timbales to the front of the group so as to provide the driving Latin rhythms that could swing the sounds of brass and winds in a new way. He was said to be able to conduct the band through his *timbale* playing, by virtue of the rhythms he punched up for the music. A large influx of Puerto Ricans and other Caribbean peoples to New York extended the market for Latin dance music, and the *mambo* scene flourished in dance halls and clubs. Tito Puente brought on Cuban *conguero* (*conga* player) Mongo Santamaria and Willie Bobo, the New York-born *bongocero* (*bongo* player), and the skills of the three players solidified a sound that prevails decades later as a model of what brilliant percussion performance can do to energize the musical "wall" of big band brass, wind, and piano.

### The Experiences

- Listen to Track # 16, and keep a steady pulse while following the repeated motifs of the horns and piano against the innovative rhythms of the timbales.
- Listen again to the recording, and tap, clap, or pat the rhythmic motif of the horns.
- Hum or sing on "loo" the horn part, while also tapping, clapping, or patting the rhythm.
- Play the piano motif, and add trumpet, saxophone, and other brass/wind instruments on the horn part.
- Invite a percussionist to play on *timbales*, *congas*, drum set or other drums.

### Recommended Listening

+*The Best of Tito Puente: El Rey del Timbal!* Rhino/WEA R2 72817.
*Essential Tito Puente.* Bluebird RCA 69243.

# TOEI KHONG

Laos

# TOEI KHONG (DRONE)

## The Tune

The popular melody "Toei Khong" is frequently played in Laos and Northeast Thailand on the *khaen*, a bamboo mouth organ.

## The Music Culture

The Lao people reside in Laos and Northeast Thailand, or Isan, as it is locally known. The instrument of their own cultural identity is the free-reed mouth organ called *khaen*, which appears as a long raft of sixteen (more or less) bamboo pipes that are connected with a small hollowed-out wooden vessel into which air is blown. Related in its acoustical principles to Western free-reed instruments such as the harmonium, concertina, accordion, and harmonica, the *khaen* uses a pentatonic scale in its melodies and multiple drone pitches. The *khaen* is played solo, sometimes in ensembles, and often as accompaniment to the *mo lam* vocal repartee style sung by male and female singers. A rise of interest over the last fifty years in Isan-derived "country music" called *luk thung*, which utilizes *khaen*, has come to appeal to Thai people and has penetrated Laos as well through the Thai media. In the 1990s, *khaen* began to be blended with drum kit and rock band instruments in a style called *lam sing*, which appeals to youth in both Thailand and Laos. The Canadian band, Asza, plays a kind of *lam sing* with an Afro-beat, featuring the traditional *khaen* melody, "Toei Khong."

## The Experiences

- Sing the melody on a neutral syllable such as "nah," and solfège syllables (beginning on "la" in "la"-based minor) or scale numbers (beginning on "6").
- Sing the cluster-chord, sounding "nah" and holding for sixteen beats as support for the melody.
- Play the melody and cluster-chord together on piano.

## Recommended Listening

+*Asza*. Pacific Line Music PM0410.
*Anthopology of World Music: Music of Laos*. Rounder Select ROUN 5119

# TOMMY PEOPLES

Ireland

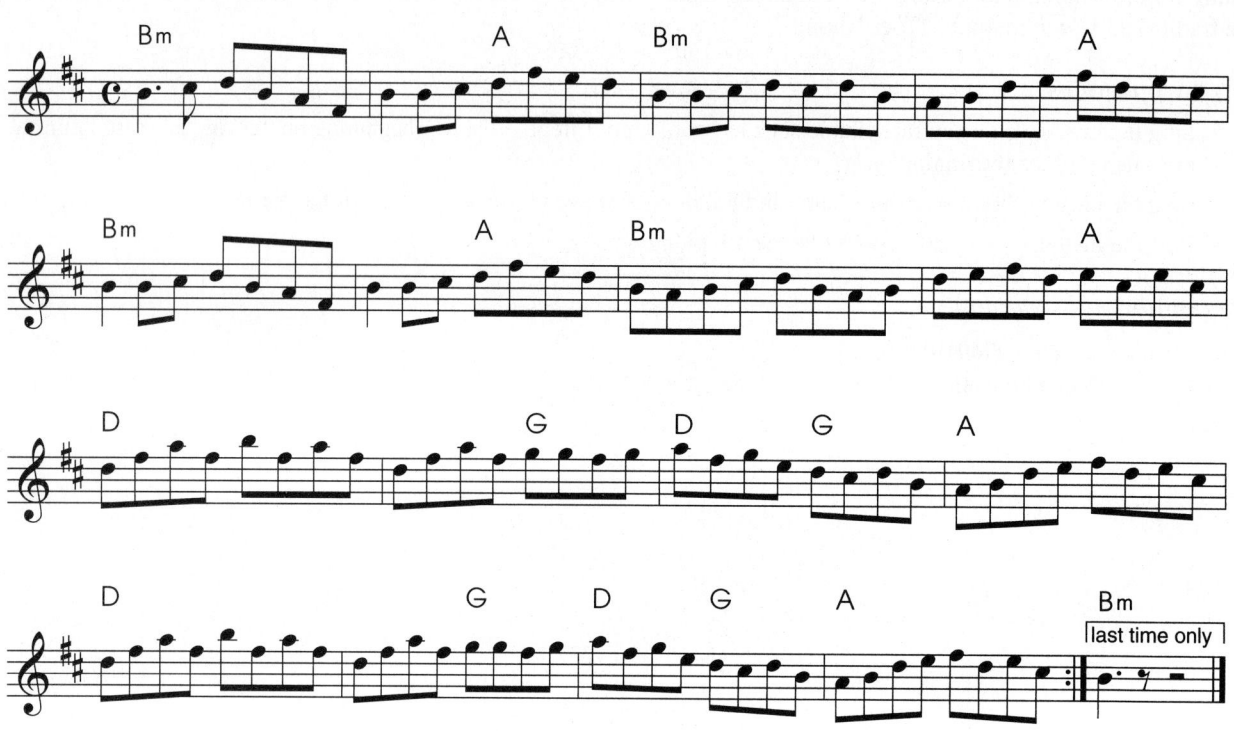

CD III, Track # 17

## The Tune

A reel associated with the Irish fiddler Tommy Peoples was given his name by the group known as Altan from County Donegal in Ireland.

## The Music Culture

Traditional music of Ireland has made a comeback in Irish contemporary culture, both in Ireland itself as well as in Irish communities abroad, especially in the United Kingdom, the United States, and Australia. Central to Irish identity itself are the sounds of pipes, whistles, flutes, fiddles, and the Irish hand drum known as *bodhran*, along with the concertina and the wooden Irish harp (which is the state symbol of the Republic of Ireland). Melodies predominate, and it is not unusual for multiple instruments to play the same or similar melody. More than half the Irish traditional melodies are in major modality, but Mixolydian, Aeolian, and Dorian modes are well represented, too. Harmonic and percussive dimensions of Irish music have developed more recently, hence the more frequent appearance in recent years of the guitar and *bodhran*. The fiddle music of County Donegal and the flute tunes of Northern Ireland form the basis for much of the music of the group called Altan, which rose to fame by the late 1980s to become internationally known for both its preservation of traditions as well as for its innovations. Named after a deep lake behind Errigal Mountain in Donegal, Altan performs reels, jigs, ballads, and even popular songs of Ireland.

## The Experiences

- Listen to Track # 17, and tap, clap, or pat the pulse while following the fiddles, accordion, and guitar.
- Listen to the recording again, and "air play" by imitating in the air the fast bowing of the fiddle across the fast-moving melody with its triadic chordal outline.
- Play the melody on violin, flute, piano, or other melody instrument.
- Play the chords to the melody on guitar, accordion or piano, using a strum or roll every two or four beats.
- Play a constant stream of eighth notes as subdivisions of the beat, on drum (hand drum, conga drum) or a flat surface (such as a table top). Accent the first of every eight strokes.

## Recommended Listening

+*The Best of Altan*. Green Linnett 1177.
*Andy Irvine / Paul Brady*. Mulligan Music LUN CD 008.
*Local Ground*. Narada 724387592728

# TURKEY IN THE STRAW

United States

*Verse:*

Well, I had an old hen and she had a wood - en leg, Just the -

best old hen that ev - er laid an egg. Well, she laid more eggs than an - y

chick - en on the farm, But an - oth - er lit - tle drink would - n't do her an - y harm.

*Chorus:*

Tur - key in the hay. (fiddle_____ ) Tur - key in the straw. (fiddle_____ )

Pick 'em up, shake 'em up, an - y - way at all, And_ hit up a tune_ called "Tur - key in the Straw."

2. Well, I hitched up the wagon and I drove down the road,
   With a two-horse wagon and a four-horse load;
   Well, I cracked the whip and the lead horse sprung,
   And I said "Goodbye" to the wagon tongue.
   (Chorus)

3. Well, if frogs had wings and snakes had hair,
   And automobiles went a-flying through the air;
   Well, if watermelons grew on a huckleberry vine,
   We'd have winter in the summertime.
   (Chorus)

4. Oh, I went out to milk and I didn't know how,
   I milked a goat instead of a cow.
   A monkey sitting on a pile of straw,
   A-winking his eye at his mother-in-law.
   (Chorus)

5. Well, I come to the river and I couldn't get across,
   So I paid five dollars for an old blind horse.
   Well, he wouldn't go ahead and he wouldn't stand still,
   So he went up and down like an old saw mill.
   (Chorus)

## The Tune

Popular as a barn dance tune in the nineteenth and twentieth centuries, "Turkey in the Straw" is a well-known American fiddle tune.

## The Music Culture

In the culture of the square-dance, tunes like "Cripple Creek," "Soldier's Joy," and "Turkey in the Straw" have fared well on the roster of music to dance to. Live music and a caller are important to the recreational event, which once transpired in barns and have moved on to community centers, grange halls, school gyms, and church basements. At one time a fiddler was the sole source of the music, but contemporary square-dance groups consist of one or more fiddles and guitars, along with an occasional banjo, mandolin, steel guitar, hammered dulcimer, and (in the northeastern United States) piano. A caller stands in front of the band, offering rhythmically delivered and melodically chanted instructions to "swing your partner," "fall back home," "do-si-do," and "circle to the left and promenade." Dance calls were first delivered by a fiddler, but later became so ornate as to take on the form of rhyming couplets that were fully sung and which then required a caller who could concentrate on multiple stanzas. Barn dance string bands of the 1920s and 30s, including their featured fiddlers and callers, became famous through their airing on radio programs like the WSM's *Grand Ole Opry* and WLS's *National Barn Dance*.

### The Experiences

- Sing the melody on neutral syllables such as "tootle" and "too," and with solfège syllables (beginning on "mi") and scale numbers (beginning on "3").
- Sing the words to the song, articulating them as they move quickly along in sixteenth-note rhythms; notice that some syllables are sustained over two pitches, and that in the chorus sections, there are instrumental solo phrases separating the sung phrases.
- Play the melody on fiddle, mandolin, guitar, piano, or other melody instrument.
- Play the chords on guitar or piano, providing at least one chord per pulse.
- Sing the melody to the rhyming words of a caller's song, with the understanding that it may be necessary to stretch and slightly improvise the melody to fit the words. As well, chant the words, stretching them across the melodic phrases.

1. Sixteen hands and circle right,
   For the train's a-comin' and I want to ride.
   Promenade your partner
   Around, around, around, around.
   (Chorus)

2. First gent pass right by the left,
   And two hands swing
   Across the hall, and cheat and swing.
   Back around your partner and do the same.
   (Chorus)

3. On your right, see the fight,
   And not go home till broad daylight.
   Back around your partner, do the same.
   (Chorus)

4. On your left, your left hand,
   Your little miss and my old man.
   Back around your partner.
   (Chorus)

5. Everybody swing and everybody whirl,
   And you all promenade the left-hand girl.
   (Chorus)

6. Same gent and a different girl
   Across the hall and chat and swing.
   Back around your partner and do the same.
   (Chorus)

### Recommended Listening

+*cELLAbration*. Smithsonian Folkways SFW 45059.

+*Progressive Bluegrass, Volume 3* (Roger Sprung). Folkways FW 02471

# 'ULILI E

Hawaii

Ho - ne a - na ko le - o e 'U - li - li e o ka - hi ma - nu no - ho a - e ka -

i. Ki - a i ma ka la - e a o ke - ka - ha, 'O i - a ka - i u - a la - na ma -

li - e. 'U - li - li e (A - ha - ha - na 'U - li - li e - he - he - ne 'U - li - li a - ha - ha na)

'U - li - li ho 'i (A - ha - ha - na 'U - li - li e - he - he - ne 'U - li - li a - ha - ha na)

'U - li - li ho - lo - ho - lo ka - ha - ka - i e, 'O i - a ka - i u - a la - na ma - li -

e. 'U - li - li ho - lo - ho - lo ka - ha - ka - i e 'O i - a ka - i u - a la - na ma - li - e.

*Listen for the sandpiper calling from the shore.*

*See how he dips and he soars across the sea.*

*He is a caretaker watching o'er the water.*

*He is at home when the coast is clear and calm, oh.*

*Sandpiper call: "Ahahana . . ."*

*Sandpiper call: "Ahahana . . ."*

*Sandpiper skitters and he skips at water's edge.*

*He makes his home along the wavy, salty sea.*

*Sandpiper soars rip in the sky of azure blue,*

*Then comes to rest his wings down on the golden sand.*

# 'ULILI E

## The Tune

On the Hawaiian islands, there is a long-standing tradition of singing and dancing—for the preservation of knowledge (such as family history and morals), worship, socialization, recreation, and entertainment. "'Ulili E" has entertainment value in its description of the endearing little bird known as the sandpiper.

## The Music Culture

About 2,500 miles west of California, people of the Hawaiian islands are linked to American history and culture as well as to the region of Oceania that lies south and west of them. Hawaii became the fiftieth American state in 1959, but was in fact formally annexed in 1898. Still, the cultural roots Hawaiians belong to another world, and their traditional music sounds more like that of the Tahitians, Fijians, Samoans, and the Maori than that of mainland North America. The *hula* (dance) and the *mele* (chant) are Hawaiian indigenous forms, and *pahu* (a shark-skin drum), the oldest instrument on the islands, is directly related to the drums of their Polynesian ancestors. When missionaries arrived, they brought with them their hymns in full-color harmonies. The Puerto Ricans brought guitars, and the Portuguese brought a lute that later became the *ukelele*. The music of Hawaii was enriched also by immigrants from Japan, the Philippines, and China, as well as from Europe and America. The emergence of *hapa haole* ("half white") songs in the early twentieth century was a phenomenon all its own, where English lyrics were merged with traditional Hawaiian. The reclaiming of a Hawaiian identity brought about a resurgence of interest in songs that utilized the Hawaiian language, such as "'Ulili E."

### The Experiences

- Sing the melody on a neutral syllable such as "lee," and on solfège syllables or scale numbers.
- Sing the lyrics, with these directives as a guide: *a* ("ah"), *e* ("ay"), *i* ("ee"), *o* ("oh"), *u* ("ooh"). The vowel-heavy language challenges the singer to articulate them as much when they run in a succession as when they are separated by consonants.
- Sing the harmony parts in lines 3–4 (the sustained upper tone and the moving lower tones) and lines 5–6 (the thirds); other parts can be added in filling out full chords, at several octaves.
- Play the chords on ukelele or guitar, using a ♩ ♫ pattern in a down, down-up strum.

### Recommended Listening

*Musics of Hawaii: Anthology of Hawaiian Music*. Smithsonian Folkways SFW 400016.
*Sounds of Hawaii. (Kealoha Kono and His Orchestra)*. Laserlight (USA) 12228

# UNCLE JESSIE

U. S.: Georgia Sea Islands

Traditional, Georgia Sea Islands, as sung and arranged by Janice Allen. Campbell, P. S., McCullough-Brabson, E., Tucker, J. C. (1994). *Roots & Branches: A Legacy of Multicultural Music for Children.* Danbury, CT: World Music Press. Courtesy World Music Press.

## The Tune

As an old African-American singing game originating in the islands off the coast of Georgia and the Carolinas, "Uncle Jessie" offers a portrait of life as a plantation worker with a boss who can be persuaded with a little magic.

## The Music Culture

Many Africans who were transported to the United States as slaves in the eighteenth and nineteenth centuries retained aspects of their cultural beliefs and practices, but none so much as those who were landed on the islands along the coastline of Georgia, and North and South Carolina. Johns Island, James, Wadmalaw, and Kiawah islands were isolated from the mainland culture, which was urban and white-dominated, and many Africans were enslaved there to work the plantations, where they grew grains, vegetables, fruit, and herbs. Their bosses were typically black, too, so there was little need to conceal or camouflage their cultural practices. As they did at home in Africa, they worshipped in ways that blended their older African prayers and rituals with Christian ones. They used herbal potions to medicate and cure, ate fish and shellfish as they did at home, and spoke a dialect, Gullah, that was comprised of African and English phonemes, words, and phrases. Their music was also blended, and Africanisms were prevalent: vocal slides and slurs, polyrhythmic clapping, stamping, and body slapping, and improvised melodies and harmonies. "Uncle Jessie" is a ring game, or singing game in the round, that refers to the boss as "coming through the field" and "looking sad," who could be charmed to overcome his sadness so as to make for more pleasant working conditions for those slaves working the plantations.

## The Experiences

- Sing the song on a neutral syllable such as "nah," and on solfège syllables (beginning on "sol") or scale numbers (beginning on "5").
- Sing the lyrics, with attention to the syncopated rhythm on the chorus section.
- While singing, clap on beats 2 and 4. Add also a stepping pattern in place, beginning with weight on the left foot:

| Step: | 1 | 2 | 3 | 4 | | 5 | 6 | 7 | 8 |
|---|---|---|---|---|---|---|---|---|---|
| | R | L | R | L | | L | R | L | R |
| | step | close | step | touch | | step | close | step | touch |

- Play the chords on piano or guitar, using an alternating pattern of root or bass tone (on beats 1 and 3) and chord (on beats 2 and 4).
- Form a circle to play the singing game, with one person in the center acting as "Uncle Jessie" while others clap, sing, and step in place. "Uncle Jessie" pantomimes the actions of the song. On the chorus ("Walk, walk, Uncle Jessie"), the center person chooses a partner. They hold hands in a skater's position, and move by sliding, stepping, and strutting in the circle center, using the stepping pattern above. At the end of the chorus, the old center person returns to the outer circle, and the partner becomes the new "Uncle Jessie."

## Recommended Listening

+*Roots and Branches: A Multicultural Legacy of Multicultural Music for Children* (Campbell/McCullough-Brabson/Tucker). Danbury, CT: World Music Press.

*Slave Shout Songs from the Coast of Georgia.* Folkways FW 04344.

*I'm So Glad I'm Here* (Bessie Jones). Rounder 2015.

# VIVA JUJUY

Argentina

*Long live Jujuy, long live the high land, long live my true love.*

*Long live the canyon and the lofty mountains, soaring high above.*

*I'll never leave you, I'll never forsake you, I belong to you.*

"Viva Jujuy" gr. 5 from MAKING MUSIC. Copyright © 2005 by Pearson Education, Inc. Reprinted by permission.

CD III, Track # 18

## The Tune

In the far northwestern corner of Argentina lies Jujuy, a province high in the Andes that borders Bolivia and Peru. "Viva Jujuy" celebrates the province, and the dramatically beautiful, deep gorge known as Humahuaqueña.

## The Music Culture

The Argentinian province of Jujuy is a mountainous region of farming and shepherding that shares with neighboring Bolivia and Peru the complex dynamics of pre- and post-Hispanic cultures. The Incan influences were strong there between 1480 and 1550, when the Spanish influences began to be felt. Roman Catholic missionaries began arriving in 1580 with their beliefs, rituals, and cultural practices. At the same time, the border crossings by workers in the mines and sugar-cane processing from Argentina to Bolivia and back ensured that in Jujuy there would be musical expressions similar to those found in Bolivia, with a combination of indigenous and Spanish cultural elements. Thus, there is in the music of Jujuy the presence of *sicu* or *zampoñas* (panpipes), *quena* (flute), *charango* (plucked lute with the body of an armadillo), and guitar, along with a pre-Hispanic transverse trumpet and the post-Hispanic clarinet. Typical dance music of the region is jubilant in character, and features pentatonic melodies in duple and compound meter.

## *The Experiences*

- Listen to Track # 18 for the sounds of plucked lutes, panpipes, flutes, and voices, while tapping out the pulse or the plucked rhythms.
- Listen again to the recording, singing lightly to the melodies that are played and sung.
- Sing the melody on a neutral syllable such as "mi," and on solfège syllables or scale numbers.
- Sing the lyrics, pronouncing "Jujuy" as "yoo-yoo" and "que" (as in "Humahuaquena") as "kay."
- Play the chords on guitar, using a ♩ ♪ strumming pattern. For piano, the chord root can be played by the left hand while the right hand plays a continuous broken-chord pattern.

- Play the melody on flute, recorder, or other melody instrument.
- Add a drum to sound every ♩. or in a ♩ ♪ rhythm.

## *Recommended Listening*

*Music of the Andes*. Hemisphere 7243 9 2910 2 8.
*Argentine Folk Songs*. Folkways FW 06810.

# VIVA LA MUSICA

Michael Praetorius

From *Music in Childhood: From Preschool Through the Elementary Grade* with Audio CD 3rd edition by CAMPBELL/SCOTT-KASSNER, 2006. Reprinted with permission of Wadsworth, a Division of Thompson Learning: www. Thomsonrights.com. Fax 800-730-2215.

## The Tune

The message of "Viva la Musica" ("long live music") is a strong and positive one that is widely embraced wherever it may be sung.

## The Music Culture

The origin of this round is uncertain, although it is usually attributed to sixteenth-century composer Michael Praetorius. The words are Italian, and yet the song is thought to have traveled throughout central Europe and into the northern lands in the fashion of an oral tradition—no notation was necessary. Its "staying power"—simple triadic melody, alternating I–V harmony, and *joie de vivre* textual meaning—brought it into circles of amateur, everyday singers. One theory is that the song made its way into the custom of "high table" at Cambridge and Oxford universities in the late seventeenth century, when formal dinners were taken in college dining halls. Faculty dressed in full academic regalia of gowns and capes assembled, not only to dine but to engage in discourse on their latest literary and scientific discoveries. Prayers were said in Latin, a blessing was offered, and then dinner was served. As the evening wore on, the meal and social exchange led to spontaneous singing, first from one table and then from another. Folk songs, including ballads, chanteys, and songs of the hunt, were the substance of communal singing, as were rounds (canons, catches, and chases) such as "Viva la Musica." (The designation, "high table," refers to the elevated stage on which the professors were seated at a table about five steps above the level of the students.) The remnants of the high-table tradition are found in the Latin prayers that are spoken before dinner, although the gowns are seldom worn and the tradition of singing common songs has faded.

### The Experiences

- Sing the melody on a neutral syllable such as "moo," and on solfège syllables (beginning on "sol") or scale numbers (beginning on "5").
- Sing the lyrics, pronounced as "Vee-vah lah moo-zi-kah."
- Sing the song in a three-part canon, with each part entering two measures after the one preceding it.
- Play the chords on piano or guitar, using two arpeggiated or strummed chords per measure.

### Recommended Listening

*Kodály: Choral Music Volume 7.* Hungariton HCD 31291

*Hindemith: Lieder, Choruses, and Canons.* Wergo WER 66422

# VOICE OF TRONG

Vietnam

Theme:

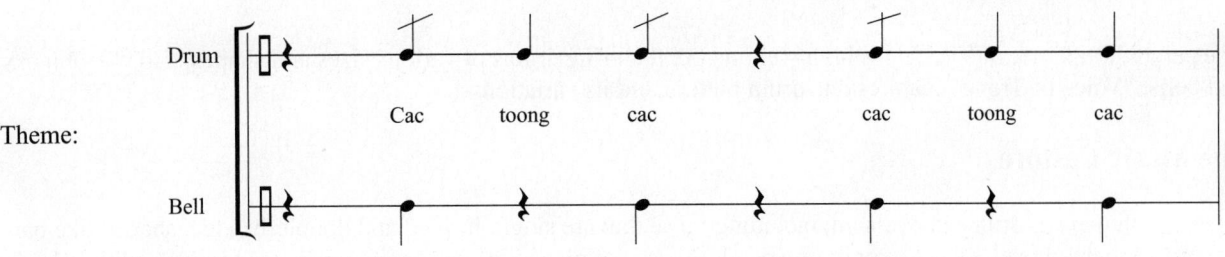

Variation 1:

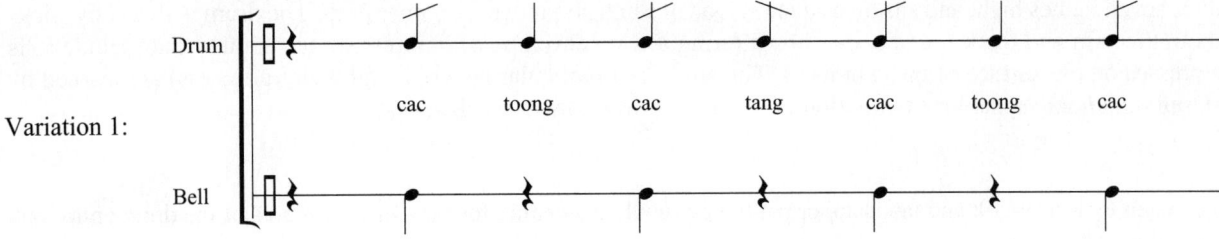

Variation 2:

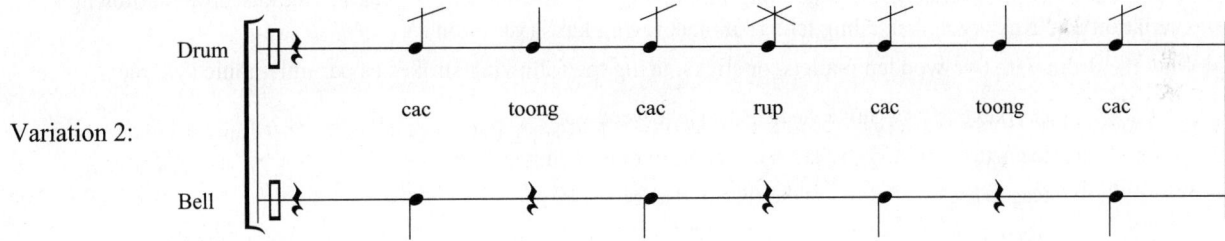

Variation 3:

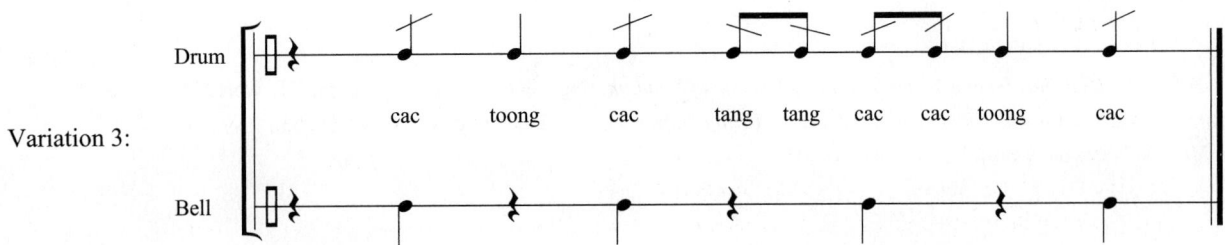

Traditional, Vietnam, as arranged by Phong Nguyen. From Nguyen, P. T. & Campbell, P. S. (1990). From *Rice Paddies and Temple Yards: Traditional Music of Vietnam*. Danbury, CT: World Music Press. Courtesy World Music Press.

# VOICE OF TRONG

CD III, Track # 19

## The Groove

The percussion music of Vietnam is highly energetic, featuring drums of various sizes and shapes, and woodblocks and bells. "Voice of Trong" features one drum pattern and its variations.

## The Music Culture

There are numerous drums in Vietnam, including those that are single-headed and double-headed, shaped like barrels or cylinders, played by sticks or by the hands. Some are played in ceremonial music, or for the traditional theater performances, and others may be traced to the court music traditions of Huế. Some drums play leading roles in orchestras and chamber groups of string and wind instruments, while others are combined with other a variety of percussion instruments in their own ensembles. While *trong* is a generic term for any Vietnamese drum, it is also a specific two-headed drum used in village ensembles with a cowskin surface and a body of a wooden box. The *trong* body is seven inches high, and sits on a square wooden stand about twenty inches high. The drum is struck by sticks on both the skin and the wooden body, thus offering a wide envelope of timbres and techniques that include rolls and presses on the surface of the skin itself. The strokes of particular patterns (and their variations) are learned by chanting mnemonic syllables in imitation of the master drummer or teacher.

### The Experiences

- Listen to Track # 19, and tap, clap, or pat the pulse while listening for the various timbres of the drum on its skin and wooden body.
- Listen again to the recording, and listen to differentiations between the theme (played first) and the three variations on the theme.
- Recite in rhythm the mnemonic of the theme and variation strokes, as indicated under the drum part. Say: "Kak towng kak" (theme), "Kak towng kak tahng kak towng kak" (variation 1), "Kak towng kak roop kak towng kak" (variation 2), "Kak towng kak tahng tahng kak kak towng kak" (variation 3).
- Play the drum with two wooden mallets, or sticks, using the following strokes as per mnemonic syllable:

|  |  |
|---|---|
| cac (kak): | Strike the mallets on the wood side |
| toong (tawng): | Strike at the center of the drum skin |
| tang (tahng): | Strike at the edge of the drum skin |
| rup (roop): | Roll two mallets on the skin briefly and stop, pressing at the center of the skin |

- To reinforce the patterns, chant each one twice and then play them twice.
- Play from start to finish, and following the third variation, invite improvisation by way of selecting from among the patterns and varying them—so long as the beat holds steady and the rhythm length remains the same.

### Recommended Listening

+*From Rice Paddies and Temple Yards: Traditional Music of Vietnam.* (Nguyen/Campbell). Danbury, CT: World Music Press.
*Eternal Voices: Traditional Vietnamese Music in the United States.* New Alliance Records NAR CD 053.
*The Music of Vietnam.* Celestial Harmonies 19903-2.

# WAI BAMBA

Zimbabwe

*"You have caught him/her! You've got him/her!"*

Traditional, Zimbabwe, Arranged by Dumisani Maraire. Adzenya, A. K., Maraire, D., & Tucker, J. C. (1997). *Let Your Voice Be Heard: Songs from Ghana and Zimbabwe* (Rev. Ed.). Danbury, CT: World Music Press. Courtesy World Music Press.

# WAI BAMBA

## The Tune

A wedding song in Zimbabwe, "Wai Bamba," is sung in joyous celebration of the event in which the bride (or groom) has "caught" his (her) partner for their lifetime ahead.

## The Music Culture

Shona is the mother tongue for three-quarters of the population of Zimbabwe, followed by Ndebele (about 15 percent), and the former colonial language (now the official language), English. The majority of Zimbabweans live as herders and farm laborers in rural areas, where indigenous cultural traditions and music styles are continued—even as a healthy industry of urban popular music has emerged in recent decades. In the village wedding celebrations, the entire village will come out to sing, dance, and play instruments such as the *mbira* (a thumb piano), *hosho* (gourd rattles), and a variety of *ngoma* (drums). Yet no instruments are necessary for the performance of "Wai Bamba" and other wedding songs. Instead, enthusiastic voices can sing together in chordal harmony that reflects the four-part hymns that were brought by missionaries. Typical of much Shona music, there is opportunity for improvisation, particularly at the close of the four-measure phrases when the sung syllables "wi wi" are replaced with whistles, claps, and chants like "hup hup." Singers will also improvise clapping and stamping patterns throughout the song.

### The Experiences

- Sing the melody in the alto line on a neutral syllable such as "wee," and on solfège syllables (beginning on "sol") or scale numbers (beginning on "5").
- Sing the lyrics, pronouncing them as "Why bahm-bah why; wee wee."
- Sing each of the remaining parts (a) on "wee" and (b) on solfège or scale numbers.
- Put the parts together, either assigning each line to sopranos, altos, tenors, and basses, or choosing one's favorite part to sing.
- Stamp and clap an ostinato rhythm while singing:

  ♩.     ♩.     ♩

  R stamp   L stamp   clap
- Improvise a clapping rhythm, or a chanted (or sung) phrase, for the last measure (of every four measures) to replace "wi wi."

### Recommended Listening

+*Let Your Voice Be Heard: Songs from Ghana and Zimbabwe*. (Adzenyah/Maraire/Tucker). Danbury, CT: World Music Press.
*Chaminuka: The Music of Zimbabwe* (Dumisani Maraire). Music of the World 093785020820

# WALKIN' BLUES

Robert Johnson

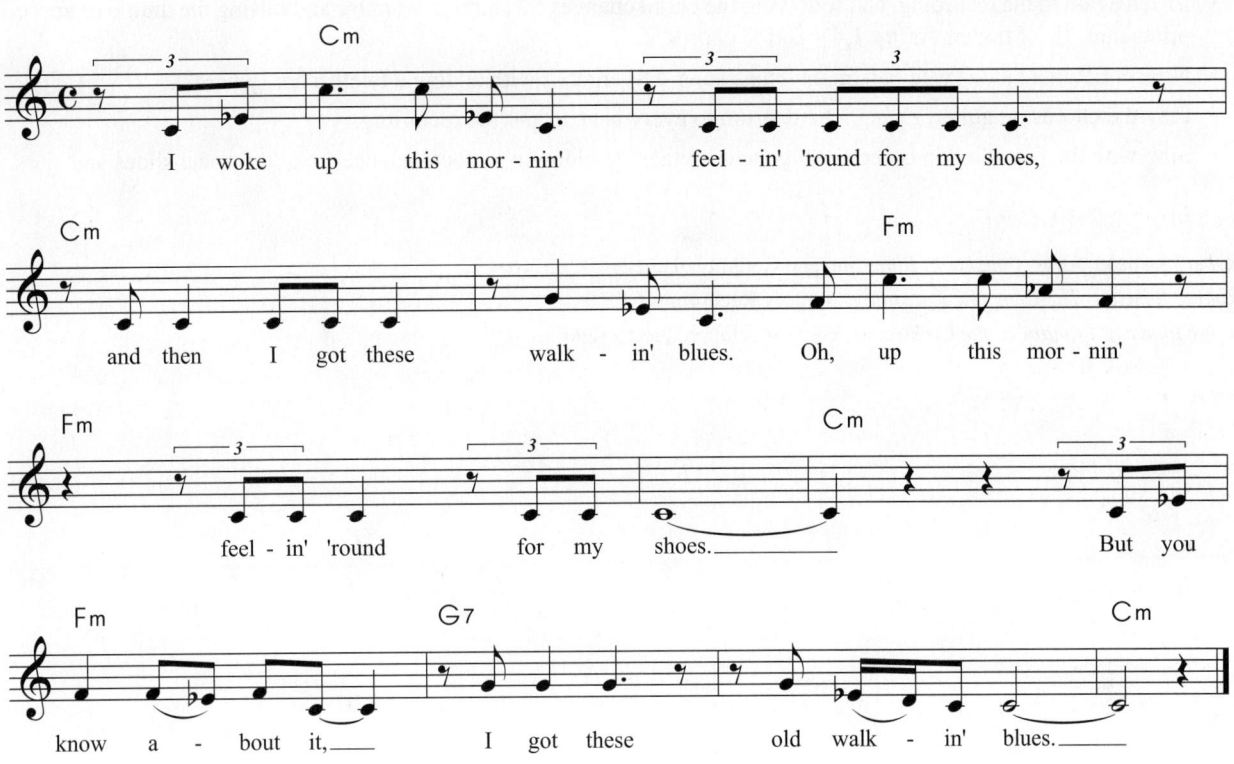

CD III, Track # 20

## The Tune

The legendary bluesman Robert Johnson (1911–1938) sang of unrequited love and difficult women, and his "Walkin' Blues" tells of the need to walk away from these troubles.

## The Music Culture

The blues is a secular African-American musical form that emerged at the beginning of the twentieth century, but which had been evolving much earlier in the field hollers of the rural south. It crystallized into a three-line stanza (of which the first two lines were identical) and a 12-bar progression of tonic, subdominant, and dominant (I, IV, V) chords. The blues featured improvisation and a flattened third degree of the scale, and blues singers sometimes employed rasps or growl techniques. Among the famous blues singer-guitarists was Robert Johnson, called "King of the Delta Blues," who set in motion the shape and style of the form for generations to come. Robert Johnson recorded only twenty-nine songs in his time, but he was active as an itinerant musician, playing in clubs throughout the Mississippi Delta. Some of his most covered songs are "Cross Road Blues," "Love in Vain," "32-20 Blues," "Sweet Home Chicago," and "Come On in My Kitchen." The style of Johnson's vocal phrasing and guitar style can be heard in the rock music of Led Zeppelin, Bob Dylan, The Rolling Stones, U2, and Eric Clapton. His voice was taut and somewhat strained, and utilized an occasional falsetto, and his guitar playing was notable for its syncopated rhythms and bottleneck slide, and its walking bass.

## The Experiences

- Listen to Track # 20, and tap the beat while following the guitar's chord progression, strong and pulsive strums, brief walking bass, and occasional melodic slides and flourishes.

- Listen again to the recording, and following the chord changes by tapping the pulse and raising the thumb or appropriate number of fingers for the I, IV and V chords.

- Notice that there are eleven bars in the blues song. Experiment with adding a twelfth bar (where?).

- Play the chords on guitar, giving a hard strum to every beat, as per the recording.

- Sing with the recording in order to gauge and imitate the blues-style vocal nuances, and the vocal slides and slurs.

## Recommended Listening

+*Robert Johnson, King of the Delta Blues Singers*. Columbia/Legacy CK 65746.

+*Robert Johnson: The Complete Recordings*. Legacy Recordings 64916

*Robert Johnson: Standin' at the Crossroads*. BMG special products 27290

# WEDDING DANCE GROOVE

Ghana

## The Groove

This complex layering of rhythms in "Wedding Dance Groove" is a prime example of the polyrhythmic sound of various types of drums, rattles, and sticks that are found in Ghana.

## The Music Culture

The Akan, Asanti, Ewe, and Ga are among the many ethnic groups of people living in Ghana, each of which enjoys a rich heritage of music that gives emphasis to membranophones (drums) and idiophones (such as bells, sticks, shakers, rattles, xylophones, and log drums). In most of these cultures, there are also horns, flutes, and even stringed instruments such as fiddles, plucked lutes, and harps. Music in Ghana serves social occasions, religious ceremonies and rituals (such as initiation practices). The songs and instrumental pieces are used to heal, to mourn, and to celebrate life passages—including the joyful celebration of a wedding dance. Sometimes, the music is composed in advance and is performed in a similar way every time, but more often, the music of Ghana is spontaneously created. Invariably, there is a balance of preconceived and practiced patterns with fresh and newly created components in children's songs, percussion ensembles, marimba bands, and in Afro-pop genres.

## The Experiences

- Keeping a steady pulse, clap, pat, or tap the six lines of notated rhythms, one after another. Note the "feel" of a seven-beat phrase.

- "Adjust" the notated rhythms to the sounded rhythms, playing rhythms on the same or similar-sounding instruments.

- With others, play the seven-beat phrases simultaneously. Select a different instrument for each line in order that it might be distinguished from the others.

- As a variation, play the six phrases in canon, with one instrument beginning as the previous one ends.

- Play the rhythms with pitched instruments, staying on one pitch for the duration of the piece.

## Recommended Listening

*Sowah Mensa: Naa Niami.* Available from nanamo@africonline.com.ghTrac

*Obo Addy: Okropong.* EarthBeat! D-2500.

## WERE YOU THERE?

U. S.: African American

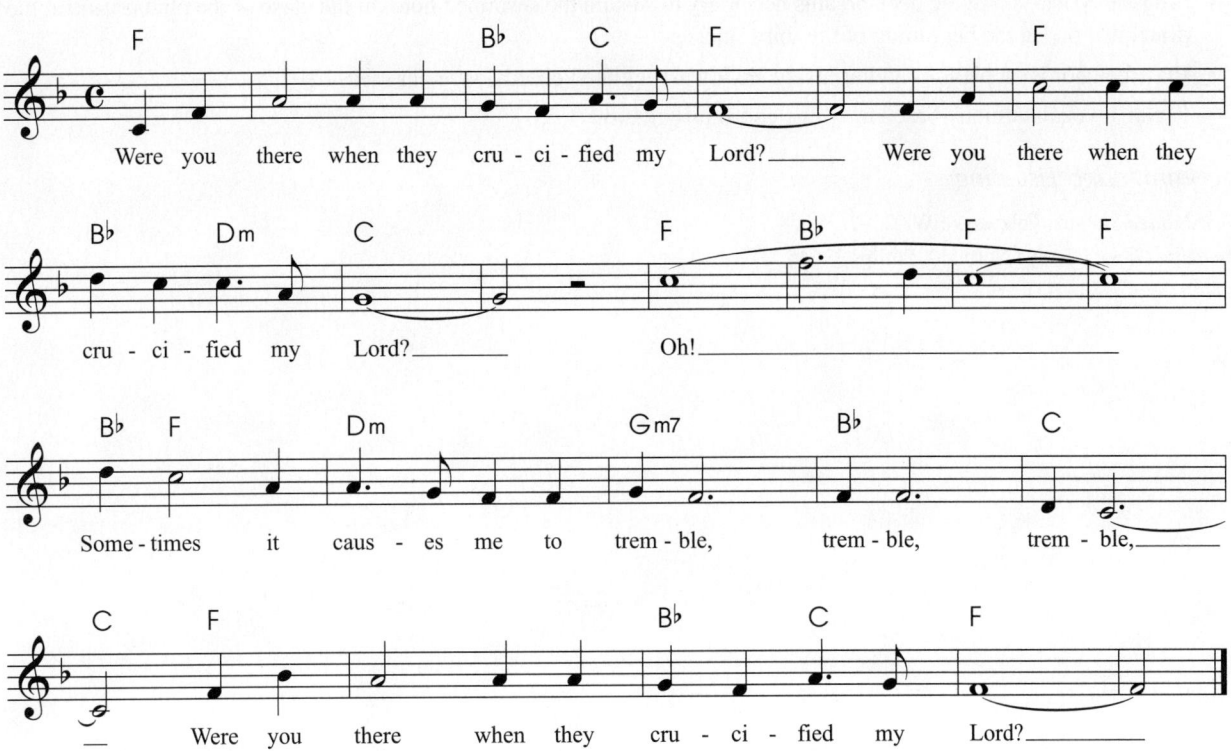

### The Tune

One of the *sorrow songs* of the repertoire of African-American spirituals, "Were You There?" is a soulful expression of the crucifixion of Jesus Christ.

### The Music Culture

The African-American *spiritual* developed during slavery as a form of religious expression, coupled with its function as a commentary on bondage. Traditional spirituals were performed without piano (or other instrumental) accompaniment, although hand clapping and foot tapping were employed for some spirituals to help swing and further syncopate the already snappy rhythms of the melodies. Spirituals fell into categories that included the fiery and fast call-and-response form, with its accompanying body percussion, and the slow and sustained sorrow songs that were almost wailed in their projection of grief. "Were You There?" is clearly the second type of spiritual, a sorrow song that covertly pays tribute to the trials and tribulations of the singer, even as it more directly refers to the suffering of Jesus Christ.

## The Experiences

- Sing the melody on a neutral syllable such as "lah," and on solfège syllables (beginning on "sol") or scale numbers (beginning on "5").

- Sing the lyrics, taking the deep breaths necessary to sustain the sustained notes at the close of the phrases and at the dramatic "oh" at the beginning of the third line.

- Play the chords on piano or guitar, using slowly arpeggiated chords once per measure.

- Create a vocal harmony based upon the chord progression.

## Recommended Listening

+*Fisk Jubilee Singers*. Folkways FW 02372.

+*Amazing Grace.* (Jessye Norman). Philips 32546.

## WHEN JESUS WEPT

William Billings

## The Tune

The early American composer, William Billings (1746–1800) wrote "When Jesus Wept" as a *fuguing tune* that functions canonically to produce rich vocal harmonies.

## The Music Culture

The British sought ways of elaborating the metrical psalmody of their Anglican parish churches, and so devised a form called *the fuguing tune* (or fuging tune) that would allow contrapuntal entries involving textual overlap. By 1750, fuguing tunes had taken hold among country church choirs in England. James Lyon's *Urania*, published in 1761, was the first American tune book to contain fuguing tunes, all of them taken from British publications. Colonial composers like William Billings took to the form, and by the 1780s, fuguing tunes were flourishing in congregational meetinghouses in New England. Billings is regarded as a founding father of American choral music. He was born, lived, and died in Boston during the colonial period (during and just following the American Revolution). He worked as a traveling singing schoolteacher, and a composer of hymns, anthems, and fuguing tunes. Despite its poignant melody and cascading harmonies, Billings' "When Jesus Wept" and all other New England fuguing tunes were eventually replaced by organ-accompanied hymns with homophonic textures.

## The Experiences

- Sing the melody on a neutral syllables such as "loo," and on solfège syllables (beginning on "la") or scale numbers (beginning on "6").

- Sing the lyrics, using the breath to support the singing of the occasional melismatic phrases of several pitches to a single syllable.

- Play the chords, strumming or arpeggiating them on piano or guitar.

- Sing the song in "fuguing tune" fashion, or canonically, with each part entering four measures after the one preceding it.

## Recommended Listening

*American Sampler: Atlanta Singers.* ACA Digital ACD CM20046

+*The Unclaimed Pint* (Sally Rogers). Flying Fish FF 0409.

+*Wake Ev'ry Breath—Music of William Billings.* New World Records 80539

# WHERE DID YOU SLEEP LAST NIGHT?

Huddie Ledbetter (Lead Belly)

2. My girl, my girl, where will you go,
   I'm going where the cold wind blow.
   In the pines, in the pines,
   Where the sun never shine,
   I would shiver the whole night through.

3. My girl, my girl, don't lie to me,
   Tell me where did you sleep last night.
   In the pines, in the pines
   Where the sun never shines,
   I would shiver the whole night through.

4. My husband was a hard working man,
   Just about a mile from here,
   His head was found in a driving wheel,
   And his body never was found.

5. My girl, my girl, where will you go?
   I'm going where the cold wind blows.
   In the pines, in the pines
   Where the sun never shines,
   I would shiver the whole night through.

CD II, Track # 6

## The Tune

Lead Belly's version of "Were Did You Sleep Last Night?" (sometimes referred to as "In the Pines") tells the story of a "black girl" who is hiding in grief and shock from the news of her husband's murder.

## The Music Culture

Numerous versions of "Where Did You Sleep Last Night" are found in collections and on recordings. Huddie Ledbetter (1888–1949), better known as Leadbelly (or Lead Belly), released an influential recording of the song in 1944. His version is based on a combination of two tunes, one that was learned (according to Alan Lomax) "from someone who took it from Cecil Sharp's collection, Volume II" (which had been sung by Lizzie Abner of Kentucky for Cecil Sharp and Maud Karpeles, in 1917) and another that was collected by Robert W. Gordon from Bertie May Moses in North Carolina in 1925. It is set in a minor key, moving in a triple meter that is punctuated by the bass-strum-strum pattern of the acoustic guitar he plays. Leadbelly's version is not from the black tradition, but was Anglo-American until he developed his rendition of it. The tune was widely copied in the 1950s, and still had staying power forty years later when Kurt Cobain of Nirvana recorded it in 1995.

### The Experiences

- Listen to Track # 6 for the sliding melody of the voice, the strummed chords, and the occasional melodic interludes between phrases that are played on the low strings. Tap the rhythm of the strum.
- Sing the melody on a neutral syllable like "noo," and with solfège syllables (beginning on "do") and scale numbers (beginning on "la").
- Sing the lyrics to the song, careful to differentiate between the F and F♯ pitches.
- Play the chords on guitar or other harmony instrument, following a basic three-beat strum.
- Explore other accompaniments on the guitar, plucking the root or bass note of the chord on the first beat of each measure, adding transitional notes between phrases, picking rather than strumming.

### Recommended Listening

+*American Roots Collection* (Lead Belly). Smithsonian Folkways SFW40062.
+*Where Did You Sleep Last Night? Lead Belly Legacy, Volume 1*. Smithsonian Folkways SFW40044.

# WILDWOOD FLOWER

U. S.: Appalachian Mountains

I will twine and will ming-le my ra-ven black hair With the ros-es so

red and the lil-ies so fair. The myr-tle so green, of an em-er-ald

hue, The pale am-an-i-ta and is-lip so blue.

2. Oh, he promised to love me, he promised to love,

   And to cherish me over all others above.

   I woke from my dream and my idol was clay,

   My passion for loving had vanished away.

3. Oh, he taught me to love him, he called me his flower,

   A blossom to cheer him through life's weary hour.

   But now he is gone and left me alone,

   The wild flowers to weep and the wild birds to mourn.

4. I'll dance and I'll sing and my heart shall be gay,

   I'll charm every heart in the crowd I survey.

   Though my heart now is breaking, he never shall know

   How his name makes me tremble, my pale cheeks to glow.

5. I'll dance and I'll sing and my heart shall be gay,

   I'll banish this weeping, drive troubles away.

   I'll live yet to see him regret this dark hour,

   Still he once said he loved me, he called me his flower.

## The Tune

The Carter family made famous a style of country music that featured autoharp and guitar, and vocal harmonies. Their rendition of "Wildwood Flower" influenced American folksingers through much of the twentieth century.

## The Music Culture

The genre known as American country music was evolving in the 1920s and 30s, and a recording session of the Carter Family and Jimmie Rodgers in August 1927 by the Victor label was a pivotal point in the transmission of folk and country sounds that could be beamed to listeners by radio and bought for family record players throughout the land. Jimmie Rodgers was an ex-railroad worker from Mississippi who played guitar and sang the songs that celebrated the ramblers, gamblers, and hoboes on the open road. The Carter Family (A. P., his wife, Sara, and their sister-in-law Maybelle) emerged from the Clinch Mountains of Virginia with a large repertoire of traditional songs—some British but mostly vintage American gospel and sentimental "parlor" songs. Their vocal harmony was marked by Sara's strong lead, Maybelle's tenor, and A. P.'s baritone or bass. Sara chorded the *autoharp,* a box-zither with twenty-one (or up to forty-nine) strings, and Maybelle was known for her "thumb-style" guitar playing. Their sound was immediately recognizable on records and radio shows, and their songs were referred to as "Carter Family songs." They disbanded in 1943, but Maybelle, later known as "Mother Maybelle," performed on the *Grand Ole Opry* radio show with her children Helen, June, and Anita (June Carter eventually married Johnny Cash). "Wildwood Flower" is widely known as one of the "national anthems" of country music, a tune that fledgling guitarists and autoharp players learn as they develop their ability to play melody and chords simultaneously.

### The Experience

- Sing the melody on a neutral syllable such as "mah," and on solfège syllables (beginning on "mi") or scale numbers (beginning on "3").

- Sing the lyrics, with attention to supporting the voice with a good breath so that it can be heard on the lower pitches at the phrase endings.

- Play the chords on guitar, autoharp, piano, or other harmony instrument. On guitar, play a pattern of ♩ ♫ that features a down, down-up stroke or the root tone followed by two quick strums of the chord.

- Play and sing in the key of D Major to adjust to a higher vocal range, using D, G, and A7 chords.

- Explore the potential for vocal harmonies, using the chords as a guide and utilizing parallel thirds and sixths.

### Recommended Listening

+*The Carter Family: Wildwood Flower.* Asv Living Era 5323.

+*Mountain Music Played on the Autoharp.* Folkways FW 02365.

+*Bluegrass* (Billie Ray Johnson and David Johnson). Folkways FW 31056.

# WITH LAUGHTER AND SINGING

Germany

With laugh-ter and sing-ing the green earth is spring-ing, The

shep-herd__ is__ pip-ing, a - gain it__ is__ spring. Tra

la la la la la la la la, Tra la la la la la la la.

## The Tune

The dancing melody of "With Laughter and Singing" seems to bubble up joyfully in celebration of springtime, and this effervescence is multipled when the song is sung as a *canon*.

## The Music Culture

Canons have been written for centuries. In the European Middle Ages, composers carefully constructed formulas as to how a second voice could be extracted from the original melody at a specific intervallic and temporal distance. There were rules for altering a given line without creating a new voice, or requirements for singers to perform a part in retrograde motion so that the imitating part started at the end rather than at the beginning of the piece. Other complexities were the mensuration canons that called for canon by rhythmic augmentation, diminution, or by proposed changes of note values. The common meaning of canon, an imitative texture of multiple voices that enter at various times, came to being in the sixteenth century, and has come to mean approximately the same thing as a round. "With Laughter and Singing" is a translation of a canon from Germany that has made its way over many decades into the English-language repertoire.

### The Experiences

- Sing the melody on a neutral syllable such as "lah," and on solfège syllables (beginning on "sol") or scale numbers (beginning on "5").
- Sing the lyrics, carefully singing through the two pitches to a syllable (in the second phrase) and holding on the fermata for twice the duration of the note.
- Play the chords on piano or guitar, one per ♩.
- Sing the song in canon, with each vocal part entering two measures after the one preceding it.

### Recommended Listening

*Kodály: Choral Music Volume 7.* Hungariton HCD 31291

*Hindemith: Lieder, Choruses, and Canons.* Wergo WER 66422

# WOKE UP THIS MORNING

U. S.: African American

## The Tune

A song of the American Civil Rights movement "Woke Up This Morning" expresses the dream of freedom and equality that African Americans rightly sought for themselves and all people of color.

## The Music Culture

Boycotts, sit-ins, and freedom rides were means of protest against the history of unjust and unequal treatment of African Americans during the period of the American Civil Rights movement, 1954–1968. Long after the Abraham Lincoln's Emancipation Proclamation, many African Americans continued to live without the means to pull themselves out of the impoverished conditions that they had known as slaves. A century later, they still had little access to the quality of schooling, jobs, and housing that whites enjoyed. For African Americans, the freedom they yearned for was defined as the desegregation of public places, such that there would be no more "separate but equal" schools, lunch counters, and drinking fountains for blacks and whites. They dreamed of a time when there would be no discrimination in hiring practices for blue- or white-collar jobs, and for a time when they would have access to registration so as to qualify them as voters whose voices could be heard on issues relevant to them as citizens of a democracy. The American dream of freedom was just that: a dream from which African Americans awoke every morning, yet still in the hope that it was on its way to being realized. Reverend Osby of Aurora, Illinois, is credited with revamping an old gospel song and shaping it into "Wake Up This Morning" during his stay in a Mississippi jail for his participation in the freedom rides. These freedom rides were a series of student political protests performed in 1961, when African American and white student volunteers rode on interstate buses into the pro-segregationist U.S. South to test *Boynton v. Virginia*, 364 U.S. 454, the law that prohibited racial segregation in interstate public facilities, including bus stations.

### The Experiences

- Sing the melody on a neutral syllable such as "mah," and on solfège syllables (beginning on "sol") or scale numbers (beginning on "5").
- Sing the lyrics, with attention to the sustained notes, the triplet figures, and the syncopations.
- Play the chords on piano or guitar, emphasizing a steady pulse by playing the chord in full or in a quarter-note rhythm of alternating roots and chords.
- Clap on beats 2 and 4 while singing.
- Improvise a vocal harmony for the sections, "stayed on freedom" and "hallelu."

### Recommended Listening

+*Sing for Freedom: The Story of the Civil Rights Movement Through Its Songs*. Smithsonian Folkways SFW 40032.

+*The Pennywhistlers*. Folkways FW 08773.

# WOLF AND TURTLE SONG

Apache

CD III, Track # 21

## The Tune

Irene Poolaw sings the "Wolf and Turtle Song" in the Apache language, one of a vast repertoire of Apache songs that celebrate the natural world, including animals.

## The Music Culture

The Apaches ranged over southeastern Arizona and northwestern Mexico, but may have arrived there only a few decades before the Spanish. They had been hunters, living on wild things, and were nomadic and yet successful at herding sheep, goats, and cattle. Considered a powerful tribe, the Apaches were constantly at enmity with the whites and the Mexicans who at one time controlled much of their territory. The U.S. Army found them to be fierce warriors and skillful strategists in their various confrontations in the nineteenth century, led by the most famous of them, Mangas Coloradas, Cochise, and Geronimo. On their final surrender in 1886, the Apache were placed on reservations in Arizona, New Mexico, and Oklahoma. The legends of the Apache are similar to those of the Navajo, and in fact they speak a Southern Athabascan language that is related to the Navajo language. They have medicine "sings," and have amassed a repertoire of songs about wolves and eagles, their horses, and the sheep, goats, and cattle they herd.

### The Experiences

- Sing the melody on a neutral syllable such as "bah," and on solfège syllables (beginning on "la") or scale numbers (beginning on "6").
- Sing the lyrics, using the following pronunciation:

  Bah day chah,

  Tre-ten gole,

  Boh ta nee-shay

  Beh-nez ka-nay oh.

- Play a drum and shaker on the quarter-note beat, twice per measure.
- Play the melody on flute or recorder, or various other melody instruments
- Play the chords on guitar or piano, although such harmony is not traditional to the Apache people.

## Recommended Listening

+*A Fish that's a Song* (Irene Chalepah Poolaw). Smithsonian Folkways SFW 45037.

# WONDROUS LOVE

John and Charles Wesley

2. And when from death I'm free, I'll sing on, I'll sing on;
   And when from death I'm free, I'll sing on.
   And when from death I'm free,
   I'll sing and joyful be,
   And through eternity, I'll sing on, I'll sing on.
   And through eternity, I'll sing on.

## The Tune

The thrust of the text for this old American hymn is to beg forgiveness for human errors so as to attain salvation.

## The Music Culture

Hymn singing has long been important to the liturgical services in American Protestant churches. As early as the arrival of the Pilgrims and Puritans in the early seventeenth century, singing was integral to worship. Then, it was the singing of psalm tunes that filled the congregational meetinghouses, with singers following the leader's (or their own) beating of the meter. Yet with churchgoers unable to read music, the diversity of tunes was reduced and only those remembered few melodies were applied to the multiple psalms. By the eighteenth century, singing schools with itinerant teachers were established in towns and villages, where the devout could gather in the evenings to learn music notation so as to increase the number of melodies sung, and to develop their singing voices. Tune books were published at this time, carrying notation for the syllabic psalm tunes and the more elaborate fuguing tunes.

New hymns were written based on folk melodies, too, with a considerable number of them set in the Mixolydian and Dorian modes. Folk hymns emerged, too, such as "Wondrous Love," which is likely to have been based on a folk balled tune called "Captain Kidd." By the 1730s, John Wesley and his brother Charles began writing hymns that eventually replaced the psalm-singing and fuguing tunes, and in the decades that followed they produced a body of several thousand hymns that were borrowed by other Protestant denominations. Whether sung by a choir or the entire congregation, hymns then, as now, were central to institutionalized devotional practices.

## The Experiences

- Sing the melody on a neutral syllable such as "lah," and on solfège syllables (beginning on "la") or scale numbers (beginning on "6").
- Sing the lyrics, with attention to the smooth rise and fall of the melody across the four-measure phrases.
- Beat the time while singing, by tapping out the quarter-note pulse with a pencil or hand on a flat surface.
- Play the chords on piano or guitar, one chord per every two beats, or as a continuous stream of pitches in arpeggiated or broken chords.
- Sing a vocal harmony that corresponds to the chordal progression, experimenting with triads and open fifths.

## Recommended Listening

+*American Angels*. (Anonymous 4). Harmonia Mundi HMU 907326.

*American Sampler: Atlanta Singers*. ACA Digital ACD CM20046

# THE WREN SONG

Ireland

The wren, the wren, the king of all birds, Saint

Ste - phen's Day was caught in the furze, Al - though he was lit - tle, his

hon - or was great. Jump up, me lads, and give us a treat!

2. As I went out to hunt and all,

   I met a wren upon the wall.

   Up with me wattle and gave him a fall,

   And brought him here to show you all.

3. I have a little box under me arm,

   A tuppence or penny'll do it no harm.

   For we are the boys that came your way,

   To bring in the wren on St. Stephen's Day!

## The Tune

On December 26 each year "The Wren Song" and a small bird in a cage are featured in parades in Irish towns that continue a tradition dating back to the Middle Ages.

## The Music Culture

While the British celebrate December 26 as Boxing Day, people in County Kerry and the Dingle Peninsula in southwestern Ireland are reviving the "Hunting the Wren" custom. A gang of people take to the roads dressed in straw suits and masks, or with faces blackened. They process to the accompaniment of musicians, hunting for the bird that they call the traitor and the infidel. Legend has it that St. Stephen, the first martyr (whose feast is celebrated on December 26), was once hiding in a bush from his enemies when he had his whereabouts betrayed by a chattering wren. An old Druidic custom developed of spearing the wren and fastening it to the top of a pole, but that has disappeared in favor of carrying a small bird in a cage, or even an artificial bird. The Wrenboys (and now girls, too) are quite the spectacle in the parade, dressed in full regalia, singing, high-stepping, and dancing. Pennywhistles, pipes, fifes, and drums sound through the streets of the parade for the hunt, and the paraders take up a collection for a dance party in a local hotel or public house where traditional Irish musicians play.

## The Experience

- Sing the melody on a neutral syllable such as "bah," and on solfège syllables (beginning on "sol") or scale numbers (beginning on "5").
- Sing the lyrics, bouncing lightly in the 6/8 metric scheme. Note the meanings of Old English terms: furze (grass or weeds), wattle (poles used to catch the wren), tuppence (variation of twopence, the sum of two British pennies).
- Play the chords on guitar or piano, in an arpeggiated pattern that features one chord tone per beat—and six per measure.
- Add a two-measure ostinato rhythm on hand drum:
- Play the melody on flute, pennywhistle, or recorder, as interludes between the sung verses.

## Recommended Listening

*Songs of Ireland*. Monitor MON 61447.

*Traditional Music of Ireland: The Older Traditions of Connemara and Clare*. Folkways FW 08781.

# XIAO QI CHE

China

Xiao qi che di da di | man men kai hua er shi yi. | Er wu liu er wu qi

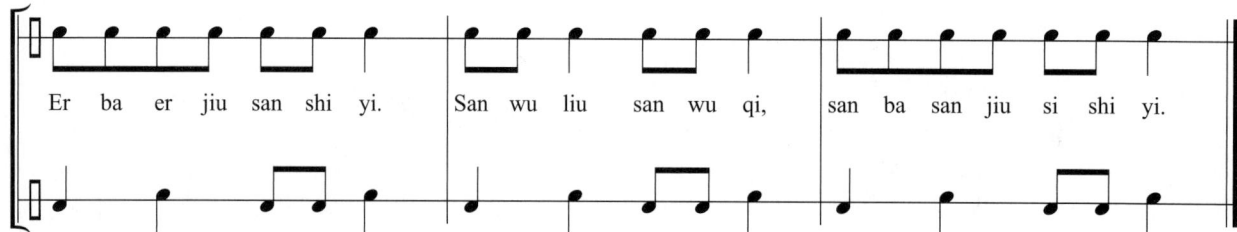

Er ba er jiu san shi yi. | San wu liu san wu qi, | san ba san jiu si shi yi.

*Little car, di da di, Flowers blooming twenty-one.*

*Two five six, two five seven, Two eight, two nine, thirty-one.*

*Three five six, three five seven, three eight, three nine, forty-one.*

## The Groove

Even as children continue to chant and sing their counting-out rhymes, some of the repertoire is borrowed and arranged for popular genres. "Xiao Qi Che" is a technologized rap-style arrangement of a traditional Chinese children's rhyme.

## The Music Culture

The lore of children, including their chanted and sung verse, has staying power across many generations. As well, the rituals, verses, rhythms, and melodies make their way forward into a child's life, and are never completely lost on adults who then transmit them to their own children. Occasionally, this lore of nursery rhymes and playground chants becomes all or part of a new artistic expression: verses appear in novels, plays, and films, and musical segments emerge in popular music and symphonic compositions. Gao Hong, a highly regarded performer of the Chinese *pipa* (a pear-shaped lute) and an enthusiastic educator now directing the Children's Chinese Music Ensemble in the United States, resurrected a Chinese children's counting-out rhyme and offered it in rap style. "Little Car" fits within the larger category of Mandarin pop music, in which Chinese lyrics are coupled with the essence of popular music.

## The Experiences

- Create a rhythmic track to accompany the verse, using drum set and/or instruments such as *djembe* and *conga* drums, sticks, bell, and shakers.
- Convert into children's counting game by gathering in small groups, stacking fists vertically one on top of the other, designating a counting-out person who taps one fist after the next (each to a pulse) up and down the column of fists. On the final pulse and syllable ("yi"), the last fist tapped goes "out" of the column and the chant resumes until, through repeated chantings of the verse, there is only one fist winning fist that remains.

## Recommended Listening

*Yin Tsang: For the People*. Scream ASIN: 788005537.

*50 Popular Chinese Childrens' Songs, Volume 1*. China Spout MC 5032.

# YEYSH LANU TAYISH

Israel

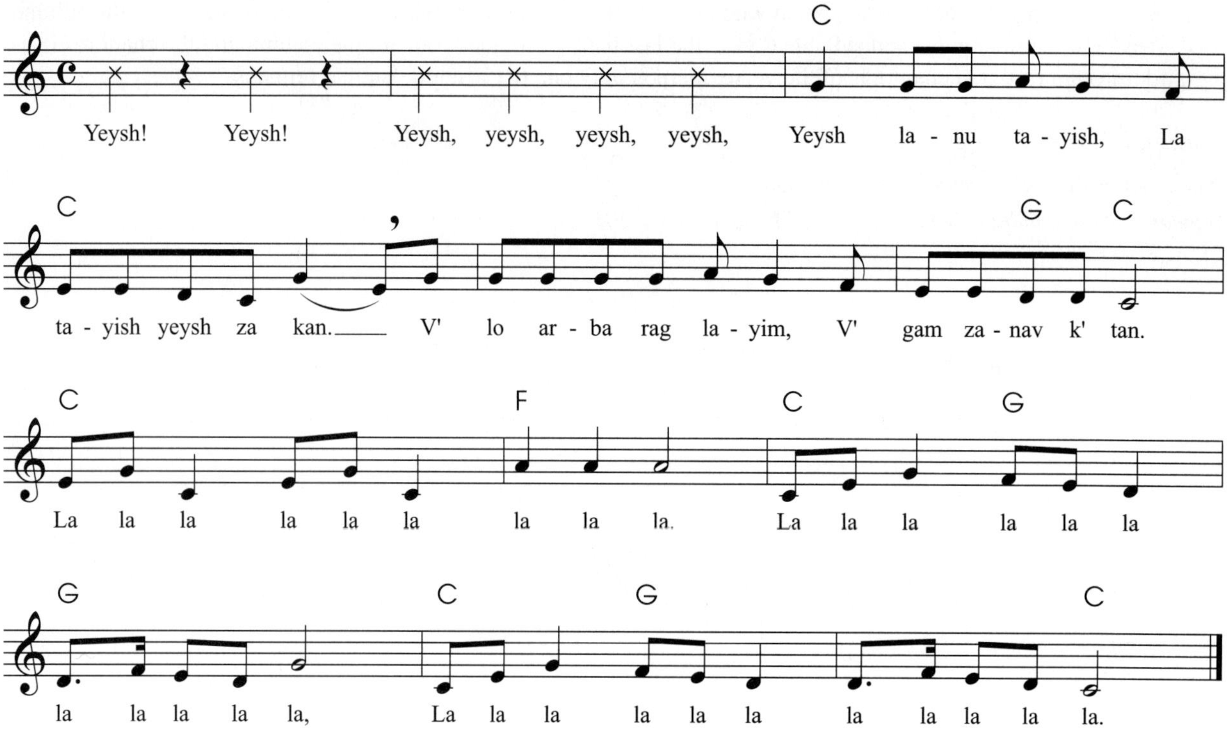

*Yeysh! Yeysh! Yeysh, yeysh, yeysh, yeysh, Yeysh la - nu ta -yish, La*

*ta - yish yeysh za kan.___ V' lo ar - ba rag la - yim, V' gam za - nav k' tan.*

*La la la la la la la la la. La la la la la la*

*la la la la la, La la la la la la la la la la la.*

*We have a goat.*
*He has a beard.*
*He has four legs,*
*And also a little tail.*

## The Tune

Popular with children in Israel, "Yeysh Lanu Tayish" is a song in Hebrew about a goat. It is danced in two facing lines of facing partners that gallop up and down the aisle and under a human-made arch.

## The Music Culture

From the land of Canaan, to Israel, then Palestine, Israel became an independent nation in 1948. Arriving from Morocco, Tunisia, Yemen, Russian, Spain, Romania, Ukraine, Poland, Austria, Germany, France, Ethiopia, and the United States, Jewish people came to the eastern Mediterranean to build the modern nation of Israel: its cities and frontier towns, schools, scientific institutes, and high-rise apartments and office buildings. Multiple languages are still heard on the streets of Israel and across the airwaves, including Hebrew, Arabic, English, and Yiddish (among settlers from Europe). Yet despite the diversity, music has played an important role in the unification of people from the Jewish Diaspora to Israel. There are professional orchestras, youth orchestras, choral groups, and chamber groups, as well as music education programs that begin in early childhood to develop skills for singing, listening, and playing classroom instruments such as recorder. Children learn folk songs, even as adults participate in folk music and dance as means of expressing national pride. "Yeysh Lanu Tayish," a folk melody of German origin, combines the harmonies of Western Europe with singing in Hebrew, and with the rousing movements of a folk dance. It is well known in Jewish youth groups, and by children as young as preschool age. The words may be composed, and have been attributed to Yitzchek Alterman.

## The Experiences

- Sing the melody on a neutral syllable such as "la," and on solfege syllables (beginning on "sol") or scale numbers (beginning on "5").
- Sing the lyrics, noting these points as guide to pronunciation: "yeysh" ("yaysh"), "v'lo" ("vuh loh"), "v'gam" ("vuh gahm"), "k'tan" (kuh tahn).
- Play the chords on guitar and piano. Strum in a down, down-up ♩ ♩♪ rhythm on guitar. For piano, play an alternating root-and-chord pattern on the piano.
- Play the melody on recorder, clarinet, violin, and accordion, alone or all together.
- Perform the dance in partners arranged in two facing lines.

| | |
|---|---|
| Mm. 1–2: | Head couple holds hands, moving them up and down to "yeysh" chant. |
| Mm. 3–4: | Head couple gallops sideways down the aisle between the two lines. |
| Mm. 5–6: | Head couple gallops sideways back up to original position. |
| Mm. 7–12: | Head couple forms an arch. All partners pass under together, then separate to either side and walk rhythmically down the outside of the left and right lines. They rejoin as partners again and gallop back up the middle. Head couple also separates and goes around the outside down to the end of each line. A new head couple begins the song anew. |

## Recommended Listening

+*Roots and Branches* (Campbell/McCullough-Brabson/Tucker). Danbury, CT: World Music Press.
*Israeli Children's Songs*. Folkways FW 07226.

# YE JALIYA DA

Mali: Mandinika

Ye ja - li - yaa da_____ Al - la le - ga ja - li - yaa da.

Ye ja - li - yaa da_____ Al - la le - a ja - li - yaa da.

*The professional musicians make beautiful music.*

## The Tune

Among the Mandinka of West Africa there are skilled musicians known as *jali* who play a variety of instruments and sing songs of praise and historical narrative. "Ye Jaliya Da" calls attention to their music and musical roles.

## The Music Culture

In Mali, the professional musician of the Mandinka people is called *jali*, and his (or her) predominant musical genre is known as *jaliyaa*. From the thirteenth century onward, *jali* enjoyed permanent patronage by district chiefs and even the emperor of Mali, with the power to criticize as well as to praise societal conditions and circumstances. While music and its sources are much more diverse among the Mandinka today, and is available on radio and television and in hotels and clubs, *juliyaa* is still the music for the social class that includes politicians, businessmen, and religious leaders and is standard for weddings, child-naming events, and religious celebrations. A male *jali* learns to sing and to play one of three melodic instruments, depending on his family lineage: a twenty-one-stringed bridge harp known as *kora*, a five-stringed lute known as *konting* or *nkoni,* and a xylophone with gourd resonators known as *balafon. Jali* women are highly trained singers, and they play only a tubular iron bell. Their *jaliyaa* is a repertory of praise songs that celebrates the achievements of past heroes and contemporary figures.

### The Experiences

- Sing the melody on a neutral syllable such as "yay," and on solfège syllables (beginning on "la") or scale numbers (beginning on "6").
- Sing the lyrics, pronouncing them as "Yay jah-lee-yah dah, Al-lah leh-gah jah-lee-yah dah." Sing with gusto, in an outdoor "calling" voice.
- Perform the repeated phrases as solo and group, or as two antiphonal groups.
- Play the chords on guitar or piano, strumming or rolling them twice per measure, with the understanding that such harmony is not typically found in the traditional music of the Mandinka *jali*.

### Recommended Listening

*Kora Music from the Gambia.* Folkways FW 08510.
*Ancient Heart: Mandinka and Fulani Music of the Gambia.* Axiom/PGD 510148.
*Mali Lolo! Stars of Mali.* Smithsonian Folkways SFW 40508.

# YO, MAMANA, YO

Mozambique

Yo ma - ma - na yo, Yo ma - ma - na yo,

Un - ga fam - ba u - ni si - ya U - ni si - ye - la visi - wa - na.

*Oh, Mama,*
*Oh, Mama,*
*You left me alone*
*With my suffering.*

Traditional, Mozambique, as sung by Salomao Manhica. From Campbell, P. S., McCullough-Brabson, E., Tucker, J. C. (1994). *Roots & Branches: A Legacy of Multicultural Music for Children*. Danbury, CT: World Music Press. Courtesy World Music Press.

## The Tune

"Yo, Mamana, Yo" is a children's lullaby of the Ronga and Shangana people of Mozambique.

## The Music Culture

Located on the southeastern coast of Africa, Mozambique is an ethnically diverse country where mother-tongue languages and cultures of the Ronga, Shangana, Tswa, Chopi, and Tsonga stand side by side with the influences of the Portuguese, Arabs and Swahili. The Portuguese colonized Mozambique beginning in 1492. Following liberation in 1975, Portuguese remains the official language for government and business even as English is fast becoming the language of choice among students. Yet as the country has modernized, the majority of children learn the age-old traditions of their communities. Perhaps the best-known music from the region is that of the xylophone orchestras of the Chopi people, which has been documented for the last century for its rich textures, driving rhythms, and virtuosic melodies. There are in Mozambique superb drummers, as well as players of bone, wood, and bamboo flutes; gourd and clay ocarinas, panpipes, one-string musical bows, and board zithers. There is also a strong tradition of singing (including the yodeling of central Mozambique) and dancing. All of this musicianship begins at home, in the arms and on the backs of mothers, fathers, siblings, and other family members, when even infants hear the lullabies and work songs in the local language and musical style of their own families.

### The Experiences

- Sing the melody on a neutral syllable such as "mah," and on solfège syllables (beginning on "sol") or scale numbers (beginning on "5").
- Sing the lyrics, articulating clearly the swift-moving consonants in measures 3 and 4. Pronounce *a* as "ah" and *i* as "ee."
- Play the chords on piano or guitar, stressing the feeling of triple meter by accenting the first beat of each measure.

Yo

tián.

zar.

Traditional, Ecuador,
Danbury, CT: World

**The Tune**

During the Chri
ration for the m

**The Music Cu**

Much of the mu
whole communi
seasonal cerem
with the exciten
ing the nine day
Christmas vigil
(Christmas). In
of San Sebastiá

## The Experience

- Sing the melody on a neutral syllable such as "nah," and on solfège syllables (beginning with "sol") or scale numbers (beginning with "5"). The top of the two-part notation is the melody.

- Sing the lyrics, noting these points for pronunciation: "Indiecito" (een-dee-ay-cee-toh), "vengo" (ben-goh), "vigilia" (vee-hee-lyah).

- Sing the lower harmony line with the melody.

- Play a guitar strum that features the plucked root or bass note followed by the down-up stroke of the chord with this rhythm in each measure:

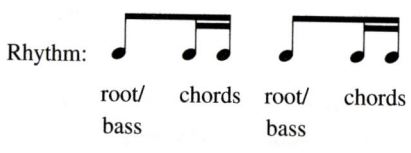

Rhythm:

root/    chords    root/    chords
bass               bass

- Play a two-measure ostinato on a drum:

- Play the melody and harmony parts on recorder, flute, or other pitched instrument, as an interlude to the singing.

## Recommended Listening

+*A Singing Wind* (Brennan). World Music Press.
*Bolivia Manta* (Tinkuna). A.S.P.I.C. X55511.

# ZANE NIL ABEDEEN

Palestine

Ah   ya   Zane,        Ah   ya   Zane,        Ah   ya

Zane___ nil___ A - be - deen:   Ya   ward,   Ya___

ward___ im - fet - tah,   bay - nil - be - sa - teen.

*Zane from Abedeen,*
*You are my best friend.*

# ZANE NIL ABEDEEN (DRONE)

## The Tune

"Zane Nil Abedeen" is an Arabic-language song known in various regions of the Middle East, including Palestine, about a best friend named "Zane" (a man's name) from Abedeen.

## The Music Culture

The music of Palestine consists of rich variety of songs and dances. There is a repertory of sung verse, much of it freely improvised in stanzas of four or eight lines with a metrical syllabic refrain. There are also open-air responsorial songs, and songs for wedding processions. Dances include the *dabka* or chain dance, and a dance for men with swords who advance towards a woman soloist. A number of instruments are found in Palestine, including a single-reed clarinet with double pipes called the *mijwiz*, a reed flute with six holes known as the *shabbaba,* and a metal goblet drum, the *darbukka*. Yet songs sung a cappella, joined only by hand clapping, are common at school, at play, and in the home. As is the case throughout the Middle East, melodies are based upon modes that are constructed of pitches of various sizes, including 1/2, 3/4, whole, and 1 1/2 tones. "Zane Nil Abedeen" is a melody in Hijaz mode.

## The Experiences

- Sing the Hijaz modal scale—D–E♭–F♯–G–A–B♭–C♯–D—repeatedly, with attention to the augmented seconds between the second and third and between the sixth and seventh pitches. Use neutral syllables, numbers, or solfège as in a "la"-based minor.

- Sing the melody on a neutral syllable such as "yah," and on solfège syllables (beginning on "fa") or scale numbers (beginning on "4").

- Hum the melody, clapping in between the phrases.

- Sing the lyrics, pronouncing "Zane" as "zahn." The song is translated as "Zane from Abedeen, You are my best friend."

- Play the drone pitches on piano, sustaining them with pedal through four beats.

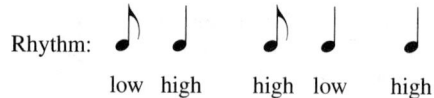

Rhythm:　　　low　high　　high　low　　high

- Add an ostinato rhythm on drum, such as a goblet drum or hand drum, finding lower and higher pitches to play:

## Recommended Listening

*Folk Music of Palestine.* Folkways FW 04408.

*Palestine Lives!: Songs from the Struggle of the People of Palestine.* Paredon Records PAR 01022.

## ZUI ZUI ZUKKOROBASHI

Japan

Zu - i  zu - i  zuk - ko - ro - ba - shi  go - ma  mi - so  zui!  Cha - tsu - bo  ni  o - wa - re - te

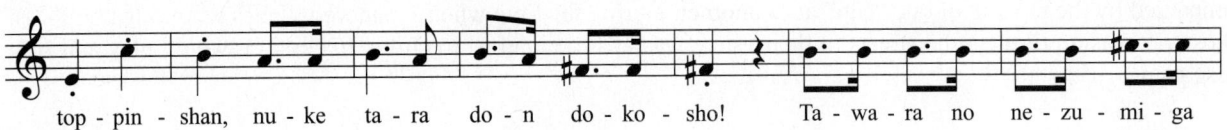

top - pin - shan,  nu - ke  ta - ra  do - n  do - ko - sho!  Ta - wa - ra  no  ne - zu - mi - ga

ko - me  kut - te  chu!  chu,____ chu,____ chu!  Ot - to - san  ga  yo - n - de - mo,

ok - ka - san  ga  yo - n - de - mo  i - ki - ik - ko  na ____ shi  yo.

I - do - no  ma - wa - ri - de  ot - cha  wa - n  ka - i - ta - no  da ____ re?

*Soy bean paste,*

*Take tea leaves in a chatsubo bowl,*

*When the entourage comes through,*

*Run into the house, shut the door and play inside.*

*When the entourage passes, let's go outside again.*

*The mice in the rice case are eating rice,*

*Squeaking "chu, chu, chu!"*

*Mother calls, father calls, but of course we're not going home!*

*Who broke the rice bowl around the well?*

Traditional, Japan, as sung by Mayumi Adachi. From Campbell, P. S., McCullough-Brabson, E., Tucker, J. C. (1994). *Roots & Branches: A Legacy of Multicultural Music for Children*. Danbury, CT: World Music Press. Courtesy World Music Press.

## The Tune

A Japanese children's singing game "Zui Zui Zukkorobashi" references soy beans, tea leaves, rice bowls, and parades of the lord of the village that passed through the streets centuries ago, while the children played.

## The Music Culture

Children of Japan sing songs of three types: *warabe-uta*, traditional singing games; *shōka*, songs for educational use; and *dōyō*, songs for children composed by professional musicians. Of these, *warabe-uta* are songs orally passed from child to child, some of them many generations old. There are ten classifications of these songs, including those for counting-out, teasing, picture-drawing, skipping rope, hand-clapping, and play with bean bags, ball-bouncing, and rock-scissors-paper hand games. Most *warabe-uta* melodies are simple in structure, usually within the range of a sixth, in duple meter, and with lyrics that are syllabic. Unlike the songs of school or those composed for children, the singing games tend to be based on one or two tetrachords, are often pentatonic (or tetra- or tri-tonic) and not in Western major or minor modes, and are not harmonized. "Zui Zui Zukkorobashi" is a counting game for children's amusement, where their hands are shaped into loose fists to resemble cups, and counting is accompanied by the tapping of one "cup" after another. During the time when Japanese villages were ruled by lords, whose procession through the streets to their estate was of little interest to children, children would play and sing these games.

### The Experiences

- Sing the melody on a neutral syllable such as "zoo," and on solfège syllables (beginning on "la") or scale numbers (beginning on "6").

- Sing the lyrics, noting the following pronounciations: an *n* alone sounds like "innnn," while *a* = "ah," *e* = "ay," *i* = "ee," *o* = "oh," and *u* = "oo."

- Play the singing game in small circles of three, four or five people. Form hands into loose fists in the shape of cups. A counter is designated to tap on one fist per pulse while the group sings. On the last pulse, the person last tapped must tell a joke, sing a song, or take that hand out of the game. The game winner is the last person with an untapped hand.

- Explore the accompaniment of the melody with two or three pitches from the melody, clustering together on the piano. Note that for measures 1–11, there is one pitch-set (A, B, C, E, and changeable F and F♯), and for measure 12 and onward there is another pitch set (A, B, and changeable C and C♯).

### Recommended Listening

+*Roots and Branches* (Campbell/McCullough-Brabson/Tucker). Danbury, CT: World Music Press.
*Traditional Folk Songs of Japan.* Folkways FW 04534.

# ZUM GALI GALI

Israel

1. *Pioneers work hard on the land;*

   *Men and women work hand in hand.*

2. *As they labor all day long,*

   *They lift their voice in song.*

From *Music in Childhood: From Preschool Through the Elementary Grade* with Audio CD 3rd edition by CAMPBELL/SCOTT-KASSNER, 2006. Reprinted with permission of Wadsworth, a Division of Thompson Learning: www. Thomsonrights.com.  Fax 800-730-2215.

## The Tune

"Zum Gali Gali" is a song of the making of Israel, when people worked together to create cities and towns in the desert where no urban settlements had previously existed.

## The Music Culture

The modern nation of Israel arose as a result of the return of Jews from Europe, North Africa, Arab countries, and the Americas. The great Diaspora that had sent them scattering and settling in communities for centuries in other parts of the world was reverting itself in the twentieth century, when land was provided and the gates were opened for the Jewish people to construct a nation. The Ashkenazi people traveled to Israel from Europe and the Americas, and the Sephardic peoples arrived from Greece, North Africa, Spain, and Portugal. Likewise, the Jews migrated to Israel from Syria, Lebanon, Iraq, and other Arab countries. They converged upon the desert land as pioneers, working to build homes, hospitals, schools, factories, and office buildings. (Some formed autonomous, self-sufficient communities called *kibbutzim* (singular: *kibbutz*) of like-minded people who lived, worked, and shared specific goals and values.) Israelis today are quick to acknowledge their pioneers, and to revere them for the nation they established.

### The Experiences

- Sing the melody on a neutral syllable such as "zoo," and on solfège syllables (beginning on "la") and scale numbers (beginning on "6").
- Sing the lyrics, articulating clearly on the quick-moving words. For singing Hebrew, follow this pronunciation guide: "hek-ah-lootz leh mahn ah-voh-dah" and "hek-ah-lootz leh mahn hahb-too-lah." Note that the words of a first two-measure phrase are placed in reverse order from the second two-measure phrase.

- Play the chords on guitar, piano, or other harmony instrument, producing chords (or partial chords, or pitches of broken chords) in an eighth note rhythm. For example,

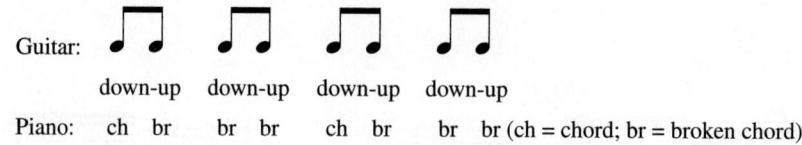

Guitar:

       down-up   down-up   down-up   down-up

Piano:   ch  br      br  br     ch  br     br  br (ch = chord; br = broken chord)

- Sing the verse and refrain together, as partner melodies, to create harmony.

## Recommended Listening

+*Songs of Work and Play*. Folkways FW 77870.

*Israeli Children's Songs*. Folkways FW 07226.

## ZUNI SUNRISE CALL

Zuni

Nah  ay  loh ah  noh ay  loh ah,  Wah  ah  day  oh  nah  wee

yahn nah lay  Ah____ day oh  na  wee  yahn na lay  Nah yah nah ah wee  oh,____

mee tehn lah lay,  nah yah nah ah wee  oh, ____ mee tehn lah lay.

## The Tune

Whether sung or played on a pan-Indian wooden flute, the melody of "Zuni Sunrise," recorded by Chester Mahooty and the American Indian Dance Theater, evokes the peace and radiant beauty of a New Mexican sunrise.

## The Music Culture

Continuing today is the traditional Native American practice of performing sunrise songs at dawn in thanksgiving for the coming of another day. The new sun is considered by many tribal groups to be sacred, and a vessel of powerful forces that directs life itself. The Hopi present their newborn children to the sun at dawn. The Navajo believe that sunrise is the most sacred time of day, when the spirits are alive and energized, and able to help those who are awake. For the Zuni, sunrise is a fresh and peaceful time to quietly reflect upon and give respect to the earth, animals, and people. The vocables transliterated in "Zuni Sunrise" have no literal meaning, and are traditionally thought to stem from a time when people and animals spoke to one another in an ancient language that is now lost. The melody of this song and other sunrise songs are played on Native American flutes of cane and wood, particularly the red cedar which has a spiritual significance. R. Carlos Nakai, one of the most recorded and most revered Native American musicians, is credited with reintroducing the cedar flute. He plays his own sunrise songs and other works of his creation.

### The Experiences

- Tap, pat, or clap the pulse (quarter notes), or subdivision of the pulse (eight notes), while silently reading the melodic notation.
- Sing the melody on a neutral syllable such as "loh," and on solfège syllables (beginning on "mi") or scale numbers (beginning on "3").
- Sing the melody on the vocables, as noted.

- Play the melody on flute, recorder, or other melody instrument.
- Play a rattle accompaniment, swirling them without accent, continuously.

## Recommended Listening

+*Stroutsos: The Native Heart.* Makoche Records MM0142
*Canyon Trilogy by Carlos Nakai.* Canyon Records-610
*A Native American Odyssey.* Putumayo PUTU 144-2.

# Glossary

**Agogo bells** Iron double bells played in West Africa (for example, Ghana); these bells play unchanging constant time lines over drums.

**Alap** An introductory non-metric section in North Indian Hindustani music that establishes the tonal structure of a *raga* prior to the entrance of *tabla* (drums), meter, and fixed and improvised sections.

**Arabesk** A style of Turkish urban popular music that originated in the 1970s in the recording studios of Istanbul. It is Arab-influenced and is stylistically connected with music of the Egyptian cinema.

**Arca** Follower to the leading pan-pipe (*ira*) in the interlocking parts of Andean music in Peru, Bolivia, and Ecuador.

**Arpa** Spanish (and Italian) term for harp.

**Ashik** In Turkey, a folk poet.

**Asoto** A large (ten feet high) Haitian drum.

**Autoharp** A box-zither with 21 (or up to 49) strings. It has been used in the United States as a folk and bluegrass instrument.

**Axatse** A gourd with an external net of beads used to support and amplify the rhythm of the *gankogui*, the bell which provides the essential rhythmic pattern of a West African drum ensemble.

**Bachata** A form of slow and romantic folk music whose prominent sound is the Latin American-style guitar, originating from the Dominican Republic. It is closely related to the *bolero* and has been influenced by the *merengue*.

**Bajo sexto** Twelve-stringed bass guitar used in Mexican music, primarily in norteño music of northeastern Mexico and in "Tex-Mex" and "conjunto" music of south Texas.

**Balafon** A pentatonic or heptatonic xylophone of West Africa.

**Balalaika** A long-necked lute with triangular body and three strings, played first by Russian peasants and then elevated to artistic stature.

**Ballad** A short popular song that may contain a narrative element. It is known throughout Europe since the late Middle Ages, combining narrative, dramatic dialogue, and lyrical passages in stanzaic form sung to a rounded tune, and often includes a recurrent refrain.

**Banda** A brass-based form of traditional Mexican music.

**Bangzi** A pair of wooden clappers used typically in Chinese folk music and opera.

**Basso continuo** An instrumental bass line which runs throughout a piece, over which the player improvises ("realizes") a chordal accompaniment. It is used in almost all genres of music in the European Baroque Era.

**Bata drums** A family of three double-headed tapered cylinders, with a slight hourglass shape originating from the Yoruba people in western Nigeria. With varying sizes that produce differences in pitch, they are named according to size: *iyá*, the larger drum, considered the mother; *itótele*, the medium-size drum, and *okónkolo*, the smaller or baby drum. They are carved out of solid wood, not built from staves.

**Bateria** A Brazilian musical group, the percussion band of a Samba School. Outside Brazil, the term "bateria" is also sometimes used loosely to mean any musical ensemble that plays samba.

**Berimbau** A single-string percussion instrument, a musical bow, from Brazil.

**Bluegrass** A form of American roots music with its own roots in the English, Irish, and Scottish traditional music, with influences also of rural African-American, jazz, and blues. The name of the genre is derived from the Blue Grass Boys, the name of Bill Monroe's band. Like jazz, bluegrass is played with each melody instrument switching off, playing improvised solos in turn while the others revert to backing; this is in contrast to old-time music, in which all instruments play the melody together (or one instrument carries the lead throughout while the others provide accompaniment.)

**Blues** A secular African-American vocal genre, often in 12-bar structure, utilizing AAB form, and accompanied by acoustic or electric guitar, or piano.

**Bodhran** An Irish frame drum ranging in anywhere from 10" to 26" in diameter, with most drums measuring from 14" to 18."

**Bolero** A 3/4 dance that originated in Spain in the late eighteenth century.

**Bomba** One of Puerto Rico's most famous musical styles. Although there is some controversy surrounding its origin, most agree that it is a largely African music. The rhythm and beat are played by a set of hand drums and a maraca. Dance is an integral part of the music: the dancers move their bodies to every beat of the drum, making bomba a very wild and rich dance.

**Bongo** Two small drums made of wood, metal, or composite materials, attached by a thick piece of wood. The history of *bongo* drumming can be traced to Cuban music styles and are heavily used in genres like Latin jazz, *salsa*, *bachata*, *merengue*, *son*, and *mambo*.

**Bongocero** In Cuba and throughout the Caribbean, a *bongo* player.

**Bossa nova** A style of Brazilian music created by João Gilberto and first introduced in Brazil by Gilberto's recording of "Chega de Saudade" in 1958, a song written by Antonio Carlos Jobim, first released as a single, and shortly thereafter as the album by Gilberto, bearing the same title as the song (1959).

**Bouzoúki** A stringed instrument with a pear-shaped body and a very long neck used in modern Greek music and Balkan folk music. The *bouzoúki* is a member of the "long neck lute" family and is similar to a mandola. The front of the body is flat and is usually heavily inlaid with mother-of-pearl. The instrument is played with a plectrum and has a sharp metallic sound.

**Cabasa** A gourd with an external net of beads used in West African percussion ensemble.

**Ca-khee** A three-stringed crocodile Thai zither.

**Caixa** Snare drums used typically in *salsa*.

**Cajones** A wooden box drum played by slapping the front face with the hands. A musical instrument used both in Cuba and in coastal Peru.

**Call-and-response** A succession of two distinct phrases usually played by different musicians, where the second phrase is heard as a direct commentary on, in response, to the first. A technique used in choral singing of many peoples, especially in African and African-American cultures.

**Calypso** A style of Afro-Caribbean music which originated in the British and French colonial islands of the Caribbean around the start of the twentieth century.

**Cancion** A genre of Latin American music. A song characterized by romantic sentimentality and pathos divided nearly always in long stanzas with the same number of verses.

**Cancion ranchera** A song in triple waltz meter or in slow and fast tempo versions of duple meter; a genre of the traditional music of Mexico.

**Canon** Imitation of a melody by one or more voices at fixed intervals of pitch and time.

**Cantus firmus** A term, associated particularly with European medieval and Renaissance music, that designates a pre-existing melody used as the basis of a new polyphonic composition. The melody may be taken from plainchant or monophonic secular music, or from one voice of a sacred or secular polyphonic work, or it may be freely invented. Cantus firmus com-

position is now understood to encompass a wide range of rhythmic and melodic treatments of an antecedent tune within a new polyphonic texture.

**Capoeira** Martial art/dance of Brazil.

**Catch** From the late sixteenth century through the nineteenth century, a kind of English round for three unaccompanied male voices.

**Changgo** Korean hour-glass drum.

**Charango** A guitar-like instrument made from the hard-shelled body of an armadillo, especially prominent in Andean tradition of Bolivia and Peru.

**Chace (or Chase)** A finite canon in three parts that was popular in the fourteenth century.

**Charleo** "Buzzing" sound of marimbas in Central America.

**Chaya** A traditional dance song of Argentina.

**Chimurenga** A style of music associated with Thomas Mapfumo of Zimbabwe, who mixed traditional Shona and Western styles in songs that achieved wide popularity among the protest movement against white minority rule.

**Ching** Thick brass hand cymbals used in traditional Thai music ensembles.

**Chocallo** A metal shaker, usually consisting of one or more tubes of tin or aluminum, but sometimes in the shape of a maraca, and containing beads or beans. The *ganzá* (chocallo), which has a sound resembling that of a maraca, is an important instrument in Brazilian music, especially *samba*, and is often used in Latin jazz.

**Chula** Call-and-response song used in capoeira (an Afro-Brazilian martial art form) to give thanks to God and one's teachers.

**Ch'usok** Korean mid-autumn festival at which song and dance are prominent.

**Claves** A percussion instrument (idiophone), consisting of a pair of short, thick dowels. Normally they are made of wood but nowadays they are also made of fiberglass or plastics due to the longer durability

of these materials. It is commonly used to play repeating rhythmic figures in Afro-Cuban music such as the *son* and *salsa*.

**Columbia** A style of *rumba* in Afro-Cuban culture that is fast, aggressive, and competitive, generally danced by men only, occasionally mimicking combat or dancing with knives.

**Conga** A tall, narrow, single-headed Cuban drum of African origin, probably derived from the Congolese *makuta* drums; a common drum throughout the Caribbean and in Latin American jazz and dance music.

**Conguero** In Cuba and throughout the Caribbean, a *conga* player.

**Coro** Spanish (and Italian) term for chorus.

**Corrido** Mexican-American narrative ballad.

**Corridos** Call-and-response songs that are sung while *capoeira* (Afro-Brazilian martial art form) is being played.

**Cowboy songs** A type of song describing cowboys and their life. Such songs began to appear in popular newspapers, as broadsides, in magazines (such as stockmen's journals), and in songbooks in the late nineteenth century; they became increasingly romanticized when they were taken over by Tin Pan Alley songwriters (such as Billy Hill) and by Hollywood composers. They are generally written in ballad style, but are melodically and structurally indebted to traditional popular, folk, and religious songs.

**Cuarteto** A musical genre born in Córdoba, Argentina. It is almost always upbeat; its rhythm is similar to that of Dominican *merengue*.

**Cuatro** A small four-stringed plucked lute similar to the Spanish *vihuela*.

**Cui'ca** Friction drum used in Brazil primarily in Rio de Janeiro-style Carnaval *samba*.

**Cumbia** Originally a Colombian folk dance and dance music and is Colombia's representative national dance and music along with *vallenato*. *Cumbia* is popular, widely known in the Latin music mainstream (except Brazil), South America, as well as Central America and Mexico, with lots of regional variations and tendencies. The traditional instruments of *cumbia* were mainly percussion; different types of drums, claves, and a *guiro,* and woodwinds; including flutes. Modern *cumbia* includes instrumental mixing; guitars, accordions, bass guitar, modern flutes, and modern deep-toned drums and other percussion. The basic rhythm structure is 4/4.

**Dabka**  Chain dance common in Palestinian, Lebanese, Syrian, and Jordanian villages and cities.

**Daff (defi, deff, duff)**  Round single-headed frame drum originally Persian or Kurdish, used in Sufi music.

**Dan bao**  A Vietnamese one-stringed zither.

**Dan tranh**  A plucked zither of Vietnam; the national instrument of Vietnam .

**Daoúki**  Deep-toned drum.

**Daoúli**  Large cylindrical double-skin drum found in Greece. It provides rhythmic accompaniment to double-reed wind instruments and may also accompany the bagpipes.

**Darbukka**  Metal goblet drum of Arabic origins commonly associated with Middle Eastern music, often as the lead percussion voice.

**Dastgah**  Mode or melody type used in Persian music.

**Décima**  A verse form, commonly sung, comprising ten lines (rhyme scheme *abbaaccddc*), which develops a theme introduced by a quatrain (rhymed *abab*). Textual material may be set or improvised, religious or secular. In Venezuela *décimas* are sung in parallel thirds and accompanied by the *cuatro* (small four-stringed guitar) in primary triad harmony to either *merengue* or *joropo* rhythms. The *décima* is common throughout Latin America and is particularly characteristic of Argentine and Chilean *payas* (*payadas*), *tonos* and *estilos*.

**Degung**  A type of gamelan found in Sunda, the mountainous region of west Java. It is tuned to a pentatonic scale, and features gongs and chimes (metallophones).

**Dholak**  Double-headed cylindrical or barrel drums of South Asia.

**Dhrupad**  A type of vocal composition in North Indian art music, and the style in which such compositions are performed. The composition has two or four rhymed lines of verse, in Hindi, usually on religious (Hindu or Islamic) or philosophical themes.

**Di-tse (or di)**  Chinese transverse flute.

**Doyo**  Songs composed for Japanese children by professional musicians.

**Dutar**  Long-necked two-stringed lute found in Central Asia.

**Er-hu**  A two-stringed Chinese fiddle used as a solo instrument as well as in small ensembles and large orchestras.

**Fandango**  A Spanish couple-dance in triple meter and lively tempo, accompanied by a guitar and castanets or *palmas* (hand clapping); a style of flamenco music and dance.

**Flamenco**  The generic term applied to a particular body of *cante* (song), *baile* (dance), and *toque* (solo guitar music), mostly emanating from Andalusia in southern Spain.

**Fugue**  A form of imitative counterpoint, in which the theme is stated successively in all voices of the polyphonic texture.

**Fuguing tune**  An Anglo-American psalm tune or hymn tune, designed for strophic repetition, which contains one or more groups of contrapuntal entries involving textual overlap.

**Gaida (or Gajda)**  A bagpipe from the Balkans in southeastern Europe, especially Bulgaria and the Republic of Macedonia.

**Gamel**  Haitian water drum.

**Gamelan**  Musical ensemble of Indonesian origin typically featuring a variety of instruments such as metallophones, xylophones, drums, and gongs; bamboo flutes, bowed and plucked strings; and vocalists may also be included.

**Griot**  A West African poet, praise singer, and wandering musician,

considered a repository of oral tradition.

**Guaracha**  A musical form that originated in Spain, and evolved largely in Cuba. Traditionally an early form of peasant street music with satirical lyric content somewhat in the *son* rhythm style. In Cuba it is now used as a loose term for a general, medium-tempo *son montuno* or a little brighter-style tune or groove. Guaracha derived from the fusion of a vast cloud of rhythms during the mid-1950s in Cuba. It started as a descarga-like music (in fact, called *descarga*) provided by various bands.

**Guiro**  A notched scraper commonly used in Latin American music.

**Guitarrón**  A large, deep-bodied Mexican bass guitar used in *mariachi* bands.

**Gusle**  A single-stringed bowed lute of southeastern Europe, used to accompany epic songs.

**Haka**  A Māori posture dance accompanied by chanted vocals.

**Halaam**  Plucked lute of sub-Saharian Africa; ancestor of the African American banjo.

**Halk muzigi**  Turkey's folk music.

**Hapa haole (half- foreign)**  Songs about Hawaii by Hawaiian composers using English-language lyrics.

**Harmonium**  Small reed organ invented in Paris in 1842. It is now commonly used as a drone instrument in many genres of Indian music.

**Hocket**  The alternating back-and-forth sharing of the melodic pitches by two voices or instruments (or group of instruments). In Western classical music, hocket was used primarily in vocal music of the thirteenth and early fourteenth centuries. The term is also used in describing music of the Indonesian *gamelan*, Andean panpipes, and many African cultures.

**Hora**  A popular circle dance in Israel.

**Hosho**  A Zimbabwean gourd rattle used to accompany Shona music.

**Hsiao**  Chinese end-blown vertical bamboo flute.

**Huapanguera** A large Mexican guitar with eight strings and eight to ten frets.

**Hula** Generic name for Hawaiian dance, sometimes applied loosely to other dances of the Pacific Islands.

**Imzad** A one-string fiddle used by the Tuaregs who live in Algeria, Tunisia, Libya, Mali, Niger, and Burkina Faso.

**Ira** Leading panpipe in Andean music.

**Jali** Professional musician of the Mandinka people of West Africa.

**Jaliyaa** Predominant musical genre of the *jali*.

**Jarana** A small guitar-shaped fretted stringed instrument from the Veracruz region of Mexico.

**Jarocho** Traditional music style from the Veracruz region in Mexico, typically played by an ensemble consisting of a *harp*, a *jarana*, and a *requinto jarocho*.

**Jhaptal** A ten-beat rhythmic cycle in north Indian music.

**Juapango** A term for peasant or rural Mexican music that is known for its plucked *rasgueado* technique on the instruments of the guitar family.

**Jubilee** A term synonymous with spirituals, more commonly used in the nineteenth century.

**Kanari** Haitian drum made from a clay pot.

**Kankani** A language that is spoken in the Western region of India, south of Bombay and along the coast of the Bay of Bengal.

**Kantele** A plucked zither played throughout the eastern Baltic Sea region expecially Finland.

**Kappelmeister** German term for director of music; a master, leader, or director of a band, or musician in charge of a chapel.

**Kaval** An end-blown flute traditionally played throughout Azerbaijan, Turkey, Bulgaria, Republic of Macedonia, Kosovo / Albania (Kavall), northern Greece (Kavali or Dzhamara), southern Romania (Caval), Armenia (Blur) and Kurdish (Blul).

**Khaen** Free-reed bamboo mouth organ of Laos and northeast Thailand.

**Khali** Empty. In North Indian music, it implies a wave of the hand.

**Khluoy** An end-blown flute of Thailand.

**Khong wong** Circle of gongs used in the classical music of Thailand.

**Khrüng saai** Thai court music featuring flutes, strings and percussion.

**Khyal** Modern genre of classical singing in North India; its name comes from an Arabic word meaning "imagination."

**Klezmer** Musical genre traced to fifteenth-century Jewish music, now dance music for weddings and celebrations that feature Yiddish song texts, clarinet and violin.

**Kolo** Traditional circle dance from Croatia.

**Konting (nkoni)** A West African skin-faced, slender oval lute with five strings.

**Kora** A 21-stringed harp-lute used extensively by Mandingo peoples in West Africa.

**Korng tauch** High-pitched embossed gong used in the Cambodian *pinpeat* ensemble.

**Korng thomm** Low-pitched embossed gong used in the Cambodian *pinpeat* ensemble.

**Koto** A traditional stringed musical instrument from Japan resembling a zither.

**Krajappi** Variation of the *ca-khee* found in the Philippines.

**Kulintang** Name of a specific indigenous musical instrument of the Philippines (usually, a set of eight tuned, graduated gongs laid on a horizontal rack); however, *kulintang* also refers to the entire ensemble of percussion instruments which are typically played with the *kulintang* instrument of the Philippines (for example, in the Maguindanao culture, the *agung*, *dabakan*, *gandingan*, and *babendil*). *Kulintang* also refers to the music performed by the ensemble musicians.

**Laba** Chinese festival celebrated on the eighth day of the last lunar month, referring to the traditional start of celebrations for the Chinese New Year. "La" in Chinese means the twelfth lunar month and "ba" means eight.

**Lam sing** An upbeat, post-1989 Laos repartee genre that blends traditional styles and instruments with electrified ones and a drum kit.

**Laoúto** Plucked lute of traditional Greek ensembles.

**Luk thung** Isan-derived country music of Northeast Thailand.

**Luogu** Music of parades, street festivals, and religious rituals of Chinese origins consisting of drums, cymbals, a variety of gongs, and various other percussion instruments.

**Mahoori (or Mahori)** Thai court music.

**Makam (or Maqam)** In the Middle East, in Turkey, melodic modes upon which improvisation is based.

**Mambo** A Cuban musical form and dance style.

**Mariachi** A type of musical group, originally from Mexico. Usually a mariachi group consists of at least two violins, two trumpets, one Spanish guitar, one *vihuela* (a high-pitched, five-stringed guitar) and one *guitarrón* (a small-scaled acoustic bass), but sometimes featuring more than twenty musicians.

**Marimba** A wooden xylophone with resonators under each bar.

**Mbira** Thumb piano classified as part of the lamellaphone family found throughout many regions in sub-Saharan Africa and in Latin America.

**Mbube** A form of South African vocal music, made famous by the South African group Ladysmith Black Mambazo. The word *mbube* means "lion" in Zulu [1]. Traditionally performed a cappella, the style is sung in a powerful and loud way.

**Mele** Chant of Polynesian and Hawaiian origins.

**Merecumbe** Rhythm fusing the *cumbia* and the Columbian *merengue*.

**Merengue** Lively, joyful music and dance that comes from the Dominican Republic.

**Mestizos** A term of Spanish origin used to designate the people of mixed European and indigenous non-European ancestry.

**Mi gyaung**  Variation of the *ca-khee* found in Burma.

**Mijwiz**  Single-reed clarinet with double pipes mainly found in Syria, western Iraq, Lebanon, northern Israel, and Jordan.

**Minyo**  Japanese or Korean folk songs.

**Mohori**  Court ensemble of Cambodia.

**Molam (mawlum)**  Laos vocal repartee style sung by male and female singers.

**Montuno**  In salsa, the repeated part of the song, like a chorus/refrain in popular music, in which the soloist and choir perform in a call-and-response style.

**Musica tropical**  Synonymous with *salsa* music which refers to a diverse and predominantly Caribbean and Latin genre that is popular across Latin America and among Latinos abroad.

**Narrative**  A long song that tells a story; it may or may not be accompanied.

**Nigun**  A Hebrew term meaning "humming tune." Usually, the term refers to religious songs and tunes that are sung by groups.

**Nong-ak**  Farmer's music belonging to the Korean folk tradition.

**Noteña**  A genre of Mexican music with the accordion and the *bajo sexto* as the most characteristic instruments.

**Ngoma**  A common term (with many variants) used generically for many kinds of drum among the numerous Bantu-speaking peoples of central, eastern-central, and southern Africa. Equally widespread is its meaning of performance and participatory events that embrace music, dance, and dramatic expression.

**Nong-ak**  In Korea, music of rural peasants that include farmers' percussion music, work songs, dance music, and songs of celebration.

**Nykelharpa**  Keyed fiddle of Scandinavian origins used traditionally in Sweden.

**Old-time music**  A form of North American folk music, with roots in the folk music of many countries,

most notably: England, Scotland, Ireland, and the African continent. This musical form developed along with various North American folk dances, such as square dance. The genre also encompasses ballads and other types of folk songs. It is played on acoustic instruments, generally centering on a combination of fiddle and banjo.

**Opera buffa**  Comic opera which arose in Italy and gained popularity in the eighteenth century.

**Ozan**  Music of folk poets of the Anatolia region of Turkey.

**Pahu**  A sharkskin drum of the native Hawaiian people.

**Pandeiro**  Small hand frame drum used in a number of Brazilian music forms, such as *samba*, *choro*, and *capoeira*.

**P'ansori**  Korean stylized dramatic narrative form for solo voice and drum.

**Patois**  A language considered as nonstandard.

**Pin**  Four-stringed lute of Laos and Lao people in Thailand.

**Pipa**  Pear-shaped plucked lute of China and Korea.

**Pisik**  Traditional Inuit song form from Alaska and northern Canada.

**Piupiu**  Maori skirts traditionally made from long fibrous leaves that are scraped, buried in a muddy marsh so as to dye them dark brown, and then washed and curled into slender tubes.

**Poi**  Maori word for ball, the action of juggling with balls on ropes, held in the hands and swung in various circular patterns.

**Polska**  A Scandinavian folk dance performed in couples or group, often in 3/4 meter.

**Polyphony**  A term used to designate various important categories in music: namely, music in more than one part, music in many parts, and the style in which all or several of the musical parts move to some extent independently.

**Powwow**  A gathering of North American indigenous people for social purposes, and to sing, dance, and drum.

**Protest song**  A song intended to protest perceived problems in society

such as injustice, racial discrimination, war, globalization, inflation, social inequalities. Protest songs are generally associated with folk music, but in recent times they have come from all genres of music. Such songs become popular during times of social disruption and among social groups.

**Qawwali**  The devotional music of the Sufis of Pakistan and northern India.

**Quan ho**  A competition song that is particular to the northern province of Ha Bac near Hanoi, Vietnam.

**Quena**  Traditional cane flute of the Andes.

**Quinto**  Conga drums of Cuba, typically about 11" across.

**Rabab (or Rebab)**  Bowed-string instrument originating in eastern Persia, now Afghanistan.

**Raga**  Melodic modes used in Indian classical music.

**Rai**  Music genre that mixes together Algerian local traditions with the influences of rock, soul, funk, and *reggae*.

**Ramwong**  A Thai popular partner dance that moves around a large circle with a shuffling step and graceful upturned hands and fingers.

**Ranaat**  Thai wooden xylophone of 16 or 21 keys; see *roneat*.

**Ranchera**  Songs literally once sung on a Mexican ranch, typically in the style of a waltz, polka or bolero.

**Rasgueado**  A technical strum in flamenco guitar that uses the back of the fingernails on the right hand in sequence to give the impression of a very rapid strum.

**Reco-reco**  A Brazilian wooden scraper.

**Reel**  A traditional Scottish folk dance.

**Reggae**  A music genre developed in Jamaica. Reggae may be used in a broad sense to refer to most types of Jamaican music, including *ska*, *rocksteady*, and *dub*. The term is generally used to distinguish a particular style that originated in the late 1960s. Reggae is founded upon a rhythm style which is characterized by regular chops on the backbeat, known as the "skank," played by a rhythm guitarist, and a bass drum hitting on the third beat of each measure, known as "one drop." Characteristically, this beat is slower than in *reggae's* precursors, *ska* and *rocksteady*.

**Reggaeton** A form of dance music which became popular with Latin American (Latino) youth during the early 1990s and spread to North American, European, Asian, and Australian audiences during the first few years of the twenty-first century. *Reggaeton* blends Jamaican music influences of reggae and dancehall with those of Latin America, such as *bomba* and *plena*, as well as that of hip hop. The music is also combined with rapping (generally) in Spanish.

**Ritmo** A concept of polyrhythmic organization that refrers to the timing, volume, and timbre of the instruments that play it.

**Rocksteady** Name given to a style of music popular in Jamaica between 1966 and 1968. The term comes from a dance style which Alton Ellis named in his recording "Rock Steady." The rocksteady dance was a more relaxed affair than the earlier, more frantic *ska* moves.

**Romance** Signifying a ballad in fifteenth century Spain and Italy.

**Rondador** Panpipes in Ecuador.

**Rondalla** Ensemble of the Philippines consisting of plucked string instruments with percussion. The size of a *rondalla* can vary: while a small ensemble might feature eight or so instruments a large ensemble can comprise more than thirty. The common *rondalla* consists of four *bandurria* (a 14-stringed lute with a flat back), *laúd* (lute), *octavina* (small guitar) one 5- or 6-string *gitara* and a 4-stringed bass guitar. Smaller ensembles might include one of each instrument and omit the *octavina* and *laúd*, while larger ensembles increase the numbers of instruments included rather than the types.

**Roneat** Khmer wooden xylophone of 16 or 21 keys in Cambodia; see *ranaat*.

**Rota** A term used in thirteenth century England for a round or canon, a form in which voices enter successively with the same melody.

**Round** A song consisting of a single-line melody constructed so that it forms its own harmony when sung as a canon.

**Rumba** A family of music rhythms and a dance style that originated in Africa and traveled via the slave trade to Cuba and the New World.

**Salidor** Synonymous with Cuban tumbadora, a *conga* drum (see *tumbadora*).

**Salsa** A diverse and predominantly Caribbean and Latin genre that is popular across Latin America and among Latinos abroad. *Salsa* incorporates multiple styles and variations; the term can be used to describe most any form of popular Cuban-derived genre, such as *chachachá* and *mambo*. Most specifically, however, *salsa* refers to a particular style developed by the 1960s and '70s Cuban and Puerto Rican immigrants to the New York City area, and stylistic descendants like 1980s *salsa romantica*. The style is now practiced throughout Latin America, and abroad; in some countries it may be referred to as *música tropical*.

**Samba** One of the most popular forms of music in Brazil. It is widely viewed as Brazil's national musical style. The name *samba* most probably comes from the Angolan *semba* (*mesemba*), a type of ritual music.

**Samulnori (or Samul Nori)** Traditional percussion music of Korea. The word "samul" means four objects, and "nori" means play. Hence Samulnori is performed with four instruments: the *kkwaenggwari* (a small gong), the *jing* (a larger gong), the *janggu* (an hourglass-shaped drum), and the *buk* (a frame drum similar to the bass drum).

**Sarangi** Short-necked fiddle of South Asia, found both in the art music of North India and Pakistan and, in related forms, in traditional musics, especially those of Rajasthan and the Northwestern India.

**Sarod** Double-chested plucked lute, without frets, of northern India, rivaling the sitar in its function as one of the greatest lutes of the region.

**Saz** Long-necked lute found in Turkey, southeastern Europe and neighboring areas including northern Syria and northern Iran.

**Sea shanty (or chantey)** Shipboard working songs of the United Kingdom and North America. Shanties flourished from at least the fifteenth century through the days of steamships in the first half of the twentieth century. Most surviving shanties date from the nineteenth and (less commonly) eighteenth centuries.

**Setar (or Sehtar)** A four-stringed lute used in classical Iranian music.

**Shabbaba** A obliquely held, end-blown flute with six or seven finger-holes used in Iraq, Syria, Jordan, and by Palestinians.

**Shakuhachi** A Japanese end-blown flute.

**Shamisen** A Japanese three-stringed musical instrument played with a plectrum.

**Sheng** Mouth organ of the Han Chinese.

**Shoka** Japanese songs for educational use (especially in primary schools).

**Siku** Andean panpipes (see *arca* and *ira*).

**Sikuris** Panpipe players.

**Sitar** Large, fretted long-necked lute. It is a prominent instrument of the classical music of India and the northern and central regions of South Asia.

**Ska** A form of Jamaican music combining elements of traditional calypso with an American jazz and rhythm and blues sound. Originating in Jamaica, possibly in the 1950s, it was a precursor to *rocksteady* and later *reggae*.

**Son** A style of music that became popular in the second half of the nineteenth century in the eastern province of Oriente, Mexico. The earliest known *son* dates from the late 1500s. It combines the structure and elements of Spanish *canción* and the Spanish guitar with African rhythms and percussion instruments of Bantu and Arara origin.

**Son Jarocho**    Musical style developed in southern Veracruz on the Gulf of Mexico.

**Sorrow songs**    African-American spirituals that reflect both ends of the emotional continuum that begins with despair and ends with hope and joy.

**Spiritual**    An African-American song, usually with a Christian religious text. Originally monophonic and a cappella, these songs are antecedents of the blues and gospel music.

**Suling**    Bamboo end-blown flute of Indonesia, Malaysia, and the southern Philippines.

**Surdo**    Brazilian bass drum.

**Tabla**    Asymmetrical pair of small, tuned, hand-played drums of North and Central India, Pakistan, and Bangladesh.

**Tabor**    A side drum with one or more snares that has existed in Europe since the Middle Ages.

**Tala**    Rhythmic cycle in Indian musical theory and practice, and a system for organizing measured musical time.

**Tamborim**    Hand drums of 6" (Portuguese term for the tambourine).

**Tambura**    Long-necked plucked drone lutes of South Asia, found in both art and traditional musics. Tambura also refers to plucked lutes of southeastern Europe (as in Macedonia) and through much of the Middle East.

**Tar**    A lute with 26 moveable frets and six strings found in Iran and the Caucasus.

**Tarana**    A type of composition in Indian classical vocal music in which meaningless syllables are used in a medium-paced or fast rendition.

**Tejano (Tejano music, conjunto)**    Tex-Mex music featuring accordion, *bajo sexto,* bass guitar, and drums.

**Thumri**    A type of North Indian vocal composition and the style in which such compositions are performed.

**Timbalero**    In Cuba and Latin American jazz and dance music, a *timbale* player.

**Timbales**    A pair of toms (tom-tom drums) that are mounted on a stand, played in Cuba and in Latin American jazz and dance music.

**Tinde**    A drum made from a goatskin stretched over a mortar, which is played by Tuareg women of North Africa to accompany their songs and from which the names of their two kinds of songs are derived.

**Tombak (or Dombek)**    Goblet drum of Iran.

**Trong**    A generic term for any Vietnamese drum, also a specific two-headed drum used in village ensembles with a cowskin surface and a body of a wooden box.

**Tumbadora**    Conga drum of Cuba, typically 12" to 12.5" inches across.

**Turku**    Turish folk-infused urban music.

**Vihuela**    A five-stringed instrument with a vaulted back used by mariachi bands in Mexico and in Zona de Chiloe, Chile.

**Warabe-uta**    Japanese traditional singing games.

**Waiata (or Waita)**    Māori term for song and singing.

**Waita-a-ringa (or Waiata kori)**    Maori action song.

**Western swing**    A style of country music originating largely in the fiddle and guitar bands in Texas during the 1920s.

**Xing**    Pair of small bells of Chinese origin.

**Yambu**    A style of rumba of Afro-Cuban origin that is slower-paced, sparser in percussion; its dance resembles a stylized courtship.

**Yang chin**    Hammered dulcimer of the Han Chinese.

**Yunluo**    Chinese frame of small pitched gongs suspended vertically from a wooden frame.

**Zabumba**    Bass drum played with a beater, popular in the northeastern states of Brazil.

**Zampoñas**    Spanish for Andean panpipes (see sicu).

**Zourna (or zorna, zukra)**    Folk shawm of West and Central Asia, southeastern Europe and parts of North Africa. Its general form is a conical wooden tube 30–45 cm long, but its length may extend to 60 cm. It is played with a double reed and usually has a pirouette.

**Zydeco**    A form of folk music originating in the beginning of the twentieth century among the Francophone Creole peoples of southwest Louisiana and influenced by the music of the French-speaking Cajuns. It is heavily syncopated (with a backbeat), usually a fast-tempo, and dominated by the button or piano accordion and a form of a washboard known as a *rub-board* or *frottoir.*

# Appendix

Alphabetical List of Tunes and Grooves (with Meters, Vocal Uses, Keys, and Chords).

| | Meter | Vocal Use | Key | Chords |
|---|---|---|---|---|
| A la Rueda de San Miguel | $\frac{2}{4}$ | s-u | G | (G, D) |
| A Mi Querido Austin | $\frac{3}{4}$ | s-u | G | (G, D) |
| Abbots Bromley Horn Dance | $\frac{6}{8}$ | - | Dm | (Dm, A) |
| Aeyaya Balano Sakkad | $\frac{4}{4}$ | s-u | C | (C), drone |
| Afshari | $\frac{3}{4}$ | | | |
| Ah, Poor Bird | $\frac{4}{4}$ | c-r | Dm | (Dm) |
| Ajde Jano | $\frac{7}{8}$ | s-u | Em | (Em, D, G, Am) |
| Ala De'lona | $\frac{2}{4}$ | s-u | Em | (Em, Am, B7) |
| All Around the Kitchen | $\frac{2}{4}$ | s-u | Am | (Am, E7) |
| All the Pretty Little Horses | | s-u | | (Em, D, G, B7) |
| Allons Danser, Colinda | $\frac{4}{4}$ | s-u | D | (D, G, A) |
| Amores Hallaras | $\frac{2}{4}$ | | D | (D, A, Bm, E, F♯m, C♯m) |
| Andean Panpipe Melody | $\frac{6}{8}$ | - | - | - |
| Arirang | $\frac{3}{4}$ | c-r | G | (G) |
| Arkansas Traveller | $\frac{4}{4}$ | s-u | D | (D, G, A, A7, E7) |
| As I Roved Out | $\frac{4}{4}$ | s-u | Dm | (Dm, C, Em, A) |
| Atsiagbeko | $\frac{3}{4}$ | chor | - | - |
| Bach: Brandenburg Concerto No. 2, in F Major, Third Movement | $\frac{2}{4}$ | - | C | (C, F, G) |
| Bach: "Little" Fugue in G Minor | $\frac{4}{4}$ | - | Gm | (Gm, D, Dm) |
| Ballad of César Chávez, The | $\frac{3}{4}$ | s-u | G | (G, D) |
| Bambodansarna | $\frac{3}{4}$ | - | Dm | (Dm, Am, F, Em, Gm) |
| Barby'ry Allen | $\frac{3}{4}$ | s-u | D | (D, Bm, A, G, F♯m) |
| Batman and Robin | $\frac{2}{4}$ | s-u | F | (F, C) |
| Benjamin Franklin | $\frac{4}{4}$ | s-u | - | - |
| Better Days | $\frac{4}{4}$ | chor | E | (E, A, Em) |
| Billie | $\frac{4}{4}$ | - | Dm | (Dm, C) |
| Billy Boy | $\frac{12}{8}$ | s-u | C | (C, G, Am, F) |
| Bonjour, Mes Amis | $\frac{4}{4}$ | s-u | C | (C, F, G) |
| Buzzard Lope, The | $\frac{4}{4}$ | chor | F | (F, C) |
| By the Waters Babylon | $\frac{4}{4}$ | c-r | Am | (Am, C, B♭, E) |
| Caiqiu Wu | $\frac{2}{4}$ | - | D | (D, G, Em, A) |
| Cajueiro Pequenino | $\frac{2}{4}$ | s-u | C | (C, F, G) |
| Calypso Freedom | $\frac{4}{4}$ | chor | D | (D, G, A) |
| Chaang | $\frac{4}{4}$ | s-u | C | (C, G, F) |

|  | Meter | Vocal Use | Key | Chords |
|---|---|---|---|---|
| Chawe Chidyo Chem'chero | $\frac{4}{4}$ | chor | G | (G, C, D) |
| Cherokee Morning Song | $\frac{4}{4}$ | c-r | F | (F, B♭, C, Dm) |
| Cielito Lindo | $\frac{3}{4}$ | s-u | C | (C, G7, F) |
| Čija li je Taraba | $\frac{4}{4}$ | chor | C | (C, F, G) |
| Cinderella | $\frac{2}{4}$ | s-u | - | - |
| Cô Hàng Xóm | $\frac{4}{4}$ | s-u | Am | (Am, D, E, G, C) |
| Coo-Coo Bird, The | $\frac{4}{4}$ | s-u | Gm | (Gm) |
| Copland: Fanfare for the Common Man | $\frac{4}{4}$ | - | C | (C) |
| Copland: Hoedown | $\frac{2}{4}$ | - | D | (D, A), drone |
| Cripple Creek | $\frac{2}{4}$ | s-u | D | (D, G, A7) |
| Cuban Rumba Groove | $\frac{2}{2}$ | - | - | - |
| Cumberland Gap | $\frac{2}{4}$ | chor | C | (C, F, Am) |
| De Colores | $\frac{6}{8}$ | s-u | D | (D, G, A) |
| Deirdre's Fancy | $\frac{9}{8}$ | - | Em | (Em, D) |
| Do Doc Do Ngang | $\frac{4}{4}$ | s-u | Dm | (Dm, Am, C) |
| Dok Djampa | $\frac{4}{4}$ | s-u | - | drone |
| Domino | $\frac{4}{4}$ | s-u | - | - |
| Doraji | $\frac{3}{4}$ | s-u | F | (F, Dm, C, B♭) |
| Dowidzenia | $\frac{3}{4}$ | c-r | Dm | (Dm, C) |
| Down by the River | $\frac{4}{4}$ | s-u | - | - |
| Down by the Service Station | $\frac{4}{4}$ | s-u | D | (D, G) |
| Drowsy Maggie | $\frac{4}{4}$ | - | Em | (Em, D, A, G) |
| Drunken Sailor | $\frac{4}{4}$ | s-u | Dm | (Dm, C) |
| Dúlamán | $\frac{6}{8}$ | s-u | Am | (Am, G, F) |
| Dulce, Dulce | $\frac{2}{4}$ | s-u | Dm | (Dm) |
| El Barreño | $\frac{3}{4}$ | s-u | C | (C, G7, F) |
| El Juego Chirimbolo | $\frac{2}{4}$ | s-u | C | (C, G7) |
| El Rabel | $\frac{2}{4}$ | s-u | G | (G, C, D) |
| El Siquisíri | $\frac{3}{4}$ | - | C | (C, G) |
| En Cada Primavera | $\frac{4}{4}$ | c-r | B♭ | (B♭, F) |
| Erdo, Erdo | $\frac{2}{4}$ | c-r | Dm | (Dm, Am, B♭, F, Gm) |
| Fast Mambo Groove | $\frac{2}{2}$ | - | - | - |
| Feng Yang | $\frac{4}{4}$ | s-u | D | (D, A, Bm) |
| Fish and Chips | $\frac{3}{4}$ | c-r | E | (E, B) |
| Follow the Drinkin' Gourd | $\frac{2}{2}$ | s-u | Em | (Em, Bm, G, A, Am) |
| Forty-Niner | $\frac{6}{8}$ | s-u | G | (G, C) |
| Freight Train | $\frac{4}{4}$ | s-u | D | (D, A, F♯, G) |
| Froggie Went A-Courtin' | $\frac{2}{4}$ | s-u | F | (F, C7, B♭) |

| | Meter | Vocal Use | Key | Chords |
|---|---|---|---|---|
| Galbi | $\frac{4}{4}$ | s-u | Dm | (Dm, Cm) |
| Gimpel the Fool | $\frac{4}{4}$ | - | Em | (Em, F♯, B, Am) |
| Go Down, Moses | $\frac{4}{4}$ | s-u | Gm | (Gm, D, Cm, E♭) |
| Gong Xi Fa Cai | $\frac{4}{4}$ | s-u | Dm | (Dm, Gm, A) |
| Guajira Guantanamera | $\frac{4}{4}$ | s-u | D | (Em, A, D, G) |
| Haere, Haere | $\frac{3}{4}$ | s-u | F | (F, B♭, C) |
| Hai Wedi | $\frac{4}{4}$ | s-u | - | - |
| Haida | $\frac{2}{4}$ | c-r | Gm | (Gm, D) |
| Haliwa-Saponi Canoe Dance | $\frac{4}{4}$ | s-u | Em | (Em, B) |
| Handel: Minuet No. 2 | $\frac{3}{4}$ | - | E♭ | (E♭, B♭, A♭) |
| Hands, The | $\frac{4}{4}$ | s-u | - | - |
| Hashewie | $\frac{2}{4}$ | s-u | F | (F, C) |
| Hava Nagila | $\frac{2}{2}$ | s-u | Gm | (Gm, D, C, Cm) |
| Hava Nashira | $\frac{4}{4}$ | c-r | C | (C, G, F) |
| Haydn: Symphony No. 47 in G Major, Minuet and Trio | $\frac{3}{4}$ | - | G | (G, D, C) |
| Here Comes Sally | $\frac{4}{4}$ | s-u | C | (C, G, A, F♯dim) |
| Hindewhu | $\frac{3}{4}$ | s-u | - | - |
| Hotaru Koi | $\frac{4}{4}$ | c-r | - | - |
| How Can I Keep from Singing? | $\frac{4}{4}$ | chor | F | (F, B♭, C) |
| I Walk in Beauty | $\frac{4}{4}$ | chor | C | (C, F, G) |
| I Went to California | $\frac{4}{4}$ | s-u | G | (G, D) |
| If All the World Were Paper | $\frac{6}{8}$ | s-u | C | (C, F) |
| If You See My Savior | $\frac{4}{4}$ | s-u | A | (A, D, E7, Bm) |
| Ikokou | $\frac{4}{4}$ | s-u | - | - |
| In the Pines | $\frac{3}{4}$ | s-u | F | (F, B♭, G) |
| Jo'Ashila | $\frac{3}{4}$ | s-u | B♭ | (B♭, F) |
| John Wayne's Teeth | $\frac{6}{8}$ | s-u | D | (D, G, A) |
| Johnny Has Gone for a Soldier | $\frac{4}{4}$ | s-u | Am | (Am, G, C, F) |
| Joshua Fought the Battle of Jericho | $\frac{4}{4}$ | s-u | Em | (Em, B) |
| Juanatia | $\frac{4}{4}$ | s-u | Dm | (Dm, F) |
| Jubilee | $\frac{2}{4}$ | s-u | F | (F, C, B♭, Dm) |
| Jump in the Fire | $\frac{2}{4}$ | s-u | - | - |
| Kalinka | $\frac{2}{4}$ | s-u | D | (D, A, G, F♯, F♯m, Bm) |
| Karaw | $\frac{4}{4}$ | - | - | - |
| Keep Your Hand on That Plow | $\frac{4}{4}$ | s-u | Cm | (Cm, A♭, E♭, Fm) |
| Khaang Khaaw Kin Kluay | $\frac{4}{4}$ | - | - | - |
| Khmer Changkeh Reav | $\frac{4}{4}$ | - | - | - |

| | Meter | Vocal Use | Key | Chords |
|---|---|---|---|---|
| Kneebone | $\frac{4}{4}$ | chor | A | (A, E, D) |
| Kommt ein Vogel | $\frac{3}{4}$ | s-u | F | (F, C, C7) |
| Kum Bachur Atzel | $\frac{2}{4}$ | s-u | C | (C, G7) |
| Kwaheri | $\frac{4}{4}$ | chor | Am | (Am, G, C) |
| Kwa-Nu-Te | $\frac{5}{4}$ | s-u | Dm | (Dm, Gm, C) |
| K'wejina Ch'ing Ch'ing | $\frac{6}{8}$ | s-u | Cm | (Fm, E♭) |
| Kye Kye Kule | $\frac{4}{4}$ | s-u | B♭ | (B♭, C) |
| La Bamba | $\frac{4}{4}$ | s-u | F | (F, B♭, C7) |
| La Macchina del Capo | $\frac{2}{4}$ | s-u | C | (C, G7, F) |
| Lak Gei Moli | $\frac{2}{4}$ | s-u | C | (G, C, Dm, Am) |
| Las Mañanitas | $\frac{3}{4}$ | s-u | G | (G, D, D7, C) |
| Le Jig Français | $\frac{2}{4}$ | - | G | (G, F, D) |
| Let's Get the Rhythm of the Band | $\frac{4}{4}$ | s-u | Cm | (Cm, Fm) |
| Lian Xi Qu I, II | $\frac{2}{4}$ | - | - | - |
| Lo Yisa Goy | $\frac{4}{4}$ | c-r | Dm | (Dm, C, Am) |
| Loop de Loo | $\frac{4}{4}$ | s-u | Em | (Em, G, C) |
| Los Machetes | $\frac{4}{4}$ | - | G | (G, D, C) |
| Loy Krathong | $\frac{4}{4}$ | s-u | F | (F, B♭, C) |
| Lua Afe | $\frac{4}{4}$ | - | - | - |
| Maitreem | $\frac{4}{4}$ | s-u | G | (G, C, D, Bm) |
| Majka Rada | $\frac{4}{4}$ | chor | D | (D, A, G) |
| Mama Lama | $\frac{4}{4}$ | s-u | D | (D, G, A7) |
| Maramica Na Stazi | $\frac{4}{4}$ | chor | C | (C, F, G) |
| Máru-Bihág (Raga) | $\frac{10}{4}$ | - | - | drone |
| May Day Carol | $\frac{4}{4}$ | s-u | C | (C, G, B♭, F) |
| Mbube | $\frac{4}{4}$ | chor | G | (G, C, D) |
| Meda Wawa Ase | $\frac{4}{4}$ | chor | C | (C, G7, F, Dm) |
| Merengue Groove | $\frac{2}{2}$ | - | Fm | - |
| Mi Bajo y Yo | $\frac{2}{2}$ | - | Fm | (Fm, A♭, C, G7) |
| Mi Tierra | $\frac{4}{4}$ | chor | Dm | (Dm, Gm, A) |
| More Sokol Pie | $\frac{7}{8}$ | chor | Em | (Em, B, C, Am) |
| Mozart: Eine Kleine Nachtmusik (Theme, First Movement) | $\frac{4}{4}$ | - | G | (G, D7, C, Em, Am) |
| Mozart: The Marriage of Figaro (Overture) | $\frac{4}{4}$ | - | D | (D, G, A7) |
| Mozart: Symphony No. 40 in G Minor, (First Movement) | $\frac{4}{4}$ | - | Gm | (Gm, Cm, D, A) |
| Mutubaruke Emihanda | $\frac{4}{4}$ | s-u | F | (F, C) |
| My Mother, Your Mother | $\frac{4}{4}$ | s-u | - | - |

| | Meter | Vocal Use | Key | Chords |
|---|---|---|---|---|
| Nine Hundred Miles | $\frac{2}{4}$ | s-u | Am | (Am, G, E7) |
| Noble Duke of York, The | $\frac{2}{2}$ | s-u | G | (G, D, D7, C) |
| Northfield | $\frac{4}{4}$ | chor | B♭ | (B♭, E♭, F, Cm) |
| Oats, Peas, Beans (and Barley Grow) | $\frac{6}{8}$ | s-u | D | (D, D7, G, A7) |
| Oh, Freedom | $\frac{4}{4}$ | chor | G | (G, D7, C) |
| Old Joe Clark | $\frac{2}{4}$ | s-u | A | (A, G) |
| Old Roger | $\frac{6}{8}$ | s-u | F | (F, C, B♭) |
| One August Morn | $\frac{4}{4}$ | s-u | G | (G, C, D) |
| One Cold and Frosty Morning | $\frac{2}{4}$ | s-u | C | (C, G7, F) |
| Over My Head | $\frac{4}{4}$ | chor | D | (D, A) |
| Paddy Works on the Railway | $\frac{6}{8}$ | s-u | D | (D, A7) |
| Piki Mai | $\frac{4}{4}$ | chor | G | (G, C, D) |
| Poor Wayfaring Stranger | $\frac{3}{2}$ | chor | Dm | (Dm, Gm, Am) |
| Pullin' a Skiff | $\frac{2}{4}$ | s-u | - | - |
| Qiugaviit | $\frac{3}{4}$ | s-u | D | (D, A, G, Bm) |
| Qua Cầu Gió Bay | $\frac{4}{4}$ | s-u | Am | (Am, G) |
| Quien es ese Pajarito? | $\frac{3}{4}$ | s-u | Am | (Am, F, E) |
| Rabbit Dance: "Uncle Sam" | $\frac{6}{8}$ | s-u | Em | (Em, Am) |
| Reggae Groove | $\frac{4}{4}$ | - | - | - |
| Rumba Groove | $\frac{4}{4}$ | - | - | - |
| Rich Irish Lady, A | $\frac{3}{4}$ | s-u | Em | (Em, D, G, Am, C) |
| Riddle Song, The | $\frac{4}{4}$ | s-u | G | (G, C, D) |
| Rio Grande | $\frac{6}{8}$ | s-u | D | (D, A, G) |
| Rise Up, O Flame | $\frac{3}{4}$ | c-r | Dm | (Dm) |
| Sakura | $\frac{4}{4}$ | s-u | Am | (Am, E, Dm) |
| Salsa Groove | $\frac{6}{4}$ | - | - | - |
| Salty Dog | $\frac{2}{2}$ | s-u | D | (D, B7, E7, A7) |
| Samba Groove | $\frac{2}{2}$ | - | - | - |
| Sambalele | $\frac{2}{4}$ | s-u | F | (F, Gm, C7) |
| San Serení | $\frac{2}{4}$ | s-u | C | (C, F, G7) |
| Sansa Kroma | $\frac{4}{4}$ | s-u | C | (C, G) |
| Santa Clara | $\frac{3}{4}$ | s-u | A | (A, E7, D) |
| Santa Lucia | $\frac{3}{4}$ | s-u | C | (C, G7, A7, Dm, F) |
| Santo de Otavalo | $\frac{2}{4}$ | s-u | Dm | (Dm, B♭, F, A7) |
| Sarika Keo | $\frac{4}{4}$ | s-u | G | (G, C, D) |
| Savalivalah | $\frac{12}{8}$ | chor | F | (F, C, C7, B♭, Dm, Am) |
| Sea Lion Woman | $\frac{4}{4}$ | s-u | Dm | (Dm) |
| Separala Tambien | $\frac{4}{4}$ | - | - | - |

| | Meter | Vocal Use | Key | Chords |
|---|---|---|---|---|
| Shalom Chaverim | 4/4 | c-r | Dm | (Dm) |
| Shehuo Gudien | 4/4 | - | - | - |
| Shenandoah | 4/4 | s-u | D | (D, G, A, Bm) |
| She's Like the Swallow | 4/4 | s-u | Dm | (Dm, C) |
| Shi Naasha | 3/4 | s-u | C | (C, Am) |
| Ship's Carpenteer, The | 5/8 | s-u | D | (D, C) |
| Shortnin' Bread | 2/4 | s-u | Em | (Em) |
| Singabahambayo | 4/4 | chor | G | (G, D) |
| Soldier, Soldier, Will You Marry Me? | 4/4 | s-u | G | (G, C, D7, A7) |
| Soldier's Joy | 2/4 | s-u | D | (D, A7) |
| Somebody's Knocking | 4/4 | s-u | D | (D, G, A7) |
| Sometimes I Feel Like a Motherless Child | 4/4 | s-u | Em | (Em, Am, A7, B7, C7) |
| Soran Bushi | 2/4 | s-u | G | (G, Am, Em) |
| Staliá, Staliá | 4/4 | - | Em | (Em, B, Am) |
| Streets of Laredo | 3/4 | s-u | F | (F, C7) |
| Sumer Is Icumen In | 6/8 | c-r | C | (C, Dm) |
| Swing Low, Sweet Chariot | 2/4 | chor | F | (F, B♭, C) |
| Tabla Solo in Jhaptal | 10/4 | - | - | - |
| Tafta Hindi | 2/4 | s-u | Dm | (Dm, Gm, A, B♭) |
| Tamborcita | 4/4 | s-u | Dm | (Dm, F, Gm, A) |
| This Little Light of Mine | 2/2 | chor | G | (G, C, D, Em) |
| Three Sisters | 4/4 | s-u | Dm | (Dm, C, F, Gm) |
| Tihore Mai | 4/4 | chor | Dm | (Dm, C, Am, G) |
| Tinga Layo | 2/4 | s-u | C | (C, F, G) |
| Tito Timbero | 4/4 | - | D | (D, C, Dm) |
| Toei Khong | 4/4 | - | - | drone |
| Tommy Peoples | 4/4 | - | Bm | (Bm, A, D, G) |
| Turkey in the Straw | 2/4 | s-u | G | (G, D7, C) |
| 'Ulili E | 4/4 | chor | C | (C, F, G) |
| Uncle Jessie | 4/4 | s-u | D | (D, A, G) |
| Viva Jujuy | 6/8 | s-u | Am | (Am, C, F, G7, E7) |
| Viva la Musica | 4/4 | c-r | G | (G, C, D) |
| Voice of Trong | - | - | - | - |
| Wai Bamba | 4/4 | chor | D | (D, G, A) |
| Walkin' Blues | 4/4 | s-u | C | (Cm, Fm, G7) |
| Wedding Dance Groove | 7/4 | - | - | - |
| Were You There? | 4/4 | chor | F | (F, B♭, C, Dm, Gm7) |
| When Jesus Wept | 3/2 | c-r | Dm | (Dm, F, Am) |

| | Meter | Vocal Use | Key | Chords |
|---|---|---|---|---|
| Where Did You Sleep Last Night? | $\frac{3}{4}$ | s-u | Dm | (Dm, Gm, A) |
| Wildwood Flower | $\frac{2}{4}$ | s-u | G | (G, D7, C) |
| With Laughter and Singing | $\frac{6}{8}$ | c-r | F | (F, C7) |
| Woke Up This Morning | $\frac{4}{4}$ | chor | C | (C, F, E, Am, G) |
| Wolf and Turtle Song | $\frac{2}{4}$ | s-u | Am | (Am, C) |
| Wondrous Love | $\frac{4}{4}$ | chor | Dm | (Dm, C, Am) |
| Wren Song, The | $\frac{6}{8}$ | s-u | G | (G, D, D7) |
| Xiao Qi Che | $\frac{4}{4}$ | s-u | - | - |
| Yeysh Lanu Tayish | $\frac{4}{4}$ | s-u | C | (C, G, F) |
| Ye Jaliya Da | $\frac{4}{4}$ | s-u | C | (C, F, G7) |
| Yo, Mamana, Yo | $\frac{3}{4}$ | chor | F | (F, B♭, C) |
| Yo Soy Indiecito | $\frac{2}{4}$ | chor | F | (F, A7, Dm, B♭) |
| Zane Nil Abedeen | $\frac{4}{4}$ | s-u | - | drone or D, Gm |
| Zui Zui Zukkorobashi | $\frac{2}{4}$ | s-u | - | drone |
| Zum Gali Gali | $\frac{2}{4}$ | chor | Em | (Em, G, B) |
| Zuni Sunrise Call | $\frac{4}{4}$ | s-u | C | (C, Am) |

c-r: canon/round
s-u: solo/unison
chor: choral

# Chords

## 1 Chord

Aeyaya Balano Sakkad (C)

Ah, Poor Bird (Dm)

Arirang (G)

Cherokee Morning Song (F)

Coo-Coo Bird, The (Gm)

Copland: Fanfare for the Common Man (C)

Dulce, Dulce (Dm)

Rise Up, O Flame (Dm)

Sea Lion Woman (Dm)

Shalom Chaverim (Dm)

Shortnin' Bread (Em)

## 2 Chords

A la Rueda de San Miguel (G, D)

Abbots Bromley Horn Dance (Dm, A)

All Around the Kitchen (Am, E7)

Ballad of César Chávez, The (G, D)

Batman and Robin (F, C)

Billie (Dm, C)

Buzzard Lope, The (F, C)

Copland: Hoedown (D, A)

Deirdre's Fancy (Em, D)

Dowidzenia (Dm, C)

Down by the Service Station (G, D)

Drunken Sailor (Dm, C)

El Juego Chirímbolo (C, G7)

El Siquisíri (C, G)

En Cada Primavera (B♭, F)

Fish and Chips (E, B)

Forty-Niner (G, C)

Galbi (Dm, Cm)

Haida (Gm, D)

Haliwa-Saponi Canoe Dance (Em, B)

Hashewie (F, C)

I Went to California (G, D)

Jo'Ashila (B♭, F)

Joshua Fought the Battle of Jericho (Em, B)

Juanatia (F, Dm)

Kum Bachur Atzel (C, G7)

K'wejina Ch'ing Ch'ing (Fm, E♭)

Kye Kye Kule (B♭, C)

Let's Get the Rhythm of the Band (Cm, Fm)

Mutubaruke Emihanda (F, C)

Old Joe Clark (A, G)

Over My Head (D, A)

Paddy Works on the Railway (D, A7)

Qiugaviit (D, A)

Qua Cầu Gió Bay (Am, G)

Rabbit Dance: "Uncle Sam" (Em, Am)

San Serení (C, G7)

She's Like the Swallow (Dm, C)

Shi Naasha (C, Am)

Ship's Carpenteer, The (D, C)

Singabahambayo (G, D)

Soldier's Joy (D, A7)

Streets of Laredo (F, C7)

Sumer Is Icumen In (C, Dm)

With Laughter and Singing (F, C7)

Wolf and Turtle Song (Am, C)

Zane Nil Abedeen (D, Gm)

Zuni Sunrise Call (C, Am)

## 3 Chords

Ala De'lona (Em, Am, B7)

Allons Danser, Colinda (D, G, A)

Bach: Brandeburg Concerto No. 2, in F Major, Third Movement (C, G, F, Dm)

Bach: "Little" Fugue in G Minor (Gm, D)

Better Days (E, A, Em)

Bonjour, Mes Amis (C, F, G)

Cajueiro Pequenino (C, F, G)

Calypso Freedom (D, G, A)

Chawe Chidyo Chem'chero (G, C, D)

Cielito Lindo (C, G7, F)

Čija li je taraba (C, F, G)

Cripple Creek (D, G, A7)

Cumberland Gap (C, Am, F)

De Colores (D, A7, G)

Dúlamán (Am, G, F)

El Barreño (C, G7, F)

El Rabel (G, D, C)

Feng Yang (D, A, Bm)

Froggie Went A-Courtin' (F, C7, B♭)

Gong Xi Fa Cai (Dm, Gm, A)

Haere, Haere (F, B♭, C)

Handel: Minuet No. 2 (E♭, B♭, A♭)

Hava Nashira (C, G, G7)

Haydn: Symphony No. 47 in G Major, Minuet and Trio (G, D, C)

I Walk in Beauty (C, F, G)

If All the World Were Paper (C, F, G)

In the Pines (F, B♭, C7)

John Wayne's Teeth (D, G, A)

Kneebone (A, E, B7)

Kommt ein Vogel (F, C, C7)

Kwaheri (Am, G, C)

Kwa-Nu-Te (Dm, Gm, C)

La Bamba (C7, F, B♭)

La Macchina del Capo (C, G7, F)

Le Jig Français (G, F, D)

Lo Yisa Goy (Dm, C, Am)

Loop de Loo (Em, C, G)

Los Machetes (G, D, C)

Loy Krathong (F, B♭, C)

Majka Rada (D, A, G)

Mama Lama (D, A7, G)

Maramica na stazi (C, F, G)

Mbube (G, C, D)

Mi Tierra (Dm, A, Gm)

Mozart: The Marriage of Figaro Overture (D, G, A7)

Nine Hundred Miles (Am, G, E7)

Noble Duke of York, The (G, D, C)

Oh, Freedom (G, D7, C)

Old Roger (F, C, B♭)

One August Morn (G, C, D)

One Cold and Frosty Morning (C, G7, F)

Piki Mai (G, C, D)

Poor Wayfaring Stranger (Dm, Gm, Am)

Quien es ese Pajarito? (Am, F, E)

Riddle Song, The (G, C, D)

Rio Grande (D, A, G)

Sakura (Am, E, Dm)

Sambalele (F, Gm, C7)

Sansa Kroma (C, F, G)

Sarika Keo (G, C, D)

Somebody's Knocking (D, G, A7)

Soran Bushi (G, Am, Em)

Staliá, Staliá (Em, B, Am)

Swing Low, Sweet Chariot (F, B♭, C)

Tinga Layo (C, F, G7)

Tito Timbero (D, C, Dm)

Tihore Mai (Dm, C, Am)

Tulog Na Nonoy Ko (D, A7, G)

Turkey in the Straw (G, D7, C)

'Ulili E (C, F, G)

Uncle Jessie (D, A, G)

Viva la Musica (G, D, C)

Wai Bamba (D, G, A)

When Jesus Wept (Dm, F, Am)

Where Did You Sleep Last Night? (Dm, Gm, A)

Wildwood Flower (G, D7, C)

Wondrous Love (Dm, C, Am)

Wren Song, The (G, D, D7)

Yeysh Lanu Tayish (C, G, F)

Ye Jaliya Da (F, C, G7)

Yo, Mamana, Yo (F, B♭, C)

Zum Gali Gali (Em, G, B)

## 4(+) Chords

Afshari (C, D, E♭, F, G, A♭)

Ajde Jano (Em, D, G, Am)

A Mi Querido Austin (G, C, D, Am)

All the Pretty Little Horses (Em, D, G, B7)

Amores Hallaras (D, A, Bm, F♯m, E, C♯m)

Arkansas Traveller (D, G, A, A7, E7)

As I Roved Out (Dm, C, Em, A)

Bambodansarna (Dm, Am, F, Em, Gm)

Barb'ry Allen (D, Bm, A, G, F♯m)

Billy Boy (C, G, Am, F)

By the Waters Babylon (Am, C, B♭, E)

Caiqiu Wu (D, G, Em, A)

Chaang (C, G, Am, F)

Cô Hàng Xóm (Am, Dm, E)

Do Doc Do Ngang (Dm, Am, C, Am7)

Doraji (F, Dm, C, B♭, C7)

Drowsy Maggie (Em, D, A, G)

Erdo, Erdo (Dm, Am, B♭, F, A, Gm)

Follow the Drinkin' Gourd (Em, A, G, Bm)

Freight Train (D, A, F♯, G)

Gimpel the Fool (Em, C7, F♯7, B7, Am)

Go Down, Moses (Gm, D, Cm, E♭)

Guajira Guantanamera (G, A, D, Em)

Hava Nagila (D, Gm, Cm, D7)

Here Comes Sally (C, G, A7, F♯ dim)

How Can I Keep from Singing? (F, B♭, C, Dm)

If You See My Savior (A, D, E7, Bm)

Johnny Has Gone for a Soldier (Am, G, C, F)

Jubilee (F, C, B♭, Dm)

Kalinka (D, A, G, A7, F♯m, Bm)

Keep Your Hand on That Plow (Cm, A♭, E♭, Fm)

Las Mañanitas (G, D, C, D7)

Lak Gei Moli (G, C, Dm, Am)

Maitreem (G, C, D, Bm)

May Day Carol (C, G, B♭, F)

Meda Wawa Ase (C, G7, F, Dm)

Mi Bajo y Yo (Fm, Am, C, G7)

More Sokol Pie (Em, B, C, Am)

Mozart: Eine Kleine Nachtmusik (Theme, First Movement) (G, D7, C, D, Em, Am)

Mozart: Symphony No. 40 in G Minor, (First Movement) (Gm, Cm, D, A)

Northfield (B♭, E♭, F, Cm)

Oats, Peas, Beans (and Barley Grow) (D, G, A, A7, D7)

Qiugaviit (D, A, G, Bm)

Rich Irish Lady, A (Em, D, G, C, Am)

Salty Dog (D, B7, E7, A7, A)

Santa Clara (A, E7, A7, D)

Santa Lucia (C, G7, A7, Dm, F)

Santo de Otavalo (Dm, B♭, F, A7)

Savalivalah (F, C, B♭, G7, Dm, Am, C7)

Shenandoah (D, G, Bm, A)

Soldier, Soldier, Will You Marry Me? (G, C, D7, A7)

Sometimes I Feel Like a Motherless Child (Em, Am, B7, Am7, C7)

Tafta Hindi (Dm, Gm, A, B♭)

Tamborcita (Dm, F, Gm, A)

This Little Light of Mine (G, D, C, Em)

Three Sisters (Dm, C, F, Gm)

Tommy Peoples (Bm, A, D, G)

Viva Jujuy (Am, C, F, G7, E7)

Walkin' Blues (Cm, Fm, F, G7)

Were You There? (F, B♭, C, Dm, Gm7)

Woke Up This Morning (C, F, E, Am, G)

Yo Soy Indiecito (F, A7, Dm, B)

## Drone

Aeyaya Balano Sakkad

Ajde Jano

Copland: Hoedown

Dok Djampa

Toei Khong

Zane Nil Abedeen

Zui Zui Zukkorobashi

# Meter

## $\frac{2}{2}$

Cuban Rumba Groove
Fast Mambo Groove
Follow the Drinkin' Gourd
Hai Wedi
Hava Nagila
Merengue Groove
Mi Bajo y Yo
Noble Duke of York, The
Salty Dog
Samba Groove
This Little Light of Mine

## $\frac{3}{2}$

Poor Wayfaring Stranger
When Jesus Wept

## $\frac{2}{4}$

A la Rueda de San Miguel
Ala De'lona
All the Pretty Little Horses
All Around the Kitchen
All Pretty the Little Horses
Amores Hallaras
Bach: Brandenburg Concerto
    No. 2, in F Major, Third
    Movement
Batman and Robin
Caiqiu Wu
Cajueiro Pequenino
Cinderella
Copland: Hoedown
Cripple Creek
Cumberland Gap
Dulce, Dulce
El Juego Chirimbolo
El Rabel
Erdo, Erdo
Froggie Went A-Courtin'
Haida
Hashewie
Jubilee
Jump in the Fire
Kalinka

Kum Bachur Atzel
La Macchina del Capo
Lak Gei Moli
Le Jig Français
Lian Xi Qu I, II
Nine Hundred Miles
Old Joe Clark
One Cold and Frosty Morning
Pullin' a Skiff
Sambalele
San Serení
Santo de Otavalo
Shortnin' Bread
Soldier's Joy
Soran Bushi
Swing Low, Sweet Chariot
Tafta Hindi
Tinga Layo
Turkey in the Straw
Wildwood Flower
Wolf and Turtle Song
Yo Soy Indiecito
Zui Zui Zukkorobashi
Zum Gali Gali

## $\frac{3}{4}$

A Mi Querido Austin
Afshari
Arirang
Atsiagbeko
Ballad of César Chávez, The
Bambodansarna
Barb'ry Allen
Cielito Lindo
Doraji
Dowidzenia
El Barreño
El Siquisíri
Fish and Chips
Haere, Haere
Handel: Minuet No. 2
Haydn: Symphony No. 47 in G
    Major, Minuet and Trio

Hindewhu
In the Pines
Jo'Ashila
Kommt ein Vogel
Las Mañanitas
Qiugaviit
Quien es ese Pajarito?
Rich Irish Lady, A
Rise Up, O Flame
Santa Clara
Santa Lucia
Shi Naasha
Streets of Laredo
Where Did You Sleep Last Night?
Yo, Mamana, Yo

## $\frac{4}{4}$

Aeyaya Balano Sakkad
Ah, Poor Bird
Allons Danser, Colinda
Arkansas Traveller
As I Roved Out
Bach: "Little" Fugue in G Minor
Benjamin Franklin
Better Days
Billie
Bonjour, Mes Amis
Buzzard Lope, The
By the Waters Babylon
Calypso Freedom
Chaang
Chawe Chidyo Chem'chero
Cherokee Morning Song
Čija li je Taraba
Cô Hàng Xóm
Coo-Coo Bird, The
Copland: Fanfare for the Common
    Man
Do Doc Do Ngang
Dok Djampa
Domino
Down by the River
Down by the Service Station

**465**

Drowsy Maggie
Drunken Sailor
En Cada Primavera
Feng Yang
Freight Train
Galbi
Gimpel the Fool
Go Down, Moses
Gong Xi Fa Cai
Guajira Guantanamera
Haliwa-Saponi Canoe Dance
Hands, The
Hava Nashira
Here Comes Sally
Hotaru Koi
How Can I Keep from Singing?
I Walk in Beauty
I Went to California
If You See My Savior
Ikokou
Johnny Has Gone for a Soldier
Joshua Fought the Battle of Jericho
Juanatia
Karaw
Keep Your Hand on that Plow
Khaang Khaaw Kin Kluay
Khmer Changkeh Reav
Kneebone
Kwaheri
Kye Kye Kule
La Bamba
Let's Get the Rhythm of the Band
Lo Yisa Goy
Loop de Loo
Los Machetes
Loy Krathong
Lua Afe
Maitreem
Majka Rada
Mama Lama
Maramica na stazi
May Day Carol
Mbube
Meda Wawa Ase
Mi Tierra
Mozart: Eine Kleine Nachtmusik
　　(Theme First Movement)

Mozart: The Marriage of Figaro
　　(Overture)
Mozart: Symphony No. 40 in G
　　Minor, (Movement 1)
Mutubaruke Emihanda
My Mother, Your Mother
Northfield
Oh, Freedom
One August Morn
Over My Head
Piki Mai
Qua Cầu Gió Bay
Reggae Groove
Rumba Groove
Riddle Song, The
Sakura
Sansa Kroma
Sarika Keo
Sea Lion Woman
Separala Tambien
Shalom Chaverim
Shehuo Gudien
Shenandoah
She's Like the Swallow
Singabahambayo
Soldier, Soldier, Will You Marry
　　Me?
Somebody's Knocking
Sometimes I Feel Like a Mother-
　　less Child
Staliá, Staliá
Tamborcita
Three Sisters
Tihore Mai
Tito Timbero
Toei Khong
Tommy Peoples
'Ulili E
Uncle Jessie
Viva la Musica
Wai Bamba
Walkin' Blues
Were You There?
Woke Up This Morning
Wondrous Love
Xiao Qi Che
Yeysh Lanu Tayish

Ye Jaliya Da
Zane Nil Abedeen
Zuni Sunrise Call

$\frac{5}{4}$

Kwa-Nu-Te

$\frac{6}{4}$

Salsa Groove

$\frac{7}{4}$

Wedding Dance Groove

$\frac{10}{4}$

Máru-Bihág (Raga)
Tabla Solo Jhaptal

$\frac{5}{8}$

Ship's Carpenteer, The

$\frac{6}{8}$

Abbots Bromley Horn Dance
Andean Panpipe Melody
De Colores
Dúlamán
Forty-Niner
If All the World Were Paper
John Wayne's Teeth
K'wejina Ch'ing Ch'ing
Oats, Peas, Beans (and Barley
　　Grow)
Old Roger
Paddy Works on the Railway
Rabbit Dance: "Uncle Sam"
Rio Grande
Sumer Is Icumen In
Viva Jujuy
With Laughter and Singing
Wren Song, The

$\frac{7}{8}$

Ajde Jano
More Sokol Pie

$\frac{9}{8}$

Deirdre's Fancy

$\frac{12}{8}$

Billy Boy
Savalivalah

# Key

**A**
If You See My Savior
Kneebone
Old Joe Clark
Santa Clara

**Am**
All Around the Kitchen
By the Waters Babylon
Cô Hàng Xóm
Dúlamán
Johnny Has Gone for a Soldier
Kwaheri
Nine Hundred Miles
Qua Cầu Gió Bay
Quien es ese Pajarito?
Sakura
Viva Jujuy
Wolf and Turtle Song

**Bm**
Tommy Peoples

**B♭**
En Cada Primavera
Jo'Ashila
Kye Kye Kule
Northfield

**C**
Aeyaya Balano Sakkad
Bach: Brandenburg Concerto
    No. 2, in F Major,
    Movement 3
Billy Boy
Bonjour, Mes Amis
Cajueiro Pequenino
Chaang
Cielito Lindo
Čija li je Taraba
Copland: Fanfare for the Common
    Man
Cumberland Gap
El Barreño

El Juego Chirimbolo
El Siquisíri
Hava Nashira
Here Comes Sally
I Walk in Beauty
If All the World Were Paper
Kum Bachur Atzel
La Macchina del Capo
Lak Gei Moli
Maramica Na Stazi
May Day Carol
Meda Wawa Ase
One Cold and Frosty Morning
San Serení
Sansa Kroma
Santa Lucia
Shi Naasha
Sumer Is Icumen In
Tinga Layo
'Ulili E
Walkin' Blues
Woke Up This Morning
Yeysh Lanu Tayish
Ye Jaliya Da
Zuni Sunrise Call

**Cm**
Keep Your Hand on that Plow
K'wejina Ch'ing Ch'ing
Let's Get the Rhythm of the Band

**D**
Allons Danser, Colinda
Amores Hallaras
Arkansas Traveller
Barb'ry Allen
Caiqiu Wu
Calypso Freedom
Copland: Hoedown
Cripple Creek
De Colores
Down by the Service Station
Feng Yang

Freight Train
Guajira Guantanamera
John Wayne's Teeth
Kalinka
Majka Rada
Mama Lama
Mozart: The Marriage of Figaro
    (Overture)
Oats, Peas, Beans (and Barley
    Grow)
Over My Head
Paddy Works on the Railway
Qiugaviit
Rio Grande
Salty Dog
Shenandoah
Ship's Carpenteer, The
Soldier's Joy
Somebody's Knocking
Tito Timbero
Uncle Jessie
Wai Bamba
Zane nil Abedeen

**Dm**
Abbots Bromley Horn Dance
Ah, Poor Bird
As I Roved Out
Bambodansarna
Billie
Do Doc Do Ngang
Dowidzenia
Drunken Sailor
Dulce, Dulce
Erdo, Erdo
Galbi
Gong Xi Fa Cai
Juanatia
Kwa-Nu-Te
Lo Yisa Goy
Mi Tierra
Poor Wayfaring Stranger
Rise Up, O Flame

# Vocal Use

Turkey in the Straw
Uncle Jessie
Viva Jujuy
Walkin' Blues
Where Did You Sleep Last Night?
Wildwood Flower
Wolf and Turtle Song
Wren Song, The
Xiao Qi Che
Yeysh Lanu Tayish
Ye Jaliya Da
Zane Nil Abedeen
Zui Zui Zukkorobashi
Zuni Sunrise Call

**C-R (Canon/Round)**
Ah, Poor Bird
Arirang
By the Waters Babylon
Cherokee Morning Song
Dowidzenia
En Cada Primavera
Erdo, Erdo
Fish and Chips

Haida
Hava Nashira
Hotaru Koi
Lo Yisa Goy
Rise Up, O Flame
Shalom Chaverim
Sumer is Icumen In
Viva la Musica
When Jesus Wept
With Laughter and Singing

**Chor (Choral)**
Atsiagbeko
Better Days
Buzzard Lope, The
Calypso Freedom
Chawe Chidyo Chem'chero
Čija li je Taraba
Cumberland Gap
How Can I Keep from Singing?
I Walk in Beauty
Kneebone
Kwaheri
Majka Rada

Maramica Na Stazi
Mbube
Meda Wawa Ase
Mi Tierra
More Sokol Pie
Northfield
Oh, Freedom
Over My Head
Piki Mai
Poor Wayfaring Stranger
Savalivalah
Singabahambayo
Swing Low, Sweet Chariot
This Little Light of Mine
Tihore Mai
'Ulili E
Wai Bamba
Were You There?
Wondrous Love
Woke Up This Morning
Yo, Mamana, Yo
Yo Soy Indiecito
Zum Gali Gali

# Contents of CD

**CD 1**

1)  A Mi Querido Austin
(Eva Ybarra)
Eva Ybarra & Group
℗1996 Rounder Records Corp.
Licensed courtesy of Rounder Records Corp.

2)  Abbots Bromley Horn Dance
(Anonymous)
Lisle Kulbach, recorder
℗1978 Revels Records
Courtesy of Revels, Inc.

3)  Brandenburg Concerto No. 2 in F Major, III
(J.S. Bach)
Tafelmusik
℗1994 SONY BMG MUSIC ENTERTAINMENT

4)  Bambodansarna
(Olov Johansson)
Väsen
℗1997 Xource Records
Courtesy of Northside Records, Inc.

5)  Benjamin Franklin
(Traditional)
Illinois school children
Courtesy of Smithsonian Folkways Recordings

6)  Better Days
(Traditional)
Brownie McGhee and Sonny Terry
Courtesy of Smithsonian Folkways Recordings

7)  Billie
(Palmieri)
Eddie Palmieri
℗2003 Concord Records, Inc.
Courtesy of Concord Music Group

It was not possible for us to license for the CD set every song that is discussed in this book. For those who would like to hear the other selections, we've posted an iTunes list for as many of the items that are not on the CD as possible. A link to this list may be found on the e-catalog page for this book at www.prenhall.com.

8)  Bonjour Mes Amis
(Traditional, arr: Jeanie McLerie and Ken Keppeler)
Jeanie McLerie & Ken Keppeler
℗1994 World Music Press
Courtesy of World Music Press

9)  The Buzzard Lope
(Traditional)
Georgia Sea Island Singers
℗1977 Recorded Anthology of American Music, Inc.
Courtesy of Recorded Anthology of American Music, Inc.

10)  Cherokee Morning Song
(Traditional)
Walela
Courtesy of Triloka Records

11)  The Coo-Coo Bird
(Traditional)
Doc Watson and Clarence Ashley
Courtesy of Smithsonian Folkways Recordings

12)  Fanfare for the Common Man
(Copland)
London Symphony; Aaron Copland, conductor
Originally recorded 1968. All rights reserved by **SONY BMG MUSIC ENTERTAINMENT**

13)  "Hoedown" from Rodeo
(Copland)
London Symphony; Aaron Copland, conductor
Originally recorded 1960. All rights reserved by **SONY BMG MUSIC ENTERTAINMENT**

14)  Do Doc Do Ngang
(Traditional, arr.by Phong Nguyen)
Phong Nguyen
℗1990 World Music Press
Courtesy of World Music Press

15)  Dúlamán
(Traditional)
Altan
℗1993 Green Linnet Records, Inc.
Courtesy of Green Linnet Records, Inc.

16)  El Siquisiri
(Traditional)
Xocoyotzin Herrara

17)  Freight Train
(Cotten)
Elizabeth Cotten
Courtesy of Smithsonian Folkways Recordings

18)  Galbi
(Aharon Amram)
Ofra Haza
℗1984 Shanachie Entertainment Corp.
Courtesy of Shanachie Entertainment Corp.

19)  Gimpel the Fool
(Hankus Netsky)
Klezmer Conservatory Band; Hankus Netsky, conductor
℗1997 Rounder Records Corp.
Licensed courtesy of Rounder Records Corp.

20)  Guajira Guantanamera
(Fernandez—Marti)
Cuarteto Patria y Compay Segundo
Courtesy of Smithsonian Folkways Recordings

## CD 2

1)  The Hands
(Valdez)
Steve Loza Sextet
℗1994 Merrimack Records, Inc.
Courtesy of Merrimack Records, Inc.

2)  Symphony No. 47 In G Major, Minuet and trio
(Haydn)
L'Estro Armonico; Derek Solomons, conductor
℗1985 SONY BMG MUSIC ENTERTAINMENT

3)  Hindewhu
(Traditional)
Ba-Benzélé Pygmies
Licensed courtesy of Rounder Records Corp.

4)  I Was Standing By the Bedside of a Neighbor (If You See My Saviour)
(Dorsey)
Michele Lancaster with Sweet Honey in the Rock
Courtesy of Smithsonian Folkways Recordings

5) Ikokou
(J.S. Bach—Akendenqué)
Nana Vasconcelos and ensemble
℗1994 SONY BMG MUSIC ENTERTAINMENT

6) Where Did You Sleep Last Night? (In the Pines)
(Ledbetter)
Lead Belly
Courtesy of Smithsonian Folkways Recordings

7) Jo' Ashila
(Traditional, arr: Marilyn Hood)
Marilyn Hood
℗1994 World Music Press
Courtesy of World Music Press

8) Khaang Khaaw Kin Kluay
(Traditional, arr: Pornprapit Phoasavadi )
Pornprapit Phoasavadi
℗2003 World Music Press
Courtesy of World Music Press

9) Khmer Changkeh Reav
(Traditional, arr: Sam-Ang Sam)
Sam-Ang Sam and ensemble
℗1991 World Music Press
Courtesy of World Music Press

10) Kneebone
(Traditional)
Georgia Sea Island Singers
℗1977 Recorded Anthology of American Music, Inc.
Courtesy of Recorded Anthology of American Music, Inc.

11) La Bamba
(Valens)
Ritchie Valens
Courtesy Of Del-Fi Records, Inc.

12) La Bamba
(Traditional)
Los Pregoneros del Puerto
Licensed courtesy of Rounder Records Corp.

13)  Lak Gei Moli
(Traditional, arr: Han Kuo-Huang)
Han Kuo-Huang
℗1997 World Music Press
Courtesy of World Music Press

14)  Le Jig Francais
(Reed/Doucet)
Michael Doucet and Beausoleil
℗1981 Arhoolie Productions
Courtesy of Arhoolie Productions Inc.

15)  Lian Xi Qu
(Traditional, arr: Han Kuo-Huang)
Han Kuo-Huang
℗1997 World Music Press
Courtesy of World Music Press

16)  Los Machetes
(Vargas)
Mariachi Vargas de Tecalitlan
Originally recorded 1962. All rights reserved by SONY BMG MUSIC ENTERTAINMENT

17)  Maitreem
(T. Banzi—J. Banzi—K. Paramaharya)
Al-Andalus
℗1997 Koch International, LP
Courtesy of Koch International, LP

18)  Maramica Na Stazi/Cija Lije Taraba
(Traditional)
Village Harmony Singers; Mary Cay Brass, director
Courtesy of The Village Harmony Singers

19)  Máru-Bihág
(Traditional)
Ravi Shankar
Originally recorded 1957. All rights reserved by SONY BMG MUSIC ENTERTAINMENT

20)  Mi Tierra
(F. Salgado—G. Estefan)
Gloria Estefan
℗1993 SONY BMG MUSIC ENTERTAINMENT

21) More Sokol Pie
(Traditional)
Village Harmony Singers, Mary Cay Brass, director
Courtesy of The Village Harmony Singers

22) Mozart: Serenade in G Major, K. 525, "Eine Kleine Nachtmusik", I
Cleveland Orchestra; George Szell, conductor
Originally released 1969. All rights reserved by SONY BMG MUSIC ENTERTAINMENT

## CD 3

1) Symphony No. 40 in G Minor, I
(Mozart)
Cleveland Orchestra; George Szell, conductor
Originally released 1967. All rights reserved by SONY BMG MUSIC ENTERTAINMENT

2) Northfield
(Jeremiah Ingalls)
Alabama Sacred Harp Singing Convention, 1942; Paine Denson, leader
Courtesy of Odyssey Productions Inc.

3) Old Joe Clark
(Traditional)
Wade Ward
Recording provided by the Archive of Folk Culture, Library of Congress

4) Piki Mai
(Traditional)
Kiri Te Kanawa
℗1999 EMI Records Ltd.
Courtesy of EMI Records Ltd., under license from EMI Music Marketing

5) Pullin' the Skiff
(Traditional)
Ora Dell Graham
Recording provided by the Archive of Folk Culture, Library of Congress

6) Qiugavit
(Traditional)
Tudjaat
Courtesy of Rescue Records

7) Qua cau Gio Bay
(Traditional, arr: Phong Nguyen)
Phong Nguyen
℗1990 World Music Press
Courtesy of World Music Press

8)  Sea Lion Woman
(Traditional)
Christine and Katherine Shipp
Recording provided by the Archive of Folk Culture, Library of Congress


9)  Separala Tambien
(J.R. Sanchez)
Tito Puente
Originally recorded 1960. All rights reserved by SONY BMG MUSIC ENTERTAINMENT


10)  She Is Like the Swallow
(Traditional)
Karan Casey
℗1997 Shanachie Entertainment Corp.
Courtesy of Shanachie Entertainment Corp.


11)  Shehuo Gudien
(Traditional, arr: Han Kuo-Huang)
Han Kuo-Huang
℗1997 World Music Press
Courtesy of World Music Press


12)  Soldier's Joy
(Traditional)
Nashville Washboard Band
Recording provided by the Archive of Folk Culture, Library of Congress


13)  Sometimes I Feel Like A Motherless Child
(Traditional)
Mahalia Jackson
Originally recorded 1956. All rights reserved by SONY BMG MUSIC ENTERTAINMENT


14)  Swing Low, Sweet Chariot
(Traditional)
Fisk Jubilee Singers
Courtesy of Document Records, Vienna


15)  Tabla Solo in Jhaptal
(Traditional)
Zakir Hussain, tabla; Ustad Mohammed Omar, rabab
℗2002 Smithsonian Folkways Recordings
Courtesy of Smithsonian Folkways Recordings


16)  Tito Timbero
(T. Puente—E.Ortiz)
Tito Puente and His Orchestra
Originally recorded 1949. All rights reserved by SONY BMG MUSIC ENTERTAINMENT

17) Tommy Peoples/The Windmill/Fintan McManus's
(Traditional/Tourish/McManus)
Altan
℗1993 Green Linnet Records, Inc.
Courtesy of Green Linnet Records, Inc.

18) Viva Jujuy
(Traditional)
Cathy Guarjado

19) Voice of Trong
(Traditional, arr: Han Kuo-Huang)
Phong Nguyen
℗1990 World Music Press
Courtesy of World Music Press

20) Walkin' Blues
(Johnson)
Robert Johnson
Originally recorded 1936. All rights reserved by SONY BMG MUSIC ENTERTAINMENT

21) Wolf Song and Turtle Songs
(Traditional)
Irene Poolaw
℗1990 Smithsonian Folkways Recordings
Courtesy of Smithsonian Folkways Recordings